the
ROOT
of All
EVIL

ALSO BY JOYLYNN M. JOSSEL

Dollar Bill

Please Tell Me If the Grass Is Greener

World on My Shoulders

Twilight Moods

The Game

the
ROOT
of All
EVIL

JOYLYNN M. JOSSEL

St. Martin's Griffin

New York

www.stmartins.com

Library of Congress Cataloging-in-Publication Data

Jossel, Joylynn M.
    The root of all evil / Joylynn M. Jossel.—1st ed.
      p. cm.
    ISBN 0-312-32860-5
    EAN 978-0312-32860-3
    1. African Americans—Fiction.   2. Female friendship—Fiction.
3. Single mothers—Fiction.   4. Poor families—Fiction.   5. Rich
people—Fiction.   6. Authors—Fiction.   I. Title.

PS3610.O68R66   2004
813'.6—dc22   2004040539

First Edition: June 2004

Thank you to my three beautiful children.
Mommy did it, and thanks for allowing me to do it.

Thank you, Nicholas (Boogie Bang) Ross.
Thank you for sacrificing for my sacrifices.
Thank you for the love, arguments, encouragement,
disagreements, and agreements, for they each had their purpose
in the success of my debut novel. I know this now.
I love you and am in love with you.

An extra special thanks to my editor, Monique,
for not letting me go out into the literary
world with my slip showing.

Acknowledgments

I dedicate every morsel of the success of this book and my ability to make a name for myself in the literary industry to the Ross family of Toledo, Ohio. God used them to get me to recognize that support comes in a multitude of forms. A two-hour drive didn't keep them from coming to get the kids so that I could have time to write and go on book signings. Each of your genuine loving and unselfish acts plays the most volatile role in my passion as an author. Grandma Gwen, your powerful brace and character are irreplaceable. Special gratitude to Mama Ross, Aunti Nicole, Tab, NiGayle, Nichelle, Vater, and cousins Chris, Chad, and Bianca for your part in caring for the kids. Thanks to bra-bra Randy (even though after a while you started charging me money to baby-sit). Thank you, Aunt Joy, Aunt Gwen, Ms. Jawan, Ms. Dawn, and Rachel, too. I would've never been able to pick up and go do promotions without your generosity.

Thank you for lending me your angels, God.

■ ■ ■

A very special thanks to my agent, Vickie Stringer, and my PR, Earth Jallow. (Who would have thought a couple of chicks from the Midwest would grow up and bring it like this?)

Thank you, ladies.

Thank you, Traci Thompson of the Circle of Friends Book Club's Columbus, Ohio, chapter for your unselfish contribution in getting the word out about this up-and-coming new jack author.

First of All
(Don't Give It Away)

Sipping on an apple martini in a $500,000 condo, a woman would vow, and put it on her favorite auntie's grave, that she would never sell herself. Life is random and lures humanity to unpredictable acts. What a woman pronounces she won't do and what a woman will, in fact, do are two distinct conditions based on the predicament at hand. Let an eviction notice welcome her and her children home after eating Ramen Noodles for two weeks straight. What about the days of choosing between the $1.25 school lunch for the kids or the orange empty fuel light on the car? Or better yet, let her have to boil water to do a warm wash-up because the gas is shut off. See if she doesn't stamp a price tag on her forehead.

The same woman who turns her nose up at a chick who has to do what she has to do to make ends meet is the same broke-ass woman fucking for free. It's funny, isn't it? She can't even keep her cable on, but got some man laid up next to her, getting his nut off. And it's that same woman who is sleeping with every Tiwan, Slick, and Kahari for free that's tampering with the game of women who fuck for needs. Although it's probably not exactly what Iyanla Vanzant meant in her bestselling book, she was right. Don't give it away! This soon became Klarke Taylor's motto.

Klarke's stomach ached every time the phone rang. She was just shy of being three months behind on her truck payment, the same truck that broke down every other week it seemed, costing her more money in repairs and towing than it was worth. She hadn't paid her student loan since Columbus set sail. All of her credit cards were maxed, and the payment due dates had long come and gone without being satisfied. Her bank had already returned two cash-advance checks. Hell, the bank was even hounding her for the negative $287 her checking account reflected. She couldn't seem to help using her checks as if they were credit cards.

If something was on sale that Klarke just had to have, she would write a check for it, knowing she had just exhausted all of her funds. But she just had to have it. She knew she wasn't alone, though. People did it all of the time. Yes, the sweater was on sale for twenty dollars less than its regular price, but once the bank charged a twenty-nine-dollar return-check fee and the vendor turned around and tacked on another fifteen-dollar fee, it equaled out to be one sweater for the price of two. The mathematics of it all never stopped Klarke, though. Her checks might as well have been in a marathon. Whichever one made it to her bank account first was the winner.

She got into the most trouble if her daughter, twelve-year-old Vaughn, and her son, ten-year-old HJ, accompanied her on her sprees. They unknowingly acted as Klarke's justifiable accomplices to her bad spending habits. She refused to let them know how broke she was. Whatever they wanted, she somehow managed to get it.

Last winter she wrote a check for three hundred dollars over the amount that was actually in her bank account. The children had spoken endlessly about wanting a computer for Christmas. While in Best Buy they pleaded with Klarke to buy them one. She put the salesman to work like she really had money for the Compaq. He carried the computer to the register for her as she stood in line sweating bullets. She prayed that CheckRite didn't run her account and put a stop to her madness. Even more so, she was hoping the clerk didn't try to put her on Front Street if she was found out. She knew she was about to commit a crime by writing that stale check. But when it came down to it, she didn't care. She'd do anything for her children to make sure that they had whatever it was that their little hearts desired. She lucked up that time though. The next evening she won the 50/50 raffle at her company Christmas party, for which the pot was $527. She stopped at an ATM and made a deposit that very same night.

Recently the dates for all those damn credit-card deferments Klarke had charged to her debit card were coming around to kick her straight in the ass. Being something of a fashion guru, she couldn't help but shop the catalogs that frequently showed up in her mailbox. At the time of placing the order for that suede faux-fur-collared coat and two pairs of shoes from Chadwick's of Boston, the one dollar that was held on her debit card didn't do much damage. But four months later when the other $299 was deducted, it buried Klarke deeper into debt than she already was. She didn't have the money when she placed the order, but she prayed her luck would turn over the next few months and that the money would be available by the time the balance became due.

Klarke was always hoping money would miraculously appear. Every day when she got home from work she anxiously thumbed through the mail in anticipation of a surprise check. Maybe she had overpaid her taxes and Uncle Sam was throwing her a few ends. Maybe it had gone unnoticed that her mortgage escrow account was overpaid and the error had finally been discovered. Maybe someone had died and named her the heiress of a million-dollar estate. Klarke didn't give a damn where the money came from as long as it had her name on it. But every day Klarke was greeted by the same old acquaintances: Bill, Bill, and Bill.

The past three years had been hell for Klarke. It was three years ago when Harris, her husband of a thirteen-year sentence, decided to leave her for his *so-called* cousin. Klarke never saw it coming.

She and Harris had enjoyed two years of courting prior to their nuptials. She met him one afternoon while out window-shopping. Harris, almost eleven years Klarke's senior, appealed to her innocent youthfulness. And Harris dedicated their two years of courting to molding Klarke into the perfect woman for himself. And for the next thirteen years, Klarke committed herself to him and their children.

Klarke's parents were both living at the time she and Harris wed. It meant everything in the world to Klarke to have her father walk her down the aisle. He had been battling diabetes for years and had had some close calls. A year later he lost the battle. Shortly thereafter, Klarke's mother lost her will to live and allowed herself to fade away. But they had each lived long enough to see Harris take their daughter's hand in marriage. He had promised them that he would honor their daughter and take care of her. This gave them priceless peace of mind.

During their marriage, Harris provided a very comfortable life for Klarke and the children. He had been employed on the assembly line at Jeep for nineteen years, and made decent money once he was promoted to foreman. Although Harris would have liked for them to live modestly, Klarke never had a budget to adhere to. Anything she wanted she could have.

Their three-story home was part of a new housing development on the outskirts of Toledo, Ohio. Harris had wanted to purchase a base-model home so that he could customize it to his liking. The first thing he did was have a swimming pool built in the shape of a heart, to represent what Klarke meant to him.

He couldn't live without her and he wanted to make sure that Klarke was the envy of all. It wasn't because he was afraid that some young buck was going to come along and steal her away. He felt she was entitled to everything he could give her. She was, after all, his creation.

Before Klarke, Harris had mostly dated women his own age. But none of them could ever hold a candle to Klarke's sophistication. She was young in years, but intellectually mature.

Klarke never disrespected Harris's manhood. She never questioned his decisions for the family's well-being, choosing to silently correct his errors and always without argument. She just didn't find it necessary to bring his inaccuracies front and center.

It wasn't a difficult task for Harris to mold Klarke into his tailor-made queen. It was as if she had been born just for him, anyway. Knowing how to please a man came naturally for Klarke. Everything, that is, with the exception of one minor thing. The ability to give head. Getting his dick sucked was Harris's shit. Klarke, on the other hand, couldn't fathom wrapping her lips around a man's urine repository.

When Harris and Klarke were *just kickin' it*, Harris had even paid for oral sex here and there. It was nothing but a thing for him and a few of his cats to roll up to Club Diamond after work and pay for a private dance. Once the girls got to shakin' that ass, he'd tip them two Hamiltons and get three minutes' worth of head. The women there weren't the finest in town, but it was the only place he could get a decent dick suck for twenty dollars.

The Naked Glass had some dimes dancing up in there, but those pretty bitches would solicit a fifty spot before they would even consider going down. The audacity! Pretty girls know they can't suck no dick. They're too busy trying to be just that—pretty. Harris could do without the drama, but on occasion he would visit the bar. All he wanted was a good hardy blow job, but those pretty wannabe actresses and music video rats would be looking at him, trying to be sexy while doing that annoying fake-ass moan ("umm . . . umm . . . umm"). Harris was happy with an okay chick just getting down on her knees and doing her thing, slurping, slobbing—the works.

It would take eleven dates, a gift basket from Bath and Body Works, three failed attempts resulting in Harris having to masturbate, and a weekend trip to King's Island theme park before Klarke would give in to his request for oral sex. Even then, her performance was modest at best. Eventually, however, just like everything else Harris asked of Klarke, she would master it to his liking.

She even learned how to hang over the edge of the bed on her back while Harris stood over her so she could deep throat him. Klarke had read in a magazine that when a woman deep throats in that position the semen just flushes straight down her throat. No gagging, no clumps, no nothing . . . just a straight shot. If there were an Olympic category for dick sucking, Klarke would be awarded the gold on word of mouth alone (no pun intended).

Klarke did everything for Harris except breathe for him. When he came home from a solid day's work and didn't have a taste for what was on the kitchen table, Klarke never hesitated to whip him up something that would please him.

Harris got back rubs when it was Klarke's back that was aching. Klarke pampered Harris with foot massages when it was her feet that were tired. She took delight in every minute of it, though. It was her way of showing Harris gratitude for his role in allowing her to spend her days with their children instead of working a nine-to-five.

By the time Harris walked through the door in the evenings, the children's homework would be complete. Their clothes for the next day, along with his, were ironed and laid out. The children had been bathed and were ready for bed. Klarke kept the house immaculate, so it was always clean when Harris walked through the door, and the shower was running at his desired temperature. Dinner would be hot and dessert would be in the fridge. What Klarke came to find out, however, was that what she thought was keeping her husband honest, loyal, and committed was actually what made him the man of another woman's home.

When a man enters his home, he has the need to feel needed. As far as Harris was concerned, the only thing his home needed was his paycheck. He had often joked to his buddies that his wife's pretty titties hid an S. Although Klarke was exactly the woman he programmed her to be, her perfection made him feel less than a man. His castle was being reigned just fine by the queen.

Take the average married man, for instance, who is cheating on his wife. The other woman damn sure isn't as pretty as his wife, and nine times out of ten she's on Section 8. Her car is an older model that needs a new part each month, and her kids don't have a fit male figure in their lives. That's where his need to be needed is fulfilled. The man's shaft tingles when his pager goes off and it's the other woman needing him to come pick her up because her car broke down. She *needs* him to give her the money to get it fixed. His penis becomes erect when the other woman *needs* him to get her kid's school clothes out of layaway. He outright ejaculates when the other woman *needs* him to help her move from her Section 8 apartment to her Section 8 house.

Most of the time a man's unfaithfulness isn't even about sex. The man doesn't go to the other woman so that he can get his sexual needs fed. He goes to her to get his ego fed. It's called *eating out,* and that's just what Harris ended up doing.

Tionne was Harris's baby cousin. Not a blood-related cousin or even a cousin by marriage. The kind of "cousin" who grew up with the family and therefore qualifies as family. In short, the kind that it's okay to sleep with.

Klarke was never aware of the fact that Harris and Tionne had something going on. It wasn't out of the ordinary for Tionne and Harris to spend time together. Tionne was over at the house on a regular, and at Harris's mother's house for Sunday dinner after church. Klarke liked Tionne. Tionne was only a couple of years older than she was, and the two had even gone out together on several occasions. By the time Klarke found out that Harris was a clandestine adulterer, he and Tionne's love-child was going on one year old.

The affair completely shattered Klarke. When Harris told her the truth about his relationship with Tionne, she took to her bed, and it was weeks before she would regain the strength to get up again. Harris might as well have been Ike Turner and beat her ass for the past thirteen years because that's just the kind of pain Klarke felt consumed by. Her body literally ached all over. She wanted to die. She knew she had to pull it together for her children, but inside she just wanted to die.

It's a wonder she didn't get bedsores because all she did was lie in the bed crying and contemplating suicide. The house became a neglected mixture of clutter and filth. She couldn't even muster up the strength to take out the garbage. The stench had been horrible.

For the children, it had been the next best thing to being at Disneyland. Chores were on hold indefinitely, and they were left to fend for themselves, which meant a diet of ice cream, potato chips, and an array of other junk foods. Vaughn, was very mature for her age, so she kept herself and HJ situated.

Klarke wouldn't answer the phone or the door. She had changed the locks to keep Harris out and her voicemail was full of messages from well-meaning friends and family who genuinely cared about how Klarke was doing, but at the same time were itching to get the scoop. She was too humiliated to oblige them. She herself didn't understand what had happened. She certainly could not explain it to others.

Klarke was the nova of her family and friends. What everyone was working so hard to obtain had seemed to be handed to Klarke on a silver platter. On the outside looking in, she had it all: a beautiful daughter and handsome son, gorgeous home, nice vehicles, expensive housewares, designer clothes, and a few boast-worthy pieces of jewelry. Above all, it appeared that she had an admirable and faithful husband.

How could this have happened? Klarke had thought as she lay in bed crying. *I thought a woman always knew. What the fuck happened to my intuition?*

It sickened Klarke when she thought about the times she had welcomed that woman into her home, her life, and the lives of her children. She had babysat for Tionne and Harris's baby! After five weeks of not being able to eat, sleep, think, drink, or function there was only one thing Klarke could do to kick the bitter feelings and anguish behind her. . . . KICK THAT BITCH'S BEHIND!

Prior to this ordeal, Klarke had pretty much been a noncon-frontational individual. She never made a big deal over trivial mat-ters. She respected that there were folks in the world with bigger problems than hers. She appreciated life's challenges and played with the hand she was dealt. But this particular hand contained a wild card.

Klarke didn't bother to run a comb through her matted hair. She didn't bother to secure her 36 Cs with a bra. It was only 30 degrees Fahrenheit outside and she just threw on her Ohio State University T-shirt, a pair of cutoff sweat shorts, her flip-flops, and grabbed the kids and headed over to Tionne's.

After loading her children into the backseat of the Rodeo, Klarke drove calmly to Tionne's Section 8 townhouse. Klarke pulled up and parked next to Tionne's ten-year-old Toyota Corolla and told the children she would be right back.

She wanted to pull a Jackie Chan and kick in the door, which was made of a combination of metal and aluminum with chipped brown paint. Instead she knocked lightly and waited for Tionne to come to the door.

"Klarke," Tionne said, startled, when she halfway opened the door.

"I figured it's about time we talked. May I come in?" Klarke asked in her most amiable voice.

Tionne hesitated before saying, "Sure, Klarke." After another brief hesitation Tionne slowly opened the door for Klarke to enter.

"I don't know what to say to you. I can't even come up with the right words," Klarke said.

"You shouldn't have to say anything. This is entirely my fault. I'm sorry. As lame as that sounds, I truly am sorry," Tionne said with sincerity as she put her hand upon Klarke's shoulder. Klarke looked down at Tionne's hand. It took everything in her to stay calm.

Tionne gestured for Klarke to sit down at the kitchen table and offered her a soda, which Klarke accepted. She didn't know how she managed to swallow. She was so busy visualizing a fistful of Tionne's burgundy microbraids dangling from her hand.

"Where's the baby?" Klarke asked, knowing she couldn't act out if the child was in the house.

"Oh, she's with her fath . . ." Tionne said, her words trailing off awkwardly. For the past five weeks she had finally been able to freely tell people that Harris was the father of her child. It felt good after having to keep it secret for so long.

Just that quick Klarke knew the small talk was over. No *Why? How long? Does he pay your bills?* or *Did he eat you out?* At that very moment Tionne was every woman who had raped another woman of her man and family.

Klarke launched herself out of her chair and on to Tionne and began swinging. She made sure she gave Tionne a hit, kick, punch, smack, jab, sock, whack, scratch, slug, and bite for every sistah out there who had been played. It was a beat-down worthy of pay-per-view.

Klarke knocked Tionne down and sat on top of her. Locks of Tionne's braids filled Klarke's hands as she slammed Tionne's head over and over against the floor.

Tionne managed to buck Klarke off of her. Klarke came after Tionne like a raging bull and Tionne kicked her in the stomach, almost knocking the wind out of her. Klarke hunched over holding her stomach, gasping for air.

Tionne turned over and tried to crawl away, but Klarke quickly recovered and grabbed Tionne's foot and dragged her back. She flipped Tionne over and jumped back on top of her. She pinned Tionne's arms to the floor with her knees and continued to beat the living daylights out of Tionne.

After about ten consecutive blows to the mug, Klarke stood over her while she moaned and groaned.

Maybe she's had enough, Klarke thought to herself. After all, the tramp at her feet was only human. Klarke did feel *some* sympathy for her opponent. But as she stood there looking down at Tionne, she became pissed off all over again.

"Fuck that!" Klarke said and pulled Tionne up from the kitchen floor and began whaling on her some more.

Tionne was a helpless rag doll as Klarke knocked her around the kitchen, breaking a few dishes and a chair along the way. Unfortunately, Tionne didn't have a timekeeper to ring the bell, or a referee to break up the fight and declare the bout a TKO. Klarke pounced on Tionne until the blood-covered whore looked like she was near death. Klarke didn't want Tionne dead, though.

Klarke felt justified and satisfied. Each blow had been her mouthpiece. Before returning to her children, who were waiting for her in the truck, Klarke knelt on the floor next to Tionne. With her lips barely touching Tionne's swollen earlobe she asked the only question that truly mattered to her, "How long have you wanted to be me?"

When Klarke returned home, she put on her Rachelle Ferrell *Individuality* CD, ordered the children to clean their pigpens, and started working on her house. She couldn't believe how much filth and dust had accumulated. Knowing her daughter had asthma, she felt selfish for allowing it to get that bad.

She cleaned as she sang along with Ms. Ferrell. The frantic cleansing of her house was a symbol of the cleansing of her spirit.

As Klarke dusted the bar and stools she couldn't help but

admire all the expensive bottles of wine, champagne, and liquor Harris had collected over the years. Harris was so proud of this bar. As a matter of fact, he had actually taken a week's vacation from work just to customize it. He had installed a black marble floor to host the eight-seater bar and plastered mirrors above the mantel he built.

The high-priced beverages were strictly for show. Harris never intended to actually drink them. It was a silent boast, kind of like that loser who runs around the club all night with an empty bottle of Moët. Just in case everybody didn't see him and his crew sipping on it, he takes it onto the dance floor and dances with it. He thinks he looks like a baller but in actuality he looks like the man from the movie *Car Wash* who carried that bottle around to piss in.

Klarke picked up the gold-trimmed bottle of Cristal in one hand and the opal black-trimmed bottle of Dom in the other, and sang, "Eeney, meeny, minee, moe."

She looked in the mirror panel, raised the bottle of Cristal and toasted aloud, "Happy Birthday, Klarke Taylor," before drinking every single drop. Klarke felt born again. Soon she would no longer be Mrs. Harris Bradshaw. She would be unattached, a gift to bestow unto the world.

After the divorce Klarke would manage to take out a student loan and earn a two-year degree at a local community college. She began seeing a man named Rawling, who was also one of her professors. After only an eight-month courtship, the two married. Six months later, Rawling decided he needed his space, that they had married too soon. Klarke didn't put up a fight or was she bitter. She had married him out of fear anyway, the fear of being alone. They had the marriage annulled.

Klarke's marriage to Rawling was so brief that no spousal

support was awarded to her, and her second marriage had terminated the alimony payments Harris had been ordered by the court to pay. Klarke couldn't believe she screwed up that restitution. She still received child support for the children, but Klarke had become accustomed to a certain lifestyle. She had gotten used to drinking champagne when she should have been drinking lemonade. Eventually she began drinking lemonade, but by then it was too late. She should have been drinking water with lemon wedges.

1

All Work—No Play

"Miss Taylor, you have a call," the receptionist's voice said over the intercom. Klarke hated when she got a phone call while someone was at her desk. It just so happened that her boss, Evan, was standing over her with a rush print order.

Opalescent Press had just placed a print order for one of their best-selling author's books. They needed seven hundred thousand copies of his latest, *Dollar Bill*, in one week. Apparently the author was scheduled to appear on *Oprah*, so bookstores from all over were putting in orders. With Klarke being the executive accounts representative and company liaison, she was put in charge of the project.

Klarke was honored to be handling this account. Opalescent Press was a major publishing house and one of the company's largest clients. They housed some of the top authors in the United States. Klarke had just seen the author of *Dollar Bill* on a late-night television talk show. Klarke recalled that he was single and not bad looking at all. She had even imagined how nice it would be to be the woman by his side to help catch the windfall of dollar bills that he was about to come upon. On top of that, she could say the hell with her job.

She had been working for the company a little over a year and a half, ever since her divorce from Rawling. With no man and no money, Klarke had been forced to get a job.

"Can you put the call to my voicemail, please?" Klarke asked.

"Oh, go ahead and take it," Evan said.

Klarke could tell he wanted to be nosy. Not only that, but catching her on a personal call would give Evan a rise. It had only been a month since she got off probation for excess personal phone usage. Evan seemed to find personal enjoyment in reprimanding Klarke ever since she had turned down his dinner invitation.

Klarke had already pledged not to let her business relationships and her personal life mix. She knew from the moment she stepped into Evan's office for her second interview with him that he was going to test her conviction.

Instead of him coming to meet her in the lobby and interviewing her in the conference room, as he had done on the first interview, she had been instructed to go directly to his office.

Evan couldn't stop licking his lips once he laid his ocean-blue eyes on Klarke's five-feet-five-inch banging silhouette as she stood outside of his office door. He had been so excited and caught up as to the treat on the other side that he couldn't distinguish Klarke's faint knock from his own heartbeat.

He had been looking forward to Klarke's Friday afternoon appointment. Never had a black woman made this all-American white boy cream his Hanes.

Behind closed doors a cunt was a cunt, be it chocolate or vanilla (hell, strawberry and banana too, for that matter). Evan could have cared less about not being able to take Klarke home to

meet his upper-class suburban family. He only cared about satisfying his curious chocolate craving.

Klarke was a very sensual woman. It was the way she looked at
a man, the shape of her lips when she spoke, the way her bronze-
tinted puffy locks rested softly on the nape of her neck. It was the
way her Cimmerian skin looked as if gold glitter had been dusted
over it.

She made love to herself when she rubbed her legs and arms,
or grazed her chin and cheek with the back of her hand. She suspected she was beautiful, yet she wasn't entirely sure. She wore a
deliberate, smile that said, If I'm not beautiful, at least I'm
happy. Klarke felt that a person had to possess at least one of
three things in order to get by in life: money, beauty, or happiness.

As Klarke patiently waited outside the frosted glass door to
Evan's sky-rise office, Evan ran his fingers through his moussed
blond hair. He loosened his silk tie and undid the top button of
his crisp white shirt before clearing his throat to grant Klarke permission to enter.

Since her first interview two weeks prior, Evan had fantasized
about throwing Klarke on his desk, lifting her tight miniskirt,
pulling her thong to the side, and fucking the shit out of her. Or
pinning her up against his glass window and pumping her so hard
that her sweaty ass cheeks left their imprint behind. He fantasized about her sucking his erect penis until cum exploded down
her throat and dripped from between those almond lips of hers. It
was no wonder he hired her and gave her an annual salary of five
thousand-dollars more than the white girl she had replaced, who
had been there almost seven years.

Normally the administrative assistant, Renée did all the training, but Evan had trained Klarke himself. The standard one-week
training lasted almost three weeks and included five lunch sessions.

Klarke always made sure to carry a pencil and pad to lunch as a corroboration of her business-only stance. She knew her boss was feeling her and didn't want to lead him on in any way.

It was their final lunch date when Evan grabbed hold of his balls and asked Klarke out for dinner. Klarke answered him with a simple no. She didn't even give him an explanation. She didn't smile or pretend to be flattered. She simply said no, then took a bite of her turkey club and a sip of her Shirley Temple. From that point on she was no longer the house nigger as far as Evan was concerned. She was back in the field with all the rest of the black folk.

"Kemble and Steiner Printing," Klarke said in her *white* voice. "Klarke Taylor speaking."

She could feel Evan's eyes on her tongue as he listened.

It was the finance company for her Rodeo, calling to inquire as to whether or not she would be making her monthly payment.

Evan didn't even try to pretend that he wasn't paying undivided attention to Klarke's conversation. *He's probably got nut running down his legs,* Klarke thought. *At least I finally made the fucker cum.*

After a shitty day at the office Klarke hopped into her shitty vehicle and drove her regular route home. There had been an accident on I-75, so the traffic on the freeway was at a complete standstill. Klarke's seven-minute drive turned into forty-five minutes.

While sitting in traffic Klarke just happened to look over into the burgundy Nissan Maxima on her right-hand side. The gentleman driving was very nice looking. He was a bald-headed, deep-chocolate brotha. He looked to be the clean-cut type, sporting a short-sleeved, cream-colored henley. He had a thick gold rope chain around his neck with a diamond cross. Everything about him said class and money. He smiled at Klarke. His pearly whites sparkled like he was on a Colgate commercial. Klarke smiled back. He winked. Klarke blushed.

Klarke looked ahead to make sure traffic hadn't inched any. She just knew the guy was going to say, "Excuse me Miss, what's your name?" But he said nothing.

Why won't he holla? Klarke thought to herself. *Hell, it's the new millennium. Why am I waiting on him to make the first move?*

Klarke straightened up in her seat, cleared her throat, then turned to look at the gentleman. As she opened her mouth to speak nothing came out. Staring back at her was a young thugged-out looking dude with a wave cap on his head. His vehicle, a huge black Lincoln Navigator with spinners, had taken the place of the bald-headed deep-chocolate brotha's. The young man was bouncing to the song "Get Low" by Lil Jon and the East Side Boyz blazing from a huge speaker in the tailgate of his vehicle. The young man was singing along with the song word for word. All Klarke could hear was *bitch* this and *ho* that.

When the young fella caught Klarke looking at him he smiled, then licked his lips as if he could have eaten her right up. His grill had been invaded by silver. He probably received radio signals in that mouth. Other than that, he was kind of cute, in a thugged-out sort of way. It was obvious he had a nice hunk of change. If the oversized SUV didn't scream out money, then those two-carat diamond earrings did.

Klarke cracked a crooked smile at him. Maybe he wasn't so

bad. Besides, she hadn't had a good dick between her legs since Rawling. Perhaps Nelly over there could show her a thing or two. Maybe a thug in her life was exactly what she needed.

Klarke imagined being in the backseat of his Navigator, riding his young ass like a mechanical bull. He'd probably be ordering her around with words like *"shake that ass, bitch"* or *"fuck that dick, ho."* A little dirty talk never hurt nobody. Maybe Stella had something going with that getting-your-groove-back shit.

The driver in the car behind Klarke laying on her horn broke Klarke's thoughts. Traffic had begun to move again. Now even the young thug had proceeded down the highway. Klarke had just lost her chance at two men in less than five minutes. She gritted her teeth in frustration.

"From now on I am not waiting around on any man to make the first move," Klarke said out loud. "From this point on, I'm calling the shots. I'm making all of the rules to the game. Never again will I let a man have control of my destiny."

Klarke thought back to how she had been robbed of the lifestyle she had been accustomed to when she and Harris divorced. She got ill thinking about her interlude with Rawling, another man who didn't know what the fuck he wanted in a woman. Although unfortunate for him, the next man in Klarke's life would have to pay for the sins of the others.

The more Klarke thought about it, the more motivated she was to change the current course of her life's path. "Let the games begin."

And Klarke had just the game in mind. She put the pedal to the metal so that she could get home and begin executing her plan.

2

You've Got Mail

"What a day." Reo sighed as he collapsed onto the king-size bed in his suite at the Omni Hotel in downtown Chicago. He wished that for just once his publicist would get her ass on a plane and hit up two or three bookstores. A brother appreciated the seven-figure contract, but damn. After a three-month spell, his body was pleading for a break. Reo wasn't used to all the travel his five-book deal would entail. He had never been on a plane in his life and now, after thirty-three years, here he was committing infidelities on his hometown of Columbus, Ohio's, modest skyline.

Reo's complaints were short lived, however. Every time he thought about his dedicated following of readers that awaited his arrival to their town, Reo's dick got hard. He had finally done it. He had gone from a $40,000-a-year teaching salary to that of a two-time best-selling author's. Up until a year ago Reo had only dreamed of arriving at the independent African American book-stores with a line of people waiting to buy autographed copies of his books. It didn't bother him one bit that over three-fourths of them were beautiful women.

Being a bestselling author had always been Reo's dream. Tales seemed to spill out of him. He had a vivid imagination, and initially he wrote for his own personal pleasure or just to get stuff off of his chest. Then he had shared his writings with his father, who also thought that Reo had true talent.

Reo's father, who taught college English comp and was considered a respected authority in the community, helped him put together his first book, which was a compilation of short stories. In a strictly advisory role, of course. Reo laughed to himself as he remembered an incident in grade school.

Reo's sixth-grade teacher, Miss Willoughby, had accused him of plagiarism on a paper he wrote on the march on Washington, which was worth 50 percent of his grade. The teacher knew Reo's father's profession, which had been high school English teacher at the time, and had accused Reo of having his father complete the paper for him.

The teacher rejected the paper and gave Reo a week's extension to complete another one. Reo had been crushed. One word of dispute would have caused him to erupt into tears in front of the whole class. He simply took the paper back from Miss Willoughby and placed it in his book bag.

When he got home from school he fell into his mother's arms. Reo had held his tears in for two hours, twenty-three minutes, and eighteen seconds. His head was throbbing and his eyes were stinging. He could barely relay the tragedy to his mother.

Mrs. Laroque couldn't sleep that night. She must have rehearsed in the mirror a thousand times what she was going to say to that teacher. How dare someone, anyone, send her baby home in tears!

The next morning, when Reo's mother, who was still fresh with anger, had finished ranting and raving, he begged her to just allow him to write another paper. He didn't know what was worse, being accused of plagiarism or his mother being hand-cuffed and taken off to the jail for laying Miss Willoughby out.

Mr. Laroque convinced his wife to allow him to handle the situation. Reo was relieved. He knew how his mother could be. He remembered his mother clobbering the neighborhood bully's mother for cheering on her son to fight Reo. That was the first time Reo had heard the adage *the apple doesn't fall far from the tree*. But after the way his momma beat that poor woman's tail, he wasn't too sure who the tree was, his mother or the bully's.

Reo was amazed and proud at how his father handled Miss Willoughby. Mr. Laroque turned the table and told her how insulted he was to be accused of having the writing skills of a sixth grader. He then told her how proud she must be as a teacher for producing pupils who could turn out such well-written pieces of writing and how wonderful it must be to brag to her colleagues.

By the time Mr. Laroque finished swelling Miss Willoughby's head, she was inviting the family over for dinner. Reo was permitted to resubmit the same paper. He received an A+ and the chance to read it to the sixth-grade student body during an honors assembly. He had never felt more proud than to be the fruit of his father's tree.

After numerous rejections of Reo's short stories from publishing houses, Reo decided to self-publish his book. Every dime he earned was put toward the writing, editing, printing, distribution, and promotion of his book. He gave his two-year-old, fully loaded Nissan Altima back to the bank and bought a fifteen-year-old Chevrolet Chevette that didn't even have AC. He gave up his suburban German Village studio and moved back home with his mom and dad. He sold his furniture, pawned his jewelry, and even borrowed against his 401K plan.

Reo called in to radio stations to discuss his book. He wrote fill-in articles for newspapers and magazines, which helped to promote his book. He beat the pavement, visiting beauty and barber shops to spread the word about his book. He visited parking lots where conferences were taking place and put fliers about his book on all the car windshields. He drove from city to city and neighboring states doing this. He sold the book from out of his trunk and out of his briefcase. He even gave it away for free.

It was a long, hard sacrifice, but in the end it paid off. In the beginning though, it was a struggle. He lost Meka, his high school sweetheart and fiancée at the time.

Meka and Reo held the record for the longest engagement ever. It was a well-known fact that the engagement ring Reo had presented to Meka, Christmas of 1999, was really a hush ring. That year, every other word out of Meka's mouth had pertained to marriage. It had gotten so bad she had been holding out on sex. She claimed that she felt guilty having sex under the Lord's watch without even the possibility of marriage on the horizon. Reo had to do something to shut her up so he pretty much proposed under duress.

Meka was from a well-to-do family. Her mother was a doctor and her father was a lobbyist for telephone companies. Meka was a dental hygienist studying to become a dentist. She planned to open her own practice. She was the eldest of three daughters, and each of her sisters had married men who were also from well-to-do families.

Meka wholeheartedly supported Reo's publishing efforts. She wanted to see him succeed. Nothing thrilled her more than the idea of being the wife of a successful writer. She had begged him to let her give him money toward the production of his book, but he declined the offer. He had seen *Judge Mathis* one too many times and knew that a gift from a current girlfriend metamorphosed into a loan with interest upon breakup. There was no way some woman, or anybody else for that matter, was going to be able to stake a claim on his talent and success.

Meka went as far as suggesting Reo move into her loft rent-free. There was no way Reo was going to give her the pleasure of being able to put him out of *her* house every time they got into an argument. Lord knows that was a woman's favorite declaration: "This is my house, muthafucker."

Eventually, it became too unpleasant for Meka to roll in a Chevette, and shameful for her to tell people her fiancé lived with his parents. Reo's sacrifices were more than Meka was willing to make. She could not continue subjecting herself to such humiliation.

Of course, once Reo's book dominated the number-one spot on the national bestseller lists for a record fifteen weeks straight, Meka was back on his dick again, literally. As soon as she caught wind of his accomplishment she called to congratulate him.

A simple phone call wasn't adequate for Meka. She invited him to her loft for a celebration dinner with a guest list including only the two of them. With slight trepidation, Reo accepted her invitation.

When he arrived at Meka's loft he was escorted to a candle-lit dining table, where he was greeted by a small feast. Meka had never made him a peanut-butter-and-jelly sandwich before, and yet here she had managed to whip up a meatloaf, twice-baked mashed potatoes, mac'n'cheese, some collard greens, and buttered rolls.

Reo gobbled down the spread as if it were the Last Supper. They conversed while intoxicating themselves on shots of Hennessy. This was surprising to Reo, as he had only known Meka to sip on cutesy drinks such as fuzzy navels and wine coolers. As a special congratulatory token Meka decided that she would be dessert, so she excused herself from the table in order to begin her preparations.

Reo got reacquainted with the leather sofa in the den that he had made himself comfortable on many times before. He managed to flick through a few channels on the big-screen television until Meka entered the den modeling a Frederick's of Hollywood black chemise. Before Reo could even compliment her appearance, she was feeding him her tongue, nipples, and fingertips that bore the color of Cherries Jubilee polish on the nails.

Departing from their regular sexual encounters, Meka did things to him that he had only fantasized about or had seen on a porno tape. Their acts ventured on the verge of obscene. He screwed her in every position they could think of and invented a few new ones as well. He beat up her pussy like it had done him wrong. She fanatically sucked his dick, licked his balls, and allowed him to give her a pearl necklace. In other words, she let him jerk in her face. She grazed the crack of his ass back and forth with her tongue as if she was licking the ice cream from in between an ice-cream sandwich. What tripped him out was the fact that the glossy crimson lipstick on her lips seemed unaffected. He now understood why she had spent excessive amounts of money on those damn Mary Kay cosmetics. They were everlasting.

Reo had cum more in that one night than he had in his whole life. At least that's what it felt like anyway. He was almost certain that his last climax, like a twelve-year-old boy jacking off for the first time, had been dry.

Reo's mind was blown, considering Meka was somewhat of a tightass. Sex with her, for Reo, had been like a cop on traffic duty. Meka had limitations on how far Reo could insert his penis into her vagina. She preferred he be on top and properly centered.

When he was eating her out he couldn't stick his tongue inside her. He could only suck her clit. When it was time for him to cum he had to pull out because she hated cleaning his fluids from inside of her. One would have thought she hired Paula Abdul to choreograph their lovemaking.

Everything about Meka was predictable, from the way she wore her hair in a tight, low-maintenance bun to the white French cuff shirt and navy bottoms she sported. But on that night it was safe to say that Meka had let her hair down. It also explained those shots of Hennessy she had taken. Like a call girl about to take on her first trick, she needed the liquor to both warrant and excuse her conduct.

After their sexcapade, Meka rested on Reo's chest and they both dozed off for a while. When he woke up, Reo slid from underneath the sleeping beauty and began putting his clothing back on. Meka slowly woke up when she heard him moving around.

"Where are you going, sweetie?" she asked with a yawn.

"It's late. I better get going," Reo answered.

"You don't have to go."

"Yeah, I know," Reo said as he sat back down on the couch. "I want to go."

Meka's mouth dropped open as she sat up. "What do you mean you want to go?"

Reo could tell she was shocked and disappointed. Nonetheless he proceeded to put on his socks and shoes.

"It was good seeing you again. Dinner was lovely and dessert was extraordinary. Thank you."

"Whoa. Hold up. Thank you? Thank you? Is that all I get is a thank you?"

Reo ignored her, a smirk on his face as he searched for the keys to his new Escalade. Meka felt disgusted. Here she had done things that were sure to make her sick to her stomach in the morning, things she would deny ever doing on a stack of Bibles, all in hopes of reeling Reo back into her life. But from the beginning Reo saw right through her scheme. She was just too damn predictable.

"You ate my food. You drank my liquor. You screwed me all night long and all I get is a lousy 'thank you.' Hell, I didn't even get to cum."

Reo knew she was getting ready to recite the angry woman anthem *"You can't even fuck. You don't even make me cum. That's why you have a little-ass dick . . . blah blah blah."*

"Well, what were you expecting?" Reo said before she could get warmed up.

Meka just sat there looking at him, dumbfounded. She couldn't very well tell him that she had expected to pussy-whip him back into a relationship with her. She couldn't tell him that she had expected to get back with him and spend all of his new money.

"I don't know, a little respect maybe?" Meka said, putting her clothes back on. Reo couldn't contain his laughter. "What the hell is so funny? Did I just tell a joke? Am I on fucking Def Comedy Jam?"

"Respect . . . that's funny coming from a woman who just licked my ass clean."

Meka could not have slapped Reo any harder without hurting herself. But he saw it coming and braced himself for the impact. He knew he deserved it, but it felt good to finally take charge. Throughout their relationship, just to keep the drama at a minimum, he had allowed her to belittle him and boss him around. It was fair turnabout.

Meka decided to turn on the waterworks. Reo chuckled under his breath as he headed to the door.

"I ate your food because I was hungry. I drank your liquor because I was thirsty. Hell, I screwed you all night long because I was horny. Now I'm leaving because I'm finished. In other words, my dear, you've just been humbled."

The gray marble tabletop clock missed Reo's head by only a centimeter as he closed the door behind him, shattering into a million pieces, right along with Meka's pride.

That was the last time Reo hooked up with Meka. Strange, but he had missed the hell out of her, too, because as far as intimacy was concerned, Meka had been all his body had known for a long time.

Finding female companionship wasn't a challenge for Reo. Women came in droves. But what Reo soon found out was that love didn't come at all. Most women Reo encountered already knew him as Reo Laroque, the national bestselling author. When they were talking to him, they were talking to the dollar signs in his bank account. When they were fucking him, they were actually fucking his wallet. So Reo never took any of the women he had hooked up with seriously. Lately, though, Reo had been truly longing for a genuine woman to call his own. One who could care less about Reo the bestselling author, but care, instead, about Reo the man.

Eventually Reo rolled out of his hotel bed and jumped into the shower. He knew the Omni was very efficient when it came to service, so he decided to wait and order from the in-room dining menu after his shower. He didn't want to risk not hearing the server's arrival.

After scrubbing his five-feet-eleven-inch frame with his Mambo body wash, Reo moisturized his ebony-toned body with the matching lotion. He massaged his scalp and *good hair* with a Carefree moisturizer and edged up his goatee.

After ordering a Cobb salad and a glass of champagne, Reo pulled out his laptop to check his e-mails. His inbox was always full of fan mail, so he had to keep on top of it. Book clubs and bookstores alike e-mailed invitations for Reo to sign and do readings for them. Reo scrolled down immediately deleting the spam. He didn't have time to waste viewing unsolicited long-distance plans or pharmaceutical specials for Viagra.

After reading and replying to several e-mails, Reo then checked his private e-mail address. One e-mail in particular caught his attention, with the subject heading "Boston Airport." Reo didn't even bother looking at who the sender was. He knew it was from his publicist. Whenever a book signing had been scheduled for him, the city in which the book signing was to take place was always in the heading.

"Isn't this just great?" Reo muttered. "Another damn signing. In Boston no less."

From: KAT@myworld.biz
To: RLQ812@sunset.com
Subject: Boston Airport

Hey you!
I hope all is well. I noticed that you had "accidentally" left the business card I gave you on the restaurant table. I'm assuming the rush of hearing the last boarding call for your flight was the reason you forgot it. I had a good time talking to you. I can't believe we lost track of time. Funny how time flies, huh?

I was cleaning out my briefcase and I found the piece of

paper you wrote your e-mail address on for me. I just wanted to drop you a line and let you know that it was a pleasure meeting you. I never knew a layover in the Boston airport could be so exhilarating. I'm referring to my time spent with you, of course. :-)

Once you get settled into your new apartment and office in New York City, perhaps you can call me sometime. I would love to keep in touch. Let me know and I'll give you my number again.

Sincerely,
Your newfound friend

A warm feeling came over Reo. He couldn't explain it. It was as if he wasn't reading the e-mail, but as if the voice of the sender was speaking the words directly to him.

Then there was a the knock on the door. "Room service," a voice called. Reo walked over to the door to look through the peephole. He opened the door. A tall, fair-skinned girl with medium length, dark brown hair rolled in his order. She was checking out Reo so hard that she couldn't keep from bumping into the bureau with the cart.

"Thank you, um, Jheri," Reo said, reading her nametag.

"You are so very welcome Reo—I mean, Mr. Laroque, sir."

"Reo is fine."

"Yes, sir. I mean, Reo."

Reo quickly signed the receipt and handed it to the girl. She took the receipt, but just stood there like she had shitted on herself and couldn't move.

"Do you need anything else from me?"

"Uh, no sir—I mean, Reo."

Becoming a little annoyed by the starstruck server, Reo walked over to the door and opened it for the girl.

"Oh, I'm sorry. Yeah, all I needed was your autograph—I mean your signature."

"Very well. You have a good evening."

Reo couldn't believe the girl just kept standing there. He was hoping she didn't become as bold as the cleaning lady at the Royal Sonesta Hotel in the New Orleans French Quarter. That woman had actually gotten butt-ass naked and laid herself out on the bed for Reo to have his way with her. The little Latino woman hadn't even spoken good English. All Reo understood was *"boom boom."*

"As a matter of fact there is something I need from you," the girl said as she began to dig in her bra. Reo grabbed her arms and pushed her out of the room.

"You are a beautiful young lady with a lot going for yourself," Reo said, his tone scolding. "Don't you dare degrade yourself or your body."

The girl's eyes filled with tears as she held the dollar bill in her hand that she had pulled from her bra.

"I'm so sorry, Mr. Laroque—I mean Reo, sir. I usually never do this, but I just really wanted you to autograph this dollar. I'm in college majoring in journalism and I just really admire your writing style. *Dollar Bill* was magnificent and . . . I'm just so sorry." The girl cried as she hurried down the hall and around the corridor out of Reo's sight.

Reo just stood there in awe before bursting out laughing. "When did I become so vain?" He laughed.

Reo closed the door, returned to his laptop and reread the e-mail that was still on his computer screen. Although it was pretty simple it was sweet. Reo made his living creating fantasy. Maybe this time, instead of creating a fantasy for millions of readers, he could create a little one for himself.

He sipped on his champagne, hit reply, and began to type.

3

Window Shopping

Klarke always wanted what she either didn't or couldn't have. Which was why she and her lady friends, Jeva and Breezy, would spend hours consoling one another's monetary shortages by window shopping. They truly found comfort in it.

It became a third-Saturday-of-the-month ritual for the girls to spend the afternoon window-shopping. They would get up that morning, get their fake workout on (that five minutes they relayed to each other as twenty), chase the workout with a bowl of cereal, shower, then squirm into some little number guaranteed to highlight all the assets—going braless, pantyless, or both.

Window shopping wasn't fun unless the sun was cooperating. If clouds even teased with the threat of rain, their monthly excursion was put on hold. There was something about the sunshine that complemented a woman's scent, her body, and her hair. They knew the sun was the true pimp. Nothing was quite as good at showcasing a woman to her best advantage.

Klarke, Jeva, and Breezy always met at the same location, but Klarke was always the last to arrive. She did it on purpose. She knew she was the finest of the three and loved walking onto the scene like Dorothy Dandridge in *Carmen*. It's kind of like a bachelor party. A couple of modest madeup dolls go shake their ass for a few minutes, and then the main attraction comes out to give the bachelor the time of his life. Klarke was saving the best for last.

Klarke possessed the average 36 C bust, but her legs were her true assets. They went on for days. Her fair complexion was clear and she always wore light makeup.

At thirty-four, Klarke knew it took just a little more effort to be sexy than it had two babies ago. But being average just was not an option for her. Even when she was younger, she always had to be the exception.

Klarke's clothes had to be the best, and always worn with class. She could have on the exact same outfit as both Jeva and Breezy, yet one would never notice it. Klarke liked to be a little different when it came to her wardrobe. She was good for wearing a tie-back sweater backwards, or a long skirt as a tube dress. Her fashion style was a perfect mixture of funky and classy. She always stood out.

Jeva and Breezy were fine as well. Klarke didn't keep company with people who didn't complement her own flavor.

Jeva was a cute half Caucasian, half Hispanic *mami*, Colombian. She was only five feet tall with straight black hair down to her buttocks. Besides her slanted bedroom eyes that drove men crazy, her stand-out feature was her deep dimples that were visible even when she wasn't smiling.

Because Jeva had been given up at birth, she had never known either of her parents. When Jeva turned eighteen she had gone to the Welford Child Placement Agency, the place that handled her initial foster-home placement. She was hoping that there was some information on her biological parents that would allow her to find them. The agency had nothing. As a matter of fact, Jeva's records had been lost. There was no explanation. They were just gone.

All Jeva knew was that her mother was Colombian and her father was white. This information was given to her by one of her many foster moms. That was always one of the first things people wanted to know when they took in her exotic features, her nationality. It was also the reason she would get beat up by the other girls. Boys tended to get soft in the head over a pretty, exotic-looking little girl, but the girls would be hating! No matter where she was she just never fit in, so she was constantly in and out of foster homes.

In the homes a kid was either black or white. Jeva didn't even fall in between with her Hispanic bloodline and features. After so many years of being teased, if Jeva was asked what she was she would reply that she was a honky spic. The sad thing about it was that she would say it with such pride. It was like a little black boy being asked what he was and replying conceitedly, "A *nigger*."

Going on twenty-nine, Jeva still struggled with identity issues and hated that she would not be able to share much about herself with her own daughter, Heather. She was just happy to be raising her in a two-parent home. Jeva wasn't married to Lance, her husbfriend. But when she wasn't working as an amateur photographer, she was working on getting Lance to marry her. At this point, though, her efforts hadn't even gotten her a hush ring.

Breezy, on the other hand, knew she was all woman and then some. She was a thick, full-figured woman with a cute face. There was no jiggle in her walk. She was more than enough woman for more than one man, which was why she divided her time between two of them, one of whom happened to be married.

Her short, boblike haircut molded her round face becomingly.

Her men swore she had the most voluptuous ass on earth, and her full breasts could make a grown man cry. Her ghetto vocabulary was a repellent for unwanted conversations with men. But sistah knew how to shut the fellas down with just a few choice words from her ghettosaurus.

You either loved Breezy or hated her. It was as simple as that. She had a fresh mouth and could get real cute sometimes. She really wasn't that ghetto, but she was used to being hard as a way of keeping people at a distance and out of her business. There was only so much of Breezy's life, especially her past, that she was willing to share, even with her girlfriends.

Breezy had worked hard mentally to close a few chapters in her life. She'd dealt with many tragedies, the most devastating being the events that led to the incarceration of her father and her mother eventually divorcing him. Breezy had taken the divorce hard. To this day Breezy and her mother didn't even speak. Breezy blamed her mother for abandoning her father when he needed her the most.

If it had not been for Breezy, her father would have never been incarcerated in the first place. She never spoke of the actual events, but in the back of her mind, she was afraid of loving a man so much and then losing him, the way she lost her father. So, Breezy used men instead. No love, no loss.

When Jeva and Breezy arrived at the Cheesecake Factory they knew that they were going to have to wait the standard thirty minutes for Klarke's arrival. They sat on the patio at their designated table, sipping on drinks and killing time with their latest gossip.

"So, what's been going on with your husb-friend, Lance?" Breezy asked.

"Same old, same old. Still no ring. I give up. I'm just going to leave it alone."

"I've been telling you that for years. He takes care of the baby and he fucks you right. What do you need a ring for? You and Klarke kill me with that marriage hoopla."

"Well, there are some women out there who are still traditional and want more than sex out of a relationship, thank you very much," Jeva said smartly.

"You mean there's actually more to a relationship than sex?" Breezy joked. "Oh yeah, how could I forget? Money!"

"See, that's your problem," Jeva began to preach.

"What, what's my problem, Jeva? Don't hate because my kitty is made to purr on a regular."

"Hold up now, Lance can handle his business."

"I know."

"How do you know?"

"I figured he must be putting it down for you to be with him this long as pressed as you are about marriage."

"If getting laid is so important to you, then why do you have all those vibrators, beads, and finger puppets and stuff? I mean, like, I'm surprised you haven't been diagnosed with carpal tunnel."

"Ha, ha. But, anyway, all that stuff is backup," Breezy said, waving a hand. "I've had some doozies before, or—what's that word for a firecracker that won't pop? Oh yeah, a dud. I'm talking the kind where you get down on your knees and just ask God, Why did you only give him five inches? Couldn't you have at least made it fat?"

Jeva laughed. "You're going to hell, Breezy. Straight to hell."

"That's cool with me 'cause I know ain't no fucking going on up in heaven, that's for sure, and I gots to get mine."

"You know what? I'm getting away from you," Jeva said

scooting away from Breezy, "because when that bolt of lightening comes down, I don't want to be nowhere near you."

"Too late for all that," Breezy said. "The Lord already knows that you and I are cut from the same cloth. But like I was saying, there was this one guy that I only did it with once. I swear I couldn't even tell he was inside of me. I can't help but laugh every time I think about it. I mean, this fool knew damn well that he had a little dick. I can't even believe he pursued me the way he did."

"I don't know why men do that. They know they got a little dick and then on top of that they ask you do you think they have a little dick. Why is it a man needs a woman to confirm that?" Jeva asked inquisitively.

"And little-dick men know they talk big shit. Hell, they light-weight scare a bitch off, but at the same time, they leave you curiously hanging on the edge of a wet dream," Breezy said.

"Umm hmm. Already been there and done that. Remember Kent? I thought he was about to tear it up. He came in less than two minutes, no exaggeration. After he came, he licked my cat, my ass, sucked my titties, the works. I couldn't get over the size long enough to concentrate on any trick he pulled out of his hat. It was like sitting in a lecture hall in school trying to hold in a laugh. The kind of laugh that you know once you get started, there ain't no stopping. The condom was even baggy." Jeva laughed.

"Oh, girl, not the baggy condom."

"Yes, the baggy condom."

"See, FUBU sleeping on that one. They should come out with the platinum baggy condom," Breezy said, laughing.

"You know," Jeva said, agreeing, "I was afraid it was going to come off inside of me. I had never clinched my pussy muscles so tight in my life trying to grip that little muthafucker."

Jeva and Breezy high-fived as they tried to contain their laughs. Then Klarke finally arrived.

"Did I miss something?" Klarke asked, hanging her purse over the back of her chair and taking a seat.

"Nah," Jeva answered still laughing. "Just one of our short-short man stories."

"Don't dog out the short-short man," Klarke stated with authority in her tone. "They are some of the nicest men out there."

"Yeah," Jeva said. "They don't mind spending that extra dollar bill either."

"Shit, they don't have a choice but to be nice," Breezy said, rolling her eyes. "They have to wear their wallet on their dick in order to make up for the missing inches. The same reason why ugly people have to be nice . . . how you gonna be mean on top of ugly?"

The girls laughed as Chauncy, their usual waiter, came over to take their orders. The girls decided on their main entrées as well as an appetizer. Jeva couldn't peel her eyes off of Chauncy's butt as he walked away.

"He's sooo cute." Jeva sighed.

"He's sooo a waiter," Klarke added.

"I'm not into white boys, but he is a cutie," Breezy said with an attitude.

"What's the matter with white people?" Jeva asked.

"Oh, Lord, here we go again," Klarke and Breezy said in unison, slumping down into their chairs.

"Now see, there you go. I didn't say anything about white people. All I said is that I don't do white boys," Breezy said, knowing she was hitting a sore spot with Jeva. "I don't have anything against white people. Hell, I even had dinner with a white man when I was in Vegas."

Jeva took offense. "Basically you are saying that you are prejudiced. What's the difference between a black man and a white man, hell, a Latino, Asian, or Indian for that matter?"

"About three to four inches," Klarke joked to break the building argument between Jeva and Breezy.

The girls laughed and things relaxed a little.

"You always get so serious," Breezy told Jeva.

"Ah, you know how she is," Klarke said. "She got that identity crisis thing going on."

"Will somebody pleazze help Orphan Annie over here find her real parents?" Breezy said loudly as if she truly wanted a response from the other patrons.

"Y'all stupid," Jeva said cracking a smile. "You never know. Maybe someday I just might find them."

"Yeah, and maybe your father reads," Breezy said.

"And betcha your mother sews," Klarke replied.

Klarke and Breezy continued together in song as they butchered part of the chorus from a song in the movie *Annie*.

"Maybe she's made you a closet of clothes."

Jeva blushed. "The hell with the both of youse."

"You know we love you, girl," Klarke said as their shrimp cocktail appetizer arrived.

The girls nibbled on their entrées just enough to satisfy their buds, but were careful not to overstuff themselves. They still had to hit the mall and couldn't be weighed down.

The girls left Chauncy his regular 15 percent tip, touched up their faces in the ladies' room, and headed toward the mall to begin their window-shopping excursion. Klarke stopped outside Structure and looked in the window.

"Umm, I'll take that right there," she said, pointing toward a rack of linen short outfits.

"Too cheap," Breezy said and tried to pull Klarke away in order to proceed to the next store.

"Hold up. Let me go see for myself." Klarke broke free of Breezy's grip and entered the store. She made her way over to a rack of linen shirts and shorts. The gentleman who was standing at the rack couldn't help but notice Klarke as she stood there in her hot pink chiffon dress that hit just below her knees.

"Linen is nice," the gentleman said in a baritone voice. "It's soft, but a tad craggy."

"Yeah, that's what I like about it too," Klarke said, looking up from the linen shirt she was caressing. She couldn't help but notice the gentleman's extra thick eyebrows. They seemed to be growing together.

"Shopping for your husband?" the gentleman asked, trying to determine if he had any chance in the world at hooking up with Klarke. Klarke didn't hear him, though. She was so taken by his woolly unibrow. She just couldn't manage to take her eyes off of it. It looked like a big coochie sitting right in the middle of his forehead. The sound of his voice grew farther and farther away as she stared at his coochie face. She couldn't fight the urge any longer. Klarke raised her hand to finger his brow, but not before Breezy stepped up and grabbed her.

"Hey, the men went to get the car. They're going to pull around and pick us up at the door so we better get going," Breezy said.

"Oh . . . well, excuse me, ladies," the gentleman said. "And by the way, your men are quite lucky." He walked away.

"Oh my God, did you see that?" Klarke asked Breezy, still slightly dazed.

"Yes, I did, and did I not try to warn you about Sasquatch?"

"All you said was that he looked cheap. You didn't say anything about him having a crotch on his face."

. . .

"This is the best Cinnabon I've ever had," Jeva said, licking her fingers. "We ought to come window shopping twice a month."

"Not if you had witnessed what Breezy and I just did," Klarke said.

"What happened?" Jeva asked, looking at them.

"I'll tell you after you finish eating. I wouldn't want it to ruin your appetite," Klarke said.

"Come on, tell me," Jeva insisted, her tone childlike.

"We just saw a man with a coochie," Klarke blurted out as she and Breezy fell into hysterics.

"I can't take you two anywhere," Jeva said, shaking her head.

"Oooooh-wee," Breezy said, interrupting. "Look over there in Nordstrom. I gotta have that. Ladies, follow me." Breezy led the girls over to the store. There was a huge shoe sale going on, so there was quite a crowd.

"Excuse me, sir," Breezy said tapping on the male clerks shoulder. "Do you have this in my size?" She held up a chestnut pair of boots with spiked three-inch heels.

"What size are you?" the clerk asked politely. Breezy was captivated by his immediate attentiveness, not to mention his fine-ass physique. He wasn't too buff, but cut just right. He had wavy black hair that was slicked back, and beautiful brown skin. He had a tight shaved mustache and beard. Breezy imagined using her toes to play with his facial hairs. Each hair tingling her toes, arousing her.

"I'm not sure. What size do you think I am?" Breezy said seductively, smiling at him.

"Hmm, why don't we just get that shoe off and take a measurement?" he asked, returning her smile.

Breezy sat down as Jeva and Klarke checked out the shoe selection.

The clerk removed Breezy's strappy sandal with sensuous ease. He delicately placed her foot on the foot measurer. She looked up and thanked God that her feet were freshly pedicured. She had just visited the walk-in Super Nail shop around the corner from her house. Her toenails sported a water marble design that cost her an *extra fifteen dolla*.

"Umm, a nine and a half," the clerk said.

"How ironic. I was thinking that same thing about you," Breezy said, looking at his crotch.

"Excuse me?" he said, his tone suddenly outraged.

"That you're probably about a nine and a half, too." All of a sudden it was like the clerk turned into Sybil. He stood up, popped his neck, and snapped his fingers in circles as he checked Breezy.

"Nuh uh, Miss Thang, no, you didn't. No, you did not just go there, okay?" the clerk said.

"My fault. I'm sorry. Calm down, *Chanté*."

"Oh, you got jokes. Listen up everybody. The lady here got jokes."

It only took seconds for the manager to hurry over. Klarke and Jeva joined the roundup, too.

"We apologize for our friend," Klarke and Jeva explained, using their mother-hen voices as they pushed Breezy away. "She sometimes doesn't realize what she's saying. We do apologize."

"Don't apologize for me. Hell, he should be flattered someone like me tried to hit on him," Breezy said, smacking her lips and rolling her eyes.

"Girlfriend, please," the clerk said, sucking his teeth. "Women like you kill me."

"Look, let's just go, Breezy," Klarke said, continuing to push Breezy away.

"Women like what?" Breezy asked, getting louder.

"Women who think they can turn somebody like me out," the clerk told her, rolling his eyes.

"You are taking this to a whole 'nother level, trust!" Breezy shouted.

"Yeah, yeah, yeah. Say that, but you are just afraid that if I had your man in a dark room after two drinks he might let me please him better than you can. I know your kind," the clerk said.

"Oh, my goodness!" Breezy said in her Shanae-Nae voice. "No, he didn't! Oh my goodness! You really need to calm down. All of this is not even necessary. I'm sorry that I mistook you for a man."

"Oh, no problem, dear heart. I'm sure people mistake you for a lady all the time until you open your mouth," the clerk said.

"Okay, see, Chanté, now you are hitting below the belt. I would return the blow by hitting you below the belt, but it probably wouldn't even have an effect on you, now would it?" Breezy said.

"Let's get out of here," Klarke said, and this time she and Jeva succeeding in removing Breezy from the store.

"That raggedy queen," Breezy huffed when they were finally out of the store.

The girls sat down on a bench outside the store, Klarke and Jeva relieved that they had gotten Breezy out before she managed to catch a case.

"He wasn't raggedy when you were about ready to let him lick your toes," Klarke said. "And he wasn't raggedy when you were screaming *Ooooh-wee, I gotta have that!*"

"You have to keep in mind that gay men get flak all the time," Jeva said, calmly. "He just had his guard up, that's all. His anger wasn't aimed at you, Breezy. It was for all the ignorant folks he's had to deal with on a regular."

"Is that you talking or that shrink you used to see?" Breezy asked, glaring at her.

"Go to hell," Jeva said, about to get loud too.

"Will you two stop it?" Klarke shouted. "I'm so sick of this shit. What are we doing? I mean really. Once a month we get dressed up, come to the mall, and hope we apprehend our very own Donald Trump. We're so frustrated with our imperfect lives that we're even starting to take it out on each other."

"Well, what do you suggest?" Breezy said sarcastically. "Next month we pack a picnic basket and take a trip to the Land of Oz? Oh, I know, and you can be Dorothy."

"That fly-ass mouth is going to get you in trouble one day," Klarke said, glaring at her.

"Well, you had your Donald Trump," Breezy said, smacking her lips.

"Yeah, and I lost him to a woman like you," Klarke replied, snapping her neck.

"Please, Klarke's right. This is crazy," Jeva said. "Why don't we just join a book club or something?" Klarke and Breezy paused and gave Jeva a disbelieving look.

"Is her dumb-as-rocks routine for real?" Breezy questioned and the three began to laugh. "Don't book clubs have men in them?" Breezy said. "Meeting up with a room full of women every month, and at the rate I'm going with men, them hoes might start looking good to me. Coochie must be the thing anyway. We done met two men with coochies in one day."

"You are just plain ignorant." Jeva laughed.

Klarke's laughter faded and tears filled her eyes. "I'm sorry for snapping at you, Breezy," Klarke said with watered eyes. "It's just that shit gets so hard. I can barely keep my head above the water, you know? This is supposed to be the time when we make fun of our have-nots and love lives and lack thereof. Shit ain't supposed to seem so bad. My misery just hasn't been up for company lately, I guess," Klarke said.

"Harris didn't deserve you and neither did Rawling," Jeva told Klarke. "Your true Prince Charming is going to find you one day. He's searching for you just as persistently as you are searching for him."

"Well, I'm about to give his ass a little help," Klarke said suddenly determined.

"Sounds like you've got something up your sleeve," Breezy said, licking her lips, eager to get the 411.

"It's in the works. But I don't want to jinx myself so I'm keeping it on the low-low for now," Klarke said, winking. "Let's just say that computer I bought the kids last Christmas is coming in handy."

"Well, I'd like to think I've found my Prince Charming, but I don't know," Jeva said, uncertainly. "Lance just isn't feeling the marriage thing. He won't go back to school and finish college. He's content with his lifestyle. I just want so much more."

"Besides," Breezy added. "You done gave him almost five years of your life. If that man died tomorrow or even if he just walked out of your life, you wouldn't get a dime. An investment with no return. At least with Klarke, she *was* getting money for herself and she got the house and stuff."

"Yeah, but paying the mortgage, utilities, and all the other luxuries that come along with being a homeowner is another story," Klarke said with a sigh. "Whoever said owning your own home was an asset is a liar."

"You need to get yourself a sugah daddy like me," Breezy bragged. "Klarke, I know you have a problem with the fact that one of the men I'm seeing is married, but hell, I got bills. He takes care of them."

"Aren't you the one who swore back in the day that you would never be with a man just because he had money? There's just so many men out there who are not married who will take care of you, Breezy," Klarke said.

"Who? Where they at? Do you mean men like Chanté over there?" Breezy said, pointing at Nordstrom.

"Yeah, Klarke," Jeva said. "No offense, but you've lived the good life. You at least know what it tastes like. You lived it for thirteen years. That's more than Breezy and I can say."

"And she can live it again. Next time just don't fall in love with the fucker. As a matter of fact, you might as well had stayed with Harris in the first place," Breezy said.

"What are you talking about?" Jeva asked in disbelief.

"Love and money are like oil and water. They don't mix," Breezy answered.

"I don't know, Breezy," Jeva said, shaking her head. "I can't back you on that one."

"How could you? Lance ain't got no money. I'm not clownin' on him or anything, but the only way you're going to live the good life with Lance is if he hits the lottery," Breezy said. "He's a tennis shoe hustler. He makes enough money hustling weed to buy a pair of new Jordans, then he's straight until the next style comes out. Hell, he's got to be the last weed man on earth selling nickel bags."

"I don't care about all of that. I guess that's why I'm just not fine with window shopping anymore," Jeva replied.

"Yeah," Breezy said. "You spend the day looking for something that you can't have."

"In the end, though," Klarke said, "when you think about all the headaches you're leaving behind, you wish you could donate all that other shit that you actually did buy to Goodwill."

"Well, I'm going to hang in there with my man for now. In the meantime, I'll think of some way to rope his ass in," Jeva said.

"Just remember what I said," Breezy said in a very serious tone. "Love or money . . . when you seek them both you're seeking a headache. It has to be one or the other, love or money. You can't have both."

4

Part-Time Pops

"Mom, do we have to go?" Vaughn asked, stomping her foot with a broken-up look on her face.

"We're not going through this again, Miss Thang," Klarke told her. "Get your stuff together. Your dad will be here any minute."

"But Dad's never even there. He's always at work and we're stuck with Tionne and I can't stand her."

"I think she's kind of nice," HJ said as he licked the cream from the middle of the Oreo he had managed to separate.

"You only like her because she sneaks your fat butt extra Ho-Hos," Vaughn said, poking HJ in his belly as if he were the Pillsbury Doughboy. They both giggled.

"Mom," HJ said. "What's a home wrecker?"

"Pardon me?" Klarke asked, shocked.

"What's a home wrecker? That's what Vaughn said Tionne is."

It seemed as though every other week, when it was time for the children to go stay at their father's house, HJ had a new word he needed defined, thanks to Vaughn. The last time it was *mistress*, and the time before that it was *Jezebel*.

Klarke and Harris had joint custody of the kids. They alternated living one week with Klarke and one week with Harris. Joint custody usually worked out so that one parent had the children for six months and the other parent for the other six months. The court finds this less disruptive for the kids. But since Klarke and Harris lived in the same school district and they never once had a problem with arrangements, the courts allowed for their every-other-week arrangement.

It was always a battle getting the children prepared to spend a week with their father and Tionne. The children loved their daddy to death, but Tionne's presence caused tension, not so much with HJ as with Vaughn.

Vaughn, being the oldest, understood more about the divorce and the circumstances surrounding it. Still, being a child and not understanding her father's role in the matter, she placed all the blame on Tionne. It didn't make things any better when they found out that they had a little sister, either. Vaughn was crushed to know that she and her mother were not the only women in her father's life anymore. It was as if they had both been replaced. She was no longer Daddy's little girl.

Vaughn had always craved attention. When she had been a toddler she had refused to accept the birth of her little brother. Whenever anyone was cooing over the new baby boy, Vaughn would do something disruptive, like pee her pants, just to turn the attention on herself. She was no longer the star of the show, and HJ being a junior was a double whammy. She didn't like it. Eventually, however, she adjusted, but it had taken a long time.

Klarke decided to overlook HJ's question and ask one of her own.

"Do you both have all of your schoolbooks? I don't want Tionne having to bring y'all back here every other day to get something."

The children always managed to leave something behind so that they would have reason to come back to the house before their week was up.

"I think I left my spelling book upstairs," HJ said, and dashed up to his room to retrieve it.

Vaughn waited until HJ was out of sight, then turned to her mother and said, "Mom, I don't want to go this week. Why can't we visit him every other weekend like other kids do?"

Klarke couldn't help but laugh at that one. She walked over to Vaughn and kissed her on the forehead. "I love you, too."

The doorbell rang and Klarke yelled for HJ. She walked over and opened the door. There stood Harris, looking his handsome mature self. Tionne was waiting in the passenger side of the "his" of their "his" and "her" Lexuses. She waved at Klarke and Klarke nodded with a cordial smile, feeling like she was in a Lifetime movie.

"Dad!" HJ exclaimed, bumping past Klarke to get to him.

"Hey, buddy," Harris said hugging him and kissing him on the head. "You all set?"

"Yep. I almost left my spelling book. Oh, and Vaughn," HJ said pointing to a purple duffel bag he had laid at his mother's feet, "you almost forgot your gym bag again."

"What were you doing in my room?" Vaughn said angrily, knowing that HJ's courtesy had just eliminated a trip back home during the week.

"The word is thank you," Klarke said brushing her finger down Vaughn's nose.

"Well, if you two have everything, then let's get ready to roll," Harris told the children.

"If by chance they did forget something, just call me and I'll bring it over," Klarke said. She kissed the children good-bye and watched as they headed to the car. Harris lingered behind.

"So how are you?" he asked in a soft tone, trying too hard to be sexy.

"Good, I'm real good," Klarke replied in a nonchalant tone.

"Are you sure?" Harris said with a fake concern that Klarke saw right through.

"I'm not your responsibility anymore, Harris. I thought that would make you happy, a burden off of your shoulders," Klarke said, fluttering her eyes, waiting for Harris's next remark.

"Klarke, you were never a burden," Harris said, looking into her eyes. "You were anything but a burden."

"Just spit it out. What is it you want to say? Every week you are standing at my door pretending to be concerned about my well-being. What, you gonna take care of me, Harris? You want me to be your kept woman now?" Klarke, knowing that she had gone too far, lowered her head and bit her lip.

"Are we ever going to be friends again?" Harris asked. By this time Klarke could see Tionne getting impatient waiting on Harris.

"You better get going. Tionne doesn't look too happy with you standing here talking to me." They both looked at Tionne, who was sitting in the car with the boo-boo face.

It was always obvious how insecure Tionne was with Harris being around Klarke. Hell, she had won the man, but she still saw Klarke as a threat.

"Just let me know if you ever need anything, Klarke. I do still have love for you."

"So, if I said I still had love for you, too, and fell into your arms with promises to take you back, would you leave her?" Klarke said, batting her eyes.

"In a heartbeat," Harris said, shocking Klarke.

"No wonder your girl is sitting out there looking so insecure. Does she know she don't have her shit locked down? Does she know that you still love me and would come back to me if I'd take you?" Klarke asked, knowing what his answer would be. Harris just stood there without words. "Men. You are all the same and you never change. Get your sorry ass off of my doorstep."

Klarke closed the door as Harris walked away. God knows she wanted to say, "Baby, I do love you. Come back home where you belong." But she refused to ever give him the chance to hurt her again. Even if she would have loved to fuck him just to spite Tionne.

Klarke missed the lifestyle Harris had given her. She just couldn't go back to Harris, not after the way he had hurt her. Besides, she had her mind set on fresh bait, something bigger and better.

5

Meow

"So, how is the Opalescent job coming along?" Evan asked Klarke as she poured her afternoon cup of coffee.

"The shipment is going out today and I'm going to track them on Thursday," Klarke answered.

"Make it Wednesday," Evan said, grabbing himself a cup of coffee as well.

"Whatever you say, boss," Klarke said enunciating the *b* and letting the *s* sound roll off her tongue.

"Is there a problem with Wednesday?" Evan asked, almost daring Klarke to say yes.

"No, not at all. As a matter of fact, I always say, why put off until Thursday what you can do on Wednesday?" Klarke walked away, putting a slight switch in her ass.

She knew if Evan was going to even try to get the last word in, that swing in her hips would shut him up for sure. She sat down at her desk and prioritized her assignments as she did every Monday afternoon. Her Monday mornings were spent checking her voicemail messages and e-mails. She got out her follow-up list and took a sip of her steaming hot coffee. No sooner than she could put the cup back down, Evan was at her desk.

"Klarke, can I see you in my office, please?" Evan asked.

"I'll be right in," Klarke responded. She placed her cup of coffee on her electric coffee warmer with a sigh. Evan loved tearing her away from her work for some dumb shit.

Just as Klarke approached Evan's office she could hear her phone ringing. She knew the call would go to her voicemail, so she continued into Evan's office.

She hated being in his office alone with him. Every time she set foot inside he was trying to get to her. Besides, she could have had on a snowsuit with a floor-length parka and still would have felt butt ass naked with the way Evan stared at her. Evan wasn't a bad-looking white man by far. If a sistah was going to get with a white dude, he'd be the one.

Evan was about six foot even with beautiful ocean-blue eyes ringed with black. He had shiny light blond hair, his roots just a shade or two darker. He was well built and quite fashionable. The three thousand dollars' worth of dental work gave him a near perfect grill. His breath smelled of the Altoids he kept on him at all times and last, but not least, his pockets were deep.

None of this mattered to Klarke, though. The fact that Evan was non–African American didn't even play a part in her decision not to get with him. She was firm about not dating anyone she worked with, especially her boss. She simply felt that mixing business with pleasure was begging for trouble.

When Klarke got to Evan's office he ordered her to close the door behind her. As she did Evan's phone buzzed and the receptionist's voice came over the speaker.

"Mr. Kemble, is Klarke in your office by any chance?" the receptionist asked. "She has an emergency phone call. It's about her daughter."

Klarke felt her heart begin to race. She quickly picked up the phone. "I'm here, I'm here. What happened?" Klarke asked frantically.

"Your daughter's school called," the receptionist said. "Apparently she had a serious asthma attack and had to be taken to the hospital."

Klarke could hardly breathe herself after hearing those words. She raced out of Evan's office, grabbed her purse from her cubicle, and dug for her truck keys. She rushed through the office lobby and out to the elevator doors. She pushed the Down button continuously, but the elevator was taking its sweet time coming. Klarke opted to take the stairs down to the parking lot.

When she got outside, Klarke frantically searched for her vehicle. Her mind went blank. She couldn't find the Rodeo anywhere. She tried to calm herself down so she could think straight, but that didn't work. She had to have walked up and down every single aisle in that parking lot, but still the truck was nowhere in sight.

Klarke ran back inside the building. The window at the receptionist's station had an aerial view of the parking lot. She had a better chance at spotting her vehicle that way. The receptionist was puzzled to see Klarke coming back.

As Klarke came through the lobby doors Renée was coming around the corner with Evan right behind her.

"More trouble with the truck?" Renée asked. "I saw the tow truck racking it up and taking it away."

Klarke knew she hadn't scheduled for anyone to pick her truck up for repairs. Then it dawned on her what had happened. Of all the times in the world the finance company decided to make good on their threat to repossess her vehicle, they picked now, when she needed it most.

Klarke's eye flooded with tears. She just stood in the lobby trying not to cry.

"Let me grab my keys," Evan said. "I'll take you to the hospital."

By the time Klarke made it to the hospital, Harris and Tionne had already been there over an hour. Another damn accident on 75 had held Klarke and Evan up. Evan let Klarke out at the emergency-room entrance. She went straight to patient information to find out where Vaughn was. The nurse saw how distraught Klarke was and called for a candy striper to show her to Vaughn's room.

Klarke felt as though she was lost in a Roman maze garden with all the twists and turns the candy striper took her through. One more turn and she was going to yell at him if he even knew where the fuck he was going, but within seconds she saw Harris and Tionne standing in the hallway outside of Vaughn's room.

About three Mississippis before Klarke reached Harris and Tionne, the doctor approached the two. The doctor grabbed Tionne's hand and said, "Your daughter is a strong girl. She's going to be just fine."

As if things weren't bad enough, Tionne attempted to take pleasure in the moment by thanking the doctor, but Klarke stampeded onto the scene.

"I'm her mother," Klarke said almost out of breath. "My daughter, she's going to be fine?"

"Klarke," Harris said as he hugged her. "Our baby's going to be all right." Klarke fell into Harris's arms with tears of relief.

"You two don't know how lucky you are that her school was aware of her asthma condition," the doctor continued. "They knew exactly what was going on and called nine-one-one immediately. They saved your daughter's life."

"When the school called me," Tionne said, "they said that she started getting short of breath. She told the teacher that she had left her inhaler at her mom's house."

Klarke planted her forehead in the palm of her hand. She knew Vaughn had deliberately left it in order to have a reason to come back home. All of this was becoming far too much for Klarke to bear.

"Can we see her?" Klarke asked the doctor.

"Yes," the doctor replied. "Don't be alarmed when you see her. She has tubes to assist in stabilizing her breathing, but she's just fine."

They all entered the room and upon seeing her baby girl in such a condition, Klarke almost fell to her knees. Instead she just pulled up a chair beside Vaughn's bed and held her daughter's hand for the next couple of hours.

Harris and Tionne tried to get her to go down to the cafeteria with them to grab something to eat, but Klarke refused, almost becoming aggravated by their pestering.

"I need to be here when she wakes up," Klarke said.

"Honey, she's going to be all right," Harris said to Klarke.

"She needs her rest. Go home, get changed up, get some rest, and come back in the morning," the nurse said with authority. "If anything changes, anything at all, I promise we will call."

"Thank you," Harris said to the nurse. They gathered up their things in order to leave. "HJ is at Momma's. We have to swing by and pick him up. Klarke, are you okay to drive?"

"Oh, man," Klarke said as she had forgotten all about her lack of transportation, "I got dropped off here. The truck is gone . . . well, it's a long story. I'll tell you about it later."

"We'll take you home," Harris said.

"No, thank you. I have no desire to take a backseat to her again," Klarke said, pointing at Tionne, and exited the hospital room.

Klarke decided to pay a visit to the ladies' room before calling a taxi. She went back over to the patient information desk in the emergency room lobby and asked where the pay phones were. The receptionist pointed Klarke in the right direction, and as Klarke headed over to the pay phones she saw Evan sitting in the waiting area flipping through a magazine.

Klarke couldn't believe it was him.

"Evan," Klarke said walking up to him. He immediately rose to his feet.

"Klarke, how is she? How is your daughter?"

"She's fine. She's going to be okay. Evan, what are you still doing here?"

"You didn't think I was going to let you walk home, did you?"

It was pouring rain when Evan drove Klarke home. Initially Klarke just sat there and traced the raindrops down the window with her index finger. Her mind was full of so many things—first and foremost, Vaughn's health. But the scene at the hospital had aggravated her situation with Harris and Tionne all over again.

"Why do men cheat?" Klarke asked Evan suddenly.

Evan remained silent, not sure if Klarke was just thinking out loud or if she truly wanted him to answer.

"Why?" she asked again.

"Because we can," Evan said calmly. "Not me personally," he added quickly. "I've never cheated on a woman."

"Please, you're with a different woman at every company affair."

"But none of them are my wife."

"Here we go with that male way of thinking."

"No, seriously. I didn't take vows with any of those women."

"Yeah, but a woman assumes."

"Then they shouldn't," Evan interrupted. "No one should ever assume anything."

"That's not right, Evan, and you know it," Klarke said.

"What's not right is women thinking they can dictate how the male population is supposed to act, how we're supposed to feel, and how we're supposed to think. Men and women do not think alike." There was a brief silence as Klarke pondered over Evan's words.

"I would have rather not known," Klarke said.

"What?"

"I would have rather not known that Harris was cheating on me. As crazy as that might sound, I wish things could have continued on as they were than to go through all the pain and devastation I've had to go through. I'd still be the good little wife, and Harris would still be screwing around behind my back. But at least I was happy."

"Women are always saying how they want honesty," Evan said. "You swear you can handle it and you dig for the truth. Y'all dig in our pants pockets, in our cell phones and e-mails for the truth. Some women even go as far as checking the mileage on a man's car for the truth. They want to know why, if he was just going around the corner to get a pack of cigarettes, there were thirty miles put on the car. Now, when a woman starts questioning a man about the passenger seat being reclined, it's time to let her go." Evan laughed.

"I didn't have to look for the truth. It smacked me right upside the head. Harris just flat out told me one day. It was eating him up, he said."

"Well, women are always saying they'd rather hear it from the man than find out some other way. That's bullshit. It doesn't matter if the bullet hits you close range, three feet, or six feet. Once it hits, it's going to hurt either way."

"Turn here," Klarke said pointing. "My house is right there. The brick house on the right." Evan pulled up in Klarke's driveway and put his car in park.

"Are you going to be all right?" Evan asked in a sincere tone. It was a tone he had never addressed Klarke with before.

"Yeah. Thanks for the ride, Evan. I don't know what I would have done . . ." All of a sudden Klarke broke down crying. Evan, not knowing what to do or how to comfort her, just looked at her with sadness.

"Klarke, I'm sorry all of this is happening to you," he said. "I know I've been an asshole. And I know that you know I've been an asshole on purpose. It's just that, when you rejected me—oh, man. That cut like a knife. You're a class act, Klarke."

"I've been called a lot of things, Evan, but never in my life have I been called a class act." They both began to laugh.

"I guess that was quite white of me." They laughed again.

"Well, thanks again," Klarke said.

"Sure, any—" Klarke's sweet peck on Evan's lips put a halt to his words. The kiss shocked Klarke herself just as much as it shocked Evan. Quickly Evan returned the kiss with one of his own, and then another one, followed by yet another one, each one deeper and sweeter than the last.

■ ■ ■

Klarke was up bright and early the next morning. She showered, dressed, and put on a pot of coffee. She wanted to hurry and get to the hospital to see Vaughn, but she also had to contact the finance company to discuss getting her truck back. She planned on being at the hospital all day and didn't want to call them to discuss it there. She dug through some paperwork and collected all the information she would need before making the call.

She poured herself a cup of coffee and walked around the island that separated her kitchen from the living room. She placed her coffee by the phone on the end table, sat down on the couch and proceeded to put her documents in some kind of order. Once she located the phone number of the finance company, she picked up the phone to make the dreaded call.

"This is Klarke Taylor, and I'm calling to discuss my account. Yes, it's account number 555 . . ."

"Good morning. Oh, I'm sorry I didn't realize you were on the phone," Evan said, coming down the staircase and entering the living room.

"Oh, good morning," Klarke said, quickly hanging up the phone.

"Is everything okay?"

"Oh, yeah. Everything is fine. Finance company," Klarke said, gesturing to the phone, then hanging it up.

As Klarke sat there looking into Evan's eyes, which she had never allowed herself to notice were so hypnotizing, all she could think was, What have I done?

Klarke's body quivered as she remembered how Evan had popped one of those famous Altoids of his in his mouth and then proceed to lick and suck her. The curiously strong mint's coolness had provided a delightful delayed reaction. Even after Evan made her climax, her clitoris had still been tingling. Klarke had then proceeded to lay him on his back and take out years of sexual frustration on him.

Klarke had been on a couple of dates since her stints with Harris and Rawling, but she had never gotten close enough to anyone long enough to sleep with them. She was so busy trying to regroup and get her life together that sex had simply not played a starring role. Of all the times for it to make a cameo appearance, Klarke couldn't believe it had been with her boss.

Klarke got up from the couch to go into the kitchen to fix Evan a cup of coffee, giving him a quick, nervous kiss on the cheek on her way. Evan accepted it for what it was and smiled.

As Klarke poured the coffee Evan took her place on the couch and fingered through the papers she had left by the phone.

"You have a nice home," Evan said, making conversation.

"Thanks," Klarke said as she carried the cup over to him.

"Thank you," he said taking it from her.

"Well, I don't want to rush you out of here or anything, but I really need to get to the hospital," Klarke said as she wiped her sweaty palms on her jeans.

"Oh, no problem," Evan said taking a sip of his coffee and placing it down on the table. "I'll take you."

"Oh, no, that's okay. My girlfriend is coming over to pick me up," Klarke said nervously. "You sit right there and finish drinking your coffee."

Just then she heard Breezy pull up. She raced to the door and held up her index finger to let Breezy know to wait a minute, that she'd be right out. There was no way she was going to explain to Breezy the white man sitting on her couch.

"Well, that's her," Klarke said, panicking as she grabbed her purse and her keys off the key hook Vaughn had made in woodshop class. "Uhh, towels and washcloths are in the closet in the master bath. Anything else you need I'm sure you'll find easily. You can just push this bottom lock and let yourself out, okay? Okay then, I gotta go. Good-bye."

Klarke detested leaving Evan alone in her home, but it was either that or deal with Breezy. Just as she closed the door behind her, Breezy got out of her car.

"Whose cat?" Breezy called, referring to Evan's money-green Jaguar in Klarke's driveway.

"Shhh," Klarke said, waving her hand in a shushing motion. "Are you trying to wake up the whole neighborhood? Come on, let's go." The two then got into the car and pulled away.

"How's Vaughn?" Breezy asked.

"She's well. I called the hospital this morning and she'll probably be released this evening."

"I can't believe she left her inhaler at your house."

"Yeah, me neither."

"She just won't get used to the arrangement you and Harris have, huh?"

"Vaughn's just stubborn. You know how you Leos are. It's either your way or you make a way."

"That's how us lionesses are." Breezy smiled and patted Klarke on the leg. "It's going to be okay. Everything is going to work out for you."

"Yeah, it better," Klarke said, deep in thought.

"What is this master plan you've got cooking?" Breezy asked, her curiosity getting the best of her. "You act like it's going to change the world."

"It is. My world."

"Well, spit it out."

"It's nothing really. I just decided that sometimes even divine order needs a shove here and there. Breezy, this lifestyle just isn't me. I mean, sure I have the house still, but this working and trying to make ends meet shit is for the birds. It frightens me that I'm feeling this way."

"Why? You're not embezzling money from your job or anything like that, are you?"

"No, girl, because you know me. I've always been happy with what I have. It just so happens that now I want more. Knowing that there are people doing far worse than I ever will has always kept me grounded and humble. I mean, I don't have the bug as bad as Jeva, but I want the fairy tale, too. And Jeva was right. I had it. I had it fist-tight and yet it still got away. I swear, if I could do things over, this time around, I don't care if he moves the ho in our house like she's Shug Avery from *The Color Purple*. As long as he's taking care of my children and me, I'll have no complaints. He can do whatever his heart desires."

"Who is this he?" Breezy asked.

"The answer. Just as long as everything falls into its proper place, he is my answer to a secured life. I just hate that it has come down to this. Me, Klarke Annette Taylor, being crafty. Who would have thought it?"

"Sounds like you're convinced that your strategy is airtight. But whatever happens, don't sweat it, mama," Breezy said. "It's like I told you. Yes, you probably should have just stayed with Harris in the first place. Women bounce from man to man before they realize that it's the same shit, different man. Harris, no doubt, took care of you. But you'll get a different man who can give you the same shit. Granted, you are still going to have drama, but at least you'll have shit. You know what I'm saying?"

Klarke looked at Breezy as she drove, an intense and serious look on her face. Breezy took her eyes off the road momentarily to return the acknowledgment. They both started laughing.

"I don't know where you come up with half the material that comes out of your mouth," Klarke said smiling.

"It flows like a gift from God, baby."

"Umm, I wouldn't go giving God credit for what comes out of your mouth." They laughed and continued on to the hospital.

"Hey, baby girl. You feeling all right?" Klarke asked Vaughn as she kissed her. "You had me scared to death."

"Yeah, I'm feeling all right," Vaughn answered, then turned her attention to Breezy, who was standing behind Klarke with a gift bag in her hand. "Hi, Auntie Bria."

"How's my mini me?" Breezy said hugging her.

"Fine. Whatcha got in that bag?"

"My lunch for work today," Breezy joked. "What do you think? It's for you."

"Oh, thank you!" Vaughn said as she took the bag and pulled out the latest in the Cheetah Girls book series.

"No problem," Breezy said winking at Vaughn. "Well, I have to get going to work, but I had to stop by to make sure you were okay first."

"Thank you," Vaughn said, flipping through the book excitedly.

"Call me tonight, Klarke, so we can talk about that cat," Breezy said, rolling her tongue inside her closed mouth and pushing it against her jaw.

Vaughn looked up from her book. "Oh, wow! We have a cat?" she asked.

"Bria Nicole Williams, I will call you tonight for sure," Klarke said, using Breezy's full name—as she did whenever Breezy had gone too far, even for Breezy.

Klarke shook her head and sat in the chair next to Vaughn's bed.

"Meow," Breezy joked as she clawed her nails down the air and walked away.

"Are you and Daddy mad at me?" Vaughn asked.

Klarke looked at her in surprise. "Now why would we be mad at you?"

"Because it's all my fault I'm in here. I didn't take my inhaler to school with me. I had some at Daddy's. I hid them because I wanted to come home for the ones at our house."

Klarke began to smooth her hand through Vaughn's hair. "It doesn't even matter, sweetheart. But now do you see how serious asthma is, girl? People die from attacks like this, Vaughn. It's not like a stuffed nose that comes along with a common cold. We're talking about your ability to breathe." Vaughn put her head down in shame. "I'm not trying to fuss you out. I just want you to know that you can't play with this, okay?"

"I know, Mom. I'm sorry."

Klarke and Vaughn were still embracing when Harris entered the room, dressed for work. Seeing him in his uniform brought back memories. She remembered laundering them every week. She would inhale Harris's scent before throwing them into the washer machine. She felt the heat on her fingertips that the iron expelled as she laid them out for his workday. She remembered how fortunate she thought she was back then.

"How's one of my favorite girls?" Harris said as he walked over and handed Vaughn a teddy bear and bouquet of sunflowers.

"Thanks, Daddy," Vaughn said. "Oooh sunflowers! They're so beautiful."

"They're strong like you, Princess," Harris said as he kissed Vaughn on the forehead, then turned his attention to Klarke. "How are you doing, Klarke?"

"Much better now that my baby is up and about," Klarke said in a pleasant tone. "Where's HJ?"

"Oh, Tionne drove him to school for me. She'll be up here to see you after she drops him off," Harris said to Vaughn.

"Hey, little chiquita!" Jeva said, suddenly breezing into the room. "Hey Klarke, Harris."

"Hello," they each said.

"How are you feeling, baby?" Jeva said to Vaughn.

"Oh, I really feel great now. Mom got a cat!"

Jeva stayed at the hospital visiting Vaughn with Klarke for a few hours. She had taken a sick day from work only because she had exhausted all of her vacation days. When it was time for her to leave, she offered Klarke a ride home. Klarke accepted. She kissed Vaughn good-bye, promising to call her later that night. The doctor had been in to see Vaughn and was going to release her from the hospital. Klarke and Harris decided that Vaughn would return to his house to finish out her and HJ's week there.

Harris hugged Klarke good-bye, and just as he was doing so Tionne entered the hospital room.

"I'll talk to you later," Klarke said, brushing past Tionne on her way out.

"Excuse me," Tionne muttered under her breath. She smiled when she saw Vaughn. "Hey, Vaughn. How you feeling?"

"Ah, so-so," Vaughn said, turning her back on Tionne.

"Your brother said to tell you hello." Tionne continued her attempt to make conversation with Vaughn. "He was really worried about you."

"Did you give him a Ho-Ho to calm him down?" Vaughn asked smartly. "I know how him and Daddy both are really fond of *Ho-Hos*." Vaughn exaggerated her pronunciation.

"Tionne, how about some coffee?" Harris asked, in an attempt to referee. "Let's go down to the cafeteria and grab a cup."

"Sure," Tionne said. "Vaughn, would you like anything?"

"Daddy, would you bring me back some Skittles?" Vaughn said, ignoring the fact that it was Tionne who had made the offer.

"I'll check with the nurse and make sure it's okay," Harris replied.

"Thanks, Daddy."

As Harris and Tionne exited the room Tionne could hardly keep her composure. She had been waiting for an opportunity to let her feelings be known.

"I know Klarke has her acting that way toward me," Tionne said angrily.

"Please, Klarke's not like that. She'd never badmouth us to the kids. Those kids mean more than anything in the world to Klarke. Klarke does everything she can to try to make Vaughn happy with our situation. Do you think it makes her happy to send her children somewhere she thinks that they hate being?"

"Well, aren't we all defensive of the former Mrs. Harris Bradshaw?"

"Look, I'm not going through this with you every time you start feeling insecure," Harris said sternly.

"Well, I'm only what you make me," Tionne replied.

"And what is that supposed to mean?"

"If you wouldn't make me feel so unsure of myself when it comes to you and Klarke then we wouldn't have this problem," Tionne said raising her voice. "It's like you do it on purpose. I walk into the room today and she's in your arms."

"Oh, T, come on."

"And yesterday, did you have to call her honey?"

"I didn't call her honey," Harris argued.

"Yes, you did."

"Look, my child is in the hospital and you're worried about me and Klarke having something going on. Go on with that bullshit, T," Harris said angrily. The more Tionne spoke, the more pissed off Harris became.

"Well, do you have something going on?" Tionne said, continuing to push Harris's buttons.

"Damn it, Tionne, stop it!" Harris said through clenched teeth. "I said I'm not going through this with you."

"You can't even say it. You can't even just say that you two aren't fucking because it's true. You're still fucking her. Just say it, Harris. I'm not going to get mad."

Harris paused before turning to Tionne. He had put up with her crazy accusations for three years now and it was time to put it to a stop.

"This isn't about Klarke and you know it," he said, his voice low and intense. "This is about you and how you and I ended up together. What, Tionne? You think Klarke is on some reciprocity kick . . . that she's going to do the same thing to you that you did to her? You want to brand her as some woman focused on trying to rope in a man at any cost. You want to see her as some woman with nothing better to do than to be hugged up on and wait to be called honey by someone else's man. Think about it. It's not Klarke at all you're looking at. It's yourself you see."

Tears filled Tionne's eyes. "I can't believe you just said that to me," Tionne said as she began to cry.

"Look, baby," Harris said holding Tionne's arms and looking into her eyes. "I'm not trying to hurt you. I just had to put it out there. We can't change how our relationship started. It's a choice we both made. We knew what we were getting into when we decided to be together and you have done nothing but carry around a load of guilt. Feeling guilty about a wrong does not right the wrong or make it any less of a wrong. It's time to move on now. Do you understand what I'm saying to you, woman?"

Tionne was too choked up to respond. Harris had read her like the morning news. For the past three years she hadn't allowed herself to fully enjoy being with Harris. She had never wanted God to see her happy with another woman's husband, a man she immorally and maliciously stole from another woman, to say the least. All she could do was bury her head in Harris's chest and cry. He squeezed her tight and they headed for the cafeteria.

6

A Few Good Men

Klarke thanked God she lived only a few miles from her office or she might not have been able to afford the taxi fare to work. She hadn't yet found the time to contact the finance company for her truck to make arrangements to get it back. Who cared if it broke down constantly? This was the last year of payments before Klarke would own the truck free and clear. She would be damned if she would give up ownership on the truck this late in the game.

When Klarke walked into the office she felt as if everyone could tell she had slept with the boss. She felt as though any whispering at the water cooler that day would be about her and Evan's sexual encounter. Klarke thought that it was possible Evan had kissed and told, but then again, he probably wanted to keep their escapade just as much of a secret as she did. The last thing Evan would want is for any of his good old boys finding out is that he boned a sistah.

"How's your little girl?" the receptionist asked in a concerned tone.

"She's fine now, thank you," Klarke answered with a smile.

"Is she out of the hospital?"

"Oh, yes. She's doing good."

When Klarke got to her desk there was a bouquet of flowers and a card expressing the sentiments of Kemble and Steiner Printing. She knew Renée had ordered them because Renée always ordered the floral daisies from Kroger for any occasion. It was like her own personal trademark.

Klarke sat down at her desk. She could hear Evan fumbling around in his office and her stomach turned queasy. She wasn't looking forward to her first face-to-face with Evan since having sex with him.

Klarke decided to call the finance company. She followed the correct prompt to reach a live collection representative. She proceeded to give them her account number and held patiently while the rep pulled up her information.

"Miss Taylor," the collection rep said, "how can I be of assistance?"

"I need to know what I need to do to get my truck back," Klarke said.

"Hmm," the rep said punching away at the computer keyboard. "I guess I'm a little confused. My records show that your truck was returned back to the point at which custody was taken. Let me see what the deal is with that. It will be just a moment. I have to change screens."

Klarke was completely baffled at this point. She had no idea what was going on.

"Just one more second," the rep assured Klarke. "Our computers are running a little slow today."

Klarke was becoming a tad antsy. There was nothing more

nerve-wracking than being on a drawn-out personal phone call at work.

"Okay, here we go," the rep continued. "Yep, just what I thought. Miss Taylor, the past due amount was paid by wire, as was the remaining balance on the note. You should receive your original title in the mail within two to three weeks. Is there anything else I may assist you with?" The line was dead silent. "Miss Taylor, are you there?"

"Yes. I'm sorry about that. I'm still here," Klarke said, stunned.

"Is there anything else I may assist you with?" the rep repeated.

"No, I'm fine. Have a good day."

Klarke hung up the phone and sat at her desk, confused. She went to the receptionist's station to look out the window and into the parking lot. Lo and behold, there sat her Rodeo in one of the visitor's parking spots.

"I can't believe he did this," Klarke said aloud to herself thinking about Evan. "That son of a bitch is trying to keep me quiet. Why else would he spend almost four thousand dollars to get my truck back for me?"

"Did you say something?" the receptionist asked.

"Oh, I was just talking to myself," Klarke answered as she began to walk away.

"As long as you don't start answering yourself," the receptionist said.

Klarke smiled at her, hating how people always said that type of stupid shit. That and *Is it cold enough for you outside?*

Evan had more money than he knew what to do with. The thought of him using his money to get what he wanted in life gave Klarke a bad taste in her mouth. It was one thing for a person to have money, it was another thing for a person to have money and throw it around in the face of people who didn't. Now more than ever she wished that she hadn't slept with Evan. It would be difficult, but Klarke would somehow manage to avoid the subject matter as well as avoid Evan himself.

The alarm clock on the mini refrigerator in Klarke's bedroom went off at 6:00 A.M. She sighed, remembering that that same *buzz beep buzz* used to be music to her ears back when she was with Harris. It was her call to get out of bed and be the perfect wife and mother that she was—iron clothes, prepare breakfast and lunches. Of course that was when she was able to be back in bed by 9:00 A.M., too.

When the children first started going over to Harris's, Klarke would hit the snooze button two and three times before finally getting up. Not having the motivation to jump out of bed and get them ready for school, Klarke would try to catch a few extra zzz's. Being regularly tardy for work earned her a written warning. It got to the point where Klarke had to start plugging in the alarm clock across the room so that the snooze button would be out of her reach.

There were many times she tried to drown out the annoying sound of the alarm by burying her head in her down feather pillows. But when that wouldn't work, the purpose for putting the clock across the room in the first place prevailed. She would stagger over to the clock and shut the alarm off. Only once did she return to bed after shutting the alarm off, and ended up oversleeping, so eventually she moved it back over by the bed.

As Klarke reached over to turn the alarm off she knocked over the book she had been reading, *28 Days* by Nina Tracy. It was a collection of true erotic kiss-and-tales that Klarke regularly masturbated to. Unfortunately, the Dixie cup full of water that was sitting on top of the book went tumbling too. "Damn it!" Klarke yelled, sitting up.

She walked into her master bedroom's private bath to grab a towel. She relieved herself, washed her hands, and untied the silk Louis Vuitton scarf she had around her hair. As she proceeded back to the bedroom to clean up the spilled water, she shook loose her curls.

As Klarke soaked up the water she remembered why the cup of water had been there in the first place. It was for the birth control pill she had forgotten to take. Klarke quickly headed back toward the bathroom to retrieve another cup of water so that she could take her pill. Before she could do so the phone rang.

Klarke looked at the digits on the clock that now read 6:10 A.M. "Who died or who is in jail?" Klarke said as she read Breezy's name on the caller ID box.

"Hey, girl, it's only me. I've got Jeva on the line, too," Breezy said.

"Hey, girl," Jeva chimed in.

"What do y'all want at six o'clock in the morning?" Klarke asked.

"Meow," Breezy purred.

"I know you didn't call me this early for that," Klarke said.

"And I know you didn't not call me like you said you would, so that must mean it's something juicy," Breezy said. "That's why I have Jeva on the line. You can just tell us both so you don't have to repeat yourself. Then you can be on your merry little way to work."

"Come on, Klarke," Jeva said. "Spill the beans. Whose Jaguar was in your driveway and how long had it been there?"

"Forget all that. Did you finally get laid?" Breezy asked.

"You two need to get a life," Klarke said.

"Will you just spit it out, damn it?" Breezy stated.

"Okay, okay," Klarke said. "Yes."

"Yes, what?" Jeva and Breezy said at the same time.

"Yes, I got me some," Klarke said bashfully.

Jeva and Breezy couldn't contain themselves. They cheered like Laker Girls. Klarke just sat on the phone, embarrassed.

"Well, who was it?" Jeva asked.

"And was it good?" Breezy added. The girls waited impatiently as silence reigned.

"Hello, anybody there?" Breezy sarcastically asked.

"I'm still here," Jeva answered.

"Not you, dodo. Klarke," Breezy said.

"Ohhh, can't you guys wait until the next time we're at the Cheesecake? We'll have something to talk about. It will be a great conversation piece."

"You expect us to wait that long?" Breezy asked in disbelief. "Now don't make me come over there. Who was it, Klarke?"

"Okay, okay, it was Evan, my boss," Klarke said reluctantly. The girls each screamed at the top of their lungs. Klarke and Breezy could hear Lance in the background yelling for Jeva to keep it down.

"You didn't!" Jeva whispered.

"I knewed it!" Breezy exclaimed. "You gave him some *Boyz N the Hood* pity sex?"

"Evan lucked up on some life-crisis drama sex like Cuba." Jeva laughed.

"What were you thinking?" Breezy asked. "Bitch, Halle

already got the Oscar for screwing a white man, so what's your excuse?"

"I knew I should have never told you two." Klarke sighed with regret.

"Then you should have gone with your first instincts," Breezy said, "'cause I ain't never letting you live this one down, Lisa Bonet."

Jeva laughed. "I had almost forgotten about that movie. What was it called again? Oh yeah, *Angel Heart*. What about that one with Angela Basset and Robert De Niro?"

"*The Score!*" Breezy shouted.

"Whitney Houston and Kevin Costner in *The Bodyguard*," Jeva added.

"Yes, good one!" Breezy exclaimed.

"All right, already!" Klarke shouted over Jeva and Breezy. "This isn't a game show. This is my life. Now, will you two shut up and let me finish?"

"There's more?" Breezy asked.

"This is getting even better," Jeva said.

"Y'all, the man done got my vehicle back for me. The balance is paid in full." All the girls yelled and screeched with excitement. They went ballistic with joy.

"You done turned your first trick," Breezy said proudly.

"What the hell are you talking about?" Klarke was stunned by Breezy's comment.

"Look at it any way you want to, but when you fuck for a deed or a need, it's just like turning a trick," Breezy explained. "There's a world full of women out there turning tricks as we speak and they don't even know it. Wives, too, for that matter."

"Okay, Breezy," Klarke sighed. "You are not making me feel

any better about this. I had no idea that man was going to pay for my truck."

"Then you are one up on the game," Breezy said. "It's like serendipity. You were going to sleep with the man regardless, right? It just so happens that you got something in return. You got a fuck and a truck." The girls laughed hysterically.

"How was it?" Breezy just had to know. "I mean how was it doing it with a white man?"

"In complete honesty, it was the bomb," Klarke said licking her lips.

"Hmm, so there are a few good white men out there after all," Jeva said dryly.

"Well, now that Breezy done broke the game down to me," Klarke said, "there's always been a few good white men out there. Ben, Andrew, Abe, and all the rest of those fuckers who make the world go round. Sistahs better recognize."

"That's my girl," Breezy said proudly. "That's my girl."

Klarke had just logged off of her computer when Harris dropped the kids off. She could hear them coming in the door, so Vaughn must have used her key.

"Mom!" the kids shouted. "We're home."

"Hey, babies," Klarke said, coming down the steps to give them a kiss and hug. "Hello, Harris."

"Klarke," Harris said, standing outside of the door. Klarke peeked around him to see Tionne waiting impatiently in the car as always.

"You're not allowed to come into the house? I mean, hell, it did used to be your house. Let me guess," Klarke whispered in his ear to keep the kids, who were on their way up the steps, from hearing. "She's afraid you might come inside for a quickie."

Harris sighed. "Klarke, not you too."

"What's that supposed to mean?" Klarke asked sharply.

"Nothing, Klarke. Nothing at all," Harris said, putting his head down.

"Oh, she's been riding you, huh? And I don't mean that literally."

Klarke looked outside at Tionne, who appeared to be holding something in her hand and scrutinizing it. After all these years Klarke still hated the sight of that woman.

"See you next week, Klarke," Harris said, not ready to deal with Klarke's temperament. "See you next week, kids."

"Bye, Daddy!" they yelled from their bedrooms.

Harris returned to the car where Tionne was waiting for him, their daughter was in her car seat, sound asleep.

"What the fuck is this, Harris?" Tionne said, waving in his face what she had retrieved from out of his glove box. "What the fuck is this?"

Harris buried his head in the palm of his hands and took a deep breath. He had some explaining to do.

There was no way Klarke was going to be able to avoid Evan. Today was the monthly departmental meeting. Klarke had even considered calling in sick, but she knew that would only mean Evan briefing her one-on-one when she returned to work.

The meeting actually went quite smoothly. Klarke managed

not to make eye contact with Evan. She made sure she sat on the same side of the table as he did, but a few chairs down. That way she wouldn't even accidentally look at him.

As her luck would have it, after the meeting, Evan asked her to stay behind in the conference room because he had a few questions regarding her monthly accounts.

Klarke made her way over to the pitcher of ice water to pour herself a glass. She waited for her sidebar with Evan as her coworkers cleared the conference room.

"Did I do something wrong?" Evan said, almost heartbroken. "Do you feel as though I took advantage of you? Talk to me, Klarke. I know you've been avoiding me and I just don't want this to start affecting our work relationship. You are the best at what you do." He flinched. "Oh shit, not in bed. I mean, you were good there too, but that's not . . . well, you know what I mean."

"Evan, it's nothing personal," Klarke said softly, looking down at the floor.

"I can finish this one for you: Evan, it's not you. It's me," Evan said coldly. "So, how did I do?"

"What do you want me to say, Evan?" Klarke said, throwing her hands up. "Let's get together the second Friday night of each month and have sex?"

"No, I don't want you to say that. I want you not to treat me as if I gave you an STD or something."

Klarke laughed. Evan stared at her momentarily, then began to chuckle himself.

"I'm sorry, Evan," Klarke said, bringing her laughter to an end. "It's just that you are so melodramatic."

"Well, it must be a white thing," Evan said looking at her with those hypnotizing eyes.

"Don't look at me like that, please, Evan," Klarke said, blushing.

"Like what, Klarke? Like this?" Evan moved in to kiss her. Fortunately the conference room door was closed. The last thing Klarke needed was to be seen getting it on with her boss in the company conference room. "Maybe if you didn't taste so good, not wanting you would be a lot easier. I wish you didn't taste so good."

"Umm, it must be a black thing," Klarke said as she lifted her skirt and sat on the conference table.

Evan felt so good inside of Klarke that she didn't give a damn if he did have the audacity to offer her some sort of purse to keep quiet about their sexual relationship. It wasn't even worth mentioning at that point. Hell, he could pay her house off for all she cared. After experiencing the most heated and passionate one-and-a-half-minute encounter ever, Klarke straightened herself out while Evan buttoned up his pants and proceeded to leave the conference room.

"Evan, wait," Klarke said. "I just want to say thank you for everything, and I do mean *everything*."

"No, Klarke, thank you," Evan said, winking.

Klarke almost broke her leg trying to get to the phone. After four rings it went directly into her voicemail, and she wanted to catch the call before it did so.

"Hello! Taylor residence," Klarke said in a lively tone.

"Taylor residence . . . aren't we perky?" Harris asked.

"Oh, hey, you!"

"Damn, what's his name?" Harris asked.

"Oh, please."

"Oh, please nothing, I know when Klarke's been done up right," Harris joked.

"Stop it! I'm not going to talk sex with my ex. Now, why are you ringing my phone?"

"I was wondering if the kids can stay with you again this week?"

"What's up?"

"Ahhh, nothing, I just have to put in some long hours at work again."

"You haven't had the kids in a month. Harris, what's really going on? Is it you and Tionne?"

There was silence on the phone. Klarke could tell that if Harris spoke at that given moment his voice would have probably cracked. He eventually did speak.

"It's more like me and you," Harris said a bit desperately. "Klarke, just say the word. Rescue me."

"I'm not going to do that, Harris," Klarke said firmly. "I can't do it."

"You can't or you won't?" Harris asked sharply.

"Come on now," Klarke said, trying to stay composed.

"I mean, everything is all wrong. I'm supposed to be with you. Woman, you never even accidentally washed one of my good shirts, that's how perfect you were."

"I'm not perfect, Harris. I never was and never will be. But I loved you so much that even knowing that nobody is perfect, for you, it was still worth trying for all of my life."

"Can I come over just to talk?"

"Oh, no, you don't, mister."

"I'm serious, Klarke. We've never really talked."

"Because there's nothing to say. You have Tionne. You jeopardized everything for her. You got what you wanted. Talk to her."

"I can't talk to her," Harris said sadly. "There's been a lot of tension between us. Besides, I don't want to talk to Tionne. I want to talk to you. The way things are now between us, I never wanted it to be like this."

"Then why did you bother telling me about Tionne? Why didn't you just fuck her a few times behind my back and stay married to me?"

"You wanted the divorce," Harris said in a bold tone. "All I've ever wanted was you. I didn't want to let go of you. You cut me off when you filed those papers."

"Do you blame me? Was I supposed to stay with you after you dropped that bomb on me?"

"I never thought you would leave me. It was killing me inside, having a child outside of my marriage. I was sick, Klarke, both physically and mentally. My doctor told me I had to come clean."

"Oh, your doctor told you, not your conscience. Harris, what do you think you and I could really be? I'm so bitter it's not funny. You had a child with that woman while you were still married to me. I love that child to death and you know it, but I could never accept her like I could any other stepchild."

"She loves her Aunt Klarke, too," Harris said sincerely.

"She is my children's sister. You know I love her. She has nothing to do with this trifling mess but because of that child, Tionne will always be in our lives. You're asking too much of me."

"Just tell me you love me. That's good enough for me," Harris said, almost begging.

"I can't even give you that, Harris."

"Then tell me you don't and I promise, I'm done pushing the issue forever."

"I'm done giving you what you want. I'm done saying what you want to hear. That's another woman's job now."

"I'd die for you Klarke," Harris said passionately. "I'd die for you."

"I'll talk to you later," Klarke said as if she hadn't heard a word he said. "I'll let the kids know they won't be coming to your house this week. Good-bye."

After hanging up the phone, Klarke went into Vaughn's bedroom. She was listening to her headphones and studying from one of her schoolbooks.

"How in the world can you understand what you're reading while singing 'Baby, baby, baby, baby, baby'?" Klarke asked Vaughn. Then she walked over to her, removed one of the earphones from her ear and repeated herself.

"Oh, Ma, please," Vaughn said rolling her eyes. "You do everything to music, clean the house, take a bath. If you had a boyfriend you'd probably . . ."

"All right already," Klarke said in a firm tone.

"I wasn't even going to say nothing like that," Vaughn said in an assuring manner.

"Well, one never knows when it comes to you. I think I'm going to cut out you spending the night with Breezy anymore."

"You crazy, Ma." Vaughn giggled.

"Crazy about you," Klarke said rubbing her finger down Vaughn's nose. "Your dad called. He has to work long hours again."

"You mean he's still at the hotel."

"What?"

"That's where he goes when him and Tionne are having it out.

They mostly argue about why he hasn't married her yet. She thinks Daddy is still in love with you. If he marries her then he'll never have a chance at getting back with you."

"How is it you know so much?"

"They talk too much around me. Besides, he always works long hours and it never stopped us from going over there before. Think about it, Ma," Vaughn said, putting the headphones back on her head.

Klarke left Vaughn's bedroom and went into HJ's, where he was tracing a picture of Sponge Bob Square Pants.

"Hey, little man," Klarke said to HJ.

"I heard. No Daddy's house again," HJ said sadly.

"I'm sorry," Klarke said, patting HJ on his head.

HJ didn't respond. He laid down on his bed silently.

"Baby, what's wrong?" Klarke asked him.

"I think I owe Vaughn a million dollars and I don't have it to give to her," he said.

"What are you talking about?" Klarke asked.

"Vaughn told me that Tionne and Lil' Sissy would win Daddy, so not to get too comfortable. She said it was only a matter of time before Tionne would put his head in the clouds with a whip, or something like that. I bet her a million dollars that that wouldn't happen. Where am I supposed to get a million dollars, Mom?"

"Come here for a minute," Klarke said to HJ. She sat down on his bed and signaled for him to sit next to her. "Your father would never turn his back on his children for any reason whatsoever. Do you understand?"

"Yes," HJ said looking down at the ground. "I guess."

"You don't have to guess," Klarke reassured HJ. "Your father loves you very much and he always will no matter what."

Klarke kissed HJ on the forehead and hugged him tightly. She wished Vaughn would stop poisoning him with her own bitterness. She couldn't believe that after three years Vaughn was still this bitter. But then again, why wouldn't she be? Like mother, like daughter.

7

The Pretender

From: RLQ812@sunset.com
To: KAT@myworld.biz
Subject: Boston Airport

How are things going with you? I'm not quite used to life in the Big Apple. Everything has been so hectic that I haven't been able to get a phone line yet. I'm at a training site so I have no idea what my office even looks like yet. My only means of communication has been this laptop I'm working from.

What I do know is that it's great to hear from you. I'm so glad you decided to e-mail me. You don't know how many times I've kicked myself for leaving your contact information behind.

I look forward to hearing from you again!

Reo had no idea who KAT@myworld.biz was, but that didn't stop him from replying to the e-mail that she had sent him. *What if KAT is a man?* Reo suddenly thought. It was too late. He had already hit the send key after spell-checking the e-mail. Reo wasn't going to let whomever KAT was think he needed Hooked On Phonics.

He could feel it in his gut that KAT was a woman. Reo receiving that e-mail was no accident as far as he was concerned. That e-mail could have been misdirected to anyone in the world, yet it showed up in his e-mail box. It was pure fate that a slip of a keystroke landed Reo his mysterious penpal. He wasn't going to disregard fate. Besides, what harm could there be in a little game of cyber charades?

Reo thought about the consequences of his stepping on the toes of someone else's hookup. What if KAT had realized her error and had e-mailed who she meant to e-mail in the first place? Well, it was too late now. He just hoped he had gotten to her first.

"Be careful, man," Nate, one of Reo's writer friends, told him as they were playing a game of chess. "I met a freak on the Internet once and couldn't get rid of her."

"It ain't even like that, partner," Reo said as he studied the chessboard contemplating his next move. "The e-mail wasn't even intended for me. It wasn't any of that freaky fan mail or chatroom mumbo jumbo. It was sent to my private e-mail address, not the public one for fans."

"I hear you, dawg. I'm just saying, you have no idea who you are communicating with in the cyber world. It could be some inmate named Bruce."

"Man, you read the e-mail. You know it's straight."

"I don't know nothing. Why do you think I'm telling you to be careful? You need to ask her name, address, social, blood type . . ." Nate went on as Reo laughed.

"I can't ask her name. You know how women are. If you

remember anything about them at all it better be their name and their birthday. She would be offended if I were the person she thinks I am and I don't even remember her name. She would be pissed. Besides, I already e-mailed her pretending to be that person."

"You should have kept it real, man. You should have replied by saying that the e-mail was misdirected to you, blah blah blah. Ain't you got no game, nigga?"

"I guess I just didn't want to take that chance. She might have thought I was some freak. Then I really wouldn't have had a chance with her."

"What makes you so sure she's someone you would even want to kick it with?" Nate said making his next move. "Don't tell me you believe in that fate shit."

"Yeah, I guess I do. You don't?" Reo said, making a not-so-well-thought-out move.

"Nah, I believe in God, so be careful . . . and checkmate."

From: KAT@myworld.biz
To: RLQ812@sunset.com
Subject: Getting To Know You

Hey, you.

I wasn't sure I had the correct e-mail address there for a minute.

Well, I'm glad things seem to be working out for you. I would expect some chaos after such a big move. It's a little slower here in the Midwest (see, you should have relocated here).

Did I tell you how much I enjoyed conversing with you? It's so hard to find a man with something worth listening to to say.

Half of the men I meet don't have anything to say at all. That probably sounded rehearsed, huh? I hate it when men tell me stuff like: "You have intelligent conversation . . . most women I meet are airheads." LOL.

Do you know what? I would love to know more about you. So tell me something, what's your favorite song, movie, book, food . . .?

My favorite song is "Ribbon in the Sky" by Stevie Wonder. My favorite movie is "Love and Basketball" and my favorite book is "Shattered Vessels" by Nancey Flowers. I absolutely love no-bake cookies.

Besides working, I like spending time with my children, my friends and myself. There's nothing like "self time." You know how us women are, a long candlelit bubble bath and a good book . . . we're in our world (LOL).

Write me back when you get a chance.

P.S. Don't wait so long this time (smile).

"Mom, you didn't have to cook all of this grub," Reo said as he kissed his mom on the cheek.

Whenever Reo was in town, he ate dinner with his mother and father every Sunday. It was a tradition. Before he got involved in the literary game he and Meka had never missed a Sunday.

"Good, because I didn't," his mother replied. "Your father cooked today. He put it in the Crock-Pot before we went to church. Which reminds me, you haven't been to church in a while."

"Momma, you know I'm always out of town on weekends."

"Well, you're in town this weekend."

"Mom," Reo said, as if begging for a break.

"I mean it now, Reo. Don't think you got it going on so much you can't come to church and praise the Lord. Sure, you've been blessed with a lot of nice things. You've shared your blessings unselfishly, too. Your father and I are more than grateful for this fancy house you bought us, the maid, cars, and everything else. But remember, son, He giveth and He taketh away."

"Hey, now," Reo's father said as he entered the kitchen.

"Hey, Pops," Reo said as he hugged his father and kissed him on the cheek.

"Is your momma Bible-beating you?"

"She was fixin' to throw a couple of jabs," Reo said as he balled his fist and did some play fighting by punching the air.

"Umm hmm," Reo's mother continued. "Make fun all you want. Remember that pair of pliers that made all that money entertaining folks and then went bankrupt?"

"Momma, what are you talking about?" Reo asked.

"Don't play stupid with me," she said. "Some people relish in monetary and material things and think that they are set for life. Next thing you know, zip, zero, zilch."

"But pliers, Momma?" Reo said.

"You know the guy. He wore them trash-bag pants and had a whole army on the stage with him when he performed."

"MC Hammer," Reo and his father said at the same time.

"Whatever. Y'all know more about that worldly music than I do," his mother replied with an eye roll. "Just don't get too big for your britches. Give praise every chance you get."

"Oh, lay off of the boy," Reo's father said in Reo's defense. "The church isn't always a building with folks trying to outdress one another and speaking in tongues. The church is a man's heart, too, you know."

"Is that how you feel about our holy temple?" Reo's mother asked. "Why do you bother stepping foot in it then?"

"Do you know how many men are up in there specifically

looking for a fine woman like yourself?" he answered. "If I let you go up in there alone I'll end up a single man." He winked at Reo.

"Don't try to flatter me. It's the Lord you need to be flattering," she replied.

"Next Sunday, Momma, I promise," Reo said kissing her on the cheek. "Next Sunday for sure."

From: RLQ812@sunset.com
To: KAT@myworld.biz
Subject: Getting To Know You

You are not going to believe this in a million years. My favorite song is "Overjoyed" by Stevie Wonder. Now my favorite remix ever is Biggie's "Give Me One More Chance." My favorite movie is a toss up between "Love Jones" and "Love and Basketball." My favorite book is "Dollar Bill" by Reo Laroque. I really don't have a favorite food, but I can stand the taste of anything sweet. You're sweet, aren't you?

Did I make you blush? Good, then I'm doing my job.

When I'm not working I enjoy reading and especially writing. Looks like we have a great deal in common. So tell me a little bit more about yourself, KAT (smile).

When is your birthday? What do you like to do for fun? How many kids do you have again? How old are they? What about your family, any brothers and sisters?

I bet you think I'm writing a biography on you (LOL). I just want to get to know you better.

Talk at ya later!
P.S. I hope I didn't make you wait too long.

■ ■ ■

"It's a woman!" Reo exclaimed to Nate who had just arrived at Reo's house for a game of chess. "She likes candlelit bubble baths and reading."

"Hmm, a romantic," Nate said as he handed Reo a bottle of J. Roget.

"Man, she's the one," Reo said as he sat the bottle down next to the chess game on his Philippines wood coffee table that had once been a door. Reo admired unique furniture and laced his home with such items. The table was fixed across a sheepskin rug that he had purchased from a French flea market while on vacation with his parents in France.

"Slow down, son. Give me a light," Nate said as he pulled out his hand-rolled cigar and ran it under his nose for a whiff. Nate was one of those cool cats. He dressed crisp clean and sharp. He always smelled good. He carried around a leather flap bag to keep his personals in, versus a wallet. He had the word *classy* written all over him.

Nate and Reo became acquainted via their online writer's group, the Black Writer's Alliance. Reo had been a member for some time before Nate got his membership. When Nate joined, the welcome e-mail that was sent to all the current members showed that he lived in Columbus, Ohio, also. Reo thought it would be cool to have someone local to work with, pass ideas back and forth and edit each other's writings and whatnot. Reo hit him up offline and they'd been friends ever since.

"I just can't stop thinking about her," Reo said.

"She could be tore up, man," Nate said, lighting his cigar with the pack of matches Reo handed him that he had gotten from a club called the Milk Bar while touring in Dallas, Texas.

"Nah, she's one of the beautiful ones. I can tell by her words."

"See, that's why I write nonfiction and you write fiction. I keep it real and you make up shit people want to hear."

"What do you do before you come over to my house? Drink a gallon of hateraide? You never have anything positive to say."

"The truth ain't always positive, nigga. It is what it is. Now get pussy off your mind, get us some glasses, and let me whoop your ass in dis here game."

"Naw, you got it wrong. It's the other way around. I'm 'bout to whoop your ass."

"I didn't hear you talking trash last time you lost."

"Well, this is a whole new game and I damn near got your move sequence memorized."

"But I'm like the L.A. Lakers, nigga. I dominate back to back."

"Well, all good things come to an end," Reo said, lightweight slamming the champagne glasses down. "And stop calling me nigga!"

From: KAT@myworld.biz
To: RLQ812@sunset.com
Subject: More About Me

Hey you,

Hmm, where should I start? Let's see: No, I don't believe in a million years that Stevie Wonder just happens to be the artist of our favorite songs; yes, I'm sweet, very sweet if you'll allow my ego a moment to come out and play; and yes, you did make me blush, so job well done. Remind me to talk to you about a raise.

My birthday is February 12 (you didn't think I was going to offer the year did you?:=) What do I like to do for fun? I'm a woman. Shopping. What else?

I have two children, a preteen daughter and a ten-year-old son. I have two sisters, no brothers. My sisters live in different states. Careers, education and/or a spouse led them there. What about yourself? Do you have any siblings?

Well, Mr. Writer, since you like writing in your spare time, and I like to read, write me something. Write me something I can read during my next candlelit bath. Don't hold back.

KAT

P.S. I just love that nickname (wink).

"That was a nice sermon, Reverend Sandy," Reo said shaking his pastor's hand. Service had just ended and Reo stopped by her office to chat.

"Well, I'm glad you enjoyed it," the reverend replied sitting at her desk. "Three weeks in a row I've seen you out in the congregation. You haven't gone and run out of things to write about, have you?"

"Oh, no," Reo laughed.

"Must be a woman," Reverend Sandy said, getting serious as she looked at Reo from over the top of her eyeglasses.

"Excuse me, Reverend," Reo said surprised.

"You done found yourself a wife, Reo?" Reverend Sandy asked.

"You know what, Reverend? I think I have. The only thing is, I don't even know who she is."

"You're going to have to explain that one to me. You haven't been communicating with that Miss Cleo, have you?"

"No, Reverend." Reo laughed. "It's nothing like that. It's just that I've been communicating with this woman on the computer who I've never met in person."

"Oh, Lord. I would rather it had been some business with Miss Cleo than an Internet rat."

"Reverend, Sandy!" Reo said shocked. "And in the Lord's house at that."

"You don't think I know about all those Big Boob Bambis and Luscious Lip Lindas on those Internet pay sites?"

"Ah ha ha. It's not anything like that either. It's a woman who I connected with sort of by accident. See, she sent me an e-mail that was really meant for someone else."

"And instead of you just deleting it or advising her that she misdirected the e-mail," the Reverend interrupted, "you replied to it and now she has no idea she's not communicating with the person she had originally intended to receive that e-mail."

"Now who's been messing around with Miss Cleo?" Reo laughed.

"If this person is meant to be your wife, then you've already started off on the wrong foot."

"I know, Reverend. I just have to find the right time to work in the truth in our e-mails."

"Don't wait too long. Before you know it you'll bury yourself in lies."

"I'm going to clean it up, Reverend, and I know everything is going to work out. She and I have so much in common. She's like a gift from God. I was just starting to think that I was going to be a bachelor forever. I want what my mom and pops have. I want to come to church every Sunday . . ."

The reverend cleared her throat.

"I mean, every Sunday that I can, with my wife on my arm."

"Sounds good, Reo. I do hope everything works out for you. I'm just going to ask you to remember just one thing."

"Sure, Reverend. What is it?"

"That every gift isn't always from God."

From: RLQ@812sunset.com
To: KAT@myworld.biz
Subject: What's Your Pleasure

What's Your Pleasure?
Stark and startling I appear with all inhibitions flung
Standing before you bold, butt naked, and nicely hung
Verbalizing a sensual verse of late
Watching you bite your bottom lip, drool, and salivate
Figuratively speaking you go into a head spin and do back flips
Anxiously moving about like a cat that craves catnip
With an intensifying urge, that in time, does not ease
Because at a respectable distance my nakedness is a tortuous
     tease
Moving ever closer to you while gettin' my prose on
My nakedness grinds against your body, with all of your
     clothes on
With the inviting vibes that you're throwing, I am a receiver
I touch your forehead, you're hot, you have a fever
Feverously horny you are; my eyes you intently watch
All the while guiding my hand to a now-moist crotch
And while through your clothes, I massage your treasure
In a soft, strong male tone, I whisper, "What's your pleasure?"

I kiss you and massage your crotch a few moments more
You moan and breathe heavily from the passionate outpour

Your pussy in my hand, your tongue in my mouth, this I adore
Suddenly, your clothes magically fall to the floor
Mind opening is the mental/physical erotic ajarment
As I see the floor littered with sexy, girly undergarments
Still with a handful of twat, with a feel of derriere
I see a strapless bra here, pair of panties there
Here we be, as hot as two hot toddies
Two awaiting startling stark naked bodies
Up against one another, grinding away
Each waiting for the other to move beyond the arousing fore-
    play
With my endowed maleness stiffening, the candle is lit
Using the head of my shaft to titillate your clit
Teasing you as I tease myself, teasing measure for measure
As I hold you, and your eyes are closed, I whisper, "What's
    your pleasure?"

At the second asking, there wasn't much in the way of decidin'
Just like your eyes, the gap between your legs widened
Guiding my rod into you slowly, savoring the feel
Letting out a blow as if you're blowing hot oatmeal
We start up a rhythm, let the pace advance
Before long I'm pumping into you, and we start to dance
Backing you against a wall to which your ass, I pin
And your expression is more of a grimace than a grin
With each thrust, and intended pussy pounce
I jar your body and make your titties bounce
As I fuck your lovely femaleness, sweet and tender
We both approach the orgasmic experience to which we will
    ultimately surrender
with a mean look on your face, set like the stones of Stonehenge

Your expression is that of an angry woman out for revenge
Working this groove without a hitch
Instead of screaming my name, you yell, "FUCK ME LIKE I'M
     A BADASS BITCH!!!"

Shocked and amazed at what I was to hear
I get excited and throw it into high gear
Intensity growing hotter and bolder
So much so, you bury your head into my shoulder
One hand grabs my back, the other my ass
Grips and squeezes as I repeatedly impale you with my male
     mass
That makes you groan and utter about
And erotically, fuckingly cuss me out
"UH . . . UH, UH . . . AHHH . . . OOOOOOH!!!"
You jump, you jerk, you twitch, you squirm, you bounce, you
     squeeze, you coo
As I bring you to orgasm, to me your twat convulsions serenade
Making the neighbors blush as I juice your pussy like lemonade
I continue to fuck you with your eyes wide open, feeding my
     sexual consumption
Fucking you, loving you, as the white lava spews from my
     eruption
Slowing the pace, and still hard from these gestures
I'm ready for round two baby, so tell me . . . What's your plea-
     sure?

Once again Reo was back at the Afro-American Bookstop at the
New Orleans Centre Mall. Besides Ujamaa and Zawadi Bookstores in his hometown, they were one of the other few bookstores
willing to host a book signing for Reo when he was selling his

self-published books out of his trunk. The owner even squeezed him in during the Essence Music Festival, when author time slots were in high demand.

Today, though, was Reo's first time signing at the store when he had brought out such a large crowd.

The line stretched from the store down to the main mallway and almost to the food court. There had to be over three hundred people waiting to meet and greet him. Reo felt like the Ali of the literary world.

Of all those folks in line, one woman in particular stood out. She was with her two friends, chatting, then all of a sudden, she was staring right into his eyes.

This woman had to be one of the most beautiful women Reo had ever laid eyes on. Reo sized her up to be about five feet and nine inches tall. She had jet black, shoulder-length curly hair. She had to be about a 38 D bra size, with a waist he could almost fit his hands around . . . and that ass was banging. This chick was Bonita Applebum in the flesh.

As all the other readers in line began to notice that the guest author had arrived, Reo was followed by the crescendo of their applause. He couldn't take his eyes off of this particular woman, though.

He made his way to the table, where he was greeted by the book-store's friendly staff. He didn't waste any time prepping. He imme-diately began pen-whipping those books. Some people didn't have money to purchase a book that day. They simply stood in line to congratulate him on his success with promises to return to pur-chase his book on payday. He thanked them and supplied them with bookmarks and autographed postcards.

It seemed as though Reo had signed a million books before the woman he had made eye contact with reached him. Her two girlfriends, who were in line before her, praised and flirted with Reo. He smiled, nodded, and stared at their lady friend. He couldn't have moved the two groupies along fast enough. Then finally she stepped up to the table. Reo opened the book to the title page and smiled up at her.

"Who am I signing this to?" Reo asked her.

"Tuesday," the woman replied. "You can sign it to Tuesday."

"Is that you?" Reo asked.

"How'd you guess?" the woman asked with a sexy eyewink.

Reo smiled. "Are you from here, Tuesday?"

"Not originally. But I live here now. I was born in Atlanta."

"Oh, you're a Southern girl. With a name like Tuesday I was sure you were going to say you were from the West Coast or something."

"Don't you hear that Southern twang in my voice, mista?" she said, emphasizing her accent even more.

"Stop teasing me. As a matter of fact, don't stop," Reo said, teasing right back.

"How long are you going to be in the Big Easy?" she asked.

"I'm just in town for the weekend," Reo replied.

"Well," Tuesday said, grabbing the pen out of his hand. She dabbed the tip of the pen on her tongue and began writing on one of Reo's postcards. "This is how you can get ahold of me this weekend."

"Let me guess, you want to show me around."

She smiled seductively.

"I can show you a few things. For now though, just watch me walk away."

Tuesday handed Reo his pen back and slowly walked away with book in hand. Her white form-fitting Capri accented her hips. She was shaped like a pear, and Reo couldn't wait to take a bite.

The remainder of the book signing was like a scene from *The Matrix*. Reo was moving as fast as lightning. He moved the line right along, scribbling the standard "Best Wishes" and "Peace and Blessings."

When Reo got to his hotel the first thing he did was phone Tuesday. Of course, it was her cell phone number. She didn't pick up so he left a message. He told her where he was staying and left her the hotel phone number. He checked the messages on his cell phone and then signed onto his computer to check his e-mails.

From: KAT@myworld.biz
To: RLQ@sunset.com
Subject: What's Your Pleasure

Hey you,

What are you up to? Me, I'm just sitting here drying off. I'm still just a tad wet from that poem you sent me (wink). What can I say? You've got skills.

Did you write that poem specifically for me? I hope so. If not, there's a lucky girl out there somewhere. I'd love to write you a poem as well, only I'm not that great of a writer. I guess I'll have to show you better than I can tell you.

Whoa, it's getting hot in herre.

I hope I'm not getting too personal, but there's just something about you that makes me feel as if I can tell you and ask you anything. For instance, what's your favorite position? I like being on top, backwards. There ain't nothin' like a good rodeo show.

You'll have to forgive me. I hope I'm not offending you. I know how some men like to be the sole instigators when it comes to sex, with very little feedback from the opposing party. That's where I'm a little different than most women. I like taking charge every now and again. Maybe someday you'll find out. You never know when we just might run into each other again. It could happen.

KAT

Reo closed his eyes and cupped his pulsing manhood. He envisioned KAT riding him like he was a champion horse and she was the jockey. He decided to go for the full act so he unzipped his pants and pulled out *Simmy*. Before he could get down to business the hotel phone rang, disrupting his groove.

"Hello," Reo said.

"What are you wearing?" the voice on the other end moaned.

"Excuse me?" Reo said.

"What are you wearing? I'm wearing a black trench coat with clear high-heeled open-toe pumps."

"Tuesday, is that you?" Reo asked.

"How many women know where to find you?"

"Besides my mother, only one other woman."

"Then I'm that woman, and you know what, Reo?" she said in her most alluring tone.

"Why don't you tell me, baby," Reo said as he began to stroke *Simmy*.

"I'm right outside your door."

"Stop playing."

"Baby, I don't play. I flunked kindergarten because I don't play."

Reo walked over to the door and peeped out the peephole. There stood Tuesday. He could see the collar of her coat standing as erect as *Simmy* was. Her hair was clipped up with spit curl strands falling about. He could see the glow of her lip gloss that covered a deep path of lip liner around her lips.

"Damn," Reo said out loud.

"You didn't believe me?" Tuesday said looking directly at the peephole as if she could see Reo looking at her through it.

"No, it's not that I didn't believe you. Damn, you look good."

"I must not look good enough," Tuesday said.

"Why is that?"

"Because I'm still standing out here."

"Oh, my fault," Reo said as he put *Simmy* away and zipped his pants back up. He got so goosey acting that he pulled the phone off of the desk, which made the receiver jerk out of his hand. He picked the phone up and placed it back on the desk. "Sorry about that, I'm coming now."

"Don't cum yet. Let me in first."

Reo hung up the receiver and opened the door. There stood Tuesday in a black, three-quarters length trench coat. He followed her chocolate legs all the way down to her clear slippers. She was like a Cinderella right out of *Playboy*.

"Hi," Reo said, licking his lips.

"Right back at ya," Tuesday said as she stepped into the hotel room.

Reo closed the door behind her and began to straighten up the room a little. He walked over to his laptop to log off. KAT's message was still on the screen. He paused for a moment. All of a sudden he felt bad. He felt as though he was cheating on her and here he didn't even know his penpal's real name. Tuesday could detect the change in Reo's attitude.

"Is something wrong?" Tuesday asked.

"Uh, no. Nothing's wrong."

"It looked as though your mind wandered off there for a moment."

"No, I was just thinking of something I forgot to do," Reo said.

"Don't worry," Tuesday said as she pulled a string of condoms from her coat pocket. "I've got you covered." She grinned a naughty grin and started kissing Reo all over as she began to peel his clothing off of him.

Reo remembered that he hadn't had a chance to shower yet. As Tuesday made her way to removing his pants he grabbed both her wrists to stop her.

"What's the matter?" she asked.

"Baby, let me get cleaned up. I just got back from the bookstore and I haven't had a chance to take a shower or anything yet. I won't be long. Why don't you order room service and a movie?"

"That's fine with me. Do you need me to wash your back?"

"You save your energy for other things."

Reo handed Tuesday the room-service menu and gave her the remote to the television. He went over to the closet and grabbed some khaki shorts and a short-sleeved henley, then proceeded into the bathroom. Even though he knew he was about to get down with Tuesday, he didn't want to come out of the bathroom in the buff.

As the water from the shower massager beat on Reo's chest he couldn't get KAT off of his mind. A beautiful damn-near-naked woman was waiting on him in the other room and a stranger occupied his thoughts.

After Reo showered, performed his particulars, and got dressed, he once again joined Tuesday. Room service arrived merely seconds later. Tuesday had ordered some wine, chocolate-covered strawberries, and a cheese-and-cracker plate. They drank a couple glasses of wine, nibbled on the food, and then had meaningless conversation followed by meaningless sex.

"When is the last time you got you some?" Tuesday asked in a joking tone. "My shit is probably swollen. I'm going to have to go home and take a seltzer bath."

"I'm sorry. I thought it felt good to you," Reo said licking his lips.

"Oh, it felt good all right," Tuesday said in a sensual tone.

"Good, now maybe you can give me back my skin from underneath your nails." They both laughed as Tuesday went into the bathroom to clean up. She came back out a few moments later and put on her coat and shoes.

"It's been real, Mr. Laroque. You'll have to make sure you give me a call the next time you're in town. I'd love to do business with you again," Tuesday said, running her tongue across her teeth.

"Fo sure," Reo said.

"Your total comes to fifteen hundred dollars," Tuesday said, holding out her hand.

"That's cute," Reo said getting up and slipping on his shorts. "I'll walk you down to the lobby."

"No, you're cute, Mr. Laroque. Now, just pay your tab and I'll let Benjamin walk me down to the lobby."

Reo couldn't believe he had been bamboozled. He would have never imagined that Tuesday was a call girl. He ended up having to walk Tuesday down to the lobby anyway because he was a few hundred dollars short and the lobby had an ATM machine. There was no need for Reo to try to argue with her. All it would have done was cause a major episode, or even caught him a case. But there was one thing Reo was certain of—he was taking this one to the grave.

Nate would have never let Reo live down the fact that he had been tricked, literally. Reo had to force himself to look at the bright side. Hell, Tuesday could have turned out to be a man instead of a call girl. Reo was cool with the latter.

"Nate, man, I mean all of a sudden I just started feeling guilty," Reo said as he phoned Nate with the details of his latest one-night stand.

"All I know is if you tell me you didn't hit that because of some computer love, I'm revoking your playa license," Nate responded.

"Oh, I hit it all right. I didn't go down on her or anything like that though."

"No foreplay. She must have been a hairy one."

"You got it!"

"Will somebody please tell all these women out here that they will get a man to go down on them more often if they keep that shit bald?" Nate yelled.

"At least fade that muthafucker," Reo added.

"I ain't mad at you, dawg. So what's been up with you and your mystery woman anyway?"

"I'm still diggin' her. She must feel the same about me. We've sent each other a thousand e-mails."

"She must be married."

"Why do you say that?"

"She ain't asked for your phone number, cell number, pager, or nothing. She hasn't given you hers, either. Something ain't right."

"See, there you go. I haven't even asked her for her phone number yet, for your information," Reo said angrily. "If I try to call her then she'll know I have a phone. She'll ask me for my number. Once she finds out that I have a 614 area code she'll know something is up."

"Well, it looks like you are going to have to go to New York just to make a phone call."

"I could get me a New York cell phone and have the calls forwarded to my Columbus phone."

"Okay, you just got two points taken from your playa license. I was just going to let you off with a warning this time, but I see I got to give your ass a citation."

"I was just hypothetically speaking. I wouldn't really go through all of that."

"Well, you thought about it and that's bad enough."

"I just don't know what to do. I have to think of something quick."

"Ride the wave."

"Is that all you have to say? Nothing slick this time?"

"Do you think you might be falling in love with this chick?" Nate asked Reo.

"I know it sounds crazy, but I think so. Well, I think I'm in love with the idea of being in love with her. With her being a mystery to me, I get to make her the woman I want her to be. It's easier to like someone who's not in your face getting on your nerves every day, you know what I mean?"

"Naw, man. My wife's mean ass keeps me rooted. Do you have any idea how many times I might have made some fucked-up decisions if it wasn't for my fear of hearing her mouth? You talk about something sounding crazy, I don't even look at other women the wrong way anymore. I feel guilty when you tell me stories about you fucking."

"Persia got your ass whipped." Reo laughed. "And you haven't even been married a year yet."

"Persia don't take no shit. Out of all the women I have dated, I came to realize why my and Persia's relationship worked out so well. I realized why I never fucked around on her."

"Oh, then you better keep that under lock and key because you've got the answer to the twenty-five-million-dollar question."

"I'm serious," Nate said.

"So, tell me. What did Persia do to keep you an honest man?"

"It's what she didn't do," Nate answered.

"And what was that?"

"Compromise. She never compromised for me."

"What?"

"She never compromised herself. I ain't talking about small shit like I want cheeseburgers and she wants hamburgers so hamburgers it is. I'm talking about stuff other women compromise every day."

"Like what?" Reo inquired on the edge of his seat.

"Well, take a woman whose dude doesn't come home until four o'clock in the morning. His lying ass tells her that he was just out driving around, listening to his music. She accepts it. She knows damn well it's a lie, but yet she accepts it. She might fuss and argue about it, but in the end she accepts it and then her man turns right around and does it again. This time his lying ass talkin' about he went to the Waffle House after the club. She accepts it. She compromises her beliefs and what she knows to be true."

"Okay, I'm feeling you," Reo said.

"Now take the woman who has the potential nigga," Nate continued.

"Who's that?"

"That nigga that ain't got nothing but potential. He ain't got a car, but he has the potential to get one. He ain't got his own house, but he has the potential to get one. Hell, the potential nigga ain't even got a job, but he has the potential to get one."

"Okay, okay," Reo said.

"His woman is letting him drive her car around and live up in her house rent free. When she goes out of town she actually leaves this nigga money to kick it with while she's gone. Now she wants to cry and complain to her girlfriends because she compromised her own shit. A woman should never ever compromise herself for no man. Once she starts, it never stops. It's like letting a man hit her. If she allows it once, he's going to do it again."

"That's true."

"A lot of niggas get confused as to what a good woman is. They think that a woman who is always compromising for their sorry ass is a good woman. They think that her allowing him to get away with so much dirt makes her a good woman. They got it wrong. A good woman is going to keep that ass in check."

"Some men do have it twisted. Because a woman allows for some man to hit on her don't make her a good woman. Because a woman allows for some man to spend all her money up and cheat on her don't make her a good woman," Reo added.

"Like you say in your book, homie. It makes him a dawg."

"That's the most sense you've made in the two years I've known you."

"I'm not the author of *The Rule Book* for nothing," Nate said in a confident tone.

From: RLQ812@sunset.com
To: KAT@myworld.biz
Subject: The Poem

I'm glad you enjoyed the poem. Of course it was written especially for you. You told me to write you something so that is exactly what I did. Your every wish is my command. But on another note, me personally, I like to hit it from the back. I like to lay my prey on her stomach and enter. I like to pin her arms down and plant kisses on the nape of her neck. I like to cum deep. Did you feel that?

This doesn't seem quite fair. I want some reciprocity, some quid pro quo, a tit for a tat . . . write me something. It doesn't have to be publishing quality. Just write me something my imagination can dance to. I want to know more than just what you like. I want to imagine what it's like to be inside of you. So tell me, what's it like?

Also, e-mail me a picture of you. I need a new screen saver.

From: KAT@myworld.biz
To: RLQ812@sunset.com
Subject: The Poem

Hey you,
Imagine this: You ask what it feels like to be inside of me.
Well, with words, it's hard to explain.
Imagine the wind grazing a leaf.
Imagine clouds releasing rain.

And every move you make, like a Broadway production, is cho-
    reographed so well.
Imagine a flower blooming.
Imagine rolling off your tongue a secret you promised not to tell.

It's a desired imprisonment, the weight of your body holding
    down mine.
Imagine the anchor of a glass ferry.
Imagine a cork securing the freshness of a wine.

I anticipate the pliant kisses you apply upon my portions
within your reach.
Imagine the landing of a snowflake.
Imagine the fleecy skin of a peach.

The moisture created between us two when we become one is
passionate and warm.
Imagine mist on a 110-degree afternoon.
Imagine the sticky honey of a comb where bees swarm.

Each time we climb the mountain it's like the first time no
matter how many times before we've reached the top.
Imagine waking up every morning.
Imagine if the Earth's rotation just stopped.

Imagine what it feels like to be inside of me.
Imagine that.

Attachment: Photodoc.1

From: RLQ812@sunset.com
To: KAT@myworld.biz
Subject: Picture

The picture you sent is stunning. You are so beautiful. Your
pretty brown eyes sing songs. I fell asleep to the rhythm.
    The same way I feel like I've known you all of my life, I feel
like I've seen you before. It must have been in my dreams.
    My imagination did more than a jig to your words. Damn,

girl. My water bill isn't going to be nothing nice with all the trips to the cold shower you've sent me on. This is crazy, the way I'm feeling about you. This is crazy!

From: KAT@myworld.biz
To: RLQ812@sunset.com
Subject: Picture

Hey you,

Thanks for the compliment. I'm blushing again.

You have seen me somewhere before, Silly, the Boston airport. Your sense of humor is just another attribute that's making me fall head over heels for you.

I'm glad you liked the poem, but I have a confession to make. I got it out of a book of poetry by Joylynn M. Jossel titled "Flower in My Hair." But just because I didn't make it up myself doesn't mean they weren't my words. I was thinking them, it's just that she beat me to the punch in writing them down.

You never did tell me about your family, if you have children or any brothers and sisters. Mr. Reciprocity, how about a picture of yourself?

KAT

From: RLQ812@sunset.com
To: KAT@myworld.biz
Subject: Hello

I wish I did have a pic to send you right now. I'll have to unpack and find a good one or get one taken just for you. Yeah, that's what I'll do. I'll go out and get one just for you, KAT, to go along with that poem I wrote just for you.

I'm an only child. I don't have any children, although my parents are hounding me about getting a girlfriend to at least get the ball rolling. They want me to give them some grand-children soon.

From: KAT@myworld.biz
To: RLQ812@sunset.com
Subject: Hello

Hey, you.

Well, you answered my next question, which was going to be are you married. One never knows.

An only child, huh? You must be spoiled rotten. But that's okay, I'd love to spoil you too.

From: RLQ812@sunset.com
To: KAT@myworld.biz
Subject: Single

Nah, I'm not married. I was engaged before to my high school sweetheart. It's a long story. I'll tell you some other time.

From: KAT@myworld.biz
To: RLQ812@sunset.com
Subject: Single

Hey you,

Actually, I'm not too fond of hearing about exes. I find that in the future that does damage to a relationship. Frankly, I don't give a damn about her. You're my concern now.

But just so that you know. I've been married before, twice. It's my past. I have no intentions of showering you with details of my ex-lovers. I hope you'll spare me the same.

From: RLQ812@sunset.com
To: KAT@myworld.biz
Subject: Friends

Who do you keep company with? Do you have many friends?

From: KAT@myworld.biz
To: RLQ812@sunset.com
Subject: Friends

I have two best friends, Jeva and Breezy. Breezy and I have been friends the longest, for about ten years now. Breezy met Jeva a few years ago and we've both been friends with her ever since.

What about you?

From: RLQ812@sunset.com
To: KAT@myworld.biz
Subject: Friends

My closest partner is named Nate. He and I have only been friends for a couple of years.

Do you tell your girlfriends about me? What do you tell them?

From: KAT@myworld.biz
To: RLQ812@sunset.com
Subject: Conversation Piece

You're not vain are you (LOL)? You just got straight to the point.

You want to know if you're worthy of girl talk, huh? Allow me to put your mind at ease. You are a great conversation piece. I tell my girlfriends all about you. Of course, they think I'm crazy. They don't understand how I can possibly dig you as much as I do just from communicating mainly over the Internet.

Why don't you call me? My number is 419-777-9311. You can even call collect.

What about me? Am I a good conversation piece?

From: RLQ812@sunset.com
To: KAT@myworld.biz
Subject: Conversation Piece

You are more than a good conversation piece. Woman, I've even talked to my reverend about you.

People think I'm crazy too. Hell, sometimes I think I'm crazy. It's amazing that two people can become so close. The written word is a true gift from God. Look at how much we're learning about one another just by writing each other back and forth. Some married people don't know as much about each other as we know and will continue to learn.

I was with my ex for years and I'm learning more about you than I knew about her. It just goes to show you how one can benefit from being confined to one source of communication.

P.S. That's the last you'll hear about my ex . . . I promise! What do you do for a living besides sit around looking beautiful?

From: KAT@myworld.biz
To: RLQ812@sunset.com
Subject: Work

I do work for a printing company.

From: RLQ812@sunset.com
To: KAT@myworld.biz
Subject: Work

You mean like Kinko's?

From: KAT@myworld.biz
To: RLQ812@sunset.com
Subject: Work

Pretty much.

Reo had to buy himself some time and continue ignoring the fact that KAT had e-mailed him her phone number. Once he researched the 419 area code and discovered that Klarke resided basically in his own backyard, he knew she was heaven-sent. Toledo was only a two-hour drive from Columbus.

Reo didn't know how he was going to get out of not calling KAT. He knew from the moment she provided him with her phone number, every time her phone rang she would be expecting his voice on the other end. If only he knew what would show up, if anything, on her caller ID box if he was to call her. What if it showed up "Ohio Call?" She might think he was some stalker calling from her own basement.

Not wanting to appear as though he was a bugaboo anyhow, Reo stalled on calling KAT. He proceeded with the e-mails as if she had never supplied him with her phone number. They continued e-mailing back and forth and forth and back. He decided that he would wait for her to bring it up again.

8

It Takes Two

Breezy couldn't decide whether to wear her low-cut black Donna Karan dress or her paisley-printed Spiegel skort set. She never knew what Hydrant had in store for her when they went out. One time she got all decked out in her Armani skirt suit and to her surprise he took her on an evening picnic by lantern in the park. It was quite romantic of him, but it pissed Breezy off that she had wasted the most expensive outfit in her closet. Not that she had paid for it or anything like that. It's just the fact that she wouldn't be able to wear it again on a date with him, plus she had wanted to be seen out on the town in it.

On another occasion Breezy decided to sport the hottest little Baby Phat outfit she could fit her body into. The hookup brought out all the flavor in her, but no one ended up seeing her in that outfit either. Hydrant waited until he got to Breezy's house to pick her up for the date to decide he wanted to spend the evening cuddled up. He could be such a softy at times, but damn, how Breezy loathed wasting good outfits, especially that Armani one.

Breezy had lucked up on the Armani garb on a trip to Las Vegas. Breezy's job sent her to an insurance fraud seminar at the Bellagio hotel last winter. All expenses were paid. It only cost her eight hours a day of being bored out of her mind with lectures.

During one of the seminars the lecturer asked a question regarding red flags on fraudulent claims. Breezy raised her hand to answer the question, which she correctly did. She was given a $250 gambling chip. Breezy hadn't really done any gambling that entire trip, but since it was no money out of her pocket, she decided to play the slots. Breezy randomly picked out a $5 slot machine and put in a single coin. Her dad had always told her to find one machine, and if it paid off after the first few spins, stick with it all night.

On Breezy's first spin the son of a gun went jackpot. She couldn't believe it. She was jumping up and down screaming and causing all sorts of commotion. There were jealous onlookers who were down to their last dime and here she came out of nowhere to win five thousand dollars.

Breezy was escorted to the cashier, where she eagerly collected her winnings. She was glowing like a full moon at midnight. This radiance attracted an older-looking gentleman who was playing the blackjack table. As Breezy walked by, he neglected the dealer and did a one-eighty to speak to her.

"Congratulations to the lady," the gentleman said. Breezy couldn't help but notice that he was playing with a stack of chips identical to her $250 chip. She also couldn't help but capture a glimpse of his Rolex watch.

"Good evening," Breezy said.

"Do you think you could step over here so that some of your luck could rub off on me?" the gentleman joked.

"That means I'd have to rub on you."

"Whatever works. But seriously, I'm going broke here. I guess gambling just isn't my thing. While I still have a penny to my name let's say I treat you to dinner tonight."

"Oh, I get it," Breezy said, pretending as though she hadn't noticed his stack of chips or his expensive jewelry. "You just saw me win all of that money and you're inviting me out to dinner. Let's see if I get this right . . . we'll get to the restaurant and you'll say you forgot your wallet and I'll end up paying for our three-hundred-dollar meals. Well, let me save you the time," Breezy said as she stripped her wad of money of three one-hundred-dollar bills and threw them at the gentleman's feet. She then walked away. She knew he wouldn't be far behind. There was no way her sassy ass didn't just make him bust a nut. So she walked away praying he'd bring her back that three hundred dollars.

"Hold up, now," the gentleman said as he signaled for one of the men with him to watch his chips. He leaped from the stool, picked up the three hundred dollars, and went after Breezy. "Don't be so mean, Miss Lady. Here, you dropped something."

He handed Breezy her three one-hundred-dollar bills.

"Thanks," she said, taking it and then turning away to continue her strut.

"Just dinner," he said, hurrying after her. "I'll send a car for you out front in two hours. It will take you to the Stratosphere. Meet me in the line for the restaurant On Top of the World."

"You took a gamble coming after me, huh?" Breezy asked, stopping in her tracks.

"Yes, I did," the gentleman said approaching her.

"In that case, you're right, gambling isn't your thing."

Breezy continued to walk away with a killer grin on her face. The gentleman followed close behind her.

"How do you know I'm even staying at this hotel?" Breezy

said as she once again stopped in her tracks, nearly causing him to run into her.

"Because we all are. I've only been in seminars with you for the past three days."

"Commissioner of the Nevada Insurance Department," Breezy said, realizing who he was. "I'm so embarrassed right now."

Breezy held out her hand to shake the commissioner's hand. His strong grip and mature features sent a faint shiver through Breezy's body. His jet-black hair with strands of gray was very becoming.

"Don't be. You are in Sin City, after all. You can't just be accepting dinner invitations with any ole body," the commissioner said, kissing Breezy's hand.

"I would love to go to dinner with you, Commissioner, but this is our last night here. Look at me. I'm a mess," Breezy said, pointing at her business-casual attire. "The only other outfit I have to wear is what I'm wearing on the plane home tomorrow."

"Hmm, I guess we do have a problem. Here, take this," he said, handing her his hotel cash card. "Stop off at one of the hotel shops. Grab yourself something nice to wear. Charge it to my room. Two hours," he said, walking away.

This was Breezy's lucky day. She would have been a fool to stop off at any other shop but Armani's. She felt like Pretty Woman. The suit she picked out was sharp and the commissioner was pleased. They had a lovely dinner as the revolving restaurant allowed them to see the glittering, flashing beauty of Vegas.

The commissioner didn't even try to push up on Breezy. It might have had something to do with the fact that he had a wife at home. Nonetheless they shared hours of conversation before they parted, with him giving Breezy a simple kiss on the cheek outside of her hotel room door. The next morning upon checkout, a dozen red roses with a card that said *Have a safe flight*, signed by the commissioner, was left for Breezy at the front desk.

Breezy never communicated with the commissioner again. She never forgot him, either. She thought about the commissioner every time she opened her closet and looked at that Armani suit. And tonight was one of those times as she contemplated what to wear on her date with Hydrant.

Hydrant could care less about what Breezy was wearing, but she really wanted to look good for him. Most important, she wanted to look good for herself. Why she tried so hard to impress Hydrant was beyond her own reason. Hydrant was cool people, but he lacked the class that normally attracted Breezy to her men.

Hydrant fooled Breezy by looking so fly the night she met him. The diamonds in his ears lit up the joint. Breezy was certain he had a little *amour propre*. She met him at a First Friday happy hour affair. He was styling a royal blue suit with matching gators that had all the women sniffing behind him.

Breezy loved how he was shooting all the females down with suavity. She felt as though she was looking at the male version of herself. He felt the same way about Breezy as he noticed her putting the fellas in their place.

Breezy, being the intrepid woman that she was, stepped to Hydrant because she had to have him. They ended up exchanging phone numbers and hooking up.

The first few times they got together it had been something simple, like him renting a video and the two of them watching it at Breezy's apartment. Other than that, Breezy would perhaps make dinner and Hydrant would clean up the kitchen afterward.

Breezy had never met a man she didn't have to pick up behind. Most men felt that a woman shouldn't mind cleaning up behind them, or that it was her inborn duty. Hydrant took pride in his surroundings and respected Breezy's dwelling.

Her place wasn't that big anyway, so it wasn't like Breezy would have had to break a sweat or anything if she had to pick up after him. Breezy's apartment was more expensive than her salary as an insurance claim tech could afford. But it was conveniently located near the major malls and theaters. She paid far more in rent than it was worth. Her two-bedroom, two-and-a-half-bath place was nice though. She made sure, during her apartment hunt, to get a two-bedroom, just in case she ever accidentally got pregnant or for whenever her imprisoned father was released from jail, whichever came first.

Tidiness was a must for Breezy. Her mother had been strict with her when it came to cleanliness. Hydrant, having been raised the only boy of six children, inherited most of his tidy habits from his sisters. If Hydrant was drinking a beer and failed to use the coaster, he would grab a paper towel and clean up the mist. He cleaned out the shower after every use and wiped down the sink after shaving or brushing his teeth.

When Hydrant dusted he would even go as far as dusting Breezy's picture frames. Breezy had a picture of herself in a wooden frame engraved with her name that was a magnet for dust. He maneuvered the dust rag through every nook and cranny of the frame. For one reason or another, Hydrant's neatness turned Breezy on even more.

After the sixth or seventh date or so, Breezy slept with Hydrant. That was all it took for Hydrant to lasso Breezy in. She had met her equal in bed. Hydrant was the first man to ever fill her up and satisfy her. As a matter of fact, that's why Breezy gave him the nickname Hydrant instead of using his real name, which was Kristopher Long. She told him that was exactly what his dick resembled, a big ole fire hydrant.

After that, all Breezy and Hydrant did was hook up to have sex, and neither of them thought of their relationship beyond that. What did the two have to offer one another besides some good, down-and-dirty sex?

Once Breezy finally did come out of hibernation with Hydrant, she found him to be, in the words of Eddie Murphy, *just a regular ole cracker.* There was nothing major wrong with him. Breezy just found him not to be her typical flavor at all. Klarke had advised Breezy not to pick up any of those men at First Fridays as they were, in her opinion, nothing more than dressed-up thugs.

Hydrant wasn't a thug, but he wasn't the Mr. Suave she first thought him to be, either. As it turned out, that royal blue suit and matching gators Hydrant had been sporting on the night Breezy met him were his only nice fits. Breezy got so tired of seeing him in that getup every time they went out that she broke in a credit card just for him.

Breezy felt as though she was stepping down from her throne to be with Hydrant, but that in the end, he would be worth it. He was like a starter home, a fixer-upper. Breezy had her work cut out for her, but the dick was worth the effort. He was down to earth and lacked drama, no wife, no ex-wife, no babies, and no babies' mammas. For Breezy, being with Hydrant meant that she would have to get used to not getting what she wanted when she wanted it, which was usually right that damn minute. She wasn't accustomed to a man telling her "wait until I get paid." Those words gave her an allergic reaction. She got this sudden tic every time Hydrant would mouth those words.

Breezy tried giving Hydrant up many times. She stopped taking his calls and answering the door if he stopped by, but by then
it was too late. She had grown attached to him. They had spent so
much time together that they could finish each other's fly-ass sentences. There were things she did adore about him, like his romantic side and his obsession with pleasing her. Even if he
couldn't get her what she wanted right then and there, he would
always come through eventually.

Breezy craved Hydrant like a pregnant woman craved ice
cream. When she had to be done up just right, she knew Hydrant
was the go-to man. It was unspoken, but they sort of fell into being a couple.

There was Guy, on the other hand. Talk about a knight in
shining armor. This man didn't even give Breezy a chance to ask
him for anything before he was showering her with her desires.
Guy's generosity was always right on time.

Money was time as far as Guy was concerned. He gave
Breezy money as a substitute for the time he couldn't give her.
Guy was one of those career-oriented, loving, devoted husbands
and fathers. There appeared to be a shortage of those types of
men.

Guy picked up Hydrant's slack, material-wise. Although she
did care for Guy, Breezy didn't feel for Guy half of what she felt
for Hydrant. Sometimes she got so confused and indecisive between the two that she didn't know which way was up.

Breezy never allowed herself to get caught slippin' though. If
she did, she always managed to slither her way out of any farce.

Just last week she was supposed to meet Guy for a drink. After
twenty-four hours of a Hydrant fix, she was worn out so she left
Guy a voice message on his cell phone saying that her car had

broken down and she couldn't meet him. She went on and on about how she was plagued with a headache because of the stress of finding out that her car, which he paid the down payment on, was going to cost over $1,500 in repairs.

Guy stopped by Breezy's house bearing a basket he had made up with Tylenol, chocolate bars, and tea. It was one of Guy's typical sweet gestures that Breezy was hoping he didn't try to pull on this particular occasion. Since he came bearing gifts, Breezy felt obligated to let him hang out for a spell. Guy tried not to push up on Breezy, but he couldn't resist with her gallivanting around in that oversized University of Toledo sweatshirt, panties, and white bobby socks. She looked like a little college freak to him. He had to try to get some. He ended up saying to her what every guy says, but never really means: *Let me just eat you out. We don't even have to do it.*

Guy could eat the hell out of some coochie and Breezy could barely resist the offer. *It won't hurt if I just let him eat me out,* Breezy thought. She gave in to Guy by climbing on him and placing her thick juicy pussy on his face. She had barely straddled him before he sealed his serpent tongue behind his teeth and pushed her off of him.

"What the fuck?" Guy said as he rolled out of bed in rage. Breezy stared up at him, clueless. She thought that maybe she had started her period without knowing. That had happened with them once before.

"I can't believe you are fucking somebody else! And on top of that, you let me stick my tongue in your pussy after some muthafucker's dick been up in it."

"Guy, I don't know what you are talking about, baby," Breezy said, keeping her cool. Besides, she knew there was no way in the world Guy could have known she had just had sex with Hydrant. She figured he was just testing her.

"Next time wash your fuckin' pussy out a little better so that I won't smell and taste the rubber from the condom."

"You're married, for Christ sakes," Breezy said, not fazed that she had been busted. "You fuck somebody else on a regular. Do you mean to tell me that you've never come over here after sticking it to your wife and then stick it to me? You're a goddamn liar if you even try to tell me you haven't. As a matter of fact, you fucked her before coming over here tonight. My pussy is laced with gold, but there ain't no way you just want to eat it unless you done already got you some."

Not only did Guy finish eating Breezy's coochie until she juiced all over his face, he left her two thousand dollars to repair her perfectly running Benz.

Breezy could do no wrong when it came to Hydrant and Guy. They would believe her if she told them that water wasn't wet. She had a way of always turning the dice when it looked like she was about to throw craps. She played men like they were dice. And although she cared for Hydrant, he was one of them potential men, and potential wasn't paying any of Breezy's bills. She would have been stupid to stop fucking with Guy in order to be with Hydrant . . . stupid and broke!

"Damn, Hydrant, you're early," Breezy said in a smart aleck tone, opening the door with only her skort on. "I'm not even finished getting dressed yet."

"It's cool. I was thinking we should stay in anyway. I'll whip up something to eat and get a movie off of pay-per-view," Hydrant said.

"Are you turning into a hermit or something? That's all you want to do anymore is lay up in my house. I've worked hard all week. I want to get out of here and go do something."

"Well, go ahead. Call up your girls. I don't mind," he said in a laid-back tone, kicking off his Timberland boots and flopping down on the couch.

"Then you won't mind taking your ass back home, either," Breezy said sharply, walking into her bedroom.

"Oh, it's like that?" Hydrant asked in a cool voice, following her. "Baby girl, don't be like that."

"Get away from me, Hydrant. I don't feel like playing," Breezy snapped.

"You know you ain't doing nothing but turning me on," Hydrant said, kissing on Breezy as she tried to push him away.

"I'm serious. You are making a habit out of having me get dressed only for your ass to show up looking like a scrub trying to lounge around in my shit."

Hydrant was speechless. It was like those words had been longing to erupt from Breezy's mouth. He left her standing in the bedroom as he went to put his shoes back on.

"I fucked up. I'm sorry," Breezy said, approaching Hydrant.

"Naw, ma, you straight. Do your thang, I'm out."

"Hydrant, don't go. Really, that just came out all wrong."

"I know you well enough to know that nothing comes out of your mouth wrong. Just tell me this, how long have you been feeling like that? How long have you been feeling like I'm just breathing up your air?"

"I don't, baby. I just got mad. I wanted to go out and you keep doing this. I mean, if you don't have the money to take me out then . . ."

"Listen to you, Breezy. Listen to what you sound like. You got a brotha, a damn good brotha, trying to be hugged up under your black ass. You wanna lightweight bitch about me showing up early. I am not one of these *I'm on my way niggas* that got you waiting up all night for me. And fuck going out all the time. You think I give a damn about being seen by the okee doke Negroes in this town? I'm all about you, and you ain't trying to have that. I'm trying to give you me, my time, my heart, and your ass worried about a nigga's pockets. You want to be treated like a hoe, Breezy? You wanna trick? What's up? I can do that shit. Hell, pimpin' ain't easy, but it fo sho is fun, so just let a brotha know if that's what you want in this relationship. We can play games if you want to. I'm cool with that. Just let me know the rules. I'm just here to accommodate you, love."

No man besides her daddy had ever brought Breezy to tears. There she stood before Hydrant, unable to blink for fear the tears would come rolling down. The little voice in her head kept telling her to say something to him, but she was speechless. The little voice told her to get down from her high horse and walk over to that man and put her arms around him. Hopefully by doing so he would put his arms around her and make her feel the way she'd needed to feel for years. Instead she let him walk right out of the door.

"Ahh, he'll be back," she said to herself, knowing in her heart that this was the last straw for Hydrant. They had had that same argument five times in the past four months already. They might have just had it for the last time.

Just needing to be needed and to release some of her pent-up feelings, Breezy decided to call Guy's cell phone to see what his plans were for the night, to see if he could get away.

"Hello," a woman's voice answered.

"Hello," Breezy said, completely stunned.

"Yes?" the woman said, daring Breezy to ask for Guy.

"Is Guy available?" Breezy asked in a cool tone. She couldn't hang up because she was sure her name and phone number was visible on the cell phone caller ID.

"Who wants to know?"

Breezy had no idea what she was supposed to do or say. What if it was Guy's wife? Of course it was his wife. What other woman could have been answering his phone? If she hung up, for certain this person would call her right back.

"I'm wanting to know," Breezy, starting to lose her cool.

"I don't have time to play these games with you bitches. If you are woman enough to call another woman's husband, then be woman enough to identify yourself."

"I'll try calling him another time," Breezy said nonchalantly.

"The hell you will!" the woman exclaimed. "I got your name and your phone number right here on this caller ID screen. All I have to do now is call Pizza Hut to get your address, you dumb bitch. So, you just try calling my husband again. You've been warned."

The phone went dead. All Breezy could do was sit there and stare at the receiver in her hand. No sooner than Breezy hung up the phone did it ring. Guy's cell phone number was on her caller ID box. She let the phone ring so that it would go to her answering machine. Her machine was in her bedroom, so she rushed into her room to see if the caller was going to leave a message.

"Breezy, pick up," she could hear Guy say. "I know you're there. Pick up."

"Guy, what the fuck, yo!" Breezy said snatching up the receiver. "Your wife has your cell phone. You getting sloppy on me?"

"Look, you nasty-ass ho. I'm not going to tell you again to stop calling my cell phone," Guy yelled into the phone.

"Guy?" Breezy said, shocked.

"I told you I didn't want anything to do with you. Do you honestly think I'd jeopardize my wife and family for someone like you? Get over it. I don't want you, so stop calling my phone."

Guy hung up the phone in Breezy's ear. She couldn't believe this was happening. Then she took a deep breath. He was probably saying all of those things for his wife's benefit, but it didn't keep Breezy's emotions from doing backflips. She was heated. She wanted to call him back and cuss him out royally, but she couldn't let him know his theatrics had gotten the best of her. Breezy threw the phone across the room in anger and began to pace the floor.

"That punk!" Breezy screamed. "He doesn't know who he's fucking with. I'll turn his world upside down." Breezy continued to pace. Then she tried to call both Klarke and Jeva to school them on what had just gone down, but neither was available. She left them messages and fell asleep waiting on either to return her call. At about 1:30 A.M. Breezy was startled out of her sleep by a knock on the door. She made her way, bleary-eyed, to the door.

"Breezy, open the door. It's me, Guy," he said in a loud whisper.

"You've got some nerve," Breezy said as she opened the door only as wide as the chain would allow.

"Come on, now. I'm not going to talk to you standing out in this hall. Baby, open the door and let me explain what happened."

"I can put two and two together. You don't have to explain anything to me. You had to impress the missus at my expense. I bet she fell for it and then you two had make-up sex. Now you're here trying to clean shit up with me just like the last time. Well, I'm sick of this, Guy."

"She's my wife, Breezy. You chose to be the other woman."

"Get it right! *You* chose *me* to be the other woman. Don't act like you walked up to me and said, 'Hi, my name is Guy and I'm married. Will you be my mistress?' Shit didn't happen like that."

"Once I did tell you that I had a wife I didn't see you breaking it off with me. You kept right on screwing me, taking my money and accepting gifts. I give you the world. I love you to death, Breezy, but she's my wife, the mother of my children."

"Since when do you give a fuck about having a wife? Certainly not when you're laid up with me. Tell me all of the bad things you told her about me this time. Tell me, Guy."

The neighbor across the hall opened her door to see what the commotion was about. Guy turned to her and gave her an everything-is-okay smile, and she closed her door.

"I'm not going to stand here in the hallway and argue with you in the middle of the night for all of your neighbors to hear. I care about you and I wanted to at least show you the courtesy of coming here to talk to you in person. I'm tired of this shit, too. I can't do it anymore. I can't do this to you. We have to cool it for a while. I have to take care of home. I'm about to lose my family."

Breezy could hear her heart beating in her chest, the sound drowning out anything else Guy had to say. If anything, Guy should have been leaving his wife for her. Who in the hell did he think he was, coming to her door to throw her away like a used-up hussy?

"So you think it's that easy, Guy? Do you honestly think that I'm going to allow you to throw me away like I'm nothing?" Breezy said. "You've got another thing coming. You know me better than to think I'm going to go out like that."

"It doesn't have to be like this," Guy said in a soothing tone. "Don't say things you might regret."

"After all is said and done, you'll be the only one doing the regretting," she said through the cracked door. "Imagine how your wife would react if she just happened to find out every little detail about us. The car, the money, the jewelry, clothes . . . the abortion . . . I wonder who'd be regretting what then."

Guy kicked the door in, catching Breezy off guard, the chain shooting across the room. Breezy backed up toward the couch as Guy lunged toward her with rage in his eyes.

"Look you, little tramp bitch," Guy said, grabbing Breezy's chin with his hand. "You've long been bought and paid for. I don't owe you shit. Your worst fucking nightmare would be to fuck with my family. You got that? Do you?"

Breezy had the heart of a gang member during initiation. She was unaffected by his threats. What she couldn't stand was his hands gripping her pretty face. She went way down in her chest and hacked up a nice-size glob of spit and landed it right in Guy's face.

"Before you go making idle threats you better think twice about all that you have at stake," Breezy said, with her face still in Guy's grip. "Me, on the other hand, I don't have shit to lose. This little stunt of yours—kicking my door in, putting your hands on me—it's already going to cost you."

"Do you think I give a shit about that?" Guy said as he pulled out his wallet and began to lay bills out on Breezy's coffee table. "I waste more money in a month than you net in a year. You could live off of what I throw away, you cheap bitch. You gonna try to swindle me? Is that what you saying?"

Breezy was beyond angry. For the second time in a twenty-four-hour period a man had brought her to tears. Only these were tears of anger. They were tears laced with revenge. The other times when Guy would disrespect her, she knew he hadn't meant it. He had done it before, when his wife got ahold of his pager, and the time she got ahold of his old cell phone. She called every number he had stored in that phone, one of which was Breezy's. She knew he had to put on a show for his wife. But this time his words were swords.

Breezy began to laugh. She laughed hysterically. Guy just stood there watching her as if she were a madwoman escaped from the loony bin.

"Bravo!" Breezy yelled as she began to clap. "Bravo! Encore! Encore!"

Guy was completely lost at this point. He stood there shaking his head in disgust at Breezy.

"I knew I should have never fucked with you," he said.

"Why?" Breezy asked, putting her hand on her hip. "I wasn't worth it? I wasn't worth what is about to happen to your life? You know what? If I were you, Guy, I wouldn't be going out buying a rabbit anytime soon." Breezy snickered in reference to the infamous boiling rabbit scene in *Fatal Attraction*.

"You're crazy!" Guy said. "Look, we're both a little high-strung right now. Let's just cool off and give this thing some time."

"What's the matter, Guy? You afraid I'm going to go kidnap your kids from school or something?" Breezy laughed.

"I'm warning you, Breezy—"

"No, bitch, you've been warned. Now you shut the fuck up and listen to me. Like I said, I don't have anything to lose. You on the other hand have a wife, kids, and a career. None of that means shit to me, but I would like to know what it's all worth to you?"

"You really think I'm going to cave in to your ass? Do you think I'm going to stand by for one moment and let you blackmail me? This is cute, Breezy," Guy said as he headed for the door to leave. "I don't have time for this. You take care of yourself."

"1234 Rinterace Lane, Toledo, Ohio, 46789. Wife, one Eleanor

Gainer; children, one Whitely and Cal Gainer, school . . . ."

"Okay, okay," Guy said, throwing in the towel. "Fuck it. You win, okay? I don't even care. It's not worth it. You're not worth it. I just want you completely out of my life. What do you want? Money, sex . . ."

"Sex." Breezy laughed. "Don't flatter yourself."

"Then, what? What is it going to take for me to never have to lay eyes on you again, to never have to hear your voice or your name? What is it going to take?"

"What's it worth to you, Guy?" Breezy asked greedily. "What's it all worth?"

"Are you okay?" Klarke asked as she and Jeva stormed into Breezy's apartment.

The door was open as Breezy poked and picked at the door chain with a screwdriver. She was going to have maintenance do it, but didn't want to have to wait the entire weekend for it to be repaired.

"When I got your message I thought Guy had beat your ass or something," Jeva said with much concern. "What happened?"

"He tried to play me, so now he has to pay me," Breezy said, smacking her lips.

"What happened this time?" Klarke sighed. "Did his wife get ahold of his pager or cell phone again?"

"You know how sloppy he is," Breezy said as she continued to mess with the door. "He just went overboard this time. He tried to treat me like I wasn't shit to him."

"You know he'll be right back over here next week," Jeva said rolling her eyes.

"He sure in the hell will. To pay my rent," Breezy said proudly.

"And why is that man paying your rent?" Klarke asked glaring at Breezy.

"Because all of a sudden he wants to spare his wife's feelings and shit on me. Nobody shits on me," Breezy said with conviction.

"Wait a minute. Let me get this right," Klarke said, hoping she hadn't heard what she was hearing. "Is this something he's doing to stay on your good side or are you pulling a Michael Jordan mistress stunt?"

Breezy confirmed the latter with the look she gave Klarke.

"Girl, that's extortion!" Jeva exclaimed.

"Not to mention you are talking about this man's family," Klarke added.

"Fuck his family!" Breezy said angrily. "He doesn't care about them, so why should I?"

"Baby girl, don't do this. I know you are pissed right now, but don't do this. You might as well go into the jungle and try to take a male lion's female and cubs," Klarke said in a comforting tone.

"What was that, Klarke?" Breezy said, putting her hand up to her ear. "Did I hear the pot calling the kettle black? Quit acting like you don't have your own little twisted game of ransom going on."

"What I'm into is different," Klarke said in her defense. "It's nothing compared to what you are doing. I'm not breaking any laws."

"What are you doing?" Jeva asked Klarke, her eyes wide.

Klarke paused, then proceeded with her spill. "There's this account at work. It involved an enormous print order for Reo Laroque's book."

"Who?" Jeva said, frowning.

"That fine-ass author that was on BET?" Breezy asked.

"Yeah, that's him," Klarke paused again to gather her thoughts. "I had seen him on television and then the print order for his book landed on my desk. I felt like it was destiny or something. I had worked up this fantasy of being his wife, never having to worry about working for the man or money again. It was like a sign."

"So you called him up?" Breezy asked.

"Not exactly," Klarke said, slowly. "I sent him an e-mail."

"I'm sure he gets e-mails all of the time. What was so special about yours?" Breezy asked.

"It was mysterious." Klarke smiled. "I pretended to be sending an e-mail to some man I had met in a Boston airport. I didn't want him to know that I knew who he was. I mean, like you said, Breezy, I'm sure he gets tons of e-mails from groupies."

"So when he got the e-mail what did he do?" Jeva asked. "Did he respond and tell you that you had sent the e-mail to him by mistake?"

"No, he did exactly what I thought he'd do," Klarke said as a devious grin took over her face. "He pretended to be the person that I met in the Boston airport. And I've been playing the game right along with him."

"Well, have you heard from the guy from the Boston airport?" Jeva asked with great concern.

"Were you not listening, Edith Bunker?" Breezy asked, exasperated. "There never really was a man in the Boston airport."

"Oh," Jeva said, nodding. "Oh, I get it."

"Why didn't you just show up butt-ass naked on his door step? That's what I would have done. You would have left a hell of an impression. I mean, why use the computer? What if he had deleted the e-mail and not have responded?" Breezy asked Klarke.

"That wouldn't have happened," Klarke answered. "I knew the e-mail route would be the most effective in this case. Reo writes fiction, which means he's into a good fairy tale, just like me. He likes a good story. And besides, do you know how many people meet over the Internet and marry? It's today's reality whether you want to believe it or not. Besides, he spends more time on his computer than he does breathing. I know that much about him just from all of the research I did on him."

"Research, huh?" Breezy said.

"Aside from the fact that I've seen him on television and heard a couple of his radio interviews, I've read all his books, I have every newspaper and magazine article that's ever been written on him. Girl, I even know this man's favorite song."

"Is that where you got his e-mail address from?" Jeva asked. "His books?"

"No," Klarke said. "Everybody and their mama has access to that e-mail address. We had his personal information, which included his personal e-mail address, in our system at work for some reason. It was right there at my fingertips."

"Damn," Breezy said. "And I thought I was good."

"We've been corresponding with each other back and forth for about a month now," Klarke said proudly. She then told them how she planned to play upon Reo's sensitivity and his emotional needs. Ultimately, Klarke would catch Reo offguard, get inside of his head and his heart, possess his mind, and then work on the physical aspect once she had him right where she needed him, which was cupped inside her gentle palm.

"So you see, I'm not putting anybody at risk," Klarke said. "What you're doing, Breezy, is putting a man's entire life at risk. What you're pulling could cost him everything."

"Well, his wife finding out the real-deal Holyfield will cost

him more than I ever will," Breezy said going back to fixing the
door.

"You don't think that Guy might try to get stupid on you?"
Jeva asked.

"It doesn't matter what I think," Breezy said. "I got a
9-millimeter in my nightstand drawer that knows he won't."

9

Once Upon a Time

Jeva had already been waiting twenty minutes for Lance to pick her up from work before she called Cassie, the sitter who took care of their five-year-old daughter. This was the second time this week Lance had been late picking her up from work. She had gotten just as used to making the call to the sitter as the sitter had gotten used to receiving it.

"Cassie, hey, it's me, Jeva."

"Lance late again, coming to get you?" Cassie said presuming correctly.

"You know it. He kills me, not answering his cell phone. That means he's on his way and just doesn't want to hear me cursing him out until he gets here." Jeva laughed.

"Don't even worry about it. Your little Heather is asleep anyway."

"Thanks, girl. I'll be there as soon as I can."

"All right, peace," Cassie said as she hung up the phone.

At least once a week Lance was late picking Jeva up from work. They were a one-car family and Lance was always on call for his job as a maintenance man, so he had custody of the vehicle most of the time. Lance's inability to be on time was just one of his flaws that never bothered Jeva for long.

Thank goodness she was blessed with a baby-sitter like Cassie. Cassie lived at one of the properties Lance did maintenance work for. Cassie worked with far fewer marbles than Jeva, but she was great with kids. Klarke and Breezy referred to Cassie as a wigga, a white girl with intentional versus natural-born black characteristics. She was known to get her hair done up in a French roll or even braided and beaded. Lance had gotten her number from the laundry room bulletin board at the property.

Lance did maintenance work for two Eastside Toledo apartment complexes. His work schedule was from 8:00 A.M. to 5:00 P.M. but those hours weren't engraved in stone. If there happened to be an emergency after five, then he was required to go take care of it. He got paid overtime on those occasions.

On the side, he was supposedly a hustler. He was always in the streets making runs to deliver his weed, yet never had anything to show for it. Last year Jeva had to borrow eighty dollars from Breezy to keep her phone from being disconnected. The electric had already been disconnected, but God forbid the phone got turned off. Folks will talk in the dark.

Jeva and Lance had been playing house for about five years. Lance had promised to marry her after her daughter was born. Her daughter would be two years old by the time they planned for a romantic getaway to the Bahamas, during which they would exchange wedding vows.

Jeva had stopped using birth control about three months prior to their wedding date. She wanted to perhaps conceive on their wedding night, which was one of Jeva's biggest problems, she always expected some fairy-tale type stuff to happen. Every step she took in life was supposed to get her closer to that happy ending that all little girls grow up reading about in those damn Disney books.

Lance had really wanted a second child, a son. Making Lance happy was what made Jeva happy. He had been hounding Jeva for over a year to have another baby. Jeva refused to have another child out of wedlock, so Lance knew it was a no-win battle unless he agreed to marry her.

Besides, Jeva had been so caught up in her photography and landing high-profile photo jobs that she couldn't even think of fitting in another baby. This photography thing was new to her and she enjoyed it.

A man she did a bachelor party for back when she used to dance for a living turned her on to it. He supplied magazines and newspapers with photos and articles, mostly fillers. He ended up leasing a studio with state-of-the-art equipment so he could do layouts.

Shortly after Jeva had her daughter, he had contacted her to dance at one of his boy's parties. Jeva told him that she was no longer dancing, but was instead seeking out a new gig.

He had recently decided to hire a couple of independent freelancers and was willing to give Jeva a stab at it. Compared to the fast and easy money she had made dancing, the money from the photography gig was shitty, but it was morally honest.

The gentleman she worked for was now one of the main go-to guys in the industry for fillers in magazines and newspapers. Although most of Jeva's assignments were local, she did well and it kept her busy.

Jeva's exotic look always attracted the male entertainers when she was given a major event to cover, which gave her easy access to photo shoots.

She landed some high-priced photos with her slanted *mami* eyes and petite figure. What would Jeva have looked like being sent off to do a shoot at John Blassingame's *Black Men* magazine anniversary party, for example, big as a house with Lance's off-spring? How would her pop-belly tear the Morris Chestnuts and Nellys away from conversation, and Cristal for a couple of quick camera shots and standard interview questions? Come to think of it, she probably would have gotten more action from the fellas. Men were able to pick up the scent of the wet cream of pregnant pussy like wild animals.

As it turned out Jeva found out she was pregnant a month be-fore their getaway. It wasn't the fairy-tale conception she had mentally worked up, but there was nothing she could have done about it. Let Jeva tell it and she knew the exact night she got pregnant. It was the night she and Lance were supposed to go see Maxwell in concert. Alicia Keys was the opening act.

Maxwell came down with a flu bug and canceled the morning of the concert. Jeva heard the cancellation on the radio while working on a layout. She didn't share this bit of information with Lance, though. They had already booked Cassie's baby-sitting services for the night, so Jeva decided to take advantage of that.

When Lance got in from work, Jeva directed him straight to the shower. He was late getting in so they would have missed Alicia Keys's performance anyway.

Jeva laid out the most elegant picnic setting in the middle of the living room floor. She had spread a Mexican blanket out, which was a souvenir from a trip she had taken to Cancun. The wicker picnic basket, which was a house-warming gift when she moved into Lance's home, was filled with sandwiches, potato chips, and Chips Ahoy cookies. All were freshly packed in Ziploc baggies.

The flare of the apple pie–scented candle flickered off the glasses filled with chilled Asti. Jeva had spread herself out on the blanket in her Daisy Duke denim shorts and checkered haltered top. She had even stopped at a craft market and bought a bale of hay.

When she heard the shower water shut off, she went into the bathroom to retrieve her man. Butt-naked and wet, with only a towel wrapped around his waist, Lance was escorted to the personally prepared indoor picnic.

They made love for what would have been the duration of the concert. It was such a beautiful evening of lovemaking, almost dreamlike. That's why Jeva claimed it as her evening of conception.

Jeva getting pregnant before she and Lance had the opportunity to say "I do" was a lifesaver for Lance. He came up with 101 reasons why they shouldn't get married after all (he wasn't ready, he wanted a big fancy wedding, he couldn't get off work for the trip, etc.). He wanted a baby, a son. He was getting what he wanted out of the relationship, so why take it further?

Jeva couldn't believe he was pulling such a stunt. They argued over the subject matter for months. Jeva felt used and like she had been tricked into thinking that Lance truly wanted her as his wife. She became indecisive as to whether she wanted to give birth to another child without being married. She didn't want to be a breeding ground for any man.

She cried to Klarke and Breezy almost every night. She couldn't believe what was happening to her. She felt like a teen in trouble. For Jeva, there was no feeling worse than the initial pain of discovering someone didn't love her as much as she loves them. Lance's bailing out on their nuptials told her that he didn't feel the way she felt for him.

Jeva thought about getting an abortion. She had actually gone to the clinic to have the procedure done twice, but changed her mind each time. She was finally so far along that when she made up her mind to have it done, she had to go to another city. No doctor in Toledo would touch her with a ten-foot pole.

She told Lance that she miscarried. There was no doubt in her mind that the truth would have sent him packing. After that horrifying experience she felt lucky to have been put up for adoption.

Jeva could hardly contain her anger as Lance drove up. She had stood there over thirty minutes waiting for him. He was acting as if he had just come from the Mardi Gras with the music in the car bumpin' as he rocked his head to each boom of the bass.

Even rugged and scroungy from a hard day's work, Lance still looked good to Jeva. He had dry loop curls that covered his head, and rugged bronze skin. He was six feet, nine inches tall with a medium-cut build. He had appealing brown eyes that he always squinted because he wouldn't wear the glasses his optometrist had prescribed. People always told him that he looked like the guy who played Jason in the movie *Jason's Lyric*.

"I see that somebody needs a watch for Christmas," Jeva said smartly, getting into the car and slamming the door.

"Hey, how was your day?" Lance asked in a pleasant tone.

"Why do you do that?" Jeva asked with a puzzled look on her face.

"Do what?" Lance said, squinting his eyes as he pulled off.

"Act like pulling up almost a half hour late isn't nothing. Why don't you try apologizing for a change, or is that too much like right?"

"And what's an apology going to do? Make the thirty-minute wait feel like fifteen instead?" Lance said, shaking his head.

"You don't have to act like such an asshole, Lance," Jeva snapped.

"Who in the fuck do you think you're talking to? I work hard just like you. Don't even come at me like that. Your ass can walk home next time," Lance said catching a major attitude.

"That's so uncalled for. You don't have to talk to me all disrespectful."

"You're the one who called me an asshole, and it's not the first time. What if I always called you a stripper or a ho?"

"In so many ways you do. Every time we argue that's the first thing that comes out of your mouth: *You were just a stripper when I met you.* How many more years are you going to throw that in my face?" asked Jeva, as if she were sick and tired of Lance's comments. "Every time we get into it it's like you get your jollies off by reminding me about my past. I know what I used to do for a living, Lance. I don't need you to remind me."

Lance turned up the music and continued to drive. He sought pleasure in tuning Jeva out. Her lips were moving. Her neck was twisting. Her head was bobbing. Her finger was pointing and yet he could hear nothing but his music. After several minutes of wasting her breath Jeva turned the music down.

"Do you want to just call it quits, because I'm sick of being treated like a nobody?" Jeva asked.

"Girl, stop talking crazy. You know you ain't going anywhere. What? You going to go stay with Breezy for a week like you always do? You'll be right back home." Lance laughed.

"You think everything is funny. If you don't straighten up, one day you're going to come home and find me gone for good."

"Then why are you with me, Jeva? If you are so determined

to leave me, why are you laying up with me every night?"

"Have you ever heard of that thing called love?"

"Jeva, I'm trying real hard to love you," Lance said seriously.

"What's wrong with me, Lance?" Jeva asked.

"Nothing is wrong with you. You just need to chill out."

"Then why do you make loving me sound like you're training for the heavyweight title of the world? Loving a person should be easy. Loving *me* should be easy. Chinese arithmetic is hard."

"Baby, loving you and dealing with you are two different things."

Jeva was starting to become emotional. Lance knew what this meant. She was beginning to think about her birth parents. That is what always followed their arguments. She would forgive Lance for not loving her because her own mother and father didn't love her. If they had they would not have given her up. Lance pulled into the parking lot of a convenience store and put the car in Park.

"I don't want to keep going through this with you, ma. I know how you feel and before you start telling me that I don't, just listen," Lance said, rubbing Jeva's hand. "I know how you feel because when you hurt, I hurt. I feel the same pain you do. When you close your eyes I see your darkness. Jeva, I know you said that you are giving up the search, but baby, we've got to find your parents. It's eating away at you and it's not good for our relationship. You don't know who you are. We're going to force that child placement agency to locate some type of paperwork on you. It's impossible for them not to have a single document on you or your parents."

"No, Lance." Jeva began to cry. "I already told you it's useless. It only makes things worse getting those letters from Welford Child Placement Agency telling me, once again, that they came up with nothing on my parents. It tears me apart."

"Then we'll hire a private investigator. I'll work longer hours to pay for one. I'll invest in some chronic instead of that weak shit I been pushing and flip my ends. Hell, I'll go find them myself if I have to. We've got to do something."

Jeva looked at Lance. "You'd do all that for me?"

"Did you think I wouldn't?"

"Let's go get the baby," Jeva said as she kissed Lance, and they drove off.

The following two weeks Jeva put the wheels in motion toward finding her biological parents, investing all of her time in just that one task alone.

"When is the last time you washed clothes and when is the next time you plan on washing again?" Lance said as he threw clothes out of the dirty hamper in search of a work shirt.

"Oh, honey, I'm sorry," Jeva said, jumping up off the bed, leaving a stack of letters, envelopes, and stamps behind. "I've been so busy writing letters to the agency and to the media about the agency, as well as talk shows, that I haven't gotten around to washing clothes."

"And you want me to marry you," Lance mumbled under his voice.

"Excuse me?" Jeva said, putting her hand on her hip and rolling her eyes.

"You won't even wash clothes. We done ate out all week. I need a woman who is going to take care of little shit, like her house, and hell, her man."

"You are like Dr. Jekyll and Mr. Hyde, I swear. You are the one who pumped me up to get on top of finding my birth parents and you won't even be supportive."

"If I had known I'd have to wear dirty clothes to work then I would have suggested otherwise."

Jeva stomped away from Lance. She didn't want him to see her cry. She flopped back down on the bed and continued stamping and sealing envelopes. Tears flowed from her eyes as she did so.

"Will you stop crying?" Lance shouted. "You're like a big-ass baby. I don't know who's worse, you or Heather."

Jeva had been nibbling on a piece of pecan cheesecake she had left over in the refrigerator from the Cheesecake Factory. She was so furious and overcome by emotion that, without thinking, she scooped up a mess of it and threw it right at Lance. He had been looking down, buttoning his shirt, but just as the cheesecake flew across the bedroom he looked up. It hit him dead smack in his face.

It was too late when Jeva realized what she had done. She covered her mouth with her hand in surprise. Lance stood there scraping the cheesecake off of his face. Jeva tried her hardest to hold in her laughter but didn't succeed. Lance looked at her and ran over to the bed and jumped on top of her.

"You think that was funny, huh?" Lance said, smearing it on Jeva's face.

"Lance, don't!" Jeva said, laughing.

"Mmm, mmm. I want you to know what it feels like to wear cheesecake."

Lance sat on top of Jeva and pinned her arms above her head. He proceeded to rub his face against hers. When he released her arms, she scooped up some of the cheesecake off of Lance's face with her index finger. Jeva then seductively sucked it off of her fingertip.

"Mmm, it tastes even better on you." Jeva smiled.

"I know where it will taste even better," Lance replied as he gave Jeva a seductive look.

Lance lifted up the white dress shirt of his that Jeva was wearing and pulled down her white Victoria's Secret Body Glove panties. Lance then proceeded to smear his face all over Jeva's pussy. He ate her out until her cream slid down his throat.

Lance planted a hard kiss on Jeva's clit and then on her mouth. He winked at her and then got up and proceeded to go clean himself up.

Jeva watched him walk away, mesmerized. Then she collapsed backward onto the bed and smiled.

"Mmm, I love me some him," she said to herself. "I love me some him."

The Check Is in the Mail

"Okay, what did I miss?" Klarke asked as she flopped down into her chair at the Cheesecake.

"If you would stop trying to be the Terrell Owens of the clique," Breezy said, "you wouldn't have to ask that question every time you meet us."

"What does that mean and who is Terrell Owens?" Klarke asked, crossing her legs.

"He plays for the Forty-niners. People think he's always doing things to purposely make himself stand out," Breezy said.

"If you ask me, he can. Hell, he's one of the top five receivers in the league. They need to leave that boy alone, him and Keyshawn." Klarke and Breezy looked at Jeva with squinted faces, repelled that Jeva knew just a tad too much about football.

Jeva shrugged. "I can't help it. Lance and I watch football all of the time together. Anyway, Klarke, Breezy was getting ready to talk about Hydrant."

"What about him?" Klarke said, making eye contact with

Chauncy to signal that he could now bring her a Shirley Temple.

"He still hasn't called her or nothing," Jeva said.

"Can you blame him?" Klarke was quick to ask.

"Y'all, he was laying on the couch all wrong," Breezy cringed. "I just snapped."

"Girl, you stupid." Klarke laughed.

"You know how it is when you just look at a man and get mad? I mean he just be laying there on my couch . . . wrong. It's like he can't do nothing right, not even lay on the couch right."

"You are so wrong!" Klarke chuckled. "And that's just what women like you get."

"I'm not trying to hear you say that shit one more time, Klarke," Breezy said seriously.

"Slow down, baby. That's not even where I was about to take you," Klarke said. "When I said women like you, I meant women who hinder a man. A brotha lets a sistah know his shit isn't all in-tact, but yet y'all got to have him and y'all got to have him right now. Y'all don't want to wait until he comes through and gets himself together . . . so scared the next chick is going to stick her claws into him. Breezy, if that man is supposed to be in your life, he's going to be in your life. You don't have to hold onto him so tight that you start to suffocate yourself with his presence. Let him go. Let him handle his business without worrying about hav-ing to be up under your ass, trying to please you. Do you think that makes him feel good? Do you think that makes him feel like a man?"

"Well damn! I guess you told me," Breezy said, pulling her head back and staring at Klarke. "You think you the funkin shiznit now, huh? Your little scam with Reo Suave is turning you into a philosophizing brute."

"It's taught me a thing or two," Klarke said, smacking her lips. "Not to mention I also went to college and learned a few things there too."

"Oh yeah, miss college girl. I forgot you went to community college. So you completed the thirteenth and fourteenth grade. Big deal!" Breezy joked.

"Have I ever told you how much I hate you deep down inside?" Klarke snarled.

"You know you love me," Breezy said, puckering her lips and making a kissing sound.

"I'm not all that hungry today," Jeva said twisting up her face.

"Me either," Klarke agreed. "What about you, Breezy?"

"I'm not starved or anything like that. I can grab something in the mall if you two are ready to raise up out of here."

"Check please," Klarke called to Chauncy as the women prepared to go window shopping.

"I don't see anything worth admiring today," Jeva said as they walked through the mall.

"Yeah, I could have skipped this, stayed home and watched Lifetime all day," Breezy added.

"Face it, girls," Klarke said. "We've outgrown window shopping. There's no fun in it anymore. It only highlights what we're supposed to be forgetting about."

A quad of men who looked to be younger than the women walked past them and made eye contact. Breezy said hello and the men responded. One of them decided he wanted to take that simple hello to another level.

"Damn, y'all looking good," the idiot boy said as he pranced around. "Woooo, weeee. Do y'all got men? Hot damn! Hell, and if y'all do, are y'all allowed to have friends? You can never have too many friends."

"Come here, baby. Let me tell you something," Breezy said in her most seductive voice.

The men all looked at one another as if they weren't sure who Breezy was directing her words toward.

"Yeah, you," she said, pointing at the idiot boy. "Don't be sceered."

He looked at his crew as if he had just been a made man by the Godfather himself. He held his head high and walked with a slight pimp over to Breezy. She leaned into his ear and whispered, "Men like you are the reason sisters don't speak."

"Excuse me?" he said jerking away, but Breezy jerked him back.

"Baby, let me give you a little bit of priceless advice. From now on, when a woman says hello to you on the street, don't assume she's interested in you, wants to fuck you or even wants to know your goddamn name. Just say hello and walk away. This is the new millennium. If a woman is interested, oh, you'll know. Trust me. But that shit you just pulled, that little crackhead version of the *American Idol* show, it's not becoming of the male species. Now, if any of us had been interested in you, you just blew it. You look quite fuckable, too. Nonetheless, next time, take heed to what I just told you and you might land you some pussy. Now run along and enjoy the rest of your afternoon."

Breezy kissed him on the cheek, wiped her lipstick off of him and shooed him away with her hand. His boys praised him once he returned to their circle, none the wiser that he had just been shut down.

"You are so wrong," Jeva said to Breezy in complete disbelief as they continued walking through the mall. "You done probably scarred the boy for life."

"Women need to start correcting men's behavior," Breezy said as if she was fed up. "When they act like two-year-olds, then they need to be scolded like two-year-olds. I'm sick of it."

"See what I mean?" Klarke said shaking her head. "This is getting tired. I won't be doing too much more of this shit anyhow. Jeva is right. We're going to have to join a book club or something if y'all trying to see my ass every month."

"The girl even has the mouth of a sailor now," Breezy said referring to Klarke. "You must be handling your business after all with the novelist."

"What can I say? I got him, girls," Klarke said as they high-fived each other. "I can just feel it. He's diggin' me tough. He's a busy man. Why else would he spend so much time e-mailing a complete stranger?"

"That shit actually worked? When you go back to work on Monday, flip through them files and get me the e-mail address of a best-selling author. He could be the answer to my caviar dreams and gated-community lifestyle," Breezy said seriously.

"You know," Jeva added, nodding.

"I'm serious," Breezy said.

"This man's e-mails . . . I'm telling y'all. I don't need an erotic book, magazine, a dirty movie, a vibrator, a nothing to get off anymore. His smooth words alone satisfy my pleasuredome and cause me to orgasm," Klarke bragged.

"Then print them muthafuckas out and let me have a look," Breezy said. "My battery expense is more than my damn electric bill."

"So, are you going to meet him in person or what?" Jeva asked.

"Soon," Klarke answered. "I mean we haven't set anything up, but I'm just about ready to pull his ho card."

"Men are so predictable it's ridiculous," Breezy said, shaking her head. "He fell for everything, hook, line, and e-mail, just like you said he would, Klarke. You da bomb."

"I don't see how he's going to possibly agree to meet with you knowing he's not the person you think he is that he doesn't know never existed in the first place," Jeva rambled on.

Klarke and Breezy couldn't make heads or tails out of the point Jeva was trying to get across.

"How does Lance deal with you?" Breezy asked. "You're like Chrissy Snow."

"I swear I was thinking the same thing," Klarke laughed.

"Now that's a scary thought," Jeva said.

"Boo!" Klarke said. "Anyway, I know he's going to agree to meet me in person, then he's going to toss and turn all night trying to figure out what to do. The next day he'll send me an e-mail telling me the truth and my work will be done. I'll meet him, give him a little of this Ill Na Na and be living back in the land of La La in no time. Just like you said, Breezy, men, there're so predictable."

"Klarke Annette Taylor, that's what I'm talking about, damn it," Breezy said giving Klarke multiple hand smacks. "Men have been burning us for ages. It's time we throw a bucket of water on their eternal flame of dawgin' us out. It's our turn to rule the world."

"There is just one thing that could be a minor setback," Klarke said. "My period is a week late."

"Oh, girl," Breezy said like the actress on the cell phone commercial. "You're shittin' me."

"How you just gonna throw that in there like it's nothing?" Jeva asked Klarke.

"Y'all know I take the pill to regulate my cycle. I missed a pill or two and I think my body just got off track," Klarke said, pretending that she wasn't that worried.

"What if you are pregnant?" Breezy said putting her hand over her mouth. "Girl, what are you going to do?

"I'd get an abortion," Klarke said without hesitation.

"I don't know about an abortion for you," Breezy said. "I don't think you could live with that choice, Klarke."

"You and I both have had an abortion before," Jeva said. "Sometimes it's the answer."

"Don't use Klarke's situation to justify ours," Breezy said. "And besides, what I got was an abortion. What you should have gotten was ten to life."

"Breezy!" Klarke said in shock.

"You remember how far along she was," Breezy said in her I-don't-give-a-damn tone. "She had to leave the state. One more week and she probably would have had to leave the country to get it done."

"I know you think your little remarks are cute, but they're not. That's hurtful, Breezy," Jeva said sadly. "And I didn't have to leave the state. I only had to go to another city."

"I don't want to talk about abortion anymore," Klarke said in a regretful tone. "I shouldn't have even said anything."

"Yeah," Jeva said. "Let's not jump to any conclusions. Just make a doctor's appointment and see what's going on."

"I made one for next month. That's the earliest my OB/GYN could get me in," Klarke said. "And I don't trust the accuracy of those home-pregnancy tests."

"Well, I'd be calling every day to see if there are any cancellations," Breezy said. "You don't want to wait too long or you might end up having to leave the state. I mean the city."

"Ha ha," Jeva said.

"Anyway," Klarke continued. "I got to get a handle on this. I can't chance blowing it this far into the game."

"Just make sure you do handle it and I'm here if you need me," Breezy said.

"You are risking something, Klarke," Jeva said sincerely. "I've been thinking about it, about you and Reo. You're taking a risk that you've probably never even thought twice about."

"And do tell," Klarke said opening her hand, giving Jeva the floor to speak.

"Falling in love. You're taking the risk of this man falling in love with you. This could cost him his heart. Or you could fall in love with him. It could cost you your heart."

"Yeah, yeah, yeah," Breezy said, swinging her hand back and forth. "Men don't know nothing about love, not until somebody dawgs them out that is. Hell, Guy's wife has me to thank for his newly devoted monogamous relationship with her. By the time I drain that son of a bitch, he'll wish he had stayed true to his vows in the first place."

"You still taxing him?" Jeva asked.

"I don't look at it like that," Breezy replied. "I took him for a ride, or two, or three or four or five . . . hell, he's just paying the fare."

"Some people grow up Baptist, others Lutheran, some Apostolic or what have you. I grew up Catholic. Breezy, your domination is M-O-N-E-Y," Jeva said, shaking her head.

"It's a very old religion," Breezy said, smiling. "I thought you knew."

"Amen," Klarke witnessed, as she waved her hand in the air.

"You two are tripping," Jeva said. "Money has your minds twisted."

"Don't forget where you came from, Darling Nikki," Breezy said to Jeva.

"Hey, I might have slid down a pole or two back in the day, but I never turned a trick," Jeva said in defense.

"How do you explain Lance?" Breezy asked.

"Well, Little Red Corvette, I met him at the bar I danced at, but it wasn't via sex for hire or anything like that. We just got to talking and formed a friendship. One thing led to another."

"What's with the Prince songs as metaphors?" Klarke laughed.

"Prince done told everybody's life story. If you can't find yourself in one of his songs, then you haven't lived," Breezy said. "I'll be a Little Red Corvette anytime. After my contract with Guy expires, you never know, I just might own one."

"Which one do y'all think I am?" Klarke asked.

"'The Beautiful Ones,'" Jeva and Breezy said at the same time.

"I guess I am a heartbreaker in the making," Klarke said.

On the way to her truck, Klarke saw Evan coming toward her. There were two other gentlemen with him.

"Mr. Kemble," Klarke said. "Hello."

"Miss Taylor," Evan said nervously.

"Out doing a little shopping?" Klarke asked.

"Uh, yes. Our mother's birthday is next week and my brothers and I decided to hit the mall together to see what we could come up with."

Klarke looked at Evan's brothers, then looked at him, waiting for an introduction. When Evan caught Klarke's subtle hint, he said, "Oh, where are my manners? Klarke, I mean Miss Taylor, this is my brother Elliott and my brother Eric."

Elliott was the spitting image of Evan, only about three inches taller, and Eric was shorter than Evan, with dark brown hair and dark brown eyes.

"Triple E, huh?" Klarke said, shaking their hands. "Well, it was nice to meet you."

"Same here," the brothers said as they looked at her admiringly.

Klarke could see that Evan felt really awkward standing there.

"Well, you all enjoy yourself," Klarke said, waving and walking away.

"Miss Taylor," Eric said, "we could use a woman's touch. Why don't you join us, and then afterward we can all just hang out? You know what I mean?"

From the look in his eyes and the tone of his voice, Klarke knew that Evan had shared their encounter with his brothers. How he explained it was beyond her, but they seemed to have taken it as if Klarke was some free-for-all tramp.

"I don't think so. I've been in that mall a while now," Klarke declined with a smile.

"But you don't have any bags," Eric said.

"Yeah, well, my girlfriends and I did a little window shopping."

"You didn't see anything you liked?" Eric asked as he raised his eyebrows.

"Nah, not really. Thanks for the invite, though," Klarke said, walking away.

"Then what do you say we just skip the shopping and get right to the hanging out?" he asked, grabbing hold of Klarke's arm.

Klarke was starting to lose her patience with him.

"Do you mind?" Klarke said looking down at his hand on her arm.

"Oh, pardon me," Eric said, letting go and backing away.

"You gentlemen enjoy your afternoon," Klarke said, cutting her eyes at Evan.

Klarke walked away feeling the burning sensation of three pairs of eyes on her back. She was so pissed she wanted to cry. No, what she really wanted to do was spit in Evan's face.

As she fumbled for her keys Klarke was startled to see in the reflection of her tinted window a figure coming up behind her. She turned around in panic only to find Evan standing there. She rolled her eyes at him, turned back around, and inserted the key into the door.

"Klarke, I know what you're thinking. My brother just acts that way. He's the youngest and he's in college. He's a little immature," Evan pleaded as Klarke proceeded to climb into the truck and roll the windows down.

"Well, I wonder where he gets it from."

"Klarke, please."

"So, you didn't tell them about us? They don't know that you and I have . . .?"

"No, I didn't tell them, but they know me. I'm sure they could sense that something was up. Why, Klarke? Are we some secret, under lock and key? Are you ashamed of what happened between us?"

"Don't try to flip the script on me, Evan," Klarke said as Evan stood there looking puzzled.

"You're beautiful even when you're pissed off," Evan said, trying to pull a smile out of Klarke.

"You know what, Evan?" Klarke said as she started up the

truck and began to back out of her parking spot. "You're a class act."

Minutes later as Klarke sat at the red light waiting for it to turn, she looked in the rearview mirror at herself and cringed. She had *known* better than to have sex with Evan. Here she had gone to bed with a man she wasn't even in a relationship with. Her vision blurred as her eyes filled with tears.

"If I'm pregnant, I'll die," Klarke said to herself. "I will absolutely die."

She began to sob uncontrollably.

"What's happening to me? You're not me. Who are you?" she said to the mirror. "How in the hell did I go from a housewife to a ho? God, help me. Tell me what to do with myself. Just one word. Please, God."

Klarke was in the basement folding a load of laundry when she heard the doorbell ring.

"Just a minute!" she yelled. The doorbell rang again.

"I'm coming!" Klarke said as she went over to the door and opened it.

"Tionne, what are you doing here?" Klarke said, surprised.

"I've just got to get some things off of my chest, Klarke," Tionne said.

Tionne's chin trembled in an effort to hold back tears. Klarke stood there, waiting for Tionne to gain her composure and state the purpose of her unannounced visit.

Klarke was surprised by Tionne's appearance. Tionne had always made it a point to look her best when knowing that she would be seeing Klarke. But now her hair was pulled back in a dried-out ponytail and it looked like she hadn't run a comb through it in days. She was sporting a wrinkled black jogging suit and some regular white leather Keds with no socks. This was the first time Klarke had ever seen Tionne without makeup on. There were visible blemishes on Tionne's face that Klarke had never known existed under the smoothly applied cosmetics she always wore.

"Look, Klarke, I'll just get right to it," Tionne said, wiping her eyes. "Are you and Harris trying to get back together?"

At first Klarke looked at Tionne, dumbfounded. Then she exploded with laughter.

"You've got some nerve," Klarke said in disbelief. "I honestly can't believe that you've come to my home with this. On a bad day I would tell you to go fuck yourself and have this conversation with your man. And he is *your* man now, Tionne. But since you done drove all this way to ask me that question I suppose I'll answer it. *No*, Tionne. I have no intention whatsoever of getting back with Harris."

"And is that how Harris feels, too?" Tionne asked.

"You've got to be kidding me." Klarke grinned, putting her hands on her hips. "Ask him. I can't tell you how Harris feels."

"Well, you're going to have to tell me something," Tionne said, digging into her purse. She pulled out a piece of paper and unfolded it. "Something's going on, or is Harris just running around paying off people's truck notes now?"

Klarke took the piece of paper from Tionne and skimmed it. Sure enough, it was documentation that Harris had paid off Klarke's truck note. Klarke's mouth dropped in shock.

"I found it in the glove compartment of his car," Tionne said as she studied Klarke's reaction. "Don't tell me you didn't know."

"Honestly, I had no idea Harris was the one who had paid this.

I thought it was my boss," Klarke said still stunned. "Please, Tionne, come in."

Tionne came inside and sat down on the couch. Klarke fixed Tionne a glass of ice water and sat down next to her.

"I don't want to seem cold," Klarke said, "but you and I aren't friends. We are cordial to one another, but that's where it stops. I see you're going through some things and I'm only doing what any decent person would do. I'm listening. I just don't want you to say too much or the wrong thing to me."

"I understand," Tionne said, taking a sip of her water. "This is my karma, Klarke. It's everything I did to you ten times over. I'm sorry, Klarke. I'm so sorry. I'm sorry, not because it's all coming back to me now, but because I knew Harris didn't love me. He didn't love me like he loved you. He cared for me, but that was about it. I knew he didn't want me and I just had to have him. When you filed for divorce and he came to stay with me, do you know how many times I put my ear against the bathroom door and listened to him cry in the shower over you?"

"I don't think I need to hear this," Klarke said, getting up from the couch.

"Even back when I stopped taking the pill and got pregnant on purpose, he didn't want me," Tionne continued. "He went as far as giving me money for an abortion. I took the money, but as you know I didn't get the abortion."

"Tionne, really, I don't think I'm the person you should be sharing all of this with."

"No, you are exactly the person I need to be telling this. Klarke, do you love my child?"

"How can you ask me that? You know she doesn't have anything to do with what went on between you, Harris, and myself. I've never mistreated her and never will," Klarke said taking offense. "My beef has always been with you, Tionne. What's strange is that I probably wouldn't have even been mad at you if you were just *the other woman*. But when you decided to take on the role of my friend—laughing in my face, going out with me, coming over to my house and having me baby-sit your and Harris's love child, you crossed the line. Otherwise my only beef would have been with Harris. Harris took vows and made a commitment to me, not you. You didn't owe me shit. Harris did. I'm not like most women who fly off the handle and set out to beat the mistress down. But you, Tionne, you pretended to be my friend. You played me and that hurt."

"You're right. I think I better go," Tionne said as she walked over to the door to let herself out. "Can you not mention to Harris that I stopped by?"

"No problem," Klarke said. She closed the door behind Tionne.

Klarke recognized that look of devastation in Tionne's eyes. It was that same look that had been on her face when she found out Harris had cheated on her.

"So what's wrong with Tionne?" Vaughn said, coming down the stairs.

Klarke turned around in surprise. "Oh, her and your dad are just going through some things," Klarke said casually.

"Ooooh, did they break up?" Vaughn asked eagerly.

"Come here," Klarke said, sitting down on the couch and patting the spot next to her for Vaughn to join her. "Baby, your father loves you. Your father would love you no matter who is in his life. Do you understand what I'm saying to you?"

Vaughn nodded. Klarke kissed her on the forehead, smiled and got up to go in the kitchen to get dinner started.

"What about you?" Vaughn asked, causing Klarke to turn around and face her daughter.

"What about me?" she asked.

"Will he love you, too, no matter who is in his life?"

11

Your Place or Mine

From: KAT@myworld.biz
To: RLQ812@sunset.com
Subject: Meet Me Halfway

Hey you,

I hope you don't take this the wrong way. I enjoy your e-mails. I really do. I race to my computer in hopes of seeing your e-mail address in my inbox.

I honestly feel as though I've known you all of my life (okay, maybe just for most of it . . . smile) but nonetheless, when it comes to you everything about me seems to pour out. I don't hold back with you.

This cyber shit has to stop, though.

I gave you my phone number and it has yet to ring with you on the other end. Maybe you're not a phone person. If that's the case, just say so.

I guess what I'm really trying to say is that I won't even be satisfied with your calling me at this point. I need to see you again. I don't care when or where. We can meet each other halfway if you like. I just need to luxuriate in your words face-to-face.

I've been waiting for months for you to get around to mentioning that you perhaps wanted to see me again and you never have. So I figured I'd come on out and say it (crossing my fingers that you want to see me too). It's kind of like a couple who's been dating for a while but neither wants to be the first to say "I love you."

Anyway, think about my proposal and let me know how you feel about it.

KAT

From: RLQ812@sunset.com
To: KAT@myworld.biz
Subject: Meet Me Halfway

I'd love to meet you face-to-face. You name it.

"Come on, Dad. You're the only one who can tell me what to do," Reo said to his father.

"You don't need me to tell you what to do. You knew what you should have done a long time ago when the girl first sent you that e-mail," Mr. Laroque said.

"This woman may very well be your future daughter-in-law," Reo said. "She could be the mother of the grandchildren you and Mom have always wanted. You gotta help me out, Dad. Give me some of that *if I were you, this is what I would do* fatherly advice."

"If I were you I would have never pretended to be someone I wasn't. Ain't you got no game, son?"

"Thanks for nothing, Dad," Reo said, frustrated.

"Anytime, son, anytime," Mr. Laroque said, hanging up the telephone in Reo's ear.

Reo didn't know what he was going to do. Hell, yeah, he wanted to meet KAT face-to-face. He had only wanted to do that forever. But either he would have to tell her the truth or he would have to let her go. Or perhaps he could block out her e-mails, ignore them all together. Eventually she would catch on and let him be.

Reo knew it was immature and self-serving of him to continue this masquerade with KAT. He couldn't help it, though. He felt in his heart that KAT *was* meant for him.

He decided to sleep on it. Hopefully the answer would come to him in the morning.

From: RLQ812@sunset.com
To: KAT@myworld.biz
Subject: Confession

Before you tell me when and where you want to meet face-to-face, there is something I need to confess. I'm going to get right to the point as you often do. I know I never used your phone number to call you. I know I've never sent you that picture that I said I would either. It's not that I didn't want to. I didn't want you to find out that I'm not the man you think I am. Literally.

I don't know who you shared moments with in that Boston airport, but ever since you first e-mailed me I've been wishing that it had been me. Through your words, KAT, I've grown attached to everything about you.

Through your words I know how you brush your hair. I know

how you stretch and rise out of bed in the morning. I know that you brush your teeth in circles. I know that you collect figurines of elephants. Damn, you got me, girl. You have truly become a part of me.

I'm going to be sitting on pins and needles awaiting a response from you. If you never want to communicate with me again I'll understand. If that is the case, just hit your reply button for this e-mail with "Return to sender" in the subject line. If that's not the case, 614-576-9322. Ask for Reo.

Reo sat outside his publicist's office, boiling mad. He couldn't believe she had scheduled for him to visit over a dozen different bookstores in one month. She had left him a voice message informing him of his tour schedule and had avoided his phone calls since doing so. Reo decided to pay her a surprise visit.

"Mr. Laroque," the receptionist said. "Carla will see you now."

"Thank you," Reo said as he went into Carla's office.

"Hey, Reo," Carla said as Reo entered her office.

"What's wrong, you can't call nobody?" Reo asked.

"You so crazy," Carla said getting up to close her office door and lock it. After doing so she removed the red-and-black sheer scarf she was wearing around her neck. She undid the top button to the jacket of the red suit she was wearing.

"No, you are the one who's crazy if you think I'm going to spend all of next month packing and unpacking while bookstore hopping. I'm no bookstore ho, Carla."

"What's the problem?" Carla asked. "At first you couldn't get enough of arriving in different cities with a line of women waiting on your ass."

"That was then and this is now. I don't need to do all of this anymore."

"Oh, I get it. You think you're Omar Tyree now . . . or Michael Baisden? Well, let me tell you this, those brothas have been in the game far longer than you have and they are still putting in work. Don't ever think because you hit the best-seller lists that you no longer have an obligation to the readers out there," Carla said as she went to the mirror that was hanging above the couch in her office. She licked her fingertips and dabbed down a piece of hair that was disfiguring her Anita Baker short-short hairdo.

"I'm not saying that," Reo said. "What I am saying is that I don't have to get down that hard in the paint. All of those signings, Carla, in one month. Come on now!"

"Okay, Reo. Let's just sit down and talk about this calmly," Carla said as she grabbed Reo by his tie and led him over to the plush couch in her office. Carla began tasting Reo's lips with a nibble here and there.

"Uh, Carla," Reo said, pushing her away. "I already told you. We are not going there. I'm sorry about that night I came onto you at Marlon Green's book release party. I don't know what I was thinking, but I'm not trying to screw around and mess up our business relationship."

"You don't really mean that. Quit playing hard," Carla said, grabbing Reo's penis through his pants. "Oh, you're not playing. You really are hard."

"Damn it, Carla," Reo said, pushing her hand away.

Just then Reo's cell phone rang. He normally turned it off when he was going into a meeting, but he had been so pissed that it had slipped his mind. He looked down at the phone and the caller ID read "Unknown ID". Reo decided to let it go to voicemail. He pushed the Off button, or at least he meant to, but he had hit the green Okay button instead, which answered the call.

"Damn," he muttered then put the phone to his ear.

"Hello?" Reo heard a voice through the receiver say.

"This is Reo speaking," he said.

"Well hello, Reo speaking," the voice on the other end said.

Reo's heart began to race. "KAT, is that you?" Reo asked.

"I guess you don't have many women calling you, huh?" she said.

Reo dropped the phone down to his side. He closed his eyes and lifted his head up to the sky.

"Thank you, God," he said. "Thank you, heavenly Father."

"Hello? You still there?" KAT said.

"Yes, yes, oh, I'm sorry. Can you hold on one more time?" Reo asked.

"Certainly," KAT replied.

Reo covered the phone with his hand and whispered to Carla, "Just forget it, Carla. I'll do the signings. "I'll do a hundred signings."

Reo jetted out of Carla's office, leaving her standing there in his smoke. Back out in the lobby Reo took a deep breath and then placed the phone up to his ear.

"KAT, I do apologize," Reo said.

"Did I catch you at a bad time?" she asked.

"You couldn't be more perfect. I mean with your timing, that is."

"Hmm, okay. So, do I call you out of your name for having me think, all of this time, that you were someone other than yourself, or do I blow you a smooch through the phone and tell you how flattered I am for you doing so?"

"I would like that very much."

"Which one, to be called out of your name or blown a kiss? Knowing you, you would probably enjoy both."

By the time Reo had made it to his home, he and KAT had

talked and laughed for over an hour. Reo had driven all the way home from Carla's office before he knew it.

They were like a couple of high school sweethearts who had found each other again.

KAT was vague about her previous marriages, but went into great depth with tales of her children and the wonderful relationship she'd had with her parents before they passed. Reo told KAT about his struggle and the sacrifices he had made to become a writer and his relationship with his parents, especially his dad.

"So, we've graduated from e-mail to the phone," KAT said. "Does that mean I'm going to have to talk to you on the phone a few months before we get to actually meet one another face-to-face?"

"I'd enjoy nothing more than verbal relations with you, but I'm shooting for a personal encounter. You say when and where and I'll have airline tickets delivered to your front door," Reo said.

"This 614 area code is Columbus, right?" she asked.

"Yes," Reo said.

"That's only a two-hour drive, max."

"Then I'll send you a gas card, a rental car voucher, or something."

"Why is it you automatically assume I should drive to see you versus you come to see me?"

"I know you, KAT. You wouldn't have a man come to you. You wouldn't play that. No good mother would. I don't see you having that when it comes to your children."

"Yeah, I did right by calling you," she said proudly.

"I take it I gave you the right answer," Reo said, smiling.

"You did. There's nothing more attractive than a man who knows how to respect a woman who has children. Remind me to give your momma a great big hug and kiss for bringing you up right."

"Damn, girl, you already trying to meet my momma? Uh oh, I think that was my other line," Reo said as they both laughed.

"Oh, my, Reo. You are so crazy."

"About you," Reo said on a more serious note.

"Well, I better get off this phone."

"Yeah, but it's been a pleasure talking to you, KAT. But before I let you go, can I ask you something personal, and this is quite embarrassing?"

"What is it?" she said.

"Your name. What's your real name?"

"Klarke. Klarke Annette Taylor."

"I did it!" Klarke exclaimed to Jeva and Breezy, who were at her house preparing to watch *Sex and the City*.

"What are you talking about?" Breezy said. "Did you fart or something?"

"Why are you so stupid?" Klarke laughed. "No, I didn't fart. I mean I did IT . . . I got Reo to arrange to meet me in person."

"I never doubted that you would," Breezy said.

"You a bad woman," Jeva said, smiling. "I don't know how the two of you pull this kind of stuff off."

"Skills, baby," Breezy said. "It's called skills."

"I guess I don't have those type of skills," Jeva said.

"Damn skippy you don't," Breezy said, "or you wouldn't move in with me once a month to get away from Lance, only to keep running right back to him. I'm glad I don't mind my own company. Being alone is all right by me."

"I can't imagine raising my daughter without Lance. It's harder when kids are involved. There is a stronger bond," Jeva said.

"Bullshit, and I'm sick of women using that lame shit as an excuse to stay with a man," Breezy said. "Just because you have a baby with him doesn't mean you love him more than a woman who doesn't have a baby with a man."

"You don't have any kids, Breezy, so you don't understand," Jeva said.

"So you mean to tell me if Klarke had been married to Harris for thirteen years and not had any children by him that your five years with Lance would hold more weight because you two have a daughter? That's crazy. Why don't y'all baby mommas stop using the kids and that bond shit as an excuse to stay in a relationship and be treated like shit?"

"Excuse me," Jeva said dropping the knife she was using to cut the vegetables for the veggie tray. "I'm going to go check on my little Heather."

As Jeva headed up the steps to check on her daughter who was playing with Vaughn and HJ, Klarke went at it with Breezy.

"Sometimes you go too damn far," Klarke said. "You know how sensitive Jeva's feelings are."

"And you know how I am," Breezy explained. "If I'm going to have to tiptoe around her then maybe you two should just hang without me."

"See, now you are talking crazy," Klarke said. "Just try to be a little more diplomatic, why don't you?"

"Whatever," Breezy said as Jeva came down the steps.

"Yeah, whatever," Klarke said.

From: KAT@myworld.biz
To: RLQ812@sunset.com
Subject: Columbus Trip

Hey you!

I booked the rental car. I pick it up next Friday at 5:30 P.M. I can hardly wait. I should arrive in Columbus at about 8:00 P.M.

From: RLQ812@sunset.com
To: KAT@myworld.biz
Subject: Columbus Trip

I'm attaching your hotel itinerary. I got you a suite at the Double Tree downtown. I hope that is okay. If not, let me know and I'll change it to the hotel of your choice.

I'll be out of town from Tuesday to Friday, but my flight arrives back in Columbus at 3:00 P.M. Is 9:00 P.M. an okay time to meet me in the hotel bar? We can enjoy a cocktail and then go somewhere for dinner. I know of a nice steakhouse downtown. Would you like steak? What about alcohol?

From: KAT@myworld.biz
To: RLQ812@sunset.com
Subject: You

Hey you!

I think nine o'clock will be good. Steak sounds great. I don't drink on a regular, but when I do, you know Passion Alizé does the trick for me.

I can't wait to see you, Reo. Which leads me to the million-dollar question: How will I know who you are?

From: RLQ812@sunset.com
To: KAT@myworld.biz
Subject: Me

You just will!

The night Klarke was to meet Reo for the first time she skipped lunch and left work an hour early. She decided to pick up the rental car and load up her travel bags, so that once Harris picked up the kids she could head out straight for Columbus.

Klarke had definitely overpacked, but not knowing what-all Reo had in store for her, she didn't want to take the chance of not having the appropriate attire. Before loading her bags she double-checked the contents one last time. She removed the lingerie from her bag as it didn't coincide with her plan not to give Reo any. She replaced it with a nice long satin gown and robe set.

Hell, I'm not even going to put myself in a position where he sees me in my sleepwear, Klarke thought as she exchanged the long satin gown-robe set for a two-piece, black-and-white Chicago White Sox pajama-short set.

"There, all set," Klarke said to herself as she proceeded to carry her bags out to the car.

As she was coming out the door Harris pulled up and got out of his car.

"So what's taking you to Columbus?" Harris asked, coming up the driveway.

"Business," Klarke said, winking an eye.

"Business, huh?" Harris said, taking the bags from Klarke's hands and putting them in the rental car trunk for her. "I find that hard to believe."

"Well, believe it," Klarke said, slamming the car trunk down.

"Daddy, Daddy!" the kids yelled, bursting through the front door.

"Hey, Vaughn, Junior," Harris said, kissing and hugging them. "HJ, why so much stuff? You act like you don't already have an entire wardrobe at my house."

"This is my PlayStation stuff," HJ said, holding up a red-and-black duffel bag.

"Okay, well, load up," Harris said as the kids gave Klarke hugs and kisses good-bye and headed for their father's car. "Do you have your cell phone on you?"

"Of course," Klarke said. "Vaughn has the hotel information where I will be staying, so if anything comes up just holler."

"Be careful," Harris said. "Traffic is hell."

It was 8:15 P.M. when Klarke checked into her hotel. The bellboy waited patiently as the receptionist at the registration desk informed Klarke of her suite number and provided her with a key. The bellboy then escorted Klarke up to her concierge tower suite.

Klarke tussled with the key card to the suite. It took her three attempts to get the green light to enter the room. She stepped aside and allowed the bellboy to carry her bags into the suite. She dug into her purse for some one-dollar bills in order to tip him a dollar per bag. As she located the money the bellboy approached her, wishing her a comfortable stay. She handed him his tip and proceeded into the suite.

"Damn!" Klarke shouted.

As she walked through the lounging area of the suite, the aroma of scented candles hypnotized her. She turned off the lights to get a better effect. The scene was absolutely dazzling.

There was a basket of fruit and a bottle of her favorite alcoholic beverage, Passion Alizé, on the kitchenette table. As she proceeded to the bedroom she noticed different colors of rose petals covering the floor. The petals trailed to the Jacuzzi that was off to the side.

"I can't believe this," Klarke said, stunned. "Oh, my goodness."

The Jacuzzi was full of water and petals were afloat. Klarke dipped her fingers into the Jacuzzi to make a tiny splash. The water was still hot. On a marbled shelf along the Jacuzzi were a basket of Hershey kisses and a small envelope addressed to *KAT*.

Klarke picked up the envelope and was greeted by its wonderful scent. She swiped the card underneath her nose and inhaled the pleasant odor of what she later learned was Issy Miyake. She opened the envelope to find a message that read, *Let's make it 9:30 P.M.*

Klarke knew that was her sign to get butt naked and enjoy the Jacuzzi before meeting Reo at the downstairs bar.

Klarke's clothing lay on the floor where she had once stood. She had gotten both feet into the water before deciding to go retrieve the bottle of Alizé from the kitchenette table.

Since she was out of the water she grabbed a hair twisty from her toiletry bag and scooped her locks up.

For the next half-hour or so Klarke soaked in the Jacuzzi. She envisioned being able to engage in such treatment on a regular basis. She had to play her cards right with Reo. She just had to.

As Klarke made her way through the hotel lobby to the bar area, all eyes were on her. The gold-sequined gown she wore flickered in the eyeballs of every man, and woman for that matter, that was fortunate enough to catch a glimpse of her. Her three-and-one-half-inch gold pumps with a clear heel made her foot arch high like a Barbie doll's.

The trail of Issy Miyake from the bottle she found in her hotel suite bathroom, along with some other bath and body products, only reminded her audience of the lovely vision that had seemed to vanish too quickly.

As the view of the bar became clear to Klarke, she noticed that all of the men sitting at the bar were white, so she knew none of them were Reo. She had studied the picture of him in the back cover of his novel, but everything on her mind seemed to have gone down the drain right with the Jacuzzi water.

It was 9:50 P.M. when Klarke swallowed the last sip from her Shirley Temple. Reo was a no-show. She kept checking her cell phone to make sure she hadn't missed the call telling her he would be late. Although thirty minutes was the official wait time, twenty had been sufficient, so Klarke scooped up her matching sequined evening bag and left the bar.

Klarke went to the registration desk to see if a message had been left for her. She was hoping that there were no mind-readers in the lobby. As beautiful, calm, and relaxed as she appeared on the outside, on the inside she was pissed the fuck off. Here she had driven two hours to see this man and the asshole didn't have the decency to show up, let alone call her to say he was going to be a no-show. If Reo had, in fact, bitched out on her, to Klarke, that was months of work down the drain (with the Jacuzzi water).

"I'm Klarke Taylor in 2218," Klarke said to the clerk at the desk. "I was wondering if by chance I had any messages?"

"Miss Taylor," a voice called from behind Klarke. "Are you Miss Klarke Taylor?" the voice asked.

"Who wants to know?" Klarke said, turning around seductively, assuming the voice belonged to Reo.

The voice belonged to a man who appeared to be a limousine driver. He had on a black cap, very dark sunglasses and a driver's jacket. "Oh, I'm sorry. I thought you were someone else," Klarke apologized.

"No need to apologize, ma'am," the driver said tilting his hat. "I have a message for you from a Mr. Reo Laroque. Regretfully, Mr. Laroque will not be able to join you this evening. He missed his connecting flight and won't be able to get put on another one until early morning."

Klarke tried to maintain her calm, but her skin tone quickly went from a caramel sundae topping to that of strawberry. *This is just what I get,* Klarke thought to herself.

"Mr. Laroque felt that there was no need for you to miss out on the dinner reservation, so he hired me to see that you get transported and well taken care of," the driver continued.

Although it was a nice cover-up on Reo's part, it was still somewhat of a turnoff to Klarke that he didn't phone her and explain the situation himself. Nonetheless, Klarke hadn't eaten all day and was starved.

"Well, I guess there's nothing I can do about it," Klarke said, trying to emerge as the passive individual she had always been. "I knew I should have taken those flying lessons; then I could have picked Mr. Laroque up myself."

"I'm sure Mr. Laroque would have liked nothing better than to be chauffeured home, via air, by such a lovely pilot."

"Thank you." Klarke blushed.

"Shall we?" the driver said, holding out his arm for Klarke.

"Yes, we shall," Klarke said, allowing the driver to guide her to the limo.

Once the driver got Klarke safely tucked into the limo, he walked around to the driver's side, made a call on the CB, and drove off. The driver rolled down the black-tinted partition that was separating him from Klarke.

"The bar is full for you, Miss Taylor," the driver said. "Please feel free to help yourself. And again, Mr. Laroque sends his apologies."

"Did he say what time in the morning?" Klarke asked.

"Excuse me?" the driver said.

"Did Mr. Laroque say what time I should expect him in the morning?"

"I'm afraid he didn't share that information with me, ma'am."

Klarke sat back in the cushioned leather limo seats, comfortable but extremely disappointed. She had to remind herself that this was business. She looked herself over and could have spit at the fact that Reo wouldn't get to see her in her delectable evening dress.

As the driver watched Klarke through his rearview mirror he could tell she was discontented. Although he was only the bearer of bad news, he felt like he had thrown the knockout punch.

The driver began to make small talk with Klarke in order to get her mind off of Reo's absence. He asked her where she was from, if she was married, and if she had any children. They compared and contrasted Columbus and Toledo, and the driver even gave Klarke tips on where to shop while in Columbus.

They looked at one another's eyes through the rearview mirror, in conversation the duration of the drive. Klarke could barely see the driver's eyeballs but could feel when he was watching her. The driver even swerved a couple of times in an attempt to be attentive to Klarke.

Ten minutes after leaving the Doubletree, the limo pulled up to a quaint steakhouse that was camouflaged by the downtown strip buildings. The driver parked and walked around to let Klarke out of the limo.

"Thank you," Klarke said, taking his hand.

"Right this way, Miss Taylor," the driver said. "I'll see that you are seated properly."

The driver escorted Klarke into the dimly lit steakhouse. There were only a few patrons, but it looked to be the exquisite type of place where crowds didn't lurk. It had a cathedral ceiling with heavy satin drapes that made love to the windowpanes.

"Reservation for Miss Taylor," the driver said to the Maître d'.

As Klarke looked around, she forgot all about Reo standing her up. It was safe to say that he had made amends for his absence with the premeditated hospitality.

The Maître d' asked Klarke to follow him to a table. Klarke was led, with the driver following close behind, to an angelic table setting in the rear corner of the restaurant. A dozen long-stemmed roses were laid across the table, as well as a chilled bottle of Chardonnay.

"Miss Taylor," the driver said, "Everything looks to be in order. I shall wait for you outside. Please take your time and enjoy your dinner."

A saxophone player walked over to Klarke's table and began to blow a smooth melody belonging to one of Brian McKnight's songs. Klarke put her hand over her heart and smiled at the driver.

"Are you sure you want to miss this?" Klarke asked. "I'd hate for you to be sitting out there all alone. Perhaps you can join me. Have you eaten yet?"

"Oh, Miss Taylor, that is kind of you. I don't think my wallet could afford it. But not to worry, Mr. Laroque has taken care of your tab for the night. Do enjoy," the driver said, walking away.

"Then perhaps we can share mine," Klarke said, sad to see the driver walk away. She could only imagine how he must feel, working for peanuts while seeing to it that rich egos got everything their hearts desired.

The driver turned, walked back over to the table, and snapped his finger for the hostess. He removed his hat and began to remove his jacket as the hostess hurried over to take his personals.

"So, I take it you'll be joining the lady tonight, Mr. Laroque?" the hostess said to the driver.

"I certainly will," the driver replied, removing the dark shades and handing the items to the hostess.

Completely astounded and caught offguard, Klarke's eyes filled with tears as she bowed her head at the sight of Reo standing before her. She had to be dreaming. There was no way this was real.

"Baby, don't," Reo said, wiping her tears.

"I don't know what to say," Klarke said to Reo, choked up. "No one has ever done anything like this for me before."

"That's why I'm here," Reo said caressing Klarke's face. "To do things for you and to you that no one has ever done before."

Reo took a small box that was sitting in his chair and handed it to Klarke. Inside was a miniature hand-carved wooden elephant. It was absolutely beautiful. Klarke couldn't hold in her weeping. Underneath that phony limo driver garb stood one of the most handsome men she had ever laid eyes on. Reo's eyes were warm like marshmallows in hot chocolate. His lips were luscious and moist and could only benefit her. His skin was flawless and his manner was that of a veritable esquire.

There Reo stood, not ashamed of the game he played and not afraid of winning it. He went out on a limb and placed his lips against Klarke's. She pressed closer to him and mumbled, "Now I wish I had packed the lingerie."

. . .

As difficult as it was not to be taken in completely by Reo's charm, Klarke didn't give him any. She had promised herself that she wasn't going to have sex with him the first time she met him face-to-face. She had come this far and refused to mess up now. She wanted to keep him guessing, wanting to know more and more.

Reo's strong hands and mellow touch made it almost impossible for Klarke to keep her panties on. Just the way Reo played with her hair made her panties wet. Yet, she couldn't give her body to him. Not yet.

Klarke and Reo started meeting one another whenever they could. Either she would drive to Columbus or they would meet halfway at a lodge. They had grown so fond of one another that the two-hour distance between them was intolerable.

After several more rendezvous Klarke finally gave Reo the green light to drive to Toledo to be introduced to her children. She felt that the time was right. Harris and Rawling were the only two men the children had ever seen their mother with, so Klarke had been a tad leery. She hadn't wanted Reo to visit until she had her game locked airtight. She didn't want her children to grow fond of Reo only for her to rip him out of their lives, as they had accused her of doing with Rawling.

After her second divorce Klarke realized that when couples parted, it deeply effected the children.

After her divorce from Rawling, Vaughn and HJ had fought a lot with one another and had been cutting up in school. Klarke had had to sit them down and ask what was going on with the two of them. She was heartbroken when they had accused her of husband-hopping—even if they hadn't used those exact words. After that Klarke made sure to never have men in and out of her life or the lives of her children.

Klarke felt that Reo was a shoo-in however. He was so genuine and he enjoyed doing nice things for Klarke because he admired and respected her, not because he was trying to prove something to her.

To get the kids used to the idea of a new man in their mommy's life, Klarke started bringing up her *author friend,* Reo's name. She placed his books in the living room and in the bathroom in an attempt to familiarize the children with him.

When Vaughn finally asked if she could meet Reo and interview him for a paper she had to do in school, Klarke had been elated. The timing couldn't have been more perfect. Klarke okayed it with HJ, who gave his two thumbs up, and immediately invited Reo to visit.

Klarke had wanted to plan Reo's visit to the tee. She wanted them to spend the day at an amusement park, go to the movies, eat pizza, and everything else kids love to do, but Reo wasn't hearing it. He told Klarke that he just wanted to spend time with the kids and get to know them because they were a part of the woman he had fallen in love with.

Klarke was so nervous that she was running in circles. Reo was due to arrive at her house any minute and the cake was still baking. Earlier she had turned the oven on before taking her shower but had forgotten to put in the cake.

"Mom, just go put on your makeup," Vaughn told her, exasperated. "When the timer goes off I'll take the cake out."

"Okay, honey," Klarke said as she headed up the stairs. "Set it on the cooling stone and be careful."

"Mom, I just turned thirteen, remember? I know how to take a cake out of the oven."

When Klarke got to the top of the steps, she stopped to check herself out. That was when she noticed a stain near the crotch area of her one-piece white pantsuit.

"What in the hell?" Klarke said, as she suddenly realized that she had gotten her period. At first Klarke didn't know whether to jump up and down because it meant she wasn't pregnant with Evan's child or to be pissed off for ruining her $155 pantsuit. She decided to go with joy.

"Thank you, God," she said looking up at the ceiling. She then hurried to find another outfit to wear for the evening.

No sooner had Klarke run up the stairs than Vaughn heard a car pull up in the driveway. She ran to the window and saw a white Escalade in the drive. Vaughn went over to the door and opened it as Reo walked up the pathway with a bouquet of flowers in hand.

"Are you Mr. Reo?" Vaughn asked.

"I am," Reo said with a smile. "You must be Vaughn."

"I am. Pleased to meet you," Vaughn said, opening the door wider.

"I'm HJ," the little boy said, running over to shake Reo's hand.

"Hello, HJ. It's good to finally meet you both. Your mother has told me a lot about you two."

"Do you have presents for us?" HJ asked and Vaughn elbowed him in the chest.

"Pardon me?" Reo asked in surprise.

After giving Vaughn a stern look HJ said, "Well, in the movies the new boyfriend always comes with gifts. You know? To get the new stepkids to like him."

"You'll have to excuse him, Mr. Reo," Vaughn said, rolling her eyes. "He's an idiot."

"Am not," HJ said, indignant.

"Are too," Vaughn said.

"Okay, you two," Reo said, laughing. "Sorry, little man, but I didn't bring gifts. I'm a rookie at this."

"Ah, that's okay," HJ said.

"Do you have any kids?" Vaughn came right out and asked.

"Uh, no," Reo said with a smile.

"So that means no baby-mama drama, right?"

Reo laughed. "You are too much."

"Those flowers are lovely," Vaughn said, sniffing the bouquet in Reo's hands. "And they smell good. Are they for my mom?"

"As a matter of fact, they are," Reo said, pulling a hot pink daisy from the bunch. "But if I had any idea that you were going to be even lovelier than your mom described, I would have bought you a bouquet, too. Hopefully this will do for now."

Vaughn smiled a genuine smile as Reo tapped her nose with the daisy. She took it from him and gently inhaled.

"Mom will be down in a moment," Vaughn said. "She's putting on her face. Do you want a glass of water?"

"Yes, please," Reo said with a smile.

Vaughn went into the kitchen to get a glass of water for Reo. The timer went off for the cake, so she took it out of the oven and placed it on the cooling stone.

While they waited for Klarke to come down, Vaughn and Reo watched and coached HJ on a video game he was playing. The three laughed and talked for a good while before Klarke came down the steps. The children were enjoying Reo so much that neither of them thought twice about notifying Klarke of his arrival.

"Well, how long have you been here?" Klarke asked as she entered the living room.

"I don't know. I lost track of time," Reo said, rising to hand Klarke the flowers and kiss her on the cheek.

"Thank you, sweetheart," Klarke said, with a huge grin on her face. "I'm so glad you're here. Did you check into the hotel yet?"

"Yeah, I stopped there first before coming here."

"You didn't call me so I guess you found your way okay."

"Sure did," Reo said.

For a moment the four just stood in the room like bashful classmates at a school dance. Klarke wanted so badly to put her arms around Reo and welcome him with a big kiss. Instead, she suggested they all sit down for dinner.

No one could have asked for a more perfect evening. The fried chicken was golden and crispy. The mashed potatoes had not a lump, and the gravy was a creamy, smooth shade of brown. The gravy Klarke had made from the fried chicken grease was just right. The green beans were seasoned to taste, and the rolls were buttery and soft.

The children took to Reo like they had known him all of their lives. He played some more video games with HJ and helped Vaughn ice the cake.

Around eleven Reo decided it was time for him to leave. The children—and Klarke—hated to see him go. He promised them he would return first thing in the morning to whip them up some breakfast.

Klarke sent the kids off to get ready for bed while she walked Reo to his truck. It was the first moment they had alone.

"Looks like they adore you," Klarke said.

"Man, they are great," Reo said. "You are great. You raised some beautiful children, KAT . . . no lie."

"Thank you."

"So, do I need to stop off at the grocery to pick up items for breakfast?"

"That depends on what you are making."

"Do the kids like pancakes?"

"Vaughn does, but not HJ."

"Does HJ like eggs?"

"Yes."

"Okay, a pancake breakfast for Vaughn and an omelet delight for HJ."

"Sounds great, but what about me?"

"For you, I'll really have to exercise my culinary skills. How does a Reo on a stick sound?" Reo said to Klarke, pulling her close to him.

"Stop teasing me," Klarke said.

"That was wrong of me, huh?" Reo said, giving her a peck on the lips.

"Yeah, you know we can't get down this go-round."

"I'm always getting down with you even when you're not around."

"You writers always have some creative shit to say," she said, giving Reo a deep French kiss. "I'll see you in the morning."

"All right, Miss Lady," Reo said unlocking his door. "Oh, what about breakfast? Do I need to stop and get anything?"

"I have everything you need right here." Klarke winked.

. . .

The next morning Reo was at Klarke's door bright and early. She had no idea he would be arriving at 8:00 A.M. She jumped out of bed to look out her window and there his Escalade was, parked in the driveway. Her head hurt and her stomach was queasy, probably because she had jumped up from a deep sleep too fast. She had been dreaming about Reo.

In her dream Reo was away on a book signing and she was vacationing at some ocean-view beach house. She called him and told him how much she missed him as the waves slapped against the shore. The next thing she knew Reo was at the beach house eating her pussy like no one had ever done before.

The dream was so real that as Klarke ran down the steps, she could feel how moist she was between her legs.

She straightened herself up as much as any woman at eight in the morning could do. She stuck a piece of mint chewing gum in her mouth and opened the door.

"Good morning, early riser," Klarke said to Reo, who was holding a bag of groceries in his hand.

"Good morning to you," Reo said, kissing her on the forehead.

"You just had to stop at the grocery store anyway, huh? Man, you are so hard-headed."

"I had to make sure I had my secret ingredients." Reo winked.

"Well, excuse me," Klarke said, clearing the way for Reo.

"You just go on back to bed and let me do my thang."

"Do your thang where? In the kitchen or in my bed?" Klarke teased as she headed back upstairs.

Klarke rested for about twenty more minutes before getting up to get herself together. She could hear conversation downstairs and knew that the children had gotten up and joined Reo in the kitchen.

The aroma of buttermilk pancakes, bacon, sausage, omelets, biscuits, and hashbrowns filled the house. Klarke couldn't wait to get her eat on.

When Klarke got downstairs, Vaughn, still in her pajamas, was pouring glasses of orange juice and HJ, showing off his new Spider-Man sleeper, was laying out the silverware on the huge dining table, which was an old conference room table she and Harris had bought from an auction. She had dressed up the table with a long black runner and placed an Indian chunky wooden candleholder on each end. Klarke couldn't help but smile at the Norman Rockwell scene.

"Good morning," Klarke said, smiling.

"Good morning," the children responded happily.

"I see you had help," Klarke said to Reo.

"Oh, yeah. I couldn't have done all of this without them," Reo replied with a smile. "Everything is ready, so let's chow."

The four hurried to sit down and Klarke, Vaughn, and HJ began to scoop up food onto their plates. Reo sat back and stared at them. Realizing that he was staring at them, they all stopped what they were doing to stare back.

"May I bless the food?" he asked.

Klarke smiled. "Certainly."

Klarke and the children weren't very religious, but they were believers. Klarke almost felt embarrassed that she had never raised her children to take time out to give thanks. Lord knows she should have. Sometimes their meals were indeed a blessing. Klarke felt joyous that someone was in their lives to now teach them about prayer. Better late than never.

From that point on, Klarke and the children always blessed

their food. Vaughn even did it at school. The school had the nerve to phone Klarke at work about it. They felt as though Vaughn could influence the other children with her religious belief.

The day after the phone call, Klarke sent Vaughn to school with a sign she had printed up on her computer at work. Klarke placed it in an envelope and ordered Vaughn to give it to the school adviser who had phoned her.

There was an acknowledgment of the phone call in the envelope. Included was the sign, which read "SCHOOL ZONE: NO DRUGS, WEAPONS, OR GOD ALLOWED."

The next time Reo came to Toledo to visit Klarke and the kids, they shared the experience with him. He told them about the time that his father had to get with one of his schoolteachers. Reo advised Vaughn to continue praying whenever she felt the need to communicate with God.

Reo was so moved by his deep influence on Vaughn and HJ that he took them each out to purchase their first Bible. He gave them a brief overview and went over the first book of the Bible with them. The children enjoyed the lesson and the comparisons to real life that Reo made.

"This is like reading a fairy tale," HJ said to Reo.

"Yeah," Vaughn said, nodding. "This is a good book."

Reo winked. "That's what most people say."

"How's my favorite girl?" Reo said, hugging Vaughn as she ran down the driveway to meet him at his truck.

"Hi, Mr. Reo. Is that HJ's present?" Vaughn asked, knocking on the wrapped gift box Reo was holding.

"It sure is," Reo said, kneeling down infront of Vaughn. "But this is for my favorite girl."

Reo handed Vaughn a mood ring that he had picked up from the Atlanta Underground while in the ATL on a book signing.

"It's gorgeous!" Vaughn said, thrilled.

"Just like you," Reo replied. "Now, where is the birthday boy?"

"He's inside the house playing. Come on." Vaughn said, pulling Reo by the hand.

Reo could tell by all the cars parked outside that most of the guests had arrived. When he walked through the door he saw little boys and girls running everywhere. Breezy was playing Pin the Tale on the Donkey with one group, while Jeva was preparing a tub of water for a game of Bobbing for Apples.

Klarke was in the kitchen talking with one of the parents, while holding a little girl who looked to be about four years of age. Reo's face lit up at the sight of his KAT. Her hair was pulled up in a curly ponytail. This was his first time seeing her in a pair of jeans, and oh how they showed off her figure. Her gray turtleneck sweater fit her like a glove. She was an extremely beautiful woman. Reo had never felt so lucky.

"You must be Reo," Breezy said, holding out her hand.

"Breezy," Reo said, shaking her hand.

"Finally we meet. Though it's not like I don't already know everything about you," Breezy said.

"Same here," Reo said. "Klarke has shown me every last one of her photo albums."

"She didn't narrate the pictures from my twenty-fifth birthday party, did she?" Breezy asked. "I'll kill her if she did."

"Not to worry," Klarke said coming up behind them. "I gave him the edited version."

"HJ will be glad you made it," Klarke said, kissing Reo.

"That's my cue to scram," Breezy said, walking back over to the game of Pin the Tail on the Donkey.

"I've missed you," Reo told Klarke.

"Ditto."

"Who's this cutie?" Reo asked referring to the child in Klarke's arms.

"Oh, this is the kids' little sister," Klarke said, kissing her on the cheek.

"Harris's daughter?" Reo asked, with raised eyebrows.

"Umm hmm," Klarke said, looking down at the little girl.

"Is he here?"

"HJ's actual birthday was three days ago. He had his party for HJ last weekend. Besides," Klarke said in a low whisper, "I'm not so sure his woman would approve of him hanging out with his ex."

"Oh, he's got baby-mama's drama, as Vaughn would say," Reo said, watching for a moment as Klarke rubbed her nose against the little girl's, making her smile. "You are a beautiful woman," Reo said, his voice low and intimate. "And I mean that in every way possible."

"You two going to join the party?" Jeva said, walking into the kitchen with an empty potato chip bag. She threw it in the trash.

"Oh, Jeva, this is Reo. Reo, Jeva," Klarke said introducing them.

"Finally I meet the man who keeps a smile on my girl's face," Jeva said, hugging Reo.

"It's good to finally meet you too," Reo said.

"Where's the birthday boy?" Reo said, looking around.

"Oh, he's somewhere," Klarke said, looking for him as the phone rang. "He's right there getting his picture taken with the clown."

"I've always wanted a picture with a clown," Reo said jokingly and walked away.

"Taylor residence," Klarke said, answering the phone.

Jeva waited patiently as she watched Klarke's mouth drop open. She put her hand on Klarke's shoulder and asked if everything was okay.

"Take the baby," Klarke said, handing the child to Jeva.

Klarke continued to listen to the caller as her eyes filled with tears. "What's wrong?" Breezy walked over and asked, sensing something was wrong.

"I don't know," Jeva said, worried. "Here, take her and let me see what's going on."

Breezy took the little girl from Jeva and rejoined the party. Klarke placed the phone back in it's receiver and stood there.

"Klarke, what's going on?" Jeva asked.

"It's Tionne," Klarke said, her voice filled with shock. "Harris just found her dead. She hung herself."

Klarke didn't feel comfortable going to Tionne's funeral. There had been so much bad blood between the two. She was worried that Tionne's family would be upset if she showed up.

Instead, Klarke cooked and received food from visitors at Harris and Tionne's house while the funeral was taking place. Once Harris and the children, Tionne's family and friends, started arriving, Klarke left.

On her drive home Klarke thought about Tionne's last visit to her house. She remembered how Tionne had wanted her to reassure her of the love Klarke had for her and Harris's child. There had been a desperate devastation in Tionne's eyes. Never in a million years would she have thought that Tionne would kill herself.

Klarke realized that Tionne had chosen the day of HJ's party to do it because none of the children would be home. She didn't have to worry about one of them finding her.

Klarke pulled her car over to the side of the road and gave thanks to God. She thanked him for making her a strong woman. She thanked him for getting her through this devastating time in her life. She asked Jesus to represent her before God by closing her prayer in his name. She wiped the tears from her eyes and continued her drive home.

Klarke had called into work the day of Tionne's funeral and informed the receptionist that she needed to take a funeral day due to Tionne's death. She ended up calling in the day after as well. She just needed time to herself. The day she did return to work, she wished that she didn't have to.

"I heard about what happened," Evan said as he walked up to Klarke's cubicle. "Your ex-husband's wife. I'm sorry to hear that."

"Thanks," Klarke said, not looking up at Evan.

"How are the kids doing?"

"They're fine."

"How are you?"

"I'm fine too," Klarke said, still not looking up.

"So, is this how we are going to deal with this?" Evan asked.

"Deal with what?" Klarke snapped.

"With us. I mean, look at you, Klarke. You can't even look at me. You're ashamed."

"Me, ashamed?" Klarke said, looking up at Evan. "You're the one who tried to act like you barely knew me in front of your brothers, and besides, I don't see you inviting me to Momma Kemble's house for dinner."

"Is this what all of this attitude is about? Dinner? Hell, you can come tomorrow if you like," Evan said, throwing his hands up. "Because this is bullshit. You're treating me like shit has got to stop. I mean, we can go back to me being the asshole white boss and you can be the bitchy black girl if you like, but let's decide what it's going to be."

"Hold it right there!" Klarke said, standing up. She looked around to make sure she hadn't drawn anyone's attention with her outburst, then sat back down calmly.

"No, you hold it," Evan said in a sharp tone. "Look, Klarke, all I want to do is—"

"What? All you want to do is what?" Klarke said with attitude.

"Forget it," Evan said walking away. Evan was tired of saying what he thought Klarke wanted to hear. Yeah, maybe at first being with Klarke had something to do with Evan being turned on by the novelty of being with a black woman. However, he had no idea he would want more from her. Not just more sex, which he wouldn't have refused, but more from her as a person.

Klarke sat at her desk overwhelmed by everything that was going on in her life. She got up and went to the copy room and grabbed some empty Xerox paper boxes. She returned to her desk and began packing up her belongings.

She didn't stop to think of the consequences. She just knew she didn't want to be there anymore.

Once Klarke was finished packing up her desk she went into Evan's office. She didn't rehearse what she was going to say to him or how she was going to say it.

"I'm leaving," Klarke said almost under her breath.

"For lunch, for good, what?" Evan asked baffled.

"For good, I think," Klarke answered confused. "I don't know. I just need some time."

Evan got up to close the door.

"No matter how you feel about me on a personal level, as your employer, I won't let you go. I'll accept the fact that you don't want to have a personal relationship with me, but I refuse to let one of the most valuable assets of the company walk away. Now, I understand you have a lot going on in your life so I'm willing to grant you leave—paid leave—but I won't let you go permanently, Klarke. I won't."

"Evan, why are you making this so hard?"

"You're the one making everything so hard. You're the one who wouldn't even give us a chance. It's obvious we're two very different people from two very different walks of life, but can't we at least start over and try to be friends? We can then just go from there."

"Evan, you and I both know that curiosity got the best of you. You've wanted to climb in bed with me the moment you saw me. You didn't want to marry me, or make me your girlfriend for that matter. You wanted to screw me and so you did. Get over it already. I did."

"You're so cold," Evan said shaking his head. "You're cold and you're wrong. What's happening to you, Klarke?"

"You don't know me, Evan."

"You won't let me know you. You act like I have some hidden agenda."

"You people normally do," Klarke mumbled under her breath.

"Just go, Klarke. You win. Just go. If you are standing here saying hateful things in order to make this easier for yourself because you know you are wrong, then just go. I'll have Renée draw you up some type of severance package. We'll say you were terminated. No need for your kids to go hungry just because their mother wants to be a bitch."

"Or is a severance package your discreet way of trickin'?" Klarke said, storming out of Evan's office.

Klarke carried the Xerox box full of her belongings from work into the house and dropped it right at the door. She slugged over to the couch and threw herself down. Just as she decided to get up and get a glass of Alizé, the phone rang.

Klarke looked at the caller ID and saw that it was Reo's number. She took a deep breath and then answered the phone.

"Hello," Klarke answered.

"I just called your office," Reo said, lightweight frantic. "They said you were no longer with the company. What happened?"

"Baby," Klarke said as her voice began to break up. "I'm tired. There was just so much going on there and . . ."

Klarke began to cry.

"Don't cry," Reo said in a soothing tone. The sound of her tears broke his heart.

"I don't know what I'm going to do!" Klarke cried. "My life is just so crazy! It's always been so crazy. And just when I start to think that everything is going to be okay."

"You don't have to worry 'bout a damn thang," Reo said in a strong, comforting tone. "You've got me in your life now and I ain't going nowhere. I got your back."

12

The Sin Is Pride

In the maternity ward of Columbus Hospital, the doctors on staff were having a hard time with one patient in particular.

"Push! Just one more push," the nurse pleaded.

"The head is out," the doctor confirmed. "Just one more push and you'll be all done. I promise. Just one more push."

"You said that two pushes ago, damn it!" the angry pregnant woman yelled. "This is the last goddamn time I'm pushing. If the baby doesn't come out, then you are going to have to figure out some other way to get it out."

One more push and the baby left its mother's womb. The doctor cut the umbilical cord and offered the new baby girl to the nurses to clean up. The nurse placed the tiny little girl on her mother's chest just long enough for her to take a good look.

The nurse used a nasal suction to clear the baby's throat and nostrils of fluids. The baby girl didn't cry once throughout all the tossing and turning—that was, until they put those darn droplets into her eyes. She had an infant tantrum then.

The nurses seemed rough and relentless as they scrubbed her tiny body clean of her mother's blood. Once the nurses pampered her by shampooing her curly black mane, the little diva relaxed and found some serenity in the entire transition. Nonetheless, if the baby girl had had the strength she would have scratched those bitches' eyes out for fucking up her nine-month siesta.

It was obvious that the young sprout was going to be just like her mother. From the moment the baby girl was rolled into the nursery it was like the other babies immediately fell silent. It was as if she had been born to rule the world.

Others would see her as another statistic, a little black child born without a father to pen his name on her birth certificate. In this case, though, the mother would not have wanted it any other way. She stood to gain more from the father's absence.

"Hey, Mommy's little pot of gold. I can't wait to tell your daddy that you are here," Meka cooed to her new baby girl. "You look so sweet, yes you do. But then again, revenge always has been sweet hasn't it?"

Meka had put her body through nine miserable months of hell in the name of revenge. After her and Reo's lovemaking finale, finding out that she was pregnant was the worse news Meka could have received.

Not only had Reo made her feel like a third-rate slut after a night of explicit sexual acts, but he also thought he had heard the last of her. After that night he never even bothered to call Meka to see if she was still breathing.

Of course Meka, being the kind of woman she was, told everyone that it was she who wanted nothing more to do with Reo. She told her friends and family that success had gone to his head, that he was a changed man. She had even insinuated that he had become violent with her. Everything except the truth . . . that he wanted nothing more to do with her saddity ass.

Meka hadn't been out of the hospital a full day before she phoned her attorney's office. She had had her attorney draft the paternity suit papers against Reo before she had even started showing. Now she wanted to finalize things.

Whenever she would suffer morning sickness or have to purchase bigger clothing, Meka would pull out her copy of the million-dollar paternity suit and know that her discomfort was not in vain.

Reo was going to pay dearly for what he had done to her. He would regret thinking he was Mr. Big Shit.

She had put up with him when he was just a nobody. How dare he settle into a storybook lifestyle and leave her behind? She deserved to be on his arm when he was rewarded the Pulitzer or the NAACP award for best mainstream fiction author. Some trophy tramp would enjoy what she well deserved and was born to be a part of.

Meka never did believe that she was supposed to spend any portion of her life working. It didn't matter how much money her paycheck would be worth, she deemed herself worthy of marrying big money. She had it in the palm of her hands, on the tip of her tongue, at her fucking feet, and she blew it. If only she could have held on for a little longer. But now she was man overboard. The hell with that. She was going to get hers.

"Darling, are you sure you're doing the right thing?" Meka's mother said as the two sat in the baby's nursery while she cuddled her grandchild.

"It's just like you to be on his side, Mother," Meka said. "You don't know the real Reo Laroque. He was just putting on a show for you and Daddy."

"It just seems that something like this could ruin the relationship this little bundle of joy here needs with her daddy."

"By the time I get done with him, Mother," Meka said, "we'll be able to buy her a new daddy."

"You're acting like this baby is more of a meal ticket than your daughter."

"Mother, need I remind you of how you got Daddy to marry you?"

Meka's mother gave her an evil look then got up and took the baby over to the changing table. "You shouldn't believe everything your Aunt Margaret tells you."

"I'm sorry, Mother, but I just hate when I feel like you're against me."

"I'm not against you. I've never been against you. You are my baby. It just doesn't seem right. I mean, you never even bothered telling Reo that you were pregnant. You act as if he abandoned you in the delivery room. I don't understand why you are not even giving him a chance to accept the baby into his life."

"Some things aren't meant to be understood, Mother," Meka said. "Some things are just meant to be."

The doctor had ordered Meka to take care of herself for the next six weeks, but after a week Meka was out and about. She couldn't think straight until she met with her attorney to give the go-ahead on the filing of the paternity suit papers.

"Do you think I should ask for two million?" Meka asked as she lunched with her attorney at the Olive Garden. "I'm sure by now he's got some cute little Barbie he's promising to spend the rest of his life with. The last thing he needs right now is a baby with a touch of baby-mama drama in the equation."

"I work for you," her attorney replied, slinging her butt-length brunette hair over her left shoulder. "You know this Reo far better than I do. What do you think keeping you and your daughter out of his life is worth to him?"

Meka dipped a breadstick in some tomato sauce and nibbled off a piece. She thought about what her resurfacing in Reo's life with a child would do to him.

"Yes, let's go for two million," Meka said, nodding slowly.

"We can negotiate down to a million if all else fails. In the meantime, what you might want to do is take out a million-dollar life insurance policy on your daughter. You never know what could happen between now and then," Meka's attorney said.

"That sounds like a good idea. You are amazing," Meka said, smiling.

"Do you remember that black model guy who started off dancing on that stupid underwear commercial or something like that?"

"The one on the soap opera now?" Meka asked.

"Yes, that's the one. I got the mother of his twins five million dollars," Meka's attorney said proudly.

"Wow, he must have hated her," Meka said.

"No, not really. He hated the idea of his wife finding out about her."

The two laughed. They finalized the specifics of the suit and discussed some interesting ways of serving Reo with the paternity papers.

13

Daddy's Coming Home

The guard frisked Breezy thoroughly. She had gone through the metal detector and had also been subjected to the wand. After visiting her father in the Chillicothe prison for the past fifteen years she was used to the tri-search her body was put through. This could have all ended five years ago, but more time had been tacked onto her father's jail sentence due to his poor behavior.

Breezy didn't mind the depressing atmosphere as she walked through the prison halls. After all, it was her fault he was in there.

"Daddy," Breezy said as her father joined her at the round mint-green table, sticky with leavings of visitors over time.

"Hey, sweetie. How's my little girl?" Mr. Williams said, kissing Breezy, his thick black mustache scratching her cheek. Breezy loved how he had grown his mustache in prison. It made him look refined. Jail hadn't affected his good looks one bit. He still had skin the color and smoothness of honey. A person could melt in the serenity of his hazel eyes. When he had first gone to prison, he had started losing his hair. Breezy had suggested that he shave it bald, so he had. You could see yourself in his shiny head.

"I'm fine. How are you doing, Dad?"

"I'm locked up." He laughed. Breezy didn't find it amusing. "Sorry, honey. How's work?"

"Tiresome. But you know how it goes. We's gots to do our part for Mr. Charlie in order to live in this great land of his," Breezy said in her Kizzy voice.

"Good old U.S. of A," her father said.

"Yep, but I wouldn't want to live anywhere else." She paused. "I hear Ma was asking Uncle Rudy about you."

"Was she?" Mr. Williams said, a smile creeping across his face. "Your Momma is always going to be my girl. Even though she couldn't find it in her heart to wait for me, I love her. How is she and that new husband of hers doing?"

"Beats me," Breezy said huffily. "I hardly talk to her. She don't call me, so I don't call her."

"You can't be like that," Mr. Williams said sincerely.

"I'm like this because you're not. I hate her for you. It was supposed to be until death do you part, not a lousy jail sentence."

"I wouldn't call ten to twenty-five years lousy," Mr. Williams said. "I hate to see my little girl so angry. I don't know where all that hate in you comes from."

"My father is locked up. My mother is off gallivanting with a man half her age. I spend more time working than living. Hell yeah I'm angry."

Mr. Williams put his hand on hers and looked Breezy in the eye. There was something about looking into her daddy's eyes that always made her get teary.

"I know you blame yourself for my being in here, honey. Whether you want to admit it or not, I think that's where a little bit of that anger comes from. I just want you to know that after what that boy did to you, to my little girl, I'd kill him dead all over again," Mr. Williams said, slamming his fist onto the sticky table, causing the people next to them, as well as Breezy, to jump.

"Daddy," Breezy said, looking around to make sure the guards didn't come over and try to end their visit. They had done that a time or two when Mr. Williams had been giving them trouble.

"Listen to me. I don't mind the fifteen years I've spent in this hellhole. I don't mind it at all. If that bullet hadn't killed that boy, I'd happily serve fifteen more years after serving this term because I'd go finish the job."

"I don't want you to talk like that, Daddy. Don't say those types of things. If that's what you said to the parole board, then you can hang up ever getting out of here."

"When you have a child you'll know what I'm talking about. You'll understand this feeling."

Breezy broke out into a sweat as she thought about that unforgettable evening her freshmen year at college. She and a few of her friends had gone to Gino's Pizza and Sports Bar to watch their school's football team play against a rival team. About an hour into the game there had been a disturbance on the field. Some madman had run out onto the field and gunned down the star football player, Judge Callaghan.

It had been gruesome. Judge had been sitting on the sidelines with his helmet off when a bullet entered his head. Brain matter and blood spattered nearby teammates' uniforms and faces. The media had assumed it was rivalry-related as they commentated the event. As the camera zoomed in on the assailant being wrestled to the ground, the person's identity became clear to Breezy. She watched helplessly as her father was handcuffed and escorted off the field by police.

Emergency medical technicians raided the field in an attempt to save Judge, but Judge was pronounced dead at the scene. It was later reported as a vigilante killing. The details of the accused's daughter having been raped by the victim headlined every television channel and newspaper.

The news story brought so much negative attention to Breezy and her family. It was like a tornado funnel had sucked them all in. Their lives had gone under a microscope.

Breezy stayed on top of her father's case every step of the way. She wanted to make sure he was being represented to the best of that public defender's ability. She dropped out of college, and had never gone back. The second-degree-murder verdict earned Breezy's father ten years minimum in prison.

Mrs. Williams, five years after her husband being incarcerated, would eventually lose their home and go on to remarry a couple of years thereafter. She didn't even have the decency to tell her father to his face that she wanted a divorce. She just stopped visiting or accepting his phone calls altogether.

When Breezy's father had received the divorce papers in the mail he had been heartsick. Breezy didn't even know about her mother's intentions. She talked to her every day and never missed Sunday dinner, and not once had her mother mentioned that she intended to leave her father.

Breezy's instincts told her that her mother was seeing someone. Not that her mother wasn't already a beautiful woman, but each Sunday there would be something more and more striking about Mrs. Williams's appearance. One week she had a new hairdo, and the next week she had on a new Sunday's best. Breezy knew a new man was behind the change.

Breezy knew that her mother had needs. She never dreamed in a million years that she would leave her father, though. Breezy programmed her mind and her heart to agree on never forgiving her mother.

After Mr. Williams got over the initial shock of losing his better half to a free man, he gave his wife his blessings to move on. Breezy had had next to no contact with her mother since the divorce.

"So do you know the exact date that you will be getting out of here if the board approves your release?" Breezy asked.

"No, I'm not sure," Mr. Williams replied as he pulled on his three-inch beard.

"I see you got a couple gray hairs in that beard," Breezy said, pulling on it herself.

"Yeah, your pops is getting old."

"You are still the finest old man around," Breezy said. "Remember how all the women in the neighborhood tried to befriend Ma in order to get to you?"

"Now, go on girl." Mr. Williams blushed.

"Please, I take after you so I know you're not a modest man," Breezy said. "Everybody else in here writes letters home asking folks to send them soap, deodorant, and cigarettes or to put money on their books. But you, you want a sistah to buy designer-scented shaving creams and deodorants. You want CK drawers."

"Oh, Bria," Breezy's father said, putting his head down sadly.

"It's almost over, Dad. You'll be free and at home with me before you know it."

"I don't know if I'm going to have to go to a halfway house or not first."

"I don't see why they wouldn't let you come live with me. I've got the spare bedroom waiting for you."

"We'll see, love. We'll see," Mr. Williams said. "Any perspective son-in-laws I need to know about?"

Breezy snickered. "After years of dating, Dad, I've learned the hard way that there is only one man I don't have to tolerate, but just love."

"Oh, yeah," Mr. Williams said. "And who's that?"

"My daddy."

14

The Envelope Please

Jeva was speechless when she went through her mail and found the letter from Welford Child Placement Agency. She knew that inside that envelope was the answer to her questionable life. She stared at it for an eternity before laying it down on the kitchen table.

"Baby, are you okay?" Lance asked, peeking in the kitchen at her.

"It's here. The letter from Welford. It's here," Jeva said, staring at it as if she were hypnotized.

"Do you want me to open it for you?" Lance asked.

"Choca milk," Heather said to her, handing Jeva her favorite sippy cup.

"I'll get it for you, Heather," Lance said, taking the cup from her to rinse it out.

"No, I've got it," Jeva said. "I'll do it."

Jeva decided to see her daily routine through before opening the letter. She fixed her daughter a cup of chocolate milk and started the preparations for dinner. She washed a load of clothes and set a bath for her and her daughter.

Bathtime was mommy and daughter time each evening. It made up for the guilty feeling Jeva had about being away from her daughter all day.

While they bathed Lance mixed the spaghetti noodles Jeva had boiled with the meat sauce she had cooked.

After dinner the family of three watched some television and put together a couple of puzzles with Heather. Once Lance tucked Heather into bed for the night, Jeva made her way back into the kitchen to keep company with the envelope.

"Dear Lord," Jeva prayed. "I know whatever is inside this envelope is what is written for me and my life. No matter how I might feel about it, I know your plan for me is divine. I open my heart and ask that you guide me and give me strength to deal with what is in store for me. I say this prayer in the name of your son and my savior, Jesus Christ. Amen."

Dear Ms. Jeva Price:

We are pleased to inform you that the result of our search for your file has been successful. Your natural parents were located and have responded to your inquiry as to their whereabouts and the possibility of a meeting. Please know that their wishes are just that, and not those of Welford Child Placement Agency.

Your natural parents request that the meeting occur in a public place. This location has been decided by them to be Hollingwood Park in Toledo, Ohio. They will expect you on Saturday, the 27th of this month, at 2:00 P.M. If you are not available on this date and or time, please notify our agency. A new date and time will be mediated for both you and your natural parents.

We do wish you the very best.

■ ■ ■

Jeva had arrived at the park an hour early. She didn't want to risk getting stuck in traffic, her car breaking down, or any other obstacle that might hinder her from this moment that she had waited a lifetime for.

Once Jeva got to Hollingwood Park, she took a seat at the first vacant park bench she came to. She watched the parking lot and primped herself every time she saw a car drive up.

Two o'clock had come and gone as Jeva waited impatiently on the bench. It was hard for her to keep from crying every time she thought of the possibility of her parents not showing. She pulled the letter out a thousand times to double-check the date and time. Finally a tall, slender gentleman wearing a black suit approached her.

"Ms. Price, I presume," the gentleman said.

"Yes," Jeva said standing up. She knew this man wasn't her father because he was Oriental. If she knew nothing else about her natural father, she knew that he was white. She smiled nervously and waited for the gentleman to speak.

"I'm Mr. Christian, a representative of the Dawsons."

"The Dawsons?" Jeva said confused.

"That would be the family name belonging to your birth mother and father."

"Is something wrong? Are they dead?" Jeva asked, panicked. "Oh God, they're dead, aren't they?"

"They are very much alive. Ms. Price, they wanted me to share some things with you. Please sit down."

Jeva sat on the bench and the gentleman sat down beside her. He pulled an envelope out of his inside coat pocket and placed it between them.

"Your father is a very positive and powerful figure. Your mother is a loving supporter. You have five younger brothers and sisters who are all either in college or have graduated college and are doing quite well for themselves. There is no history of cancer, diabetes, MS, high blood pressure, or any other serious hereditary disorders." The gentleman babbled on endlessly as if he had a tape recorder down his throat and had hit the play button. It was becoming clear to Jeva that she wasn't going to meet her natural parents that day or any other day.

"Sir, I appreciate all of this information, but all I want to do is meet my parents. I want to look into their eyes to be able to know whose mine are like. I want to hear their voices. I want to ask questions I've never been able to get answers to."

"They were young. They didn't know what their relationship would entail. Their families would have frowned upon such circumstances as an unwed pregnancy. In addition to that, they were from two very different backgrounds."

"Will you stop it already?" Jeva said, her voice rising. "Sir, Mr. Christian, I'm very sorry. I truly am. It's just that you have no idea of how long I've dreamed about this day. Do my parents, or don't they, want to know me?"

"Ms. Price, they are asking that you cease all efforts involving contact or face-to-face meetings with them. They do not wish to know you. They are afraid your surfacing would cause confusion to their lives and the lives of their children."

"My surfacing," Jeva said. "You say that as if they drowned me and my body is now afloat."

"Ms. Price, please understand that three decades ago they were young and lived different lives. They send their regrets. They know how this must make you feel. They decided that sending a representative on their behalf would be best as, over the years, you have failed to back off of your efforts in finding them."

Jeva expected nothing like this. Her eyes swelled with tears. This was like a nightmare coming to pass. She wanted someone to pinch her.

"I can't believe this," Jeva said, rising up from the bench.

"Please, sit down, Ms. Price," the gentleman said. "I just have a couple more items to go over."

"I've heard enough," Jeva said as she began to storm off.

"Please, Ms. Price," the gentleman said, grabbing the envelope off of the bench and going after her. "This is from your parents. Please take it."

Jeva took the envelope from the gentleman's hand. "At least they were kind enough to send pictures," Jeva sarcastically remarked. She looked inside the envelope and found a very thick stack of brand-new crisp one-hundred-dollar bills.

"This is really crazy," Jeva said angrily. "A payoff? I'm their firstborn, for Christ sakes!"

"Please take it," he said calmly, set on finishing his monologue. "By now you should have received a document from United City Bank . . . the document that pertains to a trust fund set up under your name. This trust will allow you to live a more than comfortable life."

"I don't get it," Jeva said. "What's the catch?"

"There is no catch, only a stipulation," he said. "You must agree to relinquish your search to find your birth parents. As I stated before, they have no desire to associate with you. As your parents, though, they do wish for you to have a comfortable life. That's why they have made these arrangements for you. Just make sure you have read over the material carefully, especially the disclaimer, which you are required to have notarized. Keep in mind that any breach on your part will result in your paying back the monies put up, and possibly a lawsuit against you."

"Did they give you any other instructions?" Jeva asked.

"Like what?" he asked, confused.

"Like, for you to take note of what color my hair is and my eyes; how tall I am; how do I wear my hair?" Jeva began to cry. "If I have a pretty smile? Don't they want you to be able to ramble off particulars to them about me?"

"I'm sorry, Ms. Price," the gentleman said as he walked away.

"Don't they even want to know if they have grandchildren from me?"

"There's plenty in that envelope and the trust to take care of any existing and future children you might have. Good day, Ms. Price."

At this point Jeva didn't want someone to just walk up to her and pinch her, she wanted them to shake her. She had to be sleeping. This had to be a nightmare. She couldn't have waited all of her life for this moment, for such crushing pain.

Jeva stared at the envelope filled with money. She wondered if her parents were perhaps somewhere in the park staring at her. She gazed around to see if anyone looked peculiar. After a few moments Jeva, with envelope in hand, walked over to the trash bin. She dropped the envelope inside the trashcan and watched the lid swing back and forth. She stuffed the wad of hundred-dollar bills that she had taken out of the envelope down in her purse and headed for her car.

Jeva drove home, and as she pulled up to her house she saw Lance standing on the porch. He had just put Heather down for a nap and was waiting on the porch for Jeva when she drove up. Jeva walked to the porch in a zombielike state. She didn't even walk up all five steps to get to where Lance was standing. She stopped and sat down on the first step.

Jeva didn't even have the desire to cry anymore. Hell, her parents were strangers, and had been for almost twenty-nine years. She could survive it. Lance, sensing that things didn't go how Jeva hoped and dreamed they might have, joined his woman on the steps and put his muscular arms around her frail little body. She felt like a corpse in his arms.

"Baby, are you okay?" Lance asked. When he didn't get an answer, he continued to rock her. "What's that?" he asked, referring to the wad of hundred-dollar bills stuffed in her purse.

"I guess it's back–child support." Jeva snickered, still in somewhat of a daze. "They didn't want me, Lance. They didn't want to know me. My own mother and father. All I've ever wanted was to be able to call someone Mommy and Daddy . . . just to be somebody's little girl."

Lance squeezed Jeva even tighter as he kissed her on the forehead and whispered to her, "I'll take care of you, baby. You can call me Daddy."

15

It's a Girl

"Mom and Dad, this is her," Reo said, walking through the front door of his parents' Victorian home, which he had purchased for them. "This is Miss Klarke Taylor."

"It's so good to finally meet you," Mrs. Laroque said, walking over to the door to greet them. She hugged Reo and then gave Klarke a hug and kiss on the cheek. "You have made my son so happy. I've never seen him this happy before. He even comes to church now every Sunday that he's in town. I reckon he's giving thanks to you."

"Oh, Mrs. Laroque," Klarke said, hugging her once again and even tighter.

"Honey," Mr. Laroque said jokingly to his wife as he approached them, "you better be lucky our son set eyes on her before I did or you might have been replaced."

"Oh, Mr. Laroque," Klarke said, hugging him too.

"Klarke, we're so pleased you could drive up to join us this Sunday for friends-and-family day at church," Mrs. Laroque said. "Where are the little ones?"

"They fell asleep on the way. They're out in the car," Klarke said, smiling.

"I'll go carry them in," Reo said.

"It's about time to go," Mrs. Laroque said.

"So why don't you just load them right into that big ole semi of yours? We can all fit in it. There's no need in taking two cars."

Everyone climbed into Reo's Escalade and headed to the church. The service turned out to be lovely. Reverend Sandy discussed fornication and babies being born out of wedlock. She touched upon couples taking vows but not seeing them through to the end. The main lesson was forgiveness, how forgiveness is an ingredient for a successful marriage or any relationship for that matter. Klarke felt like everyone in the church knew Reverend Sandy was preaching to and about her.

The children especially enjoyed Sunday school. Vaughn was really taking to the Christian way of living and wanted to absorb all that she could. She even asked Mrs. Laroque if they had a church in Toledo. Mrs. Laroque promised to ask the Reverend to suggest a nice Baptist church that Klarke could attend with her children in Toledo.

Everything was falling into place far more smoothly than Klarke could have ever visualized. There was only one occurrence she hadn't prepared herself for . . . falling in love.

Reo sat at his computer, frustrated. He tapped his freshly manicured nails on the Kartell Maui table that his computer sat on. The deadline for his next novel was right around the corner and he couldn't figure out how to wrap up the storyline. He was undecided as to whether he wanted to add another twenty thousand words to the story or leave it open for a sequel.

Reo got up from the computer chair and flopped down on the rattan chair that hugged the corner of his study. He let out a sigh of relief when he heard the doorbell ring. It was just the time-out he needed.

Reo exited the study and made his way down the long corridor of his oversize ranch house. He stopped at the rusty, gold-trimmed vintage mirror that hung on the wall to make sure he looked suitable before answering the door. Outside the door stood a young man around twenty years of age, wearing a velour olive-green Outkast jogging suit with white K-Swiss kicks. He was holding a vase with a mixture of beautiful pink-and-white blooms. Three pink balloons wavered above his head, which was adorned with jailhouse braids.

Reo opened the door, leaving the security storm door locked.

"May I help you?" Reo asked.

"Delivery," the young man said in a *duh*-like manner. "I need you to sign for this."

Reo opened the storm door, took the pad the young man handed him, and signed his name. He dug into his wallet and pulled out a dollar bill to tip the young man with.

"Naw, I'm straight, cuz," the young man said, handing him the delivery. "You keep that. I'm going to rob Fifth Third Bank at three o'clock P.M. for some real money."

Reo closed the door behind the sarcastic smart-ass chump. He admired the lovely arrangement, wondering who it could be from.

He pulled out the letter-size envelope that was tucked gently in the flowers. "Congratulations!" was written on the outside of the card. Reo double-checked the delivery ticket to make sure the delivery guy had delivered him the correct item. Reo's name and address was written in the "deliver to" column, so he opened the envelope.

Mr. Reo A. Laroque
5437 Easton Trails
Columbus, OH 54237

RE: CASE No. DR0356852
Dear Mr. Laroque:
I represent Ms. Meka Tarrant in the above referenced case. Please read the attached complaint and suit. You or your attorney may file an answer with the Franklin County Court of Domestic Relations or contact me at my office in regards to a settlement.

Very truly yours,
T.C. Bowens, Esq.

"I think if half of the men in this world got paternity tests done on the kids they've claimed as their own, they would be very surprised at the outcome," Nate said. "Just calm down until you get the results of the paternity test, man."

"Do you know what this shit could do to my life?" Reo said in a rage. "That fucking bitch!"

"Whoa, hold up. She didn't plant a seed in a pot of dirt and grow that baby on her own," Nate said. "Just relax before you say some foul shit that you can't take back, especially if that child does turn out to be yours."

"What am I supposed to tell KAT?" Reo said.

"You tell her the truth. You tell her the truth and you tell her now. Don't drop a bomb on her like it's been dropped on you. If she's the beautiful woman you claim her to be, then she'll understand and she'll be by your side to support you through this drama. It's not like you planned all of this."

"I don't understand why Meka waited so long. Hell, the kid is probably walking now."

"Do the dates match up?" Nate said, looking over the suit papers again.

"Yeah, man. Actually they do. *Fuck!*" Reo shouted.

"Is everything okay in here?" Persia asked, coming out of the kitchen with two glasses of lemonade.

"I'm sorry, Persia. I didn't mean to disrespect your home," Reo said, rubbing a hand over his face.

"Is there anything I can do?" Persia said, setting down the glasses and then putting her hand on Reo's shoulder.

"You can make me understand the game," Reo said putting his head down to his knees as tears filled his eyes.

"The game?" Persia asked, confused.

"The game women play," Reo answered.

"Now I know how Jennifer Lopez feels," Klarke said, stroking her hand down one of the gowns in the dainty little bridal boutique. Klarke, Breezy, and Jeva had passed the shop that sat right outside of Nordstrom in the mall a thousand times. This time Klarke insisted that they stopped in to take a little peek. "I can't believe I'm getting married for a third time, but this one just feels so different."

"He hasn't even asked you to marry him yet," Jeva said, exasperated. "And you got me and Breezy up in some bridal shop. You're going to jinx yourself, girl. Remember when I did the same thing the year I thought Lance was going to propose to me on Valentine's Day?"

"Girl, you even started getting quotes on invitations and writing out your guest list." Breezy laughed.

"But I can feel it coming," Klarke said in a dreamy tone. "I know that he's going to ask me to marry him. And to think I almost fucked up everything when I thought I might have gotten myself pregnant by Evan."

"Can you imagine having to explain that little white baby to Reo?" Breezy asked, poking out her lips and rolling her neck. "You would have died if your period hadn't come."

"Well, that little white baby would have been a product of something that took place before you and Reo even met face-to-face," Jeva said.

"I know, but still, who wants to start a relationship with someone only to find out that there will be a new addition to the relationship? I mean, come on. Remember when that girl told Hydrant that she thought her five-year-old child was his? Him and Breezy fought about it until the paternity test came back verifying that he wasn't the father. I think it's different when you get into a relationship knowing that the person has x number of children versus finding out after the fact."

"Well, I love kids. So something like that wouldn't matter to me," Jeva said, throwing her hands up.

"Yeah, well," Klarke said in a carefree manner, grabbing the gown she had been admiring off of the rack, "I don't have to worry about that now."

Klarke held the dress up and stared at it. It was a snow-white beaded-and-lace tube gown.

"Excuse me," Klarke said to one of the store clerks. "May I try this on?"

"Certainly," the clerk responded as she led Klarke into the fitting room.

"Make sure you come out so we can see what you look like," Breezy shouted.

"I can't believe that she is trying on a white gown," Jeva said, feeling more than just a little jealous.

"There is no force greater than the will to get even," Reo's attorney said to him. "Revenge is the mother of all."

"So, are you saying I should just give her two million dollars just like that?"

"Reo, the DNA test results conclusively prove that the baby is, without a doubt, yours."

Reo shook his head, feeling dazed. "I'm just going to go over there and talk some sense into Meka."

"You know I've advised you against doing so."

"Well, now that I know that the baby is mine I have to communicate with her. It's my child."

"For two million dollars you can walk away," the attorney said. "That has been your thing all along, that you've wanted a way out. We could probably even talk them down to one million. By agreeing to her terms you can buy your way out of parenthood. You can leave that part of your life behind. When the child turns eighteen, we can't prevent her seeking you out, but for now, this buys you years to build a new life."

"I don't know," Reo said, unsure.

"It's up to you. It's unfortunate that men are put in these positions every day. You can't stop a woman from having an abortion and you can't stop her from having the baby. Your entire life is affected by the decision she makes."

"I can't believe this is happening to me," Reo said again.

"Well, just think about it for a few days, but you're going to have to get back to me soon. She could have a change of heart and decide she wants three million or that she wants you to be the father of the year."

"I'll give you a call in a couple of days," Reo said, standing up.

"Just keep in mind," the attorney said, "you have the golden opportunity to buy your way out of a situation that you had no control over."

"You're wrong on that one," Reo said, staring into his attorney's eyes. "I could have controlled my dick and kept it in my pants."

"Thanks for coming over, Dad," Reo said as he and Mr. Laroque sat down on the couch. Reo tossed one of three gold raffia cushions that decorated the couch out of his father's way so he could sit more comfortably.

"Well, it sounded urgent when you called me," Mr. Laroque said.

"I have a problem, Pops." Reo sighed.

"Women trouble, huh?"

Reo took a deep breath. "It's Meka."

"Meka. I haven't heard that name in a long time."

"She had a baby, Dad. My baby."

"Son!"

"I know, Dad. She kept the pregnancy from me. I had no idea. I just found out myself."

"But why?" Mr. Laroque asked.

"This is why," Reo said, handing his father the paternity suit papers.

"She's lost her mind!" Mr. Laroque exclaimed. "You're not going to sell the rights to your child!"

Reo looked away and then looked back at his father.

"Son, you didn't," Mr. Laroque said, his face filled with shock and disappointment.

"No, Dad. Not yet anyhow."

"I can't believe you are even considering such a thing."

"Dad, do you have any idea what it would do to my life right now to bring Meka back into it? Meka and a baby?"

"*Your* baby. Your baby, son. What's Klarke say about all of this?"

"Nothing," Reo said once again, lowering his head.

"You mean you haven't told her? That poor girl."

"Well, I didn't want to tell her if that baby wasn't even mine. I didn't want to get her all worked up over nothing."

"Tell her, boy. You mark my words, not telling her would be one of the worse things you could do."

"I just need to think about everything, Dad. Can you do me a favor and not tell Mom about any of this, not until I make a decision as to what I'm going to do?"

"If that's what you want, son," Mr. Laroque said, standing up from the couch and heading toward the door. "I'll keep it from your momma. You can keep it from Klarke and whomever else you feel like. But you can't keep it from God."

After talking with his father Reo paced the floor for hours. He didn't know what to do about Meka, the baby and, most of all, KAT.

There was no way a baby would fit into the picture of his life with KAT. And there was no way in hell Meka fit into it, either.

Reo searched deep within himself for a solution to his dilemma. The longer he kept the situation from KAT, the harder it would be for her to be understanding. Besides, keeping secrets did nothing for a relationship but hurt it. The last thing Reo wanted to do was hurt KAT. So after hours and hours of soul searching Reo made a decision. He hoped it was the right decision. Just as long as the old cliché, what a person doesn't know won't hurt them, was true, then everything would work out just fine.

16

The World Is Mine

"We've gotta stop meeting like this," Reo said as he sat down at the barstool next to Klarke at Club 504. A local entertainer, Middle Child, was about to perform. It would be her last performance in Columbus for a while as she had just signed a record deal with a major label.

Comedian Steven G was emceeing that night, and had just commented on the fine woman sitting alone at the bar—Klarke.

"I'm sorry that my meeting with my attorney kept me from being here on time. Have you been waiting long?" Reo asked.

"That's okay," Klarke said. "I'm sure you'll make it up to me, and you can start by buying me a drink."

"Bartender," Reo said, "another Shirley Temple for the lady, please."

"Make that a glass of Passion Alizé with ice," Klarke said. "What's wrong with you? Don't you know that when a man is buying a lady a drink we upgrade? Besides, I want to get a nice buzz. That way you can take advantage of me." She smiled.

"Light on the ice and heavy on the Passion," Reo said to the bartender.

"To answer your question, I've only been waiting here about fifteen minutes or so."

"How was the drive? Did you run into any traffic?"

"My drive was fine. There was an accident coming in off of Twenty-three, but other than that, everything was smooth."

"We're putting far too many miles on our vehicles with all of this driving back and forth."

"Am I not worth it, Mr. Laroque?"

"Oh, you're plenty worth it, but I was thinking next time we meet somewhere different. Let's fly to a destination and meet there. You know, save some mileage and prolong those warranties."

"And where do you have in mind?" Klarke asked.

"Las Vegas."

"I've never been there before," Klarke said as the bartender set her drink in front of her.

"Don't worry. I've been there a couple of times. I'll be your tour guide," Reo said as he lifted Klarke's drink from the napkin, sprinkled salt on the napkin, and placed the drink back down. "We'll start off by checking into the Rio hotel. We can get massages, enjoy the sauna, and then hit the strip. We can check out Rodman's club, get married, eat at a seafood buffet, and of course, gamble."

Klarke sat her drink down calmly, and tried to reassure herself that she wasn't hearing things. She was almost certain Reo had slipped in a marriage proposal. This is what she had hoped for. This was the climax and conclusion of a well-thought-out script, all rolled into one.

The feeling of finally getting the proposal was nothing like she thought it would be. Where in the hell were all of the warm emotions that were taking over her body and mind coming from? This shit felt like love, true love. She was speechless and couldn't even bring herself to look up from her drink at Reo.

"Baby, what's wrong?" Reo asked, wrapping his hand gently around the back of Klarke's neck and wiping her tear with his thumb. "Don't cry. I want you to be my everything. I want to look in the mirror and see you, the man you've made me."

Reo reached into his pocket and rolled a ring down to Klarke, then took her drink and stole a sip. Klarke captured the ring in the cup of her hand as it made its way past her. She gasped at its beauty. The ring hosted tapered baguettes on each side of the band. The cut was perfection. The color and clarity were crisp, and the carats totaled seven.

"Baby, I know you've been through a lot," Reo said in a low, deeply emotional tone. "But I love the woman that life has made you into. I love you. I wanna be more than your man. I want to be your everything."

This was one of those times in a person's life where the devil is on the left shoulder and the angel is on the right. The devil was throwing confetti and humming the wedding song, while the angel was kneeled in prayer asking God to give Klarke the heart to tell Reo how she had manipulated him to this point.

Yes, a marriage proposal was exactly what she wanted, but she never imagined she would feel so bad about it.

She had fallen in love with Reo. She slipped the ring on her finger and turned to him with a smile. "When do we leave for Vegas?"

Reo's face broke out in a wide grin and he slid his arm around her and kissed her until she couldn't breathe. When he finally let her up for air he shouted, "Champagne for everybody! She said yes!"

The patrons clapped and shouted their congratulations. Middle Child stopped the song she was singing and serenaded them with a song selection titled "I Feel You," declaring the future Mr. and Mrs. Reo Laroque.

Three months after accepting Reo's proposal, Klarke was still on cloud nine. She had counted the days to their Vegas wedding date. It seemed like it took forever, but the big day was finally right around the corner.

Nothing could have made Klarke happier than the fact that she was on a plane to marry the most loving man in the world. The kids were thrilled. If her children hadn't loved him, then she wouldn't have been able to go through with it. But Reo treated them as if they were his very own.

Vaughn was especially excited about her new family. When Klarke asked for her blessings in the marriage, Vaughn only had one stipulation, and that was that Klarke promised that no one would break up their family this time. This was a promise that Klarke was glad to make.

Their first day in Vegas was awesome. Klarke had never been pampered so much in her life. Reo had arranged for them to receive the deluxe spa package, which included Swedish massages, facials, manicures, pedicures, lunch, use of the steam room, and aromatherapy showers. That night Reo saw to it that Klarke had dinner at the Top of the World Restaurant that Breezy had bragged about so much.

The next day was their wedding day. Klarke stayed up the night before staring at the ceiling while Reo stared into the night sky.

They each were pondering over their own dirty little secrets, secrets that could mean the difference between the beginning of a new relationship with one another or its end. But they were determined. The taunting thoughts of the night before didn't keep either of them from the intentions of going ahead with their wedding vows.

Reo got up at the crack of dawn to shower and prepare himself for his wedding day.

Klarke was up shortly after. She prayed the entire time she was in the shower. She thanked God for Reo and asked him to understand her deceptive means in gaining Reo's love. Her tears mixed with the water streaming down her face. How crazy was it for her to ask God to forgive her for a wrong she planned to do ahead of time? But she knew that if Reo wanted to marry her then it was part of God's will. Maybe telling him the whole truth was the right thing to do after all.

Klarke rinsed the soap off of her body and wrapped herself in one of the thick cotton English robes the hotel had provided. Klarke called out to Reo but there was no response. Where was he? She needed to tell him now before she chickened out. She assumed he must have stepped out of the room for a moment.

Klarke stared at the long silver evening gown that was hanging in the closet. She had purchased the gown years ago because it was on sale for 50 percent off. It had been in her closet for ages without an occasion to be worn. Since she wasn't having a big church wedding, where she would be seen by her friends and family, she had decided against going all out on a bridal gown, figuring the evening gown would suffice. It looked as though the gown wouldn't have its occasion after all.

Klarke walked away and headed toward the bed, where she discovered a snow-white beaded-lace tube wedding gown laying across the bed. It was the identical dress she had tried on in the bridal boutique with Jeva and Breezy. Klarke couldn't believe her eyes and had to pinch her own self to make sure she wasn't dreaming.

Beside the dress lay a card and a single red rose, hosted by a stem and some baby's breath. Klarke picked up the card and read it:

> *I hear it's bad luck to see the bride*
> *before the wedding, so I'll meet you*
> *in the chapel in an hour.*

> *P.S. A little bird told me you admired this dress.*
> *And you might want to check the closet*
> *for the matching slippers, Cinderella.*

Klarke was ecstatic. Reo was her prince, her knight in shining armor, her everything. There was no way she was confessing now. She was Reo's and Reo was hers. If she had to live with the lie so they could be happy together, then so be it.

Once Klarke got dressed and put her makeup on, she clipped the red rose and baby's breath and pinned it in her hair with a hair comb. She felt like the most beautiful bride in the world as she made her way to the chapel. She had never felt so loved before. She had never loved a man like she loved Reo.

When Klarke entered the chapel she couldn't believe her eyes. Not only was the decor of white sheer heavenly, but the cathedral ceiling was to die for. There was a stunning baby grand piano with a crystal candlabra filled with gold candles.

But the most stunning detail, which left Klarke breathless, was the sight of Jeva and her daughter Heather, Lance, Breezy, Vaughn, HJ, Mr. and Mrs. Laroque, Nate, Persia, and of course, Reo.

Klarke almost fell over, she got so weak in the knees.

Reo had flown in everyone close to them to share in their union. Breezy, Jeva, and Persia were each in tangerine matching gowns. HJ was in a black tux holding a ring pillow. Vaughn was in a beautiful tangerine junior bridesmaid's gown, while Jeva's daughter was in a cute, lacy, sheer white dress holding a basket of tangerine rose petals. Mrs. Laroque was in a lovely cream suit, and all of the men were in black tuxedos.

No one would have known this was Klarke's third marriage by the way she boohooed throughout the brief ceremony. One would have thought she would have been a pro at it by now.

Not to take anything away from how she felt about Harris and Rawling, but this time nothing or no one was going to keep her from living happily ever after. Nothing and no one!

"So, the son of a bitch decides he's going to run off and get married to live happily ever after?" Meka shouted, slamming down a magazine that had reported on the details of Reo's wedding. "I can't believe this is happening!"

"This doesn't affect our case at all," Meka's attorney said, handing her the settlement papers. "All you have to do is sign right here on the dotted line next to where Reo signed and all of this will be over. You'll be one-point-five million dollars richer."

The attorney's words couldn't soothe Meka, nor could the idea of her being a made millionaire. Deep down inside, Meka was hoping that once Reo found out he had a child that he would come back begging to be in her life again. His marriage eliminated any chance of that happening.

Money was no longer a leading contender in Meka's fight to get to Reo. Love was taking over, perhaps tainted with a little jealousy. Meka realized that she had never actually stopped loving Reo. It had been anger that had kept her from telling him how she really felt about him. Pride had kept her from apologizing for not sticking by his side.

Now, Meka wanted her man back.

"To hell with these papers," Meka said. "I'm not letting that son of a bitch off that easy."

"What are you talking about?" Meka's attorney said, wide-eyed. "We've won. Don't you get it? You're getting exactly what you wanted."

"No, I'm not. He won. He wants me out of his life forever. He doesn't want me or his baby."

"I know how you must feel," Meka's attorney said soothingly. "It will pass."

"No, it won't pass. I won't let it," Meka said, grabbing her jacket and purse, leaving the papers behind free of her signature.

"Now you wait a damn minute," Meka's attorney said, grabbing her arm. "I've worked very hard on this case, forever. You can't just walk away from it now. Do you know how much time I've invested for your greedy ass?"

Infuriated, Meka snatched her arm from her attorney's grip and sucker-punched her dead in the nose. Meka watched her fall to the floor while blood oozed from her nose. "Bill me," Meka said, storming out of the office.

Reo and Klarke decided that they would keep both of their homes until they had a new one built for them and the children. In the meantime, Reo would commute back and forth from Columbus to Toledo. Of course he spent most of his time in Toledo with Klarke and the children.

Reo always made sure he was in Toledo whenever it was Vaughn and HJ's week with Klarke. By the time Reo would arrive in Toledo on Sundays, the children were normally already home. On this particular Sunday Harris kept them late because he had tickets for the Universal Soul Circus.

"How long before the kids come home?" Reo asked Klarke as the two put together a five-thousand-piece puzzle at the dining room table.

"I'm not sure. Why?" she asked absently.

"Because I want to make a baby," Reo said smiling.

"Boy, you are so crazy," Klarke said, pushing Reo off of her and planting a puzzle piece in its place.

"I'm serious. Let's make a baby, a little girl."

Reo stood up, picked Klarke up, and carried her over to the chaise longue. He began kissing her passionately while unzipping her pants. Klarke tore Reo's shirt off of him and began kissing his chest and licking his nipples.

"Oh shit," Reo moaned as he slid inside her. "You are so wet."

Feeling him inside her reminded Klarke of an Arrested Development song titled "Natural." Tears slipped down her cheeks. She was deep inside Reo's love.

"Oh, yes," she cried, pulling Reo even deeper inside of her.

As Reo pumped in and out of Klarke, he lifted her shirt up over her neck and removed her bra. With each thrust he watched her titties jiggle and erotic expressions move across her face.

Although Reo and Klarke had made love many times, it always felt like the first time. Reo always came quick round one, but he was always up for it during round two.

"I love you, baby!" Reo said as his penis jerked semen inside of her vagina. "I would die for you."

"Oh, you feel so good!" Klarke screamed as she placed her feet behind Reo's neck and allowed her pussy to stroke up to his belly button and down to his upper thighs as she released her own passion juices.

"I really do love you, Klarke," Reo said.

Reo rarely called her anything but KAT. Klarke just looked at him and said, "I love you, too."

A knock on the door jolted them both to their feet.

"Vaughn must have left her key," she whispered.

The two were in a race to get their clothes on. Reo went over to the kitchen sink to wash his hands as Klarke answered the door.

Standing there was a woman with her hair pulled back in a bun. She had on a white blouse with some navy khakis and a black leather jacket. She had a diaper bag over her left shoulder along with a duffel bag. In her right arm was a baby. "Is Reo available?" the woman asked with a fake smile.

"May I tell him who's here for him?" Klarke asked with a perplexed look on her face.

"Tell him it's his baby's momma," the woman said.

Reo had raced to the door as soon as he heard Meka's voice. His heart almost stopped beating when he saw her standing there with the baby.

Before he could say anything Meka handed him the baby and left the bags at his feet.

"How come you look so surprised?" Meka asked Reo as if everything was just okey-dokey. "Did you really think I'd take your two million dollars in order for me and my child to stay out of your life?"

Reo looked up at Klarke, who just stared in shock.

"KAT, let me explain," Reo said desperately.

"Oh, she doesn't know about our baby, Reo?" Meka asked with a rehearsed surprise look on her face. "Even after the paternity test proved she was yours you still didn't let the Mrs. in on your nasty little secret?"

"Why are you doing this?" Reo asked Meka.

"No, why are *you* doing this?" Meka said, holding back her tears.

Just then Harris's car pulled up. Vaughn and HJ, followed by Harris, walked slowly up the walkway, sensing the tension in the air.

"Is everything okay, Klarke?" Harris asked.

"Sure, yeah . . . uhh, I'll call you," Klarke said.

Taking the hint, Harris kissed the kids good-bye and left.

"Come on, kids," Klarke said. "Let's go upstairs."

HJ proceeded to go up the steps, but Vaughn wasn't going anywhere until she got some answers.

"Whose baby?" Vaughn asked.

"These your stepkids?" Meka asked Reo, who didn't reply. "Well, this here is your new baby stepsister," she told Vaughn.

"Is that true, Mom?" Vaughn asked in shock.

"Go upstairs with your brother," Klarke repeated.

"Oh, no, honey, I'm leaving. You all feel free to continue playing house. But it looks like you have a new addition to your little family," Meka said, rubbing her nose against the baby's as she began to coo. "Mommy loves you and she'll see you in a couple of weeks."

"A couple of weeks!" Reo shouted, startling the baby and making her cry. "Meka, you can't just abandon her!"

"Why not?" Meka said walking away. "You were willing to."

The baby's wailing filled the house. Reo stood there rocking her, hoping it would make her shut up.

"Here," Klarke said reaching for the baby. She was at a complete loss for words. She couldn't believe Reo had kept such an immense secret from her. Klarke was more disappointed in Reo than she was angry. The fact that she had her own dirty little secret is what forced Klarke to grin and bear it. "Let me take her. Vaughn, look in those bags and see if there is any milk. I bet she's hungry."

Vaughn stood staring at the baby with pure malice.

"Did you hear me, Vaughn?" Klarke asked. "Look and see if the baby has any bottles."

Vaughn proceeded to do as she was told. "There are bottles in this bag," Vaughn said carrying them over to the refrigerator. "Do you want me to warm one?"

"Yeah," Klarke answered. "Put it in the microwave for forty seconds. Make sure you shake it up really well afterwards."

"So, you got a little girl," Vaughn said to Reo as she followed her mother's instructions.

Reo couldn't even look up at Vaughn. He simply nodded. Vaughn's shoulders slumped. Reo could tell she was disappointed.

"What's her name?" Vaughn asked, pretending to give a damn.

Reo looked at Klarke as she shrugged her shoulders in ignorance at him.

For the rest of the evening Klarke tended to the baby, and she and Reo never spoke about the situation. For one reason, they didn't want the children to overhear, and for another, neither knew what to say.

"We'll have to go out and buy a crib first thing in the morning," Klarke said as she lay down in the bed next to Reo and pulled the cover over her body.

She had just placed the baby in a bassinet, which she had re-trieved from the attic, at the foot of their bed. It had belonged to HJ when he was a baby.

"Yeah, along with some other stuff," Reo replied, as if he was already exhausted from baby shopping.

"I'll make a list. I'll check the attic again to see what else I might have of Vaughn's and HJ's from when they were babies." Klarke climbed into bed, kissed Reo good night, then rolled over as if everything was normal.

Reo lay down and pulled the cover over himself. He and Klarke just lay there, listening to each other breathe.

"Why are you doing this?" Reo suddenly asked her.

"Doing what?" Klarke asked softly.

"Acting like some strange woman didn't come to your doorstep today and drop off a kid."

"Some strange woman didn't just come to my doorstep and drop off a kid. The mother of your child gave you your daughter."

"You know what I mean, KAT," Reo said.

"No, I don't!" she exclaimed, sitting up. "What do you want me to do, Reo? Send you and your child packing?"

Reo sat up too. "I want you to be mad. Hell, I'm mad and it's my baby," Reo said, his voice waking the baby from her sleep and causing her to cry. "Damn it, not again."

"What do you want me to do, Reo?" she asked again as she got out of bed, went over to the bassinet, and picked up the baby. "Do you want me to tell you how godforsaken awful you are for even thinking about paying Meka off? You want me to yell, scream, and cry? Well, that's not going to happen. You'll have to get your punishment from a higher authority on this one," Klarke said as she turned to walk out of the room, hoping that a warm bottle would put the baby back to sleep.

"I'll get her," Reo said, stopping her. He walked over to her and took the small bundle, who opened her bright sparkling eyes. She cooed and melted Reo right then and there. And right at that moment he could never imagine not wanting such a beautiful child in his life. He still couldn't overlook the hell having her in his life would bring, and Klarke couldn't overlook it either, but they could get through this. Their love was stronger than Meka's hate. They could get through this . . . somehow.

17

Happily Ever After

Jeva's twenty-ninth birthday was less than two weeks away when Lance decided he would have a small get-together to celebrate. Time was of the essence and he didn't know a thing about throwing parties so he relied upon the baby-sitter, Cassie, to arrange everything for him.

"Does Jeva like seafood?" Cassie asked Lance as she handed him a bottle of beer. Lance sat on Cassie's new three-piece, brown-and-tan tweed living-room set, which she had just purchased on credit, and started watching TV.

"Yeah, shrimp. Order shrimp for the bash. Run baby! Run baby! Run baby run. Yeah, that's what I'm talking about!" Lance exclaimed as he jumped up, almost turning over the oval glass living-room table. He always got excited when the chosen running back for his fantasy football league scored a touchdown.

"Damn you, Lance. You trying to get me kicked out of my place?" Cassie said between her teeth.

"Son of a bitch. The coach needs to trade that bum right there," Lance said, ignoring Cassie's comment.

"Lance, I swear to God if you holler one more time. My neighbor next door would just love to call the cops on me for disturbing the peace. These walls are paper thin and she's always complaining about the noise my kids make running up and down the steps. Management wouldn't hesitate putting me out, and do you have any idea how long the waiting list is for a four-bedroom down at the housing authority?"

"This is how you watch football, girl," Lance said to Cassie. "Now let a nigga be."

Since the incident with her parents went down, Jeva hadn't been herself. She had been consistently late for work and missing deadlines. This week she missed two days straight without even calling in. Her boss wanted to fire her ass, but Patty, his personal assistant, covered for Jeva. She took the heat by saying that Jeva had told her she was taking a couple of vacation days but that she must have forgotten to log them in and forward the notice to him.

Ironically enough, Jeva's boss had planned on assigning her a high-profile photography shoot that would have taken her to Jamaica. But instead of showing up for work, she stayed home in bed.

Jeva hadn't neglected work because of the money her parents had provided her with. Jeva actually enjoyed taking pictures. This was such a low point in her life right now that finding joy in her work wouldn't even have replenished her spirits.

Patty was pretty cool. She was only nineteen but always thought quick on her feet. Her uncle, Jeva's boss, hired her right out of high school. No matter what the circumstance, she had always had Jeva's back. For example, one time Lance stayed out all night and hadn't made it back home by the time Jeva needed to leave for work. Jeva had paged him on 911 until his pager was full, and of course he wasn't answering his cell phone. It was the fourth time over a two-month period that he had done this.

Jeva had run out of excuses to tell her boss. She had already used the one about her alarm clock not going off—twice, as a matter of fact. She had, too, exhausted the one about her daughter being sick. The month before that she told them the car wouldn't start. Of course she always told Patty the truth.

Jeva's inconsistency with work was the main reason why most of the time Jeva's boss only gave her local assignments. He didn't want to risk her screwing up a big money-making shoot.

On this occasion when Jeva failed to call, Patty handled it for her once again. She told her uncle that she was supposed to pick Jeva up, but couldn't find her house and didn't have her cell phone on her. Her uncle, catching on to Patty's loyalty to Jeva, asked, "Well, couldn't you have stopped at a pay phone to call her?"

"I didn't have her phone number on me, and besides, no way was I stopping at a pay phone on that side of town," Patty said, throwing in that retort just in case her uncle tried to drill her with something like she should have called information.

Patty knew she had to warn Jeva that her uncle was on the warpath. In addition, Patty had run out of excuses. It was time Jeva got her shit together.

"Hello," Jeva said, answering the phone.

"May I speak with Jeva?" Patty asked.

"Speaking," Jeva replied.

"I understand if you don't want your job, but now you are jeopardizing mine, not to mention my relationship with my uncle."

"Oh, Patty. I'm sorry," Jeva said. "You have no idea what I've been going through."

"You're right. I don't, and that's because you haven't even bothered to call in to let me know what's going on with you."

"I apologize, Patty. I really do. I'll be in Monday," Jeva said.

"Well, I won't. I'll be in Jamaica," Patty said.

"What's in Jamaica?" Jeva questioned.

"A gig that would have been yours if you had carried your ass into work!"

"Get dressed, I'm coming to take you out," Breezy ordered Jeva over the phone.

"Oh, Breezy, not today. I'm trying to rest and the phone has been ringing off the hook. I'm not up to it."

"You haven't been up to anything lately. Look, I know how you must feel."

"You couldn't possibly. Why do people always feel as though they have to say that? You have a mother you can go see every day if you wanted. Your father may be locked up, but at least you can communicate with him."

"Leave my father out of this," Breezy said in a sharp tone.

"Well, you know what I mean," Jeva said, brushing Breezy off.

"No, I don't know. I don't know about half of anything when it comes to you."

"Well, what half is it that you don't understand, the white half or the Hispanic half? Perhaps I can enlighten you," Jeva said, getting bold.

"Just fuck it, Jeva!" Breezy said, throwing her hands up on the situation.

"No, Bria, fuck you."

Jeva slammed down the phone and hunched over and began bawling. She couldn't believe she had just talked to her best friend that way when all she was trying to do was get her out of the house and cheer her up. She was only trying to do what best friends are supposed to do . . . be there for her.

She waited a couple of minutes before picking up the phone to call Breezy back. When she did she didn't even have to dial the number. Breezy was sitting on the phone. She must have been calling her back at the same time.

"Hello," Jeva said.

"Hello," Breezy responded.

"Breezy, I'm so sorry. I didn't mean to act so nasty. I know you're just trying to help."

"Look, just squash it," Breezy replied to Jeva. "It's Friday, and if you're going to play hooky from work on a Friday you might as well make it worth it. Get up and get dressed. Fuck window shopping. We're going to make a purchase."

"Girl, I'm raggedy," Jeva said. "I don't know if I can even make myself look presentable enough to leave this house."

"Then that's just one more thing we can do. Let's go to the salon and get our hair and nails did. You know that Cinnabon shop is right next door. We can hit them up afterwards."

"Okay, say no more," Jeva said.

"We're about to pull a Julia Roberts. We walking out of that mall looking brand new. New clothes, hair, shoes, the works. You with me?"

"I'm with you, girl," Jeva agreed.

"All right, I'll be there in about an hour," Breezy said.

"Okay, I'll be waiting," Jeva said. "And Breezy . . ."

"Yeah, girl."

"Thank you."

After a day full of shopping Jeva was speechless when she walked into the living room to some of her closest friends yelling "Surprise!" She hadn't suspected a thing. She couldn't believe the girls hadn't slipped up and revealed information about the surprise party.

"Thank you, guys. I can't believe neither of you peeped a word about this. You two usually can't plan anything and keep it a secret," Jeva said to Klarke and Breezy.

"Hey, you've got your man to thank for this one. We didn't have anything to do with planning this party," Klarke said.

"You mean to tell me Lance put all of this together himself?" Jeva asked.

"Yes indeed," Lance said, creeping up behind her and planting an intoxicating kiss on her neck. "You have your husband-to-be to thank for this here engagement party."

Jeva's mouth dropped open. She looked at Klarke and Breezy, and they each shrugged their shoulders to insinuate that they had no idea what was going on.

"Excuse me, everybody, excuse me," Lance said, tapping a spoon from the cocktail sauce against the crystal serving platter the shrimp was on. "I have an announcement to make. I know some of you thought this was a party to celebrate Jeva's birthday, but I lied. It's actually an engagement party. The only problem is that I left out one minor detail."

Lance pulled a small black velvet box from his pants pocket. "I forgot to pop the question. So without further ado . . ." Lance dropped to one knee and opened the box. Jeva admired the contents of the box, which was a three-carat marquis molded into a platinum band. Her eyes filled with tears of joy as she looked up at Klarke and Breezy, who each placed dark sunglasses on their faces and then yelled, "Gotcha."

Everyone in the room giggled with excitement as they waited for this production to play out.

"Jeva, will you be my wifey?" Lance asked.

"What kind of silly question is that? Yes, baby! I'll be your wifey."

Jeva was almost in hysterics. She cried with so much joy. She felt like she was Snow White and had just been brought out of a deep sleep by the kiss from her prince.

Of course Klarke and Breezy were happy for Jeva, too. They hated the fact that Jeva was going to be Lance's wife—they felt that she could do better—but as long as Jeva was happy, that's all that mattered to them.

The golden rule of not bashing one another's men didn't keep Klarke and Breezy from ridiculing Lance among each other.

"I just can't believe Lance finally proposed to her," Klarke said.

"It's a Boyz N the Hood pity proposal," Breezy said as she and Klarke began to laugh. "Him proposing was about the only thing that was going to pull her out of the slump she's been in. They'll probably be engaged until little Heather graduates college."

"Do you really think she'll fall for his game again?" Klarke asked Breezy.

"Girl, Lance is like alcohol to Jeva," Breezy said. "He impairs her judgment."

"Well, at least we know what Lance has been doing with all of the money he supposedly makes," Klarke said. "That ring is gorgeous."

"Girl, please. You know somebody's Grandmama is laying in an alley somewhere with her ring finger missing."

The two toasted their champagne glasses and laughed so hard it was almost rude. Everyone's attention turned to the two of them, from across every corner of the room. Once they noticed that all eyes were on them, they settled down and Breezy raised her champagne glass to the entire room in toast.

Almost all the guests eventually made their way over to Jeva to congratulate her and to look at the stunning stone. Last but not least, Reo sought the opportunity to bid his best wishes to her.

"Congratulations. I wish you and Lance the very best. I wish you as much happiness as KAT and I share."

"Thank you Reo. Thank you very much," Jeva said, giving Reo a nice warm hug. "Oh, I must look a mess. I've got makeup running all down my face."

"Next time you might want to try Mary Kay," Reo suggested, trying to make a joke.

"Huh?"

"Oh, nothing," Reo said as he took a sip of his champagne.

"I can't believe this," Cassie said to Lance in hysterics. "I can't believe you actually just proposed to her. What were you thinking?"

"Shhh," Lance said as he locked the bathroom door, securing both him and Cassie inside. "Do you want her to hear you?"

"Shhh, my ass. There's a party going on downstairs in the name of your engagement. You even had me plan it," Cassie said. "Oh my God, how could I be so stupid? Here I thought I was planning a birthday party for the woman I baby-sit for, and I'm planning my man's engagement party to another woman."

"I'm not your man. I'm her man. It's you I have to sneak

around with, not her. You're the other woman, so get that straight," Lance said angrily.

As Cassie began to cry Lance did the best he could to comfort her by taking her into his arms and rubbing her head. He was quite sincere. He had feelings for Cassie and didn't enjoy seeing her hurt.

"Baby, you know this has nothing to do with the way I feel about you," Lance assured Cassie.

"Then what do you call what you just gave Jeva, a fashion ring? At least that's what you told me you were getting her for her birthday. Lance, do you love her?"

"Yes, I mean, we're raising a kid together."

"I can't believe this," Cassie said.

"But I'm in love with you. There's a difference. Cassie, just trust me on this one. It's not going to change anything you and I have. You know it's only going to make it better in the end. Trust me on this one."

Cassie pulled away from Lance and wiped her tears. "Yeah, well, just make sure you pay the bill every month for that ring you got her from Bedrock on credit in my name!" Cassie exclaimed as she exited the bathroom to rejoin the party.

Lance sat down on the toilet and sighed a sigh of relief. Just then Breezy entered the bathroom. "Hey Lance, what's crackalackin?"

"Oh, Breezy, hey. Uhhh, nothing. I'm good. Everything is good."

"Is Ms. Cassie good?" Breezy asked sharply.

"What, huh?" Lance stuttered.

Breezy glared at Lance, then turned to close the bathroom door.

"Look, nigga, locking a door keeps people out. It doesn't keep people from hearing what's going on behind the locked door."

"Not today, Breezy," Lance said getting up and barging past her. "Not today."

Breezy grabbed Lance by the arm. "You tell her or I will. I think it will be best coming from you."

"Yeah, right," Lance continued for the door. "I don't know what you're talking about."

"Hey, that's my best friend and I'll be damned if I'm going to let her marry you after what I just heard between you and Cassie. Jeva can choose to get caught up in this make-believe bullshit world you try to keep her in, but this is taking it too far. I stay out of my girls' business. I've never been one to run to them like a Channel Two news reporter, but I can't let this go down, Lance."

"You fucking hypocrite. I didn't see you racing to tell Jeva shit when it was you and I talking behind locked bathroom doors. Or have you forgotten about that?" Lance said as he walked up to Breezy, putting his arms around her waist. "What's the matter? You miss Daddy? You jealous it ain't you no more?"

"First of all, that was a long time ago, Lance, over three years ago to be exact. I had only known Jeva a couple of months. We were just associates then. Now we're girls. My relationship with Jeva back then was nothing like it is now."

"Well, once you and Jeva's relationship started to become what it is, why didn't you tell her then?"

Breezy stared at him in disgust. She wished she had never slept with Lance. It should have never happened. When Breezy showed up at the house for Jeva only to find that she had gone into work to pick up some extra hours, she should have left immediately. But no, she had to sit and make small talk with Lance. She just had to have that glass of wine. She just had to have that chocolate hairy-chest hunk of a man.

She just couldn't resist. It was his fault. He should have never answered the door with no shirt on. He should have never answered the door with those boxer shorts on with his johnson just wagging in front of Breezy. That was like waving raw meat in front of a hungry pit bull.

As the saying goes, one thing led to another and Lance was tossin' it up. He had gotten on his knees, picked Breezy up and placed her legs over his shoulders, and sucked her clit like a poisonous snake had just bitten it and he was trying to save her life.

By the time Lance got finished with his rescue technique, Breezy's pussy was ripe. At first she just climbed on top of Lance with the intentions of only grinding on his rock-hard dick. They both kept whispering to each other that the act they were committing was wrong and that they couldn't go all the way. So she just grinded Lance by stroking her pussy lips and swollen clit along his penis. He had gotten her so wet and it was feeling so good that they both could have cum from just grinding. But about a minute before they both reached their climax, Lance pushed her off of him and onto the floor, where he dove into her stuff and pumped until they both screamed in ecstasy.

"Look, Lance," Breezy said, "it was only one time."

"Oh, so that's why you trippin'? Are you mad that it was only one time and you didn't get seconds?"

"Oh, please, boy, you know I could still have you to this day if I wanted. I'm the one who made sure it never happened again. You were like a dog in heat, always sniffing at my ass every time Jeva turned her head. Listen to myself. I sound ridiculous." Breezy pushed Lance off of her and headed for the door.

"Okay, I'll tell her," Lance said sincerely.

"When?" Breezy said in a demanding tone.

"Right after I tell her about us. What do you think that's going to do to poor little Jeva, your best friend?" Lance said, smiling coldly.

Breezy paused. What could she say? Lance had her right where he wanted her. There was no way she ever wanted Jeva to find out that she had been betrayed by someone else who was supposed to love her.

"You are so lucky that my heat ain't out in my trunk. I would make a trip outside just for you. I swear, I hate you so much right now, I would pump your shit with lead and wouldn't mind spending the rest of my life in the joint for first-degree murder."

Lance grabbed Breezy and pulled her close to him. She was once again face-to-face with his masculine hairy chest that his knockoff Coogie sweater showed off. The same chest that had gotten her in trouble years ago.

"Oh, baby, you know that would never happen," he said, nibbling on Breezy's ear. "Any half-decent attorney would say in your defense that it was a crime of passion. You'd only be charged with manslaughter at the very least. But a real good attorney, hell, he'll cop a plea and you'll be locked up no more than five to seven years at the most. Either way it goes, I guess that would be hard for you. I know how you like a good fuck no matter whose man's dick it is."

Lance stuck his tongue in Breezy's mouth and for two seconds she was tempted. Then she pushed him away. He grinned at her mischievously as he left the bathroom. He knew he had the W.

Breezy closed the bathroom door, then slid down it. She was so angry, yet there was nothing she could do about it. She sat there and cried. She cried hard.

Jeva frazzled her brain with wedding preparations. She had always wanted a spring wedding and the season was right around the corner. There was no way in hell she was going to wait for another year to roll around to get married. She knew she had to hurry and confirm every detail. After all, she now had the money to make it happen.

Lance was no help at all. Every time Jeva asked his opinion he would just tell her that whatever she wanted was fine with him.

"I want this to be our wedding, not just mine," Jeva said to Lance.

"I just want all of your dreams to finally come true," Lance said, kissing Jeva and caressing her bootie with his hands.

"They have," Jeva said, kissing Lance back. "They have."

Jeva got down on her knees, unzipped Lance's pants, and pulled out his penis. She began licking the shaft in preparation for the blowjob of a lifetime.

"Oh, yeah, baby, that's right," Lance moaned. "Take good care of your man. I'll take good care of you."

As Lance's penis pumped against Jeva's jaw the feeling got him to talking mad shit.

"Oh, yeah, Daddy gonna take care of you. Just think, you don't have to tire yourself with some nine-to-five anymore. We're gonna take exotic trips all over the world."

"Umm, Daddy," Jeva moaned as she swirled Lance's saliva covered penis all over her face.

"We gonna invest the money from that trust fund of yours and flip it four times over. Then we're going to fuck on a bed of money. We'll be like Whitney and Bobby." Lance laughed as he grabbed Jeva by the back of her head and rammed her head harder onto his vessel. "Umm, and after you make Daddy cum down your throat, I'm gonna finally nut my baby son up inside that tightass pussy."

"What trust fund?" Jeva asked as she gripped Lance's dick in her hand.

"You know, the one you told me your parents set up for you. Now come on, baby, don't stop."

"Lance, I never told you about any trust fund."

"Yes, you did. You must have or else how would I know about it?" Lance attempted to shove his penis back in Jeva's mouth, but she pushed herself away from him and rose from up off her knees.

She knew she hadn't mentioned the trust fund to Lance. She deliberately withheld the information as a surprise wedding gift. She would offer Lance something no other woman could, the opportunity to never have to work for someone else as long as he lived.

"No, I didn't, Lance. I know for a fact I didn't. How do you know about my trust fund?"

Lance had no answer for Jeva. He began to sweat and silently cursed himself.

"Never mind that trust fund, anyway. It's not important."

"Obviously it is. It's important enough for you to play dumb about it. I want to know, Lance, how did you find out about it?"

"It's nothing really, Jeva, but damn, if you insist."

"I insist," Jeva said, patiently waiting for Lance's explanation.

"I opened the letter from Welford before you did. I was curious. I know how you are and I just wanted to know ahead of time what I was going to have to deal with. I wanted to prepare myself to be there for you."

"I still don't understand. That letter didn't say anything about money or my parents not showing up."

"There was a second letter, from a bank. I opened it. I read about the trust and the terms. Then I resealed it the same way I had done with the letter from the agency."

"You opened my mail. You read my personal mail and then resealed it like nothing," Jeva said.

"It wasn't like that at all."

"Just stop it!" Jeva said putting her hands over her ears and sitting down on the Popason chair in their living room. "You knew they weren't going to be at the park. You knew my parents were going to be a no-show and you let me walk out that door into one of my worst nightmares. So Lance, who is it you're marrying, me or the trust fund?"

"Jeva, you know I love you. You deserved it. I knew you would have never gone to that park first and experienced the fact that your parents didn't want to have anything to do with you. If you had known beforehand what was going to happen, you would have ruined everything, and you deserved that money."

"I just needed that little something to push me over the edge, huh, Lance? Did you really feel as though I deserved the money, or was it you who deserved it?" Jeva asked. "Was that your payoff for putting up with me for all of these years?"

"I swear, it's not like that at all," Lance said.

"Once again, I was going to be your fool. Only this time I was going to take vows committing to be your fool for the rest of my life."

"Please listen to me, baby. Jeva, you know me," Lance said, getting down on one knee at Jeva's lap. "I love you so much. I want you, Jeva, to be my wifey. I want to have a son with you. I want all of this with or without a trust fund. Jeva, baby, you know me."

After listening to Lance state his case, Jeva put her hands on top of his. She viciously pushed them off of her knees.

"Oh, stop it with that goddamn wifey shit," Jeva said, mugging Lance in the forehead with her index finger. "I know you, all right. I know that you are a low-down dirty bastard. You're trash."

"I'm trash! When I met you, you didn't know who you were nor did you have a hole in the ground to shit in," Lance said to Jeva. "You were dancing in a club like some whore. I saved you!"

"There are worse things than being a stripper," Jeva said.

"Like what?" Lance asked.

"Like being broke, which is what you are. Now get the fuck out."

"This is my house. This muthafucker is in my name."

"Oh, you're right," Jeva said. "Then I'm getting the fuck out. Me and Heather are gone."

"Am I supposed to cry? We both know that Heather isn't my daughter. You were already pregnant when I first met your ass and put that fifty down your G-string. I'm the one who agreed to your little insurance scam, remember? If it wasn't for me signing that fucking birth certificate knowing damn well that baby wasn't mine, Heather, your daughter, wouldn't have health insurance to this day. So while you are at it, throw me back all those fucking premiums that got pulled out of my paycheck," Lance yelled.

"Fine," Jeva said, blowing it off like it was nothing.

"You damn right it's fine. Knowing how you felt growing up not knowing who your own parents were, you still decided to make your daughter go through the same experience. And for what, Jeva? A lousy medical bill. So make sure when you go crying to your little girlfriends you tell them that piece of truth. Tell them how you cried and begged me to pretend to the world that I was the father of your child and how you said we'd take it to our graves. Tell them how any trick you might have turned could have resulted in the birth of that baby. But I stepped up to the plate and made sure that baby was taken care of. Didn't your momma tell you about a thing called welfare, Medicaid? Oh, that's right, you didn't have a momma. She didn't want your ass and neither do I."

Jeva lifted her chin proudly. "I know you're trying to break me down. You're trying to break me down like you've done our entire relationship. But right now, at this very moment, I know that there is no way you ever loved my child or me. To say all of those things you just said, you couldn't have possibly ever loved us. People try to use the excuse that they say things out of anger and don't really mean it. All the while, it's just the opposite. Anger gives people the courage to tell the truth. But you know what, Lance?" Jeva asked. "I guess that's why it doesn't hurt for me to leave. Walking away from you, for good, feels nothing like I've ever thought it would. You always take credit for saving me and I'll give you that, Lance. You did save me. You saved me from a lifestyle that would have led me God knows where. It felt good to be saved, to be wanted. But you know what's funny? Being with the person that saved me hurt like hell. I'd often find myself weighing the odds. All the lies, the games, and the arguing, it's taught me so much." Tears slipped down her cheeks. "And what's so ironic is that out of everything, the good and the bad alike, I've learned to love myself. I've done nothing but hurt myself by being with you, so I'm convinced my days will be real cool without you. I'm crying right now because I'm happy, believe it or not. This is what it feels like to finally love myself. Besides knowing that God loves me, this is the greatest love of all. And out of all the people in my life, Lance, I have you to thank for it. So, thank you."

Lance sneered at her speech. "It's easy for you to walk away, huh? Then walk, bitch. I'm giving you the entire weekend to get your shit and walk," Lance said, slamming the door behind him, causing the picture of him and Jeva that was hanging on the wall to fall off and shatter.

Jeva just stood there, looking at the closed door. She looked around the house at everything she and Lance had shared and realized that she wanted nothing. All she wanted was to pack an overnight bag for her and her child and never return. She walked over to the CD player and fumbled through the collection of CDs. She put on Ashanti's "Foolish" and pressed the repeat button. Even if it had to play the entire weekend, she wanted that song to be the one Lance heard when he walked through that door and found her gone.

Jeva felt as though the finest hotel was more appropriate than the nearest; after all, she could afford it now. Jeva thought if anything ever happened between her and Lance she'd wallow for weeks in self-pity, but surprisingly, she didn't. She decided she would take Heather and herself on a little shopping spree.

Jeva looked up limousines in the yellow pages and arranged for one to pick them up the next morning from the hotel. They would spend the entire day going from mall to mall. Their last stop was an exclusive day spa. While her daughter was entertained in the child-care facility, Jeva got a makeover and purchased an obscene amount of cosmetics and perfumes. Her head full of straight black hair was now a head full of luscious curly locks with blonde highlights. Jeva wore herself out with all the indulging. Her next luxury would be a new car.

Fuck Lance! Fuck her parents and fuck the fairytale. It was time for Jeva to start living happily ever after in the real world.

18

Cry of the Wolf

Breezy was awakened abruptly from her sleep by a blood-curdling howl. Her heart slammed in her chest. Afraid to move, she lay frozen in her bed until she heard another scream.

Breezy slowly scooted to the edge of her bed and reached over to pull her gun from the nightstand. She cocked it and crept out of the bed. She unlocked her bedroom door and went into the hallway. Once again she heard the howl and determined that it was coming from her father's bedroom.

Her father had been released from prison only two weeks ago and was staying with her.

As Breezy opened the door to her father's room she could hear some movement and moans. She switched on the light to find her father thrashing in his sleep.

"Dad. Daddy," Breezy said as she shook her father in an effort to wake him from his sleep. "Daddy, wake up. You're having a nightmare. Dad, please wake up."

Breezy could see that her father had also been crying. Traces of tears had seeped from his eyes and formed a puddle in his ear pit. He was flinching as if he were having a seizure.

Breezy shook her father, trying to wake him. All of a sudden Mr. Williams got up and grabbed Breezy around the throat. Frantically Breezy tried to peel her father's hands from around her neck. She tried to scream "Daddy!" hoping her father would snap out of his fit and come to. But his hands tightened around her throat until there was no hope for air. He had locked in Breezy's voice with the power of his grip.

Breezy's instincts were to fight, which included hitting her father with the gun, until it came down to her last breath, and if all else failed, she'd blow her father's brains out. During the struggle Breezy lost grip of the gun and it fell to the floor and underneath the bed. She began bashing her father's head with her closed fist in an attempt to wake him. He finally opened his eyes and became aware of what was happening.

He snatched his hands from around Breezy's neck and Breezy fell back, choking and gasping violently.

"Baby, I'm sorry. I'm so sorry," Mr. Williams said as he ran into the guest bathroom to get Breezy some water. When he returned with the water Breezy had caught her breath. "Baby, Daddy is so sorry. I was having another nightmare. Daddy's sorry."

This was the third nightmare that week. This one, though, was the worst. On occasion Breezy had heard her father whimpering in his sleep, but never had he cried out so painfully. Breezy thought this time an intruder was attacking him, which is the reason she had retrieved her gun.

"It's okay, Dad. It's okay," Breezy said, massaging her neck, now bruised with the imprint of her father's fingers.

Breezy took a sip of the water and watched her father bury his head in his hands and cry. She could only imagine the pain he had gone through all of those years in prison. She had wondered, but never asked, if he had been raped, beaten, or abused. She had cried many nights at the mere thought of her father being thrown into a dark cell, nude, left to live in his own feces for days or even weeks. She knew some of her unasked concerns were where his nightmares derived from. The more nightmares Breezy's father continued to have, the more Breezy's conscience ate away at her.

"Jeva, I need to talk to you," Breezy said as she pounded on Jeva's hotel door. Jeva and her daughter had been staying at an extended-stay hotel while Jeva house-hunted.

Jeva opened the door, a frown of concern on her face. "Shhh, Heather's asleep. Now Breezy, what's wrong? What's going on?" Breezy blew right pass her and began pacing the floor.

"I can't do it anymore, Jeva. I can't live with this any longer. I have to tell my father or I'm going to kill myself."

"Look, Breezy. Just calm down and talk to me. I'm here for you. I'm here for you, girl," Jeva said as she squeezed Breezy, who was weeping frantically in her arms.

Jeva had never seen Breezy so vulnerable. She sat frozen stiff as Breezy exposed a lie she had lived with for the past fifteen years. The lie that had led to her father's incarceration.

For two hours Breezy told Jeva of how the boy she accused of raping her never actually raped her. The sex that took place between them had been consensual.

Growing up, Breezy's parents were hard but fair with her. Church and school were the only activities she was permitted to engage in. Extracurricular activities at school were thought to be a negative influence, so Breezy was never allowed to join the track team, cheerleading squad, or anything of that nature. Dating was absolutely out of the question.

Breezy's parents had sacrificed, and had forced her to sacrifice, everything in order for her to attend college. Breezy earned a partial scholarship at a university out of state. In the midst of getting accustomed to dorm life she went buck wild. Breezy was free at last from her parents' clutches and virginal way of life.

It hadn't been long before Breezy found herself knocked up. She had been only eighteen and a freshman in college. Breezy didn't know how she was going to explain her condition to her parents. She made the mistake of sharing her pregnancy with her father. When Breezy saw the disappointment in her father's eyes there was no way she could allow herself to live with being the cause of it. For the first time in her life she witnessed her father cry. Before Breezy could catch the lie she told her father, it had made its way through her lips.

Judge attended Breezy's college on a full football scholarship. He was also studying pre-law. His teammates had given him the nickname of Judge because he was the only football player who dreamed more about being a Supreme Court Justice than an NFL star. Football was Judge's mistress. Law was his true love.

Judge was the most ambitious boy Breezy had ever met. He loved football, the law, and God. Unfortunately for the both of them, his strong love of God didn't keep him from loving sex outside of marriage.

What turned Breezy on the most was the fact that when she met him, Judge, like herself, was a virgin. For a couple of months they kissed and fondled, but that was as far as Judge would go. He wouldn't even allow Breezy to suck his dick. He believed oral sex was sex and was still a form of fornication. Breezy, being Breezy, just wouldn't let up.

One evening, in celebration of Judge leading his team to the championship, Breezy lucked up on a drunken Judge at a party that was taking place at one of his teammate's homes. Judge rarely drank, if at all, but on that night he had gotten pretty full.

Breezy lured him to one of the bedrooms just to *talk*. Words led to kisses, kisses led to fondling, and fondling led to some oral acts and finally to full-blown intercourse.

Breezy had branded Judge with her pussy. He was going to be hers forever. Hell, if he didn't get drafted into the NFL, without a doubt, Judge would serve as a Supreme Court Justice someday. It was Breezy's mission to make sure she would be right there by his side.

Getting pregnant hadn't been part of the plan. Breezy was too ashamed to even tell Judge of her condition, but she needed help. She had to tell someone.

Breezy and her father had always been close, closer than the average father-and-daughter relationship. Mr. Williams had always been Breezy's best friend. She knew her father would never judge her, and that no matter what situation she got herself into he would always love her. That is why she decided to go to her father and ask for his help. She needed money for an abortion and had no where else to turn.

Had she been forewarned of the dissatisfaction and repugnance that would form within her father, she would have opted to use a hanger to rid her body of her unborn. She couldn't have guessed her father would gun down Judge.

Ironically, a few days after Breezy found out she was pregnant she miscarried the baby. By that time, she had already apprised her father of the life-altering mendacity.

"Breezy, you have to tell him," Jeva pleaded.

"I know. I know I do," Breezy cried.

"It's going to be hard for both you and your father, but you owe him that much. You owe it to yourself."

"Whoever came up with that fucked up cliché about it being better late than never," Breezy said wiping her tears, "never had to do anything remotely comparable to what I'm about to have to do."

"Dad, I'm home!" Breezy shouted as she came through the door. "Dad, where are you? I need to talk to you."

Breezy went into the kitchen to see if her father was there. When she didn't find him there she checked her father's bedroom. His clothes were laid out on the bed and she could hear the shower water running from the connected guest bath. The bathroom door was cracked, so Breezy went back into the living room.

Breezy sat down on the couch and turned on the television with the remote. She hoped that her father would hurry out of the shower before she lost the courage to tell him the truth about the rape. She twiddled her fingers, closed her eyes, and asked God for the strength to go through with the confession.

After about fifteen minutes of waiting, which seemed like forever to Breezy, who was becoming even more of a nervous wreck, she decided to go into her room to get the family photo album. She thought it would make things easier if she and her dad could reminisce over some happier times.

Breezy went to her bedroom and pulled several old photo albums from underneath her bed as well as a shoebox full of letters her dad had written her over the years. She noticed that her answering machine message light was on. It displayed that she had five messages, but when she went to play them, they were all hang-up calls.

"Hmm, that's strange. It ain't nobody but Guy's wife," she said as she piled the photo album and shoebox in her arms and headed out of her room. All of a sudden the coldest chill went through her body. She stopped in her tracks and the contents of her arms fell to the floor. She rushed to the guest room and called for her father. She knocked on the guest bath door and called for him again, but there was still no answer. She pushed the door that was partially cracked open only to find her father lying on the bathroom floor in a pool of blood, his fist clenched around his bath towel.

"What do we got, Sams?" the heavyset detective said to Sams, the rookie investigator on the scene, as he ducked under the crime-scene tape strapped across Breezy's front door.

"Oh, Detective Edwards," Sams replied. "A fatal gunshot wound to the head. It looks as though the victim might have startled an intruder."

"Who discovered the body?" Detective Edwards asked Sams.

"The victim's daughter. She's right there," Sams pointed. "The one in the middle."

"I know this must be difficult for you," Detective Edwards said as he walked over to Breezy, "but there are just a couple of questions I need to ask you that might help us find your father's killer."

Breezy didn't reply. She just sat on the couch crying as Klarke and Jeva attempted to comfort her.

"Your father's been out of prison for a little over a month now?" Detective Edwards continued as he looked down at his notepad.

"Why don't you ask her questions you don't already know the answers to?" Klarke said, glaring up at him.

"And you are?" Detective Edwards asked Klarke.

"Klarke Taylor, her best friend," Klarke said, still not used to using her married name.

"Do you own a gun?" Detective Edwards asked Breezy, totally ignoring Klarke's inquiry.

"Uhh, yes," Breezy answered, dazed. "A nine-millimeter."

"Where do you keep it?"

"Nightstand drawer, my bedroom," Breezy answered as the detective signaled Sams to go check it out.

"Now think about it really hard, Ms. Williams. Is there anyone, anyone at all, who might want to see your father dead?"

"For crying out loud," Klarke interrupted again. "Don't you think if she knew the answer to that she would have told you all about it two hours ago? The man was in jail for murdering her rapist. Why don't you go have a look at some of the members in his family and see if they weren't out for a little sweet taste of revenge?"

"Miss Taylor, is it?" Detective Edwards asked.

"Actually, I'm recently married, it's Mrs. Laroque," Klarke responded.

"Well, Mrs. Laroque, we're already looking into that as a possible scenario. Now would you be so kind as to let me do my job here?" Just then Sams came out of Breezy's bedroom, shaking his head in the negative—Breezy's gun wasn't in the nightstand. "Ms. Williams, it looks like we're going to need to ask you a few more questions down at the station."

"Oh, no, you don't," Jeva said, clutching Breezy's arm. "I've seen *Law and Order*. You're not taking her anywhere. You want us to think you are taking her just to inquire about a few innocent questions and the next thing we know we'll be putting money on her books."

"Jeva, Klarke," Breezy snapped, "I think it will be best if I go with the detective."

"Fine," Klarke said. "If that's what you want. Let's go. Jeva and I are right behind you."

"No," Breezy said. "I'll go alone."

Breezy had been down at the station for almost twelve hours. She had been asked thousands of questions, some a hundred times over, only to keep giving the same answers. She was tired. She just wanted to mourn the loss of her father. Already she missed him painfully.

"I'll ask you again, Ms. Williams," Detective Edwards said. "What did you do with your gun after you shot and killed your father?"

"How many times do I have to tell you?" Breezy screamed. "I didn't kill my father! Please, Mr. Edwards. Why won't you believe me?"

"I want to believe you. I want to help you, but you have to help me first. Just tell me the truth. Your father was having one of those nightmares you were telling me about. You thought something was wrong. You went into his room just like you had done before, with your gun in hand. It's not your fault you shot him. You had to protect yourself. You didn't know what your father was capable of. You had to kill him. It was him or you."

"No, no, no! I swear I didn't do it. That's not what happened," Breezy cried.

"Then it was an accident," Detective Edwards played. "If it was an accident then you don't have anything to worry about."

"Traces of gunpowder on Ms. Williams is negative," Sams said as he poked his head through the door.

"Can I go home now?" Breezy cried.

"Not until you tell me who you had kill your father," Detective Edwards said. "Who did you give your gun to? Ms. Williams, you were the only one in the home. You are the only one who can tell us what happened."

"Detective Edwards," Sams said. "Can I see you out here for a moment?"

"Sure," Detective Edwards said, scooting a notepad and a pencil in front of Breezy. "I'll be back, Ms. Williams. In the meantime I want you write down all the details of how you set up the murder of your father."

Breezy threw the notepad and pencil at the door that closed behind Detective Edwards.

"We don't have anything but a missing gun on her, huh, Sams?" Detective Edwards asked. "That and the fact that nothing was stolen and there was no sign of a break-in. I just have a hunch about the daughter."

"Actually, I just got a call from one of the investigators at the scene. A nine-millimeter was found under the bed in the victim's bedroom," Sams said. "It's being sent to the lab to be tested. Lieutenant Ross says we can hold her on the suspicion that her gun is the murder weapon and perhaps fluff up our other suspicions, but you know how he is. He'll only give us seventy-two hours to find hard evidence that could convict her. If we come up with nothing, then we have to let her go for now until more evidence against her develops. What do you want to do?"

Detective Edwards looked at Breezy, who was pacing back and forth, through the two-way mirror. He could see she was tired and worn out. He had asked her every question there was to ask her and yet nothing she said struck a guilty cord with the detective.

"She's not represented by counsel and she hasn't asked for a lawyer," Detective Edwards said in a conniving tone.

"Yet," Sams quickly added, "a senior law school student would know that we really don't have anything factual against her."

Detective Edwards thought for a moment before saying, "we'll just have to take that chance. Let's book her."

Klarke, Reo, and Jeva looked like three angels standing side by side as Breezy walked outside of the Lucas County jail. It had been a long seventy-two hours.

When Breezy reached the three of them they all put their arms around her.

"This wasn't exactly what I had in mind when I said I wanted a gated community lifestyle," Breezy said.

The three drove Breezy home. When Breezy walked into her apartment she was greeted by tossed and broken furniture. Furniture had been turned over and some seized as evidence. There were shattered picture frames and broken drawers. The Lucas County Police Department had no mercy in their search of Breezy's home for evidence. Nothing was worth salvaging.

Her father's blood had dried and seeped into the cracks of the bathroom floor tiles. Breezy fixed up a concoction of baking soda and water and scrubbed away the blood.

When Breezy arrived back at work her desk had been cleared and her nametag had been removed from her office door. Supposedly she was being terminated for no-show call. Her arrest had been on every six o'clock news channel so she was certain her place of employment knew of the ordeal she had to contend with. She knew this same ordeal was the true reason behind her being fired. She was too drained to try to even fight it. She loaded her belongings into her car and never looked back.

A tip had been phoned in to Detective Edwards, putting Guy at the scene of the crime on the night Breezy's father was murdered. The female caller stated that Guy had mentioned something about an attempt to shut up his mistress, only to have his plot interrupted by an unexpected occupant, Mr. Williams. Supposedly Guy had contacted the caller's boyfriend in hopes of hiring him to finish the job. Detective Edwards felt that the call might have had some validity to it so he got his brother, Judge Thomas Edwards, to issue a warrant to search Guy's vehicle and home. Lo and behold, traces of Mr. William's blood were found on Guy's car steering wheel and on an article of Guy's clothing that was retrieved from his home.

"So, what do you have to say for yourself?" Detective Edwards said to Guy as he sat down at the table in the interrogation room.

"I don't have shit to say until my attorney gets here," Guy responded as he slammed his cuffed hands down on the table. "You sons of bitches better get prepared for the lawsuit of your lives."

"No, you better get prepared to spend the rest of your life in jail. As a matter of fact, I'll help you prepare," Detective Edwards said as he threw a tube of Vaseline at Guy. "I sometimes get chapped lips, but I figure you're going to be needing this far more than me."

Detective Edwards began to laugh, and Guy went ballistic. Guards had to come into the interrogation room and settle him down.

"Now, are you ready to talk? I can't help you unless you talk to me. You can wait for your attorney in CB7 with bootie-snatchin' Bill if you like," Detective Edwards said.

"Fuck you!" Guy shouted. "This is bullshit."

"No, fuck you. And that's just what's about to happen if you don't start talking. Now did I hear you say you would like to waive your right to an attorney and tell me why traces of the victim's blood were found on your steering wheel and on the sleeve of one of your shirts?" Detective Edwards roared, becoming highly frustrated.

"Listen, I'm telling you the truth. I don't know how anybody's blood got anywhere. I was with my wife the night of the murder. I already told you that. She's my alibi. Call her and ask her."

"Oh, I don't think you want me to do that." Detective Edwards snickered.

"Call her and you'll see for yourself, you fat son of a bitch!"

"For your information your wife is in the next room, and her story ain't matching up with yours."

"Quit bullshitting with me, detective. You wanted me to be straight with you, well, don't insult me by playing games with me."

"Oh, you think I'm playing games?" Detective Edwards said as he pulled out a tape recorder and hit the play button.

Guy almost shit his pants when he heard what sounded like his wife's voice spilling out information about his relationship with Breezy. His wife stated that Guy told her that, after the incident with the cell phone call, he was going to take care of Breezy once and for all. She went on to give blow-by-blow details of how she herself suspected her husband of the crime. Guy's wife danced around vouching for his whereabouts the night of the murder.

"So just tell me the truth," Detective Edwards said after hitting the stop button only a quarter way through Guy's wife's spill. "We already have another witness, a neighbor, who heard you break in Ms. Williams's door one night. This witness says prior to the door being bashed in she saw a heated argument take place between you and Ms. Williams."

"This is bullshit!" Guy yelled.

"Your fingerprints are all over the apartment, not to mention the blood evidence. So tell me, are you ready to make a deal now?" Detective Edwards asked. "I can have the district attorney here in no time."

Guy was denied bond. The evidence that continued to pile up against him was a guaranteed conviction. His lawyer begged him to take a plea, but he refused as he maintained his innocence.

When his lawyers attempt to point the finger at Breezy failed, Guy quickly started talking deals, but by this time the DA had him by the balls and had called off all deals.

Once she was certain that Guy was going to be convicted, his wife decided to visit him at the downtown jail, where he was being held while awaiting the outcome of his trial.

"Was the pussy worth all of this, you cheating bastard?" Guy's wife asked as she sat down her small, slender frame.

"Baby, why are you doing this to me? How the fuck you going to put a block on the phone so that my calls don't go through?" Guy inquired.

"It doesn't feel too good to be played, now does it?" his wife asked.

"Baby, honey, this is much more serious than an infidelity. Is that why you telling the cops all that bullshit? You trying to get back at me? Okay, baby, you win. I'm sorry. I'm a sorry-ass bastard. Now come on. You've got to tell them the truth."

"Truth? Since when do you know anything about the truth, Guy? Look, I'm not here to tell you how much I love you and how I'm going to see to it that you get out of here. I'm not even going to bullshit you like that. I just wanted you to know that divorce papers are being drawn and the kids and I are going to Arizona to visit with my parents for a while."

"What?" Guy yelled. "Baby, please. Come on now."

"You look so cute when you beg," his wife said. "Reminds me of the sweet young man I married. It's a shame how some cute little pups can grow up to be big ugly dawgs."

"Fucking bitch!" Guy mumbled under his breath.

"I'll be that," his wife said, jumping up. "I'll be a fucking bitch. But I'm a free bitch. You, you're behind bars for God knows how long. You jeopardized everything for a piece of ass. How did it feel when that detective told you they found the victim's blood on your steering wheel and on your shirt? You felt like someone was playing you, didn't you? Good, because now you know how it feels. I'm sorry things turned out this way. It wasn't supposed to be the old man, but when there's interference and one doesn't have a plan B, shit happens. One sometimes has to make do with the situation at hand."

"You fucking set me up!" Guy began to yell hysterically. "You fucking set me up! Who was it? Who did you get to do the deed? I know you didn't have the guts. Was is that little pretty muthafucker who lives next door? Do you think I don't know about the two of you creeping back and forth across the lawn every afternoon while I'm out breaking my back at the job. Or is it his son? Yeah, you nasty ho, I know about him, too. It's funny how some little girls grow up to be women and others grow up to be hoes."

The guards had to run over and subdue Guy. He started going crazy. Once they finally got him settled down, tears of complete detestation for his wife rolled down his face. He was breathing as if he had just run a marathon.

"How could you do this to me?" Guy pleaded with his wife. "Why, why are you doing this to me, baby?"

"Why am I doing this to you? I gave you fifteen years, most of my youth, and all of my adult years. I gave you beautiful children, washed your nasty drawers, and this is how you pay me back, by running around keeping some tramp on the side. She's not even as fine as me, Guy," his wife scolded. "I had been faithful to you for all those years until you started playing me like an idiot. I had needs, too. But just remember, you started it, Guy, and I'm finishing it."

"You'll burn in hell for this," Guy said as the guards began to haul him away.

"Was it worth it, Guy?" his wife repeated while the guards carried Guy away. "Oh, Guy, just one more thing. This Bria, Ms. Williams person, she's a little thick for your taste, isn't she? That picture of her in the wooden frame with her name engraved on it . . . well, let me just say that you could have done better."

19

Son of Satan

There was a loud banging on the door. Klarke and Reo both sat up in the bed.

"Damn!" Reo said wiping his eyes. "Who is that?"

"I don't know," Klarke said, looking at the clock that read 9:00 A.M.

Vaughn suddenly burst through their bedroom door.

"Mom, Reo," Vaughn said in a panic. "There's police everywhere!"

Klarke and Reo both jumped up out of bed and hurried to put on something decent. Klarke threw on a long pink satin robe. Reo grabbed a dark blue, plaid pajama shirt that was hanging over the footboard of the bed. It matched the pajama pants he was wearing.

The two, followed by Vaughn, couldn't get down the steps quickly enough, each stumbling over one another.

Reo made it to the door first. He opened it to find four officers and a swarm of police cars.

"May I help you?" Reo asked, puzzled.

"Yes," one of the officers replied. "We're responding to a nine-one-one call we received from your neighbor. Do you mind if we check in the back, your swimming pool?"

"Sure," Reo said with a perplexed look on his face. He moved out of the way and let the officers inside. Klarke led the officers to the back patio door and opened it for them. Reo, Klarke, and Vaughn followed the officers out to the back patio. What they saw was wrenching.

The police taped off the swimming pool area of Klarke's home. It had been two hours since they had responded to the neighbor's 911 call. The neighbor had reported seeing what appeared to be a small child floating facedown in the pool.

"I don't understand! I don't understand!" Reo cried.

Several officers had to restrain him as he tried to go after the deceased baby. He completely lost his mind as he watched his lifeless baby girl being dragged out of the pool.

"Oh, baby. Oh, my God," Klarke said trying to comfort him.

Nothing anyone could do at that point could calm Reo down. He finally fell to the patio ground. The officers released him into Klarke's arms. She knelt beside him and hugged his head close to her bosom as tears slipped down her cheeks.

"I'm so sorry, baby, I'm so sorry," Klarke said over and over again.

"I don't understand. I don't understand how this happened. My baby girl," Reo said, clinging to her. "It hurts, KAT. It hurts."

Vaughn and HJ were in the kitchen awaiting the arrival of their father. Vaughn was hugging HJ tightly as he tried to understand the entire scene.

"Everything is going to be all right," Vaughn said rubbing HJ's head. "Everything is going to be all right."

The police officers had asked if there was anywhere the children could go to get them away from the tragic scene. Vaughn suggested their father be phoned. She read her father's phone number to the female officer, who called, explained the situation to Harris, and asked him to come pick up the children.

The police asked Vaughn and HJ a few questions while they waited for their father. Neither Vaughn nor HJ had any knowledge of how the baby might have drowned in the pool.

"The baby is dead, isn't she?" Vaughn asked the female officer. "Is there any way they can make her come alive again? I mean dead is dead, right?" Just then Harris came through the front door.

"Vaughn, HJ, are you all right?" Harris asked, hurrying over to them and hugging them tightly.

"Yes, Daddy," HJ said. "The baby couldn't swim."

Through the sliding patio doors Harris could see Klarke holding Reo. He headed toward them but was stopped by an officer.

"I'm sorry, sir, but you're going to have to stay inside," the officer said with his hand across Harris's chest. "And you are?"

"I'm Harris Bradshaw, the children's father," he said, pointing to Vaughn and HJ. "I just wanted to let Klarke know I was taking them with me."

"Wait right here. I'll go tell her," the officer said, walking over to Klarke. Klarke looked up at Harris as the officer pointed to Harris. Klarke nodded her head that it was okay for Harris to take the children.

"Come on, kids. Let's go," Harris said.

"Sir, could I get you to write down your name, address, and phone number?" the female officer asked. "We might have a few more questions to ask the children."

tion down and handed it to the officer.

"Sir," the officer said before Harris and the children headed out of the door, "this is the card of the detective who will be leading this case. If the children say anything to you that might be helpful, please give him a call anytime. His cell phone number is on the back of the card."

By this time Klarke had managed to finally bring Reo to his feet. A police officer noticed that she could barely handle Reo's weight and assisted her in getting him into the house and sitting him down on the couch.

"Can somebody just tell me why?" Reo said distraught. "I don't understand. I don't understand."

Klarke's heart was broken as she witnessed her strong husband melt down. She tried to empathize by imagining if it had been one of her own children and knew that there would be nothing she could do to ease that kind of pain. "Oh, God!" Reo exclaimed. "Has anyone called Meka yet?"

"A six-month-old baby didn't just hop out of her crib and decide to take a swim," an officer said to Klarke and Reo as they sat hand in hand. The officers had been drilling them on the last time they had each been with the baby. They had even called Vaughn and HJ to ask them questions before finally sending an officer over to Harris's house to question them in person.

Meka arrived with her mother and one of her sisters shortly after Reo's mother and father had arrived to the house.

"You bitch," Meka yelled as she lunged at Klarke. "What did you do to my baby? What did you do?"

Everyone hurried to hold Meka back. Reo grabbed her and held her tight as they each cried an ocean of tears.

"Reo, my baby," Meka cried. "Please, where's my baby?"

"I'm so sorry," Reo said. "I'm so sorry."

The two clutched each other and embraced. The emotions were so heavy that there wasn't a dry eye in the room. Even the huskiest officer was in tears. There was something about the death of a child, an unexplainable death at that, that tormented one's soul.

"How'd she get in the pool, Reo?" Meka asked. "How did my baby girl end up in that woman's pool?"

"I don't know," Reo answered. "I don't understand."

"Were you that afraid that my daughter would put a dent in your happily-ever-after life with him?" Meka said to Klarke, referring to Reo. "Were you afraid there wouldn't be enough room in his heart left for you, or enough money left in his bank account, you greedy bitch? I know your kind."

Meka again launched herself at Klarke. Meka's angry words to her cut like a knife. She didn't blame Meka, though. She, too, would be just as devastated if it had been a child from her own womb. She was, in fact, hurting deeply too.

"I didn't know where else to go," Klarke said, standing on Harris's porch.

Meka and her family as well as Reo's parents were staying at the Clarion hotel for the night. Officers and the media had swarmed Klarke's home until she couldn't bear to stay there.

Klarke wanted desperately to be by her husband's side, but she knew he wanted to mourn with his family and the mother of his child. Meka was already blaming Klarke, so she knew her being there would have only made things worse.

Both Jeva and Breezy offered for Klarke to stay with them, but

Klarke wanted to be with her children. She hadn't even thought about calling Harris to ask if her camping out there would have been a problem.

"As long as I have a roof over my head," Harris said, "you always have someplace to go. Come inside, Klarke."

"Where are the kids?" she asked.

"Asleep," Harris answered. "It's having a strong impact on Vaughn. I've never seen her this way before. This whole thing is just surreal."

"Harris, I don't know what happened. Words can't explain how confusing this all is to me."

"Klarke, you don't have to explain yourself to me. I know you. The truth will make itself known."

"I hope so, Harris. You should have seen how Meka, the baby's mother, came after me. And I could see it in everyone's eyes. I could see it, Harris." Klarke cried. "Everyone in that room felt the same way she did."

"She blames you?" Harris asked.

"Yes, but I swear to God, Harris, I would never—"

"Shhhh," Harris said, holding Klarke tightly. "You don't have to say it. I know the kind of woman you are, Klarke, and it's not the kind of woman who is capable of killing a baby, or anyone, for that matter."

"Now all I have to do is convince the rest of the world of that," Klarke said in a hopeless tone.

"Look at me," Harris said, pulling Klarke's face close to his. "Anyone who knows you knows you're not capable of such an act."

"I shouldn't be dumping my load on you. I know you are still trying to cope with Tionne's death. How are you dealing, Harris?"

"Oh, man. I might as well had been the one who put that rope around her neck because I feel as though I took the life out of her."

"How can you say that?" Klarke asked. "You took great care of Tionne. She had everything she wanted."

"Except for me," Harris said sadly. "For some reason I never could give her all of me."

Klarke and Harris sat there looking into each other's eyes. Harris's support was exactly what Klarke needed at that very moment. The two moved closer together until their lips just barely touched. Harris proceeded to stick his tongue into Klarke's mouth, but she pulled away.

"I better go call Reo," Klarke said as she got up to make her call, leaving Harris alone on the couch.

20

Love or Money

"I'm supposed to be your friend and I feel so useless," Jeva said to Klarke as they strolled through the mall, along with Breezy. "I see your pain and there's nothing I can do to ease it. Same goes to you, Breezy."

"You just being my friend, being by my side," Klarke said to Jeva, "is enough for me. That's all I need right now."

"Ditto, girl," Breezy added.

"Why are we bothering with this mall today?" Jeva inquired.

"With all the crap that's going on in our lives," Breezy added, "we're at the fucking mall. Typical women."

"Breezy's right," Jeva said. "Klarke, do you really think it looks good for you to be cruising the mall while your husband is mourning the loss of his child?"

"What can I do, Jeva?" Klarke asked. "Meka wants my head on a platter. Reo and his parents are spending all of their time with Meka and her family. I have to let Reo deal with this the way he needs to. Do you think I don't want to be by my husband's side? This is just all one big mess. Once again a dream come true has turned into a nightmare."

"My life is in shambles too, girl," Breezy said, "but you know I got your back."

"Did you find another job yet?" Jeva asked Breezy.

"Nah, but I'm looking," Breezy replied. "That unemployment check don't even cover my Hudson's charge card bill."

"Hey, isn't that the guy from your company Christmas party?" Jeva asked Klarke.

Klarke looked across the mallway only to see Evan. He was looking casually fine and laughing it up with some woman who was clinging to his arm.

"That's my boss," Klarke said surprised. "I mean my ex-boss."

"Who's that woman he's with?" Breezy asked. "Klarke, she looks just like you."

Evan spotted the threesome staring at him and walked over to them with a comforting smile.

"Hello, Evan," Klarke said.

"Oh, Klarke," he said embracing her. "How are you?"

Klarke looked over Evan's shoulder at the woman who did seem to hold an uncanny resemblance to her. She couldn't help but notice the shiny engagement ring on the woman's finger.

"Klarke, this is Aliyah," Evan said.

"Pleased to meet you, Klarke," Aliyah said. "You are right, Evan. She and I do look as though we could be twin sisters."

Klarke smiled, then turned her attention back to Evan and reacquainted him with Jeva and Breezy.

"How are things at Kemble and Steiner?" Klarke asked.

"Not the same since we lost our number-one executive accounts representative," Evan said. "I just want you to know that when everything blows over, and I know it will, your desk will be waiting for you."

"Can it be waiting for me inside of an office this time instead of a cubicle?" Klarke smiled. "I mean, come on, I'm an executive accounts rep, for pete's sake."

"You got it," Evan said. "It's really good to see you, Klarke."

"It's good seeing you, too."

Evan kissed Klarke on the cheek, nodded at Jeva and Breezy, and walked away.

"You must have put it on him, girl," Breezy said. "He must crave chocolate now."

"Y'all stupid," Klarke said.

"Hell, you could have just kept screwing the boss and got what you wanted out of life," Breezy said.

"Is that what you think this is about?" Klarke said. "I love Reo. Loving him wasn't part of any plan."

"That's not what she means, Klarke," Jeva said. "Come on now, y'all. Each other is all we have right now. We almost lost Breezy to the system and now Klarke is up to bat. We need each other now to lean on more than ever."

"Jeva's right," Breezy said. "I don't know what I would have done without you all."

"Klarke, do you really think they might try to pin this on you?" Jeva asked.

"I don't know, baby," Klarke said putting her arm around Jeva. "All I know is that Reo and I have been made out to be like the Ramseys. You know, I never had been able to sympathize with that family until now."

"Reo ought to make a book about our lives," Breezy said.

"Yeah, it would be a guaranteed bestseller all over the world," Jeva said.

"I'm scared," Klarke said out of nowhere. "I'm scared."

The girls all hugged each other as if they had been college room-mates and were packing up to go their separate ways. Their lives had all done a 360-degree turn. Although Jeva was starting to find comfort and love within herself, she could hardly bask in the glory of her new days as she watched her best friends' lives become ruin.

"Will you guys say a prayer for me?" Klarke asked Jeva and Breezy.

"Sure," they said.

"I mean right now," Klarke said.

"Right here in the middle of the mall?" Breezy asked.

Just then a girl in a low-cut open-back halter top with painted-on tight jeans walked by. She was sporting three-inch heels and an up-do with spritz spit curls hanging down.

"If she ain't embarrassed to walk through the mall looking like that," Breezy said, "then we sure shouldn't be embarrassed to bow our head in the name of the Lord in the mall."

The girls laughed as they bowed their heads in prayer.

"I don't have nothing," Breezy wailed as she stacked boxes of her belongings, which consisted of some clothing and a few personal items. Breezy had been unable to maintain her bills and had received an eviction notice. Jeva was helping her pack.

All the high spirit that made Breezy who she was had been lost. She didn't go out and seek another job as was stipulated for receiving unemployment compensation benefits.

"I can't believe I'm moving back home with my mother. I'm thirty years old. That's thirty years of my life wasted, gone. I had to beg her, but I don't have anywhere else to go. I wish I had my daddy," Breezy cried.

"I'll take care of you. We can be roommates—you, Heather, and me. We'll need a big house, compliments of my birth parents of course." Jeva smiled. "There's nothing more I'd like than to live happily ever after with my best friend."

Breezy hugged Jeva. She loved her so much. She knew she didn't deserve Jeva's friendship or financial support, not with the secret of betrayal she had kept from her. But with Lance out of her life Jeva would never have to know the truth.

The more Breezy thought about it, after all she had jeopardized and lost, she wasn't going to make the same mistake twice. No amount of money or lifestyle in the world was worth spending years torturing herself with lies. Nothing was worth robbing herself of quality of life with a clear conscience. Besides, she feared God wouldn't be willing to forgive her for the same deliberate mistake. Even if telling Jeva about her and Lance meant that she'd have to live the rest of her life in a homeless shelter, she had to tell her the truth.

"Jeva, you've really been there for me and I really do appreciate you for that," Breezy said. "I know I don't show it. I know it seems like I'm always coming down hard on you. It's just that you are always so easygoing with life. I wish I could be that way. It makes me jealous sometimes. I get angry. I get mad for not being able to be more like you in a sense."

Breezy paused and then looked up at Jeva. "I need to tell you something. After you listen to what I'm about to say, if you decide never to be my friend again, I'm just thankful for all this time I've been fortunate enough to have you in my life. You've always had my back." Breezy began to sob.

"Breezy, what are you trying to tell me?" Jeva asked.

"It's about Lance," Breezy said putting her head down.

"Breezy, you know what? You don't even have to go there,"

Jeva said, putting her index finger over Breezy's lips to shush her. "Like you told Lance yourself, a locked door only keeps people out. It doesn't keep them from hearing what's going on on the other side of that door. I know. I know about you and Lance."

Breezy couldn't believe Jeva had overheard her and Lance's conversation and had never said one word about it. She couldn't believe Jeva remained such a good friend to her knowing how she had backstabbed her by sleeping with Lance. Breezy broke down.

"I don't understand," Breezy said, shaking her head.

"Lance was a man, a sorry man at that. Not that I didn't love him, and not that hearing you two discuss your fling didn't hurt like hell. Do you know how hard it was to go back down to that party with a smile on my face after hearing that my best friend had slept with my fiancé? When I wasn't smiling I was crying. Not because I was elated with the fact that I was about to become this happy bride, but because I was absolutely beside myself," Jeva said as she caught a couple of tears from making their way down her face.

"Then I don't understand why you stayed with him, knowing . . . and why you remained my friend."

"It's like you told Klarke, she had the fairy tale once and chose to give it up. Well, I wanted it and I was willing to compromise everything, including myself, to have that fairy tale and to hold on to it at all cost. I didn't want to be like Klarke and Harris."

"So you would have married Lance and pretended that every-thing was just fine?" Breezy asked.

"Isn't that what a fairy tale is . . . pretending in a make-believe world?"

"I love you so much, Jeva," Breezy said, hugging her and rubbing her fingers through her hair.

"I love you too. You know that," Jeva responded.

Breezy pulled away from Jeva and looked into her eyes. She didn't know why she was so blessed to have such a beautiful person in her life. Filled with emotion she kissed Jeva softly on the lips. Jeva sat there, shy.

"I'm sorry," Breezy said, pulling away. "I don't know why I just did that."

"It's okay," Jeva said, putting her hand on Breezy's shoulder. "It's okay."

Breezy kissed her again, only this time it was a much welcomed and bracing kiss.

21

Seek and Ye Shall Find

"Miss Taylor. I mean, Mrs. Laroque," Detective Edwards said. "So we meet again, and under similar circumstances."

"Detective Edwards," Klarke acknowledged.

"Mr. and Mrs. Laroque," the detective said to Reo and Klarke, who entered his office arm-in-arm. "Please have a seat."

"Thank you," Reo said as he and Klarke sat down.

Although this was Reo and Klarke's third time being questioned about the death of the baby, it was Detective Edwards's first stab at them. Each time the questions were the same, only worded differently. It was obvious Detective Edwards's goal was to now catch Reo and Klarke in some type of lie. Reo and Klarke had been questioned both together and individually in an attempt to find incriminating flaws in their stories.

"So can the two of you start by telling me the last time you each saw the deceased alive?"

Reo broke down at the thought of his child being labeled *deceased*. It broke his heart.

"She was in our bed with us," Klarke said. "At about ten

o'clock that night we took her into the spare room and put her in her crib."

"We," Detective Edwards said. "The both of you walked her into the room."

"No, it was just me," Klarke answered.

"I see," Detective Edwards said. "About how long would you say Mrs. Laroque was absent from the bedroom when she left to put your daughter in her crib, Mr. Laroque?"

"I don't know, about ten or fifteen minutes or so," Reo said. "She went downstairs to get something to drink."

"I noticed the minirefrigerator in your bedroom was fully stocked," Detective Edwards said.

"I wanted water," Klarke said in a defensive tone.

"There are Dixie cups next to the bathroom sink in your master bedroom private bath," Detective Edwards drilled.

"I wanted ice water," Klarke added.

"So did Mrs. Laroque come up with a glass of ice water?" Detective Edwards asked Reo.

"I drank it downstairs," Klarke interfered. "There wasn't any need to bring an empty glass upstairs."

"After your wife left the room with your daughter at ten o'clock P.M.," Detective Edwards asked Reo, "when was the next time you saw your daughter?"

"Being pulled out of the pool." Reo cried.

Detective Edwards supplied Reo with a box of Kleenex and continued his questioning.

"Let's see, prior to Mrs. Laroque you were Miss Taylor. Is that correct?" Detective Edwards asked Klarke.

"Correct," Klarke responded.

"And prior to that you were Mrs. Rawling Davis, and before

that you were Mrs. Harris Bradshaw. So Taylor is your maiden name, correct?"

"Correct," Klarke said, looking at Reo, who was quickly becoming enlightened on some minor details of Klarke's history.

"Where are you employed?" Detective Edwards asked Klarke.

"I'm not," she responded.

"Oh, yeah, I see, you were formerly employed at Kemble and Steiner Printing, is that correct?"

"For a short period, yes."

"Two and a half years, if you want to call that short," Detective Edwards said.

Klarke could all of a sudden hear her heart beat. There was absolutely no way out of the heated brew she was about to find herself boiling in.

"Kemble and Steiner," Reo interrupted. "You were the accounts rep. My publisher uses Kemble and Steiner to print my books. I used them when I self-published. Your picture was on the Web site. I remember seeing it when I was researching and getting printing quotes."

"Pardon me," Detective Edwards said, looking back and forth at Klarke and Reo. "Am I missing something here?"

"Detective, I think I'm the one who's missing something," Reo said. "Klarke, what's going on?"

"I can explain, Reo, but not now. Let's answer the detective's questions first. We'll talk at home," Klarke said as her eyes began to water. Right then and there Reo released her hand from his. Right then and there she knew she had lost him.

"A deliberate stranger," Reo said. "That e-mail was on purpose. You deliberately planned all of this. Your company has my personal information in their records. I can't believe it. What did you do, research me? I bet you probably studied every article that was ever written about me." The look on Klarke's face confirmed his suspicions.

"Hmmm, articles," Detective Edwards added. "I guess that would explain this box we found in the attic of your Toledo home."

Detective Edwards pulled a Xerox box from underneath the table and placed it on the table. Klarke's eyes bulged. Detective Edwards proceeded to empty the contents of the box onto the middle of the table. There were several clippings from magazines and newspapers. Reo picked up a videotape that was labeled "Reo Laroque television interview." The tape was dated two months before Reo had ever even met Klarke.

Reo stood up and buried his face in the palms of his hands. It was as if the room was spinning around while his body was still. All of the thoughts going through his head had to be impossible, Reo prayed. There was no way the scenario forming in his scrambled brain could have been played out against him by the woman he trusted with his heart.

"Please tell me this is all a coincidence, please, Klarke."

"Mr. Laroque, can I get you something to drink?" the detective asked, seeing that Reo was becoming a little woozy.

"No, no, detective," Reo said finding his seat again.

He looked up at Klarke with shame, humiliation, and embarrassment. She read everything he was thinking about her in his eyes. She looked away from Reo. She was weakening, not even finding enough strength to look him in his face.

"Reo, it's not like that at all," Klarke said. "I swear I love you. I swear my love for you was not part of the plan. It's real. Come on, Reo, it's me, KAT."

"I gave you that name. Don't you use that fucking name." Reo paced. "So is it true? Did you deliberately seek me out? Look at me, damn it. Did you?"

Klarke looked up at Reo without saying a word. Her actions said it all. The detective was on cloud nine as he watched what felt like an episode of the *The Practice* play out before him.

"I can't believe it. You set me up," Reo said.

"Please, Reo, you're my husband now. I know you know I love you. I know you feel this shit."

"Oh, you love me, do you? And so does every other bitch out for my bank. *Fuck!* How could I have been so stupid? I should have known. I mean, when you e-mailed me that picture. I knew I knew you from somewhere. I knew I had seen you before."

Klarke's stomach began to turn with the world. She placed her hand over her mouth and began to gag. Detective Edwards quickly retrieved the trash pail for her. Just as he placed it in front of her she threw up her entire breakfast.

"I'm the one who needs to be puking," Reo said to Klarke. "You make me sick."

"Would you two like a moment alone?" Detective Edwards asked.

"Yes," Klarke said while at the same time Reo replied, "No."

"Continue your questioning please, Detective," Reo said. "I'd like to finish up here so I can go to Mrs. Lar . . . I mean, Miss Taylor's home and pack up my things."

The detective went over his notepad and proceeded with his questioning.

"Your first marriage ended because your husband was unfaithful," Detective Edwards asked Klarke.

"That's one of the reasons," Klarke said.

"Well, in your divorce decree it's the only reason stated. Your former husband, Mr. Bradshaw, committed adultery with his cousin?"

"She wasn't his blood cousin," Klarke said.

"I'm sure Mr. Bradshaw would be proud that you are defending him. But anyway . . . so the scenario with Reo having a child come into your life was like déjà vu, huh."

"I don't know what you're talking about, Detective," Klarke said.

"Your first husband, didn't he have a child outside of your marriage that you had to play mommy to?"

"I know what you're trying to do, Detective, and you're wrong. I heard about the million-dollar life insurance policy Meka had on the baby. It's all over the news. Why don't you go badger her?"

"I can't listen to this," Reo said.

"Don't you want to get to the bottom of this?" Detective Edwards asked, checking his cell phone, which had just vibrated.

"This is Detective Edwards," he said in a professional tone.

"Detective Edwards. My name is Harris Bradshaw," Harris said quickly. "I don't know if you know who I am, but I—"

"Of course I know who you are," Detective Edwards said, cutting Harris off, glancing over at Klarke. "How ironic you should phone me. Your ex-wife and I were just speaking of you. She's with me now."

"Klarke is there, with you!" Harris said excitedly.

"Yes, as a matter of—"

"May I speak with her please?" Harris said in an almost begging tone.

"Sure. One moment," the detective said, handing his cell phone to Klarke.

"Hello," Klarke said, puzzled.

"Klarke, it's me, Harris," Harris said, frenzied and speaking quickly. "I'm here with Vaughn and, and . . ."

Harris couldn't catch his breath.

"Harris, calm down. Just calm down and tell me what's the matter with Vaughn."

Klarke listened intensely as Harris rambled on and on. She advised Harris that she was on her way to his house and to just stay calm until she arrived. Klarke then ended the call and handed Detective Edwards his cell phone back. Detective Edwards spoke hellos into the receiver only to find that the line was dead.

"I've got to go," Klarke said, jumping up.

"I still have quite a few more questions," Detective Edwards said.

"Then they'll just have to wait. It's my daughter," Klarke said as she began to become panicked and impatient. "Unless you're arresting me I'm leaving. I have to get to my daughter."

"Calm down, Mrs. Laroque," Detective Edwards said. "I'm going to have to ask you not to leave town. You either, Mr. Laroque."

"I need to go home," Reo replied. "Home in Columbus. I promise not to leave the state, Detective, but I've got to get home. I need to be with my family and my daughter's mother."

"Please understand, Mr. Laroque, if we have to join forces with the Columbus Police Department to keep you under surveillance, we will."

"Do what you have to do, Detective," Reo said. "Just find out what happened to my daughter."

Klarke felt in her heart that this moment in that interrogation room would be the last time Reo would be by her side and on her side. Without her husband, her other half, her equal, Klarke felt as though it was her against the world.

■ ■ ■

"God comes up with mysterious ways to humble folks," Nate said to Persia as they stood in the dining room at Meka's parents' home. Reo had just finished praying in the nursery with Meka when he joined Nate and Persia.

"How you doing, man?" Nate asked Reo.

"Not good, but I'm trying to hang in there."

"How's Meka?"

"Terrible. She says she doesn't blame me, but I blame myself. I didn't even want to have anything to do with that baby at first." Reo began to cry.

"Don't do this to yourself, man," Nate said. "None of that matters. What does matter is that you came around and did the right thing."

"I was forced to do the right thing, but not on my own will. God is punishing me," Reo said.

"Don't put this on God, son," Meka's mother said, entering the dining room. "Always keep in mind that there was another angel with spiritual force thrown out of the heavens. Satan is an attention-getter, son. He's always competing with the Lord. Don't blame the Lord for Satan's work."

"I'm so sorry," Reo said, hugging Meka's mother.

"We don't blame you. We know that you didn't have anything to do with this. It was all her. Now just stay strong while the police do their business," Meka's mother said, kissing Reo on the forehead and walking away.

Reo was a little affected by the remark Meka's mother made blaming Klarke. Nate could sense this.

"You don't think she did it, do you, man?" Nate asked. "I mean, black people don't do that kind of stuff."

"That's what everybody said before the sniper incident, too," Reo responded.

"You claim to know this woman. You've spoken of her as if you two share the same heart. Do you believe she's capable of something this heinous?"

"There's a lot I didn't think she was capable of, Nate."

"You're avoiding answering the question," Nate replied.

"I mean, Nate, people do things all of the time that they, or the people who know them, would have never thought they were capable of doing in a million years. Circumstance and option are a muthafuck."

Detective Edwards was surprised to see Klarke return for questioning escorted by her attorney. He wasn't surprised at all that Reo wasn't with her.

"Tell it to me straight, Gary," Klarke's attorney said to Detective Edwards. "What do you have on my client?"

"It's mainly circumstantial, but it will hold. Especially our Xerox box full of documentation your client was keeping on her husband. I think a sympathetic jury will see it as premeditation," Detective Edwards said. "Your client is looking at the death penalty."

Detective Edwards went over the evidence with a fine-toothed comb with Klarke's attorney. He detailed how Klarke's character would be shot to hell by just mentioning the scheme that she concocted to gain the attention of Reo and his bank account.

"Here you go, Edwards," Sams said, handing him a piece of paper.

"Here's our warrant for your client's arrest right here," Detective Edwards said to Klarke's attorney. "The grand jury has indicted her."

"Don't worry," Klarke's attorney said to her incoherent client. "Mrs. Laroque, are you okay?"

By the time Klarke regained consciousness several people were standing over her. The shock of hearing that she was going to be officially charged with the murder of the baby was unbearable. Her attorney got Klarke to her feet and made sure that she was okay.

"Mrs. Laroque," Detective Edwards said. "I'm sorry we have to do this now, but you have been charged by the State of Ohio with the murder of the deceased child. This is very serious. As you know, you face the death penalty. Help us now with the details and we'll see about a life sentence."

Klarke looked at her attorney, still slightly disoriented, while her Miranda rights were read. Her attorney's expression showed agreement with Detective Edwards.

"May I talk to my client alone for a few moments?" Klarke's attorney said.

"Sure," Detective Edwards said, clearing the room.

"Mrs. Laroque, everything is circumstantial, so if you know anything at this point, if you can recall any single incident that might support a claim of innocence, now is the time to reveal it."

"I don't understand what they want from me," Klarke said.

"They want a guilty plea to spare your life."

"If I plead guilty, then what?" Klarke asked. "Will the case be closed forever?"

"Yes, but you will be spending the rest of your life behind bars. Do you know what happens behind bars to people who commit crimes against children?"

"Do you know what happens to children behind bars?" Klarke asked.

"I don't get it, Mrs. Laroque," her attorney said.

"Do you have any children?" Klarke asked.

"Excuse me?" Klarke's attorney said.

"Do you have any fucking children?" Klarke yelled.

"No," her attorney replied.

"Then you'll never understand."

Klarke entered her guilty plea like a true soldier. She didn't stutter or hesitate as Meka, Reo, and their families pierced her body with their eyes. Klarke didn't even break down and cry when she saw Meka snuggled tightly in Reo's arms as he comforted her pain.

All Klarke could think about were her children, who she made Harris promise would not be in the courtroom to witness their mother being sentenced to live the remainder of her natural life behind bars.

22

Echoes of Thunder

Klarke lay in her cell in disbelief. She couldn't believe for the rest of her life freedom would be a former companion. She tried to think positive thoughts. She thought of what a good father Harris was, and what a good father Reo would be to their baby, who she would give birth to in a few months. Finding out she was pregnant while in jail was devastating, but Klarke still managed to think of every positive thing about her being incarcerated that she could. Although positive thoughts weren't going to change the scenario, negative ones would have only made it worse.

Throughout the hearing and her court appearances, Klarke had pretended not to see Harris in the courtroom. At each court appearance, unlike Breezy and Jeva, who sat directly behind Klarke, he sat in the back of the courtroom, pulling out his handkerchief every now and then to wipe his tears. He never set out to make eye contact with her anyway. He couldn't bear seeing the mother of his children shackled in a prison uniform. After receiving her life sentence, though, Harris made it a point to visit

Klarke before she was transferred from the county jail to the women's penitentiary.

"You always did look good in orange," Harris said. Klarke laughed to keep from crying. The laughter almost turned to tears, but she fought them off.

"My babies. How are they?" Klarke asked.

"Good."

"You're lying."

"Huh?" Harris said.

"Harris, you're lying. I know when I'm being lied to now. I guess I've been doing so much of it myself lately."

"HJ hates the world and Vaughn cries herself to sleep. Then she wakes up crying," Harris said, starting to break down.

"Don't do that, damn it. Don't do it." Klarke said once again, fighting back tears.

"She'll pull through it. She's strong, remember? Like a sun-flower."

"I don't, Klarke. I don't know if this is the right thing to do."

"Harris, don't," Klarke said, cutting him off.

"You're no killer, Klarke."

"And neither is our daughter," Klarke affirmed. "Look Harris, let's not do this. I'm here. The case is closed. I copped a plea and I'm here."

"You call that a plea? You're in here the rest of your life."

"Yeah, but I could have gotten the electric chair."

"But you don't belong here and we both know it. Hell, I've done worse things in my life than you've ever done."

"Why do people on the outside always say that to a locked-up convict? That shit ain't soothing. I'm in here, damn it, and you're out there. There are two types of people in this world, those who get caught and those who don't. No matter which one of those people you turn out to be, you just live with it. Let me live with it, Harris. For the sake of our daughter let me live with this. Whether I take the fall or not, either way it goes I lose my daughter. Just walk away from this."

Klarke looked around at the guards to see if any of them was dipping in on her conversation with Harris.

"I'm just trying to help. I have to help. This is my entire fault. If I had ever thought for one minute this is how things would end up, I swear to God . . ."

"Harris, this is not your fault," Klarke assured him.

"Do you know what Vaughn said to me, Klarke? She said, 'Daddy, you used to call me your favorite girl, then when you and Tionne had another daughter I became *one* of your favorite girls.' She said, 'Daddy, Reo called me his favorite girl, too.' "

"Don't do this to yourself, Harris, and I mean it. Where is the strong man I knew years ago?" Klarke asked.

"He's slowly being chiseled away." Harris spoke in the third person. "He keeps losing the women he loves."

"You're on the outside. You're all our children have to get them through this now, to get them through life. You have to be strong. It will make my days in here a lot easier knowing that you are out there being strong for our children."

Up until now Klarke had not shed a tear, but she could no longer hold them in. The tears flowed like the rhythm to a favorite song. She cried hard, the sniffing, the snorting, the snot, the works. She cried a lifetime worth of tears.

"Oh, baby, I'm so sorry," Harris gulped as he accepted her invitation to cry. "What the fuck happened?"

"You tell me."

Harris couldn't even look at Klarke. There was something else causing his tears. There was something deep-rooted that he could no longer contain.

"This is all my fault. You wouldn't even be here. You would have never met that Reo and you would have never had to scheme in order to get a man to take care of you."

"Damn it, will you stop it? I made my own choices, Harris. You act as if you put a collar around my neck and walked me through life."

"Rawling. He was a decoy, Klarke," Harris said. "It was an arrangement. That's all it was. Who knew it would lead to this?"

"Okay, I'm getting confused. Harris, what are you saying? Harris, what did you do?" Klarke asked, not sure if she truly wanted to know the answer.

"I met Rawling out one night. A couple of dudes from work and I had gone to Club Diamond, and Rawling was in there with a few friends of his own. One of the guys I was with knew one of the guys he was with, so we all congregated. We got to drinking and talking and your name came up. I started talking about my ex, you. When I said your name he mentioned that he had a student in his class named Klarke. It didn't take us long to realize it was you."

Harris could hardly speak he was so choked up, but somehow he managed to continue.

"It was just talk at first. I wasn't serious, but then Rawling called me on it. It just seemed so harmless at the time. I would give him money to pursue you. The two of you would get married, he would decide that marriage wasn't for him and file for an annulment. I would be free of my debt to you. No more alimony payments."

■ ■ ■

"She is one fine woman," Rawling muttered to Harris. "I must admit, I've wanted to tutor her ass several times. How did an old cat like you get a woman like Klarke?"

"Yeah, she is fine, huh? But she ain't two thousand dollar-a-month fine." Harris took a sip of his Beefeaters and Coke as he glared at the chocolate piece of ass that was slowly bouncing down to him. The okay-looking dancer dropped her ass to the black marble floor. It was the same floor that had enticed Harris to install marble under the bar at the home he had purchased for Klarke and the children. The dancer stretched her legs from underneath her into a split. She popped her pussy in the air, pulled her g-string to the side and separated her pussy lips with her fingers. Harris was overly generous when he planted Abe's face on her coochie, considering he noticed what he thought might have been a vaginal wart.

"Is child support included in that?" Rawling asked.

"I wish it were," Harris replied.

"Damn, now I see why them rich white men be killing their hoes. Exes are some costly muthafuckers."

"It would cost more for me to have her killed. I'll settle for paying someone to marry her."

"Too bad OJ didn't think more like you."

"OJ didn't have nothing to do with that, man."

"Oh, you really think so?"

"I know so. It's public record . . . not guilty. The legal system is a godsend when it's jailing black folk. But all of a sudden it needs to be reevaluated when it's setting them free."

"We are surrounded by naked women and we are sitting here talking about a big-ass ashy dude." The two couldn't help but laugh and seal it with a high-five.

"You're crazy," Harris said.

"I'm crazy. Hey, man, you are the one acting like Robert Redford, making indecent proposals and shit," Rawling said to Harris.

"I know, but I wasn't serious. I don't expect you to marry Klarke."

"Why not? Women do it all the time. They running around marrying these little African dudes for fifteen thousand dollar minimum to keep the little bastards in the country."

"I guess it's no different from back in the day when young men knew they were going to get money for marrying a girl. A dowry," Harris said.

"It could have worked. It would have taken a little time. You know how women are after a breakup? They love telling a brotha they just got out of a relationship, that the timing is bad, they need time for themselves, et cetera. It's hard to break that wall down. I was liable to charge you another five grand for that alone. I am a fine muthafucker though. It probably wouldn't have taken too long."

Rawling drank the last sip from his beer, pulled $30 out of his wallet, and laid it on the bar. "I have an early class to teach tomorrow so I guess I better hit the road. It was nice meeting you, Harris, man."

"Yeah, you too, man. Take it easy." Harris stared at his glass momentarily before turning toward the exit door to summon Rawling. "Hey Rawling!" Harris's voice barely made it over the Drawz version of "Thin Line Between Love and Hate" that was pounding from the jukebox. "Let me buy you just one more drink."

Klarke was speechless. She had no words for the brick Harris had just busted her upside her head with.

"How much?"

"What?"

"How much did you pay him? Never mind. Because you know

what? No amount of money in the world is worth being in here."

"Baby, I'm going to get you out of here. I'm going make shit right. I owe you. I'll get the best lawyer money can buy," Harris continued. "We'll find a loophole, or some technicality to get you off. We'll appeal. Maybe Jeva and Breezy might have an idea."

"No!" Klarke interrupted. You are not to talk to Jeva or Breezy about anything."

"They are your best friends."

"Vaughn is my daughter. The fewer people who have to take this to the grave, the less we have to worry."

"Then I'll get you out of here on my own."

"You're talking crazy, Harris. I made a plea; there is no appeal. You know there is nothing you can do for me now. This is me for the rest of my natural life, remember. I'm begging you to leave this alone. Now we both already talked about it and agreed that this was the best thing. Don't get pussy on me, Harris. Think of our daughter. Would you really want to see her here instead of me?"

Klarke faded away as a vision of Vaughn wearing an orange jailhouse jumpsuit appeared before Harris. He couldn't imagine his baby girl being locked up like an animal, but by the same token he hated the fact that Klarke would be.

"I'm the sacrificial lamb. This is how the story ends, Harris." Klarke cried. "Now you focus on raising your three children. You make sure they want for nothing, do you hear?"

"Time," the guard said as her butchlike body hovered over Klarke.

"Remember, Harris . . . shhh," Klarke said, putting her index finger over her lips.

The guard tapped Klarke on the shoulder and Klarke stood up. Handcuffs were returned to Klarke's wrists and she was escorted to the door.

Harris was losing, forever, another woman he loved. He didn't care who saw him bawling like a baby. Reality was whipping his ass as he watched Klarke being walked away in shackles.

As the guard signaled for the door to be buzzed open Klarke turned around and looked at Harris. With her hands in cuffs she raised them to her mouth and this time placed both of her index fingers over her lips. "Shhh," Klarke whispered as tears rolled down her face. "Shhh."

Hey you,

It's been a while, eleven months and two days to be exact. I know because that's how long I've been locked up in this place.

I've been doing a lot of thinking in here. It's not like I have anything better to do. I've come to the conclusion that most people who tell a person they would die for them are full of shit. What is it with society thinking they have to say what a person wants to hear? To die for someone you would have to love them unconditionally. Every love is conditional, with the exception of God's, Jesus', and a mother's love. Just know that if ever someone tells you they would die for you that it's more than likely a lie. They probably don't mean for it to be a lie, but it is, in fact, a lie with good intentions behind it.

Is there really such a thing as a good lie? I mean, some people will lie about the weather outside. They'll tell you the sun is shining with the sound of rain and echoes of thunder in the background.

A lie makes a long story short. I guess that's why men lie to women . . . why women lie to men . . . why people lie to each other. But it's funny how a person will pick the hell out of the truth, huh? Tell someone a lie and they are more apt to roll with it. Lying is hard work, though. Do you know how much energy you drain your body of and how much stress you put it through in order to tell a lie? On top of that you have to store the lie in a memory bank so that you don't slip up in the future. A born liar dies a liar.

But you know something? Sometimes lies save lives. The truth hurts, so a lie is kind of like a Band-Aid on life. It covers up some foul-ass acts.

I know you have no idea what I'm trying to say. You probably think this is a bunch of jail talk. Well, that's okay. This letter wasn't meant to heal you. It was meant to free me—my mind, anyway.

I'm hoping you don't see that this letter is from me and toss it out with the garbage before reading it. I know I agreed to let you live your life and raise our child as you see fit without any interference, so I promise I will never contact you again in any form.

You know . . . this doesn't hurt as bad as I thought it would. The entire time I was carrying our child I always knew that it would never know who its natural mother is (look who's waiving the rights to their child now). You are a good man and I know you will raise the baby to be a wonderful human being. I have no worries. Therefore I can sleep at night and live with myself for the decision I have made.

So I guess, in short, I just want to say thank you in advance. Until next lifetime, when our souls mate, I'll love you always!

KAT

As Reo finished reading the letter tears rolled down his face. He was deeply moved by Klarke's words, but still he could not let go of the fact that his baby daughter had been caught in the crossfire of her love for him.

With all of his heart, Reo knew that Klarke truly loved him in spite of her cunning means of gaining his love in return. Reo was now forced to close the book on what he thought was going to be a romance novel. He was left to raise his and Klarke's son alone.

Reo read Klarke's letter over and over again. Finally he was interrupted by a small cry whimpering through the baby monitor.

"Daddy's coming," Reo said as he carried the letter over to the garbage can. His life with Klarke, the good times, flashed before his eyes. It was those good times that reminded him of the good in Klarke, the good that their child would most likely inherit. Reo folded the letter and decided to place it inside his pants pocket.

Once he made it to the nursery, he picked his son up out of the crib and looked into his sparkling eyes that were so full of life. He had eyes like his mother.

Reo walked over to the Noah's Ark trunk next to the baby's crib. He removed the small hand-carved elephant from on top of it. It was the same elephant he had given Klarke on their first date. Inside the trunk was a picture of him and HJ with the clown at HJ's birthday party, and the paper Vaughn had written about him for school. Reo placed inside the trunk the letter Klarke had written him, with the intent of perhaps one day, maybe, sharing with his son stories about the person whose eyes he had inherited.

Reading Group Guide

1. Were you able to identify with Klarke? If so, to what extent? Do you believe Klarke did what she felt she had to do as a mother to protect her daughter?

2. Which character did you enjoy the most? Why?

3. If there were to be a sequel, what issues would you like to be addressed? And which character, if any, could you do without returning? Why?

4. Was Reo realistic? Could you imagine Reo being the perfect soul mate for Klarke as you read the story? Do you feel Reo should have stood by Klarke's side to the end despite the fact that she pleaded guilty to the murder of his baby?

5. Who do you think killed the baby and why?

6. Were you satisfied with the outcome of the book, or were you starving for more?

7. Do you feel as though karma played a role in anyone's outcome? Please explain.

8. Does the author set herself apart from other writers in this particular genre? If yes, how? If no, why not?

9. What is your take on family values and its relation to a) Klarke's choice to protect her child?, b) Reo's initial choice to forgo his rights as a father?, c) Jeva accepting money over knowing her birth parents' true identities?

*Turn the page for a sneak peek at the
not-to-be-missed sequel.*

WHEN SOULS MATE

JOYLYNN M. JOSSEL

Coming Soon from St. Martin's Griffin

Visit www.joylynnjossel.com

for more!

Speak of the Devil

Reo sat in his study at his desk, pounding away at his computer keyboard. It had been suggested by his editor that he start working on his autobiography. As hard as it was for Reo to pen some of the most painful times of his life, it was also a form of therapy for him. And that's why he was so quick to oblige. His wife had been a major part of his life since high school, and he often bounced ideas off of her and welcomed her input.

Reo had just printed out the first chapter for her to review. She sat beside him, scanning down the pages as Reo started typing away on the second chapter.

"So do you think she'll try to get back in your life?" Meka said, interrupting Reo's thoughts. She had hardly focused on anything else since finding out that Klarke had been released from prison. "I mean, to try to see Junior that is."

Reo knew that Klarke trying to see his and her son was the least of Meka's worries. Meka was the type of woman who would hand over Junior in a handbag, willingly, if it meant Klarke staying out of their lives forever. It was the thought of Klarke trying to see Reo that truly stressed Meka.

"I don't know," Reo replied as he stopped typing and stared off into space. "Knowing that KAT didn't have anything to do with the murder of our child changes everything."

"Changes everything, like what?" Meka asked, slamming the papers against her lap. "And her name is Klarke."

Before Reo could reply, their potentially explosive argument was interrupted by the ringing of the door bell.

Meka sighed. "I'll get it." She stood up and set the papers down in the chair, but before storming out of the room she said, "But our discussion is not by any means over. We'll finish talking about this just as soon as I return."

Meka left the study and headed down the hall of their ranch-style home. It was the same home Reo had purchased for himself after he received his first major book deal. Meka had made some interior changes since she had moved in. There seemed to be some kind of floral theme going on. Every hanging mirror, just about, was garnished with some wild flower or another. Even the kitchen place mats had sunflowers printed on them. The living-room furniture set even had a floral pattern. The overkill of a woman's touch didn't bother Reo, though. As a matter of fact, he hardly noticed it, since he spent more time away on book signings than he did in his own home.

"Who is it?" Meka yelled as she unlocked the door. When Meka, not waiting for a response, flung open the door, she couldn't believe her eyes. The nerve of the uninvited guest to show up on her doorstep. And on top of that, the nerve of them to look as though they had especially dressed for the occasion.

"It's me," Klarke said through the security screen door with a smirk on her face. She stood outside on the doorstep looking like she had just been ripped from the pages of a magazine. Her makeup was flawless, not too much and not too little. It was just enough to give her skin a perfect bronze tone. She had on a light brush of pink eyeshadow over top of the three silver strokes of eyeshadow. The two light coats of mascara made her eyelashes look a mile long. She wore just a hint of pink rouge on her perfect cheekbones. The pink, shimmery lip-gloss on her full, pouty lips brought out the pink in her pink and white Reeboks that Klarke had purchased specifically to match the solid pink one-piece terry-cloth pants designed by J-Lo that she was wearing.

The day before, Klarke had visited Scizzors, the beauty shop she had gone to a few times before she went to jail. The stylist, Terri Deal, had dyed Klarke's hair a dark brown and cut it into multiple long layers that flowed down her back. It was whipped into a feathered Farrah Fawcett do. Klarke held a striking resemblance to the beautiful Lisa Raye. By no means did Klarke look as though she was pushing forty. As a matter of fact, she looked as though she was barely legal.

"Is Reo home?" Klarke asked, innocently batting her eyes as if she had every right to be on their doorstep. "Tell him it's his baby's mamma."

"Speak of the devil," Meka said as she stared down Klarke with the most evil expression she could muster up.

"And the devil appears," Klarke replied with a wink.

"You've got some nerve showing up at our—my and my husband's—home," Meka said, almost through her teeth.

Klarke was shocked. No one had warned her that Reo had re-married Meka while she was in jail. She had asked that no one speak of him because he was no longer a part of her life, but damn! If she had known his intent was to marry Meka, then she might have thought twice about signing the divorce papers he served her while she was locked up. Although Klarke wanted to just fall out and cry, run away in defeat even, she just swallowed and maintained her composure.

"I don't want to cause any trouble for you and Reo," Klarke said softly, but Meka cut her off.

"The hell you don't," Meka said, bobbing her head.

"Really, I don't," Klarke said innocently.

"I see right through you," Meka said, snickering under her breath. "Do you think the fact that you didn't directly harm our child changes anything? Are we supposed to look at you as some martyr now? Do you think all of this gives you the green light to just show back up in our lives unannounced?" Meka pointed her finger at Klarke through the security screen door. "Your daughter, the child you were responsible to raise properly, murdered our daughter. No matter what excuses you try to make up or what you say, I know that the apple doesn't fall too far from the tree. You are not to be trusted. So don't show up here with your violin expecting us to weep to your sad song."

Klarke stood outside on the porch, silent, as her eyes filled with tears of pain and anger. It had taken so much courage for her to come to Reo's house. She wanted to turn the car around a thousand times as she drove from Toledo to Columbus. At that very moment Klarke knew she had made a mistake showing up there.

"You're right. I'm sorry," Klarke said as she turned to walk away. She had no right at all to be there.

"Wait a minute," Meka called to Klarke, stopping her in her tracks. Meka unlocked the security screen door, cracked it, and poked her head through it to have one more say to Klarke. "If you're thinking about trying to renege on your agreement of staying out of Junior's life, just remember, you signed papers terminating your rights as his mother. I'm his mother now. I'm the one he calls mommy!" Meka quickly pulled her head back and slammed the front door proudly in Klarke's face.

Klarke ran to the car in tears. Meka had gotten the "W" (win). She had broken Klarke down, and Meka knew it as she brushed her hands together as if she had just taken the garbage out to the curb. Meka looked at herself in the oval mirror surrounded by ivy and smiled at herself before returning to the study to join Reo.

"Who was that at the door?" Reo asked Meka as she entered the study.

"Some kid trying to sell me chocolate candy bars," Meka said as she walked over to the chair, picked up the papers, and sat down.

"Did you buy any?" Reo asked.

"You know what chocolate does to my face," Meka said with a smile.

Once again the doorbell rang. Meka quickly jumped up from the chair. "I'll get it. It's probably that kid again. You know they don't take 'no' for an answer now days."

Meka rushed out of the study and down the hall.

"Hey," Reo called to Meka. "If they have the caramel-filled ones, go ahead and buy me a couple."

Meka knew it was Klarke again, probably coming back to beg and plead. Meka swung open the door and began to scold.

"Did you not understand—" Meka started to say, but Breezy quickly put a halt to her words. Breezy pulled open the security screen door that Meka had failed to lock after her encounter with Klarke. She grabbed hold of Meka's hair, snatching her out of the door and twisting her down to the ground. Meka began to scream as Breezy tried her hardest to pull every strand of Meka's hair out of her head.

"Talk shit now, bitch!" Breezy said, snatching the bun right out of Meka's hair. You couldn't even see her face as strands of hair went awry.

"Get off of me! Stop it!" Meka screamed, clawing at Breezy's hands.

"Oh, you want me to stop?" Breezy asked as she twisted Meka's hair around a hand in a tight grip. "Say uncle. As a matter of fact, say mommy. Call me mommy, bitch. Let's see who calls who mommy around this muthafucka."

"Breezy, don't!" Klarke said catching up to her and pulling her off of Meka. "She's not worth it, girl."

Breezy looked up at Klarke, breathing heavily. It took her a minute to come to her senses, but eventually, she did. Breezy turned Meka's hair loose and stood up.

"Don't you ever fucking say the wrong thing to my friend again . . . ever!" Breezy screamed while pointing at Meka as tears of anger began to roll down her face. "She's more of a woman than you will ever be. It wasn't too long ago when you were the mother putting a price tag on her child. How easy we forget."

Meka lay on the doorstep rubbing her sore head.

"Baby, what's going on?" Reo asked, alarmed as he rushed to Meka's side. Reo came around the corner to find Meka lying between the screen door, her hair a mess, strands of hair scattered about. Reo knelt down and tried to help Meka up, but she angrily pushed him away.

"Leave me alone. I'm okay. You just go call nine-one-one," Meka said, standing up and stepping inside the door to where Reo was standing. "I want those bitches arrested for assault and battery!"

By this time, Breezy and Klarke were making their way back to the car.

"Who? Who did this to you?" Reo said as he quickly walked outside to seek out the culprits.

Klarke had managed to drag Breezy back to the car and forced her into the passenger seat, Breezy begging Klarke the entire time to allow her just one more stab at Meka.

"You only came along for moral support, remember?" Klarke said to Breezy. "Now we've probably got assault charges on our hands."

Klarke and Breezy knew they had to get out of there before the police did decide to show up. In a prestigous neighborhood such as this one, they knew it wouldn't be long before they heard the wail of the sirens.

Klarke ran around to the driver's side. As she opened the car door, she looked up only to lock eyes with Reo, who was standing on the porch. When their eyes met it was like a bolt of lightening had struck.

Klarke stood frozen, unable to move. With Reo it was vice versa. Seeing one another after all of those years was like bumping into a childhood sweetheart in the grocery store. But so much had taken place in their lives. It wasn't that easy.

Klarke wanted to throw herself at Reo's feet and beg for his forgiveness. She wanted him to forgive her for all of the lies and deception she had subjected him to. She wanted him to tell her that he forgave her for all of the games she had played. She wanted so much for him to know that although she used shady methods to plan their initial encounter and forming a relationship, that their loving each other was fate. She wanted to remind Reo of how much she loved her children, how she would do everything within her power to protect them from anything, including jail. As a father he had to know how strong of a bond a parent has with a child. He, too, would have done the same thing if he had been in her shoes. What parent wouldn't sacrifice their own freedom for that of their child's if they had the chance?

Reo couldn't explain the feeling that came over him when he looked into Klarke's eyes. It was almost as if she hadn't been locked away in prison at all, but more like she had been away on a long vacation and had finally made her way back home to him. He wanted to greet her with a warm kiss, roses, and a bottle of Alizé. But he had a new life now that had no place for her. There was no place for KAT—Klarke Annette Taylor—in Reo's life, but he couldn't say the same for his heart.

Realizing that time was of essence, that the police would probably arrive shortly, and that she had no intentions on ever going back to jail again, Klarke quickly got into the car. She fumbled getting the key into the ignition and then started the car. She pressed the gas, and the car engine roared. Klarke looked at Reo one last time, who hadn't moved an inch. She then looked straight ahead and drove away, mumbling those famous words under her breath, "I'll be back."

CPSIA information can be obtained at www.ICGtesting.com
Printed in the USA
LVOW07s2139130215

427029LV00001B/82/P

PRAISE FOR *MISSING*

"[A] smart, stylish novel . . . [Detective Sergeant Manon Bradshaw] is portrayed with an irresistible blend of sympathy and snark. By the time she hits bottom, professionally and privately, we're entirely caught up in her story, [which] ends up being as much about loneliness and longing as it is about the solving of a crime. . . . It's the ensemble cast gathered around Manon Bradshaw that's entirely convincing. With luck, we'll be seeing more of them in the future."   —*The New York Times Book Review*

"Nuanced suspense that's perfect for Kate Atkinson fans."   —*People*

"If you've binge-watched *Happy Valley*, *The Fall*, or *Prime Suspect*, have I got a book for you: Former journalist Susie Steiner's *Missing, Presumed* offers a close view of diverse British characters coming to terms with both a murder and their own imperfect lives. You might come to *Missing, Presumed* for the police procedural; you'll stay for the layered, authentic characters that Steiner brings to life."   —BETHANNE PATRICK, NPR

"The missing person in question in this wonderfully written novel is a twenty-four-year-old female Cambridge postgraduate student whose empty apartment bears signs of a bloody struggle. . . . Ms. Steiner tells her well-populated and surprise-filled story in the present tense and from five different points of view, including that of the missing student's mother. . . . The author gets inside the minds and lives of her book's socially disparate personalities with the grace of a novelist of manners, even as she pulls tight the strands of one of the most ambitious police procedurals of the year. Detective Bradshaw's biting wit is a bonus."   —*The Wall Street Journal*

"What's harder: finding a Cambridge student who has gone missing from her apartment, or finding a decent date online? Brooding detective inspector Manon Bradshaw has a ticking biological clock and a ton of pressure coming from superiors to locate the woman (hopefully alive) whose father happens to be a doctor to the royal family. Susie Steiner's *Missing, Presumed* has future BBC miniseries written all over it."   —*Redbook*

"*Missing, Presumed* is fast-paced, twisty and full of realistic characters and scenarios. With any luck Detective Bradshaw will be back in future installments, since she is a quirky, likable character, capable of carrying a series."
—*The Vancouver Sun*

"I loved Susie Steiner's detective Manon Bradshaw from her opening scene, ... an agonizing internet date. The story of Bradshaw and her team in investigating the disappearance of a daughter of the English upper class is framed as a police procedural but drenched in character and setting, with pinpoint detail that breathes life and color into every sentence."
—Raleigh *News & Observer*

"Where Steiner excels is in the depth and clarity with which she depicts her characters. Manon is sad and lonely, estranged from her sister and something of a misanthrope. But she's also funny and clever, and interesting. ... I defy you not to fall for her.... It all adds up to a world that feels much bigger than the novel in which it is contained.... Here's hoping there'll be more to come from DS Manon Bradshaw." —*The Guardian*

"This novel stands out from the pack in two significant ways: first of all, in the solution, which reflects a sophisticated commentary on today's news stories about how prejudices about race and privilege play out in our justice system; and second, in the wounded, compassionate, human character of Manon. Her struggles to define love and family at a time when both are open to interpretation make for a highly charismatic and engaging story."
—*Kirkus Reviews* (starred review)

" A vein of dark humor pulses beneath this compelling whodunit with an appealing, complicated heroine at its center." —*Publishers Weekly*

"A complex, gripping read ...The mystery behind Edith Hind's disappearance is filled to the hilt with provocative breadcrumbs, making for a page-turning literary crime novel that is nicely balanced by the all-too-relatable human foibles of lonely DS Manon Bradshaw."
—SUZANNE RINDELL, author of *The Other Typist* and *Three-Martini Lunch*

MISSING, PRESUMED

MISSING, PRESUMED

A NOVEL

· · ·

SUSIE STEINER

 RANDOM HOUSE / NEW YORK

2017 Random House Trade Paperback Edition

Copyright © 2016 by Susie Steiner

Published in the United States by Random House, an imprint and division of Penguin Random House LLC, New York.

RANDOM HOUSE and the HOUSE colophon are registered trademarks of Penguin Random House LLC.

Originally published in hardcover in the United Kingdom by The Borough Press, an imprint of HarperCollins Publishers, London, and in the United States by Random House, an imprint and division of Penguin Random House LLC, in 2016.

Grateful acknowledgment is made to the following for permission to reprint previously published material:

HOUGHTON MIFFLIN HARCOURT PUBLISHING COMPANY: Excerpt from "Little Gidding" from *Four Quartets* by T. S. Eliot, copyright © 1942 by T. S. Eliot and copyright renewed 1970 by Esme Valerie Eliot. Reprinted by permission of Houghton Mifflin Harcourt Publishing Company.

NEW DIRECTIONS PUBLISHING CORPORATION: One line from "Do Not Go Gentle into That Good Night" from *The Poems of Dylan Thomas* by Dylan Thomas, copyright © 1952 by Dylan Thomas. Reprinted by permission of New Directions Publication Corporation.

UNITED AGENTS ON BEHALF OF WENDY COPE: Excerpt from "Some More Light Verse" from *Serious Concerns* by Wendy Cope (London: Faber & Faber, 2002), copyright © 2002 by Wendy Cope. Reprinted by permission of United Agents on behalf of Wendy Cope.

LIBRARY OF CONGRESS CATALOGING-IN-PUBLICATION DATA
Names: Steiner, Susie, author.
Title: Missing, presumed: a novel / Susie Steiner.
Description: New York: Random House, 2016
Identifiers: LCCN 2015037112| ISBN 9780812987744 (trade paperback: acid-free paper) |
ISBN 9780812998337 (ebook)
Subjects: LCSH: Women detectives—England—Fiction. | Missing persons—
Investigation—Fiction. | Women college students—Fiction. | BISAC: FICTION /
Literary. | FICTION / Mystery & Detective / Traditional British. | FICTION / Crime. |
GSAFD: Mystery fiction. | Suspense fiction.
Classification: LCC PR6119.T446 M57 2016 | DDC 823/.92—dc23
LC record available at https://lccn.loc.gov/2015037112

Printed in the United States of America on acid-free paper

randomhousebooks.com

6 7 8 9

Book design by Susan Turner

For John & Deb

The end of all our exploring
will be to arrive where we started

—"Little Gidding," T. S. ELIOT

MISSING, PRESUMED

MANON

. . .

SHE CAN FEEL HOPE EBBING, LIKE THE CHRISTMAS LIGHTS ON FADE IN Pound Saver. Manon tells herself to focus on the man sitting opposite, whose name might be Brian but could equally be Keith, who is crossing his legs and his foot bangs her shin just where the bone is nearest the surface. She reaches down to rub it but he's oblivious.

"Sensitive," his profile had said, along with an interest in military aircraft. She wonders now what on earth she was thinking when she arranged it, but then compatibility seemed no marker for anything. The last date with a town planner scored 78 percent—she'd harbored such hopes; he even liked Thomas Hardy—yet Manon spent the evening flinching each time his spittle landed on her face, which was remarkably often.

Two years of Internet dating. It's fair to say they haven't flown by.

He's turned his face so the light hits the thumbprints on his glasses: petroleum-purple eggs, the kind of oval spiral they dream of finding at a crime scene. He's talking about his job with the Rivers Authority while she looks up gratefully to the waiter who is filling their wineglasses—well, her glass, because her companion isn't drinking.

She's endured far worse than this, of course, like the one she traveled all the way to London for. "Keep an open mind," Bri had urged. "You don't know where the man of your dreams might pop up." He was tall and very thin and he stooped like an undertaker going up the escalator at Tate Modern—giving it his best Uriah Heep. Manon thought that escalator ride was never going to end, and when she finally got to the top, she turned without a word and came straight back down, leaving him standing at the summit, staring at her. She got on the first train out of King's Cross, back to Huntingdon, as if fleeing the scent of decomposing flesh. Every officer on the Major Incident Team knew that smell, the way it stuck to your clothes.

This one—she's looking at him now, whatever his name is, Darren or Barry—isn't so much morbid as effacing. He is talking about newts; she's vaguely aware of this. Now he's raising his eyebrows—"Shopping trolleys!"—and she supposes he's making a wry comment about how often they're dumped in streams. She really must engage.

"So, one week till Christmas," she says. "How are you spending it?"

He looks annoyed that she's diverted him from the flow of his rivers. "I've a brother in Norwich," he says. "I go to him. He's got kids." He seems momentarily disappointed and she likes him the more for it.

"Not an easy time, Christmas. When you're on your own, I mean."

"We have a pretty good time, me and Col, once we crack open the beers. We're a right double act."

Perhaps his name's Terry, she thinks sadly. Too late to ask now. "Shall we get the bill?" He hasn't even asked about her name—and most men do ("Manon, that's a funny name. Is it Welsh?")—but in a sense it's a relief, the way he just plows on.

The waiter brings the bill and it lies lightly curled on a white saucer with two mint imperials.

"Shall we split it?" says Manon, throwing a card onto the saucer. He is sucking on a mint, looking at the bill.

"To be fair," he says, "I didn't have any wine. Here." He shows her the items on the bill that were hers—carafe of red and a side salad.

"Yes, right, OK," she says, while he gets out his phone and begins totting up. The windows are fogged and Manon peers at the misty halos of Huntingdon's festive lights. It'll be a cold walk home past the shuttered-up shops on the high street, the sad, beery air emanating from Cromwell's, and out toward the river, its refreshing green scent and its movement a slithering in the darkness, to her flat, where she has left all the lights burning.

"Yours comes to twenty-three eighty-five. Mine's only eleven pounds," he says. "D'you want to check?"

MIDNIGHT, AND MANON SITS WITH her knees up on the window seat, looking down at the snowy street lit by orange streetlamps. Flakes float down on their leisurely journey, buffeting, tissue-light. The freezing draft coming in through the sash frame makes her hug her knees to her chest as she watches him—Frank? Bernard?—round the corner of her street and disappear.

When she's sure he's gone, she walks a circuit of the lounge, turning off the lamps. To give him credit, he was stopped short by her flat—"Whoa, this is where you *live*?"—but his interest was short-lived and he soon recommenced his monologue. Perhaps, now she comes to think of it, she slept with him to shut him up.

The walls of the lounge are Prussian blue. The shelving on which the television stands is fifties G Plan in walnut. Her sofa is a circular design in brown corduroy. Two olive-green velvet wing chairs sit to each side of it and beside one is a yellow-domed seventies floor lamp, which she has just switched off at the plug because the switch is busted. The décor is a homage to mid-century modern, like a film set, with every detail of a piece. The scene for a post-ironic East German comedy perhaps, or *Abigail's Party;* a place absolutely bursting with taste of a charismatic kind, all of it chosen by the flat's previous owners. Manon bought the lot—furniture, lamps, and all—together with the property itself, from a couple who were going abroad to "start afresh." At least, that's what the man had said. "We just want to shed, you know?" To which Manon replied, "Shed away. I'll take the lot." And his girlfriend looked around her, swallowing down her tears. She told Manon how she'd collected all of it, lovingly, on eBay. "Still, fresh start," she said.

Manon makes her way to the bedroom, which at the point of sale was even more starkly dramatic: dark navy walls with white-painted floorboards and shutters; a whole bank of white wardrobes, handle-less and disappearing into themselves. You had to do a Marcel Marceau impression to discover the pressure points at which to open them.

The previous owners had a minimalist mattress on the floor and a disheveled white duvet. Under Manon's tenure, however, this room has lost much of its allure: books stacked by the bed, covered with a film of dust; a cloudy glass of water; wires trailing the floor from her police radio to the plug, and among them gray fluff and human hair, coiling like DNA. Her motley collection of shoes makes opening the cupboards additionally tricky. She kicks at a discarded pair of pants on the floor, rolled about themselves like a croissant, throws off her dressing gown (100 percent polyester, keep away from fire and flame), and retrieves, from under the bedclothes in which he has incongruously lain, her flannelette nightie.

Up close he smelled musty. And vaguely sweet. But above all, foreign. Was this her experiment—bringing him close, out of the world of strangers? Was she trying him out? Or smelling him out, as if intimacy might transform him into something less ordinary? People who know her—well, Bryony mainly—disapprove of her emotional "immaturity," but the fact is human beings are different up close. You find out more through smell and touch than any chat about newts or shopping trolleys. She becomes her mammalian self, using her senses to choose a mate. She's read somewhere that smell is the most efficient way of selecting from the gene pool to ensure the best immune system in offspring. *So she puts out on the first date!* She's a scientist at the mating frontline.

In her darker moments—and she can feel their approach even now—she wonders if she is simply filling an awkward gap in the conversation. Instead of a ghastly shuffling of feet and "Well, that was nice, but we should probably leave it there," she forces the moment to its crisis. It's like running yourself over to avoid shaking hands.

In the bathroom, she picks up her toothbrush and lays along it a slug of toothpaste, watching herself in the mirror as she brushes. Here is the flaw in her argument: the sex was pretty much a reflection of the night's conversation—all newts and shopping trolleys and a definite lack of tumultuous waterfalls or even babbling brooks, if you wanted to pursue the waterways analogy.

She looks at the springy coils of her hair, bobbing ringlets, brown mostly but with the odd blond one poking out like a rogue pasta twirl—*spit*—unruly and energetic, as if she is some child in a playground, and discordant now—*spit*—that she is on the cusp of her forties. She can feel herself gliding into that invisible—*gargle*—phase of womanhood, alongside those pushing prams or pulling shopping wheelies. She is drawn to the wider fittings in Clarks, has begun to have knee trouble, and is disturbed to find that clipping her toenails leaves her vaguely out of puff. She wonders what other indignities aging will throw at her and how soon. A few centuries ago she'd be dead, having had eight children by the age of twenty-five. Nature doesn't know what to do with a childless woman of thirty-nine, except throw her that fertility curveball—aches and pains combined with extra time, like some terrifying end to a high-stakes football match.

She wipes a blob of foam off her chin with a towel. Eventually, he asked about her name (her moment in the sun!) and she told him it meant "bitter" in Hebrew, and she lay back on the pillow, remembering how her mother had squeezed her secondary-school shoulders and told her how much she'd loved it, how "Manon" was her folly, much as her father objected. A Marmite name, you either loved it or loathed it, and her mother loved it, she said, because it was "all held down," those "n"s like tent pegs in the ground.

There was silence, in which she supposed he wanted her to ask about his name, which she couldn't really, because she wasn't sure what it was. She could have said, "What about yours?" as a means of finding out, but by that point it seemed unnecessary. She had smelled him out and found him wanting. Her mind was set on how to get him out of her flat, which she did by saying, "Right, then, early start tomorrow," and holding open her bedroom door.

She smooths out the pillow and duvet where he's been and pushes her feet down under the covers, reaching out an arm from the bed to switch on the radio, with its sticker reminding her it remains "Property of Cambridgeshire Police." A cumbersome bit of kit, and no one at detective sergeant rank is supposed to have one at home, but it is not a plaything. It is the method by which she overcomes insomnia. Some rely on the shipping forecast; Manon prefers low murmurings about road traffic accidents or drunken altercations outside Level 2 Nightclub on All Saints Passage, all of which she can safely ignore because they are far too lowly for the Major Incident Team.

"VB, VB, mobile unit to Northern Bypass, please; that's the A141, junction with Main Street. UDAA."

Unlawfully Driving Away an Automobile. Someone's nicked some wheels. Off you pop, Plod. The voice begins to sound very far away as Manon's eyelids grow heavy, the burbling of the radio merging into a pebbly blur behind her eyes. The clicks, switches, whirring, receivers picked up and put down, colleagues conferred with, buttons pressed to receive. To Manon, it is the sound of vigilance, this rapid response to hurt and misdeed. It is human kindness in action, protecting the good against the bad. She sleeps.

Sunday

MIRIAM

. . .

MIRIAM IS WASHING UP, LOOKING OUT OVER THE BLEAK WINTER GARDEN—
the lawn smooth as Christmas icing. She'd have liked a bigger garden,
but this is about as good as it gets in Hampstead.

She's thinking about Edith, her hands inside rubber gloves in the
sink, washing up the Le Creuset after lunch's monkfish stew. The pan-
cetta has stuck around the edges and she is going at it with a scourer.
She's so lucky, she thinks, to have a girl, because girls look after you
when you get old. Boys just leave home, eventually going to live cheek
by jowl with their mothers-in-law.

And then she curses herself, because it goes against all her feminist
principles—requiring her daughter, her clever Cambridge-educated
daughter, to wipe her wrinkly old bottom and bring her meals and au-
diobooks, probably while juggling toddlers and some pathetic attempt
at a career. Her own career hadn't recovered from having the children,

those three days a week at the GP surgery feeling like time-filling in between bouts of household management.

Feminism, she thinks, has a long way to go before men take on the detritus of family life—not the spectacular bread and butter pudding, brought out to "oohs" and "aahs" (which always has the whiff of *Man makes pudding! Round of applause!*), but ordering bin liners and making sure there are enough lightbulbs. When the children were little, Miriam felt as if she were being buried under sand drifts from the Sahara: music lessons, homework folders, kids' parties, thank-you notes, fresh fruit, and meter readings. It silted up the corners of her mind until there was no space for anything else. Ian sidestepped it with strategic incompetence so that his mind remained free to focus on Important Things (such as work, or reading an interesting book). It was one of the biggest shocks of adult life—the injustice—and no one had warned her about it, certainly not her mother, who felt it was only right and proper that Miriam take on the more organizational tasks in life because she was "so *good* at them." She'd better not think about it now, or she'll get too angry.

She lifts the Le Creuset onto the white ceramic draining board, wondering why people rave about the things when they are almost un-lift-able and scratch everything they touch. Ian hasn't made it home for lunch so she's eaten the stew by herself, struggling to lift the damn heavy pot in order to pour the remains into a Tupperware box and struggling also not to feel hard done by. She's alone so much these days, in part because when the sand drifts receded, along with the departure of the children, they left an excess of time, while Ian's existence maintained its steady course, which was essentially Rushing About, Being Important. She has to fight, very often, not to take umbrage at the separations and also their converse, to retain some sense of herself in their togetherness. Wasn't every marriage a negotiation about proximity?

The temptation she feels during periods when he's very busy and she's left alone a lot is to become defiantly independent, but then it's hard to let him back in. She has to make herself defrost in order to come back together. She wonders how far Edith has traveled on this rather arduous journey or whether she has even embarked on it with Will Carter. When you are in your twenties, the problem of dependence and independence can be swiftly resolved by ditching your boy-friend, and she has a feeling Edith might be on that brink.

She squeezes out a cloth and wipes the kitchen surface in slow, pensive swirls. It is a slog, marriage. How could she tell her daughter that without making it sound worse than it is? Built on hard work and tolerance, not some idea of perfection as Edith might have it. Miriam has had the thought in the past that Will Carter's handsomeness is an emblem of Edith's belief in perfection—or at least her belief in appear-ance. She hasn't realized yet that looks count for nothing, that how things appear is nothing next to how they *feel*.

If she were here now, Edith would no doubt spout forth—rather self-righteously—on all the shortcomings that she herself would *never* put up with in a marriage, as if there were some gold standard from which she could not fall. She gets that from Ian, of course. Well, life isn't like that. It is full of compromises you never thought you'd make when you were young. Marriage is good—that's what she should say to Edith: that you get to an age when your attachments are so solidly stacked around you, like the bookshelves that reach to the ceiling in the lounge, and they are so built into the fabric of your life that compro-mise seems nothing next to their dismantling. Yes, she thinks, running the cloth under the tap and enjoying the warmth of the water through the rubber gloves, with age comes the recognition that one is grateful for love.

Looking out again to the garden and squeezing the cloth, she thinks back to their evening at the theater last night, all their clever friends who loved to talk about books and philosophy. She'd wondered if they had more money and more sex (they couldn't possibly have *less* sex) and better second homes or whether they were, perhaps (*well, one shouldn't hope for these things*), secretly miserable and having affairs.

"Are we all here?" Ian said, on the snowy pavement outside the Almeida Theatre. "Ready to set off?" Miriam looked at him, her hand-some husband with his impeccable scarf in a cashmere double loop. He was commanding—*well, that's Ian of course*—but also vaguely distracted. Work, probably—it so often took over his mind. That was the cost of being married to the Great Surgeon, and she noticed, then and there, a swell of pride.

They set off toward Le Palmier restaurant, talking and laughing, arms looped in arms. Miriam walked by herself, though she was at the center of the group. She'd been crying—*Lear* always made her cry— and her body had a rather pleasurable spent feeling of release, while her stomach growled in hot anticipation of dinner. Someone took her arm—it was Patty, pressing her body close to Miriam's. She got a blast of Patty's perfume—Diorissimo—even over the cold.

"I thought that was just wonderful, didn't you?" said Patty.

"Completely wonderful. I feel wrung out, in a good way," said Miriam. "Thought Gloucester was a bit shouty, though."

"Yes, quite. Why can't they just *say* their lines? There's a sort of Shakespearean delivery, which is so irritating. Ah, here we are. I'm starving."

They handed their coats to the maître d', who bowed slightly while draping them over his arm and then hung them in a wardrobe. Their table was broad and round and the spotlights twinkled off the glasses and highlighted bright circles on the starchy white tablecloth. Miriam felt happy with her very cold glass of something dry and Argentinian (Ian being the wine expert). She watched him across the table feeling in his breast pocket and taking out a pair of reading glasses with leopard-print frames—a pair she'd bought for £4.99 at Ritz Pharmacy on Heath Street. He put them on the end of his nose in order to read the menu, while Roger talked away at him and Ian laughed at something Rog was saying. The glasses were small and feminine on his patrician face.

"Darling," she said to him, reaching an arm across the table, but with her head turned to Patty, who was talking about the play.

"Oh yes, sorry," he said, and took off the glasses to pass them to her so she could read her menu. "Come on, everyone, are we ready to order? Nothing will come of nothing, after all."

And everyone laughed.

Xanthie told the table she'd been rereading Boccaccio's *Decameron*. "It's so witty! I mean, really, I've been laughing out loud on the bus." And the way she said "bus" was like some glorious egalitarian experiment. Their laughter around the table had the tinkle of money in it.

Now Miriam is peeling off her rubber gloves as her thoughts return to her daughter, as if to a favorite refrain—her beloved topic. Yes, she hopes for more for her daughter than the things she anticipates for her. Now she frowns. It doesn't make any sense. She wants Edith to fulfill her daughterly duties (thoughtful Christmas presents, regular phone calls, eventually home-cooked meals when Miriam's in her dotage) yet at the same time she wants to liberate her; she wants for her total professional freedom and a truly feminist husband who empties the dishwasher without being asked. And mingled in, she wants her daughter to share in her suffering, the same sacrifices, and she doesn't know why. Is it a hunger for fellow feeling or a fear that Edith might succeed where she failed? That Edith might actually throw off the shackles when Miriam . . . Well, she's spent twenty-odd years effectively wiping the kitchen surfaces and doling out antibiotics for cystitis. It's so *complicated*.

She reaches into the cupboard under the sink for a dishwasher tablet, thinking about her beautiful daughter who is still young, who has a flat belly and tight little arms, who can still carry off a bikini, who has yet to fall in love, and she feels pricked with envy. Oh, Will Carter is all right, but he's a bit up himself and she suspects he isn't the One. Edith still has that ahead of her—all the pleasure and pain of it. Lucky thing. The older you get, the less choppy life becomes. But Miriam misses it too—the lurching outer edges of feeling that accompany youth. Nothing is exciting anymore, though to listen to Xanthie, you'd think reading Boccaccio's *Decameron* on the bus was euphoric. Perhaps it is only Miriam for whom life has become duller and sadder, like the silver hair on her head.

"Where've you been? I woke up and you weren't here," she says, smiling at Ian, who is coming through the kitchen doorway carrying an orange Sainsbury's bag and bringing the cold in with him. He is wearing his polo-neck sweater and tracksuit bottoms. He has that curious inability that the upper classes have to wear casual clothes convincingly. She wonders if he emerged from his mother's vagina in a sports jacket.

He comes over to her at the kitchen counter, kisses her cheek, and she smells the winter on him. "Got up early and went to the office— I've got a ton of paperwork hanging over me."

"Poor you," she says. "Shall I warm you up some stew?"

"No, no. I'm fine."

"I can microwave it; it's no trouble."

"No, I had a sandwich. Edie call yet?"

"Not yet, no."

"Tell you what, let's light a fire. It's freezing outside."

"Good idea; that'd be lovely," she says, and the house feels complete again with him in it. His smell, his bigness, his company. Married love has been a revelation to Miriam—not the lurching outer edges of feeling, no, but the sheer depth and texture of it. All her memories—twenty-five years of them, especially the really vital ones, like having the children—involve him. And loving the children. He is the only person on earth who can talk about the children with the same exhaustive gusto that she does, as if they are both examining Rollo and Edith at 360 degrees. And she is wrong to be quite so consumed by feminist rage. It's not as if he does *nothing*: the cup of tea, for example, he brings her in bed each morning; his final checks on the house at night (doors locked, lights off); the way he'll run upstairs to find her slippers when she sighs exhaustedly and says, "Darling, would you . . . ?" These are small, repetitive acts of love.

They spend the afternoon in a Sunday-ish homely fug, the log fire spitting and then dying down in the lounge. It brings back the smoked, countrified scent of Deeping, where they will spend New Year. (*Must buy lightbulbs for Deeping,* she makes a mental note to herself.) Miriam could watch those flames for hours, until her face is cooked and her eyes dried out. Ian is in and out of his study, some Mozart piano concertos drifting through the house from his iPod dock. She potters about too, tidying up mostly, putting some washing on or reading the "Review" section of the newspaper.

In the evening the doorbell goes and Miriam opens it to the florist delivering three hundred stems of scented narcissi and the fresh holly wreath for her front door. This and her mulled-wine spice and the clove oranges she makes will fill the house with festive perfume. Just as she is closing the door against the night, the phone rings and she answers it, still holding the narcissi like an opera singer at her curtain call.

"Calm down, Will. . . . No, she's not here. . . . Since when?" she says, as Ian joins her in the hallway, slightly stooped and craning to hear. "So you've just got home?"

"What's he—" says Ian, but Miriam frowns at him to shush.

"Well, she's probably out at a friend's or gone to Deeping," she says into the phone while looking into Ian's eyes.

Miriam listens, placing the flowers onto the hallway table, then she cups her hand over the phone's mouthpiece. "He says he found the door open and the lights on. She's left everything in the house—her keys, her phone, her shoes. Her car's outside. Even her coat's there."

Ian nudges her aside to take the phone off her. "Will? It's Ian. When did you last speak to her? Have you called Helena?"

She watches him frowning at the hall table, listening. Then he says, "Right, call the police. Straightaway, Will. Tell them what you've told us. Then call us straight back." He puts the receiver down.

"No," says Miriam, looking into Ian's eyes and shaking her head, her hand clamped over her mouth. "No, no, no, no."

MANON

· · ·

MANON CRIES SOME MORE. IT IS THE WAY BRYONY LISTENS, AS IF SHE HAS an arm around her, that makes Manon's barriers dissolve.

"Was he awful, then?" asks Bryony. "As bad as the last one?"

"No, that's the thing, Bri, he was all right, but that's the worst feeling, that it was just all right, nothing special. Just nothingy, like I can't ever rise to the occasion."

"Maybe you need to give it more of a go. Nothing's perfect, you know."

"He wanted me to pay more for the meal because I had wine."

Bryony is silent.

"He didn't ask me anything about myself."

"Yeah, well, that's just men, I'd say."

Manon presses her fingers into her eyes. This is what she *doesn't* want Bryony to say. People in couples, they always want you to settle for anything, as if you are a second-class citizen. Just because you're lonely, you have to make do with the scrap ends.

"You want me to make do with the scrap ends."

"We're *all* making do with the scrap ends, Manon," says Bryony. "This is something you fail to grasp."

"The sex was quite good, unexpectedly," says Manon.

"You what?"

"Well, I thought it'd be rude not to."

"Don't make a joke of it."

Manon doesn't reply.

"You don't need to do that, y'know," says Bryony, her voice full of disappointment.

"No, I know."

"When's the next one?"

"Next week. Not sure I can stand it."

"Treat it like a job. It's a game of numbers. Your lucky one will come up eventually. Only don't shag them. Not all of them, anyway."

Manon can't stand to talk about it anymore. "How are the kids?" she says. "How was your Sunday?"

"Freezing playground, eight A.M. Started to sleet but we stayed there anyway. Me and Peter had a row. Lunch at eleven. Bobby threw a cup of milk down me, then shat in his pants. The usual."

"Relaxing."

"I can't wait to go to work tomorrow, just to have a sit-down. Canteen lunch? Whaddya say? I'll buy you a watery soup to cheer you up. Or are you frontline officers too important?"

A familiar prod, beneath which is Bryony's peevishness over all the excitement she thinks she's missing out on. She's an officer at Cambridgeshire too, but mostly deskbound since the children—filing court papers or on disclosure.

"My diary is remarkably free at the moment," Manon says. "Never know what the day'll throw at me, though. So yes, great. In theory. One-ish?"

"Don't know if I can hold out that long. I'm on toddler time. And, Manon?"

"Yes?"

"You'll be all right, you know. You'll find him—the right man. I just know you will."

Manon puts the phone down and shuffles under the duvet. She turns the dial on the radio, hears the reassuring murmuring, which blends into the fuzz before sleep, when all her darkest ideas bubble up. "Victor Bravo, one–two, VB, quite concerned by what we've got here. Can I have a supervisor please and can you notify on-call SIO?"

Manon opens her eyes and sits up. She knows what the gaps mean, what Oscar One in the control room is getting at without being able to state it over the airwaves. Something serious. The balloon's gone up. Senior Investigating Officer? That's jumpy. Others will be hearing it too and start heading that way, but George Street is around the corner from her—five minutes if she jogs it. She hears DI Harriet Harper's voice over the radio, saying she's on her way.

Manon can get this; it's hers. She flings back the duvet, listening intently to the radio while she pulls on trousers with one hand, reaching for her phone with the other.

"Missing female," says Harriet on the phone. "Signs of a struggle. Meet me there."

THE COLD CUTS INTO THE short space between Manon's scarf and her hat, but the place it hurts most is her toes. Bloody Chelsea boots. She might as well have worn flip-flops, and she'll likely be out in the cold all night, at best in a stationary car with a phone pressed to her ear. She digs her hands deeper into her pockets and hunches her shoulders up to her ears, hearing the clean squeak of her boots in the fresh powder. The trees hold lines of snow like sleeves on every branch. The snow has made a rather unprepossessing urban street (one of the routes out of town and close to the railway line) prettier than it is. As she turns up the garden path to number 20—a neat little worker's cottage, identical to its neighbors—she uses a gloved hand to free her mouth of scarf, but Davy speaks first.

"High-risk misper; looks like it, anyway," he says, stamping in the snow. He claps his hands. The tip of his nose is glowing red.

"Any sign of forced entry?" says Manon.

"Door was open, but not forced. There's some blood, hallway and kitchen, not that much of it, to be fair, and there's the coats on the floor," says Davy. "Where's your paper suit?"

"Where's your scene log?" she says, looking past him into the house.

"Shit, you got me," he says, smiling, and she is reminded how good it is to be around DC Davy Walker. His simple affable kindliness. If all men were like Davy, there would be no wars.

"Can I get a suit from your car?"

"Here you go," he says, holding up his keys. "I'll start a log now. Don't tell Harriet."

She returns, rustling in white paper, her egg-shaped hood encasing her face, and holds Davy's arm as she pulls on some blue outer shoes.

"Very fetching," he says.

"I think so," says Manon, at his knees. "Who's in there?"

"Harriet and the missing girl's boyfriend. She's keen to shut the place down. I'd wait out here if I were you."

Manon straightens. "Bollocks, I won't touch anything. Why've we not got a DCI on this?"

Davy shrugs. "Christmas rota. Draper's on an aggravated burglary in Peterborough. Stanton's in the Maldives. Staffing's back to the bone."

She steps into the hallway, where the coats have dropped from their hooks like fallen soldiers. They scatter the floor. Some of the hoods retain the pointed imprint of the hook on which they hung. Light anoraks (one navy, one red), a fleece (gray), two thick winter coats of the padded kind, one an olive parka with fur trim, the other navy. Leaning against the wall is a rucksack with the handle of a tennis racket poking out; some trainers that line the skirting; a Hessian shopper with the words "Huntingdon Estates" written on it. In front of her, on the laminate floor leading to the kitchen, are a couple of drips of blood—not a copious spattering or pooling of the kind they saw in killings, but the type of blood that might come from an injury such as a cut.

Harriet appears in the kitchen doorway.

"Manon, can you come through? Watch the floor, there," she says as Manon tiptoes toward the threshold. "Don't step in the evidence. Manon, this is Will Carter. Mr. Carter, this is Detective Sergeant Bradshaw. Mr. Carter has reported his girlfriend, Edith Hind, missing. He returned home at nine this evening to find the front door ajar, the coats in disarray, and blood over there." She points to a larger spatter on the kitchen floor and some on the cupboard door just above it.

"Miss Hind's phone, keys, shoes, and coat were all in the house," Harriet says.

Will Carter is pacing, running a hand through his hair. He is preposterously handsome, wearing tracksuit bottoms and a cable-knit sweater, as if he has just stepped out of a razor advertisement. Manon glances at Harriet, who gives her a look that says, *Yes, you can shut your gob now.*

"Is there anyone she might be with—a friend or relative?" asks Manon.

"I've called everyone I can think of," says Carter. "I've called her parents; they're in London. They haven't heard from her. And her friend Helena, she was with Edith last night at a party. She says she dropped Edith back here at around midnight. Hasn't seen or heard from her today."

"When did you last speak to Edith?" says Harriet.

"Saturday early evening, just before she went out with Helena."

"Did she sound her normal self?"

"Yes. I mean, it was a very quick call."

"And, I'm sorry, Mr. Carter," says Manon, "you were where?"

"I've been away for the weekend in Stoke. Visiting my mum."

"Is there anywhere she might have gone?" asks Manon. "A favorite place? Might she have just wanted time alone?"

"I don't see where she could have gone without her keys or her phone or her car."

"Car's outside," explains Harriet.

"I've gone through the contacts on her phone, called people who were at the party on Saturday night, our friends at college. Everyone I could think of. No one's heard from her. I started to panic. Her parents told me to call the police. I mean, not that I wouldn't have called, but you never know if you're overreacting, d'you know what I mean? Can you get officers out there looking for her? It just doesn't feel right. Something's not right."

"What about her passport?" asks Manon. "Is it here?"

"I don't know," Carter says. He goes to one of the kitchen drawers.

"She keeps it in here," he says, pulling it out. He turns, holding up a small burgundy book. "It's here. There's a second home, Deeping—it's her parents' place, about half an hour's drive away, near March. Edith's got keys, but they're on her key ring, there." He points to a bundle of keys on the kitchen table amid bits of paper with numbers written on them, an open diary, and mobile phones. "And, anyway, you can't get there without a car."

"Someone else might have driven her, perhaps?" says Manon.

He shrugs. "But who? The phone, her keys—she never leaves that stuff. I mean, who does?"

"Is there any reason she might have wanted to frighten you? Were you on good terms?" asks Harriet.

Carter is shaking his head before she has even stopped talking. "No, no, she wouldn't. We were on the best of terms. Everything's good. Better than good. When will you start searching? It's freezing outside and she hasn't got her coat."

"How do you know, sir?" says Harriet. "The coats appear to have fallen all over the place."

"I checked," says Carter. "I looked through them. I don't know if I should have, but I wanted to know if she had it or not."

"It doesn't look like you've gone through them. They appear to be as they fell."

"It only took a cursory look to see that her coat is there—the green one. The parka with the fur trim."

"Might she have taken another one?"

"She hasn't, I know she hasn't, and, anyway, why would they be all over the floor like that?"

"A word, Manon, please," says Harriet, gesturing outside the kitchen. They step around the blood drips in the hallway and into the lounge next door, which is under-furnished and struggling to emerge from the miasma of an energy-saving lightbulb. They speak in low murmurs.

"Blimey," whispers Manon. "He's . . ." She blows out through her cheeks.

"Very agitated, yes. What do you think? Enough to qualify as a high-risk misper? Davy and I have done a search of the house. We need to scope this country place, Deeping, soon as."

"Anything upstairs? Any signs of struggle?"

"Not that I can make out. I want to shut the place down so we don't lose anything, get SOCO looking at that blood."

"She might have disappeared in the early hours this morning," says Manon, looking at her watch.

Harriet nods. "That's twenty hours."

They are silent. They both know the first seventy-two hours are critical for a high-risk missing person. You find them or you look for a body.

"If that blood's hers, which is pretty likely, then she could be out there bleeding in some garden or lay-by. We need dogs and we need a helicopter. I want you to set parameters for the early search. I want you to get as many bodies up here as you can to begin house-to-house, and we'll need to start scoping for CCTV."

Manon nods. "Can I have Davy?"

"Yep."

"Shame Stanton's missing out."

"That's what happens when you fuck off to the Maldives."

MANON SENDS OFFICERS STRAIGHT TO Deeping, but there is no sign of the girl there. The helicopter takes two hours to get to them from the Midlands. It hovers loudly, searching back gardens, alleys, and motorway verges for a woman in her twenties clutching an injury, or a slumped figure. The helicopter's underside is like a black insect against the navy sky, the beat of its blades rhythmic and relentless. It covers swaths of ground in a way officers on foot or in cars cannot hope to do. If its throbbing drone hasn't woken the neighbors, then the dogs will, panting and snuffling under hedges and straining up paths, the scent of Edith Hind still on their snouts from her nightdress. Or the door knocks, neighbors emerging with bed hair in the brash light of their hallways. It's clod-footed, this type of early search—urgent and messy. Manon coordinates it all on the phone in Davy's unmarked car, calling in officers from across the county, hearing them report back from house-to-house, keeping Harriet up to date back at the station, where she is re-interviewing Will Carter.

At 6:00 A.M. there is a hiatus, when there are no more calls she can make, so Manon returns home for a shower and to change her clothes. She pulls at her eyes in the mirror and sees the undernourishment of the night on her skin but also the adrenaline, which has made her pupils dilate. This is why she entered the police—cases like this. Whoppers, the ones you wait weeks or months for, a whole career, even.

Harriet is the same. She'd been made DI after her work on the Soham murders, the case that shaped Cambridgeshire policing more than any other because it was so high profile and because it came to define the battle lines between police and press. The disappearance of two pretty girls in the shimmering, lazy news lull of August. The press had been on their side for one or two days, driving the appeals for witnesses, and then it grew ferocious, like a dog unmuzzled, with resources that outstripped the Major Incident Team's. Officers suspected hacking, enraged that they had to wait days for authorization to trace phones; they found themselves showing up to interview potential witnesses, only to find reporters had been there an hour earlier. Some of the more brazen Sunday tabloids hired private detectives, and they were all over it, corrupting with their money, turning over evidence, leaving their mark.

Manon holds in her hand a photograph of Edith Hind, auburn-haired and smiling—a face almost confident, the gorgeous bloom of childhood still radiating from her skin. She is wearing a mortarboard and gown, with a scroll in her hand. Graduation day at Cambridge. Just like the photo Manon's father has on the shelf.

Yes, she thinks. *This will be big.*

She learned as much as anyone from Soham but remained a DS, because if you were smart you realized things didn't get better when you climbed the ranks. She wanted to stay on the ground, interviewing suspects, running her team of DCs and civilian investigators, not holed up in an office attending management courses and filling in Main-Lines-of-Inquiry forms. It certainly wasn't, as Bryony maintained, that she was too busy humping her way around the Internet to focus on the exams.

She's left Davy at the scene in George Street, letting in SOCO— the Scenes of Crime Officer, as it is currently known, or CSI or FSI.

She has never known an organization to love an acronym as much as the police, nor to change them so often. She longs for the day some sleepy mandarin comes up with the Crime Unit National Taskforce.

She picks up the keys to her car and goes to collect Davy, to take him to Cambridgeshire HQ for the morning briefing.

DAVY

. . .

HE STANDS AT EDITH HIND'S FRONT DOOR AND LOOKS DOWN THE PATH to the men in pressed suits with Puffa jackets over the top, loitering at the gate and stamping the snow off their boots. The frozen morning air emerges from their mouths in white clouds. You can tell they're the locals, because of the suits and the polished shoes—national press are scruffy. Chinos with round-neck sweaters in jaunty colors if they're broadsheet; rumpled suits that fall at the shoulder and concertina into creases at the base of the jacket if they're tabloid. Local reporters, on the other hand, have to live among their subjects: attend their council meetings, Christmas fairs, and sports days. A pressed suit's the least they can do.

Davy sees DS Bradshaw's preposterous car pull up just beyond the men, on the opposite curb. A seventies Citroën—long nose, sagging leather seats, spindly steering wheel with gear stick to the side. She's convinced it makes her look like Audrey Hepburn, but behind her back, the DCs at the station make reference to Inspector Clouseau, putting on exaggerated French accents and saying, "In the neme of the leur," while watching from the window as she parks. Davy doesn't care about impressions. He hates traveling in her car because it's always cold, often doesn't start, and smells vaguely of wet dog. Thank God it's usually him driving, her on the phone, in a warm and anonymous unmarked police vehicle.

"C'mon, tell us something," says one of the reporters at the gate, but Davy pushes past him.

"How long's she been missing?" asks another. "Any signs of a struggle? Has she been kidnapped?"

"I'm sure there'll be a briefing soon," says Davy, careful not to meet their eyes.

He ducks into Manon's car and looks at her, but she's counting up the men at the gate through the smears on the windscreen.

Yes, she's grumpy, but a skinny latte soon takes the edge off her, most days, anyhow—like throwing a steak into the lion enclosure. He wishes he had one to offer her now but instead he has to watch, unarmed, as she squints into the shards of broken sun. He rubs his hands together and blows into them.

Perhaps it's her age that's making her bad-tempered, and he can understand that. She must be at least thirty-nine, the loneliness rising off her like a mist. He'd be the same if he didn't have Chloe. He's seen Manon, more than once, red-eyed, coming out of the second-floor toilets, and his heart goes out to her on those occasions, watching her hurriedly wipe the snot away and try to act normal. Well, pissed off, which is normal. Him and Manon, though—somehow it works, he doesn't know how, and this seems to rankle Chloe. Even now, pulling down on his seatbelt, Davy's face falls as he remembers the time he described Manon as "good in a crisis."

"Good how?" Chloe asked, trying to seem casual about it, but he knew all about "casual" and its parameters. Chloe's questioning could put CID to shame. "You share a joke, do you? Manon make you laugh much, does she? I'd use straighteners on those ringlets, if it were me." Whenever Davy makes a positive comment about her—and Davy works hard at being positive about pretty much everything—Chloe's face can darken as fast as the April sky.

"She sometimes sees things that others don't," he'd said on this particular occasion, shovel in hand, cheerfully digging himself deeper into the pit. "Makes connections. Bit left field sometimes."

"Well, I don't see how that's any more than most women have got—intuition. I mean, I can make connections between things if I want to," Chloe said, then barely talked to him the rest of the day.

Manon puts the car in gear, her eyes still on the men, saying, "Four. Just the locals."

"'Course it's the locals. Still early doors."

"Won't be long before they ring the tabs. This time of year, missing girl. Nothing like a festive stiff to warm the cockles of your front page."

"She's probably just got a new boyfriend—done a runner," says Davy.

"Leaving her phone and keys and the door wide open? I don't even go to the toilet without my phone. And what about the blood? No, I'd say she's definitely come to harm."

She's put her aviator shades down, pulling out from the curb. Davy looks at her and shakes his head.

IT'S ONLY A TEN-MINUTE DRIVE to the station from George Street. They jog up the steps of Cambridgeshire HQ, a festival of sick-yellow brick squatting in an acreage of car park. For Davy, climbing these steps with an important job to do makes him inflate with pride and elation. He wishes someone could see him, Detective Constable Walker of "Cambridgeshire Constabulary: supporting law-abiding citizens and pursuing criminals relentlessly since 1974." This mission statement is actually on the Cambridgeshire police website, but it could have been something Davy came up with.

When he brought Chloe for a tour of HQ, he was smiling to himself the whole time, and even though she described it as "a cross between a Travelodge and a conference center," it hadn't dented the dignity of his calling. She said the reception, with its curved wooden desk, spider plants, and smell of brewing coffee, reminded her of an STD clinic, but what he saw—what he was so proud of—was the electronic notice board announcing the life-and-death work going on here (*2:00–4:00 p.m., conf. room 3: crime data integrity working group; protocol*

*briefings: ambulance teams, Hinchingbrooke; UK cross border agency; 4:00–
6:00 p.m., Commissioner*). So much sexier than the jobs he could have
had: regional manager for Vodafone or selling fridges in Currys, like
his school friends. Which would you rather? Flogging some twenty-
four-month contract with three thousand free minutes or wondering
whether the Dutch woman got on a train to Brighton to kill herself
there or whether she was murdered? Human stories, base and sexual. The police operated in the seedy lowlight: drug runs, burglars in
botched stickups, murderers who said they were nowhere near the
scene but whose smartphones provided a handy GPS map of their
movements. Boyfriends controlling girlfriends, friends paying off debts,
love triangles, honor killings. That, or: "Would you like to extend your
warranty on this microwave for an extra two years, sir?"

"Look at you, Davy," Chloe had said, as he showed her the forensics
lab and the phone-tracing department. "You've really drunk the Kool-
Aid, haven't you?"

Davy and Manon enter the MIT department just as Harriet is
gathering team four for her briefing: DC Kim Delaney, DC Nigel Williams, Colin Brierley—a retired DI, now civilian investigator who runs
the tech side—and a couple of other DCs.

They fall in behind their desks, shaking off their coats.

"You're going to have to hit the ground running, Stuart, I'm afraid,"
Harriet is saying as Manon shakes hands with the new recruit—an
extra civilian investigator to type interviews into the HOLMES computer system and listen to Colin's un–politically correct diatribes, lucky
chap. "Baptism of fire. These guys will show you the ropes."

Davy nods his most welcoming nod at Stuart. Sometimes CIs were
retired officers, like Colin, sometimes young, like this one, fresh from
a three-day induction course. They were cheap and they didn't leave
the office.

"Right, everyone," Harriet continues. "Edith Hind, twenty-four,
Cambridge postgrad student, missing from the house she shares with
Will Carter in George Street. Parents have driven up and are waiting
downstairs, so let's get a family liaison officer with them ASAP. Main
lines are as follows. One: scene and examination. SOCO are in. I've
just had a call from them: two wineglasses—one clean on the kitchen
worktop, the other broken in the bin with traces of blood at its edges."

"She could have been waiting for someone," says Manon.

"That was my thought," says Harriet. "Two wineglasses out ready for a rendezvous, one of them becomes a weapon. We'll see what forensics tell us on that score.

"Two: search ongoing, including dogs. Polsa should be on board by midday today. That's Police Search Adviser," she says to the new chap. "The search teams, in other words. Three: house-to-house. Four: FLO and victimology. Five: media. We'll get a photo of Edith out this morning. I'm meeting with Fergus in an hour to discuss press strategy. Six: intel work. Colin, you've got her phone and her laptop. Let's trace her car reg on ANPR—that's Automated Number Plate Recognition, for our new recruit here. And Will Carter's too, while we're at it. I want all of the council's CCTV looked at. Seven: persons of interest. That's Will Carter, obviously, and Helena Reed, the friend she was with on Saturday night. Is that enough to be getting on with?"

"Hypothesis, boss?" asks Nigel. Manon says he's needy, always looking to senior officers for answers. Davy would never express something so judgmental, though it's fair to say Nigel is permanently exhausted since having the twins.

"I would say she's opened the door to someone she knows or at least to someone she wasn't immediately afraid of. The blood indicates an injury, possibly when someone tried to remove her from the house. The amount of blood doesn't suggest a murder on site; it's more likely it's come from a cut of some kind. A sexual encounter of some sort? He makes advances, she's not keen, and there's a blow from the wineglass in the tussle. All supposition at this point. We are within the golden hour, so let's press on."

MANON
. . .

SHE PULLS OUT A SWIVEL CHAIR AND WHEELS HERSELF NEXT TO COLIN, who smells woody—from the obscure brand of cigarettes he smokes.

"What's her phone telling us, then?" she asks.

"In terms of the victim's usage, nothing past eight P.M. on Saturday night, when she texts the friend, Helena Reed," says Colin.

"What does she say in that last text?"

"'There in five. E.'"

"Anything else?"

"Before the party she does some texting. Someone called Jason F."

Manon reads Colin's screen.

What time u getting there? E.

Later, somewhere to be first.

Don't be long, will you?

Why not?

Wouldn't like you to miss anything . . .

"There are others too," Colin says. "She texts her tutor, Graham Garfield, to say, 'Hope to c u tonite.' He replies, 'What's going down?' Trying to pretend he's not fifty-seven, if you ask me."

"And she says?"

"'Karaoke, tequila, and bad behavior.' To which he replies, 'On my way!'" says Colin.

"What about Facebook?"

Colin clicks on his screen and up pops a collage of Edith—her neck, her arms, brown legs crossed, laughing, her head thrown back. Edith cuddling a cat. Edith in cutoff shorts. Edith wearing a Stetson. Black-and-white, some with colors blown out by Instagram, which gives them a smoky, seventies sheen. Beneath these are comments to the tune of "Gorgeous!" and "Beautiful, beautiful girl" and "Stunning." Each photo is "liked" by Will Carter. In a few she's in a living room, stretched out on the sofa with her feet in Will Carter's lap as he nurses a goblet of red. In many of the images, another girl is somewhere off-center or in the background, curled in an armchair, reading; just a half of her face, a lick of her hair.

Over four hundred photographs.

"They're all of herself, pretty much," says Colin.

Edith's posts are random music lyrics, Bruce Springsteen mostly. The odd literary article about Seamus Heaney or Toni Morrison. "Bo Diddley is my new jam." "Nick Cave is my new jam."

"She has four hundred and eighty-two 'friends,'" Colin adds, drawing quote marks in the air.

"D'you know how many I've got?" says Manon, a yawn stretching her face, while Colin scrolls down. "Four. One's my dad. One's the electrician. I'm not even sure I know the other two."

"She's a member of these groups," says Colin, clicking again. "Guerrilla Gardeners."

"What do they do?"

"They grow food on communal ground. Recipes ... Here's a photo of a hot pot they made using free veg picked from a community wasteland garden. She's a member of Cycle Power—a lobbying group that aims to ban cars."

"Scroll up a minute. What's that?" says Manon, pointing at the screen.

Colin clicks on the image and Manon reads Edith Hind's caption:

Bunting made from recycled copies of the FT. Happy Christmas, planet!

She and Colin look at each other.

"It's a wonder she wasn't murdered sooner," says Colin.

"Those are exactly the sorts of thoughts I want you to keep to yourself," Manon says, rising. "Keep at it, Colin. Her hard drive, Google searches, matches on all her phone records." And then she marches across MIT to Harriet's office.

"So what was the interview with Carter like?"

"Seems genuinely worried," says Harriet, hitching at her bra strap. "Keeps crying, pacing, asking for an update on the search. We need to be all over his weekend in Stoke. We can ask the Hind parents a bit more about their relationship, and the friend, Helena, whether there was anyone else in the background, boyfriend-wise. Tabs are already ringing the press office, Fergus said."

"It won't be like Soham," says Manon. "Not in this climate, not after phone hacking. Things have changed."

"Don't bet on it, not with her parents being who they are."

"Who are her parents?"

"Sir Ian and Lady Hind. He's an ear, nose, and throat surgeon. Fits the royal grommets or something."

"Oh God."

"Yup. We have to tread carefully; the type who'll complain over anything."

"Is it a ransom job, then? He must be worth a bit."

"We'd have heard from them by now. Anyway, I'm not handing this to any centralized fucking crime unit, no way."

She gets up, pacing behind the desk, as if the speed of her thoughts is physical. The wings of her jacket are pinned back by her hands on her hips. She's full of fire, unbridled. If Manon ever went missing, she'd want Harriet to head up the search.

"Once Polsa's on board, the pressure will ease off a bit," Harriet says, as much to herself as to Manon.

The police search adviser and his specialist teams knew how to find people, or at least where to look. They would take the search farther and wider than that clumsy first night: across meadows, along railway tracks, into woods, behind the doors of lock-up garages, in attics and cellars, and soon enough down below the opaque surface of rivers.

Harriet looks at her watch. "Eight-thirty. If she went missing shortly after midnight on Saturday, then we're talking thirty-two hours. It's sub-zero out there."

"I'll send someone to bring in the friend, Helena Reed, shall I?"

"Yup. I'll go and talk to the parents. Urgh, this is the bit I hate—they'll be frantic. Then I'm meeting Fergus in the press office. We'll probably do a short briefing at eleven, just me and the agencies and locals. Got to get those photos of the girl out and an initial appeal. We need to look at her bank activity. Can you start someone on that?"

MANON AND DAVY SLIP INTO interview room one, where Sir Ian is pacing in a navy wool coat.

"So, hang on a minute, you're saying there isn't a DCI on duty to run the search for my daughter?" He has an imperious face, straight nose, pale eyes, and thin lips. Charles Dance without the ginger coloring.

"DC Walker and DS Bradshaw enter the room," says Harriet to the recording device. "It's quite normal, Sir Ian, for a DI to run a case such as this. If you'd like to sit down, there are a number of things we'd like to ask you."

"What I want to know first is who is conducting the search. Who is *actually* out there in the snow, searching for her, because if she's injured—"

Lady Hind, who sits at the table opposite Harriet, takes his hand and holds it to her cheek, then kisses the back of it, and this seems to give him pause. Her hair is gray, in a straight bob, with a beautiful streak of white framing her face. Her coat hangs expensively, her fingers glinting with diamonds.

"Sit down, darling," she says, her voice quavering with suppressed tears. "We must help them in any way we can."

Sir Ian takes up a chair next to his wife.

"Thank you," says Harriet. "Edith's phone shows a few missed calls from you over the course of the weekend, Sir Ian. Were you having trouble reaching her?"

"We always have trouble reaching her, don't we?" he says to Lady Hind. "She's terrible at calling back. So we call, and we call." At this he gives Harriet a strained smile. "We were anxious to know her plans for Christmas, weren't we, darling?"

"She hadn't told you her plans for Christmas?" Manon asks, directing the question at Lady Hind.

"Edith's fond of prevaricating. She can be . . . noncommittal, would you say, Ian? With us, anyway. We'd agreed she and Will would spend Christmas with us in London and then she'd said, 'You never know,' or something to that effect."

"You never know what?" asks Manon.

"I took it to mean she couldn't be certain Will would join us."

"So there was trouble between them?" Harriet says.

"No, not trouble," says Lady Hind. "Ambivalence, I'd say. They're only twenty-four, after all. They're not married."

"And this ambivalence," says Harriet, "would you say it was more on her part than his?"

"Yes," says Lady Hind.

"Has there been any violence between them—heated rows, say? Would Edith have reason to be fearful of Mr. Carter?"

"No, no, no," says Sir Ian. "It's not like that. It's ordinary stuff. Will is a marvelous fellow, devoted to Edie."

"But if he sensed her feelings were cooling, perhaps—"

"Detective, we are not that sort of family. I'm sure you deal all the time with people whose lives are chaotic, who drink and brawl and abuse one another. But none of us—these things are not part of our lives, our experience. I'd be very surprised if Will is involved in this."

"Right," says Harriet. "Can you think of anyone who would want to harm Edith?"

The Hinds look at each other, their expressions bewildered. "No, we really can't," says Lady Hind. "Can you tell me, how do you . . . Please, you have to find her, I can't . . . The thought of her lost, you see . . ." Her eyes brim as she looks at the officers, one to the other.

"I'll explain how we go forward from here," says Manon. "Search teams will work in concentric circles out from the house and, at the same time, we'll be building a picture of Edith, working outward from her most intimate circle—yourselves, Will Carter, Helena Reed. We'll look at all aspects of her life, based on what you tell us, her phone, computer, bank cards. So it's important you leave nothing out."

"She doesn't have any bank cards," says Sir Ian. "She feels the whole banking industry is corrupt. According to Edie, if none of us used banks, then the whole global economic collapse wouldn't have happened. It's not a view I share, but she holds these beliefs very strongly. If she could pay everyone in muddy vegetables and repaired bicycle tires, she would, but her landlord wouldn't have it."

"OK, so how does she live? Where does her income come from?" asks Harriet.

"Me," he says. "I give her a MoneyGram transfer via the post office every month—fifteen hundred pounds on the first. She pays the rent on the cottage in cash to the landlord—that's seven hundred fifty pounds, I think. He lives next door. I pay the utilities directly from London. The rest she lives off."

"So there would've been quite a lot of cash in the house," says Harriet. "She would have been seen collecting wads of it at the post office. . . ."

"Look, I feel it's risky," says Sir Ian. "And I've argued with her about it. I've said I'd rather she has a bank account into which I can transfer the funds. But she just won't have it. She says someone has to break with the status quo. I think she'd prefer not to receive any money from me, to do everything her own way, on her own terms. Twenty-four-year-olds are like that. So I don't argue with her, because I want her to have my help."

"Also," says Lady Hind, "and we discussed this, oh God, endlessly, because it worried us, but we reason that seven hundred fifty pounds goes more or less straight to the landlord, so it's not as if it's all under the bed."

"You get to a point," Sir Ian adds, and it's as if he and his wife's sentences are a continuation, "where you don't want to fall out with your children, because you don't want to lose them. The balance of power shifts, you see. I want her to have my money and these are the terms on which she'll have it."

"How many people know about this cash arrangement?"

"Well, Will, of course. We have sort of been supporting Will by default, because he lives in the house and we pay for the house," says Lady Hind. "As to others, Edith doesn't keep quiet about her views. She's quite vocal."

"So this weekend," Harriet says, "there should have been how much in the cottage, at a guess?"

Sir Ian glances at his phone. "It's the nineteenth, so she's halfway through the month," he says. "Christmas is a bit more expensive, so I'd imagine no more than three hundred pounds. Surely not enough for someone to . . ."

"You'd be surprised," says Harriet. "Why not pay her rent directly? Why not transfer that, like the utilities?"

"The landlord gives her a slight reduction in return for cash-in-hand. I assume he's fiddling his taxes somewhat."

"Fifteen hundred pounds is a generous allowance," says Manon. "Is she extravagant?"

"Quite the opposite. Edith believes in treading lightly on the earth."

"But she has a car."

"An electric car," says Lady Hind. She swallows, and Manon sees she's keeping down a swell of desperation. "A very old electric car. A G-Wiz. It used to be my run-around. Edith needed it when she moved to Huntingdon—to get to lectures and supervisions at Corpus and to Deeping, which is only half an hour from here."

"We'll need to take a closer look at Deeping; I hope you don't mind—get our forensics teams out there," says Harriet.

"It's almost impossible to get to without a car. Middle of the Fens, about three acres," says Sir Ian. "Quite a rough place, really. Edith loves it there but, like I say, without the G-Wiz . . ."

"She might have gone with someone else," says Harriet.

He nods. "Would you like my keys?"

"No, it's all right, I've got Edith's set. Can I ask, is there any way she could gain access without her keys? A spare set at the property, perhaps?"

"Yes, in the porch, high up. If you feel along the architrave, there's a key resting there for emergencies," says Sir Ian. "The house is in the middle of nowhere. Hardly anyone even knows it's there, so we're quite lax on security."

Harriet is writing in her notebook. She looks up and says, "Now, we just need to get an account of your movements over the weekend so we can eliminate you both from the inquiry."

"Yes, of course," says Lady Hind. "We were at the theater on Saturday night with friends. *King Lear* at the Almeida. After the theater, we went for supper at Le Palmier—six of us. We left there about midnight. Yesterday, we were at home mostly, with the fire on—it was so *cold*. Ian went to the office briefly in the morning, didn't you? I made a monkfish stew for lunch. In the afternoon, we pottered about at home, reading; I watched bits of a film—one of those World War Two black-and-white ones. Ian was in and out of his study. In the evening, I took a delivery from my florist—she was getting all her Christmas orders out, hence why she was delivering so late on a Sunday. Then—this was about nine—Will rang, worried sick about Edith."

"And your friends at the theater," Harriet says. "Could we have a list?"

"Rog and Patty," says Sir Ian, looking at Harriet's notebook. "That's Roger Galloway and his wife, Patricia. I'm sure their security detail will confirm everything for you."

Manon, Davy, and Harriet shoot a glance at one another and Harriet says, "A word outside, you two."

"Don't say anything," hisses Harriet, like an angry swan. "Don't fucking say anything until we're in my fucking office." Manon is right behind her as she pelts up the staircase. *Those,* she thinks, *are some mightily clenched buttocks.*

Once in her office, Harriet turns, breathless. "Fuckety, fuckety fucking fuck," she says. "Right, I've thought of a name for this case. We're calling it Operation Career Fucking Suicide."

"Let's just calm down," says Manon. "So he was at the theater with the home secretary. All that means is that his alibi probably stacks up."

"Ye *think*?" says Harriet.

"It probably is quite tight, to be fair," says Davy.

Manon and Harriet look at each other, Harriet turning up her palms.

"Right," she says, "so if we thought the press were all over it before, we should see what happens when they get hold of this. Not just the Royal Family, but 'Did the home secretary interfere with the investigation in any way?' Well, that'll be *The Guardian*. Before I know it, I'll be in front of some sodding select committee at the House of Commons having my career buried under a steaming pile of procedure. I predict a call from Galloway to the commissioner in"—she looks at her watch—"oooh, the next couple of hours?"

This was the nightmare of being the SIO: pressure from every quarter, having to make decisions about which lines to investigate in what order of priority, trying to work out which information is important and which can be discarded, and all those decisions being scrutinized from above and often from outside.

"Let's not get bamboozled by Ian Hind," says Manon. "We still need to confirm their movements."

This appears to have a calming effect on Harriet, who takes a deep breath and allows her shoulders to drop.

"Yes, right. You're right. Let's put a call in to Galloway's security detail. I want you two to drive out and scope this country pile, Deeping. See if that key's been disturbed. And I want CCTV from the post office on the first of December—see who was looking over Edith's shoulder when she picked up all that cash. Get Kim to check whether the landlord was paid his rent. I'm assuming he was interviewed during house-to-house. This is looking more like aggravated burglary by the minute."

Manon and Davy make for the door.

"And from now on," Harriet calls after them, "we treat Sir Bufton Tufton downstairs with the utterly slavish deference he so richly deserves."

* * *

ON ONE OF THE RARE occasions Harriet had come to Cromwell's and got drunk, she'd told Manon she had two consolations in life: swearing and Elsie.

Elsie was ninety-three, with Parkinson's. She lived in a care home, which had been raided by Harriet during an investigation into abuse of the elderly. Elsie had been in better shape then, standing with the help of a frame in the pink, overheated hallway. She'd regarded Harriet with beady, critical eyes—they all saw it. It was as if the team stood still, as Harriet and the old girl locked on to each other. *Some enchanted evening.*

Elsie shuffled into the room to be interviewed, her shins thick, the color of pine in tan tights, chenille slippers on her rigid, calcified feet. Harriet asked Elsie if she had been mistreated by any of the staff at the home. "Don't be *silly*," Elsie barked, and Harriet had been momentarily chastened. The balance of power was all with Elsie, who snapped and criticized ("Ever done this before, dearie?"), but Harriet persisted. Nightgowns removed how? What if the soup was unfinished? And if you wet the bed?

Gradually it emerged that Elsie believed her forgetfulness merited the odd slap. Her shaking hands drove them mad, you see. She couldn't dress anymore: "Well, that's bound to get their backs up. Who'd want to dress a scrawny old bird like me?"

Harriet said to leave it there just for now, and she fled the room. When Manon next saw her, she was leaning against a panda car, smoking a cigarette, looking furious and tearful at the same time. This is what Manon likes most about Harriet—no, not likes, understands: she isn't on an even keel. She feels the work in every fiber and it hurts her.

"I'm going to shut that fucking place down," she said, the cigarette tight between her fingers. "And that manager's going to prison."

Harriet got Elsie out of there by nightfall, much as she protested. The care home was taken over by new owners and the manager received a year's sentence for willful neglect, which was suspended "for previous good character," so she walked free, confirming all Harriet's suspicions that the courts are "a fucking joke."

Manon knows that Harriet and most of their colleagues cleave to the view that criminals either get off or get off lightly, that the system is stacked against the police. She's aware that if police officers were allowed to draw up the legislation, it would probably contain the words "and throw away the key." What worries Manon is she's joining their ranks. It can often feel as if they're fighting a tide of filth and losing; you only needed to do a week in child protection to lose any liberal tendencies you ever had.

Harriet became Elsie's visiting daughter, because Elsie had no children of her own—she was twenty-five when the war took the boy she loved, at Arras in 1940. His name was Teddy and she kept a photo of him by her bed, but Manon thought he was more an emblem of what had gone wrong. Elsie had had an abruption in her life. Grief had held her up, during which time she worked in a munitions factory and discovered how much she liked to work, when it had never really been an option before. When she emerged from mourning after the war, she found herself looking at a timer where the sand was running low.

"There were no men left," she told Harriet, laughing. "None who wanted an old spinster in her thirties like me, at any rate. It just never happened for me, the family thing."

Harriet called on Elsie every week and Manon occasionally went with her, witnessing between them a conspiratorial warmth. Elsie looked at Harriet with mischievous eyes, saying, "Thrash you this time." They played cribbage, or bridge when they could make a four with other stooped residents in the care home, though death often intervened ("Wilf not here?" "Not anymore, no."). Blackjack, beggar-my-neighbor, Sudoku, and crosswords. Then, as Elsie became more vague—the shaking and the vagueness accompanying each other as if staying fixed in thought and deed was ungraspable—the games became more infantile: Guess Who?, Connect Four, puzzles, and pairs.

Elsie humanized Harriet, who had a tendency to be hard. She was the obligation that made her feel stretched and needed. Her joyful complaint. That drunken night when Harriet had confided in Manon (her kindred spirit in singleness and childlessness), she said, "When you don't have kids, everyone assumes you're some fucking ball-breaking career freak, but it's not like that. It's more, y'know, a cock-up. It's something that happened *to* me. Elsie gets that. Plus, I really fucking hope someone will visit me when I'm pissing my pants in a care home."

* * *

DAVY AND MANON DRIVE OUT of HQ car park in an unmarked car that wears its snow like a jaunty hat, but as soon as they turn out of the gates, they slow to a halt. The traffic is always terrible on Brampton Road, a permanent feature of their forays out on jobs, but this queue has been made worse by the diversions set up around Edith Hind's house on George Street, combined with considerable rubbernecking from the fine folk of Huntingdon. Davy taps on the steering wheel with his gloved hand, a marker to Manon that he is unperturbed.

"This'll take hours," says Manon, slumping down into the passenger seat and wedging her feet onto the dashboard, her knees up. She has her phone in her lap, texting Bryony.

Can't do lunch. High-risk misper just blew up in my face. M

"Sarge," says Davy.

"Hmmm?" she says, and she looks up to see Davy casting anxious glances at her feet and at the spotless fascia of his glove box.

"You couldn't—" Her phone bleeps.

No worries. Am loving my court papers. Nothing cd tear me away. Not even pepper-flavored water. B

"Sorry, what?" she says to Davy.

"Your feet," he says, with another furtive glance at the offending boots, as if they might detonate.

"It's not even your car," she says, her fingers working on her phone. But she takes her feet down.

Tomoz maybe. M

Is Harriet losing the plot?

Yep. Crapping herself. Victim's family mates with Galloway.

Holy shit.

Yup.

At least your career isn't in cul-de-sac. May chew arm off if have to do more filing.

Go away, please, am in middle of Very Important Investigation.

All right, Mrs. Big Tits. Laters. PS: It's always the uncle. Or the stepfather. Or the boyfriend. Or possibly a complete stranger.

"How was the date, by the way?" Davy asks.

They are moving now—*at last*—having turned off onto the A14 toward the Fenland village of March.

"Don't ask."

"Can't have been that bad."

"Can't it?"

"Well, then, there'll be others—other responses to your ad."

"It's not an ad, Davy. I'm not selling roller blinds. It's a profile."

And what a work of fiction that "About Me" section is.

Genuine, easygoing. I love life and laughter, a bottle of wine with friends, cinema, and walks in the countryside.

Passionate about what I do. Looking for someone to share all this amazing world has to offer.

Age: 35

Looking for: fun/a long-term relationship/let's see what happens

Likes: sunshine, the smell of fresh coffee, walks on the beach

Dislikes: unexpected items in bagging area

Manon cut-and-pasted most of it from someone else's profile— a woman called Liz Temple from Berkhamsted, who claimed life was not about "sheltering from the thunderstorms" but "learning to dance in the rain." Except the bagging-area joke—that was Manon's and she was pretty pleased with it, feeling it made amusing reference to emotional baggage, of which there was a surfeit on the Internet.

Were she to tell the truth, her profile would go something like:

Misanthrope, staring down the barrel of childlessness. Yawning ability to find fault. Can give off WoD (Whiff of Desperation). A vast, bottomless galaxy of loneliness. **Educated:** to an intimidating degree. Willing to hide this. Prone to tears. Can be needy. Often found googling "having a baby at 40."

Age: 39

Looking for: book-reading philanthropist with psychotherapy training who can put up shelves. Can wear glasses (relaxed about this).

Dislikes: most of the fucktards I meet on the Internet.

"Mustn't give up, Sarge," says Davy.

"Like I'd take relationship advice from you. Still treating you mean, is she?"

"She keeps me on my toes."

"That's one way of putting it."

Davy is twenty-six but seems still a boy, has been in the force since eighteen, and something about him is irresistible to Manon. He has this naïve intensity—like an only child, neither at home with the adults nor one of the children—and those enormous ears always on the alert. His friendly demeanor and positive outlook have earned him the nickname "Silver" among the DCs. Silver Lining, the boy who's always looking on the bright side. He thinks the world might still come right if he just tries hard enough—which he does, all the time, mentoring at youth centers and looking out for every troubled child who crosses his path. But every silver lining has a cloud, and that cloud is Chloe.

Manon has seen them together more than once, though she and Davy never socialize outside the safety of office dos, Davy being of a different generation and this gulf becoming canyon-like outside the familiar hierarchies of work. One evening, however, they found themselves in the same pub, the Lord Protector on Mayfield Road. Manon was in a group from the station—a rowdy bunch, all pissed and telling terrible jokes ("Invisible man's at the door. Tell 'im I can't see 'im. Hahahahahaha."); Davy sat in a quiet corner with Chloe. Table for two.

Manon had watched them as the hubbub went on around her: Davy all animation, eyes on Chloe as if she were lit by some celestial cone, describing something to her. Chloe was looking over his shoulder, her face unmoving. She was a woman in a perpetual sulk and Davy was forever chivvying her out of it.

"Face like a slapped arse," said Kim Delaney, looking across the room with Manon. "Dunno what he sees in her."

But to Manon it makes perfect sense. Davy's at his best when rectifying. He often comes into the office with a carrier bag destined for the youth center where he volunteers—"Choccy Weetos for Ryan," "Rex needs socks"—and the brightness in his eyes tells her how much satisfaction this tenderness gives him. Warming up a frozen, miserable girlfriend is his destiny. If Davy got together with someone indomitably cheerful . . . well, Manon doesn't know what he'd do with himself. End it all, probably.

"I believe this leads to the abode," he says, as they turn down a wooded track. Bare tree branches bend over the car and verges rise up on either side. The sky seems to darken as the countryside burgeons around them.

"Drop the Shotley guff, will you?" says Manon irritably. Davy loves the jargon they inculcate at police school. He's forever saying the suspect "has made good his escape" with his "ill-gotten gains."

"Bit peckish?" says Davy, reaching into his pocket for a rich tea biscuit, which he hands to her.

"This place is a bit Hansel and Gretel, isn't it?" says Manon, eating the biscuit and peering up at the menacing tree fingers that reach for one another above the windscreen. The car is rocking over stones.

"Shouldn't be far down this track," says Davy.

The track is bordered by logs, sawn ends forming a honeycomb grid. Their tires plow through mud, which splinters with ice in places. The light lowers a notch, soaked up by the seaweed-gloss leaves on a row of bushes—rhododendrons, Davy says—ribboned with snow.

He is hunched toward the windscreen as they emerge in front of an ivy-clad house, broader than it is tall, with a pitch-roofed porch and a carport to the side. The house is ensconced in countryside, the woodland growing denser and darker to the sides and behind them.

With their arrival, a sensor light has clicked on above the front door—a rectangle of fire in Manon's eyes. The ivy running up the walls of the house is straining in at the windows, whose wooden frames are painted grayish green.

"Glad I'm not Polsa having to search this place," she says.

Davy turns off the engine so that all they can hear is its ticking and a blackbird, its lonely cry seeming to tell them the place is deserted.

Manon pats along the high shelf of architrave in the porch, and there it is, among dust and dead insects—the key. She puts it in an evidence bag, then uses Edith's set in the lock. The brass knob, green-gold, is icy even through her latex gloves, and its round skirt-plate rattles loosely. They step into a black-and-white-tiled hall with slate-blue walls. The house smells of wood smoke and the outdoors—an oxygenated, muddy smell that is not quite damp. An umbrella stand is filled with brollies and walking sticks, and to their left—Manon peers around the door, painted mustard yellow—is a boot room, wallpapered with Victorian images of birds, as if in a shooting lodge. She squats next to a line of Wellingtons—one black pair and three green—and touches the mud that cakes them.

"Davy?" she calls, and he appears by her side. "Does this look fresh to you?"

She swaps places with him and follows the hallway to a baronial-scale lounge. The ceiling is double height, the walls blotchy with blood-red lime wash. There is a grand open fireplace with white stone surround—the sort you could rest an elbow on when you came in from fishing in the Fenland rivers. A charred black scar runs up the back of the brickwork in the hearth. Manon squats beside the grate but it contains only the cold, crocodile husks of burnt-through logs.

The fire is surrounded on three sides by red sofas patterned with fleurs-de-lis and collapsing with age and gentility. She can imagine the Hinds reading their Dickens hardbacks or their subscriptions to *The New York Review of Books,* fire roaring and some string music playing in the background.

From the lounge is a staircase leading up to a minstrels' gallery and, off it, the bedrooms. Manon is feeling her way, the house cast in shadows. Swaths of muddy colors curling up the staircase or viewed through an open bedroom door: mustard, rose, slate blues, and gray, one leading on to the next. She pushes open a door to a vast bedroom— Ian and Miriam's, she assumes, because it is furnished with a grand French bed, its headboard framed in ornate gold and upholstered with gray linen. There is an imposingly dark French armoire too, its bottom drawer slightly open. Manon walks to the window—a long cushion in the same gray linen has created a window seat with two Liberty-print pink blossom pillows at either end. From here she can see the front drive and their car, and she has an urge to go toward it, to drive away.

She jumps at the sound of a door slamming, and her heart thuds in the shadows of the mansard window.

"Boss?" calls Davy, entering the room.

"Have you checked all the downstairs rooms?"

"I have."

"Right, well, let's check the rest of the rooms up here and the outbuildings. Then Polsa can take it from there."

"Not a bad little bolt-hole," says Davy.

Manon shivers. "Gives me the creeps."

HELENA

· · ·

THEY'VE LEFT HER WAITING IN INTERVIEW ROOM TWO, AND IN THE WAIT-ing, she can't help but rehearse what she'll say, though she fears the re-hearsal will make her appear guilty, like trying to make your face seem natural when going through passport control in Moscow or Tehran—the more you think about it, the more rictus your expression becomes. Not that she's ever been to those places, but even in the queue at Brit-tany Ferries she has made a point of catching the immigration officer's eye and smiling, so as to say, *You won't find any contraband in my backpack*.

The strip light above Helena's head fizzes then plinks, as if there's an insect dying inside it. She's always rehearsing, having imaginary conversations in her head that preempt real encounters—like she's re-hearsed her return to Dr. Young's couch after the Christmas break and how she'll tell him all that has happened with Edith. She used to re-hearse her sessions so much that when she first started with Dr. Young, it had taken quite a long time to get her to diverge from the script and "allow things to emerge," as he put it.

Helena hears a door slam somewhere in the corridor, brisk footsteps, and her heart quickens at the prospect of someone coming in. She sits upright, brushes at her skirt, but the footsteps clack past the door and drift away. She slouches again. They are keeping her waiting deliberately in this empty room with only a Formica table with metal legs and blue plastic chairs—two on the other side of the desk to where she is sitting, so presumably there will be two of them. Outnumbered by detectives. She's never met a detective before.

"Hello," she mouths, picturing herself half-rising and putting out a hand. "I've never met a detective before." Then she catches her reflection in a pane of brown-colored mirror set in the wall, her lips moving soundlessly (or like a psychiatric patient, depending on who's watching). *Is* anyone watching?

"I wanted to get Edith home safely," she murmurs, her eyes flicking to the mirrored wall. "I never imagined that home wouldn't be safe, that something could happen to Edith *after* I had dropped her home to George Street." No, saying that seems to implicate Will. She must phrase it some other way. Just go back to the beginning. Keep the narrative simple.

Edith had shouted, "Geronimo!" and tipped back another tequila shot, one of many she drank at the Crown that night. Then the barman rang last orders.

Helena told Edith they should go, it was 11:30 P.M., they'd miss the bus back to Huntingdon otherwise. And, anyway, she was tired—hot, tired, and fed up. The Crown was heaving; she was jostled by the crowd—townies, rowers, Corpus postgrads like herself and Edith.

What are you studying, Miss Reed? she imagines being asked. *Psychology. I'm a psychology fellow. My PhD is on gratification and its links to obesity.*

The door opens and a woman walks in—disheveled, with a mass of curls. Behind her is a young man, about Helena's age, with an open face and friendly, sticky-out ears.

"Sorry to keep you waiting," says the woman, holding out her hand. "I'm Detective Sergeant Manon Bradshaw; this is Detective Constable Davy Walker. We just need to ask you a few questions."

"No, I mean, yes, of course." Her heart beats so hard she fears it might be audible. While they set down notepads and fiddle about with a recording device, Helena puts a hand to her cheek, hoping the heat she can feel there is not visible. "I don't know anything," she blurts.

"If you just wait a moment," says DS Bradshaw. "We can begin once I get this machine set."

A long beep is emitted from the recording device.

"Most postgrads live in Cambridge, don't they?" asks DS Bradshaw.

"Yes. Most, but not all. There are apartments for married couples and single rooms provided by the college, but we—Edith and Will, and later myself—moved out toward the end of our undergraduate degrees. To Huntingdon."

Edith and Will, and later myself. It would be foolish to mention how they teased her about her own move to Huntingdon. Edith was always teasing.

"It's cheaper," Helena remembers saying to them, rather defensively. "And I like the quiet, y'know? Being in halls can be so . . . claustrophobic. I'll definitely get more work done here and the commute's easy-peasy."

"It's all right, Hels," Edith had said, not even looking up from chopping vegetables. "We know you're our stalker."

"Wouldn't your Christmas do normally be in the college? In Corpus Christi?" the detective asks.

"Well, yes and no. The graduate bar can be a bit damp. Jason—Jason Farrer, he's an English PhD like Edith—wanted something a bit livelier. They can be a bit socks-and-sandals, the postgrad lot."

"Socks-and-sandals?"

"Yes, you know, drilling down into the minutiae—sex life of chives, that kind of thing. All very nerdy. They're not the best at letting their hair down. Jason arranged the Christmas do—he chose the Crown."

"And Edith, how did she seem?"

"Well, drunk, to be honest. She wanted to do karaoke. She was doing tequila shots. I told her we should go—this was about eleven-thirty, last orders." Helena stops.

DS Bradshaw waits. "How did Edith react? Did she want to leave?"

Helena thinks back to Edith sticking out her tongue in Helena's direction, then swiveling on the balls of her feet to the makeshift dance-floor-cum-karaoke stage.

"Miss Reed?"

"Yeah, no, she was fine. She gave us a terrible rendition of 'Use Somebody' by the Kings of Leon." Helena stops again. She must be careful where this ventures.

DS Bradshaw is looking intently at her, waiting. "Something you're remembering? About the evening?"

"I'll tell you who was sniffing around that night," says Helena. "Graham Garfield, Edith's director of studies. Asked me where Will was. Bit predatory."

"Predatory how?" asks DS Bradshaw.

"Well, he's always hanging around the students, y'know? Even though they're half his age. He was watching Edith, watching her singing, and he just had this look. He saw how out of it she was."

"And what did you tell him?"

"I told him Will was away for the weekend, but that things were—are—solid between them. Edith and Will, I mean."

MANON

...

"AND YOU SAY YOU GOT THE GUIDED BUS HOME?" MANON SAYS.

Helena Reed is shifting about, straightening, crossing and uncrossing her legs. "That's right," she says. "You know, the one that runs along railway tracks part of the way, between Cambridge and Huntingdon."

She wears a coral scarf looped tightly about her neck and a camel cardigan buttoned up—a rather Parisian, precise attire. Manon has an irrational mistrust of very tidy-looking people. They work too hard at concealment, and besides, she doesn't understand how they pull it off. Manon seems to emerge from her flat, even at the start of the day, with a rogue bulging shirt button showing a flash of bra, or a smear unnoticed in the half-light of the bedroom (she often finds herself wetting a bit of toilet roll in the second-floor toilets and going at a stain, only to lace it with beads of wet tissue).

Helena's knees are pinned together and her pencil skirt is smoothed tight (Manon covets the idea of the pencil skirt, much as she covets the idea of being a tidy person, but hasn't the knees for it). Helena Reed is held in, Manon decides, and rather concerned with what others see, though as soon as Manon passes this judgment, she wonders if it isn't genetic—the whole personal-tidiness thing. One is destined to become one's mother, after all. This thought makes her smile to herself—there are worse things.

"I led Edith off the bus and walked her back to George Street," Helena is saying. "It was snowing and a bit slippy—she was tipsy and rather giggly, so I had to hold on to her. And when we got to the cottage, I got her keys out of her bag to let her in."

"And you closed the door behind you?"

"Yes, it self-locks when you close it—a Chubb, you know what I mean. I led her to the kitchen, helped her to take off her coat—"

"This was the green parka, with the fur trim?"

"Yes."

"What did you talk about?"

"The night at the pub, the people who were there. She was flirting with Jason Farrer, the guy I mentioned? Bit of a lech, in my view. I s'pose I told her off a bit."

"Did you have an argument?"

"Not an argument, no. She shrugged it off, really; told me I was being an old prude."

"Did you or Edith get out two wineglasses while you were there, to have another drink?"

"No, God, no. She'd had more than enough and I was tired. I didn't even take my coat off."

"Did she seem anxious, frightened of anything or anyone?"

"No, she was happy—drunk and silly. If anything, it was me who was grouchy."

"Did she talk about Will Carter at all?"

"Not really. At one point she said I was 'as bad as Will,' meaning boring, I s'pose."

"Edith's mother mentioned a certain cooling between Edith and Will. Do you think Edith wanted to end the relationship?"

"Not to my knowledge. She complained about him sometimes,

but that's normal, isn't it? If you're suggesting that Will had something to do·with Edith disappearing, that's mad. He'd never—"

"Just answer the question, Miss Reed."

"No, she didn't mention breaking up with him, not to me."

"Did they fight—physically?"

"No, God, no. Look, it wasn't like that. Will wouldn't say boo to a goose. His worse crime is that he can be a bit dull."

"Were you aware that Edith kept a lot of cash in the house?"

"The MoneyGram transfers? Yes. We all thought it was a bad idea, but Edith's a bit of a warrior in that way. She won't be budged."

"Did you notice any cash lying around in the house on Saturday night?"

"No. It's not like she leaves wads of twenties by the kettle. She isn't stupid. She hides it in various different places. Will would know better than me. You know, a tin in the kitchen cupboard, another in the bathroom. That sort of thing."

"Who else knows about the money?"

"Only her friends. Not anyone who would rob her, I don't think."

"Going back to Jason—you say Edith was flirting with him. Flirting how?"

Helena frowns. "You know, giggling with him. I . . . I don't want to . . . I don't want to land her in it."

"I think we've gone beyond that, Miss Reed. Edith has been missing for thirty-five hours now. Time is very much of the essence."

"So, OK, Edith and Jason went outside the pub. I don't know what they were doing, maybe just having a cigarette."

"How long were they outside together?"

"Oh, not long. Five minutes. I know because I was casting about for her. I wanted to leave. She came back in, I had her coat ready, and we left pretty much straightaway."

"Thank you, Miss Reed. If you wouldn't mind waiting here for a bit longer, we may have some further questions for you shortly."

"THANK YOU FOR COMING IN, Mr. Farrer," says Manon, setting her clipboard down on the table in interview room three while Davy fiddles with the recording device, saying the date and time and names of everyone in the room.

Jason Farrer leans back in his chair, legs wide apart, one elbow bent behind him on the chair's backrest. He wears a yellow knitted waistcoat with leather buttons, brown baggy corduroys, and a checked shirt. His hair hangs in a foppish wave across one side of his face. He straightens as she takes up her seat opposite him.

"Look, I want to help in any way I can." His aristocratic accent comes as a shock—surprising to hear and awkward to deliver. He is barely moving his mouth, the words escaping out the sides.

"Bit unusual, isn't it, for postgrads like Edith and Will to live outside the town—as far as Huntingdon, I mean?" says Manon.

"Not just unusual, practically unheard of. Everyone lives in Leckhampton, where the dining room is and the bar. But they're like that, Edith and Will. Superior. Like being out on a limb." She's wrong-footed by his candor. Charmers like him normally fight hard to mask themselves with affable decency toward absolutely everyone. Then he leans forward toward her across the desk, his hands clasped, and she realizes he's drunk. Rolling drunk. The ethanol rises off him in an energetic dance with the air.

"They have a project," he says.

"I'm sorry?"

"To live truthfully. Grow food, cook wholesomely, cycle, or chug along in that trumped-up lawnmower of hers. I think they thought student digs would corrupt them. 'Course, her father pays for everything—the house, the *evil* gas and electricity. She is Will's flexible friend in so many ways."

"Who's driving this project, then—Edith or Will?"

"Oh, they're both really into it. The aim is to live a simple but, I s'pose, pure life. Made me want to self-harm. I thought it was vanity. You have to understand—Edith and Will are the most beautiful specimens Cambridge will ever produce. When they got together in our final year, it was like Kate Middleton–Barbie had found Ken."

"Sorry, I don't get it. How is growing fresh food vanity?"

"Life's a competition," says Farrer. "Their superior lifestyle was their quickest route to looking down on people. I mean, that's why people do it, isn't it? Grow loads of chard? It isn't because they *want* chard. I mean, no one *buys* chard. It's so they can tell someone else they grow chard. And that someone will go away worrying about the fact they don't grow chard."

"Except you."

"I've never wanted to grow chard."

They look at each other. Farrer is slumped, lolling with the drink. He lets out a little girlish giggle, like gas bubbles escaping—then puts a hand in front of his mouth to stifle them.

"You do realize you're being questioned in relation to the disappearance and possible abduction of a young woman," says Manon.

"Sorry," says Farrer, another little giggle escaping involuntarily. "I find it hard to take anything seriously. Look, they used to bang on about it endlessly." His words are not quite slurring but rolling up against one another, like waves swelling out at sea. "You know, 'Here's some organic muffins I made.' 'Will is at home, fashioning us a table out of reclaimed crutches.' It was tiresome."

Manon nods.

"Still, it's not enough to murder someone, is it?" says Farrer. "I mean, you don't think Edith was abducted because she had a curly-kale glut, do you?"

"You don't seem very concerned," says Manon.

"That's me all over."

"Can we go back to Saturday night at the Crown? You were with Edith at the bar."

"Yes."

"And what made the two of you go outside?"

"She put her mouth next to my ear and whispered, 'Let's go outside, Farrer.' Very sexy it was too."

"Had she been flirting with you in the run-up to that night?"

"God, no. Edith always treated me with the utter contempt I deserve. That's what made it so exciting when she came on to me."

"So you went outside. Then what happened?"

"Well, lots of heavy breathing. She was up against me, against the wall of the pub. It was freezing and dark. She was whispering sweet nothings in my ear. Then we had . . . Well, I'll protect her honor, if you don't mind. Then she suddenly stopped and went back inside."

"I'm sorry, we're going to need some detail. Did you kiss?"

"I'll say."

"Did it go further than that?"

Farrer smiles at Manon, but she has done too many of these interviews to be squeamish.

"Digital penetration?" she asks.

"You make it sound so romantic," he says.

"Answer the question, please."

"Yes."

"Consensual?"

"I had given my consent, yes," he says, giggling again.

"How did Edith call a halt?"

"She pulled my hand out from her knickers, straightened her clothes, and went back inside the pub."

"Did you follow her?"

"No, I didn't."

"You didn't want to pursue her, to finish what she started?"

"Yes, I can see how you'd think that," he says thoughtfully. "But I'm not really the type to pursue anything. I don't really have it in me."

"You're doing an English PhD at Cambridge," says Manon. "You must be able to pursue things rather vigorously."

"Gosh. 'Vigorous.' What a terrific word, Sergeant. It's certainly never been used to describe me. But you're right, of course. Poetry is my secret weapon. Give me a spot of Gerard Manley Hopkins and I soar. In all other areas of my life, I'm a total fuckup. No one believes I'll finish my PhD, least of all me."

"How did you get home from the pub?"

"I walked—well, fell, really—down Grange Road to my rooms in Leckhampton House. Porter'll confirm it, and no doubt some of your evil big-brother cameras have me weaving about the streets. And then I spent the night with the lovely Ros or Rosie—at least, I think that's her name—who happened to be in the kitchen when I got back. Your chaps are checking with her now, I believe."

"And Edith went back in to find Helena Reed."

"The Limpet. Whenever Edith turns around, the Limpet's sure to be there."

"How d'you mean?"

"Ask yourself why Helena lives in Huntingdon. I mean, Edith and Will, they're cocks with a project. But Helena? What's she doing there? Bit suffocating, wouldn't you say?"

"Go on."

"Ask the Limpet what Edith gave her as an early Christmas present."

"Why don't you stop beating around the bush, Mr. Farrer, and tell me what you mean."

He stops, looks down to the floor by his side, his arms dangling, and Manon wonders if he's going to be sick. He has the soaked-in drunkenness of someone who's been marinating in it for some time—days, probably.

"They were at it. Edith told me—when we went outside the pub together. Of course, it could be she was just trying to turn me on."

"What did she say exactly?"

"She said she'd been having it off with Helena and now she couldn't get rid of her." He lets out another high-pitched giggle.

"Did you expect this type of behavior from Edith?" asks Manon.

"Well, no, it wasn't typical. But Cambridge is full of people toeing the line, swotting in libraries to please Daddy, and then rebelling and taking up crack or throwing themselves out of a tower. You know we actually have a *day* called Suicide Sunday. It's a fucked-up place, once you get under the skin of it. I figured Edith had just freaked out like the rest of us."

THE ADRENALINE HAS SWEPT AWAY Manon's tiredness as she and Harriet pummel down the stairs toward interview room two, back to Helena Reed.

"Is he reliable?" Harriet asks, pushing through the double doors.

"No, not at all. He's drunk and feckless. But I don't think he's got any reason to lie about this."

"Unless he's covering his own tracks."

"Let's just see what she has to say."

Helena looks up at them as they enter the room. Kim is standing by the wall with her hands clasped behind her back.

"I told you, we're friends," says Helena. She unloops her coral scarf and places it on her knees. The color is high in her cheeks. "I've known her since our first day at Corpus. Sorry, may I have a drink of water?"

"Just friends?" asks Harriet, leaning both elbows on the table and scrutinizing Helena.

"I don't know what you mean," she says. She looks up as Kim places a plastic cup in front of her. "Thank you."

"Jason Farrer says you and Edith were lovers," says Harriet.

"Well, Jason Farrer's lying," she says. "He's not exactly trustworthy."

"He says Edith told him, when they went outside the pub together."

She is looking wildly now at the two of them sitting opposite her, and Manon senses she cannot see them. Her skin has taken on a sweaty sheen.

"Oh God," she whispers, covering her entire face with her hands.

"Were you jealous when Edith went outside with Jason Farrer?" asks Harriet.

Helena keeps her face covered.

"Did you confront Edith about it when you got home to George Street? Things get a bit heated?"

"No, no, no," she says, still with a hand shielding her eyes, her face directed at the door, away from their gaze. "It wasn't like that.... It was ... I don't know how to explain it to you, because I don't understand it myself."

"Helena, do you know what has happened to Edith?" asks Harriet.

"No, I don't. I swear I don't."

"Do you think Will Carter found out about your affair?"

"I don't think so, no."

"How long have you been lovers?" asks Manon gently.

"Lovers?" says Helena with a soft laugh. "You make it sound so enchanting. It was one night—well, a night and a day—it happened twice, that's all. A mistake, a terrible mistake. The first time she seemed affectionate, at least. She said, 'It's always been you.' But then, last Wednesday, she was out of it. I couldn't even tell if she loved or hated me. Please, I don't want anyone to know." She starts to cry. "My parents ..."

"It's all right," says Manon. "We're asking you solely for the purposes of this investigation. There is no reason for your parents or any-one else to find out. Did Edith instigate it, the relationship?"

Helena nods, the back of her hand to her mouth, her chin trem-bling.

"And when was this?"

"A week ago. I mean, the Saturday before this one."

"So that would be the tenth?"

"I s'pose. She came to my flat late—about two A.M.—she was drunk, and she, well, she kissed me."

"And did things progress?"

"Yes, but I've never been with a woman before," Helena says in a rush.

"And after that Saturday?" says Harriet.

"She came again on Wednesday in the day. She was much more distracted, much more . . . not herself at all."

"Not herself how?"

"Sort of reckless. Kamikaze. I felt as if she was using me, as if she hated me. She wouldn't look me in the eye. She'd brought a bottle of wine and we ended up in bed. When I said, 'What about Will?' she snapped, 'It doesn't fucking matter.' Then she left very suddenly, as if she'd changed her mind."

"Did you want things to continue? Is that why you went home with her on Saturday after the pub?"

"I don't know what I wanted. I felt, feel, confused. Chewed up and spat out, if I'm honest. I feel . . . mortified. I never thought anyone would find out. I swear to you, I left her in her kitchen. We didn't even talk about it. I didn't even have the guts to mention it. I wish I'd left her in Cambridge now. I wish I'd come back to Huntingdon by myself."

HELENA

• • •

STANDING ON THE STATION STEPS, SHE BLINKS INTO THE LOW SUN, WHICH flashes off the car roofs like knives. She can see slices of Will Carter striding toward her—his hair, his chin, a black donkey coat and scarf, but not his eyes.

Will bedded down in her lounge in the early hours of this morning, after his police interviews were done, and when she'd gone in to draw the curtains at around 7:00 A.M., while he was in the shower, the room smelled thickly of unfamiliar male. She folded his sleeping bag and laid the pillow neatly on top, and when he came in to get dressed, she retreated to the kitchen to brew them a pot of strong coffee. They sat at the breakfast bar, hollow-eyed, going over the night's events.

He won't want to stay with her after this. She can't make out his expression—is there mistrust already?—because of the distorting shards of sun. She can hardly breathe at the thought of what he is about to find out. He jogs up the station steps.

"Are you all right?" he asks, taking her elbow. "You look awful."

"It's just," she says, "a bit rough in there. Scary. What's happening."

"I know. They want to re-interview me for some reason, God knows why. I've told them everything about five times already."

"I guess new stuff keeps cropping up," she says. She is grateful to the flash and glare for obscuring his face.

"Well," he says, "I'll see you back at the flat. Is it OK if I stay another night with you? Our house is cordoned off."

"If you want to—why don't you see how you feel?" She puts both hands over her forehead to create a visor. "Listen, Will, the police—they're saying all sorts, trying to poke about and stuff. Don't listen to them—I mean, not all of it can be true."

"What sort of things?"

"I'm just saying, some of it is just trying to get a rise out of you, y'know? See how you'll react."

"I don't understand," he says.

"Doesn't matter, forget it."

"Look, I better go in. I'll catch up with you after."

Helena strides headlong into the light, taking wide steps because the tarmac is flat and predictable, and with some steps the sun recedes and she can see, only for it to flash off a wing mirror or window—like peering through the slats of a blind. He'll be going into an interview room, greeting the officers who will tell him what she and Edith have done together behind his back. He might look toward the station steps, to where they have only just spoken, run a hand through his hair in shock.

A tree provides welcome shade and she can see gridlock on the road into Huntingdon. She reaches the concrete underpass, the sun slanting against its elephant gray-green hulk. The cars are bumper-to-bumper into town, and as she reaches the top of George Street, she can sense a frisson in the air. Perhaps it is the drivers craning to see what the holdup is; the hooting of horns, as they grow tired of the delay; the slowing pedestrians on the pavement. Helena has to weave through a throng as she nears the house itself and then she is in front of the familiar gate, which she has pushed open without thinking so many times, now cordoned with police tape and guarded by a WPC in a fluorescent windcheater and regulation black trousers, her radio crackling with blurred voices.

Ten feet farther down the road is a group of men—they appear from this distance to be a black huddle, like a murder of crows landed on crumbs, but as she gets nearer, Helena sees there are one or two women among them. She sees the cameras slung over their shoulders, like handbags, and the notepads. They are laughing, at ease. One of them smiles at Helena as she edges past them on the pavement and she increases her pace, pushing her chin down into her scarf. She edges around the next group—two women with toddlers playing about their legs, and a pensioner with a square wheelie shopper. "Was at the university, apparently," is all she catches, to which one of the women says, "Terrible."

Helena stops herself from breaking into a run. Her heart pounds at the thought of the women turning to look at her in horror, their faces ghoulish with opprobrium, the cameras pointed at her with sudden piercing focus.

Her breathing returns to a more normal rhythm once she is safely inside her flat, until she becomes aware of the beeps coming from the answering machine in the lounge. She unwinds her scarf. Perhaps it is Dr. Young. Perhaps he has heard about Edith's disappearance on the news and has rung to check she is all right. *Beep*. She holds the scarf against her chest. Or her father. If it's her father, she can call him back, tell him what's happened, and ask to come home for the weekend to Bromley, get away from all the intrusion and the questions. *Beep*.

What if it's Edith herself, explaining away all the confusion in that breezy way she has—"Lighten up, Hels"—like the time she'd rung on the intercom at 2:00 A.M. Helena answered the door irritably in her tartan pajamas and, when she saw Edith swaying there, said, "Is anything wrong?"

Edith, breathing tannin from some Shiraz or Merlot, her gums stained black, giggling and pushing her way through to the lounge. Edith's tiny lace bra was lilac with a diamante stud at its center and so pretty against her skin. Her bones were delicate, breakable, her breasts neat and perfectly round, her arms beautifully thin. Helena found she could circle her thumb and middle finger perfectly around Edith's wrist like a bracelet. And Edith held out to her in those lovely hands the promise of excitement and discovery, as if the only thing holding them both back was the smallness of Helena's horizons.

"Let's loosen you up a bit, Hels," Edith murmured, biting at the corner of Helena's mouth while her hands worked down the buttons on her pajamas.

Helena walks slowly to the lounge, placing her scarf on the end of the sofa, unbuttoning her coat. She presses play on the answering machine.

"Hi, this is a message for Helena Reed. It's Bethan Jones from the *Mail on Sunday*. We're doing a special piece on Edith Hind and I wondered if you wanted to tell us, you know, what she's really like—as her best friend. It'd really bring the piece to life. I'm sure you're worried about Edith and obviously coverage like this raises her profile, so if you wanted to talk, you know, to help the police appeal, then you can get in touch with me at _____. I really look forward to hearing from you, Helena. Thanks, then. It's Bethan Jones, by the way."

DAVY

. . .

HE LOWERS HIS HEAD TO THE LEFT, FEELING THE LONG STRETCH DOWN
the side of his neck, then to the other side. His body is beginning to
take umbrage at having been in a broadly vertical position for more
than twenty hours. Evening now—a full night and day on shift—and
they're waiting for the 6:00 P.M. briefing. Only last week he'd heard a
radio program about research showing the toll night shifts take on the
body, tearing through its natural rhythms, giving you cancer.

He increases the stretch by placing a hand on the top of his head
and pulling gently. Even while doing this he wants to go to sleep. One
side, then the other. He sees the department tilted on its side: Kim
pouring herself some stewed coffee, Stuart sitting next to Colin, Harriet and Manon up front by the whiteboard, all of them gathering lu-
gubriously, waiting for Fergus. Things are heating up in the press office.

Thirty-six hours missing. You'd expect a body or a firm sighting
by now, or an injured girl, limping away from whatever trauma has be-

fallen her. But this? Murkier and murkier it's getting, and Davy doesn't like the look of it.

He's just come from interview room three, where Will Carter kept running a confused hand through his hair and saying, "Edith? And Helena?" As if he and Manon had totally lost their marbles. "No," Carter mumbled. "No, I don't think that can be right."

"Helena confirmed it to us," Manon said, without nearly as much sympathy as Davy would have liked.

He's seen it all before, of course, but that doesn't make it any less depressing—watching people reassess their entire surroundings as if buildings have been moved or reconfigured, roads diverted. The people they think they know have hidden lives: other women, other men, money stolen, debts hidden, a previous life in a cartel or on the game, children fathered in secret. It exhausts as well as fascinates him, churning it all up with their big stubby stick. "Can't you all just keep it simple?" he wants to sigh. "Can't you keep it buttoned, keep your fists out of it, stop drinking, stop *shagging*? Isn't life complicated enough?"

And here was Will Carter, bewildered. He wasn't standing up all of a sudden, like most of them did, trying to turn the table over and shouting, "You're having a fucking laugh!" or kicking a chair. No, he was rather genteelly running a hand through his hair, saying, "Edith and Helena? Seriously?" And just looking mildly shocked.

"Looking back," Manon said to Carter, and Davy thought, *Go easy, now, the man's had a shock,* "can you see evidence of that relationship?"

"We were always together, always close, the three of us. I never questioned it. Shows what a fool I am." And Carter laughed in a self-deprecating way, which once again made Davy think, *You poor chap.*

Manon didn't seem to share his sensitivity. "Perhaps you did know, Mr. Carter," she said, "and became incensed by it. Jealous. Perhaps you came back early to confront Edith about it."

"No. I honestly didn't know. And it makes me look like a total chump. And I know there are people who think you should know—you know, the inner workings of your nearest and dearest. But the fact is, if they don't tell you . . ."

"Did you have the feeling that Edith was going to leave you?"

Christ, Davy thought, *give the man a sodding break.*

Carter blew out through his cheeks. "No, no, I didn't. Are you

going to tell me I'm wrong about that too? Listen, I can live with infidelity. A fling with Helena—it wouldn't change how I feel." And his
eyes brimmed with tears, fat droplets swelling to their bursting point
but remaining just there, on the brink, beneath his slate eyes with their
brown flecks. "But please don't tell me she didn't—doesn't—love me
anymore. Please don't do that, not with her missing."

Davy had put a hand on Manon's arm.

"No, of course not," said Manon softly.

And Davy exhaled, feeling reassured she would not go in and sock
him with the Jason Farrer fumble. *One infidelity at a time, eh.*

"MONEY," HARRIET SAYS, BENDING HER middle finger down in her new
list of priorities. "Edith didn't use banks. There was no cash in the
house when we searched it. Now, that either means Edith spent it all, or
it was on her when she was abducted, or it was stolen and that her disappearance is the consequence of an aggravated burglary. Nigel, where
are we with CCTV from the post office on the first of December?"

"Owner doesn't know how to burn it onto a DVD," says Nigel.

"Well, go down there and do it for him," says Manon. She and
Harriet exchange irritable glances.

Nigel shrugs. He's been destroyed by life with newborn twins,
thinks Davy, and now he's too tired even to take umbrage. "Have a
dig," his dead eyes seem to say, "I don't care, as long as I can lie down."

"Manon, can you take us through Will's journey to Stoke and back,
please?" says Harriet.

"We've got him traveling to Stoke, as he described, on Friday evening. He's picked up by ANPR at three points on his outward journey,
and obviously his mother confirms his stay."

"Well, she would, wouldn't she?" mutters Harriet. "Sorry, carry on."

"She says he left her house in Stoke at five-thirty on Sunday evening. He says he took a longer route home because of Sunday road-
works, which means his journey took closer to three hours, getting
him back to George Street at eight-thirty. He then spent half an hour
searching the house for Edith, calling various people such as Helena
Reed, before phoning her parents and then us at nine. Now, we haven't
got that return journey on camera. Might be that the cameras are out

on this route, we're checking that, or that he was tailgated by a lorry or something, or that mud splashed on his plates, which prevented a reading—"

"Or that he was at home murdering his girlfriend," snorts Stuart, with rather more confidence than is merited for a first day in the office, if you ask Davy, which no one ever does.

"Ah, Fergus," says Harriet. "The floor's all yours."

Fergus Kelly, a neat man in spectacles, never a speck on his suit. He has worked in the press office for ten years, including through the mayhem of Soham, which shook him more than the rest of them because it laid waste to half his contacts and all the unsaid niceties that had previously governed the flow of information.

"So, the tabloids are well and truly on to this now," Fergus says, pushing his glasses up his nose. He has a fresh outbreak of acne on his chin, incongruous for a man in his forties but understandable when you combined stress with the heavily refined carbohydrates served in the canteen. One of his daughters has cerebral palsy. Davy doesn't know what's made him think of this, but something about Fergus being under pressure doesn't seem fair. "Obviously we can use the press interest to flush out information, but we need to control it—all inquiries must go through the press office. The Hinds have agreed to do a press conference at eleven tomorrow and we may wheel Will Carter out to see how much he sweats. Obviously, in the first days, the press tend to be very helpful in promoting the police line. It's after a couple of days," he rubs the sweat at his brow, "when there's nothing new to report, they can become quite . . ." He coughs into his fist. "It's important there are no leaks," he adds, making eye contact with every member of the team, especially the new recruit, in a way that is pleading rather than authoritative. "And that we stay in control, as I say, of the flow of information."

MANON
. . .

MANON RUNS HER TRAY ALONG THE COUNTER, LOOKING INTO RECTANGU-lar metal pans of beans, sausages, watery mushrooms, tomatoes from a tin, and scrambled eggs that have congealed into a solid square. A permanent breakfast offering in a lightless room, at 8:00 on a Monday evening, for people who have ceased to observe normal day and night patterns.

"Hello, missy," says Larry from behind the counter. He is from Gabon. His name can't be Larry, but he allows it, this lazy Anglicizing of his name. "You look tired, dahling. Is long shift?"

Larry is smiling at her. He is always smiling, even though he works punishing hours on minimum wage, serving cheap food to an almost entirely white Cambridgeshire police force. Occasionally she hears him speak a beautiful African French to a female colleague behind that divisive counter. Manon often resolves to ask him about Gabon and how he came to Huntingdon, but there never seems to be a right time.

"Big case, Larry. No rest for the wicked. Beans and sausages, please."

She takes her tray to an empty table and looks up at the television, which is bracketed near the ceiling. Sky News is rolling out a stream on Edith Hind's disappearance. The red ticker along the base of the screen reads: *Huntingdon latest: 24-year-old Cambridge student Edith Hind missing. Father is Sir Ian Hind, physician to the Royal Family.*

She goes to get the remote control from another table. Around the room are a smattering of officers on the case or supplying auxiliary support, including Stuart, who has a habit of catching Manon's eye in a way she finds faintly inappropriate. Davy is a couple of tables away. He picks up his tray and moves over to Manon's table, looking expectantly at the telly as she flicks over to Channel 4+1 for the news.

"Officers say they are very concerned about a twenty-four-year-old woman who went missing from her home in Huntingdon on Saturday night," says the presenter ("very concerned" being code for "we think she's dead"). "As Cambridgeshire police launch a manhunt, we have this report."

Their home-affairs correspondent is stood in the gray slush outside Edith's house. The blackness of the winter night is lit around him, white puffs emerging on his breath and flurries of sleet blowing about behind his head.

"Police are investigating what happened to Edith Hind after she got home from a party in Cambridge on Saturday night." Manon saws into a processed sausage, its meat sickening-pale. *Purest eyelid and spine,* she thinks. "The postgraduate student was shown on CCTV laughing and singing at the Crown pub in Cambridge with friends. She and her friend Helena Reed then made their way back to Edith's house, here in George Street, and said good night. What happened next is a mystery.

"DI Harriet Harper, of Cambridgeshire's Major Incident Team, is urging anyone with information about Edith to contact the dedicated inquiry line. Edith's parents and her boyfriend, fellow Cambridge graduate Will Carter, will be issuing an appeal for information tomorrow morning."

The food is filling up Manon's belly with warmth, which spreads up to her temples and fills her with an intense desire to sleep. She wants to eat more—as she always does when she works a punishing shift—as if she can replace a soft bed with carbohydrates. She spoons in some beans.

"She put up with me," Will Carter told them when they re-interviewed him in the light of the Helena Reed revelation. Manon found herself staring at him with her mouth ajar, and when she looked over at Harriet, who had joined her and Davy halfway through the interview, she had the same expression on her face. *You cannot be real. You are a pretend boyfriend, created by DreamWorks.*

But it wore off, his handsomeness and its presence in the room, which initially made Manon wind one of her curls about a finger and Harriet hold her stomach in. The two of them questioned him about every aspect of his life with Edith, and though his barriers were down, and they were in the midst of the biggest case either of them had seen in years, nevertheless his answers had a curiously narcoleptic effect on them both. Manon rubbed her eye, which felt as if a bit of grit was caught in it, and cast a look at Harriet, who was stifling a yawn.

"Shall we break for coffee?" Harriet had said at one point, and they convened in whispers next to the coffee machine in MIT.

"Every time he speaks, I want it to be over," said Manon, her eyes glazed.

"Yes," said Harriet. "It's not boring, but it's like you just can't keep your mind on him at all. I found myself thinking about some shopping I have to pick up. Fascinating, isn't it?"

Carter described how he and Edith had met—the May ball, the velvet dress she wore with a sweetheart neckline, and her reciting Yeats to him across a lawn with her stilettos in one hand and a bottle of Beck's in the other.

Manon takes another bite of sausage and looks at Davy—or through him, more accurately. He is saying something about phone numbers, a number that was found on Edith Hind's phone.

Soon there would be flowers—either at the site where a body was found or outside the house—from members of the public who wrote cards saying "you're safe now" or "rest in peace" or "looking down from heaven." They scare her, these tragedy tourists, as if they are hungry for catastrophe, a line from the inside of them to the inside of suffering—like a hook inside the cheek of a fish. Manon knows death and she knows it is no rest or journey. *Do not go gentle into that good night.*

She thinks of Lady Hind's terrified face and realizes the pain for relatives of the missing is that there is no clear face to stare into—neither the abyss of death nor hope, but a ghastly oscillation between the two. If ever there was real purgatory, it's this.

"This number, unknown-515," Davy is saying, mouth full of egg, "it's on her phone twice. Edith called it on the Monday—the twelfth, I think it was—before she disappeared; that was a twenty-minute call. Then she called it again on Friday the sixteenth. That's got to be significant."

"Who's it registered to?"

"Pay-as-you-go, no records attached, purchased in cash in Cambridge. I'm trying to get more on it. Why would Edith be calling a dirty phone?"

Manon shovels in a final mouthful of baked beans. Her eye is irritable—gritty, the shards of sleep deprivation or the beginning of a sty—and she predicts that when she wakes tomorrow it will have inflated like a blister. That'll look excellent when there are scores of TV cameras about. She stops herself rubbing it, even though the urge is overpowering, and knows in about three seconds she will claw at it rapaciously.

MIRIAM
. . .

TWO IN THE MORNING, *OUR SECOND NIGHT AWAKE,* THINKS MIRIAM, noticing that she'd thought—told herself—Edith would be back with them by now. She should have been found. And she is aware that the passage of time—forty-eight hours now by police reckoning—is like a growing tumor for a missing person, as if time itself drains the life from their bodies. She cries every hour or so about the things Edith might have experienced. Or be experiencing still. Her own daughter and she can't make it stop, can't protect her. And then her mind can't bear it and it clicks into a numb state.

The hotel room at the George is overheated in the way hotel rooms often are. Airless, the windows impossible to open, the curtains like lead. They'd pushed dinner around their plates out of a vague respect for life's little routines but eventually left the dining room when their awareness of the television and newspaper reporters sitting at adjacent tables became too much: constant furtive glances, the way conversation dropped when they walked by, and the lowered gazes when she accidentally met their eyes. It was dirtying.

When she's not crying, she feels disconnected, as if the hubbub is happening to someone else: the news reports, the cameras outside Edith's house, the sheer drama of it. She is discombobulated when they are in the public eye, walking in and out of the police station or up the hotel steps, white lights shining in her face, camera flashes exploding. She allows herself to be carried along by Ian's hand on her arm. Propelled by him. She doesn't know what she'd do without him commanding everything.

After dinner she had a bath and, lying there, had thought about what she should wear for the television appeal. Is it wrong that she cares about what to wear to appear on national television? She found herself wondering which outfit was more slimming—the navy jacket or mustard waterfall cardigan? How could she think about any of this (even idly wondering which seemed more grief-stricken)? Yet the mind must chew on something, else it will chew on itself.

Lying in the bath, she heard Ian on the phone to various people—to Rollo, about how soon he could fly back from Argentina ("I'll pay for a first-class ticket, if that's all that's available. . . . Yes, yes, OK. So you'll be home by Wednesday evening? . . . Yes, I wish it were sooner"). She got out of the bath at this point, wrapped a towel around herself, and took the phone from her husband.

"Is that really the earliest you can come, darling?" she said to Rollo. "I'll feel so much better when you're home. Did she say anything to you? . . . No, well, OK, till Wednesday then. And, Rollo? I love you, darling boy." Just the sound of his voice was a bolster to her tremulous heart.

Then Ian spoke to DI Harper and to Rosemary from the practice, telling her he wouldn't be working for the foreseeable future and not to talk to the press.

Ridiculous trains of thought, wondering if she has somehow caused this. Was this her *fault*? Had she been remote as a mother? Because Edith was always overdramatizing her feelings, as if to make herself heard over a din. And this . . . event seems to Miriam somehow typical. Her eldest had never realized that a simple statement of fact was enough; it had to be "the worst time ever" or "*literally* a nightmare." Edith was always poorer, ill-er, more unhappy, than the next person. It had made Miriam all the more aware of Rollo's understatement; when he rather queasily said as a child that he didn't feel quite right, she would rush to feel his fevered brow. When Edith wailed that she was *dying*, Miriam rolled her eyes and packed her off to school. And so are our children formed and, yes, it was always going to be Edith at the center of a drama—*a police hunt, for Christ's sake.*

She screws her eyes tight, her head tipped back, and tears squeeze from their corners, because she loves the bones of Edith and is critical only as if she is a part of herself. This separation is like a rending of her flesh.

She sits up. *We have to* do *something.* She hears a sound and looks across the bed, sees Ian's back through the charcoal dark. He is sitting on the side of the bed in his vest. He has his elbows on his knees, his head in his hands, and he is crying. Quietly, so as not to wake her.

She climbs over the bed to him and rubs his back.

"I thought she'd be at Deeping," he says. "Lying on her bed with headphones in her ears, reading a book. That she'd look up and wonder what all the fuss was about."

"Let's go there now, see if she's turned up," says Miriam. "I can't stand doing nothing. I've just got this feeling—that house, she loves it there. It would draw her, if she was in trouble, I mean."

"The police don't want us there. Forensics are all over it."

"What if she's been run over, what if she's injured somewhere? And we don't know. Ian, we *don't know.*"

"That's why they've used sniffer dogs, to locate her by the scent of blood."

"You know an awful lot all of a sudden," she says, and it comes out more harshly than she intends.

"We've got to *think.* Where could she have gone?" They are both prone to this, thinking their way out of their predicaments, as if sheer force of intellect could control the random world.

"France? I mean, I know we haven't been for years and years, but she does speak the language."

He shakes his head. "Border control—she hasn't got her passport, remember? You should ring Christy and Jonti."

"Yes. They won't know anything, but yes. She hasn't seen Jonti in years. Does Rollo have any ideas?"

"No, he says not, but he says he's setting up a Find Edith Facebook page or something. I wish it didn't take so long for him to get here. Miri," he says with a sudden gasp.

"I know," she says.

They are in this together; they love Edith together with lion-like force. Whatever rows there had ever been between them evaporated when Edith tottered toward them on chubby legs or made a funny face or delighted them in the myriad ways she did, and they would find themselves looking in the same direction, grinning stupidly at their girl. Together. Thank God they are together. The only person in the world who feels as much terror as she does is here, by her side.

She starts to cry. "If she's not all right, then I will never be all right."

"Darling Miri, come here," says Ian, taking her in his arms. "We'll find her. We'll keep on looking until we find her."

MANON

• • •

ENGINE'S OFF AND THE WIND SQUALLS ABOUT THE CAR. SHE SHOULD GET out, look lively, jog up the steps ready for a new day, but instead she rests her forehead on the steering wheel.

"Morning," says a muffled voice beyond her driver's side window. Davy, of course, smiling in at her, coffee in hand, the light glowing behind those marvelous ears, like red quotation marks. She winds down the window and a tinny hail of cold rain buffets in.

"How does my eye look?" she says, trying hard to open it fully.

"Looks normal to me. I've got you this. Warm you up. Haven't we got a briefing at eight?"

"Gimme a minute," says Manon.

She winds up the window, using both hands and all the force of her shoulder. Davy has stepped back and is standing beside the car, holding her coffee like a royal attendant. She flips down the sun visor to look in its cloudy mirror. Her left eye is half closed, red, and sloping downward as if she's been punched. She opens the car door. It is perishing cold, the chill cutting into her ankles and toes and about her wrists and neck, making her hunch and tighten. She locks her car, takes her coffee from Davy, and they walk up the steps of the station.

"Come in, both of you," says Harriet, from the doorway of her office. She is pulling at her bra straps. It's as if she's never comfortable, the upholstery springing a tack.

"What's happened to you?" she says, peering at Manon's eye.

"Oh, nothing. Bit sore, that's all."

"Looks like you've been beaten up."

Harriet's jumpy. The girl has been missing for fifty-four hours now without a single firm lead but about six possible avenues for investigation. There is mercifully still no sign of their boss, Detective Chief Superintendent Gary Stanton, yet interference is palpably not far away: in the air space above them, the vague suspicion that calls might be passing between the Home Office and Cambridgeshire Commissioner Sir Brian Peabody, the odd mention perhaps at Annabelle's or in the Pugin Room at the House, perhaps some quiet pressure filtering down to the chief constable, who will certainly be taking a keen interest. "Best brains on this Hind girl, old chap. Wouldn't want a cock-up on something this big."

Manon and Davy take up seats in Harriet's office, Manon nursing her coffee with two hands.

"What's happened to her?" says Harriet, pacing. "It's like she's evaporated. There's no CCTV, no sightings. . . ."

"Where are we with the search?" asks Davy.

"Polsa's widened it beyond Portholme Meadow—more than a hundred officers in all—and sometime today Spartan Rescue are going to start on the River Ouse."

"Take a week or two for a body to float up," says Manon.

"What about that Graham Garfield chap, the director of studies?" asks Harriet. "He was sniffing about on Saturday night."

"His wife says he was home with her after the pub," says Manon.

"Think we have to be a bit circumspect about alibis given by wives and mothers."

There is silence for a moment.

"Right, the press conference with the Hinds. We're going to watch

Will Carter, see how he fares. Kim Delaney is trawling River Island for clothes similar to the ones Edith was wearing on Saturday night—jeans and a blue sweatshirt."

"Boss?" says Colin, at the door. "We've got something."

They all look at him.

"Carter had another phone. Phone mast in Huntingdon picked up activity on Saturday night from a T-Mobile number registered to him."

They all look at one another.

"What sort of activity?" asks Harriet.

"Two calls, one at five P.M., another at midnight. That's all we can tell before the full traces come in, but it puts him in Huntingdon on the night we think Edith disappeared."

"Where's the phone now?"

"Dunno; it's switched off."

"Have we tracked his car out of Stoke yet?" asks Manon.

"No, we haven't," says Harriet. "Nigel's doing some work on the smaller routes, checking alternative cameras. We need to question him on this—no more tea and sympathy."

"Hang on," says Manon. "Let's let him do the presser, see how he holds up. Then we'll ask him about what his phone was doing in Huntingdon when he says he was in Stoke."

"I want officers on the door," says Harriet. "And I want us all over his alibi. House-to-house in Stoke around his mother's address, see if anyone saw him leaving earlier than they both say. And CCTV."

MANON PERCHES ONE BUTTOCK ON the edge of Colin's desk and looks up at the monitor, which shows an empty table with four chairs behind it and microphones along the front, pointing at the chairs.

The rest of the team gathers around her: Colin in his swively chair; Kim back from River Island; Davy, of course; and the new recruit, Stuart Leach. Manon eyes him in her periphery, her eyes flicking from his shaven head to the monitor, then back to his broad shoulders in a billowing shirt (she loves a billowing shirt on a man, especially with sharp creases), his square jaw and dark eyes, which have a certain amused mischief in them. He catches her eye and smiles.

"So, it was the boyfriend, was it?" he says, and she can feel all his charm being launched at her like a hand grenade—mischief slash disrespect.

"Looks like it. We don't know for sure," she says, looking upward at the monitor and simultaneously tightening her body under his gaze. She's going to have to cut back on the Marmite toast. "Here they are."

They watch as Harriet sits in the chair to the right of the screen. The Hinds then inch into view from the left, shuffling into their seats on half-bended legs and holding hands, their gaze downward. Will Carter enters last, wearing a mid-blue shirt that brings out the slate color of his eyes. Manon can almost hear the female reporters in the room sitting up straighter. Flashes going, the electronic burr blending into the shuffling and murmuring of the crowd settling: TV news, locals, nationals, agencies, digital channels, Web reporters. Manon sees the gray hollows beneath Sir Ian's eyes. Lady Hind's are red-rimmed. They are silvery in their aging, as if covered by a hoarfrost. Carter runs a hand through his hair, and the cameras seem to flurry in response.

Harriet introduces the pertinent facts about the investigation, the timeline of Edith's disappearance, details of the police hotline. Her glance repeatedly flicks to Will, whose gaze is directed at the cameras.

Somewhere in the room, behind Manon, a phone starts ringing.

"Crikey, already," says Colin. "Here come the tank-top-wearing schizophrenics."

"Shut it, Colin," says Manon.

"It'll be the ladies offering to comfort Mr. Carter," says Kim. "Even if he's killed her, he'll get a few marriage proposals."

They watch Harriet introduce Sir Ian. There is a pause before he speaks.

"We are desperately worried about Edith," he says, lifting his gaze to the phalanx of reporters and cameras, and for a split second, utter distaste is visible on his face. Lady Hind strokes his hand. "She is a resourceful, clever, and talented girl, but the circumstances of her disappearance are obviously giving cause for mounting alarm. Edith, if you are watching this, please contact us to let us know you are safe. And if anyone out there has seen our daughter, do please contact the police."

"Mr. Carter," says a female voice. "Keeley Davis, *Hunts Post*. You must be devastated."

"I am. I'm . . . I'm . . ." Will Carter looks about the room. "I haven't slept. This is torture, a nightmare. We just want to know where Edie is."

Manon thinks she can see Lady Hind close her eyes, her mouth in a tiny grimace, but perhaps she's imagining it.

"Sorry, one more question," says pushy Keeley Davis, who will no doubt be off to the *Mail* any day now, with her tight suit and that retro Nissan she drives, the automotive equivalent of a Prada handbag. "Was there anything about her behavior in the days before she disappeared that gave you cause for concern?"

"No, not at all," says Will. He is giving Keeley maximum eye contact, furrowed and serious and frankly adorable. "This is totally out of character. We were happy, *are* happy. We're incredibly close. She is my world. Y'know, she was working hard on her PhD, looking forward to Christmas. Normal stuff."

Harriet points to another member of the audience. "Yes, Terry."

"Terry Harcourt, the *Mirror*. Sir Ian, can you tell us more about Edith—what sort of girl is she?"

Sir Ian looks vaguely lost. "Well," he says, halting for a moment as if he hasn't understood the question, "as I say, she is clever. She has a double first from Cambridge and is studying for her PhD. She is quite sporty, dedicated to the environment."

Manon watches his bewildered face as the shutters click and the flashes blind him. She knows what they want—incontinent emoting. They want him and Miriam Hind to break down over "their angel."

Harriet moves it along. "Yes, Andy, from the *Herald*."

"Sir Ian, you are physician to the Royal Family. Has the queen sent you any messages of support?"

"I don't think that's relevant to the purpose of this press conference," says Sir Ian.

"Right, yes. Nick, ITN," says Harriet, pointing to the back of the room.

"Sir Ian, you are personal friends with the home secretary. Is he putting extra resources behind this investigation?"

"I can answer that one," says Harriet. "All the resources of the police force are at our disposal in the search for Edith. This would be the case for any high-risk missing person."

"Is it true you're looking for a body?" shouts a voice into the room.

Manon sees Lady Hind flinch. The room buzzes with enlarged murmurings.

"What's your name?" asks Harriet.

"Tony Thackeray, *Eastern Daily Press*. Missing person, more than forty-eight hours, sub-zero temperatures. This must surely become a murder investigation at some point. And isn't it also true that Cambridgeshire MIT has been criticized in the past for not upscaling a missing person to suspected homicide early enough? The case of Lacey Pilkington . . ."

"*Shit,*" whispers Manon.

Sir Ian and Miriam frown at each other and then at Harriet, who says, "Our priority is to find Edith."

"Aye aye," says Colin, nodding at the screen. "Here's Officer Dibble, back from 'is holidays."

They all notice Detective Chief Superintendent Gary Stanton, who has come to stand at the edge of the room, his body leaning against the wall. The buttons on his white shirt are straining, his civilian suit sharp and navy. He has the look of a man who has just stepped off a plane: his face and bald pate basted brown like a cooked turkey and shiny with good living. His gaze is on Harriet and she bristles with it.

"We are going to have to wrap things up, I'm afraid," she says, shifting in her seat. She's eager to collar Will Carter; Manon can see it in Harriet's agitation—that's why she's closed it down so quick. "Thank you all for coming."

DAVY

• • •

"It was stolen," says Will Carter, pacing with a hand in his hair, the other on his hip. "Look, I know it looks bad, but it honestly didn't occur to me to mention it. I've been taken up with . . . just, you know, my whole mind is on Edie."

Davy is stood with his back to the wall, behind Harriet and Manon, who are sitting at the table, facing Carter. Davy has the sense that Harriet is using him as a "heavy," though he doesn't really have the face for it. He's been told he always looks faintly embarrassed or surprised, so he's trying to lean sardonically against the wall, as if he's a mass of thickset skepticism. Harriet is leaning too—back in her chair, twirling a pencil about her fingers. The disbelieving detective. Manon, however, is sat forward, her position saying, "I want to try to understand."

"Go on," says Manon.

"It didn't seem important. I forgot about it."

"When and where was it stolen, Mr. Carter?" says Manon.

"From my car. On Friday as I was preparing to leave. I left it on the seat, slammed the car door, and ran in to get my bag. I was only going to be a minute, maybe it was more like five, but when I came out, it had gone."

"Did you see anyone—running away or near the car?"

"No. I glanced in either direction but the street was empty. Maybe they were hiding behind a hedge or something, I dunno. I wouldn't have gone after them anyway. I'm a coward when it comes to things like that—I don't want to get punched. I think they must've been watching me and seized their chance when I went inside."

"And you didn't think to report it?" says Harriet.

"I wanted to get on the road—my mum was expecting me. I'll be honest, I didn't think there was much the police could do. I thought it was my own stupid fault and I had to suck it up. Anyway, I stopped at the Tesco phone shop in Kettering—it's open late—and got a pay-as-you-go, so I could give Edie a number, y'know, so she could call me in an emergency."

"Sorry, Mr. Carter, but how did you not think this was relevant to our investigation?" asks Harriet.

"I don't know. I just wanted you to find Edie. I was so worried, it didn't occur to me."

"So you phoned Edith from Kettering?"

"No, I texted."

"You didn't want to talk to her about the fact you'd been a victim of a crime?"

"I tried to call her."

"You tried to call her," says Harriet, her voice dripping with exhausted frustration.

"I did call but she didn't pick up. I knew she wouldn't recognize the number, so I explained in a text and she texted back saying 'OK.'"

He has stopped in front of them.

Davy can't see Harriet's expression, but she is probably frowning. "Forgive me, Mr. Carter, but perhaps you can see why we're confused. You say everything's perfect between you and Miss Hind, you say everything was normal in the run-up to her disappearance—"

"OK, not normal."

Harriet is gesturing at the chair in front of them, the patient mother. Carter sits at last.

"One minute everything was normal," he says, "and then it wasn't. One minute we were making dinner, watching *Sherlock* on iPlayer, and then—about a week ago, I guess—I dunno, she cooled off, like she was cross with me. Froze when I touched her. Kept saying she had loads of work on, as if she was avoiding me. I suppose that fits with what you said about her and Helena."

"Can you give specific examples?" asks Manon.

"Well, the Saturday before ... a week before ..." He colors up, doesn't know how to refer to the "event" of Edith's disappearance, which might or might not be her death. "She went out, I don't even know who with, got really drunk, and on the Sunday she spent the whole day in bed with her laptop on her knees. And then in the afternoon, about three, she put a tracksuit on and her boots and took her car keys. When I asked where she was going, she said, 'Out.' It went on like that, passing each other in the house like strangers. Then on Friday, the Friday I was going to Stoke, she was suddenly really full-on, emotional. We made love—this was in the afternoon—and I thought, oh, it's all right again, it was just a passing thing. But she started crying immediately after—after the sex, I mean—and she said, 'I'm sorry.' I suppose now she was talking about Helena, I dunno. I said, 'What for?' And she said, 'For being a bitch to you.' I said, 'You haven't been, not so I've noticed.' Which was bollocks, of course, I had noticed, but I was just glad she was back with me, I wanted to be close again, and I didn't want to argue. Anyway, it seemed to make it worse. She snapped at me, 'That's right, Will, let's tell each other lies.' I'll be honest—I didn't know what was going on."

Poor chap, Davy thinks. He wouldn't be the first man whose girlfriend was a mystery to him. What law is it that says you can't be a hapless good-looking bloke—well, a model, pretty much, actually—in the wrong place at the wrong time?

"It has taken you an awfully long time to tell us all this," says Harriet. She wants to nail him, wants his alibi broken and an arrest before Stanton can go clod-hopping all over her investigation. She'll be thinking he set up the phone theft—stopped at Kettering to buy a PAYG as part of his alibi—then slipped back early to Huntingdon to murder Edith because he was furious that she was leaving him, or being un-faithful, or both. It was often both.

"It was private, all right?" says Carter, not quite shouting but de-fensive. "My relationship with Edie is private and I didn't want to tell you lot about it."

Davy looks at the ringlets springing from the back of Manon's head and wonders what she makes of Carter. He hazards a guess: Manon would say go easy, trace the phone, track his plates, follow up on the Tesco phone shop in Kettering and the petrol stations on his return journey. Because cases, as she was forever telling him, aren't solved on hunches. They're solved with dogged, stoic donkey work.

MANON
. . .

HARRIET TAKES A CIRCULAR TIN OF VASELINE, GREEN AND WHITE, FROM
the depths of her handbag. Without looking at it, she twists off the lid
and dabs some onto her middle finger, stroking it across her lips so
they glisten. Her gaze locks on the middle distance. *These shifts are aging us,* Manon thinks. She keeps glazing over too, and when she does,
her mind returns again and again to Deeping—its painterly swaths,
colors murky and creative—perhaps because it's the polar opposite of
police HQ, all pale laminate and strip lighting. The exposure of dark
corners.

People are preparing to go home. "We can't keep you all here indefinitely," Harriet said. "Get some sleep. See you back here at seven
tomorrow morning." Coats being threaded onto leaden arms, bags
gathered, families phoned. ("Yes, Dawn, I know it's late. . . . Well, I'm
sorry, but there wasn't anything I could—shall I pick up something for
us to eat?")

"Don't walk home tonight," Harriet says, and Manon blinks into focus, sees her flicking her hair out from under her coat collar.

"No, I've got the car. Hang on, I thought Carter was our suspect."

"Yeah, well, you heard Stanton."

She'd been in on the meeting, Stanton hitching up the back of his belt, his belly its counterweight, while he told Harriet she didn't have the evidence against Carter: "No body, no forensics, no witnesses, nothing."

"We need to shake him up," Harriet said, but she was already on the back foot.

Stanton doesn't want the headlines, the payout in compensation if they're wrong, and the press going to town. His manner had said, *You've both got a bit overexcited, but now my steadying hand is back on the tiller.* "We wait," he told them. "We investigate all avenues. Trace. Interview. Eliminate."

"Just ... don't walk," Harriet is saying, covering a yawn with her fist. "You don't know—we don't know—who's out there."

"Anything on unknown-515, that mystery number on Edith's call register, Davy?" says Manon, as he walks toward them.

"Nothing," he says.

"Fancy a lift?" Manon says.

He seems to falter, then says, "OK, yes, thanks very much."

MANON'S WIPERS PUSH DOGGEDLY AT the rain but do little to dissipate the fog on her windscreen, so she winds down a window, letting in sprays of wet. Rough winds buffet the car as she pulls onto the A14 to avoid the cordon that has closed George Street and created gridlock in central Huntingdon. She'll follow the ring road around to suburban Sapley, where Davy lives. The roads roar with wetness and the damp mingles with the musty interior of her car. On the banks of the motorway, just visible in the dark, are the last sketches of snow being pummeled by the rain.

"Have you got any hobbies, Davy?" she asks, peering into the dark.

"I do, yes," says Davy. "I do my mentoring at the youth center, kids in care. I like a spot of gardening, though I haven't got a garden at the moment. I do help look after my mum's."

"See? You've got plenty of hobbies. I haven't got one."

"Why d'you ask?"

"I had to fill in a hobbies section—for the dating site—and I drew a complete blank. I literally don't have any. So I've decided to get hobbied up."

"And how is that going?" asks Davy, with a hopefulness that would imply he'd never met Manon.

"Awful. I hate it. I mean, what's the point of doing something just for the sake of it, when it isn't your job?"

"Well, to relax."

"I even went to a pottery class so I'd have something to type in. But I just couldn't get past the pointlessness of it. I mean, it's not like I'm ever going to have a pottery wheel in my lounge, to relax with."

"You don't know that. Demi Moore had one in *Ghost*," says Davy. She looks at him, but he maintains his cheerful gaze straight ahead.

"So I'm going to try Zumba instead," says Manon. "Thought I'd go tonight, actually. Help me wind down. It's been quite full-on. Do you find that—difficulty falling asleep?"

"Nope, not me. My head touches the pillow and, bosh, I'm off. Did Harriet suggest that—the Zumba, I mean?"

Manon shoots him a sharp look. "No, she did not. Why? What's she said to you?"

"Nothing, no, nothing. It's just good if we all keep fit, that's all," says Davy. "For catching villains. Ah, here we are," he says, patting his knees. Manon slows the car and Davy gets out, then leans in through the open door. "Right, well, cheerio," he says.

He waits, but she doesn't respond, so he closes the car door.

DAVY

• • •

HE'S IN BRIGHT AND EARLY, AND AS HE STANDS BESIDE HIS DESK, TAKING off his coat, he surveys the MIT department. The support and admin staff who dominate the building have subsided into a loose, festive spirit—this being the last working week for many—and this is mulling its way into the investigations team. Kim is standing on a chair, hanging some Christmas cards on a loop of string, a row of flapping birds. One of the administrators has made an attempt to stretch, between the strip lights, some accordion gold chains, one of which pings off its Blu-Tack, fluttering down against the wall.

Four days to Christmas, seventy-seven hours missing, the golden hour having ebbed away. He looks up at the television screen, which is bracketed to the wall, and sees the aerial shots of the search teams, muted on the twenty-four-hour news channel—tiny people in navy vests with "Police" on the back, or in fluorescent-yellow windcheaters, combing squares of gardens, beating bushes with sticks; white vans on street corners; and huddles of officers bent over maps or talking to residents. All of it silent while the red ticker along the bottom of the screen says, *Missing student Edith Hind, latest: frogmen search the Ouse*. The image flicks to a navy dinghy skirting the brown soupy surface of the river. Must be the worst job, he thinks; you could only ever come up with something nasty or nothing at all. Then there's a shot of the members of the public who have joined the search, forming a long line to inch their way across Portholme Meadow. Most appear to be chatting to one another, without so much as a glance around them.

He drapes his coat over the back of his chair and is about to get a coffee from the filter machine where it stews and burns, when Manon enters the room. He lifts his empty mug at her and she nods back, a thumbs-up. She seems to be walking gingerly and having trouble taking off her coat. As Davy gets her a coffee, he sees Stuart, the new recruit, approach and lift the coat from her shoulders while she winces, and they both laugh at something.

Davy doesn't know how he does it, but every time Stuart looks up from under his Disney-princess eyelashes, every woman in the room titters as if she's at a sixth-form disco. He's got so much confidence, like when Harriet had been talking to him about some quirk of the HOLMES database and he'd picked a bit of fluff off the shoulder of her jacket, and, momentarily, she hadn't known what on earth to do with herself. Davy would never have the guts to be like that with senior police officers. Marveling, he carries two coffees back to his desk, puts down his own, and hands the second to Manon, who takes it while looking at her screen.

Christmas is weighing on Davy's mind, especially what to buy his mother. Bed socks, perhaps—cashmere—or would that be too strong a reference to her bedridden years? All those weeks and months when Davy cast himself as the lightbulb to her dark recess. He wants to get her something nice, because Christmas is hard on her, the way it dredges up painful memories of when his father left, seventeen years ago. She asks Davy endless questions about his father, who continues to live happily with Sharon the lollipop lady in Kent. He couldn't, of course, go and spend Christmas with them—even though their Christmases sound rather raucous, with Sharon's extended family gathering for one long knees-up and walks along the Whitstable seafront. No, that would be a disloyalty too far.

"There's a briefing," he says to Manon. "This afternoon. Child-protection teams, multi-agency. It was on the board."

"Can't go to that," says Manon, sipping her coffee. "Too much to do."

"Boss says we have to. Three-line whip."

"What time?"

"Three o'clock. Short one, but we can't get out of it."

Davy is glad it's compulsory. They should know, his colleagues, what's really happening—what he sees at the youth center. He's been mentoring a lad called Ryan, twelve years old, who was taken into care at age ten after being admitted to hospital a second time with broken forearms. There were boot prints on his skin. Every time Ryan walked through his front door at home, he got a pummeling, if not from whichever lowlife his mum was seeing, then from his mum. She liked to put her cigarettes out on him.

Davy bought Ryan a fart gun for his eleventh birthday, which Ryan looked at with contempt, saying it was for babies and he wanted a Nintendo DS or a Wii, but Davy had ignored him, letting off the gun under the table at McDonald's so that diners at the next table began to whisper and grimace. Back at the center, Ryan started to play with the gun, parping and trumping at his friends as they texted irritably on the red foam sofas. Ryan laughed and laughed, ticklish, tearful giggling, and it was as if he was four years old, and six years old, and eleven—all the ages he hadn't been allowed to be. He loved to laugh, Ryan did, once he granted himself the freedom of it, which was hard to come by, and when the laughing overtook him, as it had with the fart gun, his face radiated like sparkling sunshine on water.

"They're sending me back," Ryan told Davy on his last visit.

"Back?" said Davy, stunned. "Where? Back to your mum?"

Ryan nodded, swallowing. "No room for me at Aldridge House no more. They cut back two of the staff—Evangeline and Bill, the only nice ones. Now there's not enough adults for all the kids—the ratio, they call it—so I have to go."

"What does your mum say?"

"Dunno, they haven't got hold of her yet. All she cares about is the money." He put on a screeching voice. "'How am I supposed to feed 'im when I got naaa money?' C'mon, let's play."

Then, when they were standing around the green baize table taking turns, Ryan returned to the subject. He had the snooker cue across his shoulders, his arms draped over it like a coat hanger, and he said, "'Least I'm not Jayden."

"What's happened to him?" asked Davy, leaning his whole body on the table to pot the red.

"He's been kicked out of Aldridge an' all. Been placed in a house with two pedos. Everyone knows they're nonces, but social services say it's all they've got. I'd rather be on the street."

"How old is Jayden?" asks Davy, rubbing chalk on the end of his cue while Ryan walks around the table, looking for angles.

"Ten."

If Davy could do what he actually wanted this Christmas, he'd spend it with Ryan at the youth center. Serving watery turkey with packet stuffing. Playing pool in his snowman tank top with a paper hat on and letting off the fart gun when Ryan least expects it.

MANON

• • •

She's yawning while the room settles. They're waiting for a morning briefing with Harriet, who is ensconced in her office with Stanton and the search adviser.

Colin is bowing his head low over the desk and muttering in Italian.

"*Posso avere quella senza aglio?*" he says to his iPhone.

"What are you doing, Colin?" says Manon, rubbing at the grit in her eye again. She pulls out her eyelid and blinks downward.

"My Learn Italian app," Colin says. "Translation—can I have that without garlic? Can't stand the stuff, nor can Gwyneth."

"P'raps Puglia isn't your ideal holiday destination, then," says Manon, the blinking not having made any difference.

"Don't see why they can't cater to our tastes," says Colin, "seeing as we're paying." He rocks back with his glasses pushed up onto his bald pate. Manon wonders: did Gwyneth look into Colin's small, bloodshot eyes and say, "You are the UKIP-voting misogynist for me"? She must have done—they'd been married for thirty-odd years. And there was luck in that; you were lucky if you could be happy with what life threw your way (even if it was Colin) instead of generally dissatisfied, as Manon is. Colin's Google searches were testament to the richness of their life together—boutique hotels in Margate, painting courses in Giverny, walking tours of the Tyrol.

"Look, here's one of the *pensioni* we're staying in," Colin is saying, scrolling through some images of wafting muslin curtains framing a view of the sea.

This is one of the many things Manon hates about the open-plan office, apart from the way it favors crazed extroverts—it throws up so much envy. She's regularly stabbed by it: envy of Colin and Gwyneth's tour of Puglia; envy of Nigel and Dawn's gurgling newborn twins; even of Davy and Chloe's Friday night takeaway in front of the telly.

Stuart is leaning against the wall, his gaze intense into the room so that every time Manon looks up, she seems to catch his eye. Only his third day in the job, yet he has a strangely dominating effect on the department. His hands had brushed her neck as he helped her off with her coat, sending a charge through her, and she made a self-deprecating reference to overdoing the exercise last night. "Won't be trying that again," she said. "From now on my fat arse stays on the chair."

Her legs and arms have seized up completely, so that she can barely put on or take off a coat, and her attempts to zip up her boots this morning resulted in her rolling across the floor in a ball like some petrified hedgehog. She takes a sip of coffee. The tiredness has hit her forcefully—a wall she must scale. It's always worse for a night's sleep, which, instead of giving the mind and body nimble new energy, seems to transmogrify exhaustion into cement.

Edith Hind is all over the morning papers, every front page carrying pictures of Sir Ian and Miriam. Most of it is straight reporting, but Manon noticed a couple of columnists in the mid-market titles commenting on the couple's demeanor. "When all a parent can say of the child they love is that they were 'very academic,' we need to look again at our value system," wrote one mop-headed moralist.

She looks down at the sheet prepared for her by Davy, detailing Edith's known movements in the week before she disappeared. ANPR cameras have picked up one trip to Deeping in the G–Wiz on Sunday, December 11, a week before she disappeared and the day after her affair with Helena began.

"Looking forward to Christmas telly?" says Davy, to no one in particular, as if trying to cheer up the room in general. "I'm going to be watching *Polar Express*."

Manon has clasped her two hands around her mug. "Did you notice," she says, "Edith Hind and Will Carter didn't have a telly?"

"It's not a human right," says Davy.

"Bloody is," says Colin, without looking round.

"I can't stand people who don't own tellies," says Manon.

"How very reasonable of you," says Stuart, his eyes meeting hers, his arms crossed over his chest.

"Shall I tell you why?" says Manon, looking back at him.

"Think you're going to," mutters Davy.

"Because they just watch loads on iPlayer and then go on and on about not having a telly to people who do have tellies."

"D'you want to know my theory?" says Colin.

"Oh God," says Manon, "close the windows, someone might hear."

"I think Edith Hind fancied a meat-feast pizza, a movie, and a good ol' shag without having to boil any mung beans or discuss the metaphysical poets."

"Right, yes, thank you again, Colin."

Harriet and Stanton have entered the department and Harriet is clapping her hands for silence and saying loudly, "Right, everybody," at which point Stanton says, "Harriet will be taking this briefing. I've got a press conference downstairs at nine. I think you should know, however, that my line will be that it is now more than seventy-two hours since she went missing and that, in our view, it is highly likely Edith Hind has come to harm."

He's reacted, Manon thinks, to Thackeray in that press conference and the criticism surrounding their last high-risk misper. Twelve-year-old Lacey Pilkington disappeared three years ago on a Peterborough estate. Stanton was SIO, then as a DCI. In a standard review, his investigation was criticized: officers had been blinded by the belief the girl was alive, which delayed appropriate action. It should have been upscaled to a suspected homicide sooner, and as a result of this misjudgment, time and evidence were lost. Stanton, they said, had become hidebound by the emotions of the victim's family. Who, incidentally, Manon recalls bitterly, were the ones who'd killed her.

"I shall also be making clear," Stanton is saying, "that the main focus of our investigation is her complex love life." He turns, nods, and says, "Thanks, Harriet," then walks out of the department.

"Ian Hind is going to *love* us," says Manon.

MIRIAM

. . .

"Not long now," says Miriam, sitting in the molded-plastic chair of interview room one. "To see Rollo, I mean." She can smell vending-machine instant coffee, dispensed in those squat brown cups that crackle in the hand.

Ian doesn't answer her. He is pacing still. She doesn't know how he keeps going; he seems to expend so much energy every minute of the day and isn't resting at night either. He has been out there, standing next to the parish priest who joined the community in prayer, doing his best to hide his distaste for the members of the public joining the search (and failing, in Miriam's opinion: she's never seen a thank-you speech so faltering and pinched), paying to print posters, T-shirts, and balloons emblazoned with Edith's smiling face and the date 12/17/2010.

He was pleased, at first, that Detective Chief Superintendent Gary Stanton was overseeing, as if someone at his own level was finally in charge—*a chap*—someone who could actually make something happen. Then he watched this morning's press conference on Sky. It caused him to puff, then stand up and walk around the room, then tut again, the tension fizzing off him and transferring itself to Miriam.

More than seventy-two hours. Edith has been gone more than seventy-two hours and there is a palpable cooling in the atmosphere surrounding the investigation. It has slowed. Officers have returned to normal shift patterns. The search is ongoing, dogged, hundreds of police inching forward with sticks or flashlights or in diving suits, but Miriam has sensed it no longer contains the urgency of searching for someone alive.

She takes a deep breath, leans her head back, and closes her eyes. She's not sure she can take another night in this town—another night sweating and dry-mouthed in that airless hotel room; another meal in the bar, at a slippery table, her clothes infused with the smell of deep-fat frying. She can't wait to see the back of Huntingdon, its dirty snow, pound shops, and gray, hunkered streets. She realizes she harbors a fantasy that when she leaves this place, she'll leave behind this nasty business—the terrible feelings, the sleeplessness, the way her mind oscillates wildly between terror and blankness. Back in Hampstead, she might return to the woman she was only four days ago, preparing for Christmas, snipping stems of eucalyptus, steeping dried figs in brandy, untangling strings of white pin lights. She feels a growing anger with Edith for putting her through this, as if she were some limitlessly absorbent sponge for her daughter's mess. And then her anger makes her cry again, because she wants nothing except to have Edith back.

"Sir Ian, Lady Hind," says a male voice, and Miriam wipes her eyes and sees DCS Gary Stanton, DI Harriet Harper, and DS Manon Bradshaw, all three reintroducing themselves.

Oh no, oh no, they must have found a body. Why all three like this? Like some ghastly triumvirate. Miriam looks up at them, a hand clasped over her mouth, her eyes flicking from one to the next.

"There's nothing new to report," says DS Bradshaw, acknowledging her terror.

"What the hell was all that this morning?" Ian is saying.

"I felt I had to say what I thought," says Stanton calmly. "I'm sorry if it was upsetting for you."

"Do you have any idea what the tabloids are going to be like after this?" says Ian, though Miriam knows that it is the "come to harm" line that has upset him more than any of the salacious things they said about Edith's love life. He cannot, will not, bear it.

"We need information. The press is the best way to flush that out."

"You effectively told the press she's dead."

"We have to be realistic. . . ." says Stanton.

"You have to find her, that's what you have to do. Find her. Stop posturing and just bloody well find her—" says Ian, stopped by tears that seem to ambush him.

Miriam's gaze has settled on DS Bradshaw, who is leaning against the closed door, her hands behind her back. Beautiful curls, unruly. She's always observing, and she now returns Miriam's gaze, though neither woman smiles.

"We feel," says DI Harper, "that you would be more comfortable back at home, rather than holed up in a hotel in Huntingdon surrounded by the press."

"What you're saying is, you're giving up," says Ian. "You're closing down the search and you don't want me breathing down your neck."

"Absolutely not," says Stanton. "This is not, in any way, a scaling down of the case. The search for Edith will continue at full tilt and you will be kept fully informed by your liaison officer."

"Great, you're sending us away with a depressed shadow," says Ian. "Do we get to keep her for Christmas?"

"Ian," says Miriam, almost in a whisper.

"Your liaison officer is there to support you. We simply don't feel it's sensible to keep you in Huntingdon," says Stanton. "But please be reassured this is not a scaling down of the case."

Of course it bloody is, thinks Miriam.

"I won't allow this to go cold," says Ian. "I won't allow you to stop searching for our child. If I have to call Roger . . ."

He is standing beside her chair, and Miriam takes hold of his hand and squeezes it, then presses it against her lips and closes her eyes tight to stop the tears from coming, because the smell of him, and the soft feeling of the hairs on the back of his hand against her cheek, and the way he is fighting so hard for them both, for all of them, is making her well up.

"I know it's hard," says DS Bradshaw, much softer than either of her bosses. "Leaving this place—it must feel like leaving Edith. But you can't stay in Huntingdon indefinitely. And your home is less than two hours away, so . . ."

"They're right, darling," says Miriam, looking up at Ian, still holding his hand against her cheek. "We're not doing any good here. We might as well go home and sleep in our own bed. But please God don't make us take that basset hound of a woman with us."

"It's for the best," says DI Harper, "and I can assure you there will be no diminution of effort or dedication."

MANON

. . .

"'THERE WILL BE NO DIMINUTION OF EFFORT?'" SAYS MANON, AS SHE AND Harriet climb the echoey staircase to MIT, without Stanton, who has gone off to stoke his belly with another large lunch. "Bit of a mouthful, wasn't it?"

"Oh, look, he gets right on my tits. I can't think straight with him looking at me, thinking"—Harriet puts on an upper-crust Sir Ian accent—"'What manner of fuckwit are you?'"

"Yes, he's a bit . . . austere."

"A bit?"

"Well, he's worried. I'd want my dad to do the same."

"S'pose. She's a bloody cold fish too."

Manon stops, a hand on Harriet's arm so that she turns on the stairs. "No, she isn't," says Manon. "She isn't at all. She just doesn't put it all out there."

"We really need to get on and identify the people in the post office queue," says Harriet. "Nigel's got the footage, but some of them are shielded by hoods or they're just standing at the wrong angle."

"We can get the staff to corroborate with their paperwork. Where's Will Carter staying?"

"Not with Helena Reed, that's for sure. We've let him go home to Stoke but asked him to stay put so we can keep him informed. The Hind brother's due in this afternoon. I want you and Davy to interview him as soon as he arrives, OK? What are you up to tonight, anything nice?"

"Another date," says Manon. "To be honest, I'd rather look at a thousand hours of local-authority CCTV."

THEY SIT IN A ROW in conference room one, waiting for the child-protection briefing, everyone on their smartphones. Manon has just received the latest demand for a dating update from Bryony. She's next to Nigel, who has turned his back to the room and is hissing into his phone, a hand cupped over the mouthpiece. Dawn, obviously. Colin is downloading confirmation of his Ryanair flights. Kim is yawning, her feet up on the chair in front. The room is an oasis of police blue—blue foam chairs, blue curtains, blue carpet—and smells of brewing coffee. It is filling up, people shuffling along the rows, slight bend at the knee: ambulance crews from Hinchingbrooke, passport control, CID. People nodding, saying hello. A few uniforms, rustling fluorescent jackets with zips and toggles and crackling radios, which make them seem larger than the rest. Amazing she can't find a date among this lot.

Davy, to the other side of Manon, is sat bolt upright, his neck straining upward so he can look at the woman at the podium, who is shuffling papers before she begins.

"You should listen," he says to Manon. "This stuff's important. You wouldn't believe what's happening out there."

But Manon is texting Bryony.

This one's a poet. Therefore not simply fucktard, but fucktard who cannot pay mortgage.

"Hello, everyone, and thanks for coming," says the mousy voice at the podium. "I am Sheila Berridge, head of child-protection services."

Manon's phone vibrates.

You don't know that. He might be laureate-in-waiting. Anyway, I admire you
for being dating daredevil. B

Manon yawns, hears the words "cross-sector involvement" and
"joined-up thinking" waft across the room toward her.

"We all need to be aware of the crisis in our children's homes and
how this spills out into all our sectors." Sheila Berridge warns of un-
precedented numbers of children entering the care system as more and
more families bump and skid below the poverty line. There are currently sixty-seven thousand children in care in England, she says.

Davy leans in to Manon, whispers urgently, "Sixty-seven thousand.
That's a city three times the size of Huntingdon."

"A city of children," says the woman at the podium, as if she and
Davy are telecommunicating, "children with their attachments broken, the majority—seventy percent—having experienced abuse or neglect. Once in care," she continues, trying to get above the shuffling
and bleeping and restlessness of the room, "many children experience
the instability of multiple short-term placements. They are more likely
to go missing, making them vulnerable to harmful situations such as
sexual exploitation."

"I see this all the time," Davy whispers to Manon, "at the youth
group. I mean, they're *children*."

"The pattern of neglect," says Sheila Berridge's harried voice, "is
getting worse. We know of gangs of men who prey on girls in care,
getting them addicted to alcohol and drugs, then grooming them for
sex. Pedophiles are operating in many care homes. This affects all of us,
every agency in this room."

Manon looks to the other side of her, away from Davy's keen expression, and sees Nigel yawning. He casts her a look as if to say, *Boring,
huh?*

"We must be aware of how difficult these children are to help," says
Sheila Berridge, her voice now raised and powerful, "and be mindful
that they *must* be listened to, however much they change their stories,
however dangerous and unpredictable they seem. We must listen to
what they tell us. We must take them very seriously indeed."

DAVY

• • •

HE SMILES AT DAVY, PROFFERING HIS HAND WARMLY. *ABOUT MY AGE,* Davy thinks, *bit younger maybe, so why do I feel inferior in front of Rollo Hind, whose face is friendly and open—unlike his father's?*

"Inferior" is too strong, Davy decides, sitting behind the table while Manon fiddles with the recording machine. There's been quite a bit of preamble, along the lines of: "Good flight?" and "Thanks for coming all this way, sir, we really appreciate it," and "How was Buenos Aires?"

Suburban, he thinks, putting his finger on it. Perhaps it's the hair. Davy's just sort of sits there, on his head—it'd be pushing it to call it a "style"—whereas Rollo Hind has a natty quiff, up from the parting, a bit rockabilly, a bit mod; dead sharp. Or the bright blue eyes sparkling out from his face, a golden shimmer at the temples. Rollo Hind seems all Hollywood, while he and Manon, their complexions the color of canteen mash, are rocking the fifteen-hour-shift look.

"You had a text conversation with Edith on Tuesday, thirteenth of December, which was quite self-questioning, wasn't it?" Manon says.

Davy has read the texts, extracted by Colin from Edith's phone, which had been conducted over WhatsApp, the free texting application.

E: Do u think of yourself as good person, Rol? I mean, do u think your goodness innate?

R: I'm definitely good, yes.

E: But don't u think everyone thinks they r good, even if they r bad? A bad person wd prob say, "I'm essentially good, but there are these extenuating circumstances."

R: Don't know what u r on about. Btw, have you seen Natalie Portman in *Black Swan* yet? She's HOT.

E: But do u think your goodness innate, or are u good because u hv been told to be good, because u r conforming to societal norms?

R: FFS, Smelly, what's brought this on?

E: Wondering: what's core, as in part of self, or what's there because society demands it. Or is goodness genetic?

R: Not in our family. Praps skipped generation?

E: Don't joke.

R: What's up with u?

E: U r lucky, Dad never expected much from u.

R: Thanks! Low expectations = freedom. Listen, am knackered, sis. Can u have yr existential personality crisis some other time?

E: No worries. Love you, Rol.

"I feel terrible about that now," Rollo says, "that I didn't take it more seriously, but it wasn't that out of character, not for Edith. I mean, she's prone to this sort of thing. She's a serious person, y'know? Gets fed up with me, says I'm glib about everything. When we traveled around Italy together, Interrailing, she was always wanting to talk about E. M. Forster and personal freedom versus duty. She likes to . . . intellectualize things."

"So she would text you existential questions like this, without preamble?"

"Well, OK, this was slightly out of the blue. I mean, it came from nowhere, but it wasn't enough to make me think . . . It didn't make me *worry*, is what I'm saying. And maybe it should've done, with hindsight. She's a student at Cambridge—they're all at it, sitting around till two A.M. pondering Kierkegaard and the essence of being. I thought it was just part of that."

"And now?"

He shrugs. "After what Mum and Dad told me, about Helena and all that, I wonder if she's talking about being unfaithful—about goodness in terms of what she was doing to Will. She would've felt really guilty about that."

MANON

. . .

SHE'S LACED THEM TOO TIGHT, THE BOOTS. THE STRINGS DIG INTO HER ankles and the cold rises up off the ice, radiating toward her face. Her fingers are cold. Her cheeks are cold. *Why have we come inside to get cold?* Her shins are painful with the tensing of her muscles. She inches forward, one foot then the other, gripping hard on to the handrail.

"Really fucking hate skating," she mutters, shuffling forward toward the poet, who is ahead of her.

He smiles. He has a meek face under a head of curls, but while her own emanate from her head at wild angles, his hang limp and wet-looking. She nods back at him, her body bent forward from the waist, her legs like scissoring crutches.

He doubles back to her, fast on his skates, and stops with a spray of ice dust, his skates a balletic "V."

"Are you all right?" he says, his hand on her arm.

"Fine, yes, all fine."

"Try to straighten up a bit. Here, take my arm."

She holds on to him, his old suede jacket rough under her hand—
she catches a whiff of mustiness from it—and tries to push her tummy
out to straighten her body, but her feet immediately slide forward and
out from under her. She hits the ice hard—right on her coccyx. She
hisses as the cold follows on from the pain, tries to get up, holding
him, but her feet are scissoring wildly and she's grasping at his smelly
jacket while he tries to keep his balance, and then her arms are actually
around his body, clambering up him until they are face-to-face.

"OK?" he says, smiling.

"Take me to the rail."

At the rail, she says, "That's enough for me," and walks through a
gap onto the rubber mat, relieved—so very *relieved*—that her feet can
grip something. "You carry on. I'm going to get a hot chocolate."

Two years of sifting through the detritus of the Internet, the sexually incontinent to the intellectually subnormal. Prior to this, she'd
spent five deluded years gambling on meeting someone "naturally,"
though there was nothing natural about turning up to every random
gathering wearing too much slap and a desperate gurn, disappointed
evenings in the pub, then clip-clopping home on uncomfortable heels.
Christ, she'd even gone for drinks with the *neighbors,* at which everyone was coupled up and about fifty-seven. With this particular outing,
she thinks, unlacing and pulling off the skates, she has plumbed a new
low.

Her feet, however, are in a state of bliss. She can walk, she can un-
tense, she is light as air. It is almost worth ice-skating for the feeling
of buoyancy of having functional feet back. Why do people do this—
create for themselves physical uncertainty when there is so much of it
to be had in daily life for free?

Her mind goes back to the child-protection woman and the sixty-
seven thousand children, as it has intermittently since she came out
of the briefing, which must be Davy's doing or perhaps the niggling
feeling that there is something she cannot see through the half-closed
smear of her sore eye—an irritation she forgets about for long enough
to stop her visiting a chemist. She resolves to sort it tomorrow.

The hangar housing the rink is noisy and smells of hot dogs and
rubber, with the odd whiff of socks. She waits for him at a Formica

table that is riveted to the floor, occasionally spots him whizzing round, pushing his body forward, confident and free. She is tempted to do a runner but, alas, here he is, edging in front of her, between the plastic stool and table, both immovable.

He smiles but doesn't say anything. She has noticed he's a man of few words and when he does speak, it is so softly that she has to crane forward, cup her ear like a pensioner and say, "What was that?"

"You're a good skater," she says.

He nods.

"When did you learn?"

"When I was young."

They look out at the rink—at the laughing skaters on faster dates.

"So you're a poet," she says.

He nods.

"Where do you write?"

"Anywhere."

"Is it lonely?"

"Not really."

"'Least you don't have to do the office Secret Santa. Thank God for Huntingdon's pound stores, is all I can say!"

He nods again. The relaxedness of his nodding says, "This silence is your failing. You should fill it." She notices she wants to dig her heels in: *I won't put you at your ease,* she thinks.

He looks out at the rink as if he's alone.

"Do they rhyme?"

"I'm sorry?"

"Your poems—do they rhyme?"

"Do you like poetry that rhymes?" he asks.

A full sentence. There is a God.

"I'm not a big poetry fan," she says, which is an out-and-out lie. She has inhaled everyone from T. S. Eliot to Wendy Cope.

You take up yoga, walk and swim.
And nothing works. The outlook's grim.

"Really?" he says, his interest only vaguely pricked. Even jabbing him with a stick doesn't work. "What do you read?" he asks.

"Thrillers. Love them. The bigger the gold lettering, the better. So how do you make a living? I mean, poetry doesn't pay, does it? Are you a poet who also serves pizza?"

"I couldn't do that. I prefer to keep my living costs down. I don't pay any rent . . . and I sign on." He takes a sip of hot chocolate. "I live with my ex-girlfriend—at least, I sleep on her sofa. She doesn't mind. We stopped sleeping together and, well, I never moved out."

"Christ, isn't that a bit awkward?"

"We're really good friends. We were always really good friends. More friends than . . ." The rest is a mumble.

Manon cups her ear. "Sorry, can you say that last bit again?"

"I said it's a bit more awkward now she's got a boyfriend."

"I can imagine."

"She likes it if I stay out—you know, in the evenings, give them some space."

Manon looks at him. Smiles. Wonders if she can make him want her. "You could always come back to mine," she says.

He looks into his hot chocolate, making her wait.

"We could," he says, as if she should do more to persuade him. Another silence that she feels the pressure to fill.

"I've got wine—a nice bottle of red," she says.

Her hand feels warm around the paper cup containing her hot chocolate, but her heart is darkening. She pictures herself writhing above him, the sex just like the skating—stilted and awkward. He will expect her to put him at his ease, then lay the failure of the exercise firmly at her door. Her life seems as if it's on a loop, round and round, nothing ever changing.

"Actually," she says, surprising herself, "forget that. It's probably not a good idea."

"But you just said—"

"Yes, I know. I don't know why I said that."

"We could just talk," he says. He has reddened.

"Talk?" she says. "I think there'd be only one person talking and it wouldn't be you."

He swallows, watches as she shuffles out between the nailed-down table and the nailed-down stool.

"To be honest," he says, "I like petite women."

"Right, of course. I should have expected that," says Manon.

THE NIGHT AIR DRIPS WITH moisture, dank and lonely. Up the broad pedestrian thoroughfare, yellow-smeared from the streetlamps, deserted
now, past the soldier on the war memorial, deep-black stone receding
into the night; only the shine on his elbows and knees and helmet are
points of light. Aimed at him on all sides, and now shuttered up behind
locked grilles, are the pound shops, one after another, which in the day
give out a tinny cacophony of jangling and kerchinging, *tink tonk, rat-
a-tat-tat,* dancing Santas, and teddies with drums.

Huntingdon. Beset with mobility scooters. Once described by a
Shakespearean drunk in the cells as "a pimple on the protruding but-
tock of England." Scene of dogged animal-rights protests outside the
Life Sciences lab. Never short on fog.

She passes the white frontage of *The Hunts Post,* which signals
the end of the high street, and into the darker residential streets, pavements glistening with rain and the last of the melted snows, the houses
either blackly empty or glowing with their curtains drawn. She hears
her own footsteps slapping on the slush and another's behind her. A
man or woman's? She can't be sure, though it doesn't have the timbre
of feminine shoes. Wide steps. A man. Seeming to keep pace with her.
She quickens, her heartbeat thudding like a bee against glass, clench-
ing her fists inside her pockets. She puts a hand to her handbag strap,
which crosses her body, pulls the bag itself to the front. Purse, keys,
phone, badge. Should she put a hand on her badge? He is still behind
her and she can hear him breathing. He has taken up a threatening
proximity at her back. The street is entirely empty, and in front of them,
the black river. She steps to the side to allow him to pass—perhaps
a businessman in a hurry. He is forced to go beyond her, a hunched
figure in a hoodie, his head in total shadow, his movements edgy, she
notices, as he turns.

"Hello, love, all right?"

She delivers a wan, businesslike smile. He is blocking her path now.

"What you doing out so late?"

"Leave me alone," she says, high-pitched and breathy. She has reached a hand surreptitiously into her bag.

"C'mon," he says. "Just bein' friendly."

Drunk? He is more quivering and energized. Drugs. Still with his face in shadow. She couldn't pick him out in a lineup.

"Can you let me pass, please?" she says, and she wishes her fear wasn't so audible.

"Where you going? Wanna go somewhere together, you an' me?"

She stops trying to edge around him, looks him in the eye, thinking, *This could be it, the moment he punches my lights out or pulls a knife.* She feels for her badge and holds it up to his face.

"Fancy being arrested, mate?" she says. "Police. Major Incident Team. I'm wondering what you know about the disappearance of Edith Hind, seeing as how you like to threaten women."

He is taking wide steps backward, his palms up. "Whoa, whoa, *whoa,*" he says. "I wasn't doing nothing. I wasn't . . ." Suddenly he turns and runs to the end of the street and onto the towpath.

It might be relief. Probably tiredness. Or hating ice-skating and the limp attacks of the poet, or having been frightened, or the flickering question of who would report her missing if she disappeared, but she shoulders into a hedge in tears.

MANON
. . .

They've made her fingertips sooty, the filth rubbing off on her. "Missing Edith had complex love life" (*Daily Mail*). "String of lovers led her into danger, say Edith cops" (the *Mirror*). Her father would say it's fair game, a big story, and why shouldn't they be all over it? Sex and death—there was no better combination for shifting copies. Being a local paper editor, he had a sneaking admiration for the tabloids, and part of Manon's problem with the press is she can see both sides.

She looks up from the pile of tabloids on her knees, peering through the car window to see a muddy sky pressing down on the flat roofs of the Arbury estate in Cambridge, built like Lego. The great thumb smudge of cloud begins to release fat droplets as she and Nigel slam their car doors and head for the block.

Day four of the investigation: interview known offenders—burglars, rapists, sociopaths, and addicts—with an MO that plausibly fits the bill.

Both of them now out of puff, they have reached the uppermost open walkway and they stop outside Tony Wright's blue gloss front door. Tony *Wrong,* as he's known in MIT. "To be fair, he hasn't put a foot wrong since he's been out," his probation officer said.

"No one's answering," says Nigel, stamping his feet next to her. He leans over the balcony and shouts, "Oi! Hop it!" to a group of kids surrounding their car, and they scatter like birds.

Manon bangs again with her fist.

"All right, all right," says a woman's voice behind the door. It opens and Manon has her badge ready, midair.

"Cambridgeshire Police, DS Manon Bradshaw and DC Nigel Williams. Tony in?"

The woman, mid-thirties, in a pink velour tracksuit, has skin the color of tapioca and oversized hoop earrings. She turns, without saying anything, to reveal the word "Juicy" written across her back in sequins. She schlumps to the lounge, where the television is on.

There is Tony, ravaged king: his face a collapsed cliff face, white hair in a loose ponytail at the nape of his neck, matching the goatee like a long drip of milk from his chin. Rounded spectacles, which make him seem curiously intellectual or like a folk-singing hippie. His tattoo sleeves are visible, creeping all the way up to his neck.

"Hiya, Tony," says Manon. They've known each other of old.

"Come in, Manon. Cup o' tea? How about you, Nigel?"

"I'm all right, thanks, Tony," says Nigel, standing with his hands cupping his testicles.

"How're the twins doin', Nigel?" Tony asks. "That's a lot o' work, twins." His Scottish brogue adds to the affable air, the gentle grandpappy. Hard to believe he broke into a young woman's flat in the dead of night, took a knife from her kitchen, which he then held to her throat, forcing her to strip. He robbed her that night, not simply of her peace of mind for all perpetuity, but of every other valuable thing in her flat too. Wright was sent to Whitemoor, the maximum-security prison just outside the village of March—a fifteen-year sentence—where he was a model prisoner, running the library. He's been out on license for eight months.

"They are a lot of work, Tony. They're wearing us out," says Nigel, smiling.

"Tae what do I owe this honor?" Tony asks. "Is there, perchance, a crime for which youse two would like tae finger me? Shopliftin', is it? Arson? Murder?"

"We want to ask you a few questions, Tony, that's all," says Manon.

"And if it isnae all right? What if now isnae a convenient time? Because frankly, ah'm watchin' *Loose Women* right now and this Coleen Nolan, she's got many interestin' things tae say."

"Do you know anything about the disappearance of a young woman from Huntingdon, called Edith Hind?"

"Now, why would ye think that?"

"Where were you on the night of seventeenth of December, Tony—Saturday night?"

"Och, that's easy; we had a lock-in an' a singsong at the Coach. You ask anyone on the estate; everyone was there. Great night, wisn't it, Lyn?"

Lyn nods, smoking.

"What time did you leave the Coach, Tony?" asks Manon.

"Aboot two A.M., wis it?" he says, looking affectionately at Lyn.

Really, butter wouldn't melt, Manon thinks, marveling. Dangerous people seldom broadcast their peccadilloes—you learned that in child protection. It's not the creepy bloke in a stained mac; it's the jolly fellow who chats to you in the queue in John Lewis.

"And Sunday morning, Tony?"

"Well, I got up, no' too early after the night before," he laughs, the phlegm bubbling in the bottom of his throat before it turns into a cough. "Sorry," he says, his hand over his mouth. "Then I went tae meet Paddy at ten, as usual."

"Paddy your probation officer?" says Manon.

"That's it. We went for a fry-up, it being Sunday mornin'. Mug o' tea, eggs and bacon, a whole stack o' bread an' butter, steamed-up windaes against the cold December morn. Lovely."

God, he's so *likable*. Must stop warming to him, immediately.

"We'll be checking all this, you know that, Tony," she says.

"Oh aye, you fill yer boots, Manon. I know you'll do yer job. Come an' arrest me when youse are ready."

"We'll see ourselves out," she says.

* * *

MANON STRIDES UP HUNTINGDON HIGH Street toward Cromwell's, dread churning at the prospect of the office Christmas "knees-up," as Davy liked to call it—already an overstatement. Just a few of them having drinks, with their mobiles on in case the duty team needs to update them. Besides, they're all exhausted. Colin will bore everyone rigid about the latest iPad upgrade; Nigel will ask if she's still single and then go on about the comfortable pleasures of being "an old married man," though he'll appear to be in no hurry to get back to "the lovely Dawn" and the twins.

She stops outside the bar, its silver lettering attempting to give it an air of modernity. It is the kind of place twenty-two-year-old boys come for stag dos when they haven't the money or imagination to reach for Bratislava. Manon scans the room as her eyes adjust to the darkness. Fruit machines glow in one corner. She spots her colleagues in another corner, Bryony at the center of the group, waving to her, then making two fingers into a gun and shooting herself in the mouth.

Manon has come later than the rest. She's been gathering in CCTV of Tony Wright's weekend, getting nowhere tracing unknown-515—the number Edith rang twice in the week before she vanished—and working out which computers Edith worked on in the college library. "Get all the data off that one," she told Nigel.

And she was still trawling through Edith's personal hard drive, reading her PhD research, her emails, her postings on the Internet, the latest one being: "'Our deepest fear is not that we are inadequate. Our deepest fear is that we are powerful beyond measure.'" Beneath it she wrote: "Not said by Nelson Mandela, but amazing anyway."

Manon was reminded of her own youthful diaries, how much she too had been in love with a notion of herself at that age, energetically self-analyzing. Edith had typed out a long passage from George Eliot's novel *Daniel Deronda,* into a Word document titled: "Just as I see it."

> . . . her horizon was that of the genteel romance where the hero-
> ine's soul poured out in her journal is full of vague power, original-
> ity, and general rebellion, while her life moves strictly in the sphere
> of fashion; and if she wanders into a swamp, the pathos lies partly, so
> to speak, in her having on her satin shoes. Here is a restraint which
> nature and society have provided on the pursuit of striking adven-

ture; so that a soul burning with a sense of what the universe is not, and ready to take all existence as fuel, is nevertheless held captive by the ordinary wirework of social forms and does nothing particular.

Edith's screensaver is a picture of a bare-breasted woman running toward the camera with her arms thrown up and the words "Still Not Asking For It" written across her chest. She is a member of No Means No—an anti-rape group. Her PhD is on the fight against the patriarchy in Victorian literature, with reference to John Stuart Mill ("The Subjection of Women") and *The Tenant of Wildfell Hall* ("the first radical feminist novel"). Her writing is impassioned, the beat of it like a fist punching the air.

"Hello, chicken," says Bryony, handing Manon a vodka tonic as they survey the group together.

Colin is talking at full tilt to Davy, who sits forward with his elbows on his knees, nodding and listening intently. Stuart, wearing a black leather jacket and black jeans, which are arousingly tight, is chatting to Nigel. Kim is knocking back a pint.

"I'm already having a bad time," says Manon.

"Oh, come on, what's not to like? It's dark, there's a faint whiff of vomit, Colin's talking technology."

"You've got yogurt down the back of your top," says Manon, picking at some dried white crust on Bryony's cardigan. "At least, I hope it's yogurt." She smells her fingers and frowns.

"Hang on," Bryony says, craning over her shoulder. "Hold this," and she hands Manon her drink. She rummages in her bag and fishes out a toy car, then a box of raisins, and finally a wet wipe. "Go at it with this, will you?"

"I put my book in the bin on the way home," says Manon, rubbing at Bryony's shoulder.

"Good for you. Is it coming off?"

They both detest MIT's yearly Secret Santa charade, organized before the Hind case kicked off, which had played itself out in the office at leaving time—everyone with their coats on. It was about as festive as a queue for the bus. Manon had received a book on dating—*Grab Your Man Before Someone Else Does*—from the cut-price bookstore in the precinct. It was still in the pink-and-white-striped paper bag, sealed with Sellotape, and the lack of wrapping put it firmly at Colin's door. Colin, whose response to every crime was to shake his head, saying, "Takes all sorts," had received a bag of Licorice Allsorts, with "Licorice" replaced with the word "Takes." ("Good one," Manon said to Bryony.) Harriet had, inappropriately enough, been given a pair of sheer stockings ("Not Stuart, surely," Bryony whispered, horrified). Davy got a nodding dog for the car. Bryony a baby's bib that said, "What happens at Grandma's stays at Grandma's."

"Shame she's in a home," Bryony whispered sadly. "What happens at Grandma's is a lot of peeing in her pants and the odd ill-timed sexual outburst."

"That probably should stay at Grandma's," Manon said.

The whole thing was like being handed a placard saying, "This is what everyone in the office thinks of you." Stuart got a seduction kit in a tiny tin (perhaps it wasn't off-target after all). Manon had been forced to buy for Kim, the office enigma. She literally knew nothing about Kim. Even her age was a mystery. So she'd bought her a bag of old-fashioned sweets and some socks. Kim seemed practical that way and when she'd opened it, she'd nodded and said, "Fair dos."

"Another drink?" says Kim now, having weaved her way over to Manon and Bryony.

"Why the fuck not?" says Manon. "We're on vodka tonics; thanks, Kim."

"Righto," says Kim, her broad back disappearing toward the bar.

"She's an enigma wrapped in a riddle, that woman."

"How did it go with the poet?" asks Bryony.

"He took me skating."

"Oh my God, you hate skating."

"Then he told me he was still living with his ex."

"This one's sounding like a keeper. Please tell me you made your excuses and left."

"D'you know what? I actually did, for like the first time ever."

"Good on you, kiddo. How did he take it?"

"Told me he preferred his women petite."

"Jeez, narrow escape, then," says Bryony, chinking her glass against Manon's. "You did the right thing."

They stand looking out at the bar. Manon feels her shoes pinching at the sides of her toes and at the heel. Kim returns and hands them their vodkas, venturing past them to her seat with her pint. You've got to like that about Kim—she doesn't impose "the chat." Manon takes a sip from the glass and realizes it's a double. She's already beginning to feel anesthetized in her lower legs and light in her head, as if her blood were heading south. She shifts on her feet.

"Christ, look at Davy," Bryony says, "listening away to Colin like he doesn't want to chew off his own arm."

"He's a lesson to us all, that boy."

They drain their glasses and new ones appear—always doubles, some with Red Bull, some with tonic. The bar seems to get darker, more blurry, the music swimming in and out of Manon's consciousness with snippets of conversation as she sways on her painful shoes, at times her eyes half closed.

She sits on the arm of Davy's chair while he fiddles about with his phone, looking up at her by way of explanation, saying, "Chloe. She likes to check up on me. Make sure I'm not getting up to mischief."

"Make sure you're not having any fun, more like," says Manon, realizing too late that she's said it out loud.

She looks to the banquette close by, where Kim is frowning and nodding, and Bryony is leaning in too close, a smudge of mascara down her face, shouting above the music in a slurry voice: "I moan about them, right, Kim. I mean, I'm never knowingly under-moaned. But fuck me, Kim—I don't mean that literally, Kim," and she burps into her fist, "but fuck me, the kids, they're everything."

Stuart is to Manon's right, seeming malevolently sober. He asks her where Harriet is.

"Got a dinner with the brass—retired plods get-together or something."

Stuart nods.

Then Davy is asking Stuart about where he's from and what he did before joining the force.

"Teaching assistant at a school in Peterborough, but it was crap."

Davy nods, his curiosity laid gently to rest like a dead cat, and the two men sit in silence, both leaning forward, elbows on knees.

"Why was it crap?" Manon shouts eventually, casting an irritable glance at Davy.

"Headmistress thought she was God's gift, lording it about."

Stuart addresses this to Davy, who nods placidly, ever the piercing observer of human interplay.

"Isn't a headmistress sort of supposed to lord it about—in her own school?" shouts Manon again, scraping a chair in to join them.

"She'd never listen to anyone's opinion 'cept her own," he says, and she sees bitterness, the charm having fallen at one corner, like a faulty curtain.

"Your opinion, you mean?"

"Yeah, my opinion. Why not my opinion?"

"Er, because you were a teaching assistant and she was the head?"

He frowns at her and then seems to remember himself, fashioning his face into an ironic smile. "What will you be up to over Christmas, then, Sarge?"

"Oh," she says, looking away. "I'm on the rota over Christmas."

MANON LIES IN BED. SHE has mascara down her cheeks and the radio burbles beside her, at too low a volume for her to make out the words. She has been lying there thinking she must turn it up so she can listen, but the thought fails somehow to translate itself into action. Her limbs are heavy, sunk into the mattress, and the room is all broken apart, the ceiling rotating at a different rate and in a different direction to the walls and floor. Her clothes lie in a hastily discarded pile next to the bed. She closes her eyes but this increases the spinning, so she opens them again. If she could just turn up the volume on the radio so she could hear Control, she might get to sleep.

Her mind is a slur, a fluid, sliding mess of thoughts taking her back through time, the door to her mother's bedroom ajar, her fourteen-year-old self, leaning on the doorframe, seeing the coroner standing over the body in the bed. Ellie was behind her, and she had pushed her sister back, wanting to shield her, knowing if she saw, she would never get it out of her head.

Forward and back, a mudslide of dark association, her mind turns to Tony Wright. Deeping and Whitemoor Prison, both in the village of March. Did Wright find his way to Deeping one night, rising out of the Fenland marsh like some twisted Magwitch?

Back again, loose and morbid. *Do not go gentle into that good night.*

The image she had shielded from Ellie: their mother's eyes open, her head on the pillow, her skin purple and mottled where the blood had stopped moving—it had gathered along the base of her like red wine in a tilted glass. Lividity. She knows the word for it now, but she didn't then. "The black-and-blue discoloration of the skin of a cadaver, resulting from an accumulation of deoxygenated blood in subcutaneous vessels."

MANON

• • •

"Is it just me?" says Harriet as she and Manon gaze at the CCTV footage of Tony Wright's various movements on the weekend of December 17–18.

"It isn't just you," says Manon.

"What the fuck's he up to?" asks Harriet.

"Guys, Kim, Davy, come and look at this."

They amble over, their faces in various states of disarray after the night before: Kim's looks like a doughnut with eyes; Davy is sporting bed hair ("Been to the Vidal Sassoon night salon, I see, Davy," says Manon). Nigel is permanently ravaged by sleep deprivation, so he looks the same as always.

They look at the screen, amid yawns and eye-rubbing.

Tony Wright traversing the Arbury's open walkways, various angles, jaunty. Coy glances at the camera. Tony Wright entering the Coach pub on the estate, a knowing smile on his perfectly captured visage. Tony Wright playing his ukulele to a packed crowd in the Coach. Tony Wright leaving the Coach at 2:00 A.M. after a lock-in (little wave). Sunday, 9:46 A.M., Tony on his way to meet his probation officer, hands in the pockets of his denim jacket. Tony and his probation officer entering the local greasy spoon.

"Talk about cast iron," says Davy.

"When was the last time the Coach had functioning CCTV, I mean with film in it?" asks Harriet.

"Never. Every nefarious deal on the estate is done in there," says Kim. "If they used CCTV, they'd have no customers."

"He wants us to know he's there," says Harriet.

"Which means?" says Manon.

"That a crime is going on elsewhere," says Harriet. They look at each other.

"Wait, this crime or another crime? Someone's kidnapping Edith Hind for him while he plays the ukulele?" says Manon, frowning.

"Rrrrrargh," says Harriet, pulling at her hair roots. "Why is he messing with my head? I don't like it. I don't like it at all. Bring him in."

"You SHOWING US YOU'VE GOT a face for radio, Tony?" asks Harriet, standing over him in interview room two, her knuckles on the table. "All that smoldering eye contact for the camera?"

"Now, I'm feelin' a lot o' negative energy coming off of you, DI Harper. I'm sensing you're really pissed off because my alibi stacks up," says Tony, smiling at her like an indulgent parent. "Did I just ruin yer Friday, did I?"

"What's going on, Tony?"

"Look, you people arrest me every time I chuff," says Tony, reasonably enough. "So these days, I walk where the cameras can see me; that way there's no confusion. I got fucked off w' havin' ma arse hauled in here and bein' shouted at fir stuff I didnae do. This is how I stop it—smile for the camera! Say cheese, Tony! S'no biggie."

"Do you know what happened to Edith Hind?" Harriet demands.

Tony leans forward, his forearms on the desk. He is looking at them over the top of his glasses. Manon avoids his gaze, focusing on his dagger tattoo, the point of its blade ending at his wrist, and for some reason she wishes Davy was in the room with them.

Tony says, very low, "Youse two want tae watch yourselves, ye ken? 'Cos youse know, an' I know, you dinnae have grounds tae arrest me. So unless youse want a whole lot o' trouble—an' I'm sayin' this for yer own good—youse need tae back the fuck off." He leans back again, friendlier now. "Now, is there anythin' else youse lovely lassies want tae talk about?"

MIRIAM
. . .

"Muuum?"

The call, which drifts up the stairs to where she lies fully clothed on the bed, is followed by stomping.

"Mum?" more gingerly at the door, and there is Rollo's darling face. Reminding her she is still a mother.

"Mum," he says, coming to sit on the side of the bed. She smiles at him, that preposterous haircut he's brought back with him from Buenos Aires—a slant upward from the parting like a wedge of cheese. "Side quiff," he'd told her, smoothing it upward with a palm.

"Can I get you anything?" he says now. "Cup of tea?" He has a hand on her shoulder. What would she do without Rollo?

"What are you wearing?" she says to him fondly, her voice tired— woolly like the thick shadows in the room. She hasn't slept more than two hours at a stretch in the twelve days since Edith went missing.

He looks down. "This?" Purple cardigan with shocking-pink trim, buttoned up over a white shirt and beige jeans that taper tightly to the ankle. Winkle-pickers. "I told you, Mum, I've got a look."

The good humor radiates from her youngest. He has been a revelation to her since the day he was born. He cracked his first joke on the breast at two months—had come off, milky-mouthed, to smile up at her, all gums, then blew a raspberry and laughed. He was his sunshine self, right from the off.

When they'd spotted Rollo down the corridor at the police station in Huntingdon, both she and Ian felt the weak gratitude of the elderly. They ran toward him and flung their arms around him, in need of holding him close. Here were reinforcements. And even though Rollo's relationship with Ian had always been strained—he was aware Edith was Ian's favorite, his academic acolyte—even Ian seemed to exhale. Later, they discussed poster campaigns and fundraisers, Rollo's Facebook and Twitter appeals forging connections and sprawling outward like blood vessels, keeping Edith in people's minds.

"Thank you, son," Ian said, rather formally, and Miriam caught him looking at their boy with a needy gaze that she shared, as if Rollo were honey and they were the bears.

They brought him back with them to Hampstead, and with his bag slumped by the kitchen counter and the glittering sheen of the beach still at his temples, the three of them sat shell-shocked around the table, nursing tea. Tea had featured heavily in the past fortnight. Miriam sometimes felt her belly sloshing with it, like a waterbed, yet still she took tea when it was proffered, for the symbolism, she supposed—solicitude, comfort, warmth. It is the English way, after all. Since December 18, she has taken it with two sugars.

"I reckon she wants time alone," Rollo said on that first night back, getting up to boil the kettle yet again, then leaning against the kitchen worktop, and she marveled at how big he was, her little one. "Time away from Will. He's enough to do anyone's head in."

"He's a decent person," said Ian.

"He's a coma-inducing bore," said Rollo.

"There are worse crimes," said Miriam.

"I'm not so sure."

"He was always very good to Edith," Ian said.

"We don't know that, do we?" Rollo said.

"The police don't think he had anything to do with it."

"Stop talking about her as if . . ." Miriam had blurted, and Rollo came over to her, cupping her head to his chest.

"This is typical Edie," he muttered. "Always hogging the attention."

THE LIGHT IN THE BEDROOM has an evening feel, though it's mid-afternoon. They hear a group of youths shout in the street.

"New Year's Eve tomorrow," says Rollo, looking toward the window.

"That's all we need," she says.

Fireworks will no doubt sputter and fizz half the night, like some war on her feelings. She'd never before noticed the forced jollity of this time of year and what injury it adds to those who are bereft: all those television adverts demanding everyone be happy.

"Are they still outside?" she asks, referring to the photographers, and he shakes his head.

"There were only two and they've sloped off," he says.

They are relieved also to be shot of Will, who arrived late on Christmas Eve and departed on Boxing Day, and even that was outstaying his welcome. Ian made them a cold collation—a "smorgasbord," he called it—for Christmas lunch, because it seemed wrong, somehow, to feast on turkey. Instead, they sawed little rectangles of cheese onto sesame Ryvitas, which shed their crumbs across the table like builders' grit (Miriam kept sweeping them into her palm, then, realizing she couldn't be bothered to get up, shook them onto the floor by her side). Pâté, which had developed a liver-red crust at its edges because Ian hadn't covered it in the fridge, pickled gherkins, and celeriac slaw, like some incongruous French picnic.

At night—endless and sleepless, all of them padding about at some point downstairs or to the bathroom—she could hear Will sniveling in the guest bedroom.

"She was in my care," Will said at breakfast. "It was on my watch."

She and Rollo had shared a wearied glance, Rollo waiting for his toast to pop up.

The phone starts ringing, distantly.

"I'll go," says Rollo, standing.

Miriam lifts herself from the pillow. "No, I'll get it. I'm hoping it's Christy."

MANON

. . .

HER CANTEEN LUNCH OF SHEPHERD'S PIE AND BOILED CARROTS HAS COL-lapsed into the four corners of its yellow polystyrene box. Brown gravy, Bisto-infused, the mince pebble-dashing her throat as it goes down. Piped mash—has it *ever* been potato? Not bad. Not bad at all.

She has pushed her keyboard to one side to make way for the rect-angular box and the *Daily Mirror,* and she scans the "News in Brief" column, seeing "Search for Edith" relegated there. One paragraph on the planned television reconstruction, which will go out in the next episode of *Crimewatch.* Twelve days missing and Edith's a NiB—a reflec-tion of the investigation's stalemate. Forensics from the scene showed only Edith's, Will Carter's, and Helena Reed's DNA at George Street, as you'd expect. The blood was Edith's but no rogue DNA on the glass shards in the kitchen bin.

"Gloves," Harriet said, "or it was someone whose DNA is already there."

Meaning Carter. They are still tracing his return journey along minor roads back from Stoke; still watching that mobile number unknown-515; still waiting for data off the Corpus college computer—everything taking an age because of Christmas rotas, skeletal staffing. Every email met with an "out of office."

"Good Christmas?" asks Marie from Accounts as she passes Manon's desk, the question she dreads and tries to shrug off.

"Yeah, good, thanks," she says, barely looking up from her newspaper and some story she's not reading about a muscled pop star on his third marriage, though it says "this time it's for keeps."

She was pulled off the Hind case Christmas Eve, onto a suspicious death. It was bound to happen sooner or later. Elderly man burned to a charcoal slump just inside the front door of his bungalow on the outskirts of Peterborough. Cover-up for a burglary, or obtaining money with menaces, or perhaps he'd done it to himself. She picked over the charred interior of the man's home and found a selection of wigs, cheap and matted—platinum blond, mostly; a rail of polyester women's dresses in a wardrobe untouched by fire; and below them a jumble of dusty high heels with slits cut in the sides and back to make room for his man-sized feet. He had worked the bins for Peterborough City Council all his life.

Manon spent Christmas Eve and Christmas Day tracing his family, and yet there were none—at least, none that said they knew him. She tried to capture CCTV, which took double the time when no one but the dimmest or most desperate was on duty, and she included herself in that. Never go in for an operation or become a victim of violent crime on a major national holiday; that would be her advice.

Still, the death of old Mr. Cross-Dresser did away with the day. She picked up a takeaway from the Spice Inn on Christmas night, stepping into the darkness of her flat and heading straight to her kitchen. She set her phone on the kitchen counter, its screen illuminated then darkening, like some sleeper rousing then turning over again in the bed, and she remembered the calls she'd ignored from her father.

Her kitchen was the one area of the flat overlooked by the mid-century modernizers: gloomy with brown floral tiles; the grouting cracked and orange behind the taps; the cupboards dark and over-twiddled with vaguely medieval handles. Bryony said she should paint the cupboards. "Cornforth White. Brighten it up no end." But Manon never got around to it. Shifts blurred into shifts, overtime into more overtime. They filled her bank account but not her fridge, so that when the tide rolled away, only empty wastes remained. A deserted life. Celery that hadn't been opened but had gone rubbery. Pants and tights spilling from the top of the basket. Apples that were woolly to the bite, so that she spat them into the bin. Manon would determinedly fill the fridge, resolve to paint the cupboards Cornforth White while the washing machine churned, resolve too to eat beetroot more and take up Zumba, only to have it all disappear in the suck and tow of the next tide.

Bloated with korma, she listened to her father's message. "Hi, lovey. Just wanted to wish you a Merry Christmas. Um, we've had a good day up here. Una cooked a terrific salmon terrine to ring the changes. So that was good. Yes. Well, don't work too hard. Call when you can, Manon, OK? Righto, then. Bye."

She had hoped for one from Ellie—even double-checked her missed calls—but nothing. So she told herself it was Ellie's fault, this silence. She called her father back, reluctantly, because he would inevitably ask for a festive-jollity meter reading and hers was set at zero, so to head him off, she told him about the cross-dressing corpse, which left him satisfyingly at a loss. She could hear Una getting restive in the background, whispering as loudly as possible, "We really must go, Robert." So Manon had said, "Go on, then. Obey her."

She wished she could call Ellie, if only to slag off Una, but the climb-down was too hard to face.

A PHONE RINGS SOMEWHERE ACROSS the room, and Manon raises her head to see Davy walking back from his canteen lunch with Stuart and Nigel. Colin is Internet shopping as usual—a TV sound bar, he says. ("You can get some real bargains in the Christmas sales.")

Manon ignores the ringing, which is shrill in the strip-lit yellow room, bouncing off the birch-laminate desks as broad as mortuary slabs.

"Sarge?" says Kim.

Manon turns. Kim is looking directly at her, the phone held away
from her body, in a way that makes the department stop.

"Spartan Rescue," says Kim. They continue to look at each other,
Manon's heart quickening. "A body. In the Ouse. Just shy of Ely. Dog
walker found it this morning."

No one moves.

"Sarge?" says Kim.

"Tell them we're on our way."

"I honestly thought . . ." Davy begins.

"Poor Miriam," says Kim.

"Poor both of them," says Colin, and Manon looks at him. Even
Colin's face has gone slack.

SHE AND DAVY JOG DOWN the municipal stairs in silence, out to an unmarked car. Everything will be new territory for the Hinds now, a life
before and a life after, and very soon that first life, the one untouched,
will recede, like some blithe foreign landscape. That first life was when
Manon used to read books with a flashlight under the duvet, the illicit thrill as her mother passed her door on her way to bed. That first
life was one of lurching passions and furies, all played out against her
mother's solid breast. Not happy, exactly—she could never understand
people who described their childhoods as happy. She looks across at
Davy driving and thinks it's probably how he'd describe his. Childhood
seems to Manon (at least, what she can remember of it) a time of frustration and effort, things that were frightening and new, and the retreat
back into familiar comforts before the next foray.

Davy has pulled out onto the A14. The sky is a fragile blue, very
far away, and the sunlight harsh and breakable and thin, sending its
glassy shards through the windscreen so they both have to pull their vi-
sors down. They begin to leave the conurbation behind, and the snow,
which has all but melted in town, gains confidence the farther they
drive out into the Fens.

And then it happened. "Sudden Death Syndrome," the coroner had
said, and everything after it was another life, a new territory, one about
to be discovered by the Hinds now that Edith was floating facedown

in the Ouse. And all the events of Manon's life were played out in its wreckage.

Much of daily life for her fourteen-year-old self and twelve-year-old Ellie remained the same. Their father had been advised to keep the routines stable for the girls' sake. School. Their bedrooms and the childish circus-print curtains their mother had chosen. Weekend swimming lessons. Crisps eaten on the backseat afterward, the chlorine rising off their wet hair, their tights twisted wrongly about their legs. Their father glancing back at them in the rearview mirror, the seat empty beside him. They wandered helplessly through it, their rucksacks on their backs, gazed at by the more fortunate, their father never quite preempting their needs, so that the shopping ran out and there was nothing to make a packed lunch with. Uniforms fished out of the dirty-laundry basket and sniffed to see if they passed muster. They appeared to be functioning, did well in exams. Manon was top in her class because work, in comparison with living, was so easy. Reading was an escape. But she and Ellie were not—and she knew this even as a fourteen-year-old—*intact,* in the way other children were. There was a surface and then there was this gulf between it and their inner lives, shattered like a broken cup.

It was as if her mother had taken with her any strategy Manon ever had for living. When she got into Cambridge to read English, it was taken as a sign of success, as if no one could see it was a refuge. She hasn't spoken to Ellie for three years now—a rift that has grown outward in layers of resentment like rings in a tree. It began when Ellie broke with their sibling protocol: the willfully immature hating of Una.

"You went and *stayed* with them?" Manon asked her, incredulous. "You didn't tell me."

"Didn't think I had to," Ellie said. "Una's all right, once you get used to her."

"Una's *all right?*"

"Yeah, she is. You know, you have to fold the toilet paper to a point after you've pulled off a sheet, but apart from that—"

"Judas."

Davy pulls up the hand brake and they sit, listening to the car ticking. In the distance she can see frogmen from Spartan Rescue, milling about on the riverbank, and an ambulance, its back doors flung wide, a red blanket smoothed flat on a waiting stretcher. She sees the pathologist from Hitchingbrooke, Derry Mackeith, talking to a uniform.

"I hate the smell of these," she says to Davy as they get out of the car.

"MIT," says Mackeith, striding toward her from the riverbank. "To what do we owe this honor?" The purple-thread veins on his nose are livid in the cold, and his breaths emerge as white puffs.

"Is she out of the water?" says Manon, trying to look past him, but the frogmen and Spartan Rescue officials are blocking her view.

"She?" says Mackeith. "It's not a she."

Manon looks at him. "What do you mean? Are you saying it's not Edith Hind?"

"Not unless Edith Hind was a young male of mixed race," says Mackeith.

"I thought—"

"Ah, yes, sorry about that. Spartan Rescue seem a bit agitated about not having found the Hind girl. False alarm. Pretty obvious the minute we hooked him out. We did try to call you. You're welcome to have a look, but I'd say you guys are not needed. He's a jumper, if you ask me. We'll get an ID from fingerprints, I should imagine. Coroner can take it from there."

Manon looks past Mackeith, and the throng of frogmen and uniformed officers has parted to reveal the body: muddied, discolored, and vastly distended. A blue marbled Buddha.

"How long ago—any idea?" she asks.

"This time of year, water's quite cold. There's only moderate decomposition. Two to three weeks, I'd say."

"Did you find a wallet, phone?" she says to the representative of Spartan Rescue, who has rustled toward them in his expensive windcheater. Navy, with pink fleecy trim.

"No, ma'am, nothing. Just the clothes he was wearing—jeans and a hoodie and some rather expensive trainers, which would've helped him sink to the bottom. If you've nothing further, we'll get him to the mortuary."

* * *

THEY STAND ON THE DOORSTEP of a sawdust-colored barn, brash new timbers bordered by prissy hedges. But when Manon and Davy walk inside, to interview the dog walker who found the body, they both look up in silent awe at the double-height atrium, thick oak beams crisscrossing the vaulted roof and cathedral-sized windows.

"We'll try not to take up too much of your time," says Manon.

"No, please. Come and sit down. Can I make you coffee?" His voice is deep and slow. He walks with a slight stoop, in his voluminous corduroys. His bowed head is gentle and apologetic.

"Coffee would be lovely, thanks," says Manon. "It's freezing out there."

"This place is amazing," says Davy, who has approached the window. The sky has turned pink, striated yellow, a radioactive lozenge at its center reflected in the river. Along its banks, leafless trees are silhouetted. The pink of the sunset—so fleshy and garish—has stretched its arm into the room, giving them all a Californian tan.

In front of the wall of windows is a refectory table with two benches, its surface strewn with newspapers. On the other side of the room, a wood-burning stove and russet-colored dog in front of it in a basket. It raised its head when they entered but lowers it again now, un-fussed.

"She's very elderly," explains Alan Prenderghast (Davy has whispered his name in Manon's ear), who is now at the open-plan kitchen area, turning levers on a complex silver coffee machine. The kitchen is a dark U-shape with slate-gray cupboards and black worktop.

"Lovely view," Manon says, joining Davy at the windows and watching the sun squat on the horizon, peppered with birds. She looks to her right and sees a frayed armchair and a pair of binoculars on a table beside it. Silence for a while, which Davy would normally try to fill, but they are both hypnotized by the stillness and scale of the house and its view.

At last, Mr. Prenderghast comes to stand next to her and is handing her a cup of coffee, froth covering its surface.

"It's my favorite thing about this house," he says, looking out with her.

Her cup's roasted smell drifts up like smoke.

"You see that field opposite—on the other bank of the river? Every winter it's allowed to flood and it fills up with literally thousands of birds. Ducks, geese, swans. Teeming with life. Great skeins of them fly in from Scandinavia. I could watch it all day, the landing and the flying off. It's a very sad view, somehow."

His voice is calm. It is as if he is selecting every word. The ravelled sleeve of care—his voice could knit it up. She looks at the view, the sunset colors like a bruise, and the bare trees. He's right—it is the saddest view she has ever seen. She wants to stay in this kitchen, which is so warm and yet so quietly morbid—silent and slow and away from the town—even though she has never been one of those people for whom the countryside is an idyll.

"It must've been a shock, finding the body," she says.

"It wasn't what I was expecting, no," he says. "I've never seen one before and it was much worse than I imagined, actually. Who was it?"

"We don't know yet. A young man. We'll have an ID by close of play today."

"Not the girl, then," he says. "The one who went missing before Christmas."

"No. Not the girl."

He nods, sipping his coffee while his free hand digs into his trouser pocket.

Davy is sitting at the refectory table with his notepad out. "Can I ask what you do for a living?" he says.

Manon has strolled over to the bookshelves, which are to one side of the stove. They are tall and crammed, with a library ladder propped against one section. *Tender Is the Night. American Pastoral. Far from the Madding Crowd. Birthday Letters. Jane Austen and the War of Ideas.*

"Yes, of course," Mr. Prenderghast says to Davy. "I'm a systems analyst at Cambs Biotech."

Freud. John le Carré. A history of Labor foreign policy in the postwar years.

"What's a systems analyst, if you don't mind me asking?" says Davy.

"Oh, it's terribly boring. I basically make the computer system work for a large pharmaceutical company—the sort of global conglomerate that *Guardian* readers hate."

"Where's it based?" asks Manon.

"Outskirts of Cambridge, toward Newmarket. One of those charmless industrial estates. But I've been working from home this week—the office is deserted this time of year."

"Did you study English at university?" asks Manon, glancing back at the bookshelves.

"No, quite a few of those are for a course I'm doing. Open University. The others are for pleasure. I wasn't . . . I didn't go. To college, I mean."

"And you were walking your dog this morning?" says Davy, pen poised.

"Yes. My usual walk, to give Nana her run-around. Well, more of a hobble these days. We took the path along the river. Nana," he says, nodding at the dog, and her eyebrows move independently at this, like two caterpillars, though her head remains lowered in her basket, "started to scratch at some tree roots close to the bank. I kept calling her but she wouldn't come away, so eventually I went to fetch her and that's when I saw it. Just the back. It was facedown in the water." He coughs. "I shouldn't say 'it'—I mean *him*."

They are all silent for a moment, in reverence for the body.

"Thanks, Mr. Prenderghast," says Manon. "I don't think we need to detain you any longer."

Davy and Manon begin to gather their coats. It takes them a few moments to re-bury themselves in scarves and gloves.

"Going out celebrating tomorrow night?" asks Davy.

"Ah yes, it's New Year's Eve, isn't it?" he says, smiling. "I'd forgotten. No, I'm afraid it's not my thing. I'm not good with crowds."

"I love a New Year's knees-up myself," says Davy.

"I'm with you, Mr. Prenderghast," says Manon. "I can't stand it."

"Call me Alan, please. I'll be staying put. Watch a film maybe."

"What, by yourself?" says Davy, appalled.

Manon casts Alan a conspiratorial look, as if they are Davy's weary parents.

He laughs. "I do think there's the most terrible fear of solitude these days—as if it's some kind of disease. People can't tolerate it. They want to be seen in a constant social whirl."

"I didn't mean . . ." says Davy.

"No, no, I was only making a general point," he says, with one hand on the open door. "I can go on a bit, sorry. I'm probably defensive. Perhaps my subconscious wishes I'd go to a party, DC Walker. Well, thank you, officers. If I can help with anything else, then do call."

DAVY

. . .

THE CYCLE PATH—MARVELOUSLY FLAT AND OPEN—TAKES HIM ACROSS the marshy flatlands of the Fens, and though it's bracing (he'd had to make himself brave the winter weather this morning), now he's out in the air and going at an exhilarating speed, there's nothing better. Davy has always kept himself active, though shift patterns sometimes intervene (especially during a whopper like the Hind case). Most mornings he runs at 6:00 A.M. or takes the bike out. He would never let himself slide, not after his mum and all that staying in bed or staring at the telly, shoving in chocolate bourbons like she was daring him to try to stop her.

This morning, Chloe had gone off to her job in Next on the high street—today being not just a Saturday but New Year's Eve, so a busy one—and he drove the car an hour out of Huntingdon, to Wisbech, so he could cycle some of the many excellent Fenland routes. He's been yearning for time to think about how to have the Conversation with

Chloe, and he's been yearning also for a feeling of movement. There's really nothing else like it, your body and your bike going at speed and the fresh scent of the countryside blowing into your lungs, big skies in an enormous dome over the flatlands, and the river like a cool gray road beside you.

He pedals harder, away from the images the river conjures of the body from yesterday—the inflammation of his flesh, his blue-purple color inhuman. Just a boy. And Davy can't help but think about Ryan—what might happen to him without the protection of Aldridge House. He resolves to put in more calls, see if the social worker can do anything. Davy must try his best to stop Ryan ending up like that boy in the river, because before you know it, it can be too late, and he finds himself in a silent argument with Chloe, because she was always saying, "You love those kids more than me," and going into a sulk.

He wheels around a bend in the towpath, following the curve of the river, loving the way the bike tilts with him on it, against the laws of gravity, almost—they should topple but speed keeps his wheels turning, and the wind roars into his face and through the bare winter trees. No, he tells himself, this thinking time is not for Ryan or the Hind case; it's for Chloe. Tonight could be the night to broach the subject of the Future, yet every time they're together and the moment seems appropriate, something puts him off: music coming on a bit loud in the restaurant; bumping into someone they know in the pub; the urgent need for a poo (his, not hers—she'd never discuss something so vulgar).

He slows his bike and looks up at a blue sign pointing left, which says MARCH. He could duck down there, have a nosey around Deeping. The case is bothering him more and more: Harriet still nagging away at the Tony Wright alibi; Will Carter far from in the clear, his return journey from Stoke still not verified. Manon reckons they should be looking more closely at the director of studies—this Graham Garfield chap—because when Davy and Manon asked about Garfield during one of their many interviews with the Hinds, they'd expressed "doubts."

"Doubts?" Manon had said.

"Well, Edith called us up very excited during the first term she had him. Said he'd told her she was exceptional—the brightest student he'd had in years," Sir Ian replied.

"Why would that raise doubts?" asked Davy, genuinely nonplussed.

"Perhaps it shouldn't have, DC Walker. But when a middle-aged man is that effusive about an attractive twenty-year-old—"

"Come on, Ian, that's not fair," Lady Hind said. "Maybe Edith was just working hard."

"Yes, maybe, but there were other reasons. When she'd been out with her peers—this was when she was an undergrad—she mentioned he was often around, in the college bar and such like. Just seemed a bit . . . creepy, that's all."

"And there's that girl he had a fling with," Lady Hind said, touching her husband's arm.

"Yes, what was her name?"

"Oh God, I can't remember. Edith told us they were sleeping together. She actually said something along the lines of 'Ew, gross.'"

"None of it, of course, was threatening," Sir Ian said. "I think he's a bit of a, well, 'pest' is the word Edith used, to be honest."

Dirty shagger, Davy thinks, wheeling away from the sign and the left-hand turn he hasn't taken to March. That's what Graham Garfield was, same thing his mum called his dad when his dad went off with Sharon—"dirty shagger" and "selfish bastard with no thought for anyone but himself."

Davy suggested they go easy on the Garfield chap, there being no law against being a dirty shagger, and it was not as if there was anything directly linking him to Edith on the Saturday night, his wife having confirmed that Garfield came home to her after the Crown.

"Remember what Harriet told us, about alibis given by wives and mothers," said Manon. "You think because Garfield reads Tennyson, he couldn't rape someone? You're a snob, Davy Walker."

"Not that, he just seems too . . . gentlemanly, like he's never had it rough."

"Posh people do fucked up just as well as everyone else," she said. "Sometimes better."

And he supposes she'd know, being half posh herself, or on the way to it after going to Cambridge. So he's trying to view Garfield in the light of Manon's mistrust—the way, for example, Garfield wore the uniform of the academic (corduroys and elbow patches) and had the books he'd written facing forward on the shelf. Manon said this showed intellectual insecurity, though Davy thought it just made him look clever. Shaved heads and tattoos, that sent a different message altogether, and he thinks of Ryan again and the rough estate he used to live on (though God alone knows where he's living now) and the unsavory men who circle his mother.

Davy's thoughts go round and round like the wheels on his bike, when he's come out here to think about Chloe, because New Year's Eve can take a romantic turn, although if he's honest, he'd rather be going out on the razz with his friends. Chloe doesn't meld with them too well, and whenever he's tried to mix the two—his girlfriend and the gang from school—he's ended up in the corner of the bar asking her over and over what the matter is. Perhaps he'll skip the Conversation, after all, there being no hurry . . .

He's forced to squeeze hard and sudden on the brakes, and he turns the front wheel sharply, the gravel spraying. A duck proceeds on its stately waddle across his path, one eye blinking at him with faint disdain, until it plops into the river to Davy's right.

MANON
• • •

SWEDISH SEASON AT THE CAMBRIDGE ARTS PICTUREHOUSE, ALL RED VEL-
vet and the smell of brewing coffee. Women wearing big beads. She
relishes the prospect of a Swedish film—it doesn't even have to be *noir*.
The Swedes are a nation who appreciate morbidity, unlike the British,
who are just as depressed as everyone else but who like to project their
darker feelings, saying to people in the street, "Cheer up, it might never
happen!" Catcalls like that make her want to take out her Taser.

She parks on a single yellow, less than a yard from the cinema's
broad steps. The cold is bitter and thin and she realizes how fed up she
is with it, how long it has been going on, tensing her body against it.
Her left eye has become reinfected, the grit scratching her eyeball. It
had recovered somewhat over Christmas and then, following the use of
a particularly unappetizing mascara, the soreness returned worse than
before, her lashes gummed with a secretion that peeled away in clumps.
It's less painful if she keeps it shut. With the other eye, she sees various

trouser legs and shoes on the cinema's white step as she joins the queue, willing it to be quick so she can get out of the cold.

"DS Bradshaw?" says a male voice.

She looks up, still with one eye shut, and there is Alan Prenderghast searching out her face.

"Hello there," she says, her neck cricked—the reluctant mole. She smiles, making a show of trying (but barely trying at all) to hide her disappointment at the prospect of him occupying her mind and preventing her losing herself in the film. And regret that she looks like she's been punched in the eye.

"So," he says. "We've had the same idea."

"Yes. The only way to spend New Year's Eve, if you ask me." She looks away from him, across the street. He strains his neck upward to look over the heads in front and see how near they are to the kiosk. They shuffle forward slightly.

"I found that, after yesterday, I didn't want to be by myself after all. I felt the need to be in the town. Among people. Alive people," he says, with a damp sort of laugh.

"Yes."

"We don't have to sit together," he adds. "I rather love going to the cinema on my own, so I do understand."

"Oh, OK," says Manon, relieved and rejected. They shuffle forward and then to the snacks counter, where she orders a real lemonade and organic popcorn and he takes a coffee, which makes her feel like a child for ordering the sweet stuff. Then he asks for a family-sized box of Maltesers.

They walk into the dark plush of the screening room, velvet seats fraying on the arms. He nods, saying, "See you later, then," and moves down the aisle. They are watching *Together* by Lukas Moodysson, about a hippie commune in the 1970s and the waifs and strays who come together there.

Alan Prenderghast sits four rows ahead and to her left, so the side of his head is visible, though not his expression. Despite her obscured view, she thinks she can see him laughing when she glances across at him during the film, which she does often, the daylight scenes illuminating his head in flickering blues. She thinks she can see enjoyment written all over his shoulders. He seems to be hugging his family-sized box of Maltesers in delight, and hugging his aloneness too, and taking pleasure in a good film with chocolate and a worn, comfortable seat, though who is to say whether it is his enjoyment or her own hopes for it, streaming forward like dancing rays from the projector.

She is ahead of him in the slow shuffling of people exiting the cinema. At the doorway, she smiles.

"I'm going for a drink upstairs if you fancy joining me," he says.

"Oh yes, that's a good idea."

The upstairs bar is art deco, with wooden tables and ferny plants in pots. She watches him bring two coffees, squat white cups balanced on saucers, back from the bar to their table and she notices how high-waisted his trousers are. His trainers are terrible too—great white ships, the kind you're supposed to play tennis in, not wear for leisure. He looks like Fungus the Bogeyman, she thinks, and she, with her half-swollen eye, like Quasimodo.

Sitting in a tree.

K.I.S.S.I.N.G.

"So, what did you think?" he says, unlooping a maroon scarf and draping it over the back of his chair.

"I thought it was fabulous. Funny, moving, great knitwear."

He laughs. "It's a very touching idea, isn't it, these misfits coming together and keeping each other company. That it's better to be together."

"Yes," she says. "But they weren't idealized. They were a genuinely motley bunch."

"It's not so easy, in real life. To make contact with people."

"No, it isn't. I sometimes think I don't actually like anyone that much. That all I ever want is to be on my own. And then I can't cope with it—with myself, just myself all the time, and it's like *I* become the worst company of all—and there's this awful realization that I need people, and it's almost humiliating," she says.

He looks at her and smiles.

"I don't know where that came from."

He shakes his head. "I totally get it. I live in that great barn and sometimes on a Sunday morning it's like heaven, sitting in front of that

massive window with my coffee, with the sun coming in, reading. And
then by eleven A.M. I'm desperate for someone to call round, but of
course they don't, because I live in the arse end of nowhere."

She laughs. "Except the police, occasionally."

"Or a corpse. Well, he didn't come knocking."

"No. Have you recovered?"

"I don't think there was anything to recover from, really. I mean,
it was shocking and I spent a day thinking about death more than
usual—and I'm someone who thinks about death *a lot*. But it's not
like I knew him or cared for him. It was the fact he was young that
bothered me."

"Yes."

"I suppose you can't talk about the case."

"No."

She rubs her eye, hard, feeling the crystals work into her eyeball.

"That eye looks sore," he says.

"Yes, I don't know what it is. Feels like I've got something stuck
in it that I can't get out. Been like this on and off for a fortnight." And
she feels the moment race toward her, unannounced, an awful parody
of *Brief Encounter,* where he will feel invited to come close to her face
and look deep into her eyes to see what's there. She hadn't intended
that at all.

"Looks like conjunctivitis to me," he says.

"Really?" she says, disappointed.

"Yes. You can get antibiotics for it over the counter."

OUT IN THE STREET, THEY find their cars are nose to tail. His is an
anonymous silver Ford, just the kind she'd expect from a systems analyst wearing tennis shoes. The seats look as if they've been recently
vacuumed.

"This is me," she says, waiting for him to comment on her seventies
mustard Citroën with the black leather seats. Waiting for him to take
in *the package.*

"This is your car, is it?" he says mildly.

"Yup." She pats the roof.

"Right, then," he says. He is digging one hand in his trouser pocket.

He brings out a handkerchief and holds it to his nose. It blooms white and big across his face, and he pushes it side to side, bending his nose. She has never seen anyone under seventy use a handkerchief.

"Do you fancy . . ." she begins. "We could . . . go on somewhere?"

He looks at his watch. "I think everywhere will be packed with awful drunkards right about now. Sorry," he says, stifling a yawn, "I'm going to have to call it a night. This is burning the candle for an old fart like me."

"Right, yes, of course. I suppose we're in opposite directions."

"I suppose," he says. "Well, Happy New Year."

She wonders if he is going to bend to plant a kiss on her cheek, but he shifts slightly. He places a hand on her upper arm and she lifts her cheek but he turns away.

She watches him duck into his warm, practical car.

MANON
• • •

BRYONY'S HUSBAND, PETER, OPENS THE OVEN DOOR WITH PADDED HANDS like paddles and lifts out an angrily spitting pan. He holds it before him, the furious beast, the God of their lunch, and the room fills with the atavistic smell of meat fat. The trail of it curls across the room to Manon in the corner armchair—the salty maple smell of the meat—and together with the dry white wine she is sipping, it works on her stomach juices to produce the sweet anticipation of being fed.

The windows of the kitchen are fogged, as if the world Bryony and Peter have created—the roast lunch, the baby she is putting down for a nap, the toddler playing Lego in the next room—has erased the outside because it is not needed. This world, their world, is inside.

"Looking good, elephant woman. Shouldn't you get that seen to?" says Bryony as she enters the room.

Manon puts a hand to her left eye. "Yeah, probably."

Bryony and Peter move around each other at the counter, a nonchalant ballet of putting forks in the dishwasher, getting out bowls, broccoli steam hitting their faces, carving the meat. And Manon watches them. Isn't this what she should have? Isn't it what she should want? She knows she comes here, like the third child, to inhale some of it, to slouch in the soft cushioning of the corner armchair, where passivity is king. Sometimes she is pricked by jealousy, or at least greed for their kind of life—not wanting to leave or not having the energy to pick herself up and send herself out into the cold world alone. She rubs the infected eye and it reopens slowly, the picture watery, as if she is looking through smeared glass. Those vicious shards of loneliness cannot seem to prick them in here, in this inner world, where someone has taken an eraser to the view. But its innerness is also airless.

"D'you know what drives me nuts?" Bryony once said. "I can't even take a shower without some kind of family summit on the logistics of being out of the room for ten minutes. Never mind pop to the shops."

It's not these notional practicalities that bother Manon. It is the loss of separateness, the dependence that might cause her to meld formlessly into someone else until she no longer knows where she begins and ends, until she is no longer capable of saying, "You might like that, but I don't like it, because I am different from you, separate from you." Or "I will not eat now. I will eat later."

"We changed the clock," Bryony is saying from across the room, sliding some cauliflower cheese from a foil tray into a serving bowl, "so it said midnight. Then we said, 'Cheers, Happy New Year!' and went to bed. About nine-thirty, wasn't it?"

"About that," says Peter. "Just think of all the poor bastards out there getting drunk and snogging strangers."

"I know, I pity them," says Bryony. "I mean, who would want that kind of sleazy, low-rent thrill?"

Manon takes another slug of wine. "I went to the cinema."

"See? She's one of us," says Bryony.

Their three-year-old son, Bobby, comes gamboling into the room on fat little legs. He is all cheeks and brilliant eyes. Manon notices Bryony's involuntary smile.

"Hello, little chap," says Manon, setting down her glass and lifting him onto her knee. She has the urge to shower him in affection, not because she loves him—she feels, in fact, an angular separateness from other people's children—but because she loves Bryony and she can make a display of it this way. "Shall we do 'This Is the Way the Lady Rides'?"

"Lady wides," says Bobby.

"Cuddle first," says Manon, and she folds the boy's solid body in her arms and luxuriates in the cashmere of his cheek against hers. She kisses him and, when he begins to struggle, squeezes him tighter. "One more kiss," she says, and then blows a raspberry into his neck, which smells of warm bread, but he is shouting, "Lady wides!"

The lunch is devoured in twenty minutes. Their lips glisten with the meat fat as they suck on bones. Bobby begins to fidget in his booster seat and knocks over his cup of Ribena.

"Come on, sausage," Peter says to him. "Let's go and watch *Top Gear.*"

When they have gone, she and Bryony pour themselves more wine and sit together at the kitchen table, strewn with cloudy glasses and smeared plates. Manon is wiping hers with a finger and licking the gravy off while she tells Bryony about the cinema and Alan Prenderghast, and it's as if she can't wait to, as if she's been waiting for Peter to take Bobby off, so she can launch into it.

"He's nice, but he's not boyfriend material," she says. "He's forty-two." She is picking at charred roast carrots, wiping the little chunks in gravy and popping them in her mouth.

"I hate to break it to you, kiddo, but you're not in the first flush of youth yourself. Forty-two is the perfect age for you."

"No, but . . . just, no. He's not, I dunno. He's really uncool. Like massive trainers, bad flappy trousers."

"So take him shopping."

"He sort of stoops."

"You've got no neck."

"He didn't go to university."

"Jesus, Manon, who fucking cares?"

"He *has* got a nice barn."

"There you go, then."

"He's just kind of . . . odd."

"Odd is good. You're really odd. It's one of my favorite things about you. Stop doing that," and she removes Manon's plate. "Ice cream?"

Manon shakes her head. Bryony yawns and stretches her arms up and forward, until her muscles judder.

"Anyway, how's disclosure?" asks Manon. "Is the filing getting to you?"

"No, the exciting news is I've been seconded—HOLMES support on a trafficking ring. Massive case, joint ops between border control and public protection. Really good."

"You mean girls trafficked into prostitution?"

"Yeah—some girls in a brothel in Luton are talking. But also just ferrying illegals in across the border. Lorries of Afghans, Syrians, wherever there's a war, basically, coming in through the ports. P&O Ferries, that kind of thing. You would not believe how leaky our borders are right now."

"Think I would."

"Anyway, it's really interesting. Nice change from *Fireman Sam*."

"They charging anyone?" asks Manon.

"Not yet. Looking at a chap—an Afghan called Abdul-Ghani Khalil." Bryony has got up, taking their plates over to the sink. "Couple of the prostitutes mentioned him, and a neighbor said he thought Khalil was making a fortune bringing people in, but not enough to charge him yet."

Manon's mobile phone has begun to vibrate across the table. "Hang on," she says to Bryony. Manon stands and her insides swim with the wine. She is loose, but she must hold it together, because Harriet is on the phone.

"Harriet," she says brightly, a finger pressing her other ear shut against the tinny sounds of *Top Gear* from the next room and the clatter of Bryony stacking the dishwasher.

"The body from yesterday, the jumper," says Harriet. "We don't think it is a jumper."

"Why not?"

"He's from Cricklewood, name's Taylor Dent."

"*Cricklewood?* How's he ended up in Ely?"

"Exactly. Can you come in? Stanton wants a briefing." Harriet hangs up. She has no time for pleasantries at the beginning and end of phone calls.

"Can you drive me in, Bri?" she says as her phone thunks to the bottom of her handbag. "I've had too much to drink."

"Yes, sure thing. Just let me put my shoes on. Don't want anyone at the nick to see me in these," says Bryony, slipping off her bright fur slippers with bunny ears—preteen pink, the color of the sunset through Alan Prenderghast's double-height windows.

"SIT DOWN, MANON," SAYS STANTON, his back to them.

Harriet is already seated on Manon's side of the desk, her crossed upper leg bouncing outward. She is reading a brown file, which drips downward at its corners.

Stanton is standing by the window, wearing a navy shirt with an ebullient floral pattern on it. Boden, from the looks of it—a Mrs. Stanton purchase, Manon guesses, fresh from the packet for a New Year's Day family lunch or knees-up with the neighbors. She imagines him dad-dancing, his teenage children rolling their eyes.

Manon has always liked Gary Stanton. He's conventional, in that suburban, slightly overweight, golf-playing way. He can rub along with the boss class without taking umbrage. As a result, he has slid noiselessly up the ranks. No flashes of brilliance. No feuds either.

Harriet hands Manon the file as Stanton turns, reaching back to scratch his shoulder blade.

"Taylor Dent," he says. "What's he doing in one of our rivers?"

"He killed Edith Hind, then killed himself?" says Harriet. "He was Edith's bit of rough, her dealer? She owed him money?"

"What if he's the link between Tony Wright and Edith?" asks Manon. "Tony's gofer."

"We need to look at all of it. I want George Street and Deeping swept for his DNA. Annoying there are no cameras around Deeping. I want you two liaising with the Met on Dent's background, links to Wright. I want interviews with the Dent family. Did he know Edith? Was there any connection through friends—a dealer, the Hind brother? Every avenue. Let's look at routes from London to here, CCTV at

King's Cross around the time he disappeared, roads, ANPR any vehicles he might have had access to."

Stanton looks depressed. Last thing he needs is a fresh murder inquiry clogging up officers' time, slowing up the Hind investigation, more forensics and an expensive postmortem draining his budget.

"Phone work," he says. "We need to check this Dent boy's number against Edith's phone and against Carter's and Reed's. Let's see if he's unknown-515."

"Will Carter's alibi holds up," Harriet says to Stanton. "His return journey from Stoke was verified by the cashier at the Texaco garage in Corby. We showed her a picture and she said, 'Oh yeah, he was *lush*.'" Harriet reaches for her bra strap, but her arm stops midair and she lays it back in her lap, like a dead thing. Has someone—Elsie?—told her she's a fidget? Still, her foot is going. Kick, kick, kick, as if the energy must escape from somewhere.

Manon has opened Taylor Dent's file and is reading. Seventeen years old from Cricklewood, North London. Mixed race. Nigerian father, whereabouts unknown. Irish mother, Maureen Dent, known alcohol and substance abuser. Taylor Dent made his money the way lots did: bit of this, bit of that. Knockoff gear, cigarettes off booze cruises sold in markets or to nefarious newsagents. If he dabbled in drugs, he didn't appear to partake in them.

"Says here he was arrested for indecency in 2008 but let off with a caution," she says, frowning.

"Had some high-profile customers," says Stanton, "who didn't wish a prosecution to come to court."

Stanton has a look of distaste. He is a man who likes to avoid confrontation, like a loyal dog tied to a railing—he does not wish to bark or snap, certainly not at the wrong heels.

"Interesting," says Manon, still reading. "Says here Dent was clean."

"Well, to our *knowledge*," starts Harriet. "A forensic postmortem will tell us more."

"Not necessarily," says Stanton, turning away from them back to the window, where the sky has darkened to a slate blue, smeared with light from the yellow streetlamps over the car park. "Toxicology will have washed away. PMs on river deaths are pretty inconclusive, in my experience. He'll have been beaten about by tree roots, got at by animals. Cause of death unascertained, I'll put money on it. To think that's what we pay them three grand for." He shakes his head.

Manon guesses he's marveling at the riches of forensics pathologists in their BMWs with cream leather seats.

"Speaking of money, the cost of the Hind investigation is getting to the point where the Home Office is going to have to bail us out. I've had a note from Sir Brian Peabody about it." He waves a bit of paper at them. "Polsa teams, SOCO, television appeals. Now this forensic PM and more officers on Dent. The profile of it, well, it's making our good commissioner jumpy."

"What're we supposed to do?" asks Harriet. "Stop looking for her? Not look as hard?"

"Just look more cheaply," says Manon.

"They're not pulling the plug," says Stanton. "But we're under scrutiny, that's all. If we had a body, then we'd have an unlimited murder budget, but Edith Hind—it's moot whether she's a high-risk misper, a suspected homicide, or even just a misper, in Peabody's view."

"Is there anyone who seriously thinks she's alive?" asks Harriet.

"Look, Peabody's just looking ahead," says Stanton. "Inquiry gets to this size, and there's always an inquiry into the inquiry, questions in Parliament about how much we spent, what result we got, and why we didn't know it was 'so-and-so' three weeks before we caught him. Everyone throwing in their wisdom with the benefit of hindsight. Doesn't help that Hind is mates with Galloway. I can see how itchy Peabody is about that. There are already mutterings about a review of our investigation by another force."

"Bound to happen, sooner or later," says Harriet.

"Manon, I want you to go to Cricklewood first thing tomorrow. Liaise with Kilburn CID. Visit the Dent family, get what you can out of the mother and the brother. Then you can pop up to Hampstead and update the Hinds."

"Perhaps she should inform Sir Ian that his dear friend's austerity budget means there aren't enough resources to find his daughter," says Harriet. "Let's see him bring *that* up at their next Hampstead dinner party."

"I'll pretend I didn't hear that," says Stanton, with a smile at Harriet that says, *We're on the same side.*

"'Least I don't have to tell them we've hooked their daughter out of the Ouse," says Manon.

STANTON CLOSES THE DOOR TO his office. They watch him turn the spindle on his Venetian blind and disappear.

"D'you need a lift anywhere?" asks Harriet, as she and Manon put their coats on.

"No. Getting the train to Bedford to pick the car up. Shouldn't take long. I forgot to ask—how was Buckaroo with Elsie? Did she throw in a custard cream?"

"Long," says Harriet, picking her bag up off the floor. "Very, very long. It's not a game I'd recommend for someone with advanced-stage Parkinson's."

"No, no, I can see hooking those little plastic . . ." They both shake their heads at the thought of it.

"I just didn't think it through," Harriet says sadly. "I'm a complete fucking idiot sometimes. She wouldn't give up, though, I'll give her that."

"S'pose you should steer clear of Operation as well."

"Anyway, how was yours? Wild partying, I bet."

"I went to the movies instead. Swedish season at the arts cinema. Bumped into that dog walker, actually—chap who found Taylor Dent."

"Oh yeah? Davy mentioned his amazing barn. Said he fancied the pants off you."

"Oh," says Manon, flushing like a marzipan fruit. "I don't think he did." And her inner world shudders as if a host of celestial doves were fluttering up inside her rib cage.

HER LONELY BENCH, POLICE BLUE, on a deserted Sunday platform; wondering what's left in the fridge for tea. The problem of food, for one: it symbolizes everything. She wants delicious morsels, yet cooking for herself is so defeating: a surplus of ingredients, the washing-up unshared, and the sense that it doesn't matter—the production of it or whether it's nice. The daily slog of being alone washes over her on the cold latticed bench, the sense of being unassisted in the minutiae:

broadband down; washing machine stuck on spin cycle. Oh yes, people spoke of the freedoms—no one to answer to!—but there was such a thing as a surfeit of freedom, a sort of weightless free fall through nothing. She wonders what Alan Prenderghast is like at fixing things or renewing roadside breakdown assistance. Masterful, if his Ford Focus is anything to go by.

There is a solitary fellow passenger two benches down, and as he turns to look at her, Manon is careful to turn her head away. Never catch their eye.

A songbird trills, curiously rural amid track and all the metal clutter overhead. The man gets up from his bench and starts toward her, carrying a holdall that looks as if it could be laden with half a torso or firearms but probably contains a mildewed towel and some unpleasantly brief Speedos. He reaches the bench next to hers just as the headlamps of their First Capital Connect train heaves into view, screeching and puffing and crawling up the platform like an elderly sex symbol keeping the fans waiting. The brakes squeal, a gush of air from somewhere.

Manon waits for the man to choose his carriage so she can choose a different one. Never board first; otherwise, they can follow you in.

The familiar blue tartan seats, the smell of warm air pumped through metal floor vents, and someone's fast food.

In Bedford she stops at her car and looks at the orange glow through the drawn curtains of Bryony's windows, imagining Bryony and Peter cuddled up on the sofa in front of the TV.

Monday

MIRIAM

• • •

A NEW YEAR AND IT FEELS SO OLD, WORN OUT AND TIN-RUSTED; 2011, fifteen days missing. Time pants away from her disappearance like a locomotive, and the rawness of it dissipates, as if this might be an acceptable new status quo.

"Right," she says to Rollo, gathering her keys from the kitchen table. "I'm off to see Jonti."

Rollo is eating more toast. It's Herculean, the loaves he can get through. "Say hi from me," he says through a full mouth.

Miriam's journey to Jonti's shop in Kensal Rise is typically vigilant. She searches every face these days, examines every doorway bed, sees Edith everywhere—the spun gold of her hair; her long, slender neck; the back of her head, beloved oval, unaware and vulnerable.

Only yesterday, Miriam had hastened across the scratched grass of the Heath to the bench overlooking the ponds, stumbling happily, she was so sure it was Edith, thinking, *Ian will be relieved.* Edith in an un-familiar coat, staring at the tall Parliament Hill houses across the water.

"Oh," Miriam said, as the stranger's face turned up to hers question-ingly. She felt furious and frowned at the woman as if it were her fault.

She looks rough sleepers in the eye, where before she scuttled guiltily past them; she seeks out faces in the hot metallic air of the Tube as commuters avoid her eye. She has visited soup kitchens in King's Cross, the other volunteers mistaking her interest for just another dose of middle-class guilt—it being the time of year for it. She has joined a support group for parents of missing children, some of whom disap-peared six years, ten years, fifteen years ago, looking at their dogged campaigns and catching herself thinking, *Can't you see they're dead?*

She is working her way through Edith's childhood friends, for con-nections, clues, anything. Pointless, really, but she does it for the sense of contact with Edith, the chance to talk about her, and for the feeling of *doing something.*

"Thought I might contact the EMFs," she'd said idly to Rollo. "Though God knows how."

"That awful bunch," he replied. And he was right, of course—the EMFs were awful, though Miriam would never have said as much to Edith. The group was given this moniker at school because they read everything by E. M. Forster and discussed it at length in cafés on Finch-ley Road, drinking lemon tea and smoking cigarettes. When Edith first fell in with them, Ian and Miriam were thrilled (Ian more so)—the intellectual set! Edith was full of literary zeal, so taken by *Howards End* and *A Room with a View, Maurice,* and *Where Angels Fear to Tread,* that she traveled by train to Firenze and San Gimignano (with Rollo as her rather Forster-ish chaperone; Miriam had insisted), writing furiously in her diary while Rollo listened to pop music through headphones that appeared to be surgically attached to his head. The EMFs turned out to be very up themselves indeed, pretentious and competitive, especially Electra, who Miriam had been sure was bulimic and who got a car for her seventeenth birthday.

Miriam preferred Christy from across the road—a few years older than Edith, who liked playing hairdressers and watching TV, and with whom Edith had a sisterly, nonchalant relationship. Last-minute sleepovers welcomed by her delightfully *laissez-faire* Spanish mother, and after-school teas in rumpled uniforms. These days, Christy has two tiny daughters, aged two and four, and a house in Golders Green.

Miriam had gone there a few days back. Christy was kind to her, of course, made her tea (*more tea*), handed her tissues, and apologized to Miriam—she hadn't heard from Edith in years. And then there was the awkward silence when Miriam became tearful. She is growing used to those too.

"It worked out for you, all this," Miriam said in a watery voice, sitting at Christy's pockmarked farmhouse table. Her fingers traced the grooves in the wood. "It could have worked out for Edith, that's what I keep thinking. For Edith and Jonti."

"Oh, I don't know," Christy said. "She was awfully critical of him. Edith's much more ambitious than Jonti."

The bell rings above Jonti's shop door, which is too minimalist to have a sign, and as it closes behind Miriam, the roar of the buses outside is silenced. They plow up and down this thoroughfare, past frayed gold velvet chaise longues and fifties Formica tables, tasseled lampshades, beaten-leather club chairs, and flaking green-painted dressers—the wares of the antiques shops that flank Chamberlayne Road.

Inside, she is greeted by the smell of sawdust and linseed warmed through the broad shop windows. She runs a hand over one cabinet— oak, she guesses—and admires its slick surface and the triangular joints that lattice together like fingers. Jonti's style is Shaker with something entirely his own. Blocky wooden rectangles with small pegs for knobs like blinking, honest eyes in a quiet face. Dressers without curls or pelmets. Stoic tables. Miriam is astonished at the craftsmanship. He has built all this from nothing. If only Edith could have had more faith.

"Jonti," she says as he enters from the back, and she is overcome with fondness for him. He has a slight stoop, is wiping his hands on the back pockets of his trousers, and wears a ridiculous beanie hat in gray wool. It is not that he is without affectation (the very location of his shop is an affectation); more that he is without guile. Jonti doesn't have a "side"—he is as plain as his furniture.

"Mrs. . . . Lady Hind," he says, checking his hands before holding one out to her.

"Miriam, please, Jonti," and she ignores his hand to hug him about the shoulders.

He had been a resident of her kitchen for long enough, an extra son when he and Edith were eighteen and going about together. When he was around—and he was around a lot—the atmosphere had a good-natured calm to it. He would lean against her kitchen worktop, his hands in the pockets of his mustard cords, and say, "Anything you want peeling, Mrs. H.?" Or joke around on the computer with Rollo, waiting for Edith to get ready.

She liked Edith when she was with Jonti; it was as if he planed down her sharper edges. Edith would rush down the stairs in a great pummeling of feet, breathless and lively, saying, "We're off out, Mum," dragging Jonti away by the arm, and Miriam would shout after them, "Have fun, you two."

Ian, of course, viewed Jonti as a dropout, and it was true he smoked a lot of marijuana (or "blow," as Edith and Rollo referred to it). He was a couple of years older, was training even then to be a joiner, as if rejecting his private school education, though that had been in the overtly liberal vein: children of singers and artists, no uniforms, and everyone calling the teachers by their first names.

When Edith got pregnant that summer, she'd already had her offer from Cambridge.

It would be quite wrong to suggest Ian made her get rid of it, but his silences over the dinner table forced them all to contemplate how seriously everything was hanging in the balance. Ian had a way of making his face say, "I am shattered by my disappointment," which could sting you to the heart. Ian was Edith's raised bar. She strained to please him, and in that striving she did well, Miriam admiring the discipline of their work together, because it counterbalanced the elastic feel of her love. Miriam was forever wavering, uncertain of where she should draw the line with the children, while Ian had been made of sterner stuff. "Never back down when it comes to children," he would say. "It's the beginning of the end." And she thought, *What* rot. *They're people— why on earth shouldn't they win sometimes? Have one over on you? Get away with it?*

Edith got her four A's and her place at Cambridge, and she had gone about with Jonti and got pregnant. Miriam stood silently beside Ian's disapproval, not because she was angry but because she felt a baby at eighteen was nothing to wish for. Edith's "death instinct," someone had said—was it Patty, who was doing a course on Freud? Miriam thought it was a more complicated mistake than that—more ambivalent, less destructive.

Miriam and Jonti sit amid the forest of turned wood in two rocking chairs. He has flipped the CLOSED sign on the door and made her some green tea, which is foul but she sips it so as not to hurt his feelings.

"I'm so sorry, Mrs. H.," he says, and she likes it that he's calling her that again. She had liked being the mother of teenagers—their sweet, ungainly hulks taking up all of her kitchen, like little children in dressing-up bodies.

"Thank you, Jonti. Your work—all this—it's so impressive. How have you done it?"

"Built it up slowly. I was an apprentice for a long time for a nice old chap in Whitechapel. I've only had this place a couple of years. There are still quiet periods where I think it's going to go belly-up, but so far I've had a lot of return business and good word of mouth, so touch wood." He doesn't have to reach far.

"Well, I'm not surprised. I mean, the craftsmanship is extraordinary. I saw Christy yesterday. She said she was saving for a sideboard. Oh, Jonti, she's got lovely children—two girls."

His face darkens and she realizes she has been insensitive. After the abortion, Edith had become dissatisfied with him. "No ambition," she'd told Miriam, and Miriam thought it was Ian talking. She witnessed Edith being cruel—putting Jonti down when they discussed politics or literature during family meals. "Like *you'd* know," she'd said to him when he'd once ventured an opinion on Iraq, and Jonti, in his mild way, had sloped off out of their lives, rather bruised but without rancor.

"I'm sorry she was cruel to you," Miriam says now.

Jonti shrugs. "It's in the past. I've made peace with it, Mrs. H. I hope she's all right, really, I do. I think about her a lot since it was on the news."

"You've not heard from her?" she asks, though it is pointless.

He shakes his head. "I'd have told you straightaway. Haven't seen her since that summer. That was not a good time. It took me a long time to, y'know, process what happened and then to let it go." Jonti's mother talking. Miriam remembers how she used to moo on about "emotional auras," with her frizzy black hair and post-divorce depressed face. She was learning about aromatherapy and healing and fed him nothing but lentils.

"But you did," Miriam says sadly. "More's the pity. I thought you two could have made a go of it."

"Did you?" he says. "You never let us know that."

"No," she says. "I didn't, did I?"

Edith has missed out on this gentle man with his big hands and his slow pace and his tolerance. She could have had that sideboard in her lounge, for starters. He would have laid her a lovely floor, put up shelves. There are worse things.

They have fallen into silence and Miriam realizes she and Jonti don't have anything to talk about. That period is gone and they can't even reminisce fondly, so sour did it turn. Another thing she has forgotten in the swim of nostalgia: Jonti is humorless. Perhaps it wouldn't have worked out between him and Edith after all—you need a sense of humor to get through marriage.

For a time, she and Jonti sit among the herd of sideboards and chests of drawers, sipping horrid green tea as the buses rumble past outside.

THE RAIN SPITS INTO MIRIAM's face, spattering the shoulders of her beige Burberry mac—too thin a layer for January—and she squints into the wind, up Chamberlayne Road toward Kensal Rise station, relieved to have said goodbye to Jonti and the guilt.

The abortion had changed Edith. Even years later it cast its sad tint, like the spring when Christy was getting married, three or four years ago now. Edith went on and on about how sorry she felt for her friend, with eyes that held Miriam's pleadingly. "Far too young. She'll come to regret it. You can't know who you are in your twenties. I'd hate to be settling down right now."

Miriam descends the steps to the overground station, for the train to Hampstead Heath, remembering times when the sadness lifted and Edith's silly, girlish joy had been allowed to escape like bubbles up the side of a glass—like the time they'd shopped in Fenwick's for outfits for the wedding. Miriam had stared at Edith in the changing rooms as she pranced and giggled, thinking how she loved the very flesh of her. You got used to that with children, love crashing over you like waves. But then Edith had picked out a shockingly expensive dress—£250—and Miriam balked, not because she didn't have the money but because it seemed inappropriate. She had a sense of obligation—to teach Edith the value of money, that she should not grow up profligate. And, as so often in her brief career as mother, Miriam had spoiled everything. She'd dithered—"I don't know, Edith, it's an awful lot"—and in her hesitation Edith read censure, or a limit on love, or some coldness that wasn't there.

No, darling, my dear one, it wasn't that. The train is coming toward her, the tears mingling with the rain on her face. *It was my own stupid inhibition. I'd buy it for you now, Edie, love, a thousand times over.*

Every fond memory is tinged like this, as if Edith can turn the atmosphere even now. In Fenwick's she had grown sullen, maintaining her dissatisfied stance toward the £80 dress that Miriam bought for her from the Oasis concession, even though she had the figure for it—Edith could carry off the flimsiest high-street fashions.

Yes, Miriam was inconsistent—she loved to buy her daughter things, to express love, but, no, she couldn't buy her everything all of the time. She frowns as she boards the train, in a silent argument with Edith or some notion of her righteousness. Well, she wasn't going to smother her spontaneity—those times when Edith was little and she'd said, "Let's go to the toy shop," just because she delighted in delighting a small person, and small people were so easy to delight, so ready to join the ride. But she'd had to say no too, and face down the hatred. This was her lot, to be so often in the wrong, and so it had been when they went dress shopping and she'd spoiled it all for Edith.

The other passengers stare at her as she presses a tissue against her eyes, trying to stop the tears and failing, knowing that her face must be a torn-up storm of anger, regret, and defensiveness.

Edith has never been quick to forgive. Is this what her disappearance is all about—one huge sulk, like the one in Fenwick's? Oh, she hopes so. She'd be happy to know Edith is alive and to never talk to her again. Anything, but not dead.

The wedding, at the church at the bottom of Church Row, had been so beautiful, Christy vastly pregnant in white, with a ring of flowers around her hair. Miriam and Edith sat together in a pew, and when Miriam looked to her left at Edith's face, the tears were streaming from her daughter's eyes, and her mouth was a soundless red twist.

MANON

$\bullet\ \bullet\ \bullet$

"So, Taylor Dent," says DI Sean Haverstock—"Havers," as he seems to be called by everyone at Kilburn CID. He is bouncing back in his swivel chair. Manon guesses he's about her age: bald, wearing a wedding ring.

"Yes," she says, "where are we with his movements in the week before he died?"

"Nowhere, to be honest, without some decent phone work. His was pay-as-you-go, basic, not a smartphone. That's disappeared. Registered activity in the North London area up until Sunday, eleventh of December, but that's as you would expect."

She nods. "That ties in with the PM's time of death."

"Phone was then either lost, switched off, or destroyed."

"Who's coming up on the call data?"

"Unsurprisingly, it was almost entirely PAYG unregistered. Dirty phones. His world—"

"We don't seem to know much about his world," she says. She wonders if Havers has made any effort at all. Has he sent detectives to interview Taylor Dent's friends and associates? Has he tickled up his Cricklewood contacts—the kinds of guys Dent would have done business with? Has he fuck.

"What about the family?" she says. "What have they told you?"

"There's a younger brother, Fly Dent, about ten. He was sheltered from the worst of Taylor's activities, it seems. Very much looked after by Taylor: he fed him, washed his clothes, got him to school on time, et cetera. Social workers are onto him now. Mother's a total case. Cheap stuff, y'know: Magners, solvents, methadone. Boy'll be taken into care, I shouldn't wonder."

"Didn't anyone report Taylor missing? Was there a misper investigation going?"

"Brother came in, yes, on the Monday—think it was the twelfth." Havers straightens and leafs through some paperwork on his desk. "It was logged, of course. But a boy like him—if we launched an investigation into every missing young man who was into all sorts, DS Bradshaw . . . He wasn't a minor, don't forget. For all we knew, he was loading up a van with fags in Spain."

Havers shrugs as if they have an understanding. *A boy like him*. He couldn't care less about the death of a boy like Dent. She can imagine exactly what type of reception his little brother got when he tried to raise the alarm.

A BUS FLIES TOWARD HER at such speed she thinks she'll be hit, but it thunders past, its warm air whipping up her hair. The smell of fried eggs and the sound of brakes squealing; past the Crown and Paddy Power and striped zip bags for the dispossessed outside the pound shop. Every face she passes, every snippet of language in the air, is from another part of the world. The shops are a motley cheek-by-jowl roll call of immigration, like strata in a rock: McGovern's Free House; Halal kebab; Bacovia *magazin românesc;* Serhat Off Licence (Polski sklep); Bosnia & Herzegovina Community Biblioteka charity shop; Milad Persian food; D'Den Exotic African Cuisine; Taste of Lahore; Bestco mini mart, where half the shelves are empty. A run-down, slip-sliding melting pot, and the necessaries blooming like lichen: pawn shop, betting shop, funeral parlor, Western Union money transfer.

She keeps walking, and where the shops thin out and the traffic roars louder still is an Ethiopian restaurant, Abyssinia, with red-and-white cheesecloth curtains in the window and beside it a gray metal door: 11A. Manon looks up and sees windows blacked by the pollution and gray nets, one pushed back by something—a sack or bag leaning against the glass. *It's going to smell in here,* she thinks, as her body tenses against it, and she's right, a combination of old frying (congealed fat, the type of smell you get from an unwashed grill pan) and damp. She's been buzzed in and she tramps up the narrow stairwell with her poloneck over her mouth and nose.

"Yes, yes, come in, come in," says a woman in a strong Irish accent. She has a ginger fuzz of hair, which is dark gray at the roots, a pale, freckled complexion in among the thread veins, and frightened eyes. She is quick, like a creature burrowing to get away.

"Mrs. Dent," says Manon.

"Dat'll be me."

"My name is DS Bradshaw, from Cambridgeshire Police. I've come to talk to you about Taylor Dent, your son."

"Taylor's gone, de Lord have mercy on his soul," she says, not looking Manon in the eye. Instead, she leads the way in, leaving the door ajar. "Sorry about de mess . . ."

The smell recedes inside the flat, overtaken by stale cigarettes, which is not unpleasant, almost warming in a way. The light is dim, the carpets dark. The space opens out into a lounge, not much brighter, the nets blocking out the light from outside. The place seems embedded with human cells. A multitude, vibrating, of people long gone, arrested or dead.

Manon and Mrs. Dent ("Call me Maur*een*") sit together on the sofa, brown floral chenille. There are open crisp packets on the floor. An overflowing ashtray. An enormous television takes up one half of the room.

"I'll clean dose up. I'll get round to it. I've got to have a camera in me stomach. A camera down in me stomach, see. I don't want it, so I don't. I can show you de letter; you might understand it. I don't understand it, see."

She gets up again, beetling off in a stooped flurry. She hasn't made eye contact and it's as if she's talking to the air, or to the flat, or to herself. Manon feels curiously invisible, not the first intruder from the state: Kilburn CID, social services, education welfare.

"I don't want it, no," Maureen says from somewhere in the hallway, and Manon follows her to a filthy galley kitchen with a full sink of dishes and every surface covered with bottles and cans (Magners, red wine, Fanta). Manon's shoes stick to the linoleum. Maureen is pulling on recalcitrant drawers, stuffed with letters and lighters, which she then can't shut. She is distracted by the discovery of a packet of John Player Blues, taking one out and lighting it, squinting at Manon for the first time.

"Where were we?" she says.

"Taylor, your son."

"He's dead. Taylor's dead, Lord have mercy on 'im. I've had a letter from de doctor; it's here somewhere." She has gone back to the drawers. "Dey want to put a camera in me stomach. Oh! I don't want it. Can y'understand it?"

She has pulled out a folded piece of paper and handed it to Manon.

"I don't understand it," Maureen is saying, beetling back into the lounge.

Manon skim-reads, sees: "Appointment, twelfth of December 2010, 10:00 A.M. Gastroscopy, Royal Free Hospital."

"This appointment was three weeks ago," says Manon, following Maureen. "Did you go?"

"Oh, tank God it's over, den. Now, who did ye say ye were?"

"DS Bradshaw, Cambridgeshire Police. We found Taylor's body."

"Oh no! Oh, Jaysus, no, Taylor's gone, rest his soul."

Maureen is contemplating her cigarette. Manon can smell the booze on her, sweated out through her freckled skin.

"Dat's his room back dere," she says, pointing her cigarette toward the hall.

"Can I have a look?"

"If you like. You're nat de first. Will I make ye a cup of tea?"

"I'm all right, thanks," Manon says, thinking of the state of the kitchen.

She walks down the hallway, at the end of which are two open doorways side by side. Through one, she sees legs crossed at the ankles. A pair of thin plimsolls, once white, perhaps, the rubber gaping where it meets the canvas. No socks. Even indoors those feet must be freezing in a January like this one. Black skin, shaded blacker at the knuckle.

She puts her head around the door and sees the boy, sitting on the mattress on the floor, his legs outstretched. There's a tiny television on the floor beside the mattress and he's watching it. The mattress—not quite a double but bigger than a single—has two sleeping bags on it. There's a melamine chest of drawers, all the drawers open, at the base of the mattress, so you'd have to crawl to get to it. The boy looks up. His hair is cut close to his head. His eyes, spectacularly dark, are enormous in his oval face. Manon is unable to speak for a moment. It's not that he's beautiful, so much (though he is); it's that he is so intensely sad.

"Hello," she says.

He looks back at the television.

"What are you watching?"

"*Dance* fucking *Download*. Piece a shit."

They look at the screen a moment, with its tinny laughter.

"My name's Manon," she says. "Funny name, huh?"

He looks up at her. She realizes he's too old and too unhappy for games.

"I'm from the police. I'm trying to find out what happened to Taylor. Mind if I sit down?"

"*Now* you wanna find out," he says.

She points at the bit of mattress next to him. He edges away to make room for her and she sinks down, sighing elaborately, the stiff-jointed grown-up. Her knees won't quite bend so she sits like him, with her legs crossed at the ankle.

"What's your name?" she asks, not because she doesn't know, but because the boy deserves some formalities.

"Fly," he says. "My name's Fly."

"Nice to meet you, Fly Dent," she says, holding out her hand to him and smiling. "Manon Bradshaw." He takes it, his palm cold and dry in hers. She looks around her.

"Did you share this room with Taylor?"

He nods.

She notices pirate stickers on the chest of drawers, silver and glittery and curling up at their edges. Skull and crossbones; cutlasses; a pirate ship. Children's stickers, the kind they get free inside magazines. The sleeping bags behind her are entwined.

"I'm very sorry, Fly. You must feel very sad," she says.

Fly looks at her. His eyes are frightened.

"Did Taylor have a mobile phone?"

Fly nods. "'Course."

"Do you know where it is?"

He shrugs. "He always had it—in his pocket. Same as dis one."

He leans back to reach into his pocket and takes out a phone, rolling it in his hand.

"Can I look?" she asks, as Fly turns back to the television.

"Taylor give it me," he says, keeping hold of the phone, "so I could call him. If I need him."

He presses some buttons and shows her. The word "Taylor" is on the screen and she presses the green call button. The dead boy's voice says, "I ain't here, innit! Leave a message and I might call you back, or I might not . . ." followed by shrieks of laughter.

"Is that you laughing with him?" she says, Fly's phone to her ear, smiling as she listens, because the laughing is infectious.

Fly nods, smiling too.

She hangs up. He has gone back to looking at the television, so she scrolls about the phone. The only number he has ever dialed is Taylor's. Twenty or thirty times. Trying to find him. Perhaps he plays it as he goes to sleep, listening to his brother's voice and the two of them laughing.

"Are you hungry?" she says.

He nods. "Taylor brought me KFC. He got the shopping from Bestco. Taylor feeded me."

"Come with me, then," Manon says, heaving herself up off the floor in an ungainly fashion.

She walks down the corridor to the lounge. "Mrs. Dent? Maureen?"

Maureen is lolling on the sofa, watching *Cash in the Attic*. She seems only semi-conscious, a tin in her hand.

"I'm just going to take Fly out for something to eat, OK?"

"You're all right, lovey, yes," says Maureen, raising her can, her chin to her chest.

Christ, thinks Manon, *I could be anyone.*

Fly is big, nearly as tall as her, but still a child. Unmistakably a child, she thinks, as she watches him pull on a thin jacket—the type a tennis player would wear onto court, and about as useless as gauze against the January chill. She knows she shouldn't be taking him out. Interviews with minors (*well, it was hardly an interview, was it?*)—there was a whole book of protocol, including never to interview them alone. No, she wasn't interviewing him; she was buying him eggs. The boy needed eggs, and this, like her taking home a police radio, was outside the bounds of protocol.

THEY ARE LOOKING OUT ON an optimistic arrangement of red plastic tables and chairs on the pavement, as if this were Ipanema, not Cricklewood Broadway. Beside them is a wire-mesh shelving unit full of Portuguese or Brazilian biscuits and cooking ingredients, mostly starch-based, as far as she can make out (everything on the shelves is yellow). There is a vast flat-screen television bracketed close to the ceiling behind them, booming out a Portuguese game show. The café owner smiles broadly at them, saying, "Scrambled?" with her pad poised.

"Fried," says Fly.

"Scrambled," says Manon, frowning at Fly. "And extra toast." A bus thunders past, slapped with an advert for Wonga. Following it is a plastic bag, bowling along in midair, its handles like beseeching arms until it hits a woman in a sari square in the stomach.

"Taylor used to go dere," says Fly, and Manon follows his gaze to a red awning on the opposite side of the road. Momtaz Shisha Café. "They all knew 'im in dere."

"Was he into anything stronger?"

"You mean drugs?" He shakes his head. "He saw Mum and her boyfriends, all dem losers. Said he'd never touch that shit. Said if I did, he'd kill me."

Manon feels a resolve hardening in the pit of her stomach. She has to find out what happened to Taylor Dent, what took him from this boy he so evidently loved.

"Tell me about the time leading up to Taylor going missing," she says. "When did you last see him?"

"Sunday, it was. We got some shopping from Bestco. He was in a right good mood. We had beans on toast, watched *SpongeBob SquarePants*. He told me to do my homework, get my shit together for school next day. He was on his phone, texting."

"Who?"

Fly shrugs. "I din know who he knowed. I mean, he knowed a lot of people—din tell me 'bout them."

"And was this on his phone, the one you used to reach him?"

Fly shrugs again. "Sometimes he had more than one. Sometimes not. The phones changed, the ones for his . . . for bidniss." He looks down sheepishly, as if he could still get Taylor into trouble with the police.

"Then what?" asks Manon.

"Then he said he had to go out. Said he be back later. Before he left, he say to me, 'Everything about to get a whole lot better, bro.' And that was it, that was the last time . . ." The tears fall sudden and fat. This is the first time he's talked about it, she thinks. He looks up at her, his huge eyes liquid with loss. "He din come back. He never came back. I woke up an' looked beside me."

She pictures the sleeping bags, one of them empty when Fly woke up on Monday, December 12. "Then what?"

"I went to school. I kept callin' him, textin' him. I thought maybe he was workin'. Straight from school I went to the police."

"What did they tell you?"

"Told me he'd turn up. Told me he not a child, so nuffin' they could do."

"Can you think of any reason Taylor might have gone to East Anglia?"

"Where dat?" says Fly, looking at the eggs as the plate lowers to the table in front of him.

"It's an area about two hours from here. Countryside. Very flat. Lots of small rivers." She can't seem to make it sound much better than that. She thinks about mentioning fog but stops short. There's a round of applause from the television, and the game-show host bellows, *"Obrigado! Obrigado!"*

"I know it don't look like much," he says, setting in on the toast, "but this is a good place. The Persian guys are good guys." He nods at Momtaz. "They gives me free tea sometimes. And the guys in Bestco. Broken biscuits, old cakes, innit. They know about Mum. They help us, 'specially Taylor."

"Did he go to school?"

Fly shakes his head. "Said someone had to get the money and it wasn't going to be Mum. He was well strict wi' me. Said I was the clever one. I was the one readin' all them books. I wish I didn't now. I wish I got off my butt and helped him."

"Helped him how?"

"So he could be proper—no sellin' and dealin' and whatnot."

"What was the 'whatnot'?"

Fly shrugs. "This 'n' that."

"Like what?"

"He din tell me; he din wan' me to know."

"Did Taylor ever mention a girl named Edith Hind?"

"Dat girl on the news? She's famous. She's on telly." And his eyes light up, as if being dead were as nothing next to the wonder of celebrity.

"Yes, did he know her?"

"Nah."

"What do you think happened to him, Fly?"

Fly looks at her, and he is all eyes, huge black pupils, wide and vulnerable. He has a way of pushing his lips out when he sniffs that is innocence itself. "He say he was sorting money for us. He say what was happening now was just, well, our luck about to change. But he din want me to know his bidniss—kept everyfing away from me." His eyes have filled up again, the wetness un-burst this time. He has the terrified look of someone who is falling off the edge of the world. "He my brudder."

"One last question, Fly. Have you ever heard the name Tony Wright?"

He thinks. Sniffs. Shakes his head. "Did he hurt Taylor?"

"We don't know. But we're going to find out, Fly. We'll find out what happened to Taylor, and whoever hurt him will go to prison, I promise you. What's happening now, with you, I mean? Have the social workers told you anything?"

He shakes his head. "I wanna stay at school, at home wi' Mum. I manage with what the guys at Bestco gimme. I went to a friend's house at Christmas. I'm all right. I don't need no care home 'n' all dat."

Manon sits back, looking at him. Looking and looking, her mind racing.

"Wait there," she says.

At the till, the café owner is staring up at the Portuguese game show, agog.

"A word," says Manon, showing the woman her badge.

She leads Manon to a corridor stacked with food, and they stand with the multicolored slats of the doorway curtain about their shoulders like plastic hair.

"I want you to keep a tab for that boy over there," says Manon. "Give him whatever he wants to eat, whenever he wants it, and send the bill to me. I can give you card details as surety."

"Is OK, your job. You will pay," says the woman, smiling. "He just a boy. I feed him, no problem."

"Right," Manon says to Fly when she gets back to the table. "Come on, we're going to buy you a coat."

"DAVY," SHE SAYS. SHE'S GASPING for breath, leaning against a wall, the phone to her ear. She's looking at the dirty Cricklewood sky, opaque as wool. She cannot seem to get a lungful. "Davy," she gasps.

"Calm down, Sarge. What is it?"

"We've got to help him."

"Who? Help who?"

"Taylor's brother, Fly. He's in a shithole and his mum's out of it, and no one's feeding him, not now Taylor's gone. Davy, he's going to get taken into care. He's ten." She feels dizzy with the lack of oxygen. A bus roars past and she cannot breathe, because she's whipped about by a gray fog of exhaust fumes, unnaturally warm. "Social workers are onto him. You remember what that woman said from child protection—what was her name?"

"Sheila Berridge," says Davy. "Didn't think you were listening."

"Fine, Davy, fine. I've changed my tune. What can we do?"

"Care's not always bad. Sometimes it's better than where they are."

"D'you believe that?"

"'Course I do. I'm not saying it's lovely. I'm not saying it's Mum and Dad and roast chicken for Sunday lunch. But people get through it. It's dry; there's food. He might get a decent foster family."

"Or he might get shoved into a massive care home that is stalked by pedos. I just want someone—a teacher, education welfare, anyone—to keep an eye on him, that's all. Free school meals, I dunno. Taylor fed him and now—"

"All right, all right," says Davy. "Leave it with me. I'll talk to my mentoring buddy. See if she can't pull a few strings down there. When did you turn so soft?"

MIRIAM

. . .

"IAAAAN!" SHE SHOUTS UP THE STAIRS AS SHE MAKES FOR THE FRONT door, rubbing her hands and thinking she must put the heating on. Their thermostat timer has not been adjusted to all these bodies being home during the daytime.

Miriam opens the front door and there is DS Bradshaw, a rumpled mass of black clothing, a capacious bag dropping off one shoulder. Her curls are pushed back from her forehead. She half-smiles a hello.

"Do come in," says Miriam, stepping back. "Gosh, it's freezing. Come on in, yes, that's it, follow the corridor straight down to the kitchen."

DS Bradshaw walks ahead of her, Miriam following and saying, "Tea?"

"Lovely, yes, thanks," says the officer, allowing her bag to slip to the floor beside the kitchen table. "Glad to see the photographers have gone."

"Yes, we are no longer of interest, thank God," says Miriam, filling the kettle at the tap. "For the time being, at least. The last of them sloped off on New Year's Eve but it was only the stragglers, to be honest."

DS Bradshaw takes off her coat, laying it gently over the back of the padded banquette and revealing only more black formless clothing. Perhaps they have to be constantly prepared for death—*harbingers at the ready!*

Ian walks in. "DS Bradshaw," he says, offering his hand. His voice these days has no uplift, no spring of humor behind it, which Miriam had always so loved in his greetings.

"Call me Manon, please."

"Yes, Manon, of course."

"Tea, darling?" says Miriam.

"Why not?"

"Can you call Rollo down?"

"Yes, of course," says Ian. "He's frantically tweeting and Facebooking," he says by way of explanation, and he disappears again to look for their son.

Miriam places a tea in front of Manon, who looks up at her, and her face is lit by the window opposite—an angry left eye, swollen, pink-sheened, and half shut.

"You'd better treat that, sooner rather than later, by the looks of it. Conjunctivitis," Miriam says, adopting her GP no-arguing voice. "Very simple—buy some chloramphenicol eyedrops over the counter. It'll clear up in a day. But make sure you finish the course. There, sermon over."

"I thought it might clear up by itself."

"Unlikely."

"How are you bearing up, Lady Hind?"

"My name's Miriam, my dear," she says. "And I'm not bearing up at all. Do you have any news for us?"

"Not about Edith's whereabouts. We have some leads. . . ."

"Leads?" says Ian, settling, with Rollo, in the chairs opposite Miriam and Manon.

Manon stretches out her hand. "Nice to see you again, Rollo. I hear you're running a formidable social-media campaign."

"Much good it's doing. There's a lot of online emoting," says Rollo, "often by strangers, which I know I should find comforting but is really quite creepy."

They smile and sip. In the sad silence of the kitchen, a fly fizzes against the glass of the window. *Tap, fizz, tap.*

"So . . . leads, you said," says Ian.

"Well, not exactly leads," says the sergeant. "Possible links that need exploring. We found a body." Then she swiftly adds, "No, not Edith. A boy—a seventeen-year-old called Taylor Dent."

"Oh, his poor mother," says Miriam, her palm across her mouth. *Poor mother, but, oh, thank God it's not Edith; thank God that wretched mother is not me.* "What has he to do with Edith?"

"We don't know yet. That's what we're investigating. He is, was, from Cricklewood, not far from here."

"I think you'll find Cricklewood is very far from here," mutters Ian.

"Did Edith ever mention the name?" asks Manon.

"Taylor Dent?" says Ian, and he searches Miriam's face. They shake their heads at each other.

"I've never heard of him," says Miriam. "How did he die?"

"We can't be sure. His body was found on Friday in the river near Ely. Did you know him, Rollo?"

"No, no, I've never heard of him," Rollo says.

"Did Edith ever try any drugs? Did she buy any marijuana from anyone, for example?"

"No," say Rollo and Miriam simultaneously.

"She had a boyfriend who smoked a bit—Jonti—but she never wanted it," says Rollo. "I know because I was with her when he was smoking."

"Might she have refused because you were there?"

"I don't think so. It wasn't a big deal—she had no moral problem with it, she just didn't like it or feel the need for it," Rollo says.

"We'll need to talk to Jonti," says Manon.

"I went to see him this morning. He hasn't seen or heard from her. But, yes, of course I'll get you the number," says Miriam, getting up to fetch her telephone book from the worktop.

The fly is fizzing its death throes again.

Ian gets up and turns to the window, his back to them. He begins to rattle—rather frantically, Miriam feels—at the window lock, trying to lift the metal arm to let the fly out.

She returns to the table, her reading glasses on, and gives Manon the number. Then she looks up irritably. "*Ian,* stop fussing and come and sit down. This is important."

"Sorry," he says. "Is this Dent boy your lead? Do you think he harmed Edith?"

"We're trying to work out whether there's a connection between the two of them first—whether they had ever met or whether they had friends in common."

"He was seventeen, you say?" says Rollo.

"A *child,*" says Miriam.

"Which school was he at?" asks Rollo.

"He'd left school. He worked the black market, basically," says Manon. "Cigarettes, counterfeit gear, stolen goods, other things too."

"I hardly think Edith would know someone like—"

"Oh, Ian, *shut up,*" Miriam says, and she is immediately ashamed. "I'm sorry," she says to Manon. "I shouldn't snap."

"It's all right," says Manon with a weak smile.

Oh, stop fucking observing us, Miriam thinks. *We are like that fly, helplessly bashing ourselves against glass.*

"We have the feeling," says Ian, "that there is information you are keeping back about the investigation."

Miriam looks into Manon's face. She can see a decision being made.

"There was another lead, which was a focus of our investigation for a time, but it has proved . . . well, it hasn't gone anywhere."

"Oh, for God's sake," says Ian, and Miriam smiles at him gratefully. At least he still has some fight in him.

"Go on," pleads Miriam.

"We have been looking at someone called Tony Wright. He was released from Whitemoor Prison eight months ago, where he'd been serving a sentence for aggravated burglary and sexual assault."

"*Sexual assault,*" says Miriam. "I was praying it wouldn't be—"

"It isn't," blurts Manon. "He has a cast-iron alibi for the weekend Edith disappeared."

* * *

SHE HAS CLOSED THE DOOR on Detective Sergeant Bradshaw and the things she shared with them about Tony Wright, the way he held a knife to the throat of his terrified victim.

Miriam and Ian stand in the cold, quiet well inside their front door. He looks at her, then frowns and turns, and in this split second she thinks she can see contempt. For what? For her upset?

He is marching down toward his study and she follows him.

"What was all that rattling about with the window? Can't you sit still for a minute?" she says, spoiling for him to swivel on his heels and give as good as she wants to give him.

"Leave me alone," he says icily. He stands behind his desk, pretending to leaf through some papers.

She walks out of the study and he shouts after her, "Where are you going—for another lie-down?" and she turns and storms back in, and when she gets there, his face is a jagged mess of fury and accusation. "Why is your distress the only thing in the room?" he demands.

"It isn't, Ian, but you won't allow me any grief at all. She's my daughter."

"And she's mine, and you sobbing or lying in a darkened room the whole time doesn't help."

"What do you want me to *do*?"

He is silent, his head bowed again toward his desk, but she knows he is fizzing and enraged just like her.

"Stop acting like this is my fucking fault," she says, and walks out again.

MANON

. . .

SHE HAS HER FEET UP ON THE BLUE TARTAN FIRST CAPITAL CONNECT seats, beside a sign saying DO NOT PUT FEET ON SEATS. She pulls at her eyelid, peeling it away from the eyeball in an attempt to relieve the scratching. The infection has moved from irritation to pain, and yet, when she has passed a chemist—on Hampstead High Street, at King's Cross station—the urgency of buying the antibiotics has gone from her mind. No chance now—it's 8:00 P.M. and she has to be in early tomorrow for the *Crimewatch* briefing.

She told the Hinds to brace themselves for renewed press interest—photographers back on their doorstep—when the televised reconstruction of Edith's last journey home with Helena Reed is broadcast on Wednesday evening. Telling them about Tony Wright hadn't been easy, despite his alibi. She recalls the look of terror on Lady Hind's face, which prevented her from describing what had become of his last victim—how he had beaten her about the head with the knife handle

so that her face was purple and enlarged. Two weeks after his conviction, she killed herself.

Manon's mobile phone vibrates somewhere deep in her bag. A
text, number not recognized.

I am toasty

She smiles. Buying the coat for Fly had brought her myriad
unlooked-for pleasures, as if satisfaction were refracted into a fresh rain-
bow. Picking out a hot-pink sequined number and saying to him, "This
is a good look for you"; his dry look in response, as if she were the sil-
liest object he had ever come across. Him picking the designer labels,
to which she would turn the swinging ticket and say, "In your dreams."
Most of all, when they had selected together a padded cornflower-blue
coat, with white stripes at the chest, she had noticed what pleasure
there was in keeping him warm: the thought of the softness of the
fleece lining against his skin, the waterproof outer layer sheltering him
from rain. It was the best twenty-five pounds she had spent in a long
time.

Shouldn't you be in bed? M

No, cos I'm not five.
Anyway, I AM in bed. I'm wearing it in bed.

She is smiling to herself, up the steps of HQ, into reception, thinking how she must type up her notes, prepare for tomorrow's briefing.
Her head is down, unaware of her surroundings, when Bob on the
front desk says, "Sarge, someone to see you."

Manon looks up, and there he is: his flappy coat, the stoop, horrifying and wonderful—Alan Prenderghast.

"Hello," he says. "I didn't expect to see you. I was just dropping
this off."

He holds out a small white paper bag, folded over at the top, with
a green chemist sign on it. Manon opens it and takes out an oblong
box. The label reads: "Chloramphenicol eyedrops, for the treatment of
conjunctivitis."

"Crikey," she says.

"I feel a bit like a criminal caught in the act," he says.

"Gosh—I haven't had time, as you can see."

"Look," he says, rather urgently, "I don't know the form for this. Am I still a witness or something, in the case?"

"No, why?"

"I was wondering if I could take you out. For dinner or something. Or a film, where we sit in the same row. Adjacent seats, even."

There is a red patch creeping up his neck.

"I don't know, I've got a lot on at the moment."

They both look down at the white chemist's bag.

"Why don't you think about it?" he says. "I'll give you my number."

He puts a hand out to take the chemist bag back off her and pats his pockets for a pen, only to find Bob holding one out to him. "I enjoyed our coffee after the film," he says, while writing on the bag against his palm.

"Thanks," she says, looking down at his writing. The numbers are all bunched up and tight. "Look, I'd better go—got to prepare for a briefing first thing. Just had a murder come in, plus it's *Crimewatch* this week," and she lays it there, her job as a police officer, which he must admire, what with his very pedestrian work as a systems analyst.

"Well, OK, then," he says, and she watches him go out of the station doors and down the steps to the car park.

When she turns, Bob is frowning.

"What d'you do that for?" he says.

"What?"

"Turn down a nice chap like him?"

"What would you know about it, Bob?"

"I know it's nice to have someone to come home to."

DAVY

· · ·

"FOR ME," KIM IS SAYING THOUGHTFULLY, "IT WOULD HAVE TO BE TUNA pasta bake with back-to-back *Place in the Sun.*"

Davy is just about to put in his two pennies' worth, which involves crackers and cheese and *Quincy,* but Harriet has shot everyone a look that says, *Shut your fucking gobs, the boss is here.*

DCS Gary Stanton has a collection of important-looking files under one arm, and his buttons are straining over his stomach. *Time to size up on the shirt front,* Davy thinks.

The whole team is gathered around a circular table, which is part of a new stratagem brought back from the States by Stanton when he went to NYPD on a skills-swap residential last autumn. For Davy, things got much more confusing after the residential, because Stanton returned armed with incomprehensible management-speak. Davy's all for a spot of police jargon, which clarifies the lines drawn between good and evil (only last night he watched a DCI on the news outside the Old Bailey telling how they'd "exposed the villain's web of wicked lies"). But this corporate mumbo jumbo—it didn't clarify; it did the opposite, scribbling over itself in loops and meanderings. It started with just having to "action" things, instead of do them; then Stanton wanted to "sunset that line of investigation," which seemed to mean not do it anymore. They had moved from breaking an alibi to "putting it on the radiator to see if it melts." But then Stanton started talking about "shifting the paradigm" in order to "leverage our synergies," and that's where he lost Davy altogether. At one point, Davy had felt quite worried about keeping up in the department, but then he overheard Harriet hissing at Manon, "What the fuck's he talking about?" and felt better.

Edith Hind has been missing for two weeks and the press have more or less shuffled off. But that's about to change with the *Crimewatch* appeal, especially if what everyone is saying is true. Stanton is about to let the proverbial cat out of the bag (his words), and they'd better all be ready.

"Right," Stanton says, sounding a bit out of puff. Perhaps he's just walked up the stairs from the press office. "*Crimewatch*. There will obviously be a massive upscaling of media interest and we can expect to be inundated with calls from the public"—Colin groans loudly—"which we need to take seriously," says Stanton. "Lot of powder, so expect some avalanches. We don't know which sighting might be significant at this point, so I want nothing dismissed, please. I don't care how left field they sound. I will also be raising the issue of Edith's love life in the appeal and the fact that she had male and female lovers. The purpose of this is not to supply fodder for the tabloids but to flush out Edith's previous lovers, be they secret or in the past."

Everyone around the table is silent. Everyone is thinking the same thing: it will incense Sir Ian Hind, who will be straight on the phone to Roger Galloway, who will be straight on the phone to Cambridgeshire Commissioner Sir Brian Peabody, who will be straight on the phone to Gary Stanton.

"I can handle it," he says mildly, as if reading their thoughts. "I've got to run this investigation with the same instincts I'd run any other, and that's with the view that she's come to harm and that a lover or sexual liaison of some kind is at the heart of her disappearance."

"Won't mentioning a female lover make things hysterical?" asks Manon.

"Unavoidable," says Stanton. "You pour milk on the step, see who laps it up."

"Sorry, what?" says Harriet.

"We need people to come forward," says Stanton. "And to be honest, we need Edith back in the public mind."

"Even if it's naked and engaging in some girl-on-girl action," says Colin, with an inadvertent after-snort.

"Shouldn't we risk-assess Helena Reed, then?" says Manon. "Her world will come crashing down when you go on telly and talk about a female lover. I'd say she wasn't the toughest person to start with."

"Yes, we certainly need to warn her. Kim, I'd like you to go round there, talk her through the whole thing. Tell her *Crimewatch* is going out on Wednesday night, reassure her we're not naming anyone, but offer her support if she needs it. She can have a liaison officer with her in her flat."

Kim nods.

"Can we please have an update on the Taylor Dent investigation, Harriet?" says Stanton.

"Right," says Harriet, with a deep sigh. "No DNA at Deeping or George Street. No phone contact as far as we know, but, of course, Dent might have had an additional phone or phones we don't currently know about. Met's looking into that one, and of course we're cross-referencing with unknown-515—the mobile Edith called twice in the week before she disappeared."

"What about the Dent family?" says Stanton. "Anything come up?"

"Younger brother, Fly," Manon says, "reported Taylor missing on Monday twelfth of December after school, so a week before Edith's disappearance. Taylor hadn't come home the night before. Went out, on some deal or other from the sounds of it. Before he left, he told his brother things were going to change, which indicates that he was going to make some money. Sounded quite pumped about it. Anyway, younger brother woke up on Monday, no Taylor in the bed next to him, got really worried but wanted to wait to see if he showed during the day. Then reported him missing, but the Met basically told him to go away and stop worrying, because Taylor was seventeen and old enough to look after himself."

"In other words, he wasn't worth investigating," says Davy, thinking of Ryan.

"Kilburn CID have got officers working their way through Dent's associates, but to be honest, they're not that easy to pin down," Manon says.

"Dent isn't coming up on any rail CCTV out of London. Looks like he must've got here in a car," says Kim.

"OK," says Stanton, hands flat on the desk as if steadying himself. "If there are no firm connections emerging between Dent and Hind, and we can't establish ownership of unknown-515, then I'm going to have to hand the Dent murder investigation on to team two. We just don't have the resources to run the two cases out of one team," says Stanton.

"But—" Manon blurts, and Davy looks at her. She's shifting in her seat, saying, "We might find . . . later, I mean . . ." but she trails off.

"Last thing, people," Stanton is saying. "Forensics Management Team meeting." Groans erupt around the room. Money talk—the FMT meetings balance investigative needs against budget. Tighten your belts, in other words. "We've been informed that we are overspending on the Hind investigation and that we should rein it in. To that end, Nigel Williams and Nick Briggs are being seconded to team two, to help on the Dent murder, while the scaled-down team continues to work on Hind."

"Sorry, boss," says Harriet, "but you're cutting our team the night before *Crimewatch* goes out and buries us in a steaming pile of false leads?"

"That'd be about the size of it," he says, up from his seat, the folders back under his arm. "This is the age of austerity, DI Harper. Haven't you heard?"

"Toast with anchovies," Colin is saying to Kim, as the room breaks up. "'Cept the oil always drips down your chin, which can greatly mar the enjoyment of *Columbo*."

MIRIAM

. . .

SHE'S AWAKE, BRUISED BY HER DREAM.

If she could, she would avoid sleep altogether, but the nights are so tortured and restless—cups of tea in the kitchen, endless trips to the loo, trying out various beds in the hope a cold pillow might do the trick—that she often succumbs to her exhaustion come late afternoon. In Miriam's dreams, Edith appears before her in altered states—wearing strangers' clothes, or with a face transmogrified in some eerie way. A shape-shifter, part gangster's moll, half ghoul.

The police have asked them whether Edith knew Tony Wright or Taylor Dent, and she wonders what web her daughter has got caught in. What does Miriam know about her own child, really? Every detail a fresh assault—the relationship with Helena, the questioning texts to Rollo. What on earth was going on in Edith's life? Any confidence Miriam ever had in herself as a mother has been eroded, and what is that confidence built on anyway, she thinks now—the luck of one's children? The DNA lottery? If they're bright and successful, you congratulate yourself. If they fall by the wayside, the world judges you. These days, she could be told anything at all about Edith and she'd be forced to accommodate it, because she knows nothing. She thought Edith loved her.

Miriam picks up the Mother's Day card, one she has retrieved from her bedside table where she treasures all the missives from her children. In Edith's neat, perfectionist hand:

Dearest Mum,

You are the tops.
I love you, and I know I never tell you that—at least, not enough.

E x

She remembers Ian's mock outrage. "Why don't I get cards like that?"

"Because her adoration of you is writ so large," Miriam said at the time. "She has to express it to me."

He has been crying in his study. She heard him on her way up the stairs an hour ago, had stopped, one hand on the banister, curious to hear his upset expressed. Man sobs are so uncommon, they were quite interesting. His were strangulated, as if his tears were out to choke him. Hers come unbidden, like a flood, dissolving her outline, and it's as if she has failed to stand up to them. A weakness of tears.

She stood listening, but she didn't go to him. The strain is widening between them, like a jack ratcheting open a notch with every day missing, every detail a fresh violence separating them. Ian's answer to helplessness is criticism, and she is its focus, implied in all his Rushing About Being Important; his interviewing of private investigators (a precaution); his poster-printing; calls to their lawyer; and complaints to newspaper editors over intrusion. He never stops, his lined face saying to her, *And what exactly have* you *been doing?*

He never acknowledges the toll on her, in part because she keeps it to herself, like the furtive trip she has taken to Huntingdon, where she walked the unsightly route beneath the concrete underpass from the station to George Street. She stopped outside Edith's house, unable to let herself in, because its interior, black with fingerprint dust, was too much a crime scene. So instead she went down to the town center, where she looked into the eyes of every person and wanted to lift her face to the sky and let out a wail because she didn't know what to *do*. The world is tipping, vertiginous, her organs plummeting away. Fear is so *physical*.

No, she hasn't told him any of this, and every time he looks for her, it seems she's lying on the bed in the dusky half-light of their bedroom, as she is now, the back of one hand resting on her forehead. She notices the wrinkles about her knuckles, pushes at a ring—a huge citrine oval, the color of honey, in a thick silver setting—with the pad of her thumb, rotating it.

It isn't just her; he's growing increasingly critical of the police, googling the officers in the investigating team in the hope of tracking their passage through the ranks of the force, the extent of their experience and training. Except all Google brings up are snippets of ancient news stories. She wonders what Ian can extrapolate from DI Harper warning the good motorists of Bedfordshire to lock their cars in 2006. His relief at having Stanton at the helm has been short-lived, Ian's current position on Stanton being that he "isn't the sharpest knife in the drawer," hence his research into private investigators.

"Why don't you talk to Roger if you're worried?" Miriam said, while they got ready for bed one evening.

"I don't want to pull rank on Stanton just yet," Ian replied. "It could do more harm than good. Keeping my powder dry for now."

Rog and Patty had been in touch, of course—an answering-machine message and a lovely card with hibiscus on it. "If there's anything we can do . . ."

She presses her hand into the back of her neck to massage it and thinks, *These things don't bring you together; they tear you apart.* There is no place else to go except toward blame, as if into the arms of a lover. If Ian hadn't pushed Edith so hard. If she, Miriam, wasn't so passive. If Rollo wasn't so *alive*. It was everyone's fault because it was no one's.

Miriam hears the bedroom door handle turn, both longing for and dreading it to be Ian, and soon enough he is sitting on the side of the bed. He strokes her arm—the one laid beside her body—and sighs deeply, but she doesn't look at him.

"I'm so sorry, Miri."

He starts to cry and she heaves herself up to look at him, curious and moved by him at the same time.

"What are you sorry for?"

"For everything ... for everything I've done," he says. He is not looking at her. He is hiding his face from her. "I haven't been a good husband to you."

"I feel as if you hate me," she says.

"Of course I don't hate you. I love you. I love you inordinately." He puts his arms around her and she lifts her face to kiss him. He kisses her back, but in a way that has a full stop at the end of it, when she had hoped it would lead on. A consummation. They need to come together and this is how husbands and wives come together, but these things are so often mistimed, their meanings taken the wrong way. How often had they refused each other out of bitterness or tiredness or standoffishness or a little bit of all three?

"Why don't I take you out for dinner tonight?" he says. "La Gaffe, or the new bistro, the French one. Might be our last chance before the oafs are back on the doorstep tomorrow."

He is a good husband. He is here and he loves her. Inordinately.

"It would seem like celebrating," she says.

"No it wouldn't. Come on. Get up. We don't help Edith by being prisoners."

Wednesday

DAVY
• • •

"COLONEL BUFTON TUFTON'S DOWNSTAIRS, AND HE'S NOT HAPPY," SAYS Kim.

"Downstairs? Ian Hind?" says Harriet.

"Downstairs. Pacing like a caged bear."

"Did we have a meeting I've forgotten about?" Harriet says to Davy, who shrugs, following her at a jog to keep up with her pelt down the stairs, while she says, "Probably here to bollock me about something." Then she stops and looks at Davy. "It'll be the female-lover line. I didn't think he knew. Guess the FLO filled him in. Shit, he'll be livid. Typical Stanton, out on a jolly when the shit hits the fan."

"Is everything all right, Sir Ian?" says Harriet, waiting for Davy to enter, then closing the door to interview room one.

He is pacing up and down, fast, exactly as Kim described, like a bear in a tight space who hasn't been fed.

"Where is Superintendent Stanton?" he says, his navy coat flying as he turns.

"He's not at HQ today," says Harriet. "What's the matter, Sir Ian?"

"You are systematically destroying my daughter's reputation."

"I don't think saying she had a female lover is derogatory, is it?"

"It's prurient," he says. Davy isn't entirely clear what "prurient" means. "It's salacious." *Ah, right,* thinks Davy, *that's what it means.* "It's dirtying her in the mind of the general public, and they don't need much assistance, let me tell you. You are riding roughshod over my family, and I—" He is stopped by a catch of emotion in his throat, except he appears to Davy to be too angry for tears.

"Sir Ian, I promise you that is not our intention. We want to find Edith and we want to find her alive. We'll do anything, anything at all, and that includes embarrassing her, and possibly you, though you have no reason to be embarrassed—"

"My wife is crying on the bed, appalled about the things you're saying about Edie, terrified about what your sergeant told us—about Tony Wright. I looked up his offenses and they're horrific."

"We have looked at Tony Wright, just as we look at all known offenders with appropriate previous convictions. It's a line of—"

"A line? You've told us some knife-wielding sexual predator might have had something to do with her disappearance and then you . . . you leave us to it?"

"Wright has an alibi," Harriet says. "A very strong alibi. We are just keeping you informed. Look, I know this is upsetting. The reason we assign an FLO is to try to contain these sorts of fears and to answer any questions you might have. Try to calm down, Sir Ian. If you'd like to sit—"

"No, I don't want to sit. Everyone's always telling me to sit or making me drink tea. I don't like our FLO, and, anyway, I want to know what you're doing, what the investigation is *doing*. I don't want to be patted by some mooning counselor who wishes to *contain me.*"

"We are looking at all avenues. Tony Wright is one of our lines of inquiry. Another is the possibility that Edith's personal life—her lovers—is at the heart of what's happened to her. We're hoping the *Crimewatch* appeal will flush out new information."

"I don't understand," he says. "Why, then, is your sergeant also talking to us about a boy—a boy called Dent, I think his name is?"

"That is another line of inquiry."

"What do you mean, 'another line'?"

"Taylor Dent's body was found in the river near Ely last week. I think DS Bradshaw informed you of that, didn't she? We are treating it as a murder investigation and we are looking into possible connections with the disappearance of your daughter. The two events had a similar time frame. It would be quite wrong if we didn't look into connections between the two incidents."

"Forgive me, forgive me, DI Harper," he says, frowning and shaking his head. "How can you possibly focus your investigation if you are vaguely looking into everything? If you have multiple lines of inquiry, if you think it might be her love life, or it might be this lowlife, or it might be the boy in the river, then what on earth is your lead? Where is your focus?" He turns, homes in on Harriet with cold gray eyes in a way that, Davy notices, makes her pretend to read some notes on her clipboard. "Inspector, is it Tony Wright or Taylor Dent? You don't seem to know. Or is it, in fact, that you're out of your depth being SIO on a case this big, and so you're frantically trying to investigate everything?" He is downright scary-furious, like a headmaster telling her off.

"I . . . we're following up all possible leads," says Harriet, fingering the corner of a page.

"Which is it?" Sir Ian booms. His knuckles are on the desk and he's looming over Harriet. It's as if he's about to bang on the table.

"It's hard to say exactly," says Harriet. "At this point, multiple avenues—"

"You're supposed to be leading this inquiry, so lead it. Is it Taylor Dent or is it Tony Wright?"

"To be honest, neither of them is holding up that well under scrutiny. But if I, I, I—if I had to, well, I'd say Wright is a stronger lead, but his alibi—"

Sir Ian exhales, straightens, and more gently says, "Right, so shouldn't you be putting all your resources into Tony Wright, then, DI Harper?"

Ian Hind marches out of the room and out of the station, into his Jaguar, and back to London, they hope.

Davy waits with Harriet outside interview room one. She is leaning against the corridor wall, head back, blowing out through pursed
lips. "Fuck," she whispers. She opens her eyes and looks at Davy, still
with her head back. "That was me at my finest. Watch and learn, Davy
Walker."

"You certainly gave him what for."

"I did, didn't I?"

"At least he knows who's boss," says Davy.

Kim is walking toward them, back from visiting Helena Reed.

"How was she?" asks Harriet.

"Yeah, all right. She's a bit out of it. I'm not sure she quite understands what it means in terms of the press an' that."

"Did you make her aware?"

"Did my best. I told her she might want to lie low, go and stay with
family. Told her officers could sit with her if she wanted. She said she
couldn't go to family, was shifty about why, and said she didn't need
our support."

"OK, write it up, will you?" says Harriet.

MANON
· · ·

THE PHONES ARE SHRIEKING, OVER AND ABOVE ONE ANOTHER, LIKE WAIL-ing babies demanding immediate attention. She has 148 unread emails in her inbox. The chorus, persistent and shrill, of keyboards clacking, voices, and mobiles bleeping is drilling into her frontal lobe and trans-forming itself into piercing pain downward toward her left eye. The department has gone into overdrive since *Crimewatch* was broadcast last night.

Girl matching Edith's description spotted walking south out of the town; girl matching Edith's description seen walking west out of the town; girl matching Edith's description spotted in Manchester; in Glasgow; in seven separate locations in London. All would have to be followed up. TI. Trace and Interview. Nothing ignored.

The sound has been muted on the television, but there is Stanton, giving more interviews, the red ticker tape running along the bottom of the screen saying, *Det. Ch. Supt. Gary Stanton, Cambridgeshire Police:*

"Missing Edith had lesbian relationship. Complex love life at heart of investigation."

"Sorry, why have you been put through to this department?" Davy is saying into the phone. "No, no, I don't want to give you the inside story." Waits. "Righto, yes, thank you, putting you through to the press office, caller," he says, pressing various buttons on his handset and slamming down the receiver with uncharacteristic annoyance. "Why aren't they putting these calls through to the media team? Why are they coming through to us?"

"Because they lie to switchboard, that's why," says Harriet.

Colin is in his element, leaping up every five minutes. "This one says the immigrants are to blame. If we didn't let them flood our borders . . ." He shakes his head, saying, "Classic."

Manon is leafing through the pile of newspapers splayed across her desk—across all the desks—every one of them leading on the Hind investigation: "TRAGIC EDITH HAD FEMALE LOVER; EDITH'S LESBIAN TRYSTS"; "MISSING EDITH HAD SECRET GIRLFRIEND, SAY POLICE." Even the broadsheets are carrying it on the front page. *The Telegraph* takes the opportunity to rerun a vast photograph of Edith in her mortarboard, something for the brigadiers to gaze at while imagining her disrobed and in a steamy same-sex clinch. *The Guardian* displays its usual distaste by running it as the third story, at the bottom of the front page: "PRESS FRENZY OVER 'FEMALE LOVER' IN EDITH INVESTIGATION." It got their juices going—girl-on-girl action. Better than that: posh-girl-on-girl action. She prays no one puts two and two together and gets Helena Reed. The Met has had to deploy a protection team to Church Row in Hampstead, where the Hinds are being ferociously doorstepped.

Fergus has walked in. Dark wet patches are leaching through the cotton of his gray shirt at the armpits. His acne outbreak has reddened. He pushes his glasses back onto the bridge of his nose.

"A word, everyone, if you don't mind."

The department settles, people perching or stood still, but for the phones, which keep on crying out.

"We need to be very mindful of attempts to infiltrate this investigation," he says. "Most of you will have taken calls from reporters this morning. They are hungry, very hungry indeed—under a lot of pressure for a follow-up to today's revelations. I would strongly advise you not to exchange any details about the case when you are on your mobile phones."

"Are you saying we're being hacked?" says Stuart.

"I wouldn't rule it out," says Fergus, and he pushes his glasses up again, the sweat making them slip. "Just to be on the safe side, don't talk about it on the blower. If you're talking to each other, don't mention names or details, and don't talk to your family and friends about it, OK? Thanks, everyone."

The room breaks up, louder than before. Manon needs to escape the increased decibels, the heightened heat and velocity in the air, the pain shooting across one side of her brain.

"I'm going to the canteen, Davy. D'you want a coffee or anything?"

"This is an almighty mess," says Davy, and she is startled, not only to hear him express something so despairing but to see the broken expression on his face. "I mean, what was he thinking? This isn't how we find out what happened to Edith. It's just exploiting her."

"Normal to shake things up at this point," she tells him. "Eighteen days missing, everyone's forgotten about her a bit. We've got fuck-all credible leads. Stanton's just swirling his stick in the sand. Tea? Bacon butty?"

On the way down the stairs, she texts Fly.

How is the coat?

Coat is good, but it making me shoes look bad.

She nudges Bryony, who is ahead of her in the canteen queue. "All right?"

"Oooh, hello," says Bryony. "All kicking off round yours."

"I know. Splitting headache. Phones are ringing off the hook."

"Any of it sensible?"

"Not so far. You know what it's like."

"Sit with me?"

"Five minutes, yeah."

They take a table in the far corner, where Bryony interrogates Manon about her love life.

"So, hang on, he came by the station to ask you out, bought you antibiotic eyedrops, and you haven't called him?" Bryony is saying, and it's doing nothing for Manon's headache.

The conjunctivitis was gone by Tuesday morning. She'd applied the first drops the minute she got upstairs to the department on the Monday evening, and the next day she was clear and evangelical about antibiotics' supernatural powers. What on earth will the human race do when this medicine stops working? Die in childbirth again. Go blind with conjunctivitis. Kidney failure from cystitis. Commit suicide during a bout of toothache. She thought about it a bit, darkly, and then on with the day! She'd been briefly full of gratitude too toward Alan Prenderghast, but this had evaporated just as fast as the infection, so that by Wednesday afternoon she'd forgotten that she was ever encumbered. She hadn't got round to thanking him, and then she didn't feel like it anymore.

It is more than that, she realizes now, sitting opposite Bryony and the pressure she exudes. She can't communicate ... what? Something nuanced and complex about why she doesn't want to get involved with him. The way she stands back from the web of interaction because she can't commit to being inside it. Her sheer ambivalence, which Bryony sees as straightforward but is anything but. Contact is difficult.

"And yet you will put out for whatever hairy sociopath comes your way on the Internet?" Bryony is saying.

Manon shrugs, as if to say, *Search me.*

"There's no helping you. I literally give up."

"I keep meaning to ring him," says Manon, and she notices how her voice sounds: slow and dissociated, as if very far away. "I just don't get round to it. I don't know why."

"I do. He might actually be nice to you. He might treat you well and give you babies."

"Come off it," she says, frowning, and she's angry now at being bulldozed. "You don't know shit about him, Bri."

"I know he's already better than the totally awful specimens you normally go out with."

Manon has stood up abruptly. She's had enough. "You fucking go out with him, then."

She walks away, hearing Bryony say, "Manon, come back, I—" before the doors to the canteen shut behind her.

HELENA

...

HER BREATHING COMES IN JOLTS, STEPPING DOWN IN HER SOLAR PLEXUS, then up again, catching in her throat. A ladder of tears. "They're coming to get me," she says. "They are com-ing to ge-et me."

"I think if we can just go back to the dream, we can try to unravel this," says Dr. Young, still the voice of calm.

"The-ey are com-ing to ge-et me. The papers ... It's all ov-er the papers ... Oh G-o-d, oh God ..." She places her palms over her face, wet and puffy from the torrent. She wants to hide, for the earth to open and for it to close over her head, welcome grave. Exposure is everywhere, about to happen. She is about to be named. She is filthy.

"The dream," he says.

In the dream, she was running down suburban streets—Newnham or her parents' street in Bromley, she couldn't tell. Breathless, her clothes torn, pursued by a flock of enormous black crows, with wings flying out behind them like academic cloaks, and angry beaks. Running and

running from them as they gained ground, and then she turned a corner and saw her parents' house, the front door of her childhood, and
she felt a surge of relief that she would be safe. They would open the
door to her and she would get inside and the crows would be barred.
She reached the front door and banged with her fists on it and the
crows were at the gate. But the door didn't open. Her parents didn't
answer, and the horror, the horror, she feels herself collapsing again,
folding in on herself. She saw her parents at the window, looking at
her from the safety of the lounge, leaving her outside to face the crows.

"They wouldn't let me in," she gasps, her palms wet over her face,
the tears seeping to the webbed crooks between her fingers. "Because
I am disgusting."

"How are you disgusting?"

"Because . . . because . . . the newspapers are saying she had a female
lover, but I'm not, I'm not . . . Everyone will think I was her lover, but
I wasn't. It wasn't like that, but everyone will think it was dirty, sordid,
that I did something to her."

"Why would anyone make that connection? Is there something
about your relationship with Edith, something about that night, that
you're not being honest about?"

"No, no, you see? You think it. You see 'female lover' and you think
of me. Her best friend, with her on the night she disappeared. It's all
over it—the innuendo."

Silence.

"But you know what *did* happen," he says. "The truth about that
night."

"Yes, I know. No, no, I don't mean that. I don't know what happened to Edith, I don't know that. You're trying to trip me up. You're
trying to get me to say I was involved."

Silence, this time of a kind that seems incriminating.

"I wonder," he says, "if you feel that I am locking you out—leaving
you to the black crows—in the gap between now and our next session
on Monday. All this press interest, the feeling you have of exposure . . .
Three days is a long time to be on your own with it all."

She is silent, except for the uneven steps of her breathing.

"We have to leave it there," he says.

DAVY

. . .

"NICE ROAD," HE SAYS. HE PRESSES ON HIS KEY FOB AND THE CAR AN-
swers with its electronic *whup-whep*. The lights flash twice and they
walk along a pavement sparkling with frost, their breath smoking and
their hands dug into their pockets. It's a relief to be out of the frenetic
heat of HQ—a million conflicting sightings of Edith and the deceiving
infiltration of reporters who are back on the story.

A ribbon of mist curls through the tops of the trees. He looks into
the front gardens: checkerboard tiling and the bare stems of magnolias
or lilacs; bicycles chained to black iron railings; bay windows so clean
they seem liquid and topped with little proud roof turrets in gray slate.

They have come to the posh part of Cambridge—Newnham—to
re-interview Barbara Garfield, wife of Edith's director of studies, after
she called and told them she had new information to share. Didn't everyone, after *Crimewatch*?

Be nice to live somewhere like this, he thinks—*so comfortable with it-*

self. Those front patches are tended by people who listen to *Gardeners' Question Time* and know the names of shrubs. He bets the houses' insides are worn but bookish, not smelly-depressing shabby, like the places they visit for work, pushing their sweaters up over their mouths and noses. No, this is easy-does-it shabby. I-know-who-I-am shabby. Persian-rug shabby.

"Grantchester Street," he says, checking in his green book.

"Left at the end here," says Manon.

They walk a little farther.

"Did you see," Davy says, "Stuart's got a new iPad?"

"That's more Colin's bag than mine," says Manon.

"Nice one, latest kind, y'know—white one, thin as you like. Says he can't get used to the touch screen. Just wonder how he afforded it, that's all. Didn't think CIs got paid that much—" He is winded by a body slamming into him from the left. Someone who has hurtled out of the gate from one of the houses they have just passed. "Whoa," he says, catching her about the shoulders. "Slow down. Are you all right?"

The girl's head is bowed, she's crying, and when she looks up, Manon says, "Helena?"

She doesn't speak. Her eyes are red raw, her lips swollen, and she is shaking.

"Helena," says Manon again. "What are you doing here? Is everything all right?"

"Everyone will know," she says, with pleading eyes. "Why did he say that, about a female lover? Why did he have to say that on telly? Everyone will know. It's all over the papers. They're going to want to know *who.*" And she collapses into Davy's chest.

"Didn't an officer come and warn you about *Crimewatch*? I thought DC Kim Delaney—"

"I didn't realize, I didn't know how huge it would be," Helena says, her eyes wide with fear. "The television. It was on the television. I don't know what I thought. . . . I didn't take it in."

"No one knows about you," says Manon. "It won't come out, about you and Edith." She and Davy look at each other over Helena's head. "No one is going to release your name, Helena. As far as the press knows, you are just the friend she was out with on Saturday night."

"Look, anyone comes after you, you call me," says Davy, pushing her away from his chest so he can dig in his pocket for a card with his number printed on it, and so that he can look her in the eye too. Tell her it's real. They will protect her. "Now, get yourself home and lay low. D'you need a car? I can get someone out here—"

"No, no," she says. She wipes the wet from her nose with the back of her hand, and the movement makes her seem like a little girl. "I can get home."

She is looking down at Davy's little white card, with its silver star symbol topped with a royal crown and the words "Cambridgeshire Constabulary" following the blue circle.

"Would you like an officer with you at your flat? We can arrange that," he says.

"Why are you here?" says Helena abruptly. "What are you doing on the same street as my, my, my friend . . . I have a friend who lives here."

"Just routine inquiries," says Manon, smiling, but this seems only to increase the terror in Helena's eyes.

"Are you sure you're all right?" says Davy. "I think I should drive you. I've got a car just around the corner."

"No, no," and she bridles, shaking Davy's hand off her shoulder. "I've got somewhere to go right now. I'm not going straight home, you see. I'll be all right." She sniffs. "It'll all blow over, right? This storm, it'll pass."

Manon and Davy watch her as she turns and scurries, hunched and quick-footed, away from them down Grantchester Street.

"Don't like the look of her," says Davy. "We should call it in. Tell Harriet she seems vulnerable."

"Yup, we'll flag it up when we get back to the office after this," says Manon.

MANON

. . .

"Have you finished yet?" asks Manon, smiling at him.

"Not yet, no," Davy says, sneezing another three times.

"Goodness me," says Mrs. Garfield. "Are you all right?"

"Do you have a cat?" asks Davy.

"Yes, oh goodness, sorry. Wait a minute, I'll put her out."

Manon takes a seat at the dining table while Davy blows his nose. They are in a sunken kitchen that gives out onto the back garden. The kitchen floor is a grid of terra-cotta squares, and the cupboards are oak. The room smells of boiling lentils and surfaces just wiped with a faintly mildewed cloth. The dishwasher is going. The round dining table, at the garden end of the room, is covered with an oilcloth in a pale-green William Morris design. On the wall is a picture of Mr. and Mrs. Garfield in shorts and sunglasses, leaning into each other.

"There, she won't bother you anymore," says Mrs. Garfield, coming back into the room and brushing at her skirt. "Though I can't guarantee her fur won't—it's everywhere, I'm afraid. Now, what can I get you to drink? Tea? Coffee?"

"Glass of water, if you don't mind, Mrs. Garfield," says Davy.

"Sergeant?"

"Nothing for me, thank you."

Mrs. Garfield runs the tap, her finger feeling its temperature, saying, "I really don't know why I rang. And you must be absolutely inundated after *Crimewatch*. The papers are full of it."

"Did you remember something that might be important?" asks Manon.

"Silly, really, and you've come out all this way. I mean, sometimes you think something's a thing, and then it isn't a thing. D'you know what I mean?"

"Something about the night Edith went missing, perhaps?" says Manon. "When your husband came back from the Crown?"

She sets the glass of water in front of Davy, who has his green book out on the dining table. Mrs. Garfield doesn't sit down with them. Instead, she returns to the kitchen counter and busies herself, clattering about with various pans and bowls. They wait.

Davy writes something in his book, the date and time probably. Manon looks out to the garden, the wet-gray paving slabs, soil silted and blown about with fallen leaves. It all seems quite dead.

Manon breaks the silence, ever so gently. "Is there something you're unsure about . . . about Mr. Garfield?"

"He wipes his Internet history," Mrs. Garfield says, without looking up, making circular motions on the worktop with a cloth.

"Go on," says Manon.

"I don't. I don't wipe my Internet history. I'm only ever on the John Lewis website, looking at table lamps. Or Amazon. I don't wipe my Internet history—it wouldn't occur to me. So why does he?"

"It occurred to you to look for his Internet history, Mrs. Garfield. Why was that?"

"He's always on his computer—lost in this world that I don't know anything about. It's like some secret door he goes through, where he's unreachable, like the screen has stolen him from me." She shakes her head, then adopts a different tone. "It's probably nothing—work or football scores. Reading the *New Statesman*. But you don't *know*, do you?" And she laughs, but the texture in the room has darkened.

"Was he with you on the night of the seventeenth of December, after the Crown?"

Mrs. Garfield nods. "As far as I know."

"As far as you know?"

"I did say at the time, but perhaps I didn't make myself clear. I was falling asleep when I heard his key in the door. I registered that and then I nodded off. I didn't actually *see* him."

"And your relationship with Mr. Garfield," says Manon. "How has that been?"

"What do you mean by that?"

"Has everything been normal between the two of you? Has he been behaving normally?"

"As far as I know," says Mrs. Garfield.

Manon waits. If she waits, something more might come. But Mrs. Garfield has become more brisk in her clattering and fussing in the kitchen area, her body language saying: *I'm really far too busy for all this.*

"Right, well, thanks very much for your time," says Manon, rising from her chair. Davy follows her cue to get up too. "I'm sure it's nothing to worry about, the computer stuff, but thanks for letting us know. And do call us if anything else comes to mind, Mrs. Garfield. We can see ourselves out."

They pull their car doors shut with a warming *shunk,* and the sounds of outside are cut off. Their coats rustle and they click their seatbelts down into the red slots.

"We going to get Garfield's laptop, then?" asks Davy, before he starts the engine.

She already has her phone to her ear, and after a short preamble— "Mr. Garfield, yes, sorry to disturb you, it's Detective Sergeant Bradshaw"—she says, "We'd like to take a look at your laptop."

"Why would you want to do that?"

"Just to eliminate you from our inquiries. It'd be best if you gave it to us voluntarily."

"I'm sorry, I do want to help in any way I can, but all you'll find on my laptop is a series of very dull essays on Tennyson's *Idylls of the King,* that sort of thing."

"We can have it back to you in a week," says Manon.

"Really, I'd love to help, but I can't manage without it for a week, and anyway, there's nothing on it. Nothing that would be of any interest to you. Look, I'm really sorry, but I've got a study group in five minutes."

"Mr. Garfield?"

"Yes?"

"I'd hate to come and arrest you at the college."

"Why would you arrest me?"

"Because an arrest gives me automatic powers to search and seize." There is silence on the line.

"I'd hate to, you know, create a scene. Uniformed constables at the porter's lodge, asking where you are. Our panda cars with their flashing blue lights outside the college—we love putting our lights on. Officers marching across the quad toward your rooms. All those students standing around watching. You know what Cambridge is like—terrible for gossip. But I'd have to do that in order to get your laptop, you see. But if you handed it over voluntarily, we could keep it all nice and quiet."

Davy starts the engine as Manon puts her mobile back in her bag. As he pulls out, he says, "To the college, then?"

"Yep."

"By the way, I've spoken to my mate—the mentoring buddy. In Brent. Said she's looking out for Taylor's brother—Fly, is it? She had meetings with education welfare and with the school, and they have agreed to work together to keep him at home with his mother."

"Great. That's great."

"Actually, she thinks he's amazing."

I know he's amazing, she thinks. "How d'you mean?"

"Well, the school said he's gifted. A great little reader. They said you'd expect a child in his situation to fall off the curve, but he's top of his class."

"Does that somehow make him more worthy of being saved?" she says, in a bid to cover an involuntary flush of pride in Fly Dent. After all, why should she feel pride? It's not as if he's hers.

"Makes him of interest to them," says Davy, eyes fixed cheerfully on the road. "My mate'll keep an eye on him. Fly's mum's really sick, you know that, right? Hasn't attended any of her hospital appointments. If she dies, he'll be taken into care. Just to warn you."

"Yes, yes, I know," she says, her hands having already dug out her mobile phone, working on a text to Fly.

How is school?

OK, if you like that sort of thing.

What did you have at the Portuguese café?

Why d'you care?

Cos I'm paying.

Oh, OK. Toast and jam.

White or brown?

Actually, it was kind of red.

Haha. White or brown toast?

Back off, DS Auntie.

DAVY

. . .

It's a short drive to Graham Garfield's college rooms in Corpus, and while Manon runs in to pick up his laptop (just her, nice and quiet, like she promised), Davy sits in his driver seat, checking his BlackBerry. His original request for information from the mobile phone company about unknown-515 had yielded nothing, but that was before Christmas, so as soon as he was back from his festive break he requested an update, and this has just dropped into his inbox.

Manon is heaving down into the passenger seat, having put Garfield's laptop onto the backseat.

"He wasn't happy," she says, breathless and rustling in her coat.

Davy is shifting in his seat, making himself more upright. "Unknown-515," he says, reading.

"What about it?"

"It's been topped up. Biggleswade, the BP service station. Two weeks ago."

"That'll have CCTV," she says. "Let's head out there."

"Shouldn't we, y'know, head back to the office, drop off the laptop, give Harriet the heads up on Helena Reed?" asks Davy.

"Nah," says Manon. She's excitable; he's seen that look before. When she gets the bit between her teeth, she doesn't want to stop. "Come on, Davy, this could be it—this could be the thing that solves it. You and me, and a collar." She lifts and lowers her eyebrows at him, a bit comedy. "To Biggleswade!" she says, raising aloft an imaginary sword.

Davy shakes his head and drives.

As they pull into the BP forecourt, Manon is already peering about its low slab of a roof for cameras.

"CCTV for December twenty-third," she says at the counter, showing her badge to the cashier. "Have you got it stored somewhere?"

The cashier, a spotty young man of about twenty, is shaking his head. "Wiped at the start of the year," he says. "I only know 'cos I was in that day."

"Were you on duty on December twenty-third?" asks Davy.

"Nope, don't know who was. I'd have to get my manager but he's not about right now."

Davy turns round at the squeak of the shop door and sees Manon already leaving. He jogs after her as she strides about the forecourt, scanning the London Road and its wide-spaced bungalows left and right.

"We can speak to the duty manager, get the rota off of him," Davy suggests to her back.

She is squinting and peering, turning this way and that. "There!" she says to him, pointing.

"What?" says Davy.

"There, can't you see it? Poking out of the ivy."

On a brick wall opposite the BP garage, camouflaged by glossy foliage, is a camera—trained on the forecourt. "Let's see what's in that one."

MANON

. . .

Back in the department, she says, "There you go, Colin, knock yourself out," and places Graham Garfield's MacBook Air on Colin's desk.

He lifts its sleek gray lid, saying, "What's he been up to, then, dirty dog?"

"It's his Web browser history we're interested in."

"All leaves a trace," he mutters, clicking about as if he's owned the laptop all his life. "Download takes time, though, going through all that data."

The room is quieter than when they left. It seems deflated with collective exhaustion, but Manon is fizzing. She wants that film, because whomever Edith was calling the day before she disappeared must hold the key, and Manon is about to get him, about to see his face. It can't be Taylor Dent, unless you can top up from beyond the grave (the phone companies are probably looking into this possibility), but it could be an associate of his.

Kim is passing round a tray of Thorntons Milk Chocolate Classics, so broad and thin it bends, crackling in her hand.

"We bumped into Helena Reed. She looked pretty torn up about the *Crimewatch* stuff. Need to keep an eye on her," Manon says to Harriet. Kim's mouth is already working on a chocolate—slow, bovine ruminations—but before passing the box on, she takes another.

"Not for me," says Harriet, taut as ever, perching on a desk, then up again, rounding her shoulders and pulling up her bra strap. "OK, let's send a liaison officer round this arvo. They can stay with her over the weekend. Make sure you put in the paperwork, all right, Manon? Who gave us those, anyway?" she says, nodding at the chocolates.

"Some old bird handed them in to reception."

"Christ, it wouldn't be hard to take out the whole of Cambridgeshire nick—you lot'll eat anything."

"Where's the menu-guide thingy?" Colin asks, the box having at last come his way.

"Speed it up, Brierley," says Stuart.

"I think I'll have … No, hang on. Yes, a Nut Caress." With a full mouth, he says, "Nothing dirty among his documents so far. Looks like he and Mrs. Garfield had a nice time in Broadstairs, mind."

"When's that CCTV footage coming in?" asks Harriet.

"Any minute now," says Manon, clicking refresh on her emails. "Council said they'd have it to me within the hour."

She creates a new email, types in "DI Haverstock," and his address at Kilburn CID fills out automatically. "Just a note," she types, "to say if anything significant comes in on the Dent inquiry, can you email me? Just keep me up to speed, that's all." Then she hits send.

She glances at Colin and Stuart—Colin half-clicking around Garfield's laptop, with the odd sideways look at Stuart's new iPad.

"I just can't get to grips with it," Stuart is saying, swiping at the screen and frowning, to which Colin says (chewing, glasses pushed up onto his bald pate), "That's normal with a new gadget. You have to hate it for a time. That's how it is."

"Here we go," Manon says to the room, opening up the new email that has just appeared in her inbox. It seems an age while the footage downloads, Harriet perching, then up again, pulling at her bra strap. Manon's mind is feeling along the possibilities: an associate of Taylor Dent; a lover they haven't been told about; a drug dealer whose previous convictions will be all over their system. They gather round Manon's screen: Harriet, Davy, Kim, and Colin. The grainy gray images flick and turn, one car, then the next. "What was the timing again, Davy?"

"It was topped up at 6:02 P.M.," Davy says.

Manon jumps along the timeline with her mouse, watching the tiny yellow numbers change in the corner of her screen. There, at 5:59 P.M., is a figure in a familiar denim jacket with small round spectacles, hands pushed into his pockets, white hair tied in a ponytail.

Friday

MIRIAM
. . .

THE PERPETUAL DUSK OF CENTRAL LOBBY—ITS OCTAGON REVERBERATING
with self-important shoes. Passes swinging from lapels or hung about
necks on ribbons. Miriam sits on a black leather button-back chair
while Ian stands nearby, reading the plate at the base of one of the
alabaster statues.

Their invitation for Rog and Patty to come to Church Row had
been politely declined, and she and Ian know why. Ostensibly, it was
because of the oafs who had returned to the doorstep—back with a
vengeance since the *Crimewatch* appeal was broadcast two nights ago.
Miriam could hear them from the bedroom, chatting and laughing,
stubbing out their cigarettes on her flagstone step. They hung their
cameras on her wrought-iron railings as if they owned the place. Their
shutters went mad every time Rosa put out the rubbish. Periodically,
Ian became incensed and put in a call to someone or other and they
retreated to the end of the street, chivvied by some local bobby, but

they soon drifted back or lurked in the churchyard close to the house.
Ian said the Press Complaints Commission was drafting a letter to editors, asking them to "respect the Hind family's privacy at this distressing time," but she'd like to see what good it would do. Everyone knew
the PCC was a toothless watchdog.

Anyway, Patty had said, "We don't want to give them more fodder
by rolling up in a government car." So here Miriam and Ian are, obe-
dient "strangers," herded through the metal detectors at St. Stephen's
Gate and waiting now to be fetched.

As they dressed this morning—Miriam rolling up a pair of 10 de-
nier tights as she sat on the edge of the bed, Ian throwing the long
tongue of his tie over itself—she said to him, "Do you think it's because
of Edith—because of what they've said about her? Do you think that's
why they refused—*Damn!*" The run in her tights felt like an injury. She
hated the slippery feel of them, and now she had to try another pair.

"That'd be rich, coming from him," Ian said.

"How do you mean?"

"Nothing."

"No, come on, Ian, you can't drop a thing like that. . . ."

"There was a lot of it at school, that's all."

If she's honest, she assumed as much, at a school like that. Dropped
off at seven years old, no one to cuddle when they fell and scraped
their knees, and homesickness considered a disobedience. The school
churned out leaders and princes, but they were men forged in the
furnace of repression. God help you if you were less than robust, if you
missed your mother desperately. When she'd seen pictures of Ian as a
boy, she knew that he was one of those sensitive ones: twiggy-legged,
with full lips that probably quivered with his tears. He hadn't even
raised the notion of Rollo following in his footsteps (apart from some
mild comments about the school's excellent facilities for sport). He
seemed to know how ferociously Miriam would guard Rollo to keep
him safely at home.

Anyway, she thinks now, these things are not so clear-cut as everyone might think. Boys experiment, girls too, evidently; their feelings
sway one way and another. All part of feeling the way toward adult-
hood.

Ian told her she was paranoid, but with Rog and Patty she has the sense of rope being let out, as if she and Ian are a boat being allowed to drift. A similar feeling with the palace, which has remained silent. It seems to Miriam that they have become tainted—the stain of life going wrong, rather like the taint of illness or disability, weight gain, depression, financial difficulty. It has the whiff of not *succeeding*—not staying sufficiently in control.

"Hello, you," says Patty, and Miriam stands, allowing Patty to clutch her arms and kiss her twice. "Rog is waiting in his office. Shall I lead the way?"

She clacks ahead of them, saying hello to various suits, down tiled corridors and then up into the realm of endless wood paneling.

Rog is out from behind his desk, crossing the acreage of carpet to where they have entered. "I thought it'd be more private here than Marsham Street," he says, reaching out his hand to Ian. "How are you holding up, both of you?"

Miriam is comforted by Roger's corpulent bonhomie. She thinks of him as a cricketer, the white cable-knit tight over the drum of his belly, jogging toward the batsman and lobbing the ball overarm. All Englishness and fair play.

"Not so well, actually," she says. "Turns out losing a child is a living torture. They don't tell you that before you have them, do they?"

Ian frowns at her while Roger coughs fulsomely into a fist. Patty has her head cocked like a therapist or an empathizing actress.

"Come in anyway," says Roger. "It must be ghastly, all of it. Drink?"

Ian and Miriam say "Thank you" and "Please" over each other. They have been here before, shortly after they won—well, formed the coalition—back in May. "The boast tour," Roger called it, laughing. He'd certainly been pleased with himself, and why not.

The room is vast, the carpet swirling away in a luxury of Persian roses, pale with antiquity. Heavy drapes and large lamps. A desk the size of a dining table. Patty is opening a highly polished rosewood cupboard to reveal a deep-set drinks cabinet—cut glasses, decanter, and all.

"Goodness," says Miriam. "Didn't think they still made those." For comforting the bereft, she guesses, or firing people. Or those long nights drawing up draconian immigration policy.

"They don't," says Patty. "This one's 1930s. Picked it up at Bonhams. I went with Sam—she's got lots more time since she left Smythson."

Miriam hasn't the energy to deliver what Patty needs. She requires admiration. Ian and Miriam have always been quick to give it, but now, standing beside Patty at the stupid Nazi-Reich drinks cabinet while Ian and Rog burble to each other on the other side of the room, and everything stripped away, she and Ian back to the bone, while Rog and Patty are still so pleased with themselves, she wonders what the basis is for any sort of friendship.

"I just don't think they know what they're doing," Ian is saying, as Patty hands Miriam a bitter lemon in a heavy, textured glass. (Not tea, *thank God*.) She takes Ian a tumbler of whiskey, which is not at all like him, but perhaps more so recently. "Saying all that stuff on *Crimewatch*, it just clouds the investigation."

Rog has retreated behind his desk for protection. "I know you're worried sick, and I can see the telly thing would have been distressing, but best thing you can do is let the police do their job."

"But there's so much confusion, you see, in the investigation. They keep looking for connections where there aren't any. One minute they say it's this criminal, Tony Wright; then it's her complex love life; next it's this Dent boy. The Edith they describe, it doesn't bear any relation . . ."

Ian's tone has become needy, and simultaneously Roger's eyes have grown cold. The trace of the bully in Roger, which is the real seat of his power—a gaze that can flash like steel, the unapologetic way in which he takes up all the air space. Miriam wonders what sort of bully—what sort of punishment he employs, these things rarely being notional, not if they're to have any heft. Perhaps the threat, simply, of being cast out from the circle of influence. The rope gets longer.

"We thought you might be able to get the inside track," Ian is saying, while looking to Miriam for support.

"I'm sure you understand, I can't meddle in police work. Individual cases—how would it *look* . . ." Roger says.

"Oh, come off it," Ian says. "I bet you meddle all the time. I'm sure you're right in there when the *Daily Mail* says you're not taking a hard-enough line."

"Ian," Miriam says soothingly. "All we want," she begins, but wonders what it is they want, really. Rog and Patty can't find Edith for them, which is the only thing that matters. Perhaps they want what anyone wants from the powerful—protection. They want Roger to oil the processes, as they would be oiled for him, to protect them from shoddiness. "All we want," she tries again, but her tears stop her and in some way save them all. "Oh God, I'm sorry," Miriam snivels as Patty hugs her. "Can we talk about something else, please? What's your news? How is Calista?"

MANON

• • •

"QUIET EVERYONE, PLEASE," SAYS HARRIET, AND THE DEPARTMENT FALLS to a hush. "As you know, Tony Wright was arrested last night at five P.M.; he's spent the night in custody, so hopefully he'll be nice and chatty this morning. His flat is now a crime scene. SOCO is still in there looking for anything that could link Wright to either Edith or Taylor Dent. We have," she looks at her watch, "six hours remaining in which to charge him with something; otherwise he walks. His brief is going to say the CCTV footage is too grainy for a firm ID and that his alibi for the weekend Edith disappeared still holds tight."

"Which is true," says Manon.

"Which is true," repeats Harriet, nodding. "So why was Edith calling Tony Wright the week before she disappeared? Twice—once on the Monday, again on the Friday."

"You don't think she was having an affair with him, do you?" says Davy.

"You'd have to be deaf, dumb, and blind to have an affair with Tony Wright," says Kim.

"Maybe," says Colin thoughtfully, as if swilling an exquisite red around his palate, "she's had enough of all the posh blokes and fancies a bit of rough."

"Yeah, 'cos it's a tough one, isn't it?" says Kim, holding both hands in the balance. "On the one hand you've got devastatingly handsome Cambridge graduate Will Carter, and on the other you've got sleazebag burglar Tony Wright. *Who to choose?*"

"There's no accounting for taste," says Harriet.

"She might find rough men exciting," ventures Colin.

"There's a lot of hope in your voice, Colin," says Manon.

"Let's stick to the point," says Harriet. "Let's say they were having an affair, preposterous though that seems—it doesn't explain how they knew each other. How on earth did someone like Edith Hind meet someone like Tony Wright? And anyway, he's still here, but she's not, so it's not like they've run off into the sunset together."

"Maybe he was blackmailing her," says Manon. "If it's not sex, it's money. Maybe he knew, I dunno, some dark secret about her and she had to pay him off. Would explain why she was calling him."

"So we need to look into his finances," says Harriet. "Any nice new tellies at his flat. I want the data off all phones and computers from his property. I want forensics from whatever vehicle he's currently using. Let's go downstairs, talk to Wright," she says to Manon. "Anything comes in from SOCO, come and get us."

"WHY DIDN'T YOU TELL US you knew Edith Hind?" Harriet says, without preamble.

"Oh aye," says Wright, and Manon can see he's rankled, he's had enough. "That girl that's been abducted? She an' I were pals! Ye wan' tae cuff me now or wait for the van tae pull up? Shall we bother wi' a trial or head straight tae Whitemoor, where you can BANG ME UP TILL I DIE?"

Tony Wright has stood up, knocking his chair backward. His solicitor, a silently composed man in a gray suit with matching waistcoat, casts him a look and he sits back down.

"Tell me about your relationship with Edith Hind."

"No comment."

"How did you know her?"

"No comment."

And so it goes on: every question, so that eventually everyone is going through the motions in a monotone, Wright not even waiting for Harriet to finish her sentences. Until she mentions Taylor Dent. At this, Wright looks genuinely quizzical, frowns, then says, "No comment" all the same. There is a knock at the door and Harriet stops the recording, and they step out of the room.

"His flat's clean," says Kim in the corridor. "I mean, nothing obvious, no items of clothing or anything belonging to Edith," she says to Harriet. "No blood on anything. Forensics'll take a bit longer, though."

"Fuck," says Harriet. She looks at Manon. They both know, unless a miracle happens in the course of the afternoon, they're going to have to let Wright go. "His brief's going to be all over this," she says, "asking what evidence we've got to sustain an arrest."

"We can't charge him with speaking to her on the blower," says Manon.

THE ONLY WAY TO COME down after a week of fifteen-hour shifts is to lose herself in a book or film, so here she is, standing on the cinema steps, head down against the cold, one hand in a pocket and the other texting Fly Dent.

What did you have at the Portuguese café?

Somefin new. She call it Manioc. She says she introducing me to new foods. Not too sure meself.

Was it nice?

Not really. It was yellow. And dry.

Do you think she could introduce you to vegetables?

We met. We didn't get on.

She shuffles forward in the queue for *My Life as a Dog,* by Lasse Hallström, reluctant to flip the phone shut, so she is scrolling back through their conversation when a voice says, "You again."

Fuck shit bollocks. She tries to think of something before looking up. He is the very last person she wants to see, not because she doesn't like him (she's all at sea over whether she likes him), but because she never thanked him, never called, and she can't bear the awkwardness. Is it too late, she wonders, as she looks up, to cough violently and pretend she's been in bed with flu?

"Alan," she says. "How are you?"

"Hurt and rejected," he says, smiling at her.

"Oh God, I'm really sorry. It was nice of you, the eyedrops, and look"—she blinks at him—"all better!"

"So I see."

"I kept meaning to call and say thanks. But work—it's just gone mental."

"Yes, your work," he says. And he's smiling ironically, as if he sees through her. And she feels annoyed at his presumption, because actually it *has* been mental.

"It affects me. It's important to me," she says.

"Yes, sir, Officer," he says, smiling again, his hands in his pockets.

"I like you," she blurts, without realizing she's saying it out loud until it's too late. The thought becomes the deed. "I sometimes show off because I like you." And as she looks at him, nothing seems honest at all, not even this.

"Swedish season," he says.

"Yes," she laughs. "Swedish season."

They stand there like that, as if they are an old couple, companionable, except her insides have clenched like an angry fist. Someone pays at the front and they shuffle forward a human width.

"Shall we sit together this time? Would you mind?" he says.

And she smiles. He has forgiven her, and she is taken up with the sensation of his proximity—a new feeling, a new smell—and interested in where it might take them.

The boy in the film is called Ingemar. His mother is dying and he keeps saying, "It could have been worse," which reminds her of Fly. She feels her phone vibrate and opens it up to see a text from him, containing a photograph of strawberry laces and the words: *One of my five-a-day.*

The cinema screen flickers black and white, colors and daylight. Words are said but she has lost track. His large hand is on the armrest between the two of them and she takes it in hers. Something receptive in her, like a flower opening, sad and vulnerable. He looks at her, then clasps her hand in return, and they both lean in and put their temples together. Her body is shaking on the inside and the vast cinema screen surrounds her with its flickering, meaningless images. She closes her eyes. His hands are big and enclosing, rough on the thumb pads. Foreign hands, new to the touch. He makes tiny stroking movements with his thumb and she can feel the aftershock between her legs. She senses the movement in the air when he blinks. He is seeking out her lips now, soft and dry, very gentle on hers, and her stomach flips over itself. She is dissolving into the dark. Alan the systems analyst, with voluminous corduroys and trainers like ocean liners. Who knew? Something unspoken, like a scent, makes her being reach toward him, and she is ardent, as if all the feelings are hers, far more than his, and she fills up all the more for it being so.

When the lights go up, their heads are still together, though her neck is hurting now and their hands have grown clammy.

"Coffee?" he says, and she nods.

They walk up the cinema stairs to the art deco café, as before. The same table but this time, when he walks toward her carrying their drinks—she's having mint tea to freshen her breath—she notices his elegant hands.

He loops his maroon scarf over the back of the chair, saying, "I loved the stuff about the dog sent into orbit by the Russians. Think of him and nothing is that bad in comparison."

Oh, she thinks, *you were concentrating.*

She takes a sip of tea.

He leans forward. "What now, Sergeant?" he says with an ironic expression, and it's as if he's saying, *Whither the rest of our lives?*

"What now indeed," she says.

They sip their drinks, each with both hands around their cups and elbows on the table, and she wonders, *Did anything happen in there? Or did I imagine it all?*

* * *

THEY LIE IN HER BED. His arm is under her neck and she is holding the weight of his forearm at the wrist. Bouncing it occasionally.

"I think you should know," she says, looking at the ceiling, "that my basic position on life is that it's shit."

"Oh, I'm with you. I only stick around for the food and, frankly, that's often crap as well."

She laughs. Bounces his wrist in her hand. "It's like, take Christmas," she says.

"Brilliant dinner, awful day."

She laughs again.

"I think part of the appeal is that slight out-of-reach quality," he says.

"You mean: 'Oooh, I'm almost having a good time. . . . Oh no, I'm not.'"

"Yes, that's it. Well, no, it's more: 'I'm going to enjoy it, I'm going to enjoy it, I'm going to enjoy it . . . Oh no, it's rubbish again.'"

"It's expectation," she says. "That's what kills off enjoyment. Holidays are stressful for the same reason."

After a time, he says, "The dog. I've got to go back for Nana—let her out."

Her insides tighten with the disappointment, but then he says, "Come with me?"

SHE OPENS ONE EYE INTO the grainy morning light, forgetful for one moment, then sees his crumpled form next to her, burrowed down into the pillow. Blissful January! The cold swirling the room, but, oh, it is warm in the bed and we are two. *We are two.* She kisses his bare shoulder, smelling his skin, malty and male, like sourdough. Alien male! This is what she needs: a person who is other.

She rolls onto her back and closes her eyes. She feels his weight upon her, his lips soft and dry, his oversweet breath, which he is trying to disguise by keeping his mouth shut, his erection against her leg.

"Well, hello," she says, laughing.

"Hello," he mumbles, as if she shouldn't make a joke of it. His voice is gravelly, his eyes closed like a little rodent, bruised and nocturnal, so she wonders if he's still asleep and wanting her out of his unconscious self, his sleepy, atavistic morning maleness. Oh, joy. *Hello, you.*

His head is in her neck as they rock together, sleepily aroused, their faces still closed up, their cells thick with half-remembered dreams.

Over and over, all day in bed, wrapped in his gray linen sheets, her on top, bare-breasted, his face burrowed there; Manon trying to ignore the stoic glances from Nana, who has wandered in like a confused pensioner in a strip joint. In the shower, him insistent behind her, the water pouring down her neck and over the hard stones of her nipples and over his hand between her legs. They cannot stop, or when they stop they seem to start all over again, and each time it is new, each time they are remembering the last time and reinventing it too.

"I'm going to give up my job and just have sex for a living," says Manon, in a shirt and knickers, her bare feet freezing on the kitchen floor.

"Me too," he says, leaning against the counter, eating toast. How is it that *not* touching, him being a few feet away, is erotic, a kind of come-on? "Our earnings might take a bit of a hit."

"Don't care," she says, sidling up to him, putting a hand down his shorts. And she leads him back to bed.

My heart has made its mind up,
And I'm afraid it's you.

She doesn't want to leave this bubble, the two of them back at her flat now, exploring each other. She doesn't want the abrasive world to shock them awake with its cold obligations. She looks at the two mobile phones, like black beetles on the side table—the work BlackBerry and the Samsung Android, which is for personal use—both switched off because when did she last have a life? When was the last time work took a backseat to the rich turbulence of her heart? She has earned this hiatus. She has earned the right to devote herself to Alan Prender*gasp* without disturbance, though the phones seem to drag her eyes to their black heft and thoughts of whether she should check in with the office, and in particular with Helena Reed.

No, she will not. Her body is her antenna now and it chooses him, again and again. And she wonders, surprised, whether this will be her undoing. How much appetite is a woman allowed these days? She towers above him on all fours, feeling like an Alice who's eaten the cake labeled "Eat Me," and now she is bigger than the room.

"COME ON, HOW MANY?"

"Not many," he says, moving her roving fingers, which have traced the line of hairs around his nipples until he's laughed and shouted, "Geroff!" then entwined them in his, a lockdown, but playful.

"C'mon, tell me," she nudges him.

"Um." He has closed his eyes, lying on his back. "Only one serious one."

"How long was that for?"

"Six months."

She doesn't comment on how slight this is for a man of forty-two. She wants him to ask about her previous lovers, the boy from university she nearly married. How much she'd loved him for seven long years, how sad she was to lose him when it petered out.

But he doesn't ask. All is new, she supposes; all is in the now. This is the new regime! Oh, hallowed bed. Who'd have thought that Alan, in all his Alan-ness, would make a right out of all those wrongs—the years alone, the terrible dates. When you meet the One, it all makes sense, it makes the cock-ups seem . . . intentional. And just in fucking time too.

Hello, you.

DAVY
• • •

EVEN MAKING THE MACARONI CHEESE LAST NIGHT, HE HADN'T FELT RIGHT.

Davy thought it would be nice to feed his mother after all she did for him and Chloe on Christmas Day. It'd been a lot of work, his mother had said (quite a few times), especially with no one to help her. He thought a macaroni cheese would be homely and filling for a January Saturday dinner, just him, Mum, and Chloe, who said it was her duty to come along—though he'd begun to have the sense that she was guarding him from his mother, didn't want them to spend time alone together, because there might pass between them a moment to which she was not privy. And then he'd caught himself having a mean thought like that. These were happening to him more and more.

He'd spooned the macaroni cheese into a square white dish and covered it so tightly with cling film that the plastic was an invisible plane. He'd straightened it so the dish was parallel with the splashback and squared up nicely beside the hob, but it didn't give him any satisfaction.

He's all out of sync with himself, he thinks now, as he peels off the cling film and pops the dish into the oven to warm and crisp up on top. He picks up his work phone and dials Helena Reed's number, because she's been preying on his mind—the way she'd slammed into him, her face full of fear. Who was she visiting, all the way in Newnham—and why had she seemed furtive about it? What "friend" had prompted such a tearful state?

No reply. This time, there is a message telling him her voicemail is full, so he can't even leave another one. It's the third time he's tried this morning.

"Just me again, Helena, checking in. DC Walker, I mean," he'd said previously. "If you get this, just give me a buzz, let me know you're all right." Still, she has his number if she needs him.

The doorbell goes.

Chloe has straightened her hair so that it hangs in sheets on either side of her face. He's always thought she looks better when she doesn't pull down so hard on the straightening irons, like in the early days when he'd pulled her back into bed after her shower so she hadn't had time for all that gubbins—the fake tan and the heavy black eyelashes, which he isn't sure are hers.

Her arms are full of the Saturday papers. "Thought we could catch up," she says, breathless.

"Put them in the lounge," he says, and they pile them on the glass coffee table, the poly-bagged glossy magazines sliding out of the folded sheaves. A tower of innuendo, he thinks, slabs of unsubstantiated hearsay. He can hardly bear to look at them.

"Right," he says, clapping his hands as the doorbell goes again. "That'll be Mum."

They settle, his mum and Chloe, around the kitchen table, and Davy says, "Who's for macaroni cheese?"

He's trying to put the uplift back in his voice, but it's not working. It's not been working for days. Manon's rubbing off on him, that's what it'll be. Her gloom, the way she sees things—always the uncomfortable underbelly, never the bright side.

Last night, as they left the office together, he said, "I just don't think we're going to get to the bottom of this one," and she put her palm across his forehead, saying, "Are you feeling all right, Davy?"

He frowned, jerked his head away, the crotchety teenager. "I mean it. It's getting me down, this . . . not getting anywhere. We've let Tony Wright go. That boy, in the river, that's going nowhere as well. And all this love-life guff. I don't like it."

"You've got to let it emerge, Davy," she told him. "Ride out the confusion, the darkness. Things will become clear, you wait and see. But in the meantime, you've got to allow yourself to be all right with the not knowing."

And all of a sudden he'd felt completely lost, like a sad hole had opened up beneath him and he was about to fall down into it.

"What's this you've put in it?" says his mother, grimacing and pushing something to the front of her mouth, out between her teeth. She picks it out with finger and thumb and peers at it. "Nutmeg, is it?" She wipes it on the table. "Didn't you grate it?"

"I did grate it, Mum. A shard must have fallen in. There's a napkin there."

The macaroni cheese is so dry he's had to carve it. Even several tablespoons of Branston pickle are doing a poor job of livening it up.

"Everyone at work wants to know the details," says Chloe. More animated, warmer, in fact, than he's seen her in quite some time. She runs a finger down the line of her hair curtain, pushing it from her eyes. "Amazing you're right at the center of it, what's on the news."

"Can't talk about it, Chlo," he says, trying to masticate a rigid piece of macaroni.

"I took some flowers—to George Street," says his mother. "Outside the house where the other bunches are."

"Why?" he asks.

"Well, you want to be part of something, don't you? And it's terrible. But to have it so near—in the same town. I didn't want to miss out. What do *you* think happened to her?"

"He knows everything, but he can't say, isn't that right, Davy?" says Chloe, winking at him.

"Dead, then?" says his mother hopefully.

"Male *and* female lovers," says Chloe. "Who'd have thought? How many?"

"We don't know."

"More than one, though?"

"We don't know."

"You do know, you're just not saying," she says, the proud wife. "Takes all sorts," she says to his mother, and they are united at last.

"Did her boyfriend know about it?" asks Chloe.

"I can't talk about it, Chlo."

"No, 'course. So have the papers been in touch with you directly?"

"All media inquiries are dealt with by the press office," he says.

"Still," says his mother, "I bet they'd give you a tidy bit of money for extra info."

"I'd lose my job."

"Not if you were nice and discreet about it."

"But it's wrong."

"Gosh, I bet her mother's shocked," says Chloe. "Imagine having a daughter carrying on like that."

"And him a famous surgeon," says his mother.

Davy is staring ahead, the room's light harsh and blue. He realizes this kitchen is about as welcoming as a dental surgery.

"They're people," he says slowly. "They're just people."

He checks his phone again for missed calls or texts from Helena Reed. Perhaps he should pop round there, check she's all right. But, then, she might have gone to Bromley to stay with her parents—get out of the heat until things calm down a bit.

HELENA
• • •

SHE CAN HEAR THEM LAUGHING LIKE DAY-TRIPPERS, SMOKING AROUND the war memorial down below her flat window, though the curtains are drawn. The curtains have been drawn against them since they gathered yesterday.

First there were only a few, but they flew down like birds on crusts, vying with one another around the narrow blue door to the side of Barclays—her front door, which has until now seemed invisible. "Helena Reed!" they called, as if she might open a window and invite them up. When she pulled aside a net to look, they locked on to her, nudging one another, shouting to her, and setting their zoom lenses for a grainy shot, so she had quickly retreated. She sat all day yesterday, and all last night, listening to the answering machine click and rewind with each new appeal from strangers luring her with false intimacy—"Look, this must be a difficult time; we can help"—while she chewed on the skin at the edge of her thumbnail. Wondering who'd released her name.

But, then, she's been waiting for this to happen, knowing it would happen, since *Crimewatch*. After slamming into those two detectives outside Dr. Young's, she's been a prisoner of her thoughts. Four days, three long nights. Would the police check whom she had been visiting in Newnham? Would they find out she was seeing a shrink and assume all manner of mental instability from that? Would they talk to Dr. Young, and would he mention her terrorized thoughts, and what on earth would the police infer? Would they inform Dr. Young that she was Edith's lover, to which he would say, baffled, "Well, she never told me that," and to all of them she would appear madder and more inscrutable, a dissembler of the facts about Edith's disappearance?

Thursday afternoon they sent someone round—"to sit with her," the officer said. A babysitter. Helena had moved round this person in her flat, trying to look natural, but inside she was gnawed at by the sensation of being observed in her own home—they were *watching* her—so she said, "You go, I'm fine, I don't need looking after. In fact, I'm going to stay with friends." Helena smiled, her hand on her open front door. The officer/babysitter said, "If you're sure?" but Helena could see she was glad. She'd received some furtive call about childcare arrangements and she couldn't get away fast enough.

Friday morning, Saturday morning, she ran out early to check the papers, dreading but assuming she would be named and surprised to find no mention of her apart from in the usual timeline descriptions. So yesterday afternoon, when the crows first gathered at the bottom of her stairs, it was as if the inevitable had taken place.

She stared and stared at the only card she had from the police. DS Manon Bradshaw. The other one—the kindly chap she'd crashed into, who'd promised to protect her—his card must've fallen out of her pocket in her rush to get home that day. DS Bradshaw appeared not to be available. Dr. Young's practice number clicked through to a machine. She couldn't think what message to leave, so she hung up.

This morning, around 10:00, there'd been a noticeable quieting outside and she braved a glance through a crack in the curtain. They seemed to have dispersed, perhaps to a greasy spoon for a Sunday fry-up, leaving one or two hapless representatives to keep watch at her front door. She chanced it, out of the need for bread and milk, running down the back staircase—concrete and municipal, the air hung with the smell of stale cigarettes—which brought her via a door with a metal push bar out by the bins to the rear of Barclays. The cold and rain drove welcome pins into her hands and cheeks as she ran, clasping her hood, to the nearest newsagent, but she was brought up short by the gray box grid outside and eight images of herself and Edith, flapping in the wind.

BEST FRIEND WAS MISSING EDITH'S LOVER

"LOVER" WAS WITH EDITH ON NIGHT SHE VANISHED

GIRLS WERE LOVERS

It was like looking at images of a very familiar stranger. She noticed how young she looked, though she felt anything but young. She wasn't nearly as fat as she assumed—rather slender, in fact. She tried to see herself as the readers of those rags might see her: unstable, predatory, sexually loose. There was a gap—the outside and the inside, and sometimes it was very wide indeed. Wide enough for you to fall through.

She'd given no thought to how she would get back in, and soon she was set upon, enveloped in bodies and voices, the smells of strangers, as she struggled for her key.

"Helena, over here!" they shouted as she barged through the black mass of jackets, arms, and shoulders, careful never to meet a face. Someone pushed a card in her hand—a blond woman, she thinks—but she was scrunching her eyes shut, trying to get through them, trying to get her key in the door without dropping the milk. This woman had got up very close and said in her ear, "We can tell your side of the story. Here's my card."

Up the stairs, she'd slammed her inner front door and leaned her head back against it with her eyes closed. Scheming lesbian Helena Reed. Jealous lover Helena Reed. Murdering Helena Reed. Edith—cloaked in all the innocence of the undead—can do no wrong, lured into Helena's crimson bed of joy. Now Helena would always be the vamp, in whatever job interview, PhD viva, applying for research funding, meeting a new man, joining a GP practice. Someone somewhere would look up from their desk and say, "Helena Reed? From Huntingdon? Weren't you a friend of that missing girl?" And the word "friend" would drip with all its sly connotations.

It was typical of Edith, blithe Edith, to leave her with all of this, while Helena did all the worrying. It had been like that from day one, the day Helena had knocked on the door across the hall at Corpus Christi. Edith shouted, "Come in!" and there she was, standing on her bed, wearing faded Levi's 501s, knocking a nail into the wall to hang up a Modigliani print. On the desk at the window was a vase of anemones, reds and purples and whites, like rich jewels. "From my mum," Edith said, breathless, still with her back to Helena. "Tea?"

Edith was breezy yet determined. She was set on her own course—like the move to Huntingdon—and you could accompany her or you could jog on. Edith, certain; Helena, anxious, following on. She sees how insubstantial she is next to Edith's luminous features, her charisma. And she hates herself for having been their lapdog. All those Saturday nights watching films on their Netflix account, Sunday lunches in their kitchen, Edith lying on the sofa, reading with her head on Helena's lap, Will sat on the floor, sipping wine. Helena, the only child in audience to the couple.

She wonders, sat here in her airless lounge while she listens to them laughing and talking on the street below, if she should call her parents. But what if they too have crows on the front step, imprisoned together, and she would have to hear it and know she was the cause? When will it end, being trapped like this, with the curtains drawn? And if she ever ventured out into the world, what would she find? She'd called the MIT offices yesterday evening, having no responses again from the sergeant's phone, and she'd got through to a duty person, Constable Monique something, who said she'd "look into it," but nothing had come of it.

"There's quite a lot of people outside."

"And what did you say your name was again, madam?"

No point calling today. Sunday was bound to be worse, and what could they do anyway? The story was out now and it couldn't be taken back in. Her own phones—mobile and landline—were filled to the brim with intrusions from people who shouldn't have her number at all, hectoring and bullying her. She couldn't bear to play them back, so she switched them all off.

During the night, by about 1:00 A.M., the crows had flown off (staying at the George Hotel, probably). Another chance: she pictured herself catching a plane to Rio de Janeiro, then another to Manaus, then a boat to where the Rio Negro meets the Solimões River—the Meeting of Waters, she'd always wanted to see that—and then deep into the tributaries of the Amazon. The world is so big and so beautiful and she'd hardly begun to explore it.

She wandered room to room, planning her escape. Where was her passport? What would she wear? Somehow, when she turned around, it was 7:00 A.M. and the crows were back on her doorstep and she didn't know how she'd get past them, let alone to the Amazon basin. She found herself staring at the back of the bedroom door—and the hook where her dressing gown hangs.

She can't see a way clear. She longs for someone—Edith, if she's honest—to throw a coat over her head and usher her through it all. She stands before the nets in the lounge, and the tears flow out of her in a great outpouring. She cries out, though it is silent, her lips cracked. She will never get out; she will never see the Amazon River. She will never be free or happy. And the girl she loves has gone.

MANON

. . .

"LOVELY TOP, KIM!"

Kim looks up, surprised.

"Stuart, me ol' mucker!"

Stuart looks at Kim, who shrugs.

"Colin," Manon says, squeezing Colin's shoulders, and it's like a puff of cigarette smoke plumes out of his sweater.

"What've you got for me today? We're going to find her, I just know we are."

She hangs her jacket on the back of her chair and reaches into her bag for her purse. She wants to eat, and she's thinking: bacon roll, sausages, egg yolk bursting over buttered toast. She is ripe with the eating; her hips seem wider, her breasts fuller. A Manon bursting forth to fruition. She is bovine, sleepy-ravenous, sensual. She wants him to move in, but he's kept his head, his beautiful Alan Prenderghast head. He ducked home last night, saying he had an early start in the morning—"need to be fresh for Monday"—and he'd kissed her, kissed her again, and they were kissing through the open door of her flat, him with his silly flappy coat on. Her lips hurt, and when the door closed, she missed the kiss they had not had. He rang the doorbell and her heart flipped over itself, puppyish and bright. She opened it and grabbed him and he was pulling his coat off and they were at it again, she in an open shirt, astride him on the corduroy sofa.

"Don't leave me," she said onto his lips.

She begins to text him, bouncing back in her chair—"Hello, you, you gorgeous chunk of hunk"—but is stopped by a thud and a billow of air toward her face.

"I take it you've seen these," says Harriet, hand on the pile of newspapers she's just slapped down on Manon's desk.

Manon straightens. Helena's face stares back at her. The headline says, "GIRLS WERE LOVERS," beneath a red masthead. The blood plummets from Manon's head, leaving it cold, fear tickling up her hair follicles. She looks at Davy, whose color has drained away.

"Who named her?" Davy asks Harriet.

"We don't know. Could've been anyone. I've sent a couple of uniforms to her flat just now, soon as Fergus showed me these. They're authorized to gain access if she doesn't respond. I've tried her phones, but there's no response and all her mailboxes are full."

"But we sent a liaison," Manon says.

"Who she sent away," Harriet says. "Told the officer she was going to stay with friends."

It might be all right, it can still be all right if Helena is found safe and well. She pictures Helena's terrified face looking up at them, tear-streaked. And the phones she turned off, how they lay immobile on the table next to the bed where she writhed, *partaking* of Alan Prenderghast.

Manon closes her eyes slowly, her body churning as shame begins its slow seep, like blood. The one time. The one time . . .

"You warned her, Kim," Harriet is saying, "about *Crimewatch*?"

"Yeah, she seemed all right about it, quite calm, but this'll be different," Kim says, nodding at the newspapers.

"And you put in the risk assessment paperwork on the Thursday?" Harriet says to Manon, who nods.

"If she said she was staying with friends," says Manon, feeling for an exit, "she won't be at the flat. When will officers be there? When will we know?"

"Dispatched ten minutes ago. They'll call me," Harriet says. "In the meantime, Colin is going to take us through Graham Garfield's hard drive in a mature and innuendo-free manner."

Colin turns to his desk. "Lots of drafts of his books on the Victorians, essays on George Eliot, work by his students, some assessment forms from the university, that kind of thing. But"—and he pulls his glasses down from his head, clicking his mouse, and the laptop's screen tessellates with Web pages, a bright and flickering collage of pornography—"he was into all sorts. Asian Babes. Big Fatties Who Want It. Frisky Housewives. A man of many interests." Colin is scrolling and clicking with great fervor. "Anyway, more significant than all that is *this*," he says, swiveling around to show everyone the screen. All Manon can see are several lines of Web links, all beginning "Facebook."

"What is it?" Manon says.

"Graham Garfield looked at Edith Hind's Facebook page five times every night the week before she disappeared. And since. Forty visits or thereabouts. Specifically, he has clicked on these pictures—selfies, I believe they're called."

He brings up several shots of Edith: eyes yearningly intense, looking straight into the lens, one with a sweater falling off her shoulder, one in which she is lying on a bed, holding her phone above her. Just you and her.

"Doesn't prove anything," says Stuart. "She put them out there. Why do that if you don't want to be leered at?"

"Proves he had an unhealthy interest in her," says Harriet.

"What sort of bloke wouldn't go clicking about on those? She's a hottie. What did she expect when she took them?" says Colin.

"Erm, freedom? Autonomy?" says Kim.

"Come off it—lying on the bed like that, all 'Come and get me,'" Stuart says.

"She might not know any better," says Kim. "Everyone's a dick at twenty-four."

MIRIAM

. . .

SHE OPENS HER EYES AND BLINKS IN AN EFFORT TO ADJUST TO THE PER-
manent dusk of the bedroom. She can hear Rosa clattering in the
kitchen. Ian will be God-knows-where, rushing about Being Important Yet Again. He's been calling in favors from his friends on the
broadsheets, old Bullingdon chums, giving profile interviews to *The
Telegraph* and *The Times*—"turning the tide," he called it. "Someone
has to set the record straight." They've promised to be sensitive in their
probing and give him copy approval before anything is printed.

Even Rollo has a sense of purpose; his father's son. He is at a meeting at the offices of a missing-persons charity, discussing a renewed online campaign involving a thousand tweets or some such. She doesn't
pretend to understand social media or why anyone would waste their
time on it, but she is very glad Rollo has it covered.

She hauls herself up off the bed, her hair damp and flattened,
pushes her feet into her sheepskin slippers, and walks out to the hall

and up a flight of wonky narrow stairs, holding tight to the gentle curve of the banister to Edith's room. On the landing between the children's bedrooms on this uppermost floor, under a mildewed skylight, is a Victorian doll's house in the architecture of their own. A Georgian house within a Georgian house. It was given to Edith when she was small by Ian's mother, Edith Senior. Ian revered the doll's house in the same way he revered his mother, had objected when Edie wanted to fill it with Polly Pockets, as if this somehow diluted its educational purity, when Miriam felt the whole point of playing was to make something your own. She'd have been rather proud if Edith had scrawled across the prim rosebud wallpaper with an indelible pen.

Ian had insisted their baby daughter be named after his mother, when all Miriam's friends were calling theirs Chloe or Jessica. These days, of course, the old dowager names are all the rage; even stalwarts of the Tory party call their children Florence and Alfred with a knowing wink. But back then Miriam had shrunk from the name—softening it to Edie—yet had borne it, like the doll's house, because she had no choice.

She lies on Edith's bed, in part to muss up the inert neatness of the duvet; gazes at the black violin case on top of the wardrobe, the clip frame leaning against the wall with a collage of photos from that Italian Interrailing trip with Rollo, the two of them smiling on the Spanish Steps. Miriam closes her eyes in order to visualize her daughter—to set her mind on her so strongly that she is all that exists—and then perhaps it will come to her: a knowledge of where Edith is and what has happened to her, as if by some supernatural telepathic intuiting. She thinks of the relatives of the missing she's seen in the past on the news, who would not give up their dogged searches even in the face of overwhelmingly poor odds. Their final argument was always the same: "If they were dead, I'd know." Or its confluence: "They're alive, I can feel it." She had always balked at the irrationality of these statements, the way people clung to a lie, yet now it makes perfect sense to her. They cannot cut the cord, not without a body. A body is what they need; otherwise these madnesses spring up like weeds, uncontrollable.

Perhaps, she thinks now, there *is* someone—a psychic or a fortune-teller—who could enter this other realm with her and tell her what has happened to her daughter. Someone with telepathic powers, who can speak with spirits or tell her the future. Not the terrible frogmen dredging rivers.

She pads down the stairs toward the sounds of Rosa emptying the dishwasher, through to the front lounge where the curtains are drawn against the rubberneckers, the lamps lit as if it were evening. Their iMac is asleep, but she only has to tap a key for it to stir into life. She daren't google "Edith Hind." She knows all manner of salacious rumor is floating about out there, just waiting to be read and wept over, vicious messages from trolls who are actually fourteen-year-olds in affluent bedrooms, their mothers grilling their fish fingers downstairs.

No, instead she types "psychic NW3" into the search field. There are fifteen serving her area, according to the Yellow Pages, which additionally provides a useful map. She clicks on solveyourmystery.com, a site advertising tarot, palmistry, and compassionate psychic readings. It is probably the word "compassionate" that secures her business.

MANON

. . .

IT TRAVELS UP HER SPINE IN A COLD BUBBLE: HORROR, CLOSE TO EXCITEMENT.

"This is a fuckup," Harriet is saying, pacing. "A massive fucking fuckup of the first fucking order."

"When did she . . . Didn't she call for assistance?" Kim says.

Time has slowed, thickening the air so that Manon can hardly breathe. There is a metallic taste in her mouth, like blood.

Davy says, "I was calling her all weekend but it went straight through to voicemail. I should've gone down there. I don't understand it—she had my number. I told her to call if she needed anything."

He is sweating, a red patch creeping up his neck.

"Apparently she rang in here late on Saturday night," Harriet says. "Call was taken by late-shift auxiliary staff, didn't know who she was, wrote a note in a book, didn't do anything about it. As with any death where there has been police contact, I am self-referring this to the IPCC, which will conduct an investigation alongside Professional Standards. Check if we did right by Helena Reed in our duty of care."

"When?" says Manon, and she is surprised her voice is audible, because she feels as if she is underwater. "When did she—"

"Sometime on Sunday. The PM will tell us more."

In the silence that has fallen over the department, Harriet tells them how it took a while for the officers to find Helena Reed. Her flat was spotless and deserted, all the cups washed up. It was, they said, how you would leave a property if you were going away, and that's what the officers thought at first.

"She's gone away, that's all, gone to stay with friends, just like she said," said the uniform.

"Hang on, in here," said his colleague.

They saw the note first, laid out on a perfectly made bed, and then they found her, hanging from the hook on the back of the bedroom door, using the cord from her dressing gown.

"Oh, sweet Jesus," Manon gasps, a palm over her mouth. It is as if Helena had tidied herself away.

The note said:

That is not what I meant at all;
That is not it, at all.

"Bloody Cambridge students," says Colin. "Why can't they leave a proper note like everyone else? You know, 'You never cared' or 'I was all alone.'"

"Someone hung her out to dry," says Davy, and Manon realizes he is staring at Stuart, his fists squeezing open and shut, almost imperceptibly, at his sides.

"We don't know that," says Stuart, trying to keep it light, but the vein standing up on his neck gives him the frozen look of a chameleon trying to blend with his rock.

"How did they know about Helena Reed and Edith?" Davy demands, and he won't take his eyes off Stuart, approaching him from across the room, and they all seem paralyzed, the bystanders. There is so much guilt by association.

"Well, it's not hard to work out, is it? Edith's best friend, with her on the night she disappears. Could've come from anyone; anyone in this building could've spoken to their wives or their girlfriends about it," Stuart is saying, stepping backward. "Or one of the students, like Jason Farrer. He wasn't exactly discreet."

"Except they don't tend to run with it unless it's come from the police, do they, Stuart?" Davy is saying, and Stuart tries to walk casually behind a desk to put some distance between himself and Davy.

"Still," Stuart says, "there's no proof that it came from us."

"I'll find out," says Harriet, "and whoever leaked it will be out on his fucking ear."

Which isn't true. Manon knows it; everyone in the room knows it, except possibly Stuart. Leaks are impossible to trace, and no journalist will ever name their source. The tabloids could have got this tidbit from anyone.

"Or she—out on *her* ear," says Stuart.

"Get him away from me," says Davy, low and quiet, watching as Stuart makes urgently for the double doors, his mobile phone already at his ear.

"Did she try you, Manon?" Harriet says. "Did you have your phone on?"

"'Course," says Manon, turning to look out at the car park but seeing nothing of the view. "I mean, reception's a bit patchy, and I was in and out . . ." Manon's face is prickled with a white heat, like an allergy.

"Hanged," she murmurs to herself. She's seen lots of victims of hanging, knows exactly what they look like—pale and bloated head to one side of the elongated neck, abrasions from the ligature. Sometimes they have fallen. Sometimes the tips of their toes touch the floor. She's surprised the hook on the back of the door held her, but Helena Reed was not a substantial person.

Manon's mind feels along the territory of the things she could have done: deployed protection to Helena's flat as soon as *Crimewatch* made mention of a female lover; had Davy escort Helena home from Newnham, right then on the Thursday, refusing to take no for an answer; monitored her work phone over the weekend, as she would normally have done, though she wasn't on call. Four days of neglect, in which

Manon did none of these things, for no other reason than she just didn't. Base, looked-for pleasures, and Manon's hunger for them at the expense of every other thought. The shame, the shame of it.

Soon, very soon, it is too much and the lines begin to shift. She tells herself there was nothing she could have done; that she couldn't possibly have known; that she wasn't on duty. Had she been on call, her phones would have been on. She tells herself defiantly, triumphantly, that her weekend was her own, this job does *not* own her, so she is not lying when she defends herself to Harriet Harper. She is telling a kind of truth.

"AWFUL," SAYS ALAN, AS THE colors darken through the double-height windows of his glorious barn. She watches the horizon, a line of fire suppressed by the blue-gray sky.

"Yes," she says. She approaches his big body, thickened by a woolen navy cardigan with leather buttons, and puts her hands on his hips, her forehead to his chest.

"Poor thing," he says, kissing the top of her head, and she doesn't know if he means her or Helena Reed.

"Worst thing is, she had nothing to do with it—just got caught up in someone else's mess."

"Mmm," he says, his chin resting on top of her head.

"She was ashamed, really ashamed," she says, and the bubble rises up into her throat and she feels she might cry out. "She just experimented, that's all, and all of a sudden it was public, and the shame of it, the guilt of it—"

"Don't cry," he says, his hand on her cheek, and she wonders if he means it as solace or whether he is actually asking her not to emote in his presence. She is descending and he is floating up, like the birds beyond his window. The landing and the flying off.

"'I am not Prince Hamlet, nor was meant to be,'" she says.

He looks at her.

"The poem. She was saying she wasn't the lead in her own play."

On the way over, she'd sat in her car in a traffic jam and she'd looked at all the little heads and shoulders in front of their steering wheels. All these people locked in their own thoughts, enmeshed in complicated lives, each of us believing we're at the center.

"Wine?" he asks, and she watches him walk away toward his gray, steely kitchen.

"Yes, please."

She sits in his sagging armchair but there is no view now that the last line of sun has been extinguished. They are together and that's a fact, and she packs her frightened, lonely feelings away. Edith, she thinks. Edith was one of those people who saw herself as the lead. Careless and selfish. Yes, there is corrosive pleasure in blaming Edith Hind. And Helena, the attendant lord, deferential, glad to be of use.

"What does it mean for the case?" he asks, bringing her an oversized goblet of red, which fills her hand. Even his *glassware* is nice.

"There'll be an inquiry. Independent Police Complaints Commission. See if we dealt with her properly, which we mostly did. But actually we didn't, of course, because she asked for assistance and the night team didn't respond, or at least not fast enough." But she stops short of the detail, both to him and to herself. "We could have stopped her" is all she whispers into her glass, taking a sip. He has gone back to the kitchen, turning his levers.

"Will you be under investigation?" he asks. "You personally, I mean."

She shrugs. "Each of us on the Hind team will be, as a matter of course. It's standard procedure when someone dies after contact with the police. Won't happen for months, though, not while the Hind investigation is still active."

He is clattering about in the kitchen. She gets up to join him there, coming up behind him and putting her hands on his hips again.

"I know you have a rule," she says, "about weeknights and everything, but can I stay? Please? Tonight? I don't want to be on my own."

"Of course," he says, and for a moment she is relieved and she hugs his back, and then she is filled with a sense of imbalance, that he is tolerating her.

He shares his steak, rare, and the brown and yellow grains of mustard trail in its wake of blood, the broccoli crisp and dark green. They consume a bottle of red, and it makes the threat of Helena Reed come nearer and Alan's unreachable quality a loneliness too far. Something about him is just beyond her grasp, though she cannot identify it in anything he says precisely. Her movements are clumsy with the wine, and with her sorrow and guilt.

She thinks they might bridge the gap in bed, that this is where the imbalance might be redressed, but he is even more distant as they come close. It is so nearly there, this almost-love, and every part of her reaches for it excessively. She towers over him, her mouth and her body, the red wine making her woolly and dark, her chest expanding so that nothing is manageable. As they finish and lie back, she bursts into tears—not demure Edwardian tears but incontinent blubbing of the kind that gives rise to rivulets of snot.

He is up on one elbow, saying, "What is it?" in a voice that, though she may be imagining it, seems on the edge of being annoyed.

"Do you feel the same way?" she says, her hand over her eyes. "Do you?"

He strokes her arm.

"I've been so fucking lonely," she says in a guttural wail, which feels good for about half a second and then feels very, very bad, because he says nothing and has lain back on his gray linen pillow, staring up at the ceiling.

MIRIAM

. . .

Twenty-three days missing and she has come so easily to this—to the door of a psychic she has found through solveyourmystery.com. Miriam Hind, née Davenport: once a scientist, always a rationalist, standing at the front door waiting for Julie, the palm reader.

Hers is a 1930s semi in suburban Hendon, its windows so clean they flash what there is of the January brightness. The doorbell a singsongy chime. When Miriam telephoned yesterday, it was in a flush of impulse—she never imagined she'd be booked in the very next day. Julie's diary was evidently not chockablock.

The remainder of yesterday, however, and the ensuing night had cooled Miriam's enthusiasm for palmistry; she'd seen how silly she was being. She is here on sufferance, because she has made the arrangement, and arrangements cannot be broken. They must be extricated from politely or adhered to (Englishness again). And yet she hadn't phoned, or texted, or sent an email to the "Contact Me" address on the website. So many ways, these days, of extricating yourself in silence.

I'll explain it's not for me, Miriam tells herself as the door opens.

"Come through," the woman says, and Miriam steps into a light, mirrored hall with new cream carpet. The heating is on luxuriantly high.

"Should I take my shoes off?" she asks, hoping the answer will be no, because bending is not as easy as it used to be.

"Please," she says. "I'll wait for you in the lounge."

Her manner, the ash-blond highlights, the taupe cardigan with sequins glinting, has all the suburban fastidiousness of a beauty therapist. Miriam follows her through to a lounge with broad doors giving out to a lawn. It smells of new carpet in here also, and there is a capacious cream leather armchair for Miriam to sink into. Communing with the spirit world is not a bad way to make a living, it would seem, even with an appointments diary as spacious as Julie's.

"So," she says.

"So," says Miriam, reserve bristling.

"I'm sensing great sadness, great pain," Julie says, her head tilted. "I'm seeing everything out of alignment."

Miriam nods. It is preposterous that she is here. She must find an appropriate hiatus in which to make her excuses. What would Ian think?

"I'm feeling that you have lost hope, lost your way in this world. The pain is too much. You are confused and unhappy."

Oh, spare me, Miriam thinks.

"You want to know what lies ahead. How it will all turn out. You want an end to the uncertainty—the miasma, as I like to call it. I can do tarot, palm, or aura; which would you prefer?"

"I don't know."

"A general reading, perhaps. You can pay with a check. I don't take cards. Or you could set up a direct debit. I recommend this to my clients—there is a reduction for three visits or more."

"Shall I?" Miriam asks, reaching for her handbag. "Now?"

She nods. Miriam writes a check, a flat fee of eighty pounds for a one-off reading. No way is she falling for that direct-debit baloney.

"May I?" Julie says, taking Miriam's hand slowly in hers, as if it were a priceless ornament, and rotating it palm-up. Miriam notices her burgundy manicure, like blood-dipped talons. "I am seeing someone you love very deeply. Someone lost to you . . ."

You are reading my age, Miriam thinks. *I am of an age for grief.*

"A daughter, a beloved daughter, whose safety is in jeopardy." *You've read the tabloids. You've seen me on the news.*

"You want to know what has happened to your daughter," she says, looking Miriam in the eye, and Miriam's heart begins to race. They both feel her hand quiver.

"Yes," says Miriam.

"You love your daughter and you are in great pain," she says. "You are tormented by thoughts of what might have happened to her. You are in an agony of uncertainty. You cannot grieve, but you dare not hope."

"Yes," says Miriam, and it comes out in a gasp, dirty with need. "Please, I . . ." Miriam is now holding the woman's hand, squeezing it.

"Your daughter is alive," she says.

Miriam stares at her.

"Your daughter is alive," she says again in an exhalation, as if she too is in pain, has taken Miriam's pain into herself.

"When will she come back?" Miriam asks. "Has she been taken?"

Julie closes her eyes, stroking and holding Miriam's hand between the two of hers. She breathes in through her nose, her eyes closed. She shakes her head.

"It's gone," she says. "Sometimes it's too powerful. Sometimes it cannot be held."

"When will you get it back?"

"You will need to come again."

DAVY

. . .

HE KNOWS HE'S GOT IT WRONG AS HE PROFFERS THE CUP TO HER, AND HE doesn't care. Manon can suck it up for once. She looks awful too, perhaps as bad as him—puffy-faced, furtive.

"What's this, Davy? I don't take it black."

"Have you listened to yourself?" he says. *Come on, if you think you're hard enough.*

"All right," she says. "Jeez, who shat in your handbag?"

He woke at 5:30 A.M., remembering abruptly, as if cut from sleep by the hard steel of his guilt. He looked at Chloe, sleeping next to him. Her hair, sticky with the various products she put on it, lay across her head like a bandage. She's been talking about "taking things to the next level" and he finds it bewildering, because even a couple of weeks ago he'd have been all for it, but now . . . How little he tells her of the fresh torments in his mind. Yet his distance seems only to fuel her enthusiasm, and he wonders idly if this is the secret about women that other men have known all along and that he's been slow to grasp. Perhaps it's what made a toerag like Stuart Leach such a success with the ladies. Stuart seems to be able to shag Marie from Accounts and then barely acknowledge her in the office.

Davy tries Ryan's social worker, Reeva Dell, again. She always sounds exhausted, a slow monotonous crawl to her voice. But, then, social services was full of depressed people.

"His mum moved, I told you—no forwarding address," says Reeva.

"Right, but she's still under the surname Wade?" he says, thrumming in his mind through the police databases he could try.

"No, no, hang on, she married someone. D'you want the name?"

"Please."

"Hold on."

Shuffling papers, clacking on a keyboard. No budget for Vivaldi. Davy wonders what manner of sociopath Ryan's mum's hooked her wagon to this time.

"Right, yes, she's going under the name Jones."

"Jones? You're kidding me."

"Why would I be kidding you, DC Walker?"

How am I supposed to trace a Jones? he thinks. And he feels like crying, or pulling the phone from its socket and a chunk of the plaster from the wall too.

"Has Ryan taken on the Jones name? Has the new local authority been notified that he was on the 'at risk' register?"

"Like I said, we don't know where they've gone. It's not like she asked our permission. The boy was returned to her, don't forget."

"Yeah, but only because . . ." Davy trails off. It's pointless hurling rocks at Reeva Dell.

"I'm sorry I can't help," she says.

"No, no, it's fine," he says.

Harriet has come to the desk he and Manon are sharing, resting her knuckles on its surface, her head low.

"Helena Reed's call log," says Harriet in a murmur so that only Manon and Davy can hear. "She tried to call you, Manon, three times."

Davy looks at Manon, but she is rummaging in her bag for her phone as if its physical presence will explain this.

"I wasn't on call," Manon says, looking up sharply at Harriet. "I have the right to turn my phone off at the weekend, to have a life. You might want to be married to this job, Harriet, but I don't. Anyway, I told you, the signal can be a bit dodgy in my flat; on and off, y'know?"

"I know you weren't on call, and this isn't part of any official investigation," says Harriet. "I'm just asking you. You know, what the *fuck,* Manon?"

"That's right, it's my fault," says Manon in a swell of tears, and Davy and Harriet watch her make for the double doors, almost at a run, and slap through them like a swimmer into the surf.

"Graham Garfield," Harriet says, louder now, so the department can hear. "What have our background checks given us?"

"One student claims he made unwanted advances, and others say he had a reputation for trying it on," says Kim. "Sounds like more of a pest than a predator. Y'know, an opportunist—he tried it on, got knocked back a few times, but every now and then he got lucky."

"Mrs. Garfield know?" says Harriet.

"Doesn't look like it."

"When we were round there she was wavering about his alibi," Davy says. "Having first said she was with him at home after he came back from the Crown, she subsequently told us she only vaguely heard his key in the door as she fell asleep."

The dank interior of the Lord Protector: sticky wooden floorboards, tinny tunes from fruit machines. Davy rotates his glass at their corner table and tries to tell Chloe what's going on with him.

He's been attempting to explain about work, how much it's a part of how he sees himself. He's trying to describe their duty of care to Helena Reed and how they'd failed her, and how he couldn't get it off his mind. They'd ticked the boxes they were supposed to tick, so why does he feel so bad?

Some part of him is taking umbrage already at the criticism that's heaped on them as officers—always the question of what they could have done better, faster, with immaculate paperwork and utmost sensitivity, what they should learn from what they've got wrong. That person on the night team, DC Monique Moynihan, will probably lose her job, and maybe that's right. But all the while it feels like a war they're fighting, without enough resources. They were only doing their job.

He's trying to form this into words to her; he needs her to understand him at this most crucial time. But when he looks up, he sees that familiar thing Chloe does with her face, allowing all her muscles to go slack in the cheeks so it's like her face is dripping, her eyes stony, like she so often made them—distant and looking over his shoulder.

Instead of chivvying her out of it, he says, "What's the matter now?"

She shrugs. "Nothing," she says. "I'm fine."

"No, you're not; you're in a huff again. What is it this time?"

She seems wrong-footed by his directness, but she maintains the hangdog slack cheeks. *The cheeks of doom,* he thinks. Bitter mouth.

"I just think it's weird, you caring so much for a dead girl. A *lesbian* dead girl," she says.

"Tell me you're not serious," he says.

Chloe shrugs again. "Your mind's always on other things: *poor Helena Reed, poor Ryan, isn't Manon the genius?* You're never here, in the moment."

"Christ, Chloe, have you ever wondered why? Have you ever thought what the moment might feel like for me?" He is rising out of his chair now, surprising himself. "Being here in the moment with you is like ... it's like being sucked down into quicksand. It's like drowning." He feels like ten-year-old Davy, pulling open the bedroom curtains with gusto, his mother in the bed, never getting up, one day to the next. "You make me suffocate, Chloe," he says, and he's letting her have it—both barrels. "You make me suffocate in the misery of it."

And he finds himself grabbing his coat off the back of the chair and walking out, and even as he's walking, he knows this is one sulk he'll never be able to rectify.

MANON

• • •

IS IT OVER SO SOON, AFTER HER STUPID OUTBURST IN BED? HAS SHE scared him off? He'd communicated with her from the very surface of himself in the morning, and she had the feeling he was annoyed that she was cluttering up his daily routine: the showering with an astringent body wash (mint—she tried it and it made her privates sting with unnatural cold), the coffee, the dark neatness of his suit. If only she could undo it—maintain her reserve—she might be transformed in his mind into the perfect lover he almost had. Un-have-able Manon. She aches for Alan Prenderghast.

"Dad?" she says, propping herself up on her pillows, the phone to her ear.

"Hello, lovely," he whispers. She hears him heaving in the bed, a groan in the background, and Una's voice saying, "What sort of time d'you call this?"

Manon looks at her watch. It is quarter to eleven.

"Hold on," he says. "I'll take it in the study."

She hears shuffling and the receiver goes down. *Click*. And then he picks up and his voice is expansive at last. "So, my darling girl, what's the news?"

"She pissed off again?"

"No, Manon, don't do that. Una was just dropping off, that's all. Don't . . . How's things? How's work?"

"Things are all right," she says sadly.

"Is the case getting you down? I saw on the news, that poor Reed girl. Stanton's taking a lot of heat."

He is always so very interested, the police his vicarious pleasure. She thinks to tell him the truth about Helena Reed, if only she could grasp where the truth begins and ends, how far her guilt seeps into the corners of it, because he would understand, would believe in her better self. He would tell her it wasn't her fault while acknowledging that some of it perhaps was. They would be silent on the phone, their receivers pressed to their ears, and it would be honest.

"Actually, Dad, I've met someone."

"Really?" he says, and his voice is genuinely taken aback. *Christ,* she thinks, *I'm not that bad.*

"So, go on," he says.

"His name's Alan. Alan Prenderghast. He's a systems analyst."

"A systems analyst?" he says, in the same voice he used to say, "It's a hedgehog, is it?" when she showed him her pictures from primary school. "What's a systems analyst?"

"I don't really know. He lives just outside Ely."

She could have added, "Drives a Ford," as if she is saying, "Darcy, yes, Pemberley."

"And you like him?" asks her father, sounding incredulous.

"Not *that* hard to believe, is it?"

"No, no, I'm sure he's very nice," he says.

Can't he hear the wonder of Alan Prenderghast, her systems analyst from just outside Ely? With the nice glassware? And Nana the dog? Can't he see how huge this is?

They are silent.

"When can I meet him, then?" he says eventually.

"When you grow some balls and come down to visit," she says, without malice aforethought, as Davy would have put it.

She pictures her father in his crumpled pajamas, cupping the phone and casting furtive glances at the study door, surrounded by tartan with stag heads poking out from the walls like surprised intruders, as if he's living some Highland fling as envisaged by Disney, except Una Simmons has the key to this particular hunting lodge. Una Simmons, their very own Macbeth of Moray, who finds ways in which his daughters—well, *this* daughter—cannot fit into their busy schedule, reasons why there isn't room for them to stay at Christmas.

"Spoken to Ellie?" he says at last, a shot back across her bows.

"No, Dad, I haven't spoken to Ellie. Better go now; it's late. You hop back into bed with Mein Führer." And she puts the phone down.

THE FEELING IN THEIR HOUSE had been that Margaret Thatcher was to blame, not just for record unemployment ("fifteen percent of the workforce," her father said, shaking his head, always behind a newspaper), but for the miners, of course, and for Murdoch breaking the print unions (a soreness close to her father's heart), and also, in some nebulous way, for what had happened in the Bradshaw family. It was all bad, Thatcher and motherlessness. Her father's sadness, in abeyance while her mother's forceful nature lit and burned the house, became their whole microclimate after she died. It was global—despair about themselves and the world. He sighed deeply at the news; he sighed at *The Guardian* and switched to the newly launched *Independent* ("It is, *are you?*") but tutted even at that; he sighed at old photographs.

Ellie and Manon listened to Kate Bush in their bedroom—well, Peter Gabriel and Kate Bush, to be precise ("Don't Give Up")—and cried copiously.

The situation continued for a good five years, during which he said he was "raising the girls," though he seemed mostly to be behind a newspaper, harrumphing. He switched back to *The Guardian* in a further state of disillusionment and became merely grumpy, muttering about the redesign of its masthead (dual font ITC Garamond Italic next to Helvetica Black! What were they *thinking?*). This seemed an improvement. He went back to writing at the *Fenland Citizen,* where he was editor (the staff having managed quite well during his Grief-Stricken Years)—book and film reviews mostly, or the odd travel piece when it was a one-nighter to Dublin or some such and the girls could be left alone.

Come 1997, their father began taking an interest in himself. He bought his first new items of clothing since the seventies—a polo shirt and some chinos. He had a haircut, without being told. He began to whistle in the bathroom, to smile and crack jokes. The root of all this did not emerge for many months and turned out not to be an organic process of healing but a woman called Una Simmons, who worked with him on the paper and wrote a household-advice column called "Simmons Solves." On the night of the general election, they traveled together to the printing presses in High Wycombe, ostensibly to make sure the correct front page went off stone, and the rest, as they say, was a Labor landslide. Things could only get better, so the song went, and they certainly did—for Manon's father, at least. And that was more or less when Manon lost him.

She puts the phone on the floor, plumps her pillow, and reaches across for the dial on the radio.

MIRIAM

. . .

"NO NEED TO CLEAN MY STUDY, CAN YOU TELL ROSA? IT'S GOT ALL MY campaign stuff—paperwork, which I don't want shuffled about," Ian says.

"Yes, of course. Where are you going?" asks Miriam. She is arranging lilies in a vase—great brutes from the Tesco Express around the corner. She doesn't even like them, their dull dark leaves and vulgar blooms, but something about buying them spoke of a reconnect with the land of the living, thanks to Julie from Hendon. Anyway, they brought scent to a winter house.

"For a quick run," he says. "You seem brighter." He is tying the laces on his trainers, toe on the cream upholstered kitchen chair.

"Can you get your foot off that?" she says.

"Yes, sorry."

She hasn't told him about Julie, of course. Julie would be taken as

further evidence of her madness. But with a single visit, Julie has made
things bearable.

"I was thinking of going back to the practice, actually," she says,
plumping the stems in a bid to make them fall about naturally in the
vase, but they are rigid as scaffolding.

"Good idea. Would do you good to be out and about. Occupy
your mind."

"Stop me thinking about Edith, you mean?"

"Thinking about her doesn't find her."

"Anyway, I haven't decided yet," she says.

Her partner at the GP practice, Raj, had called just after Christmas—
but only to tell her to take as long as she needed, that he had got in a
locum, and that if there was anything to sign (the paperwork when you
became a fundholder was beyond belief) he'd drop it round. Twenty-
four days missing; three and a half weeks of life suspended, sleepless and
confined. Like being underwater, it was quiet and engulfing, and there
was a strong desire to stay submerged rather than push up into the
brash world where people would ask how she is, how *things* are. Why
can't she stay home, arrange the house, remain loyal to Edith in her
mind, reinforced in that connection by Julie? Why wasn't that all right?

"Right," he says, pushing his keys into a shallow pocket in his jog-
gers and zipping it shut. "Won't be long."

An hour later, she has settled at her desk to tackle some neglected
household admin: a quote for contents insurance, check for the milk-
man, a meter reading. She realizes she needs a stamp and walks through
to Ian's study. He keeps a stash in the central desk drawer, among paper
clips and envelopes and those plastic label holders that clip on to hanging files. They clatter now under her patting hand. The drawer is sticky
and won't pull out fully. She shuffles and lifts at the front but can't see
any little books of stamps, so she pats her hand farther back, among the
elastic bands and stationery dust. Pens, a flashlight, her finger pricked
by a noticeboard pin; then something solid and square, which she can't
identify from memory. She brings it out. It is a Nokia. Old and chunky.
A world away from the smartphones everyone has nowadays. Grubby
about the edges of the screen. On the back are glittery pirate stickers:
skull and crossbones, a boat. A child's phone. Why would he—

She runs her thumb over the edges of the stickers and they make a flicking sound, pleasingly stiff against the pad of her thumb. She turns it over in her hand again. It's dead, of course, the battery run down. He must have found it on the ground somewhere.

She returns the phone to the back of the drawer, hearing as she does so Ian's key in the front door. She pushes at the drawer to close it but it judders and sticks, and as she pushes again, he is at the doorway, saying, "What are you looking for?"

"I just wanted a stamp," she says, unsure why she feels nervous. "Doesn't matter."

He comes between her and the desk and forcibly pushes the central drawer shut, then opens the drawer beside it and offers her a book of stamps.

"Here," he says.

MANON

• • •

SHE SMILES, CLOSING THE FRONT DOOR, AND PUTS HER FACE UP TO THE unseasonal January warmth: sharp, blinding sun, the sky too bright to look at. The air is steely-fresh in her lungs, and the river sparkles like diamonds. She wonders how he'll surprise her for Valentine's Day. Flowers? A table at a secluded restaurant? *A trip to Paris?* How quickly being alone vanishes, a country seen from your departing plane—small and far below. Even a short time makes it a distant place, as if the body is quick to relish the enveloping heat in the new territory—*love*— forgetting it is new. One week or one month is enough to make a return unthinkable.

She sinks down into the driver's seat, flipping the visor against the unruly sun, rummages in her handbag for her sunglasses, then starts the car. Has Alan noticed the pounds she must have gained with all their Sunday fry-ups and Friday-night curries? Has it put him off, the way contentment is causing her boundaries to blur? The more she expresses, it seems, the less he does, and sometimes she wishes they could return to the cinema steps, when she was demure and he was leaning in. He doesn't like to text or email. Those hearty messages are all from her, sent in a rush of feeling that doesn't need reciprocity, except that when she receives no reply she notices a darkening of her inner world. An image has stored itself in her mind: that skein of birds, landing and flying off on the bank opposite his barn, one touching down as another lifts up, as if they are set in opposition.

She slows at the traffic lights, marvels at the sun's glare off bonnets and wing mirrors, and smiles again, remembering her Sunday: head in his lap; the crinkle of the newspaper; her sleepy satisfaction as she read her book, saying, "Here's a good word—'agog.'"

"Mmm," he said, "so is 'bosom,'" giving hers a squeeze, and then they were at it again.

They are two. It'll come. He is private; he has an English reserve, which anyone would find charming. He doesn't like to text, is all.

A cloud passes overhead, its dark bulk ominous, and she lifts her sunglasses up onto her head. Still winter after all.

The lights change and she presses her foot down, the car slow to respond. He maintains his Law of Weeknights: a full eight hours, padded silk lavender eye mask on. No sleep-filled rocking, not on a Tuesday. He has got his shit in a pile, his ducks in a row. *Prim Prenderghast for Prime Minister!* He is real and they are together; and, yes, the birds do fly off, but they land also, and she just needs to give it time.

It was like she said to Bri when forced to help her move furniture around her mother's soon-to-be-rented-out bungalow:

"Loads of people like to take things slow, don't they? It's a normal part of—"

"Over there, by the wall," Bryony had huffed, with insufficient interest, Manon felt.

"It doesn't mean he's not into it. Hell, I've been in loads of situations where I've felt pressure, and it makes you back off, you know? It's just a human reaction." She was stumbling backward, the soft pads of her fingers burning under the weight of Bryony's mum's Parker Knoll. "So the most important thing I can do—"

"Coffee table now," said Bryony.

"—is stay calm and not put any pressure on him. Y'know, slowly, slowly, catchee monkey."

It is so nearly there, this almost-love, if she could only stop herself from being too much. Every part of her reaches for him, un-have-able Alan. And as she lands, he flies off.

In the wanting, in the yearning, which is so opposite to all the reluctant dates and ambivalent sex and the not-quite-liking anyone, she feels she has become more fully Manon, an ocean of Manon washing over him. Enough for both of them. She could live in the wanting. What could be more joyful than being certain of your feelings? An end to all those stop-start relationships. She feels sorry now for all those poor women out there compromising or fearful of commitment, wondering whether it would work out or if there might be someone better. She'd been like that for seven long years with the boy from university, and when they'd split up she'd had no idea if it was the right thing, but anyway, all that's behind her now.

All is perfection in the new Alan era, and everything—his big shoes, his flappy coat, his Fungus the Bogeyman head adorned with silk and lavender eye mask, his Weeknight Rules—has a rightness to it. What a wonderful father he'll make, train sets scattered across his beautiful barn. He is so *funny*. Sometimes, when he makes a joke, she laughs so hard she does a little wee, although she can't think of a funny thing he's said exactly, not a precise example.

She pulls up, nose of the car pushing at the underside of a bush, turns the key, and all is quiet. She hauls her bag onto her knees as the car ticks, feeling for her phone, the private one, just in case his love has emerged in text form, but the screen is unchanged. So she reaches out to him, as per, setting her fingers typing:

Gawd, only Tues + am already knackered. Roll on takeaway night, angel cakes. Mx

DAVY

· · ·

HE TAKES A SIP OF STEWED COFFEE AND WATCHES OUT OF THE THIRD-floor window, a hand in his trouser pocket, jangling his keys. He can see Manon slam her car door ~~and then~~ stop, holding her face to the bright sun, basking in it with her eyes closed. As if she is sodding holy.

No more crying in the car park; no more laying her forehead on the steering wheel; no more snatching the lattes from his hand or wiping away smears of mascara. These days, it is Davy who grows impatient with the traffic, as if congestion were further evidence of all that's wrong in the world. His planet's out of alignment. A girl has been missing for a month; another is dead. They haven't done their job, thinks Davy, and everything is at odds.

Manon has become ... breezy. Light. Polite to colleagues, interested in their adorable child-rearing anecdotes, when she used to make silent vomiting motions behind their backs.

"Aw, what did the twins do on the weekend, Nigel? Run you ragged, did they?"

It annoys Davy beyond measure, the bounce in her step.

They've been watching Tony Wright this past week but he hasn't put a foot wrong. The PM on Taylor Dent has come in but tells them nothing: "Whether death occurred before or after the body was immersed into water is impossible to say. Injuries consistent with river damage. Toxicology inconclusive."

The background checks on Garfield, as well as some uncomfortable questioning of the professor about his Facebook usage, were insufficient grounds for his arrest. No, it was all going nowhere. Garfield had shifted uneasily in interview but not, Davy thought, out of shame, his expression saying: *I am a man. I accept my peccadilloes; why can't you?*

The press have started to itch their beards in longer think pieces, analyzing the parameters of the investigation. The police have looked too closely at her immediate circle is the latest offering from the *Mirror*. Officers have not given sufficient thought to the possibility of a stranger, driving out of the night. A random attack.

How people love to criticize, Davy thinks, shaking his head. *It's never a stranger. Well, almost never.*

And all the while, Manon is harping on about which new restaurants to try. "I'm ardent," she told him yesterday, sitting in the car with brown paper bags on their laps from the fast-food place.

They were on a surveillance job—drugs and prostitution. His lap was warm, his mouth filled with a synthetic coating of trans fats and salt. He murmured, hiding his irritation with a full mouth.

"If there's two people, I'm always the one who's more keen."

He nodded, biting further into his cheeseburger.

"Except when I'm not," she said. "Mostly, I don't like people. And then I'm not ardent at all."

"Riveting," muttered Davy, staring ahead.

"What I mean is, it takes me ages to find someone I think is really great and then, well, sometimes I knock them over with enthusiasm."

"Like a St. Bernard."

"Bit like that, yes."

"Shall we have another cheeseburger?"

She'd nodded, chewing. "Only 99p."

"I don't think the price is the issue, is it?" said Davy.

"Get them in."

He ought to be happy for her but he isn't, and Davy is getting used to his meaner thoughts being in the ascendance. He wonders if he should apply for a transfer—move far away and start over, away from the feelings that are making the minutes and the seconds lugubrious—but he has this new connection with Stanton, like the fragile push of a shoot from a seed, and he can't pretend he hasn't harbored hopes for what it might do for his career.

Time itself has become heavy, the consistency of treacle, and yet he is sure time, for Manon, has sped up in the past fortnight. She talks about Nana as if it's *her* dog. "Nana's shedding," she says tolerantly, picking the hairs off her skirt. He pictures that stoic dog, ears like furry sails flapping at the sides of her head, and the image passes smoothly on to Chloe and those plates of straightened hair.

He misses her. He misses her, he misses her, he misses her. Some nights he cries so much his pillow's too damp to lie on. Seven miserable lonely days of missing someone he never should have been with in the first place, yet wanting her back even so. He wonders if he could overlook her lack of human sympathy and generalized air of bitterness, just so he could have the feeling of being together again. Perhaps he misses the chap he was before Helena Reed died, cheerfully intending to marry Chloe, his very own poisoned chalice. Simultaneously, like some sick, celestial seesaw, Manon's personal happiness has supplanted his own, and every day he is faced with a vision of love's smug young dream, written all over her just-had-a-shag face.

He has raked a small but pleasing harvest of earwax under a nail and he rolls it now, between thumb and forefinger, turning from the window. He looks up to see Manon come in through the double doors. She smiles at him across the room and mimes lifting a cup to her lips, mouthing, "Coffee?" at him.

"Can I have your attention, please?" says Stanton, with his ever-present files under his arm. He smiles as Davy comes near.

"Everything all right?" he says warmly, to which Davy says, "Yes, boss."

"Right, just a quick word, everyone. DI Harriet Harper is taking a leave of absence due to personal circumstances. Any issues arising, come to me or DS Manon . . ." He scans the room, then finds her. "Ah, there you are, Bradshaw."

Elsie must have died, thinks Davy. *Poor Harriet. She'll be heartbroken.*

"You two can take it from here, can't you?" Stanton says to Davy and Manon, with a hand on Davy's shoulder.

It had begun at Helena Reed's funeral on Friday. Davy stood beneath a black umbrella as the rain streamed in a wall around his personal octagon, all the mourners spattered in silver droplets, the puddles splashing at their patent pumps and polished brogues.

Manon made some excuse as to why she couldn't attend. There was a smattering of students and members of the faculty; Dr. Young, looking ashen (Davy recognized him from his police interview). Will Carter attended in an impeccable suit, which flashed through the open flaps of his black raincoat. Davy had come to admire Will Carter. He carried himself with utmost decorum; didn't overemote at the front of the church but sat with elegant sympathy, paying his respects. He looked even more handsome in mourning clothes, especially the waistcoat element, which Davy never would have thought of himself. And his socks—even his socks, visible when he crossed his legs—were a perfect shade of blue, matching his shirt and tie.

Ian and Miriam Hind attended, which surprised Davy because press innuendo surrounding Helena was still swirling, as if her suicide were part confession.

EDITH HIND LOVER FOUND DEAD

WHY DID EDITH'S GIRL END IT ALL?

Lady Hind wore a wide-brimmed hat, which forced her neighbors to duck and swerve while she remained serene. Her neckline sparkled with a collar of black stones. The Hinds cried more than was fitting for a friend of their daughter's, and Davy could see they were in some way enacting a dress rehearsal for their own worst fears. Besides, there was no way of stopping your mind from wandering at a funeral, traveling into all sorts of dark imaginings about your nearest and dearest and how they might die and how you might feel. They were riveting like that.

Helena's own parents were not present, her father having suffered a stroke during the press furor over his daughter's sexuality; her mother was described by the priest as "incapacitated." "Our thoughts are with them," he said, "and it falls to us to mourn on their behalf a beloved daughter, friend, and student."

As the congregation filed out, Davy remained seated in his pew, looking forward at the large photograph of Helena on an easel next to her coffin. He was staring at his guilt and at his failure to prevent something so wantonly destructive. And as he stared, he felt a body heave down next to him. Stanton's breathing was strained, as if the fat were squeezing the very breath out of him like a fist. They sat together, eyes trained on Helena's image—her expression smiling and innocent of what lay ahead—and there was intimacy in that pew. The constable and the chief superintendent. Then Stanton said, "Pint?" and Davy accepted the invitation, in part because, without Chloe, he had nowhere to be on a Friday night. He thought it would be one long arse ache, that pint with the boss, but as they sat at the small round table, he found he was too tired for toadying, so he looked Stanton in the eye and told him how rotten he felt about Helena Reed and how responsible. Stanton licked the foam off his upper lip and said, "If you can keep those feelings, Davy lad—and let me tell you, every minute in the police will chip away at them—but if you can hold on to those human feelings, you might just make a good copper."

Wednesday

MIRIAM
. . .

"Mum?"

It is Rollo's voice calling and she follows it into the lounge, where the curtains are perpetually drawn.

"Look at this," he says. He stands in front of the television, which is blaring the excessively jaunty theme tune to *This Morning*. The remote in his hand is still lolling at the screen. The television is never on during the day, except the odd black-and-white afternoon film when Miriam is particularly exhausted.

"Why am I watching this?" she asks.

"Just wait and see."

The set is a cacophony of exposed brick, floral wallpaper, and primary-colored soft furnishings, all yelling "CHEERFUL!" at a bruising volume.

"Here we go," says Rollo.

The presenters—a blond woman who resembles Bambi and a

white-haired, curiously ageless man—have lowered their voices to denote "tragedy item."

"A month ago, twenty-four-year-old Edith Hind went missing from her home in Huntingdon. The police still don't know what's happened to her, but since then a series of lurid revelations relating to her private life have appeared in the press. Indeed, last week, the exposure led to her best friend, Helena Reed, tragically taking her own life. Today, exclusively on *This Morning,* we have Edith's boyfriend here to talk about the girl he loves and to separate the facts from the fiction."

"That's Holly Willoughbooby," says Rollo.

"That can't be her real name," says Miriam.

"Shhhhh," says Rollo.

Holly's huge doe eyes are looking up from beneath a voluminous sweep of yellow hair. Her voice is laden with condolence, while along the bottom of the screen, Miriam notices, a ticker reveals that the next item is on flattering trousers, followed by a discussion on toddlers who bite. Something about the lighting on the show makes its world seem thin and breakable.

"You were with Edith for two happy years and presumably you had no inkling of what lay ahead. You must be worried sick about her," says the ageless man, whose bronzed skin and white hair make him seem like a photographic negative.

Will Carter smiles. He is resplendent in a slate-blue open-neck shirt, an exact match for his eyes, which, studio lit and in high definition, sparkle onscreen.

Ah yes, thinks Miriam, *of course.*

"I'm worried and I miss her like crazy," he says, "but it's also been devastating to see so many lies and innuendoes in the tabloids. It's just compounded all our distress."

"You mean yours and her parents—Sir Ian and Lady Hind," says the ageless man.

"That's Phil," Rollo says to Miriam.

"Has TV reversed the passage of time?" asks Miriam.

"It has for Phillip Schofield," says Rollo.

"I also need to set the record straight about Helena, who was our dear friend and who never did anything—never *would* have done anything—to hurt anyone. The lies about her have been astounding, with devastating consequences."

"What a heartthrob," says Rollo.

"The start of his TV career," says Miriam. They are standing in front of the television in the pretense they are not stopping, but they both are mesmerized, like babies in front of their first cartoon.

"Actually, I could see him presenting *The One Show,* or one of those nature programs like *Countryfile,* that sort of thing," says Rollo.

"Yes, but he's so boring," says Miriam. "Look, even Holly's suppressing a yawn—did you see that? Her mouth went all tight."

Rollo is looking at his mother. "I thought it was The Tedium That Dare Not Speak Its Name."

"I can admit it now."

"Well, I admire him for going out to bat for Edith and Helena."

"Darling Rollo," says Miriam, hugging him, then looking at her watch over his broad shoulder. "Oh gosh, I'm late for Julie."

"Need your fix," says Rollo, and she can hear the disapproval in his voice as she leaves the room in search of her handbag.

MANON

. . .

She strides the white expanse of King's Cross, dancing a weave through the frowning throng with their bags and newspapers, paper cups of coffee too hot to sip, and every face, almost without exception, fixed downward on a tiny screen in hand.

Manon takes out her own phone and finds Harriet's number. She will never avoid a person who has been bereaved, never put her own embarrassment before their loss, because she's been on the receiving end, has seen people cross the street to sidestep the conversation when her mother died. And yet she fears Harriet's state of mind.

She strides over the newly laid honey pavements, inset with solar lights, to St. Pancras to board the Thameslink to Cricklewood, the phone pressed to her ear.

"Turns out I'm rich," Harriet says. "Elsie had twenty grand's worth of granny bonds and she's left it all to me."

"That's something," says Manon. "How are you holding up?"

"Oh, you know."

"Mmm."

"Where are you?" asks Harriet.

"London. I've come to check on Fly."

"Good for you."

"When are you coming back?"

"Oh, I dunno. There's a lot of clearing out to do, y'know—her stuff, things to organize. Monday, probably."

In body, perhaps, but not in spirit. Manon knows what lies beneath, how people can seem normal and yet grief swirls about like an unseen tide working against the currents of life, the mourner wrong-footed by its undertow. The bereaved should wear signs, she thinks, saying GRIEF IN PROGRESS—for at least a couple of years.

The wind roughs her up on the walk down Cricklewood Lane to the Broadway, making the tops of the trees sway, noisy as high surf. She is meeting Fly at the Brazilian café, where she'll settle her bill with the owner, Neuza Lima.

She steps in, relieved to be out of the tumble of the weather, her hair falling at last.

"Hello, Neuza," she says.

"*Olá,*" she says, kissing Manon on each cheek.

"How's it been with Fly?"

"He is lovely, lovely boy. Gentle boy."

Fly has pushed the door open, sniffing in that way he has, and Manon smiles broadly at him, though he is reserved—a wan hello and then he embraces Neuza, and Manon is surprised to feel put out.

"*Olá,*" he says to Neuza.

"*Olá, meu querido,*" says Neuza, hugging him to her broad bosom. "*Bem-vindo,* both of you! Take a seat—nice one in the window. I bring you, what? Coffee? Eggs?"

The window is full of the buses rumbling up and down Cricklewood Broadway and sharp shadows in confusion with the gleam of the glass.

"How's things?" asks Manon.

He looks well. Neuza's food has filled out his cheeks and made his eyes shine, yet they are full of sadness still.

"Mum's real sick," he says. "Can't get out of bed, can't keep anything down. Doctors say it won't be long."

"Oh, Fly."

"She been offered a place in a hospice in Hampstead—Marie Curie place—when the pain gets too much, when I can't . . ."

"Do you know what you'll do when that happens?"

"I'll need to stay with someone. Social worker says it has to be someone good, a good person, a grown-up—otherwise they put me in care."

He looks into Manon's face, waiting. The room is filled with the sound of sputtering milk and Portuguese TV, and Manon turns to look for Neuza, wondering where her coffee has got to.

"Have you got a friend you could stay with—someone from school, maybe?"

"Thought you was my friend," he says. She is grateful for the approach of her latte and his juice.

"I live in Huntingdon, Fly. It's really important you stay at your school, isn't it?"

"*Obrigado,*" he says to Neuza.

"*O prazer é meu,*" she says, stroking his close-cropped hair.

Manon takes Neuza to one side and asks if she might look in on Maureen Dent, send someone in to clean the flat.

"My niece, she do it. Eight pound for hour."

"Fine," says Manon, frowning, wondering how long she can bankroll the Dent family. "Add it to my bill. Could he stay with you when . . . y'know, at the end?"

Neuza makes a mournful grimace, as if she's smelled something unappetizing. "Is no possible. Is lovely boy but my hasband, he no take in Fly. He not such a good man."

"OK, right, well, I'll think of something. For now we'll keep going with the food tab and the cleaning and looking in on them, OK?"

"*Sem problemas,*" Neuza says, and from her warm expression, Manon understands this to mean "No problem."

AT HOME AGAIN IN THE evening, in bed, she listens to the shouts of revelers across the river. A lorry rumbles down some arterial route, and its vibrations make the lightbulb rattle in its metal shade beside her head like the buzz of an insect. The phone lies on her stomach. She is worrying about Fly. She dials Alan's number.

"Hello," he says.

"Are you in bed?" she asks.

"I sure am. How was your day?"

"I went to visit Fly Dent in London. He ... he's only ten. His mum's not got long."

"Poor boy," says Alan.

"He wants to stay with me, once she goes into a hospice. He's frightened of being taken into care and I don't blame him. Don't think care would do him any good, to be honest."

"Doesn't he need to stay near to his school? Thought you said he was doing well."

"Well, yes, but he needs to be safe."

In the silence, she realizes she wants Alan to persuade her—to do the right thing, to cast practicalities aside and take Fly in, out of goodness, unalloyed. It matters where his compass lies, to which side of hers.

"It's not like I don't have the resources to look after him," she is saying, without conviction. "I've got a job, a flat. I've got money."

"It'd be a lot of disruption, for both of you," says Alan. "It's not as if he's your responsibility—not really. This is what the state is for."

"I s'pose," she says. "But don't you have to take people on sometimes? Don't you have to step up?"

"In theory," he says.

Perhaps, she thinks, grasping for hope, he is protecting their own trajectory—a chance, not to be scuppered by a ten-year-old lodger. Talk about passion killer. He doesn't want to share her (maybe).

"I went out with someone with a son once," he says. "Didn't last long."

"That probably wasn't the son's fault," she says, before she's had time to think. She wants to divert the conversation away from this dark turn. "See, that's the good thing about Internet dating—you can specify 'no kids.'"

"You've done Internet dating?"

"Hasn't everyone?"

"Seems a bit desperate," he says.

I am desperate, she thinks. *Or I was. Why lie?*

"Didn't you want to meet someone?" she asks him.

"Just rather do it naturally," he says.

"What's natural? Getting smashed and falling on someone in a bar?"

"No, what's natural is being questioned by the gorgeous Officer Dibble about a dead body," he says, sounding conciliatory.

She smiles into the warmer silence.

Then he says, "Did you tell the truth about your age, then?"

She sits up. "What's wrong with my age?"

"Well, thirty-nine—danger zone."

"I'm sorry?"

"I didn't mean . . . sorry," he says. "That was a stupid thing to say."

"What about your sperm, hobbling about on Zimmer frames?"

"Calm down."

"Whoa! *Calm down?*" she says. "I want to know. What do you mean by danger zone? Where are we heading? I mean, do we actually want the same things?"

He sighs, as if he's completely exhausted with her. "I can't do this anymore, Manon. I'm sorry."

She lies there. Stunned. Is that it, then? All finished before it even began? What has she done, with her hot head so quick to take offense?

She reaches out to turn on the police radio, hoping Control can take her back to a place of safety. Its low murmurings burble out toward her and she closes her eyes. She turns in the bed, curls into a fetal position, her hands clasped between her knees.

She thinks there will always be a gap. A sad loss of a thing that cannot be had; a will-o'-the-wisp, yearned for but never grasped. A woman who cannot be delayed for long enough. "Sudden Death Syndrome," the coroner recorded at her mother's inquest, as if the word "syndrome" made it comprehensible.

One minute you are loved, and then you are not.

Friday

MANON

· · ·

SHE MANAGED A DIGNIFIED SILENCE FOR THE FIRST TWENTY-FOUR HOURS, told herself it was a blip that could come right if she just gave him some space; he would regret what he said, realizing what a special thing they were letting go of.

But nothing.

No calls, no texts, and in his silence she has read equanimity. After a bad night, her emotions are as ragged as the Alps. Fitful sleep, wishful dreams, ended by waking to a vision of Helena Reed's body hanging from the back of her bedroom door.

Now Manon is exhausted, slumped over her desk in MIT, glancing again and again at her phone, her collapsing face resting on the heel of one hand. So far she's sent seven texts, smoked five cigarettes, and pranged the car. And it's not yet 11:00 A.M.

I'm sorry for what I said the other night. Let's not leave it like this. M

Listen, I know I can be difficult, I do know that. I just want to set things straight. M

Hey, Big Al, thinkin' about ya. [She particularly regrets this one.]

Listen, even if you're sure, let's just talk it over, as I believe a song once said.

No wonder you've never had a relationship last more than six months.

It's a fucking relief, to be honest. Cocksucker.

Please don't leave me.

There is Kim at the front of the room, writing on a whiteboard in marker pen, while Manon examines Kim's bottom. It clenches to a point at its base and then joins to two very ample, oceangoing thighs, not even the hint of a gap between them. *My bottom's probably as big as that,* she thinks. *A single person's bottom. I'm about to be forty, I will never have a baby, and I have a bottom the size of—Don't cry. Just don't cry, not in the middle of MIT.*

"Dawn's doing baby-led weaning, which is great because they just learn to feed themselves and they don't grow up with any food issues," Nigel is saying, as Davy hands Manon a coffee.

"Kill me now," she mouths at Davy.

She hears the trill of a text-message alert and her heart flips over itself just as Kim says, "Ready, everyone?" and turns to reveal her work on the whiteboard.

DAVY

· · ·

NOW WE'RE GETTING SOMEWHERE, HE THINKS, READING KIM'S LOOPING handwriting. *Five weeks missing and we've finally got some detail on Edith Hind's movements in the days running up to her disappearance.*

He casts a look at Manon, who is so slumped she's practically laid her head on the table.

"The new information is from Scope—the charity shop on the high street. They've come forward with CCTV footage showing Edith buying a whole heap of stuff on Friday, sixteenth of December, the day before she disappeared."

"Such as?" asks Davy.

"Can't say exactly. Footage is grainy and from the wrong angle to see what's on the counter. We interviewed the old dear on the till but, to use official police parlance, she's quite a few sandwiches short of a picnic."

"Wouldn't that indicate Edith was trying to disguise herself?" Davy asks.

"Not really," says Kim. "Will Carter says she was fond of buying clothes at charity shops—fitted with her environmental, y'know, what-not."

Davy glances at the board.

Saturday Dec. 10: Visits Helena Reed's flat in the early hours. Intercourse with HR.

Sunday 11: Drives out to Deeping in G-Wiz, 3:20 p.m. ANPR return into Hunts at 10:45 p.m.

Monday 12: Pays rent to landlord next door, who says she seemed "distracted." Call to Tony Wright's phone.

Wednesday 14: Visits Helena Reed's flat again. Intercourse with HR.

Friday 16: Second call to Tony Wright's phone. Shops at Scope on high st. Intercourse with Will Carter. He states she was "highly emotional."

Saturday 17: Christmas do at the Crown, Cambs. Sexual contact with Jason Farrer. Guided bus back to Huntingdon with HR.

"Well, you know the rest from here," Kim is saying.

"Fuck," Manon blurts, so the department, Davy included, turns to look at her. Her eyes brim with tears.

"Good to know I had everyone's attention," says Kim.

MANON

. . .

HER SCREEN READS "ALAN P"—SO RARE TO SEE HIS NAME ON HER MOBILE phone—and might this be the volte-face she's been waiting for? Might it be that as she lands, he flies down also, coming to a graceful stop beside her? Might this be the moment he tells her he misses her, that he wants them to be properly together, on weeknights and everything?

> I'm sorry, Manon. I have enjoyed our time together, but I'm looking for something exceptional.

In her haste to leave the room, all eyes staring at her, she trips over a wastepaper basket and slams into the sharp corner of a desk, wounding her thigh.

"Argh," she yelps, rubbing her leg and stumbling to gather her phones, her bag, her coat from the back of her swivel chair, knowing only that she must make for the double doors.

Down the stairs, not knowing where she's going or why, she tells herself she definitely won't be responding to that one. There's an end to it. That message, she thinks, lighting a cigarette on the station steps, so characteristically pinched and formal. Her only response must be an arctic silence, laced with disappointment.

Soon, when the cigarette has been sucked down to its orange stump, she's digging into her bag, a frenzy of fingers and thumbs, through furious tears that fall freely all over the little screen.

You'll have a long fucking wait, then, dick wipe cocksucking shit for brains.

THE BUZZER GOES AND SHE lifts herself from the bed. The room—the whole flat—is in darkness, and she switches on the lights as she makes her way to the handset beside the front door.

"Halloooo!" says Bryony's voice. "We're here to take you out."

Manon doesn't reply but presses the button to let them in. She leaves the door open and sits on the sofa, pulling a blanket around her shoulders as Bryony and Davy clatter in on a wave of cold air from outside.

"Listen, he's a prick," says Bryony, "top totty like you."

"He might still change his mind," says Davy, who seems back to his old self.

"Davy," says Bryony. "Let's not give the patient false hope."

"Why do none of my relationships work out?" says Manon.

"None of mine have either," says Bryony. "I just happen to have married the latest one."

"That tosser's left a space for someone better, that's what I think," says Davy.

"I love you, Davy," says Manon.

"Come on," says Bryony. "You need a drink. To Cromwell's!"

"Urgh, please. Can't we just stay here and watch *Failure to Launch*?"

"Nope, and we are not taking you wrapped in a blanket," says Bryony, pushing Manon on the shoulder, which fells her to the sofa like a chopped tree. "Go and get your glad rags on."

"Where are your rubber gloves? I'll do the washing up," says Davy.

Bryony puts the Scissor Sisters on the stereo and leads Manon into the bedroom.

"Smells like something died in here," she says. "Have you been lying on the bed crying and farting?"

Manon nods.

Bryony makes the bed and opens a window, and they select an outfit—a black tunic dress, tights, and knee-high boots—after which Bryony sits Manon down on a chair to do her makeup. Davy is clattering about in the kitchen, putting away dishes from the sounds of it. Manon has her eyes closed and feels the soft push and tickle of an eyeshadow brush, the sweet scent of Bryony's breath, and her hand on her forehead.

"I don't want to go," she says.

"Shurrup," says Bryony.

Three-quarters of an hour later, they're assembled by the front door.

"How does she look?" asks Bryony.

"Million dollars," says Davy, smiling at her.

"Davy," says Manon, "this place looks amazing."

"Well, there's nothing like a tidy-up to lift your spirits, is there?"

Manon can feel her face crumpling and Bryony notices, saying, "Hey, hey, come on, don't spoil your makeup."

THE FIRST DRINK, IN THE darkness of the bar, is like nectar. Manon begins to feel things loosen and dissipate. Who *cares*? What does it *matter*? Things *pass*!

"Fuck it!" she says, raising her glass to Bryony.

"Fuck it, indeed," says Bryony, raising hers back.

By the second drink, she is grateful to Alan for releasing her from the hell of suburban convention. All that *domesticity*. "So booorrrrring," she says to Bryony.

"Bor-ring," says Bryony.

"He wants to be friends. Texted to tell me. I mean, all of a sudden he's Texts R Us. Friends! What is that *shit*?"

"Dunno," says Bryony. "I always thought a good breakup meant never speaking to the person again, except when armed with scissors or in open court."

"'Zactly!"

She surveys the usual suspects: Colin, Stuart, Kim, and Nigel (having a quick half before getting back to "the lovely Dawn").

"The inspirational Dawn," whispers Bryony.

"The irrefutable Dawn," says Manon.

"The seriously fucking knackered Dawn," says Bryony.

"Twins woke at four this morning," says Nigel, visibly depressed and gazing into his drink.

Another reason to celebrate, thinks Manon, and orders another double at the bar. Thick and fast they come, bought by others or bought by her. She thinks life is best passed in a blur: imprecise and anesthetized from the sharper feelings. She is drowning as the gin engulfs her, swaying on the spot, the room spinning, the music pumping in time with the blood in her arteries. She can feel the beat through the soles of her feet.

Stuart is smiling, glittering at her dangerously. They appear to have been talking for some time. Bryony is nowhere to be seen.

"Christ, haven't you been fired yet?" she says, lurching toward him.

"They've got nothing on me. In fact, I'm just bedding in, getting the lie of the land, office hierarchy."

"You're all about hierarchy, aren't you, Stuart?" she says. She feels as if she can say anything, to anyone's face. "Like you're obsessed."

"Who do you rate, then?" he says, his glass raised toward their colleagues nearby. "Who's a good copper?"

"Me!" she says, close enough to put her cheek on his chest. She's tempted. Any port in a storm.

"What about Harper?" he says, and she sees that look, the same look he'd had when he had complained about the headmistress "lording it" at the school where he worked.

"Oh, Harriet's good. Very good. Sexually frustrated, though." She burps into her fist. "'Scuse me." She can't feel the bottom half of her legs. Stuart swims in front of her. "Kim's good. Solid, y'know. Unimaginative."

"Go on." This wily fox, his charm a lure into darkness.

The music is so loud, she's had to shout in his ear, to smell him. Foreign male. Exciting and dangerous. She's shouting now, just as before, but her words have a strange echo, as if they have been emitted through a loud-hailer.

"Davy'll never be a good copper," she bellows into the sudden silence. "Too busy looking on the fucking bright side."

Her eyes are half closed, her mind woolly, and she has shouted the words before she registers that the music is off. *Someone must've pulled the plug,* she thinks, too late.

And she turns, slowly, to see a row of faces staring at her. Kim, Bryony, Nigel, and Colin. Davy at the center, hurt ears pinned back. She can practically see the follicles standing up on his head.

She starts to burn. She is drunk but also painfully sober. Davy is staring at her and she doesn't know if it's simply what she has said or the fact that she has spilled it into Stuart's malevolent ear. She is so drunk that all her movements are delayed, and her eyelids half-close again, though there is panic on the inside, as if she can't persuade her body to catch up.

"Davy, I—" she begins, but the music is back on, louder than before, like she's being punched about the head, and he has walked quickly out of the bar.

Before Manon knows what's happening, Bryony has appeared, carrying her coat and bag.

"Aren't those mine?" she asks, but Bryony has taken her by the elbow, saying, "Excuse us" to Stuart.

"Oi, I was just—" Manon protests.

"Yes, we all know what you were just doing," says Bryony.

Saturday

MANON

. . .

EVERYTHING IN RUINS.

She walks the cold lounge, lighting lamps against the tinkle and spit of rain at the window.

Her pajamas stink—sweet, fetid alcohol seeping out through her skin. She sits on the curved corduroy sofa and cries.

If there was only something left: a relationship gone wrong but her work intact; her work compromised but love still offering a future. Instead, it is a desolate landscape, the death of Helena Reed at its center like a crucifixion, her head to one side. While she was with him, she could tell herself that dereliction of duty had been in aid of something; she hadn't wanted to be married to the job. Now even the job won't have her.

She sits cross-legged on the sofa, pulls her laptop onto her knees, her phones beside her. She points the remote at the TV, so the news comes on. She needs something, *anything*. She needs an idea.

She googles Tony Wright. The various reportings of his crimes pop up; a backgrounder after his conviction, in the *Eastern Daily Press*. Whitemoor Prison is highlighted in blue, and she clicks idly on the link. The Internet is a journey, down tributaries random and meandering, a journey in which you could lose hours, days, a week, and she's happy to become lost. She reads the Whitemoor Wikipedia page.

In June 2006, an inspection report from Her Majesty's Chief Inspector of Prisons criticised staff at Whitemoor Prison for ignoring prisoners, and not responding to their queries and requests for help promptly enough.

She skims the next part.

A further inspection report stated, in October 2008, that staff at Whitemoor Prison felt fear that Muslim inmates were attempting to radicalise others held at the jail. According to inspectors, officers tended to treat Muslim prisoners as extremists and potential security risks, even though only eight of them had been convicted of terrorist offences. Due to the concerns raised by this inspection, further visits by researchers from the Cambridge Institute of Criminology, commissioned by the Ministry of Justice, were arranged between 2009 and 2010 to interview staff and inmates.

Manon picks up her remote to silence the TV, as something forms, indistinct at present. Cambridge Institute of Criminology. Part of the university. Tony Wright was in Whitemoor when their inspections were taking place. Tony Wright might have been interviewed by the CIC.

She picks up her BlackBerry and finds the number of her prison-warden contact at Whitemoor, Wilco Bennett.

"Manon," he says warmly. "Long time."

"Everything all right, Wilco?" she says, making a stab at the pleasantries. She has a soft spot for Wilco Bennett: pigeon fancier, holder of socially unacceptable views, which she forgives because he's been incarcerated with sociopaths since 1989. They got to know each other during endless proceedings at Peterborough Crown Court—remand hearings, bail applications, and the attendant delays that often left them sitting on hard benches side by side beneath the courtroom.

"Your Edith Hind girl," says Wilco. "Bit of a whopper, isn't it?"

"Mmm," she says. "Can I ask a favor, Wilco?"

"Fire away," he says.

"Tony Wright."

"Prince Charming, yes."

"Can you get me his authorized visitor list?"

"'S'a while ago now, lovely. He's been out nine months."

"I know. Are you in the office or is it your weekend off?"

"No, I'm in. I'm not brilliant on the old computers; I think the AV list has to be downloaded onto the whatnot, using a doobrey." He chuckles at this. "I can never find the damned thing after that, you know? Downloaded *where*? Still, it's quiet today; I'll see if I can get someone to help me. Any particular span of time, so to speak?"

"I'd like Wright's entire AV list, if you can get it, but I want you to look at 2009 in particular. Call me back?"

"Will do."

She lies down on the sofa, her laptop at her feet, her hands between her knees. She is cold. She hasn't eaten since sometime late yesterday afternoon, before the Cromwell's debacle. She reaches back, drags a blanket off the top of the sofa to cover herself. She wonders if she should call Davy but instead turns the sound up on the TV. She lies there, looking at the ceiling, listening to the burble of the lunchtime news; always the soft stuff—items about the Royal Family or the cost of childcare, for people raising spoons of Heinz tomato soup to their quivering lips. People wrapped in blankets, just like her. She thinks about smoking a cigarette.

"Twenty refugees and the body of an Afghan man have been found in a container at Tilbury Docks," she hears the newsreader say. "A man from Ipswich has been arrested on suspicion of conspiring to facilitate illegal immigration into the UK. Abdul-Ghani Khalil, thirty-seven, was arrested alongside three men from Luton in connection with the death."

She reaches behind her head for a cigarette, which she lights without sitting upright, blowing smoke up toward the ceiling.

* * *

SHE THROWS HER CIGARETTE BUTT out of the open third of her car window, then winds it up. Sits, feeling a swell of tears rise in her chest, then lower, plus something else—a kamikaze element. She shouldn't be here alone.

In front of her, the estate road winds away into the shadowy hulk of buildings. A bin, overfull, billows with a white plastic bag stuffed in at the top. At the curve of the road is a group of youths, their hoods up, hunched, stamping foot to foot. She can't see their faces, but their bodies are febrile.

This isn't the first time she's been on the estate after dark. Last time, Manon was crouching over the body of a debt collector who'd been sent out here on her own to gather piddling sums for an insurance firm. A mother of three, smartly dressed, pootling into danger in her little maroon Fiat, wearing a white mohair sweater with a dainty gold necklace over its roll neck. She should never have been here alone, not at night, and certainly not asking for money. Twelve pounds a week she collected from the man who would eventually stab her to death.

Yet here is Manon, just like the debt collector, alone in the dark. No one to report her missing now, no police colleagues pulling out the stops. No backup.

She slams her car door and makes for Tony Wright's flat.

"To what do I owe this honor?" he says, answering the door.

"Can I come in?" she asks, and he steps back.

She hears him lock the door behind her. "Cannae be too careful. All sorts round here."

She steps into the lounge, which is dim except for a lava lamp glowing purple on a shelf, its moving globules like slow marine life. The room smells of incense and smoke.

"Lyn here?" she says, casting about. Her heart is thumping. She feels as if the ground is tipping. What is she doing here, locked inside with Tony Wright?

"No, nobody here, ma wee scone, 'cept you an' me," says Tony as he walks through to a small kitchen.

He returns carrying a bottle of whiskey and two glasses. He motions to the square table against the wall and she sits at it, a whiskey glass placed before her. She thinks about the two glasses at George Street, one with blood on its shards.

She doesn't say no as he pours; another line she's crossing.

"So," he says, raising his glass to her and smiling, with that twinkle—Father Christmas and Captain Birdseye.

"So," she says, and she drinks, hoping it will steel her nerves. The whiskey burns, a teardrop of fire descending her gullet. Her head swims and she feels sick. Perhaps he will tell her what he's done to Edith Hind, how he got away with it, and then he will kill her. Yes, that seems likely now, and she feels calm in the face of it. She doesn't care about herself. She lights a cigarette and so does he. There is so much camaraderie in lighting up together. Another protocol broken.

"Just you and me, Tony," she says. "What's the deal? Why was Edith on your AV list?"

He looks at her. Blows out smoke. "She was in the prison doin' some research, interviewin' prisoners. I dinnae remember what for, was a while ago now—2009. Whitemoor was in a right state at the time. Riots, escapes. Prison wardens were filth, abusin' us. She was askin' loads o' questions about the conditions we were livin' under in the prison. We started talkin'. And we enjoyed talkin'. So I said, if you'd like tae come back, we could talk some more."

"You were grooming her?"

"Groomin' her for what? I've no' touched her." He leans forward, jabbing the tabletop with one finger. "Ye'll get nothin' on me, 'cos I've done nothin' tae that girl. If there's a law says a lowlife like me cannae be pals wi' a classy bird like that, then show me it."

"What did you talk about, when she visited you?"

"About the prison, life inside. She brought me some books to read. *Jude the Obscure*. Well, I had a lot o' time on ma hands, but even so, I only pretended to read the books she brought me, so that she'd like me all right. I liked talkin' to her, and I liked lookin' at her. No' in a bad way—she's a fine-lookin' girl."

"So you talked literature, Tony, you and Edith Hind?"

"Ah told ye, I only pretended to read that book just so she'd keep visitin' me. Then ma mother died. I found myself in a very quiet place, ye ken? Inside myself, I mean. Edith came to see me just after. I was in a bad way; *darkness,* ken?" He beats a fist against his heart. "We started talkin' about deeper things."

"What did she call you about in the week before she disappeared?"

"This an' that."

"Ah, come on, Tony."

"Nothing special: how you doin', Tony, what's happening wi' finding work, seeing your probation officer, whatnot. She's a good person—a really good person. I never had anyone classy like her tek an interest afore. Made me want tae make an effort. Thought maybe I could have ... I don't know ..." He trails off.

"Have what, Tony? Have her money? Take her life?"

"Och, there you go again," and he gets up. Manon gets up too and they square up to each other, making the room feel small. She needs to get out of here if she's going to make it at all, but the front door is locked. Tony is reaching into his pocket slowly. She thinks of the girl, his victim, beaten with the butt end of a knife's handle until she couldn't see.

"Ye see what ye want tae see," he says, squinting as he lights another cigarette. "Ye see me, and in your view I'm no' able to change. That's fine. But I'm tellin' ye, Edith Hind has been a good pal in my life, an' even wi' all this *shit,* I'm glad I know her."

"Know?"

"Know, knew ... Ah've no idea where she is."

He has sat down again, his legs effeminately crossed, regarding his cigarette held in a tight hand.

"She's alive, isn't she?"

"I told ye, I don't know what's happened tae the girl. I hope she's alive, aye."

She has to get out of here, while the going's good. She strides for the door, tries to open it. She pulls at the door, rattling it furiously, until he comes behind her, lays a hand on her shoulder.

"Hey, hey, hey, calm it," he says, and turns her body toward his. "There's no need to be jigglin' about like that." He is so near to her she can smell him—cinnamon and whiskey. Her heart is pounding so furiously she wonders if he can feel it too. "There ye go," he says, and he opens the door onto a blast of freezing night.

She is shaking, whether with fear or with cold or with relief to have got out, she cannot tell. She is shaking so much her key will not make it into the lock of her car door. She tries again, holding her wrist with her other hand, trying to steady the aiming of the key's shaft.

Crack.

Sharp hot pain at the top of her skull. Then an ice-cold trickle down the back of her neck. Her last sensation: her legs folding beneath her.

The world tips.

Sunday

MANON

• • •

SHE IS ALL MOUTH; IMPOSSIBLY DRY, THICK AS WOOL. AN EYE OPEN TO A white room. Has she died? It is so white, perhaps this is the afterlife, in which case, it should have a better view. A broad picture window gives out onto leafless trees and the flat roofs of municipal buildings, the sky the color of porridge. She has a headache that threatens to split her skull.

"Here, you'll need a drink."

Someone is lifting her neck and she closes her mouth around a straw, the liquid so shocking it sears her temples.

"You're a lucky woman," he says.

She focuses her dehydrated eyes—first on his white coat, then the stethoscope, then his black stubble. He smells of coal-tar soap. His tie is lying on her body. He straightens, places her cup on the bedside unit, and she can see his olive skin and dark eyebrows. Albanian or Middle

Eastern, perhaps. She would like to rearrange her hair, wipe the crust from the corners of her mouth.

"That was quite a blow to your head," he is saying. "Knocked you out cold. Might have been a punch, or you might've been struck with something. We were concerned the injury might cause a bleed into your brain—that's why we kept you in overnight. How're you feeling?"

"Rough," she croaks.

He smiles. "We're going to monitor you a bit longer, run some tests. I'm going to get you some paracetamol. Expect you've got a fierce headache, right?" He is *really* nice-looking, though now she considers it, possibly about fifteen years younger than she is. "By the way, you've got a visitor."

The doctor and Harriet dance round each other in the doorway. Manon closes her eyes, her head heavy on the pillow. She feels Harriet's nervous energy lower into the plastic chair beside her bed, her hand coming to rest on Manon's.

"What happened?" Manon whispers.

"From the CCTV, looks like a kid—an addict, probably—was being opportunistic, saw you alone, liked the look of your handbag. What the hell were you doing—"

"Not Tony Wright, then?"

"No, in fact our beloved Tony came to your aid—called 999, saw off whoever'd done it. Anyway, this kid, who we will catch, don't you worry, has seriously assaulted one of my police officers and has now got himself a police BlackBerry."

"Which is passcode-locked, so don't panic. I'll give a statement to CID. Let them get on with it."

"Hmm," Harriet murmurs skeptically. "Anyway, he'll be going to prison for a *really* long time, which'll sort out his habit one way or the other. What the fuck were you doing there on your own?"

"Edith Hind was on Tony Wright's authorized visitor list in Whitemoor."

"What the *fuck*?"

Manon nods. "He reckons they were friends."

They are silent for a moment, contemplating this information.

"Edith was visiting him? Voluntarily?" says Harriet.

"Apparently," says Manon. "Wilco Bennett, one of the screws at Whitemoor, is sending me his whole file. That'll give us more."

"What were those calls about, then, in the week before she disappeared? Did Wright tell you?"

Manon has raised her head from the pillow. "He says, 'Och, this 'n' that. How youse doin'?'" She has put on an appalling Scots accent, to which Harriet grimaces and says, "Where's he from, Bangladesh?"

"Anyway, I don't buy it," says Manon, head back on the pillow. "I think something was being set up."

"Like what—a deal? A meeting?"

"Dunno. I think we've been looking at Wright all wrong. We've been assuming he harmed her, when I think—"

The door has opened and there is Davy, his expression reserved.

"I'll have to pull him in—Wright, I mean. Question him about this," says Harriet. "Anyway, I'll leave you two to it."

DAVY HAS SAT DOWN ON the plastic seat beside her bed. "Brought you these," he says, handing her garage-forecourt flowers in clear cellophane.

"Chrysanthemums," she says. She raises the bunch to her nose, sniffs. Frowns. The faint whiff of piss. She hates chrysanthemums and has evidently failed to rearrange her face, because Davy says, "Back to your old self so soon."

"Sorry," she says. "Thank you."

"'S'all right. I bought them because I know you don't like them."

Her face crumples, dissolving in a sudden well of moisture. She didn't think she had any wetness left in her dehydrated walnut of a head. "I'm so sorry, Davy. I'd never want to hurt you. You of all people, you're the last person I'd ever . . . I'd ever . . ." Childish judders, up and down. "You're the best copper I know."

"I'm not, though, am I? Always paddling too hard."

"Not lately," she says. "Lately you've seemed quite shirty."

"I'm weak," he says.

"No, you're not, you're not weak at all. Look at all the things you do for the kids at the center, giving up your own time, when I say no to Fly at every opportunity. And the guilt you feel over Helena Reed when I can't even look that in the face."

Her eyes have filled again and she seeks his face. He looks back at her and smiles, as if her tears are apology enough.

"Slept with Chloe last night," he says, sheepish.

"Oh no," she says. "That'll set you back. Comfort shag?"

He nods.

She turns her head to the window and they sit in contemplative silence.

Eventually she whispers, half to herself, "I should have 'fuckwit' tattooed on my forehead."

"Wouldn't fit," says Davy.

"Just 'twat,' then."

"That'd fit."

He leans back in his chair. She closes her eyes. She loves a silence with Davy Walker. Some people give good silence, and he is one of them.

"Being walloped really makes you feel low," she says.

"You're always low."

"I know, but more so. I feel . . ." and she starts to cry again, looking at the trees beyond her broad hospital window. She realizes they have given her this spacious room to herself because she's a police officer.

"I think you need a dog," Davy says.

"What?"

"I heard a dog makes unhappy people happy. They're good, y'know, for people who can't form proper relationships."

"You're a real tonic, Davy."

SHE LIES THERE AS THE light fades through her picture window, waiting for the handsome doctor to discharge her, thinking about Edith, about Tony Wright, the sense that he *knew* she was alive. The hospital radio burbles out the news, still leading on the Tilbury Docks container death. *Bryony will be up against it on the Abdul-Ghani Khalil evidence,* she thinks, as her mind begins its descent, merging with the news report, details of the routes driven by his trucks.

She sleeps.

MANON

. . .

THE THRUM OF HER PRINTER IS ALMOST KEEPING TIME WITH THE ACHING pulse inside her head. Manon is cross-legged on the floor in pajamas and thick socks, a blanket around her shoulders. Her back is aching, her knees stiff. The room is crepuscular but for the light from an Anglepoise that she has dragged onto the floor; it is interrogating, with its brash light, the sheaves of paper that surround her.

Paper, upon paper, upon paper, and as the printer spews out more, they flutter down, creating more chaos. "Can't get the AV list off of this," Wilco Bennett's email said, "so I'm just attaching his entire IIS file—all fifteen years of it. Enjoy!"

The Inmate Information System contained everything about the life of a prisoner: personal details, offense, sentence, possibility of parole, relationships, movements (from that spur on that wing to another), case-note information, risk assessments, courses taken, activities, paid and unpaid work, breaches of discipline, offender-rehabilitation programs.

Manon crawls across the white sea, leaving her blanket like a worm cast in sand, to where her phone has vibrated.

How's the head? I'd bring you lasagna + Nurofen but my trafficking case has proper kicked off. Bri

She's reminded to take more Nurofen, alternating them two-hourly with paracetamol, though the dull ache remains like a background noise. She pads to the kitchen, where the chill curls itself about her neck and ankles. And as she tips her head back, swallowing, she wonders what she hopes she'll find delving into Tony Wright's life inside and—also printing out in reams—the two-hundred-page Ministry of Justice report compiled by the CIC with Edith Hind's assistance. "Staff–prisoner relations in Whitemoor Prison"—a vivid portrait of prison life.

The nice doctor discharged her from Addenbrooke's last night and Harriet has forbidden her from coming in to the office. "Don't be a nutter. Stay home. Recuperate. I don't want to see you in before Tuesday at the earliest," she said.

Manon pads back to her twilit lounge, the pages crinkling under her feet. She crosses one foot over the other and lowers to the floor, pulling the blanket around her shoulders and gathering new sheaves to read.

The first three years of a long sentence are the worst, she has learned. New inmates are put on the induction spur on C-wing and are most prone to existential crises, likely to self-harm. Here are men facing fifteen, twenty, twenty-five years in prison without hope of release. They are desperate for meaning, beset by loss. Tony Wright, then in his early forties, was no exception. He cut his arms with razor blades when he could get hold of them, and blades appear to feature widely in Whitemoor.

She shuffles the papers, then glances at her watch: 4:00 P.M. She began reading at ten this morning, but she must have dozed at intervals right here on the floor, the blanket like a cocoon.

Page 20 of Wright's file: "Emotional outbursts. No reduction in Cat A status." For years he seemed to suffer the most stringent form of incarceration, every emotion deemed "risk." Stints in segregation. One suicide attempt. In conversation with his personal officer following this attempt, Tony Wright said, "I'm Spam. I'm meat in a tin."

"Don't laugh, don't look happy," he wrote in a letter home that was confiscated and kept on file, "'cos someone is looking at you on a monitor, deciding you're not suffering enough, and that someone is deciding your sentence review."

"Inmate moved to different cell every twenty-eight days," a note on Wright's file states, including strip searches and "cell turns," to prevent the formation of gang-style relationships. *Or any relationships,* Manon thinks.

Paracetamol. Cups of tea. At one point she takes a bath. Perhaps she dozes off once or twice. But she comes back to the floor, the puzzle tessellating in white across her carpet.

The CIC report describes a brutalizing regime in Whitemoor toward the back end of Wright's sentence. Staff were distant, distrustful; violence endemic. Where previously high-security prisons used to function on a known code—a gentlemanly agreement between the old lags and the screws—the modern, multicultural population of Whitemoor was viewed with intense suspicion by its staff. Prison officers were frightened by the growing Muslim population, while outside, in the run-up to a general election, the press and public were growing less liberal by the day. "Prison should be for punishment, not rehabilitation." "Offenders, particularly those convicted under the terrorism act, are having an easy ride." In response to these hard-line views, the home secretary canceled rafts of arts and education courses inside Whitemoor.

Manon looks up. The printer is growling, turning over against itself. A red light flashes. Paper jam.

She gets up, opens the printer's various drawers and flaps, pulls out an inky drum, fingers blackened, then can't jimmy it back in again. She cannot locate the jammed paper. She slaps the flaps shut again, jabs at the button angrily, turns it off, waits, then on again. She roars in frustration when she sees the red light resume its flashing and thinks she might hurl it against the wall. Then she cries. Alan could've fixed it. Alan probably has a laser jet, which never jams, because he checked its reviews on *Which?* And he probably keeps spare cartridges in a drawer. No one can help her with the printer jam. She is alone. And all this time they have misunderstood Tony Wright.

Back sitting cross-legged on the floor, she picks up another page of Wright's IIS report. Tony Wright moved to B-wing, to the spur for prisoners on the enhanced level of the incentives and earned-privileges scheme. Things seem to be improving for him. In 2005 he gets a job in the library. A note says he keeps his head down—a "loner." "Prisoner 518 focused on serving his sentence and leaving prison at the earliest opportunity." Wright has learned how to make life better for himself, plus he is nearing the end of his sentence, but in the truly repressive conditions of Whitemoor, he is living in a febrile atmosphere. In another confiscated letter, he writes: "I keep my head down. I don't talk to nobody. My personality's out there somewhere, waiting for me to grasp it when I'm out."

On the same page is an addendum: "2009, Prisoner reading Jude the Obscure by Thomas Hardy. Material confiscated: violent themes."

Manon wipes the tears from her cheeks.

Along came Edith Hind: listening to him, trying to understand him. Asking how his day was, how his life was, what his plans might be, and whether she could help him. She must've been the first person to treat him like a human being in fifteen years. Even the words, "Hello, Tony, how are you?" must've been like a long drink to a man dying of thirst.

She looks at her watch. It is 2:00 A.M. She pulls the blanket more closely about her shoulders, crawls to the last pages spewed by her now-paralyzed printer. Page 258 of Tony Wright's IIS file. "Inmate returned to C-wing, Cat A status."

Manon is frowning. What has happened to cause a setback like this?

Prisoner 518 involved in breach of prison discipline during altercation with Prisoner 678 in the gym. Sentence review frozen. In light of Prisoner 518's involvement in this violent episode, consideration of parole denied until further risk assessment has been carried out.

Who was Prisoner 678? Manon pushes at the papers around her on the floor. They slide over one another like water. She leafs, faster and faster, through the white sea, looking for an explanation for this about-turn after a decade of model behavior. Then she finds it. IIS file page 259: Prisoner 518 statement, transcribed verbatim from a record-

ing of an interview with prison staff, investigating the gym incident,
January 21, 2009.

I was workin' out in the gym by myself, runnin' on the treadmill,
when Prisoner 678 came and began working the weights next tae
me. Dumbbells an' that. We were nice an' quiet, the two of us, no'
talkin'. I seen him about but he wisnae ma pal or nothin'. Anyways, a group of prisoners walked into the gym, white guys wi' tats.
Hated the Brotherhood, these guys. Thought the Muslims had too
much power. They surrounded the lad next tae me. I'd like tae use
his name, no' his number, if ye dinnae mind, because he's a human
bein', ye ken?

So this chap, Khalil—Abdul, I think his first name is—he's carrying on nice an' quiet, lifting his weights, but ye could cut the
tension w' a knife. He an' I both knew those guys had come in here
fer violence, a "lesson" it's called in here, 'cos there's no cameras in
the gym. All the cuttin' and punchin' in Whitemoor happens in the
gym.

"Brother Khalil," one of 'em said to him. Another of them
pulled a blade. They held his arms behind his back and cut his
throat. Then they walked out.

I was still runnin' on the treadmill—can ye believe that?—an'
ma first thought was: There'll be a lockdown now on the wing. Ah
need te get ma stuff, 'cos they'll be turnin' all the cells after this.
That's what this place turned me into. That's how much o' my humanity's been sucked from me in here. An' maybe there's folk'd say
I didnae have any humanity to start with, but I had some. Anyways,
I remembered maself at that moment, an' I raised the alarm, an' I
tried to stop him bleeding to death until the medic got tae us. He's
a person. An' I'm a person, ye ken?

"Prisoner's sentence review unfrozen and all privileges restored,"
says Wright's file, "in the light of this statement and supporting statement from Prisoner 678 (A-G Khalil)."

Manon looks up, dazed. Tony Wright saved Abdul-Ghani Khalil's
life.

MANON
. . .

"THAT YOU, MANON?"

Her breath catches in her throat to hear that voice. Can it possibly be? Why now? Perhaps she has a sixth sense for Manon's heartbreak. She did when they were little.

"Hello."

"I'm . . . I'm sorry to ring out of the blue like this."

"No, no."

"Is it a bad time?"

"Um, well, I'm at work, in the toilets, actually. You might hear the echo."

She pulls at some of the rough oblong towels, jabs at the tears at the rim of her eye, and a corner of the towel pokes her eyeball. She bends over double, blinking and rubbing. The phone is heating up her ear as if it's radioactive.

It wasn't just that Ellie's truce with Una had been a treachery too

far; their rift was the calcification of years of rivalry, layers of it hardening into silence over time. Small injuries, gathering; some success Ellie
had at work, which Manon couldn't swallow; or a fabulous boyfriend;
or even just a nice holiday she didn't want to hear about. They stopped
calling and then, much sooner than Manon expected, it became too
hard to call. Their mother would have banged their heads together: "I
don't care about any awkwardness" and "Get over yourselves, for God's
sake," which would only have made it worse. But their mother is dead,
their father all the way in Scotland, which might as well be Canada,
Una having subsumed him like some mollusk who crept over the top
of him until he disappeared.

"How've you been?" says Ellie.

"Oh, you know . . ."

"No. I don't. It's been three years."

"And that's my fault, is it?"

Ellie sighs. "It doesn't matter, does it? I'm ringing to tell you something important. I've had a baby. A boy. He's three months now. Solo-
mon. Well, we call him Solly."

"A baby? You've had a baby?" The blood drains from Manon's
head. She nods distractedly at Kim, who is edging into a toilet cubicle.
"Are you . . . Where are you living?"

"In London. Kilburn."

"Wow. That's . . . terrific news."

"Yes. I wanted you to know, Manon. In case you . . . Well, perhaps
you'll come up sometime. Meet your nephew."

She pictures herself the prickly pear, lonely visitor to the pink
paradise of family life in Kilburn. The park and the swings and Sunday
roasts so newly lost to her. Wrinkled aunt.

"Well, it's quite busy in MIT right now."

"Yes, of course. Must be. You must be a DCI by now."

"Not quite."

"I better go. Solly's waking up. We've got Baby Bounce at the library this afternoon."

Manon is so jealous she cannot speak. Envy is physical, the sensation of it: difficulty swallowing, a pain around the temples, panic, and
wanting to flee the source.

"OK, well, nice to talk to you," she says. "Bye."

She takes more towels from the dispenser, knowing the tears will come again. Oh, but she loves Ellie, loves her so deeply, and now they have come to this—the slights embedding themselves into wounds and no one to knock their heads together except their better selves, which seem always to be in abeyance, held hostage by meaner feelings. On top of her jealousy, in a nauseous wave, comes guilt. My sister, with a baby and no mother to help. My sister, who I love, my love killed by jealousy. My sister, who I hate for having everything I haven't got. It is impossible to be Manon Bradshaw.

Everything is broken and she starts to cry, as Kim emerges from her cubicle to the sounds of a fulsome flush. Did Kim hear the word "unimaginative" at Cromwell's on Friday? Or is Manon blanching just at the thought?

They nod at each other silently, neither mentioning Manon's tears nor her outburst in the bar.

BACK AT HER DESK, SHE calls Will Carter on the landline.

"When did Edith first toy with the idea of criminology?"

"Summer 2009. After we graduated, none of us—well, practically none of us—knew what to do next. She decided to do a kind of work experience with the CIC—these interviews in Whitemoor—to see if it would be something she'd like to take to postgrad level. I remember she was incredibly excited about that first visit to the prison, full of zeal about reform and education, ideas about teaching a prison course in feminist literature to make rapists explore the female experience."

"She talk much about Tony Wright?"

"No, she never mentioned anyone by name. I think the visits ended almost as quickly as they began. I just remember that after a couple of trips to Whitemoor with the CIC, she became really demoralized. Said it was one of the saddest places she'd ever been in. No one treating anyone with a shred of humanity. And all these prisoners without hope and with nothing to do. She said it smelled of cabbage and bleach. She told me there was no interest in rehabilitation in prison. Just over-crowding, lack of money, and the problem of housing this jostling, violent pack of men who the state felt were uncontainable. She went to see Graham Garfield soon after and switched to an English PhD."

"So you weren't aware of an ongoing relationship with Tony Wright? That Edith was visiting him?"

"No," he says softly.

"One more question, Will. Abdul-Ghani Khalil—do you know the name?"

"The guy who's just been arrested? The body in the container at Tilbury Docks? Of course—he's all over the news."

"I wondered if Edith might have mentioned him to you."

He is laughing.

"Something funny, Mr. Carter?"

"You think she was part of a human-trafficking ring? Nothing would surprise me about Edith anymore." He sighs. "Look, I don't know if she knew Abdul-Ghani whatever his name is. But I didn't really know her at all, did I?"

No, you didn't, Manon thinks, but her mind is snagged by the ringing of her replacement BlackBerry, which is scuttling across the desk with each vibration. "I'm going to have to go, Will, I've got another call coming in. Talk soon." She puts down the landline, picks up the mobile. "DS Manon Bradshaw," she says.

"It's DI Haverstock—remember me? Havers, Kilburn CID."

"Right, yeah, hi," she says, her voice a swell of impatience. She wants to interrogate the Wright–Khalil line, see whether it leads to Edith. She doesn't want distractions.

"I've got something on Taylor Dent," Havers is saying. "Turns out he had a second phone—for his various business dealings. We arrested one of his associates and he told us about it, gave us the number. Anyway, we've got all the data off it and there's a voicemail you might want to listen to. We haven't got a clue who it is, to be honest, so I'm forwarding it to people who might, even though it's a long shot. Or would you rather I contact team two about this?"

"No, no, I can look at it," she says, simultaneously typing into the police database. "Email the audio file over. M_Bradshaw@pcn.co.uk. Thanks." Then she throws her BlackBerry across the desk.

She pulls up the call data taken off Tony Wright's phone after his arrest, highlights the numbers he called after speaking to Edith Hind—most of them dirty phones, PAYG, unregistered, no records attached.

She tries Bryony's mobile but it goes straight to voicemail.

Need to speak to you urgently. Call me. M

Can't. Massively up against it. Later.

No, Bri. It's urgent. CALL ME.

"What?" says Bri. "Can't this wait?"

"No, it can't. Are you sitting in front of the Khalil file?"

"I'm *always* sitting in front of the Khalil file. I've started calling my kids Abdul and Ghani."

"I just want to run these numbers past you. Ready?"

"What's this about?"

"Tell you in a sec. Ready? Unknown-638."

Silence as Bryony types into the HOLMES system.

"Nope."

"OK, unknown-422."

"Nope," says Bryony. "Oh, wait, hang on. Yes. That's one of his. Well, one of his associates, who basically relayed messages to him."

"Bingo," says Manon. "Fucking love you, Bri."

"What? Tell me. What's this about?"

"Tony Wright made contact with Khalil shortly after speaking to Edith Hind. Khalil and Wright knew each other in Whitemoor. One more thing, Bri. Khalil was trafficking people through ports. Dover, Folkestone, Tilbury Docks."

"That's right—goods containers and trucks boarding P&O Ferries mainly."

"And was he taking people the other way?"

"What, you mean *out* of the country? Khalil would take anyone anywhere if the money was right. I *think*—and don't quote me on this—that there's always a drip feed the other way. Y'know, people going back, thinking the Continent might offer a better deal, but border control couldn't care less about that flow so we don't investigate it. Listen, hon, I've really got to go."

"Just one more thing," Manon says. "His drop-offs and pickups—did he operate in Cambridgeshire?"

"Yup," says Bryony. "All up and down the eastern coastline—out of Felixstowe, across to the M11, down through Maidstone, and out of

Dover. Should we be interrogating Khalil on this, asking if he knows anything about the Hind girl?"

"Not yet," says Manon. "Gimme a bit more time."

"Right, look, I've really got to—"

"Yes, yes, sorry. Thanks, love. Bye." Manon lays her phone down on the desk.

Her email box says one new message. She puts her headphones on and listens to the audio file.

After a sprint around MIT, she locates Harriet in Stanton's office, sunken-eyed, clicking about at the computer. Manon is panting so hard, she almost can't get the words out. Harriet looks up.

"What is it?"

Is this a panic attack? Why won't her words come out?

"What, Manon? *Speak*."

"Audio file," she gasps. "Audio file." She is pointing at the computer.

Harriet opens up the email Manon has forwarded to her inbox and plays the audio file. She and Manon do not take their eyes off each other. The voice—patrician, superior, commanding: "Meet me at the usual place."

"It's him," says Harriet.

"I know," says Manon.

"It's fucking him," Harriet says. "What date was this recorded?"

"Sunday, eleventh of December."

"Right, I'm authorizing an ANPR trace on his plates on Sunday, eleventh of December. We need to link this Dent number back to him. I'll bet he wasn't using his normal mobile to make that call, so it'll be a PAYG, paid for in cash. Let's get a date and location for its purchase— Hampstead High Street, I'll put money on it—and let's get our voice experts matching this recording with the recordings of our interviews with him."

"Shouldn't we run it past Stanton—"

"Fuck Stanton."

MANON

• • •

SHE AND HARRIET HAVE BEEN SHOWN INTO A WAITING ROOM THAT RE-
sembles a lounge in a country-house hotel. Two leather Chesterfield
sofas face each other across a Persian rug. The smell of brewing coffee.
On a polished coffee table are arranged copies of *Country Life* magazine and *Homes & Gardens* and a generous vase of flowers. Around the
corners of the room, large lamps are lit.

"Officers," says Ian Hind, coming out from his room and bringing
with him the haste of the busy professional. "What a surprise. Do you
have an update for us? Wouldn't it be best to talk at home with Miriam?"

"Is there somewhere we could speak in private?" asks Harriet.

"Yes, of course. Rosemary," he says, peering out to where his receptionist sits at a desk in the lobby, "no interruptions, all right? Do
come through."

He shows them into another stately room, where he takes up a seat
in a leather chair beside his desk.

Harriet and Manon remain standing.

"Sir Ian," says Harriet, "I wonder if you could tell us where you were on the night of Sunday, eleventh of December."

"The eleventh of December? Well, now, that's two months ago. I'd have to consult my diaries, ask Miriam. Off the top of my head, I have absolutely no idea. At home, probably. I usually am on a Sunday night."

"You see, our cameras have snapshots of your car driving up the M11 toward East Anglia that night, in the direction of March, where your country house is."

He taps the steeple of his fingers a couple of times, turns his mouth down, looks at them blankly, as if in confusion.

"Yes, yes, that's right—I popped to Deeping. There were maintenance issues to do with the house—"

"Which you forgot to mention."

"I can barely remember making the trip, to be perfectly honest with you, but now that you mention it . . ." He gives them a condescending smile. Then looks at his watch. "Is there a significance to this, because I have a patient in ten minutes and I must look over his notes."

"One more thing, Sir Ian," says Harriet. "You have stated that you didn't know Taylor Dent."

"That's right."

"And yet you left a voicemail message on his phone saying, 'Meet me at the usual place,' on the eleventh of December, which was the date on which he was last seen."

"I'm sorry, what message?"

"Here, I'll play it for you," Manon says, opening an email on her smartphone and playing the sound file.

"Meet me at the usual place."

There is silence as the three of them listen, Hind looking at the surface of his desk, Harriet and Manon scrutinizing his face. He appears to be making a decision.

"You can't prove that's me," he says.

"Actually, we have traced the phone. It was purchased by you from Phones 4U on Hampstead High Street on the fifteenth of July, 2010. We've got a positive ID from the cashier," says Harriet.

"Look," he says, "I want to give the police absolute assistance in finding my daughter, I really do. I was talking to Rog about it only the other day—Roger Galloway, I mean. I was at the Commons and I told Roger how talented I felt the Cambridgeshire team was—you in particular, DI Harper—and that if he was looking at fast-tracking female officers—"

"Ian Hind, I am arresting you on suspicion of the murder of Taylor Dent—"

"Just a minute, Detective," he says, sitting upright. "Let's not get ahead of ourselves. I'm sure we can come to a mutually beneficial arrangement without all that caution business."

"You do not have to say anything. But it may harm your defense—"

"One call to Roger and you could move up the ranks very quickly indeed, smart pair like you. He's always saying he wants to see more women in the force."

"He should stop promoting men, then," says Manon.

Harriet sighs heavily. "If you do not mention when questioned something that you later rely on in court. Anything you do say may be given in evidence. Do you understand?"

"I can bury you too, you know."

"Do you know where Edith is?" asks Harriet.

"God, no, of course not. Look, can you sit, just for a moment?" he asks.

They nod and sit opposite him on the metal-framed chairs reserved for patients.

"I am not a bad man," he says. "It was all sort of an accident. He was blackmailing me, you see."

"We would advise you to have a lawyer present before you go any further," says Harriet.

"Yes, of course. Can I ask one thing? Don't tell Rosemary outside. There's no need to cuff me or anything, is there?"

"No, we can walk out together."

In an interview room at Kilburn station, after many hours with an expensive solicitor present, Sir Ian Hind signs a statement.

I met Taylor Dent six months previously, in June 2010. He was working on a building site opposite my home and he would catch my eye as I left the house, smile at me, barechested in the heat. I found myself attracted to him. I've been happily married for twenty-five years, but over the years I have had occasional sexual encounters with men. All very transactional—in the showers at the gym, that sort of thing. They were infrequent and never a relationship of any sort. My family are everything to me.

The encounters with Taylor were different. He awakened in me feelings I had last experienced at school. Up to this point, I had managed to compartmentalize my encounters with men from my life as a loving husband and father. But with Taylor, for the first time, something was building. We began meeting on Hampstead Heath. I didn't want Miriam finding out, so I bought a pay-as-you-go phone for the sole purposes of contacting him. I told myself it would soon be over—I would give him up, like a bad addiction—and life would return to normal. Yet I couldn't stop. It was more than just the sex, for me at least.

Taylor started asking me for money. It was never explicit, what I was paying for. I would tell him I wanted to help him when we met, give him fifty pounds usually, then it went up to a hundred pounds as he became more confident about the relationship. He was asking for money for specific things, trainers for his younger brother, that kind of thing. Then he asked if I had access to drugs at the surgery—he wanted ketamine and barbiturates. I assume he wanted to sell them on the street. I began to supply him with very small amounts, and on one occasion in late September, we took some ketamine together. The drugs made it easier for me to engage in . . . the things we were engaging in . . . the dangerous, illicit things about which I was generally inhibited.

I realized I was slipping into a lifestyle I didn't even recognize, one that threatened everything I had—my work, my family, my marriage. I told him I wanted to stop meeting, that I'd had enough. I wanted my life back, unsullied, but I suppose he'd become dependent on my money and the supply of prescription drugs.

Toward the end of November, he threatened me. He started to tell me details about my family to prove how much he knew. He said he'd tell Edith and Rollo and Miriam what I was—what I'd been doing on the Heath with him. He wanted ten thousand

pounds to keep quiet and to go away forever. I agreed to give it to
him; that's why I left that message. I agreed to hand over the money
on the evening of Sunday, eleventh of December. I wanted to pay
him off, told myself I was going resolve this issue once and for all
and then we could relax, I could enjoy Christmas with my family.

[Suspect breaks down in tears. Interview suspended.]

I got the money together and I also took some ketamine with me,
as I had often done, to the Heath. I want to be clear: my only intention was to give him what he wanted and to start anew. I felt Taylor
was a good person and that what we'd engaged in had affection in
it. I know that sounds naïve, given that he was blackmailing me,
but I felt he would take this money and that would be an end to it.

He was so manic—so bright-eyed, so excited. This was going
to change everything for him, he said, this sum of money. He had
a younger brother, as I said, and he told me this was going to make
his life different. It began to feel as if Taylor was glorying over me
and that he was happy our relationship was at an end.

I told him I had the ten thousand pounds he wanted in the
boot of my car and a little something else he might enjoy. I was
parked behind Jack Straw's Castle. He came with me to the car, I
handed him the bag of money, and he took, by way of celebration,
quite a powerful shot of ketamine from me. Then he told me that
what we had been doing repulsed him—that he was glad it was
over. "Don't have to do that disgusting shit no more," he said. He
looked at me with revulsion and I saw it was all about the money
for him.

[Suspect breaks down again. Interview halted for several minutes.]

I saw myself, tiny and humiliated. He never loved me; he never
even *liked* me. I revolted him, as did all the things we'd done. Something came over me, some powerlessness that transmitted itself into
pure rage. I've never felt so white hot with anger before. I pushed
him into the open boot of the car and slammed its door down
on him. I got in the car and started to drive, no idea where, just

anywhere. I found myself traveling the route to Deeping, which is like second nature to me. It was as if the car were driving itself. You know what it's like when a route is embedded in your brain— you can find yourself following it while your mind is entirely elsewhere. Before I knew it, I was on the M11. On that journey I thought: *I can drive him out of London and leave him stranded, without the money.* Ketamine is a potent analgesic—it causes sedation and amnesia while maintaining cardiovascular stability. He would be lost. And he would forget.

When I got to Deeping, I opened the boot and he was unconscious but alive; I checked. Ketamine, as I said, is an anesthetic: it leaves you dissociated, feeling as if you have no control over your legs or any movement at all. I went into the house and put the bag of money into an upstairs bedroom; I don't know why, to put it somewhere safe, out of his reach, I suppose. I thought I would return to get it later.

After putting the bag in the bottom of the wardrobe, I returned to the boot. I felt in his pockets to retrieve his mobile phone. I knew the phone could incriminate me, in terms of contact between myself and the boy—nothing else, you understand, just contact—and I was also taking away his means of getting help. I wanted him to take a long time getting home.

I got back in the car and drove along a dirt track—it was incredibly muddy—which runs across our land and over into the neighboring farm. I stopped in a wood beside a river and hauled him out of the boot and left him there, semi-conscious, on the ground, about ten feet from the water's edge. I did not put him in a river or drown him or cause his death. He must have come round, groggy, stumbled about, and fallen into the river later.

A week after that awful night, we were informed of Edith's disappearance. I was horrified; I still am horrified. I love my family. I would never do anything to hurt them. I know nothing of what's happened to my daughter and I am desperate to get her back.

In my haste to get back to Miriam that night—the night with Taylor Dent—I left the money in the bedroom at Deeping. When officers went to search the house, after Edith disappeared, I was sure they'd find it and ask what I was doing with ten thousand pounds stashed in a plastic bag in the bottom of a wardrobe. I had a plan to tell them (and Miriam) that I was paying cash for some building work to Deeping and that's why the money was there. I waited and waited but no mention of the money ever came. Of course, I couldn't bring it up or ask what had been found at Deeping; it would have raised too much suspicion.

MIRIAM

· · ·

SOME PEOPLE WILL SEE IT AS RUNNING AWAY, BUT WHAT DO THEY KNOW of all she's been through? A day can feel like a year. The minutes vibrate like dying wasps. Even the seconds are shuddering, giving up as they fizzle toward a strange, unnatural calm—as if petrifaction is taking place. This might be running away, yet it is so much more than that.

She waits at the baggage carousel, which is sparsely dotted with business-style cases, the type that resemble a shoe box on wheels. Executive luggage going round and round in La Rochelle arrivals. It's a strange hangar-like space, which in August throngs with pink Britons hauling folded prams off the rubber belt, sweating mothers and fathers carrying toddlers and more weight than they'd like, burgundy passports at the ready. She and Ian had been among them, all those years ago. Rollo in tears over something or other, wanting to ride in the trolley perhaps; Edie perched on the metal edge of the carousel, reading, as usual. Ian scanning the belt through the jostling crowd for their motley collection of bags. But this is January, blown about by rough winds and only a smattering of passengers—the odd French businessman, eager to get outside and light a Gauloise.

The sky is filled with voluminous clouds, which seem to boil up over the flat Vendée countryside. She drives under a canopy of trees, out of Fontenay-le-Comte, the roads smooth and empty. This is a spacious country. She is relieved to be away from tight little England and the reporting of Ian's arrest. Soon there would be the prying do-gooders, friends letting out the rope. Yes, it is a relief to be in this empty land where no one knows who she is, much less cares about the depravities of her husband. Former husband, she should begin to think of him but can't. She should have known, that's what she returns to again and again: she should have known. When DS Bradshaw rang on her door last night, Miriam experienced the slowing of time, like déjà vu. The detective stepping inside the front door, saying Ian had been arrested on suspicion of murder, seemed like a repetition of an event that had already happened, time on a loop, elongated like a stretched rubber band. She nodded, giving the outward appearance of having taken in what DS Bradshaw was telling her, but Miriam felt as if she were below the surface—perhaps of a lake—the sounds slow and lugubrious. Thoughts not keeping pace, quite.

She went to Ian's study, felt about in the desk drawer for the Nokia phone, the one with the child's pirate stickers all over it, which should have rung alarm bells when she first discovered it but didn't, she supposed, because Miriam had silenced them. You hear what you want to hear. See what you want to see. The phone wasn't there, of course. She felt about, instead, for keys to the safe-deposit box they kept behind the books in the lounge. You could always find the green metal box behind *Gray's Anatomy*.

"Are you all right?" DS Bradshaw asked, watching her with a look of intense concern. "You seem ... calm. Can I help you with something?" she said, confused as to what Miriam was doing pulling books from the shelves.

At last, she unlocked the box and there it was—the phone, among some foreign currency and a Rolex given to Ian by the Sultan of Brunei. He hadn't tried very hard to hide it.

"I imagine you'll be needing this," Miriam said, handing the phone to the detective.

"Thank you," she said.

"Is it the boy's?" Miriam asked.

"I don't know. Possibly." DS Bradshaw studied Miriam's face, then added, "There's something else I need to talk to you about." The detective told Miriam she thought Edith was alive—"I don't say that lightly, Lady Hind"—and that she may have been smuggled to France by a man called Abdul-Ghani Khalil.

"The Tilbury Docks case, the murder," Miriam said.

The detective said she thought Edith had been put in contact with Khalil by Tony Wright, that the phone calls between Edith and Wright had been to establish a pickup point on one of the motorways outside Huntingdon. Wright would have known how to avoid the CCTV cameras; Khalil would have known how to get her across the border without detection.

"But *why*?" Miriam asked.

"People want to disappear all the time. Commonest thing there is. Can you think of somewhere in France she might have gone? To hide?"

Miriam's mind felt about among her memories, like her hand patting in the central desk drawer, as she processed the idea. "Possibly. I don't know."

"I need you to give me a list of places she would know—places you've been on holiday, where there might be a connection for Edith—so that we can inform Interpol."

"Let me go," Miriam blurted, and she held the detective's gaze as intensely as she was able. "Let me go, please."

"I'm sorry, I—"

"I'm just asking you to delay, that's all. Hold back; give me some time. A day or two, that's all. I have an idea, but I might be wrong. Let me go and see if I can find her, coax her back. Our family's been through enough, don't you see?" She was holding the detective's arms, squeezing them, not letting her look away.

"I can't delay Interpol," the detective said, "but they'll be fairly ineffective without strong leads—a place to start, I mean. France is a big country. You'll have a head start if you don't delay, but I should warn you, my DI knows about the Wright–Khalil connection. They'll be interrogating Khalil on this. He might put a pin in the map for them."

Miriam nodded. "I understand," then led the way to the front door and closed it on the sergeant. Then she sank down to the coir matting in a puddle, her cheek on its coarse weave, smelling the boot dust and feeling the freezing winter air roar in under the door's brush strip. She went to bed soon after, her paralysis at war with the urging of the detective to make haste.

Lying in the bedroom, the dancing light playing through a chink in the curtains, she replayed the years of her marriage as if running a cinefilm in her mind. *Did he ever want us? A wife and children?* All the holidays—was he trapped, restless in every one? All the times he'd gone away for a conference or to play badminton with Roger. All their tendernesses, their various strains. The arguments and the reparation. She ran them all through a new filter, like a computer program adjusting the figures. She observed, and observed again, as if she might make the oscillation settle.

She cried, as the evening melded into night; cried then became still—cataplectic, almost. When she finally drifted off to sleep, the cinefilm began again, searching for clues in the crackling faded images of family life.

In the morning she heaved a suitcase down the stairs, Rollo's perplexed expression looking up at her.

"I'm sorry to leave you with all this," she said.

"Where are you going?"

"I can't tell you."

"Well, can I come with you?"

"No," she said, her palm to his cheek. "Darling Rollo. You must stay here. Go and visit him in prison. He needs you."

THE ROAD DOWN INTO VOUVANT winds beneath trees in leaf, past Monsieur Ripaud's riding stables, where Edith had gone on her first hack through the Forêt de Mervent without, Miriam had been horrified to learn from Ian, a helmet.

"Where do you think we get the phrase *laissez-faire* from?" he'd teased, bringing out the smelly cheeses that had filled the fridge of their holiday *gîte* with a sharp odor. "She survived, didn't you, Edie?"

"Ew, socks!" Rollo yelled whenever the fridge door opened and the smell hit him.

It was the summer Edith seemed to discover passion after passion—reading and horses, primarily—subsisting on a diet of French bread (soft white pillows torn from the middle) and peaches, which leaked rivulets of juice down her chin and onto her top. She hadn't wanted Miriam to wash the trousers she rode in, because they smelled of Artur, the horse she now ardently loved.

Miriam drives the car up the steep incline to the car park, in the shadow of the medieval Melusine tower. She pulls her coat from the backseat. The wind roars through the trees as she walks to the wall at the edge of the car park, peering over to the distant water below. Gusts stipple its surface into hurrying slicks like scales. She pulls the coat tightly around her and turns toward the *bar tabac,* where a carousel of postcards looks as if it might keel over in the wind.

"*Une Anglaise?*" says the man behind the bar. "*Elles sont partout.*"

"*Oui, mais une Anglaise qui habite ici?*" says Miriam. "*Il y a depuis quelques mois?*" She's fumbling about for idioms, like rummaging in an old suitcase. The words are there, but not necessarily in the right order.

"*Bof,*" he says, turning down the corners of his mouth. "'*Sais pas.*"

Miriam orders a coffee and surveys the room—a dark space with an enormous television bracketed to the wall, showing some sport or other with periodic cheers. A smattering of people, mostly watching the TV. She decides to take a table outside, despite the cold wind.

She holds down the flapping page of the guidebook she has purchased at Stansted for the purpose of finding accommodation, as the barman sets down her cup and saucer. Her leather-gloved hand rests on a page titled: "The Legend of Melusine."

According to the story, Melusine is said to have murdered her father and, as punishment for this, the lower half of her body was changed to that of a serpent every Saturday evening. Not long after, she met Raymond of Poitou, and when he asked to marry her, she agreed on condition that he would never gaze upon her on a Saturday evening. Everything was fine for several years and the couple lived in the château at Vouvant, but one night he broke the promise and saw her in the form of part-woman, part-serpent.

Typical view of female sexuality, Miriam thinks. *Serpent indeed.* She looks up to see a group of cyclists, just beyond the cluster of outside tables, in full professional gear—Lycra leggings, cycling gloves, stream-lined helmets, and wraparound mirrored sunglasses, which give them the silvered look of houseflies.

When, during a disagreement, Raymond called Melusine a "ser-pent" in front of the court, she assumed the form of a dragon and flew off, never to be seen again.

"Excusez-moi," says a man's voice, and Miriam looks up from her reading. He says he heard her in the bar, asking about a girl—*une Anglaise*—and from his rapid French, she gleans he knows of one.

"Jeune?" Miriam asks, squinting up at him, a hand over her brow.

"Oui, eh bien, dans la vingtaine je suppose," he says. *In her twenties.* His directions come in a rush that she tries very hard to follow: *"Tout droit, à gauche, en bas, par la rivière."*

She is discombobulated. She hadn't quite expected this journey to yield fruit. A flight away from the chaos in England, a pilgrimage into her family's past, yes. But might Edith *actually* be here?

Miriam hastens in the direction in which he has pointed, walking in the shadow of the shops, past the fruit and vegetable shop and the green-gloss *pharmacie,* around the corner to the Place de l'Eglise, past the *mairie,* stuck with a limp French flag, and, opposite it, Vouvant's twelfth-century church, broad steps leading up to twin arches.

She can't unravel any of the man's directions from here, and as she turns, examining each possible route, she notices an elderly woman carrying laden bags, who is walking slowly with a rolling gait. The woman is breathless with the exertion as Miriam approaches her.

"Rivière?" Miriam asks, pointing down one of the alleys off the Place de l'Eglise.

The woman nods. *"Oui, en bas,"* she says.

EDITH

. . .

A DAY OF SHARP SUN, SO BEAUTIFUL I'M TAKEN WITH THE IDEA OF OPEN-
ing up the tall windows in the bedroom. I spread them wide, setting a
cushion on the Juliet balcony, thinking of Lucy Honeychurch opening
her shutters at the Pension Bertolini.

The sun cooks my face but the breeze is still fresh, so I'm wrapped
in my thickest cardigan. I fetch my copy of *Jane Eyre* but I don't read.
I look out instead, calm for the first time in more than five weeks,
perhaps because I haven't done my Internet searches today. Head back
against the window frame, eyes closed, my eyelids glowing red with the
brightness, I hear the *patter-pat* of shoes in the alley below.

Slowly I straighten, squinting, to see the top of a head beyond the
wall. Gray hair. Something familiar about it, then a face upturned and
her eyes meet mine, and I am stabbed by familiarity and the shock of
love. Beloved face. I drop *Jane Eyre* and it falls from the balcony like a
shot bird.

I launch haphazardly into the dark interior of the flat, pummeling down the stairs to open the door to her. What is she doing here? How much will she hate me for what I have done? How much does she know, and how, oh, *how on earth* will I tell her? The secrets I have harbored; the secrets that will destroy her. The secrets I have been running from for five long weeks.

I unbolt the door and there is her ashen, accusatory face, and she has aged ten years since I last saw her. *My fault.*

"How could you?" she growls.

"Mum, I . . . I can explain. I can, Mum," I say. "You don't understand. . . ." But my words are stuck. "I never wanted to hurt you. . . ."

"How *could* you?"

"There are so many things you don't know," I cry. I cannot gather myself, cannot prevent myself crumpling.

"I thought you were *dead*," she says. Her eyes red-rimmed, now brimming, her forehead furrowed with disbelief and anger. There is nothing worse than seeing your mother cry and being the cause.

"Come in," I say, and I pull her toward me, take her in my arms, and she emits a cry of pain, her body heaving into mine. Her shouts, animalistic, are embarrassingly loud, bouncing off the alley walls. "Come in," I say. "I'll make you some tea. I can explain, I can explain why. . . ."

She snivels, reaches into her bag for a tissue, and wipes the wetness from her eyes and nose.

I lead her up the dark stairs to my apartment, wondering where I can begin. Explaining my disappearance means telling her things about our family that she shouldn't have to know. I don't know where I can start without hurting her, but I have hurt her already. I bring her into the lounge, take her handbag gently from her and lay it on the sofa, then guide her to a seated position.

"I don't know how to tell you," I say. I pace. I cannot look at her. She is looking up at me like an expectant child. "I know things, I saw things—"

"He's been arrested," she blurts. "You don't know, do you? Your father was arrested yesterday for the murder of Taylor Dent."

I stare at her. It doesn't have to come from me, like some malicious lie I've made up, some perverse thing I've imagined to cause her pain. I don't have to be the one to break it and yet I wish he hadn't been caught. I wish she didn't know, that he had got away with it, that they could still be together, and that I could have paid the price instead.

"Taylor Dent? Was that his name?" I whisper. "I didn't know."

"You saw," she says. "You saw it happen, at Deeping."

I nod, both of us now in a quiet daze.

"I still don't understand," she says. "Why run? Why did you want us to think you were dead?"

"I didn't!" It comes out hysterical, and I am losing myself again. I want to tell the truth but I don't know if I can. "I didn't, I didn't, I didn't!" I am shouting and pacing. "I wanted to disappear. I wanted the ground to swallow me up. I couldn't keep his secret and I couldn't turn him in. I couldn't go back to Will and I couldn't face Helena either."

"Helena—"

"I know," I wail, fists to my stomach. "Helena, oh, Helena." It comes out of my belly like fire, my guilt, my sorrow. How much I am responsible for. "She's dead and it's my fault. You don't have to tell me, Mum. You don't have to show me what I've done, what a mess I've made. I *know*."

"Edie," she says gently. "Edie, calm down. Come sit."

We light a fire. We gingerly hold cups of fennel tea, as if they might break. They warm our hands and we lean into each other, staring at the flames as they crackle and dance. She is sitting with her knees together, more formal than me. My legs are curled beside me. There has been a lot of silence, the two of us allowing ourselves to exhale.

She is wearing a shirt with a navy William Morris design, swirling leaves and seedpods. My head is leaning on her shoulder. I stare at the pattern on the fabric, the pendant that nestles in the soft wrinkles of her chest. I am moved by her fastidiousness, how smart she looks. Her rings gleam on her fingers, but the skin on her hands is reptilian and her face is dragged downward with sorrow and exhaustion. My poor mum. My tears fall again, and she kisses the top of my head.

"Can you tell me what happened?" she asks.

"I went to Deeping on a Sunday, early December, it was. In the afternoon. Got there about three—it was still light. I needed somewhere to think, away from Will. I was thinking about splitting up with him." I look up into her face. "You knew that, didn't you, Mum? I think you had an inkling that I was going to end it with him. Things had started with Helena, confusing stuff, and I didn't know if it was a symptom of wanting to leave Will or whether it was the start of something real with her—you know? I was really confused about it all, needed some headspace, away from both of them.

"I'd more or less decided to sleep there. I was lying on your bed—you know how I love it in your bed. It started to get dark and I fell asleep. I woke to clattering sounds downstairs. The house was pitch dark by now and I sleepily thought: *Ah, Mum and Dad are here.* But then I snapped awake. I'd spoken to you—remember?—and you told me you were staying home that weekend. Dad had too much work on so you weren't coming to Deeping. I froze, thinking it must be an intruder moving around downstairs. We're so lax about security at Deeping. I'd locked the front door on arrival—I'm always nervous being in the countryside by myself—but all the same, that key in the porch . . .

"There were footsteps coming up the stairs. My heart was pounding; I was terrified. I slipped off the bed and climbed inside your wardrobe, pulling the door closed and your clothes in front of my face. The intruder came into the room, right up to the wardrobe. I thought I was dead, but he pulled the drawer at the bottom and shoved something into it. I stayed there, cowering, as the footsteps receded. I heard more clattering downstairs, then the front door closed. I crept out of the wardrobe and onto the window seat. The sensor light had come on with his movement and I saw Dad open the boot of his car. I saw a body in the boot—a boy—"

"Taylor Dent," says Miriam sadly.

"I didn't know his name. I've tried to find out since then—I've googled missing people and murders in East Anglia—but there's been nothing about a black boy killed in or near March. His death seemed to go unreported."

"Unlike yours," said Miriam.

"Yes," I say, sitting upright. "In the weeks that followed, I was everywhere, but there was no mention of him." I slouch back down, against her shoulder. It is easier to tell her my story if I don't look into her face. "I watched from the upstairs window. I was shaking. I mean, you don't put someone in a boot unless you're doing wrong by them. The boot is where you put animals, not people."

"Hadn't he seen your car?"

"I parked right at the end of the carport. You know how short the G-Wiz is—he can't have seen it from the drive. My heart was thudding. I knew it was really bad—a boy in the boot. Dad was going through his pockets and the boy's body was rocking, unconscious or dead. He searched until he found something I couldn't see—a phone or a wallet—which he put in his own pocket. My mind was racing, thinking, why does someone go through a boy's pockets—a boy who's unconscious or dead? There was no explanation except the worst explanation.

"Before I could run down to him, demand an explanation, the doors of the car had slammed shut and he had driven away. I went to the drawer at the bottom of the wardrobe to see what he'd stashed there. It was piles and piles of money, bound together with rubber bands in a plastic bag."

"So you took the cash?" she says. I nod and she smiles wanly, saying, "At least it stayed in the family."

"I thought about all the things I could do: return to George Street and Will; pretend I hadn't seen anything; tell the police what I'd seen; tell you; go to Helena. And not one of them seemed possible. I was butting up against each option and it was like being in a dodgem car, hitting the buffers. I thought about flying to Buenos Aires to find Rollo, and then I thought about telling him. The awfulness. Then I wondered if anyone would believe me. I wondered if I would seem mad, the destroyer of our family life. I wondered if in fact I *had* gone mad and all of it was an apparition, that I should be sectioned. I looked at the money and I thought about disappearing. And it made sense. All I knew, Mum, you have to believe me, was that I wanted to run. My only impulse was to disappear, not to hurt you."

"But you did hurt me. You hurt me very deeply, Edith."

"I couldn't bear knowing something that would destroy you; I didn't want to keep his secrets but I didn't want to betray him either. I couldn't go back to Will and I couldn't bear Helena, the confusion of that. I was trapped, d'you see? When I looked at the money he'd left, I knew that was my way of disappearing. Money could make it happen. I could vanish, I knew people who could help me—"

"What people?"

I get up. I can't look at her. "Another tea?" I say, taking the cup from her hand.

"What people, Edith?" she says.

"Never mind that. You don't need to know what people. That money could make me vanish, as if the ground had opened up, and that's what I wanted."

I come back into the room with two steaming-hot mugs. "What's happened to him? Where are they keeping him?" I ask.

"He's in Littlehey. Rollo will visit. We've retained lawyers at Kingsley Napley."

"Is he all right?"

"I haven't seen him," she says, and I can see the torment written on her face. "I will, though." She looks up. "I will see him. He's still my husband."

Her look is defiant and I stare at her. "After everything he's done . . ." I begin.

She frowns. "I won't explain myself to you, Edith," she says. "I won't justify how I feel to *you*."

We are silent again, but it is not a comfortable silence.

MIRIAM
. . .

SAYING IT TO EDITH IS THE FIRST TIME SHE HAS ALLOWED HERSELF TO have the thought, and she is surprised by the force of her conviction. He is still her husband. One event cannot wipe away twenty-five years. Yes, she will visit him in Littlehey. It may take her some time; she may feel furious, betrayed, ashamed. But she won't abandon him. Friends may let out the rope, but she will not.

"How did he die?" Edith is asking now. "Taylor Dent. What did Dad—"

"Drowned," Miriam says. "In the river close to Deeping. I don't know what his injuries were. He'd been on drugs—ketamine—which may have been what caused his death when he hit the water. Paralyzed, effectively. Anyway, it'll all come out in the trial."

"So he might have been alive in the boot of the car?" Edith says, and Miriam can see the slow dawning on her face. "I could have helped him, if I hadn't stayed hidden."

"A lot of things would have been different if you hadn't stayed hidden," Miriam says, and she can't keep the censure out of her voice. Relief that her daughter is alive is giving way to hot fury, the kind she remembers from when Edith was little—those times when she lost sight of her in a park or on a beach and had to search wildly, shouts becoming hysterical and other mothers helping with instinctive urgency. And then when Edith or Rollo was discovered, nonchalantly playing inside a hedge or squatting in the sand, how she would tear a strip off them and make them cry, that they might experience a tiny millisecond of her fear. "Don't you ever, *ever* do that again." At the same time holding them very, very tight.

"How *could* you stay away?" she asks now. "How could you? You must've seen the scale of the manhunt, what the police were doing. You must've known everyone thought you were dead. That we thought you were dead."

Edith starts to cry again. "Don't you see? It had all gone too far. It had gone too far for me to come back. . . ." She is gulping, and Miriam wonders if it is guilt that's catching in her throat. "It was a thing I couldn't undo, and then Helena died. This whole series of events was set off by me and I didn't even . . . I didn't expect it. The bigger it became—all over the news, the number of police officers involved—the more impossible it was for me to come home."

"You couldn't send me an email, a postcard, telling me you were all right?" Miriam asks.

Edith turns away. There is something in this question she cannot answer.

"Edith?" Miriam presses.

EDITH

. . .

I CAN FEEL THE GAPS IN MY STORY, HOW THEY MUST SEEM TO HER. I CAN hear how lame my explanation must sound. And yet, in the quiet of the French countryside, the days went by. The more you don't make contact, the more impossible contact becomes, as if silence can enlarge like a seep of blood. And in the solitude I found space. Freedom. Something heady and illicit. I didn't *want* to return. I can't say that to her. It is a selfishness too far. Her face, the color of the ash in the grate, would look at me with too much sorrow and disappointment. Well, I've been disappointed too.

"He let me down," I whisper. "He wasn't the person I thought he was. He set such high standards for me and all the while—"

"People have inner lives, Edie; you're old enough to know that."

"But why would he kill a boy?" I say, and in saying it, I've answered the question to myself.

She looks away. I can see she is ashamed.

"Mum?"

"They were . . ." she begins. "They were having a relationship, it seems."

"A relationship?"

"Yes," she says.

"Is he . . . ?"

"Is he what?" she says, looking at me sharply. "Gay? Straight? Are you? Is anyone just one thing?"

"How can you forgive him?"

"Who said anything about forgive?"

"You seem . . ." I begin, but I can't find the right word. Accepting?

"Perhaps I don't set my standards for people quite as high as yours," she says.

"He has always been the one with impossible standards," I say. "The one who set the bar so high when all the while he . . ." I begin to cry: corrosive, satisfying, righteous tears. "I wasn't even allowed to keep my baby, settle down with Jonti, lead an average life. Oh no, that wasn't good enough, when all the time he was . . ."

She looks up, shocked. "You could have kept the baby, Edie. We never made you—"

"That's not how it felt," I say, and I am dealing in half-truths. "It was made clear to me that it would have been a failure. There were so many expectations."

"I never knew you felt that way about the baby, darling. We didn't see it as making you get rid of it. We saw it as helping you make a sensible decision—for your life. And maybe we were wrong. I saw Jonti recently, when I was searching for you. And the thought occurred to me that the two of you could have made it work. He's a decent chap. But we honestly thought we were doing right by you, Edie. There's lots of time to have a baby; you don't have to do it at eighteen, when it's so hard. That's not expectation—that's love. We wanted the best for you. I don't mean Cambridge; I mean I didn't want you depressed and alone at eighteen with a screaming infant on your hands."

She is looking at me now, with the concern I have longed for. She says, "Oh, I know Ian can be exacting and I can see you might think we wanted you to be perfect. God, maybe there was narcissism in it.

I mean, which parent doesn't want to say, 'My daughter's gone up to Cambridge'? But that's nothing next to loving you, Edith."

"How was I supposed to know what I wanted when your expectation was so *huge,*" I say, in a wail. "When all I ever wanted was to please you? Why is my life defined by pleasing you, when he . . . when he . . . he's done something so immoral!"

It has backfired.

She has stood up and I can see the rage popping at her temples. Her words come out in a low growl, only just suppressing the violence I can see she feels toward me. "You are the child of a *man.* An ordinary man, who has strengths and weaknesses and who descended into a crisis. Yes, he's done something terrible, for which he will face a very harsh punishment.

"And you are *my* child, Edie, though you show me no love at all. *You* have to decide who you are. You have to decide, Edie. It's not enough to say we made you this, and we made you that, and expectation took away this and pressure demanded that. Stand up and be counted. And if your love ends the moment you find out your parents are people, then, my God, there really is no hope for you."

"But he's fallen so short," I say quietly. A damp squib.

"So have you, Edith."

We are silent. Mum has dropped onto the sofa. Her eyes are glazed. She stares into the fire and then says, "'Love is not love which alters when it alteration finds.'" She looks at me. "He's your father and you should stand by us, as we stand by you."

MANON

...

"Fly? Fly! C'mon. Homework."

He groans from somewhere beyond the hall and she waits, looking at the dappled garden, the sun playing through the fingers of the lime trees. Honeyed patio stones radiate with the heat of the day.

"Fly! Come on, stop wasting time."

He joins her at the kitchen table and hauls his school bag onto his knee with am-dram weariness. His white school shirt has a pen leak at the pocket, a blot of black checkering into the cotton. He smells of sweaty boy. She makes a mental note to buy him some shower gel.

"What treats do your teachers have in store for us this evening?" she asks.

"I have to, like, write a persuasive argument for something, like a party political fingy."

"Broadcast. Party political broadcast. OK, any ideas?"

"Like why I should be allowed to watch TV after school like them other kids."

"*Those* other kids, Fly. You're not going to be very persuasive with grammar like that. Go on, then, write it as if you're persuading me."

"No one can persuade you of nothin', DS Auntie."

"DI Auntie, to you."

He splays across the table like a broken umbrella, chewing the end of his pen. He whispers to himself when he starts to write. She gets up to stir the lamb stew, which is bubbling on the hob.

"If you finish that, you can go out for a bit," she says, her back to him.

"Serious?" he says.

"Serious."

It gives her pleasure to surprise him with a loosening of his restrictions, even while she knows that same pleasure will tighten to anxiety as she waits for him to come home. She can hardly refuse him these forays: along Mill Lane to the newsagent, where he can buy pick-and-mix; to sit on the swings in Sumatra Road; up to Fortune Green, where friends from his school congregate in the park and scale the wire fence into the play center. He is about to turn twelve, is well over five foot, and now walks to school alone.

"No hoodie, though," she says, thinking of the group of them, how they scare people on the bus. They are so tall and so burgeoning male.

He groans. "Why?"

"One, because you'll boil in this heat—even if your trousers are right down below your bum, which makes you look completely ridiculous, by the way, but we've had that conversation—and two, because I don't want anyone mistaking you for something you're not. You are a lovely, gentle, well-mannered boy, Fly. Don't give anyone any reason to think otherwise."

"Why should I be stopped from wearing an item of clothing just 'cos of the color of my skin?"

"Maybe that should be the subject of your persuasive argument," she says. "Oh, and Fly? No smoking in the cemetery. And don't come the innocent with me—I know you've done it."

"Whatevs," he says in a whisper. His disdain is gossamer light, and she thinks she can detect beneath it his pleasure at the tight boundaries she lays.

"And I want you back by six o'clock sharp for supper. Ellie and Sol are coming."

"OK," he says. "Can I feed Solly?"

"I'm sure Ellie would be delighted," she says, smiling at him. "What d'you reckon—rice or couscous with the stew?"

"What's couscous?" he says, his eyes down to his books again.

"The grainy one, yellow."

"Yeah, that one."

The room is full of pale May light and the smell of cooking meat, and she is struck by how far they've come in their journey to being a family of sorts.

She hadn't thought any of it through. Fly's mother's illness had been swift and brutal. Three months after Ian Hind's arrest and four months after Manon first met Maureen, the stomach cancer killed her, without pause for admission to a hospice. Manon traveled to London without a plan, telling herself whatever happened next would be temporary. She and Fly stayed with Ellie—necessity being the mother of reconciliation—in her little two-bed flat on Fordwych Road, which ran like a vein on the border between Kilburn and West Hampstead. Far from a pink paradise, Ellie had broken up with Solly's feckless father during pregnancy and was tearfully battling sleep deprivation without respite.

It was cramped. The baby shared Ellie's bedroom, Manon was in the spare room, and Fly was on a put-you-up in the lounge, which he diligently tidied each morning before anyone was up. In this she saw all his worry about the precariousness of his situation.

Those two months living like that—using up all Manon's annual leave and numerous days owing from years of night shifts and weekends on duty—allowed Fly to complete his last term at primary school, where the teachers were invested in him. And it allowed Ellie the odd night off. Ellie and Manon had some understanding of what Fly needed most—the importance of keeping to existing routines after the death of one's mother.

"It's nice—having you around," Ellie said. "He brings out good things in you, Fly does."

But the person who brought out the best in all of them was Solly. How that baby delighted them, Fly especially, who lay next to Solly on the carpet and tickled his toes, blew raspberries on his tummy, and covered his own face with his hands, removing them to say, "Boo!" and Solly's chuckle would ring out, its music like a belly-burst of joy. Squawking, guffawing, high notes like piano keys—it was impossible not to smile when Solly laughed, and he appeared to spend most of his day laughing.

When all her leave was used up, Manon's hand was forced.

"I'll ask Fly to stay with friends," she told Ellie, "just while I square things in Huntingdon. I don't expect you—"

"Don't be silly. He has to stay here," Ellie told her. "Solly loves him. And anyway, he mustn't be uprooted too much, not after what he's been through. I like the company, to be honest. How long will it take you? When will you be back?" And there was fear in Ellie's eyes that they might be separated again.

"Not long," Manon said, telling herself the changes she was about to make were temporary—a stint in the Met while she sorted out a permanent arrangement for Fly, in a foster family or some such.

EDITH HIND RETURNED TO THE UK with her mother, attending Cambridgeshire Police HQ voluntarily. She wanted to explain, she said. She wore a white shirt buttoned to the top, its pointy collar ever so prudish, navy cigarette trousers over nerdish brown brogues, and glasses with thick black frames, which Manon thought were probably an affectation. The whole ensemble worked to create the impression of a serious young woman genuinely troubled by circumstances unforeseen. Despite the demure librarian outfit, she was breathtaking: glossy auburn hair curling beneath her pointed chin; skin like alabaster; slim and graceful. Manon couldn't stop staring, as if she were hungry for more of her, and she wondered if Edith's beauty meant she should face greater censure. Or perhaps less. Did Manon want someone so beautiful to get away with it or did she want to enviously punish her?

She and Harriet sat on the other side of the table to Edith, who was flanked by Miriam and a very expensive lawyer.

"I want to hear this," said Davy, who stood with his back to the wall. Everyone else, including Gary Stanton, watched the interview in the video room.

"Miss Hind," Harriet said, with unctuous politesse, "there were traces of blood in the kitchen of your home in George Street—along a kitchen cabinet and some pooling on the floor, plus some drips of blood in the hallway of your home. Can you explain how they got there?"

"Yes, yes I can," she said, pushing copper ropes of hair behind one ear. *Adorable.* "When I got back to the house with Helena, I found I was much drunker than I realized, swaying and stumbling, struggling to stay upright, to be honest." *Innocent little laugh.* "In the kitchen I poured myself a glass of wine—this was after Helena had gone—but in picking it up, I knocked it, hard, on the worktop and it smashed in my hand, cutting me across the palm. I was shocked by the amount of blood—it literally gushed from my palm. I stared at it for a moment, in that drunken way, as if it belonged to someone else, and in that time it splashed down the kitchen cupboard and onto the floor. I did a rather poor job of cleaning up the broken glass. I put the bloodied shards into the bin and got myself a new wineglass down, which I never used in the end. I stumbled upstairs, holding my bleeding hand—which is why there were drips on the hallway floor—and managed to knock the coats off their hooks as I staggered up to the bathroom for a bandage. I'm sorry," she said, looking Harriet in the eye, "if this was misconstrued as an injury following an act of violence. I had no idea it would be."

"Why did you leave the door to your house open?" Harriet asks.

"What?"

"Will Carter says that when he returned home, he found the front door ajar. Why is that?"

"I didn't. I closed it. I thought I did, anyway. Look, I was all over the place that night. I'd had too much to drink. And I was frightened about what I was about to do—I was heading into the unknown. I knew how dangerous the journey could be. I went back and forth, stumbling about. I thought I closed the door, but maybe in my haste, in my panic, I didn't pull it firmly enough behind me."

"So you have stated that you walked out of Huntingdon, out

toward Papworth Everard, and on the A428 you waited in an appointed lay-by until a truck pulled up beside you. Appointed by whom?" said Harriet, looking at her notes.

"Abdul-Ghani Khalil."

"The back of the lorry was opened by a man you didn't recognize, and you got in. Inside were several other stowaways of various nationalities. You were driven to what we can only guess was a port—you have stated that you could feel the sensation of the lorry boarding a ferry and driving into the hold. You were let out of the lorry in a lay-by just north of Calais in France."

"Well, no, it was an *aire*," she said, the "r" rolling in a pointedly French way.

"I'm sorry?" said Harriet.

"I was let out in an *aire*—a French service station. I was desperately stiff and needed the loo. This was where the transfer took place—to a car, driven again by a man I didn't know. He took me as far as Nantes. I paid him the cash as agreed—four thousand pounds."

"Agreed by?"

"Abdul-Ghani Khalil," she said.

"How did you meet Abdul-Ghani Khalil?"

"No comment."

"Were you introduced to Abdul-Ghani Khalil by Tony Wright?"

"No comment."

"Did you meet Abdul-Ghani Khalil when you were visiting Tony Wright in Whitemoor Prison?"

"No comment."

"Did you pay Tony Wright to effect an introduction to Abdul-Ghani Khalil?"

"No comment."

"Did Tony Wright give you instructions for a pickup that led to you being smuggled across the border illegally?"

"No comment."

"Why did Tony Wright's number appear twice on your phone in the week before you disappeared, once on the day before?"

"We're friends."

"What sort of friends?"

"Just friends. Have been ever since I visited him in Whitemoor. I was upset about what I'd seen at Deeping involving my father. I wanted to talk to him about it."

MANON WASN'T IN HUNTINGDON FOR long. Once she returned to North London, there was a work hiatus while she applied for jobs, in which she ate into her savings and the income from letting out her Huntingdon flat (no point selling, given how this was a temporary situation). She took a six-month let on a flat, five doors down from Ellie's, and installed herself and Fly in it. She double-checked with the agent: "So it's one month's notice on either side, right?"

During this time, she sat her inspector exams and Fly fell apart.

Perhaps it was the move to a separate flat (Manon felt they couldn't keep imposing on Ellie, who wanted to move Solly out of her bedroom). Or the transition to a vast and terrifying secondary school close by. Or just an accumulation of experiences too complex for him to manage. But all of a sudden they were alone together in the face of Fly's rage and sorrow.

"He's started wetting the bed, having night terrors," she found herself confiding to Miriam, during the hours waiting at the Old Bailey for Ian Hind's various pre-trial hearings, either sitting on the benches outside Court One or nudging a tray along silver track lines in the canteen. "I'm so knackered—up five or six times a night, changing sheets. Trying to calm him down."

"Like having a newborn," Miriam said.

It was ironic to be leaning on Miriam, who had aged but was also serene with Edith back at home. It hadn't taken that much to persuade Edith to return with her to London, Miriam said. She had a conscience, under all that self-serving narcissism.

"And I say that with great affection," Miriam said with a smile. "Told her it was better to go back voluntarily than be dragged back by Interpol. Told her you had made the connection with Abdul-Ghani Khalil and had mobilized French police. It was only a matter of time. She started sniveling, of course—that child is a master of self-pity—but I reassured her we'd hire good lawyers and a PR man to handle the newspapers."

Everyone at Cambridgeshire wanted to charge the girl with wasting police time, perverting the course of justice, and anything else they could throw at her for sparking a five-week investigation at a cost of around three hundred thousand pounds of taxpayers' money. But the Hinds' legal team, numerous and dark-suited, formulated a robust defense stating it could not be proven that she "intended" the police to infer she had come to harm. The blood, the fallen coats, the door left ajar, were all the accidental detritus of a night of panic and duress. She had merely fled the source of her distress—the crime committed by her father, whom she neither wished to shelter nor betray. The fact that Cambridgeshire Police had upscaled it to a high-risk misper could hardly be laid at young Miss Hind's door. Psychiatric reports stated she had suffered "mental anguish" in rural France.

"Anguish my arse," Harriet said.

In the opposite corner were the prosecution arguments: why did she stay away when she saw, by reading UK press reports online, the scale of the manhunt? How could she justify not telling anyone she was alive and well, even if she didn't wish to return?

A judge looked at the arguments and deemed there was a case to answer, the outcome yet to be determined in court.

At the Old Bailey, as legal wheels turned ever so slowly in proceedings against Ian Hind, Manon sought Miriam's wisdom about Fly, which probably broke some protocol to do with "sides," but neither woman cared.

"All I know is I can't take much more," Manon said.

"He's not doing it to spite you," said Miriam.

"No, I know, but I can't understand what's going on inside him."

"No, I never knew what was going on in my children either," said Miriam, and Manon was surprised to be taken as a fellow mother. "It sounds to me like he needs to know that you'll stick with him, however bad it gets, just like a mother does with a newborn baby."

She had no idea if Miriam was right but she did stick with him, though not out of nobleness. Out of exhaustion and inertia. This was not a situation she could easily unpick.

She swapped notes with Davy too, who had seen it all before at the drop-in center.

"Firm boundaries," Davy told her. "It's still love, it just doesn't waver. These kids can't take any flip-flopping. Scares the life out of them."

He is so wise, now-DS Davy Walker under Stanton's kindly wing, and resolutely single, having once more extricated himself from Chloe's clutches following the comfort shag. His life is MIT, bike rides, and his volunteering at the youth center. "More than enough," he told Manon when she'd asked if he was seeing anyone.

Poor Stanton. A standard review of the Hind investigation by Bedfordshire Police found that "Detective Chief Superintendent Gary Stanton overreacted in upscaling the disappearance of Edith Hind to a high-risk misper, later a suspected homicide, as there was insufficient prima facie evidence that Miss Hind had come to harm."

"He can't win," Davy told Manon, as if he were defending his own father. "First Lacey Pilkington, where he's told he should have upscaled it sooner, and now this. I don't know how he keeps going."

"Thinking about his pension, that's how," Manon said.

She hadn't thought it through, the situation with Fly, though she spent quite a bit of time wondering if she could get out of it. How she might tiptoe away.

Then Fly got ill.

Winter and a fever took such strong hold of him it was medieval, and no amount of paracetamol or Nurofen seemed to bring his temperature down. His heart raced like a mechanism about to spring out of its holdings. Manon couldn't get through to the GP practice— just endless ringing or the engaged signal—so in desperation she rang Miriam, who drove round, parking Ian's incongruous Jaguar next to the skips of Fordwych Road. She checked his vital signs.

"Can eleven-year-olds get meningitis?" Manon asked.

"You've been on the Internet," Miriam scolded. "Never look on the Internet for medical advice. You'll diagnose yourself with cancer. Look, you were right to call me—it is a very high temperature and we do need to keep an eye on him."

They sat together briefly in Manon's lounge on a sofa draped with a cheap cream throw and lit by a tiny lamp on a shelf. Miriam seemed more relaxed than Manon had seen her, though she wouldn't take her coat off.

"How's Ian coping with Belmarsh?" Manon asked.

"Do you know, he's all right," she said, sounding amused and surprised at the same time. "He's reading a lot. Teaching an anatomy course to other inmates—ironic, really, as some of them have actually decapitated people. I keep worrying his imperious manner will get him on the wrong side of people—you know, he'll ask for quince jelly with his cheese and someone will punch his lights out. But it hasn't happened yet."

"The children visit him?"

"Yes," she said. "Both of them. We're all doing our time," she said. Then, rising: "Look, I'll pop round in the morning on my way to work. Then I can admit Fly if I'm worried."

Though Miriam was satisfied it was only flu, the illness raged through him for two whole weeks, like a tidal wave slapping the pier wall with all its force, his rigid body tensed against it. He shook when he stood to pee. His bedroom smelled overripe, as Manon threw open the windows and changed the sheets—a sweetness that was fetid. Eventually he could begin to read and watch TV, but he was hollow-eyed and weak. And then a terrible depression took hold and he cried for his mother and for Taylor. And he blamed Manon, resented her, because she was the nearest target for his distress. His unhappiness was so deep and wide that more than once she wondered if it would ever lift.

THE IPCC REPORT INTO THE death of Helena Reed, following contact with Cambridgeshire Police, resulted in a reg 14 misconduct notice for DC Monique Moynihan, who had taken the call from Helena on the night of January 7, 2011. In her witness statement, DC Moynihan stated that staffing levels in MIT that night were herself and two other detective constables. However, one of these detective constables had a period of twenty days' leave owing, and this officer had been advised by the division if he did not take the time off it would be lost. DC Moynihan stated that she raised concerns about the staffing levels with DI Kirk Tate but did not file a report on the matter. DI Tate did not recall DC Moynihan raising the issue. DC Moynihan had a number of investigations in progress on the night of January 7 that she considered urgent. She said Miss Reed had sounded tentative and shy but not in great distress when she had rung the department. She noted that Miss

Reed had not called 999. Immediately following the call, DC Moynihan and the other detective on duty that night, DC Lee Rayner, were called out to a reported burglary.

The IPCC additionally looked into the duty of care toward Helena Reed by MIT team four investigating the disappearance of Edith Hind. The IPCC noted that the Hind investigation was extremely high profile and required a great deal of police resource. It found that risk assessments of Helena Reed prior to the *Crimewatch* appeal on Wednesday, January 4, 2011, undertaken by DC Kim Delaney, and additionally a risk assessment filed by DS Manon Bradshaw, were adequate and adhered to professional-standards protocol. However, interviews with Miss Reed's psychoanalyst, Dr. Young, revealed that her fragile state was in excess of officers' assessments of her mental health.

The IPCC issued a learning-strategy document with a recommendation that all members of MIT team four, which investigated the Hind misper, undertake a duty-of-care refresher course and complete the two-hour training package on mental health.

MANON HEARS THE VIBRATION OF her mobile phone on the kitchen table and walks over to Fly's books, patting among the papers and crumbs until she finds it. A text from DCI Havers of Kilburn CID—her new boss.

Want you on early shift tomorrow, DI Bradshaw.

Her current arse ache, the new job. No Harriet to chat to (now DCI at Cambridgeshire, the rest of the band still together—that rankles) and a twat like Havers lording it over her. And Fly increasingly beset by the Met's stop-and-search obsession. She's told him to keep the details, to log every single incident, in a notebook in his ever-drooping jeans back pocket, and these she follows up.

"Didn't know he was eleven," said one Met officer.

"Try asking him," she replied.

"Sorry, Mrs. . . ."

"It's DI Bradshaw."

They didn't like ruffling their own, and she hoped to make it clear, at least to all the officers at Kilburn, that Fly was not to be touched. A white copper mothering a black boy—didn't that set the cat among the pigeons.

She's worried about some of the lads he's hanging out with at school. Another mental note: to make an appointment with the headmaster. Shower gel, see the headmaster, pick up fruit, bread, and bin bags. When did her lists get so *long*? She casts about for a pad and pen. Buy pad and pen for lists.

WHEN THE SIX-MONTH LET EXPIRED, she signed for another six, checking again: "It's one-month notice on either side, right?"

Life isn't perfect, she thinks, as the lot of them clatter into her kitchen. It has taken her a while to get on friendly terms with this notion. She had thought perhaps it was perfect for others, just not for her. Or that she could revise and revise and revise life, as if sitting a perpetual Cambridge exam, and it would become perfect. Increasingly, she can find no evidence of perfection in any life. There's always something: illness, divorce, bereavement, or corners of the personality that are devastating to live with. Everyone making the best of it, doing their time, together by accident—like Manon and Fly, because he had no one else and she couldn't back out of it.

"Sit down, everyone," she says. "Dinner's ready. Ellie, would you like some wine?"

"Lovely," says Ellie, and she hands the solid dollop that is Solly to Fly, saying, "Here you go, do your worst."

Fly holds Solly about his hip, smiling his hello with a kiss into the little boy's neck while Solly clutches Fly's cheeks with his fat hands and lets out a delighted screech.

Manon and Fly have bought an Ikea high chair for ten pounds to have in their flat, and a cot for when Solly stays overnight. Fly wedges Solly into his high chair, and the baby bangs on the plastic table in excited anticipation of mashed stew. Everyone is seated except Manon, who is being "mother" with a ladle hovering above the plates.

"Actually," she says, "there's something I want to ask Fly, and I wanted all of you to be here."

Even Solly, who has been waving his arms at the approach of the first of Fly's spoonfuls, stops and looks up with an expectant expression on his face, making all of them laugh.

"I want to adopt you," she says to Fly.

"You what?"

"Ada-boooo!" sings Solly.

"I want to adopt you. I want us to be . . . tied. Make it legal."

He looks at her for a moment. Then turns back to Solly with a new spoonful. "So you can nag me forever."

"So I can nag you forever, that's right."

She sits down and pushes a piece of lamb about the plate, where it gathers beads of couscous like a wet stone in sand.

"Poon!" says Solly, wrestling Fly for the spoon.

"That's right," Fly says to him. "Poon." He moons his face into Solly's, nose to nose, and the boy screeches and clutches at Fly's cheeks again with meaty hands.

"Because I love you," Manon says.

"Poon!" insists Solly.

"All right, chatty man," Fly says to him. "Here comes another one." He makes the spoon fly and Solly opens his mouth on cue. Then Fly takes a forkful from his own plate. "This stew is all right," he says. "Even though there is veg in there. Is this carrot?"

"No, no," says Ellie. "You're imagining it."

"Can I go round Zach's to play on his PlayStation after?" asks Fly.

"Nope," says Manon.

Fly has turned to take another forkful of food. He and Manon chew on mouthfuls, looking at each other.

"Why do you ask when you know what the answer will be?" Manon asks.

He shrugs. "For a laugh. I figure one day you'll slip up."

"In your dreams. What do you reckon, then, about what I just said? About becoming my son?"

"Yeah. OK."

ACKNOWLEDGMENTS

• • •

I am indebted to Detective Sergeant Graham McMillan of Cambridgeshire's Major Crime Unit for his help with this book; also to Detective Sergeant Susie Hine of Cambridge CID for advice on the first draft. Inaccuracies are mine, not theirs.

Thank you, Superintendent Jon Hutchinson, for facilitating my visits to Cambridgeshire's MCU.

For guidance on pathology, thank you, Clare Craig, consultant pathologist at Imperial College NHS Trust. For postmortem and coroners detail, thanks to Michael Osborn, consultant histopathologist at Imperial.

For Maureen Dent's Irish vernacular, thanks to Marissa McConville.

For Tony Wright's Scots vernacular, thanks to Eileen MacCallum.

For advice on criminal law, thank you, Daniel Burbidge.

The report published by the Cambridge Institute of Criminology in November 2011 into staff–prisoner relations in Whitemoor, on which Edith fictionally assisted as a researcher, is real. It is readily available online and is a riveting and humane read. Find it here: gov.uk/government/uploads/system/uploads/attachment_data/file/217381/staff-prisoner-relations-whitemoor.pdf.

Thanks, Sandra Laville, of *The Guardian,* for advice on hacking and Soham.

Thanks to Sian Rickett, Susannah Waters, Alexandra Shelley, Daniel Burbidge, John Steiner, Deborah Steiner, and Zoe Ross for careful reading and good advice. And to Katie Espiner and Andrea Walker for brilliant editing. Thank you, Eleanor Jackson, for going out to bat for me Stateside. To Sarah Ballard, thank you for everything, as always. Thank you, Tom Happold, for being my first and last reader and for all your support. And George and Ben Happold for bundling in from school and filling the house with joyful noise after the silence of the attic.

Read on for an exclusive bonus chapter that
will take you from *Missing, Presumed*
to Susie Steiner's new novel,

PERSONS UNKNOWN
· · ·

MANON

. . .

"So," Harriet said, pacing and taut as ever with nervous energy. "You know the work we do—pursuing criminals?"

This was in the back-and-forth period, when Manon was extricating herself from Huntingdon and moving to London.

"Not sure about the 'we,'" Manon said. "You seem to be mostly behind your desk, pursuing bargains on H&M."

"Management brings with it responsibility. My role is strategic, whereas you—"

"Where's this heading?" Manon asked. "Because I've got a bacon roll on my desk that's calling my name very loudly."

"Yes, right—that's where it's heading. Yes, that's exactly where this is heading."

"Toward my bacon roll?"

"Away from your bacon roll. Away from all bacon rolls."

Manon looked at her friend, palms up.

"You failed your fitness test," Harriet said.

"You're kidding me."

"I am not. You are too unfit to resume your duties."

After a silence, Manon said, "I don't understand it. I do a lot of exercise."

"A lot?"

"I'm . . . active."

"When are you active?"

"I sometimes walk to Sainsbury's."

"Right, I don't need to tell you this is a fucking fuckup. Even Colin passed. He's sixty and he smokes twenty a day. It's no good sitting your inspector's exams if all the burglars saunter away because you've got a stitch."

AND SO SHE IS WEARING a headband, which has more than a whiff of Olivia Newton John in the "Let's Get Physical" video about it, and she drinks from a neon water bottle she picked up at Pound Saver. She is crackling, what with all the fresh-from-the-packet polyester being chafed about her person. She could light up Blackpool, but instead she is about to throw some mean shapes in a community hall round the corner from her London flat, showing Angie and her Zumba class how it's done.

She hasn't told DCI Haverstock about the fitness test; figures she can fix it first.

Manon approximates a calf stretch in the far corner of a room that smells of socks, its parquet grainy with plimsoll dust. She tries to smile as a group of ladies walk in together, along with the instructor, who's carrying a ghetto blaster, but none of them acknowledges her, so she sips from her water bottle purposefully.

"God, I was so stiff from last week," says one of the women. Then she adds, "Hey, Hils, how did it go?"

Hils (Hilary, presumably) regales them with tales of a raspberry pavlova: "I managed to pick out the raspberries but leave the cream," she says, to which there is a ripple of applause. A wedding perhaps, or an anniversary party. Maybe they talk on the phone, this group, or go for coffee each week after the class. Manon sips again from her water bottle, looking out the window at the rusted green downspouts and dirty bricks and wishes she could leave.

Angie approaches. "Hello," she says. "Your name is?"

"Manon."

"Marion?"

"No, Manon."

"Right. So it's eleven pounds per class or fifty for the term."

Every fiber of Manon's being doesn't want to do this one class, let alone five. "Just the one please," she says, performing an athletic lunge to get her purse out of her bag.

"And have you done Zumba before?"

She wants to say, *Ange, mate, I catch murderers and rapists for a living.*

"Think I'll manage," she says.

The women take up their positions, one of them eyeing Manon irritably, as if to say *That's my place,* so she shuffles back, almost against the wall, and the music begins—a fast Latin beat. Angie, who is lithe, with a beautiful curved bottom and a flat stomach, clicks her fingers in a flicking-out motion and counts into the room, "Five, six, seven, eight," and all the ladies move in sync, smiling to themselves, appearing to bounce on air.

The mirror behind Angie shows her beautiful behind and the group's heart-lifting synchronicity and it shows a frantic Manon, stumbling at the back, craning to catch sight of what Angie is doing, fighting hard to copy the steps but grasping them just as the routine changes to something else.

The seconds feel like hours, a purgatory of stumble-jumping and mal-coordinated thrusting and gyrating and delayed swiveling, her face set in a rictus expression that is a mixture of confusion, panic, and intense discomfort. Her mouth is filling with a strongly metallic taste. Her chest is tightening. Her heart is like a frightened, caged animal, pounding at the bars of her ribs and pounding, also, against the voice in her brain saying, "Fucking keep going. *Do not lose face.*"

Angie is shouting incomprehensible instructions: "Around the world! And cha-cha-cha. And arms to the side! And back!"

Manon's chest is tighter than ever, her eyes fogged, her brain dizzy. The music has changed. *"Oh, what a feelin',"* sings Lionel Ritchie. She has to keep up, she says to herself, keep going, despite the fact that her heart might actually burst out of her chest. She must not lose face. She will not allow Hilary to shoot her a pitying glance during a "swivel and kick," while her ponytail flicks from side to side. It's got to be the cooldown soon. She just has to get to the cooldown. *Keep going, just keep going.* Her heart keeps pounding in her ears and against her ribs. She will not allow complete strangers to see her bent double, spitting out phlegm, her thighs cramping with lactic acid.

Manon ups her pace. She's almost delirious now with pain and adrenaline. *"Oh, what a feelin', when we're dancin' on the ceiling."* What does that even *mean*? The sweat drips from her eyebrows like water trickling from the roof of a cave. She really might die; she certainly can't speak. The other women appear to be founts of never-ending energy. One of them whoops, as if to announce that she has just been flooded by endorphins. Manon has to stop. A quick drink of water will buy her a moment's inactivity, she thinks. She drinks deep, sneaks a furtive glance at her watch. Twenty minutes into the class. Another forty to go. *Take me now, oh Lord.*

THE COMBINATION OF JULY HEAT wave and her inner combustion has created a Riyadh-level climate in which Manon's throbbing head and red ears might explode.

She had been standing at the side of the room, drinking from her by-now-empty water bottle and wondering if she needed to be carried out on a stretcher, when one of the group smiled at her. Manon smiled back, forcibly panting out the words "Great, wasn't it?" To Angie, she mumbled an unconvincing "See you next week," on her way out.

Now back at her flat, she has showered and opened her laptop, whispering to herself, "Here we go," clicking on "Details" and reading "thoughtful and optimistic." This one is musically talented (allegedly), though one person's musical talent is another person's narcissistic delusion.

She tries another one. Lithuanian. Aren't they cruel? "Bright" it says, and "very kind."

The next one lists "very good mechanical and engineering skills," and something about this sentence seems to Manon to damn with faint praise or possibly by omission. In the top left of her screen it says £850. She wonders if any of the less impressive specimens have a price reduction—a sort of sperm bargain basement. "Precious few social skills"—yours for £600. "Unexpected outbursts of violent temper, probably genetic": £250.

She is only browsing, just circling the idea for now. There is no commitment on the Internet, and this search bears no more weight than any previous one ("weight loss hypnosis" and "enema holiday" to name but two).

She clicks onto the next donor. Italian, Jewish, American. Italian could mean passion plus cookery (mind-blowing spaghetti *vongole*?), with the possible risk of attendant misogyny ("Mama, eh, I no empty de dishwasher, I am-a head-a of-a dis eh-family"); Jewishness could contribute a useful quota of persecution and guilt necessary for achievement, strong maternal attachment, and, of course, neurosis/hypochondria. ("Muuuuummm! I've found another tumor!")

And American. Well, that's the naked ambition taken care of. Yes, Italian-Jewish-American could be just what she's looking for, and so she reads on—skimming ahead to his reason for donating sperm. "I believe this is one of the most meaningful ways to do good for people. It's an honor to be able to help people with something as important as forming their families."

Christ no, she thinks. *Can't have a do-gooder like that in the family.*

Back to the list. How are you supposed to choose a genetic father? There isn't even a photograph. At least sexual intercourse involves some kind of selection, even at the most basic level. Come to think of it, quite a few of Manon's sexual selections have been based on paperthin criteria, like being in the same room.

She's brought up by the vibration of her mobile phone on the coffee table. Unknown number.

"Hello?"

"Is that Fly's mother?" says a male voice.

Fear digs in its talons. "Yes."

"It's Dave Marchant from the school. I wonder if you could pop in and see us. There's been an incident."

"Is Fly all right?"

"Yes, he's quite all right—sorry, I didn't mean to give you a fright—

but there's a matter we'd like to discuss with you concerning your son. The police are here."

Manon feels the blood in her body plummet with the weight of foreboding, mingled already with defensiveness. "Yes, of course. I'll be right there."

Dave Marchant is the head of Fly's school, silver at the temples, a slept-in face. Manon fancies him, of course. Whenever she encounters Mr. Marchant, apart from feeling schoolgirlishly flirtatious, she is rendered powerless as a pupil, overcome with the need to impress him, to be perfect, yet funny, efficient in the mothering department, yet quirkier and more interesting that the rest of the herd of tapioca parents. Parents in schools are never called by their names unless they run the PTA, being only appendages of their children. In life, she has always been Detective Sergeant Bradshaw. Officer Bradshaw. Now she is "Fly's mum."

She throws on a gray linen dress and her dusty sandals, still slick with sweat, and begins the ten-minute walk to the school.

She is perspiring before she reaches the end of Fordwych Road, her heart forcibly pumping in the heat and with the effort of bolstering herself against the implied criticism of her parenting, which attends being summoned to the head's office. She is also, while feeling distinctly weak-limbed, determined not simply to roll over. *I am not a child,* she tells herself, not at all convincingly. *I am not a child.* She will listen. She will stay calm and listen.

As she enters the room, Mr. Marchant rises from behind his desk and greets her with an outstretched arm. She shakes his hand, confused by the number of people in the room, like an ambush. She looks to her right, to the foam-block sofa pushed against the wall, and there is Fly, his huge eyes looking dolefully up at her. Guilt? Or regret? She mouths *hello* to him.

"Mrs.—?"

"You can call me Manon."

"Right, Manon, yes, this is PC Pemberton and DC Jones, and you know our deputy head Miss Cavendish, I think."

A fan is on his desk, its head turning side to side. On the floor behind Mr. Marchant's desk is a boxed bottle of prosecco half-dressed in a plastic bag. A fawning offering from a parent?

"Yes, hello," she says, wishing she'd introduced herself as DS Bradshaw. Lines of power and supremacy, who will sit and who will stand, who will *win*? Mr. Marchant is directing his outstretched hand to a chair and saying, "Please," so she sits and the other people in the room perch on various chairs brought in for the purpose. The room feels like a courtroom. She wishes more of the teachers had children themselves, so that they might know what it's like to feel on trial like this, but teaching these days appears to be a young person's game.

Venetian blinds are down against the blaze outside. The bodies in the room pulsate with heat, giving off shower gel, perfume, sweat. Manon is grateful that her hair is still damp, though the smell of her shampoo is overpowering and she feels like a truant, having taken a shower during the day. "I do work," she wants to plead in her defense.

"So, what's happened?" she asks.

"Your son," says PC Pemberton, "has been sent an indecent photograph by another pupil at the school." PC Pemberton is far too young, still enjoying the power of his uniform. He has pale hair and freckles, the Ron Weasley of local policing. She finds him attractive (is no one beyond the pale?) and notices this with weariness. Is it youth she is greedy for?

Manon frowns. "Right."

"And it is an offense to take or share indecent images if you are under the age of eighteen."

"I'm aware of that, yes," says Manon briskly. "Did Fly take the image?"

"No," says PC Pemberton. "The girl in the image, Courtney Grayson, has admitted taking the image and sending it to Fly."

"OK, so is there any evidence that Fly has shared the image?"

"No," says PC Pemberton, slightly less calmly. "We have checked your son's phone and the image has been deleted."

"Right," says Manon.

There is silence.

"Sorry," says Manon. "I'm confused. I don't think Fly can be held responsible for images sent to him unprompted. That is a matter for Courtney and her parents. He has not shared the image. He has—quite rightly—deleted it."

She glances at Fly. He is staring at her with a look of unbridled adoration.

"Absolutely, Mrs.—"

She's fed up with this. "Actually, it's DS Bradshaw, Major Incident Team." *Put that in your pipe and smoke it, tweenie.*

PC Pemberton colors up. Swallows. "We merely wanted to make your son and yourself aware of the issue to protect him from future incidents."

"If that's everything, then?" she says, rising, and the room rises with her. "Come on, kiddo," she says to Fly, and they leave the room, Manon with her hand on his shoulder, impossibly high up.

Outside in the corridor, its polished lino white with reflected glare and that indomitable school smell surrounding them—cottage pie and plimsolls—she whispers to him, "Fancy a Magnum?"

"It's like stepping under a hair dryer," she says as they walk into the heat. She pulls her sunglasses down and they trudge. Their limbs seem heavier as they wade through the thick air. They nibble on their Magnums.

"Let's cross," she says. "There's a bit of shade over there."

On the other side of the road, and without the searing burn of direct sun, he says—or, rather, mumbles; he seems incapable of speaking at a normal volume—"You were so cool in there. Epic."

"What's the thing with Courtney, then?"

He shrugs.

She has gotten used to waiting for him. Letting things come.

It needs to rain, she thinks.

Eventually, he says, "She's hot."

"She's also stupid, from the sound of it."

"Is Solly at home?" he asks, looking sideways at her, hopeful.

"Dunno."

"Could get the paddling pool out for him," he says.

"He'd like that. Have to watch him very carefully if you do."

"I know that," he says. "I always watch him. I never take my eyes off him."

"Except when you're staring at your phone," she says, smiling.

The love between Fly and Solly had burgeoned, sudden and unexpected by both Manon and Ellie. How an eleven-year-old and a baby could fall quite so deeply in love was a mystery to them both, but Fly's patience with Solly exceeded both his mother's and his aunt's. Even when Solly's fat arms flailed and he whacked Fly in the face with a metal toy car, Fly never lost it. "Oooh," he'd coo. "Gently, boy. That hurt me, you know?" And then he'd hold Solly close.

Solly's dependence was Fly's belonging—Manon could see that—while Fly and herself weaved a dance, neither quite needing the other as fully as was honest. Solly had no guile in this area: he was all need. A vast register of emotion, he swung between delight and misery, fury and curiosity, without dissembling. And he seemed able to accept comfort—the cuddles, the milk, the wiping away of tears with rocking, his head held close to someone's chest, because he didn't mind his vulnerable state. Manon wondered if Fly saw Solly's precarious position as akin to his own and whether soothing Solly was soothing himself.

No. She's wrong in this, she thinks now, as they schlump along the dusty pavements. Solly did mind being so much in need of adult assistance; this was the source of many of his epic frustrations, when he would sob himself into a ball of red fire. But what she admired in Solly was the bald expression of everything: every feeling seemed to register on his Richter scale. He was fully connected, every wire lighting a bulb. He had not yet learned to disguise himself.

Unusually, Fly interrupts the silence, saying, "Was only a bit of fun."

"Sorry?"

"Dunno what the big deal is, about the picture."

"It's not a bit of fun for the girl whose naked body gets shared all over the Internet, Fly," she says. She can feel her hackles rising. Doesn't he get it?

"Just what kids do."

"Well, it better not be what you do, Fly. It's forever, this stuff. You can't regret it later. And it's bad for all of you, but it's especially bad for girls."

He shrugs. Sniffs. And it incenses her. Doesn't he care about anything? She can feel herself going too far before she has gone anywhere, but the urge to hammer her message into him is deranging. He is lolloping beside her, trainers like boats, stooping as though he doesn't care to accommodate his tallness, with that boulder of a bag dripping off him, and his nonchalance, sagging and yet rhythmic with his step, is an affront to her. What will it take to make him realize that the world is dangerous and he is at risk?

Affection through to rage, in under ten seconds.

She wheels around. "Christ, Fly, what's going to happen to you? I mean, you're going to wreck your life if you carry on like this."

"Whoa," he says gently, and his mildness is more maddening still.

"Man up, Fly," she shouts. "I'm serious. Life's serious. You can't mess with this shit, Fly. If you'd sent on that photo, you'd be being charged right now."

Brilliant: now she's swearing at an eleven-year-old. Watch and learn, parents.

"But I didn't."

"Yeah, but it's not a bit of fun. It really isn't. I'm taking your phone away."

"Wha—"

"No arguing. I pay for that phone, and I do not pay for it so that you can play fast and loose with young women's dignity."

"Have you met Courtney?" Fly whispers, smiling at the ground.

"Stop being an—" she wants to say "arsehole," halting on the street and casting about for something suitable yet sufficiently aggressive. There are no words appropriate for eleven-year-old ears.

He has walked on, away from her along Fordwych Road, toward their flat. Head down, he has gone into lockdown.

"Fly?" she says.

But he continues to walk away.

PHOTO: JONATHAN RING

Susie Steiner is a former *Guardian* journalist. She was a commissioning editor for that paper for eleven years and prior to that worked for *The Times, The Daily Telegraph,* and the *Evening Standard*. She lives in London with her husband and two children.

susiesteiner.co.uk
@SusieSteiner1

ABOUT THE TYPE

This book was set in Bembo, a typeface based on an old-style Roman face that was used for Cardinal Pietro Bembo's tract *De Aetna* in 1495. Bembo was cut by Francesco Griffo (1450–1518) in the early sixteenth century for Italian Renaissance printer and publisher Aldus Manutius (1449–1515). The Lanston Monotype Company of Philadelphia brought the well-proportioned letterforms of Bembo to the United States in the 1930s.

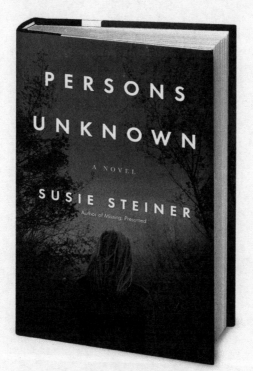